BOYCOTT

Colin C. Murphy was the Creative Director of one of Ireland's leading advertising agencies for over a decade, but left the advertising business in 2009 to pursue a full-time career in writing. He has had a lifelong fascination with history in general and is the author of *The Most Famous Irish People You've Never Heard Of,* concerning Irish emigrants throughout history who earned fame abroad but are little known at home. He has also written a light-hearted look at Irish history entitled *The Feckin' Book of Irish History*.

Boycott is his first novel. A subject he stumbled across many years ago, the Boycott incident immediately fascinated him because of the 'David and Goliath' aspect of the small Mayo community using passive resistance to take on the British Empire, and the fact that it proved to be one of the earliest examples of how the power of mass communication could bring the events in a tiny community to global attention. Between researching, writing and editing, *Boycott* has taken over two years to complete.

When not writing, Colin is often to be found wandering Ireland's mountains. A keen hillwalker, he is also a committee member of Mountainviews.ie, a free hillwalking resource for anyone who loves Ireland's dwindling wild areas. He is married to Gráinne and has a son, Emmet, and a daughter, Cíara, and he and his family are from Dublin. After his native county, Mayo is the county he loves the most, although as yet he has failed to trace any Mayo ancestors. But as he feels he must have a bit of Mayo blood in him, he intends to keep looking.

BOYCOTT

COLIN C. MURPHY

BRANDON

First published 2012 by
Brandon
an imprint of The O'Brien Press
12 Terenure Road East, Rathgar,
Dublin 6, Ireland.

Tel: +353 1 4923333; Fax: +353 1 4922777
E-mail: books@obrien.ie.
Website: www.obrien.ie

ISBN: 978-1-84717-345-4

Cover image: Wynne, Thomas J 1838-1893 The Wynne Album, National Photographic Archive

British Library Cataloguing-in-Publication Data
A catalogue record for this title is available from the British Library

1 2 3 4 5 6 7 8
12 13 14 15 16

Printed and bound by ScandBook AB, Sweden
The paper used in this book is produced using pulp from managed forests

DEDICATION

This book is dedicated to my great-grandparents, Michael and Mary Kennedy, William and Ellen Slattery, John and Margaret Murphy and Thomas and Helen Tyer, all of whom were born in the years immediately after the Great Famine and who survived through harsher times than I can imagine; but particularly to Michael and William, from Wicklow and Tipperary respectively, who were both tenant farmers during the time of the Land War.

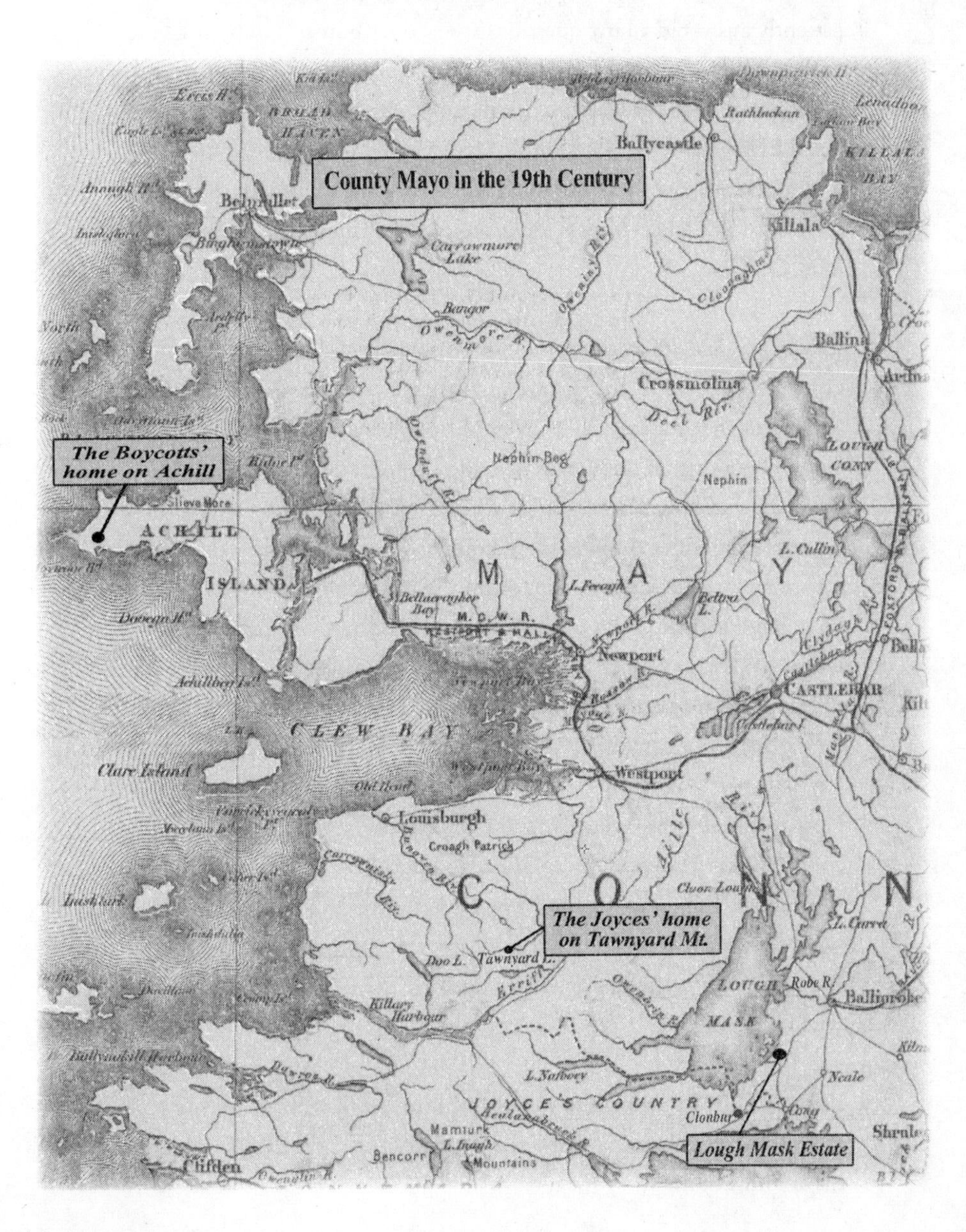

Acknowledgements

I owe a debt of gratitude to a great number of people for their help in writing this novel. Firstly to the people of Ballinrobe and Neale, who, unaware of the nature of my interest in their locality, very helpfully and patiently answered all my questions about their history and pointed me in the right direction as I tramped about their towns and environs with notebook in hand in search of local landmarks. Particular thanks to Mr Gerard M. Delaney of The South Mayo Family Research Centre, Ballinrobe, and Ms Averil Staunton of the Historical Ballinrobe website for their kind assistance in providing biographical information on Father John O'Malley.

It is impossible to create any book without having the benefit of an objective eye, and in this regard I particularly want to thank my sister, Pauline, for her patience in studying the early drafts of my work, line by line, and offering an unflinchingly critical commentary, which was helpful in the extreme. Several others also agreed to give me a critique, and my appreciation for this knows no bounds, as I am aware how difficult it is to wade though a manuscript of over seven hundred loose-leaf pages! So a huge thanks to my wife Grainne, Brendan O'Reilly, Tom Kelly, Donal O'Dea, my father John Murphy and my daughter's Leaving Certificate English teacher, Siobhan Reynolds. My gratitude also to Simon Stewart of Mountainviews.ie for his advice on historical maps of Ireland.

I am indebted to my editor, Ide ní Laoghaire, for her professional guidance, endless patience and invaluable suggestions. Also to Michael O'Brien of Brandon/O'Brien Press, for taking my novel on board, I will be eternally grateful. I also want to express my gratitude to Emma Byrne for her cover design, along with all the other staff at the press who contributed.

Lastly, I want to thank the people of nineteenth-century Neale and Ballinrobe for giving the world the 'boycott', and for writing a substantial amount of my story for me.

AUTHOR'S NOTE

Although this is a work of fiction, all of the press and book excerpts that introduce each chapter are genuine, as are the majority of those included in the body of the text, and while I have edited some of them purely for brevity's sake, I have done my utmost to ensure that I have not altered their substance. All of the events surrounding the Boycott incident in 1880 are a matter of historical record, along with many of the events described in the famine era. Also, many of the tenants who appear in the narrative bear the names of Charles Boycott's actual tenants, and most of the British Army officers, local shopkeepers, magistrates, process-servers etc are also based on real people.

There is always a danger when re-creating historical figures of either sullying their character or unjustifiably glorifying them. I have based my interpretations of all of the actual historical figures on the evidence that was available to me, although I confess that these are personal interpretations with which others may choose to differ. Some of the characters, such as that of Boycott's brother, Arthur, and the picture portrayed of Boycott's father, are composites of several people, which I have expanded on at the end of the book. I have also taken some small licence with one or two minor dates, such as the year of death of Charles Boycott's father, purely to assist the narrative, but I have tried to keep any apparent 'inaccuracies' such as these to an absolute minimum.

In certain cases the present inhabitants of some parts of Mayo or towns such as Ballinrobe may spot what appear to be discrepancies with the locality as they know it today, however landscapes, towns and place names may change considerably in one hundred and sixty years. Besides having thoroughly explored all of the areas in the book on foot, I also used a series of historical maps from the relevant time periods as references, which in some cases show distinct differences from today.

C.C.M.
June 2012

Part One

• • • • • • •

Watershed

The judgement of God sent the calamity to teach the Irish a lesson, that calamity must not be too much mitigated. The real evil with which we have to contend is not the physical evil of the Famine, but the moral evil of the selfish, perverse and turbulent character of the people.

–Sir Charles Trevelyan, civil servant responsible for the administration of relief during the Great Famine (1845–49)

CHAPTER 1

By the side of the cottage's western wall is a long, newly-made grave; and near the hole that serves as a doorway is the last resting-place of two or three children; in fact, this hut is surrounded by a rampart of human bones, which have accumulated to such a height that the threshold, which was originally on a level with the ground, is now two feet beneath it. In this horrible den, in the midst of a mass of human putrefaction, six individuals, males and females, labouring under most malignant fever, were huddled together, as closely as were the dead in the graves around.

–*The Illustrated London News*, 13 February 1847

An inquest was held by Dr Sweetman on three bodies. The first was that of two young children whose mother had already died of starvation. Their father's death became known only when the two children toddled into the village of Schull. They were crying of hunger and complaining that their father would not speak to them for four days; they told how he was 'as cold as a flag-stone'. The other bodies on which an inquest was held were of a mother and child who had died of starvation. The remains had been gnawed by rats.

–Official report from County Cork, 1847

AUGUST 1848

He had encountered the smell many times during his sixteen years. It was one with which his kind had a casual familiarity, living off the land as they did. Their closeness to the earth's coarse and cold-blooded ways had hardened them to some degree to dismiss such unpleasantries with a wrinkle of the nose and a fleeting frown before moving on. But the boy had never grown used to it, not like the others.

The smell was usually chanced upon in the woods or among the knee-high reeds that grew in wetlands, or in this case in the blossoming heather that dressed and scented the mountainside. If ever one took the trouble to investigate, which wasn't often, the reward for one's efforts was to tumble upon some small animal, usually a rabbit or a hare savaged without quarter by a fox or an eagle, its twitching remains then discarded to the mercies of the elements and the maggots. Occasionally the animal was larger, a mountain goat perhaps, although it was years since he'd seen one of those.

A subtle awareness came to him that the smell was somehow different to those he'd encountered before and, although he railed against the notion, he knew his curiosity would inevitably draw him towards its source. He tentatively rounded the small bump that rose from the slope of the mountain and stopped. A barely heard mewl escaped his lips; otherwise he was silent. He just stared.

The youth, by the standards of his peers and elders almost a man, now felt like a small child lost to its mother far from the hearth. The things before him could do him no harm and yet his fear was palpable because somewhere in his jumbling thoughts he could imagine himself coming to a similar end.

He had seen the dead before, of course; by now every Irish man, woman and child surely had witnessed the empty stare of the lifeless, for in some parts of County Mayo they seemed to outnumber the living. Each day or night brought the sound of a keening hag from a hillside or a village, keening that had echoed throughout his own home, and more than once. But death more often now did not involve the normal ritual of wake and funeral. Many had seen the fallen forms of their countrymen and women in the ditches or simply draped across the boreens, left to rot, their sunken eyes pretending to watch one's approach. Yet his previous experience of the dead had done little to steel him for this sight.

She was perhaps eighteen, not so many years his elder, although it was difficult to tell precisely, but the long black hair that in life would have almost reached her waist suggested a younger woman. God alone knew how long she'd lain here in the heather and the bog water. Her eyes were gone, pecked out by birds, and the obscene hollows in her face held his own gaze transfixed. The condition of her remains was, no doubt, due in part to the elements, but her demise was clearly the result of abject starvation. This had rendered her flesh so thin that it seemed draped on her bones the way a cloth assumes the shape of an object over which it is spread. Her very skeletal structure was defined – cheeks, jaw, ribs, shins. The fine muslin of skin was the colour of a mountain boulder and in places broken, or patchy, revealing dark red matter below. She was clothed in blackened rags that had once purported to be a dress of coarse, dyed wool, but was never more than a peasant's covering for decency's sake. Even that decency had now been shed as the gaping holes in the garment exposed her bare, decaying thighs.

But by far the most afflicting aspect of the scene was the child, no more than a withered bag of black wrinkled sacking, its shape barely defining it as human, its tiny form prostrate across its mother's sagging belly, so recently alive with the promise of new life. The black leathery lips of the baby lay an inch from the shrivelled pouch of its mother's breast, seeking nourishment that had never come. He couldn't help but wonder which of them had perished first. He hoped, he prayed to God above that it was the child. The image of the mother dead and the screaming child suckling on her cold and lifeless breast was impossible to bear.

Owen Joyce knew his mind was clinging to reason by a thread and he felt his knees weaken. His thoughts flashed to Sally, his younger sister. He'd often sat by his mother's side as she had held his sister to her breast and watched with fascination as thread-like jets of mother's milk had shot out and splashed Sally's face as she blindly sought to suckle. Sally would gurgle and he would look on in wonder, once squeezing his own nipple to soreness as he tried to create a flow of milk, much to the hilarity of the others.

His mother. Dead now. Like this young mother before him. He finally closed his eyes, swaying on his feet, trying to order his thoughts. Sally. She was why he was here, he remembered, and in the blackness behind his eyelids he saw her, now eleven years old, lying skeletal and incoherent on the straw by the hearth.

He had to find food for her – so he had sworn to his father not an hour ago. His brother, Thomas, had scoffed and been silenced by his father's glare. But he had set out nonetheless, kissing his sister on her sunken cheek and pushing through the door into the autumn sunlight. And his undertaking had led him here, to a tableau of death at its most execrable. But he needed to hasten to the lough. Sally was alive, this woman and her child were dead. In a year the bog would have consumed them, dust to dust. He turned away and looked at the slope of the hill sweeping down to Tawnyard Lough and Derrintin Lough beyond it. That was his destination. Yet his feet would not obey him. He looked over his shoulder at the girl and child. The truth of it was that he could not leave them here, exposed and naked to the rages of nature without even a holy word to mark their passing. He uttered a miserable sob.

Owen looked around. A few yards beyond the bodies lay a gash in the landscape, a bog hole. It measured maybe four feet long, less than an arm's length across, and sank no deeper than a man's thigh. He could see his own gaunt reflection in the mirror-still pool of water at the bottom.

He returned to the bodies and knelt. There was little strength in his limbs, but he suspected the remains had been reduced to near-weightlessness. Wrestling with nausea, he began to lift them both as one. One of the girl's arms, like a bone wrapped in paper, fell limply on the heather. Her head lolled backwards as he rose and the movement brought what sounded like a sigh from her open mouth, the lifeless breath so rancid it was beyond comprehension. He yelped and stumbled forward, conscious of the movement of her bones beneath the coarse clothing, his revulsion causing him almost to throw the girl's body into the hole. With an effort of will he pulled stems of heather from the bog and piled the bushy growth over the bodies until they were out of sight. It was a travesty of a burial, he knew, but the best he could fashion. He tried to recall the words he'd heard the priest utter when he'd served as an altar boy, and began to mouth the incantation through the splutters of his sobs.

'*Requiem æternam dona eis Domine. Et lux…et lux…*,' he whispered, but his brain refused to offer up more words and he quickly skipped to the end. '*Requiescat in pace. Amen.*' He blessed himself. The dead had been cared for as best he could manage; now it was the turn of the living.

Not far below he could distinguish the narrow boreen that skirted Tawnyard Hill. As he neared it he glanced over his shoulder and took in the collection of crudely assembled homes that pimpled the mountain's face. Among the highest was his own, where his father now wept as he watched the light fade from his only surviving daughter's eyes. Smoke rose from the hole punched in the rough thatch of heather twigs. None of the other dwellings showed any sign of life. The homes of unworked stone or rough-hewn lumps of turf were mostly empty shells now, the former inhabitants the victims of starvation or violent eviction.

He reached the lowland of the valley and looked out across the fields where the cottage, the place of his birth, had once nestled by the Owenduff River, before they'd been forced to depart to the near-barren higher ground. The original cottage had two rooms, a luxury unheard of, and a window! How bleak a place the world had become since those distant days, he thought, as he felt a shift of wind and stab of pain within his hollow gut.

He began to steer a path around Tawnyard Lough. A mile in length from west to east and once teeming with fish – he had a clear memory as a small boy of spotting an immense brown trout not a few feet from the shore, so close he could almost reach in and scoop it out with his bare hand. His father had taught him how to fish and he had taken to it effortlessly. He'd brought home fat, ambrosial trout occasionally, welcome company for the incessant lumper potato, or sometimes an eel or a coarse, oily fish, unpleasant yet eagerly devoured by all. Thomas, at eighteen his elder brother by two years, would on occasion look with some resentment at the food Owen brought to the table. Within a week Thomas would hunt down a rabbit and exchange it for the family's adulation, a glint of triumph in his eyes, his status as the first-born restored. Thomas was good at poaching rabbits and hares, even now when they'd almost disappeared. When they'd played together as children, he could always approach Owen from behind and leap on him, forcing him to the ground where they would laugh and roll in the dust. His brother had always been good at sneaking up on him.

Once, though, for his trouble, Thomas had earned a musket ball through his leg, luckily in the fleshy part below his arse – in one side and straight out the other, fired by the gamekeeper, Geraghty, a brute of a Galwayman in the employ of the land agent, Harris. Fortunately, Thomas had managed to flee unrecognised. After he'd fallen through the doorway in blood-soaked britches, been stripped of them and had the ragged hole in his leg scoured and bandaged, their mother had forbidden the two of them to poach game on land or water. The musket ball might just have easily have gone through his head. Owen, then aged ten, had asked his father why a man such as Harris or the landlord who paid him, Lord Lucan, would deny them the meagre extra bite of wild meat or fish when they themselves already possessed wealth beyond Owen's imagination. His father had sighed and looked into the orange flames dancing in the ingle. 'Because, Owen, to the likes of them, we're little more than wild meat ourselves.' He hadn't understood, and when he began to press, his mother had shushed him and ushered him to the straw bed across the smoky room. He had lain there alongside Thomas, Bridget and Sally and stared across the gloom at his silent mother and father, the flickering light betraying the fear on their features. In that moment he had a foreboding that some repugnant shadow would soon engulf them.

Owen rounded the sharp, easterly point of Tawnyard Lough, now all but barren of fish, its cold, deep waters exhausted of life by the numberless starving who had plucked its fruits so abundantly that no seed remained to replenish it. The tiny Derrintin Lough beyond it offered more hope, its relative remoteness from the roads a disincentive to the weak. Despite this, even its waters had been fished near to futility. Yet he had hope.

He reached the Owenduff River, which laboured to drain the two loughs of their water against the constant replenishment of the West of Ireland's rains. He waded in, the water shallow in late August but the cold still biting through his britches. His balls and *pócar* (his 'poker', as Thomas called it) shrivelled to aching tightness as the leathery soles of his feet carried him across the stony riverbed. He clambered out on the bank and rested a moment, allowing himself to be soothed by the whispers of the lazy waters.

He looked again along the valley where his home had once stood. The land hadn't always been in the ownership of Lord Lucan. He'd acquired it from another of his peers, Lord Faulks, Earl of Somethingshire in England, he couldn't recall exactly. A place of plenty, he imagined, where people dwelled in splendid homes of granite and glass, where the wood of the tables couldn't be seen for the abundance of food. At least that was the picture his father and Thomas had painted for him in recent times, their visions inspired by burgeoning bitterness.

Lord Faulks hadn't been the worst, although word had it the nobleman had never set foot in Ireland, inheriting the estate of two thousand acres from his father. It was a small estate by the standards of many of his kind. Lord Lucan had sixty thousand acres, it was rumoured. Faulks, a young man of education, was said to have been more interested in botany or biology or one of the new fields of science that were now the subject of much study in England. Life as a tenant of his had been no fairytale, but his rents were fair and any improvements to a tenant's lot brought about by his own efforts remained his own property. They had ten acres then, sufficient to exist beyond subsistence. After rent obligations had been fulfilled and mouths fed, the surplus lumpers could be sold for grain or even to buy a chicken or a pig. They'd had five or six chickens running about the house at one time, he remembered, although the taste of an egg was by now lost to his memory. Then Faulks decided to sell and Lord Lucan had emerged as the buyer. They were exchanging one preposterously moneyed lord for another. Unlikely ever to set eyes on him either. Their just-bearable lives would progress unperturbed, no better, no worse.

Then Harris had arrived, Lucan's land agent and the estate's overseer. Most of Lucan's vast holdings at that time were in the north of Mayo, around Castlebar. When the tenants met in the secret hollows of the mountain to sip their poteen, words were uttered of Lucan's ruthlessness. Around Castlebar they called him 'The Exterminator'. He'd put thousands on the roadside, left them to rot without batting an eyelid. Likely he would do the same here. The men shivered as they pulled their coats against the wind – and the fear that the whispers about Lucan spoke the truth.

At that time over twenty homes stood in the valley. All gone now, no sign even of a single stone atop another to mark the fact that people had once lived here: farmers had toiled, children had run about, families had eaten, songs were occasionally sung. Then the eviction crews had come, constables accompanied by hired thugs, bringing their machines of destruction, descending on the people, burning the thatch from over their heads, levelling the walls to the sound of screaming women and crying children, impotent looks on the faces of the men, shamed before their womenfolk.

They'd all been given a choice. They could each have plots on the mountainside, four acres apiece, rent the same as they currently paid for ten of fertile land. Or else they could have nothing. Some chose the latter, especially those with many mouths to feed. Four acres of soggy turf couldn't grow food for ten people. They'd taken the boat to faraway places, America mostly. God alone knows what became of them. A handful of the farmers had elected to stay, too long a part of the place to imagine a life beyond. Since then their four acres had become three, then two, as Lucan sought to subdivide the holdings, increase his tenantry and still extort his rents. A single Scot, Buchanan by name, was leased the land where twenty families once lived. Then the land was given over to pasture; it was more profitable.

Rested, Owen shook the memory away and moved on. He soon reached

Derrintin Lough, two jagged-edged ponds of water joined in the middle by a narrow channel, near the centre of which sat a tiny elongated island, which was more a lump of rock with a dusting of earth and a canopy of stunted trees and shrubs. The tiredness in his legs gave him pause as he looked into the peaty brown water. His limbs had been feeding upon themselves for months now, their fat burned away, languid muscle over bone all that remained. A frog croaked, masquerading somewhere nearby as grass or moss. He looked about, seized a stick and studied the reedy grass. It sat immobile, barely visible against the lush growth, alert for predators. A hind leg moved almost imperceptibly, ready to spring. The rotting stick came down on its head even as it rose into the air towards the water and it fell twitching onto the ground. He sank to his knees, grabbed it by the hind legs and held it up before his eyes. A tiny nodule of blood clung to the creature's shattered head. He shoved in into his mouth whole, bit, crunched, closed his eyes. No taste, just texture, liquid and solid, sinew and slime. It filled his mouth, spilled from his lips. He pawed at his jaw to shove the escaping tissue back in. A lump went down his throat, painfully, as his gullet had narrowed through lack of use, and he coughed, scrambling forward to the water on his knees. Cupped hands impulsively splashed the water towards his mouth, dousing the sudden awareness of his own revulsion. He hunkered back, panting and staring into space as his stomach got to work consuming the unfamiliar meat.

It was only fifty feet, maybe less, to the island. As a boy he could have swum there and back ten times over. Not now. But to fish from the shore would prove worthless and dangerous as fishing and hunting on Lucan's property was strictly forbidden. Nearby, a large lump of driftwood knocked gently against a boulder. He looked about for other people but the landscape was devoid of human life. He pulled the small pouch of rabbit hide from his pocket and tied it around his neck, stripped naked and threw his threadbare shirt, jacket and pants away towards drier ground. He pushed the log out with his toe and plunged into the water. He gasped and spluttered, clinging to the log with a stick-like arm, his nerves rebelling against the outrageous cold. He had to get moving, warm himself from the inside out. His free arm reached and pulled, reached and pulled, his legs kicking, propelling him sluggishly outward. It took him ten minutes. He scrambled up and beat his arms about him in the warm August sun, then hurried through the trees and the shrubs towards the eastern tip of the islet.

Owen emerged and looked into the black depths of the water. For months in this spot he'd baited the fish, a trick his father had taught him: maggots were frequently cast into this dark pool at the isle's tip, giving the fish a taste for them, drawing them to the spot. He retrieved the long straight wooden pole he'd secreted behind a rock. It was wrapped about with his mother's strongest thread; a bent pin was his hook. From the pouch around his neck, he spilled a handful of maggots. As he busied himself with the line he imagined his family back in their tiny cottage, his father, brother, sister, the only ones left now, probably cursing that he hadn't returned with food. In so many ways he felt he'd been a disappointment to his father. Couldn't dig a potato pit for all his worth. Cut the turf too thickly. Thatching not tight enough. Too weak to lift a rock. Run home to your mother. Hide your face inside a book. It's all you're good for.

His father had never said any of these things to him but Owen could hear him saying the words behind his furrowed brow. And then his father would turn to Thomas. Give your brother a hand, Thomas, he would say. Thomas wearing a crooked grin as he sauntered across the hillside. 'Made an arse of it again, spalpeen?' And he would ruffle his younger brother's hair, Owen shrugging him off. Yet he loved Thomas deeply.

He set aside the plumpest half-dozen maggots and cast the rest into the water, watching as they twirled and faded one after another into the darkness, then skewered one of the others on to the hook and exhaled some warm breath on the tiny doomed thing. It immediately began to wriggle furiously, as though brought to life again by his breath. He quickly cast the line while the maggot convulsed; its death dance would hopefully prove irresistible to the prey. He sat and studied the water, his naked legs dangling over the edge of the rock, and prayed that God would look kindly on his endeavour.

***

Until the moment when Owen's mother, Honor, died early in '46, he'd never seen his father weep. Weakened by childbirth and hunger, Honor faded before their eyes into a tattered rag. Patrick, the infant, had somehow survived, but only briefly. Barely nine weeks passed before they had laid him too in the earth, his father questioning God's reasoning for bringing the child into being at all.

But their father had eschewed bitterness, remained stoical. He refused to entertain any rebellious inclination towards their British rulers or resentment at their landlord or his minions. It was the early days of the famine then and many persevered in the hope that the next potato crop would bring an end to their misery. Battling with his pride, he reluctantly accepted so-called 'outdoor relief', nourishment provided mostly by the Quakers in the form of soup kitchens. Then the Poor Law known as the 'Gregory Clause' (the 'Gregory Curse' to the peasantry) had dictated that this relief would be denied to any cottier holding more than a quarter of an acre of land. The Government had effectively given them a choice: give up your land or starve. It was believed far and wide that this clause was simply a means of facilitating the eviction of tenants so landlords could grow more profitable cash crops or turn land to pasture. Michael Joyce refused to surrender his land, clinging to the hope that they would turn a corner. And despite their misery he had resisted recourse to hatred. The British hadn't brought the potato blight. Some malevolent twist of nature had thrust it upon their heads. And their treatment at the hands of the landlords was simply the lot of their kind the world over. Thomas became increasingly deaf to his father's pronouncements. And the truth was that Owen couldn't suppress his own resentment at their predicament.

Then his sister Bridget had taken ill the previous September, in the third year of the blight. The fever. Typhus, they called it. Too weak to do battle with the sickness, she had lain on the straw, by turns wailing in a tortured screech, shivering, sweating, shielding her eyes from the dim light. Each of them had cried at her side as they had listened and clasped her hand. Thomas had become enraged and dared to charge his father with finding some help. But his father hadn't rebuked him or struck him, he'd simply stared back across the smoky space for some minutes before departing into the fading evening light.

He returned some hours later and, with unmasked impertinence, Thomas asked where the hell he'd been. His father struck him with the back of his hand and then immediately sought to comfort his eldest born, a gesture shunned by Thomas.

Owen knelt over Bridget's prone form and spoke through tears. 'She's weak, Father. The pox has spread everywhere. Look at her legs. And she can't breathe.'

Michael Joyce stared at them and spoke with rage bitten down in his words. 'I went to see Harris, to plead for help. When he learned that Bridget had the fever he drew a pistol and threatened me. Geraghty escorted me beyond the gates. He told me not to return. And he said to make sure "I burned the bitch's body."'

A snarl forming on Thomas's face withered before it could rise, as Owen, conscious of a stirring in his sister's body, uttered her name aloud. Bridget whimpered and turned her head. She opened her eyes and smiled at Owen, then drew another tortured breath, the last of her twelve years of life.

The two boys sensed a shift within their father, deprived now of his wife, his infant son and his eldest daughter, a re-ordering of the rules that defined his world. He would mumble to himself that God had tested his faith beyond endurance. In those lightless days after they laid Bridget into the earth, it seemed that in his father's mind a more basic law superseded even those of God, that of survival.

It was October and winter was approaching. Once again the blight had turned their crop of potatoes to a fetid mush and the unfamiliar turnips had been ignorantly sown, their yield a fraction of that expected. Their meagre rations would hold out a month if they were lucky. Owen had been fishing from that same favourite spot in Derrintin Lough when his father had appeared from nowhere, a hundred yards away on the northern shore. He'd been on the point of calling out, but something checked him. Owen recognised that, like a timorous animal, his father was *skulking*. Crouching and watching, he saw Michael Joyce pull an object from beneath his jacket, grip it with both hands, pivot and swing, sending whatever it was twirling skyward, defining an arc towards the lough's glassy surface, the crisp hiss of the splashing water reaching his ears a moment after the event, the object lost to man's knowledge in the inky blackness of the lough.

His father fell to his knees as he pulled off his coarse woollen jacket and plunged it into the water, then his shirt, every action punctuated by a glance over his shoulder. He washed his face and splashed water on his bony chest. Owen puzzled most at the washing of his hands. If he did it once he did it six times, each time studying his palms as though for some unyielding stain. His father finally wrapped his face in his palms and across the stillness of the water, Owen shivered as the sound of sobbing reached him. He knew then that whatever malign stain troubled his father, it was not to be found on his hands.

For days after, his father was withdrawn, residing in some dark recess of human existence. And unexpectedly there was meat on the table. Boiled in the pot, a thin, flavourless broth, but greeted with jubilance. The broth was produced first on the very evening that Owen had seen him by the lough. He'd been to Drummin, he'd said, three miles to the north, a fair hike on matchstick legs and a hollow stomach. He'd bartered some venison from a traveller in exchange for an old ring. Owen thought better of questioning the implausibility of this. It seemed inconsequential when set next to the feeling of food in one's belly. Michael Joyce warned them that the subject of the meat was not to be discussed with their neighbours; desperate people, he'd muttered, were capable of anything, violence even. Owen remembered his father's eyes seeking those of Thomas as he said this, the pair sharing a brief conspiracy of thought.

A local found the gamekeeper Geraghty a week later, his body dumped beneath Tullynafola Bridge over the Glenlaur River, not a mile away. Word was about the hillside that Harris's lackey had been beaten to death with his own musket.

Four constables turned up the next day in their flat caps and dark green uniforms. The landowners harboured fears of a surge in agrarian attacks and the return of the scourge of the Ribbonmen. The Irish Constabulary had been charged with ferreting out any so-called secret agrarian societies and stringing them from on high as an example. The policemen dismounted as Michael Joyce met their eyes, then answered their questions. They searched their home, Sally looking up at them with vacant eyes as the men overturned the family's meagre possessions and held lanterns into every crevice. Michael Joyce stood stock-still and watched. The boys waited outside. The constables had been looking for the musket, Owen learned later. Find it and they find their man. But their search proved fruitless and they moved on to the next dwelling along the hill.

They subsequently learned from neighbours that the constabulary believed Geraghty had stumbled upon a poacher, had fired and missed, and the murderer had overcome him before he could reload. The attack had been frenzied. Some said Harris's gamekeeper had been struck twenty times. An unhinged mind moved among their community. A lunatic. A savage.

The subject of Geraghty was never spoken of again. To the land agent, Harris, his gamekeeper's death had been an inconvenience, nothing more. An Englishman, Burrell, had taken Geraghty's place. No one was arrested, although the constabulary did question a man by the name of Pádraig Walsh from up the valley, a suspected Ribbonmen sympathiser. But he had an alibi and no other evidence had revealed itself.

It had been a bitterly cold winter, but somehow they'd all survived. It was during this baleful period, a week shy of Christmas, that a pair of kindly Quakers appeared at their door on horseback. Owen had heard that the Quakers and others like them were often willing to provide food to the hungry for the price of their religious beliefs – to fill their bellies they must first empty their hearts of the Catholic faith and embrace Protestantism. The priest, Fr Lally, had recently warned them to resist all such temptation; it was better in the eyes of God to endure the pangs of hunger than to renounce one's faith for a bowl of soup. When the priest departed, his father spat on the floor behind the clergyman, to Owen's shock.

Yet these two Quakers made no such demands. They urged Michael Joyce to hasten to Westport workhouse or his children would surely perish. He responded that he would rather see them perish than watch their last grain of dignity stolen in such a place, begging for scraps of mercy thrown on the ground by an institution of the British Crown. The two Quakers shook their heads and handed his father a small sack of oats, not charity of the British Crown they hastened to mention, but a gift from their society on the occasion of their mutual Saviour's birth. Michael Joyce had looked at Thomas, Owen and Sally, standing shivering outside their dwelling in the crisp December air, then nodded and gratefully accepted the oats.

As the months had passed his father became more and more withdrawn. Their financial debt to Harris had long since passed beyond their means ever to repay it. This year's payment was almost due and there was no potato crop to meet it, let alone to feed them. Bridget's death had finally broken his father. Whatever last sparks of forbearance and restraint he had within him had been stamped out. His bitterness smothered his grief. The English race were bastards all, rich and poor alike, commoner and king. The Irish, their subjects, were mere chaff in their realm. Each day tons of grain were transported from Ireland's shores while her people starved or were driven onto emigrant ships. As Ireland's people had known for centuries, Michael Joyce spouted, the English only understood one language when it came to Ireland, that of the pike and the sword and the pistol. And Thomas had listened with eager ears as each spit of venom had spewed from his father's lips. Owen had felt only fear.

When Geraghty had died, Owen's fears seemed to be realised. Michael Joyce's vitriol had finally taken form. From the moment Owen learned of the manner of the man's death, he suspected that what he'd witnessed that day at the lough was his father disposing of the murder weapon – and a new sense of dread overtook him. His father, and by association his family, had crossed a line – on one side of which they were victims, on the other transgressors, sinners, murderers even. As he recalled the twirling musket fracture the glazed serenity of the lough's surface, his own innocence was shattered. The water had settled and regained its placid form, but he feared the disquiet in his own heart would ripple on to the end of his days.

***

The water rippled again now and he awoke from his reverie. The air had chilled and the sun was low in the valley behind him. The fishing line twitched and darted to and fro. He played out some slack and allowed the fish a momentary illusion of freedom before he began to ease the creature towards the surface. Gently he gathered the line, looping it about his hand until finally he caught sight of the fish's frenetic struggling. As it broke the surface he heaved upwards. The fish arced through the air and landed, flapping, a few feet away on a boulder. He'd landed a bream, barely a pound in weight. He quickly unhooked the line, re-baited it and cast, hopeful the fish had been one of a school. The sun was dipping and he still had to make his way back up the hillside, but one fish would not suffice.

An hour later and twilight had coloured the valley red. He had just crossed the boreen with his paltry catch of the bream and a small, glistening eel concealed under his jacket, when the distant sound of a scream pricked his ears. His gaze was drawn to the sight, up the valley, of black smoke creeping skywards and lingering in a brooding cloud. He understood immediately what it meant. Evictions. Harris, Burrell and their men were throwing the cottiers onto the mercies of the world. He was pondering with dread how many weeks it might be before they themselves were evicted when a voice startled him.

'Please sir. Please, in the name o' God help me.'

The frail female voice froze him to the spot. His first fleeting thought was that no one had ever addressed him as 'sir' before. He looked back to the track where a woman had risen from behind a rock. For a moment he believed God or Satan had again given life to the pitiful wretch he'd buried on the hillside earlier that day and felt a trickle of piss gliding down the inside of his leg. She was about thirty and wore the familiar mask of the wasted, along with a black scarf and a ragged dress of dark blue. In her bare arms she clutched a child of maybe six. The woman moved towards him with a pitiful gait, each step steeped in pain. He stood still.

'They've thrun us out...everyone...me home. This little one is all I have left. Me babies are dead. Me husband, he went te England te work. Please have mercy,' she wept.

'I can't help you, I've nothing.'

'Please, sir, please, I beg ye. Tim went te England. Their harvest is near done now. He'll be home with money and I'll repay any kindness.'

'I haven't anything.' He turned to leave.

The woman's wail pitched higher, panic hastening her words. 'Please, if we can only get te Westport. He'll come. She'll die soon if I don't feed her. Me name is Maebh Connor. Maebh Connor. From Glenummera, up yonder. Maebh Connor.'

Owen tried to compel himself to flee but couldn't manage it.

'Maebh Connor,' she whispered again, her voice losing hope. She sank to her knees and with horror he believed she was about to grovel for his charity, but instead she simply sat back on her heels and rested her head against her daughter's.

Owen realised he could hear his own breathing. He glanced over his shoulder up towards his home and then pulled the tiny eel from its hiding place.

'This is all I have.'

She looked up at the proffered food, reached out and snatched it. Owen watched as she bit directly into the raw flesh. She chewed and spat the mush into her hand, then began to push the half-chewed fish between the child's lips. The girl moaned and coughed, parted her lips and allowed her mother press the morsels onto her tongue.

'I have to go.'

He turned away and set off up the hill as quickly as his bony legs would permit. He thought he heard the woman call something out to him, but it was carried away on the cool evening breeze that accompanied him up the hillside.

***

As he approached the cottage through the deepening gloom, he could spy the flickering of a candle between the cracks in the half-rotted wooden door. With pride, he pulled the fish from beneath his jacket and held it aloft as he stepped through.

Thomas sat by the far wall, Sally cradled in his arms. His father sat on their sole three-legged stool, staring blankly into the empty hearth. Owen felt an instant chill as he stepped into the space, his arm slowly drooping as though the weight of the fish was too much to bear.

'She's gone,' Thomas said.

'But I've brought food,' Owen said pathetically, as if that could right anything. His father never stirred.

'She died an hour ago.' Thomas hugged his sister tighter as though afraid someone would steal her from him.

The string slipped unknowingly through Owen's fingers, the fish making a slapping sound against the hardened earth of the floor.

Thomas sniffed, stroking Sally's matted hair. 'You should have been here.'

'I went to get food.'

Thomas looked up and Owen saw rage in his brother's eyes. 'She liked you the best. And ye ran away.'

Owen fell to his knees and reached out to touch his dead sister. 'I went to find food,' he pleaded, tears spilling freely down his face.

'Ye left her dyin' te us,' his brother muttered bitterly.

'I didn't. I–'

'No food could have saved her. Ye knew she'd be dead when ye came back.'

'Why are you saying that? I wouldn't have gone if–'

'She was callin' for ye.'

Owen wept bitterly. 'Sally…'

Michael Joyce spoke then without turning his head or raising his eyes. He continued to stare into the blackened ashes of the hearth.

'We'll bury her in the morning,' he said.

Chapter 2

Achill Island is a treeless place. There are mountains beyond mountains lying against the sky, heather clad or mossgrown; there are small lakes lying at the foot of mountains or between mountains; there are dreary expanses of bog stretching for miles on each side of the road between us and the mountains, and rising out of the bog are wee bits of fields and most horrible habitations.

–*The Letters of 'Norah' on Her Tour Through Ireland*, Margaret McDougall, 1882

I may mention that Mr Boycott is a Norfolk man, the son of a clergyman, and was formerly an officer in the 39th Regiment. On his marriage he settled on the Island of Achill, and farmed there until he was offered some land agencies. After some twenty years' residence in Achill, he elected to take a farm on the mainland.

–Bernard H Becker, special correspondent of *The Daily News*, October 1880

April 1856

Captain Charles Cunningham Boycott dismounted his bay thoroughbred and landed on the Achill earth with a jubilant bounce, turning to observe as his brother, Arthur, galloped to a sliding stop ten yards away.

'Major Boycott, I believe I was twelve the last time you defeated me,' he laughed, face bright with the flush of victory.

Arthur, effulgent in his uniform of scarlet tails adorned with golden epaulets, shared the lightness of the moment and chuckled as he dismounted.

'You truly are a scoundrel, Charles. You knew full well when you challenged me that my Hanoverian was no match for your beast. This is an army horse, not a racehorse.'

Annie Boycott watched from the window as her husband Charles, Arthur's younger brother by two years, became incensed, the grin rushing from his face, shoulders sitting back as though an affront had been done to him. In the two years since their marriage she'd witnessed his abrupt mood swings and bouts of temper only too often.

'Are you suggesting I cheated?'

Annie was pleased to observe that Arthur's ebullient good humour doused the spark of Charles's emotion, as he slapped him on the shoulder and bellowed a hearty laugh.

'Charles, you really do take these things too seriously.'

A young stable hand approached and loitered, his cap clutched in front of his waist, eyes to the ground, clothing threadbare and filthy. Eventually Charles became aware of his presence and handed him the reins, barking something at the youth that was unintelligible to Annie, although she did notice a grimace flit across Arthur's face. They turned and approached the house and, anxious not to be observed peeking, Annie retreated, as quickly as her heavily pregnant form would permit, towards an armchair. She gathered her crochet things and looked up in feigned surprise as they entered the room.

'Annie!' Arthur roared, never a man to observe strict formalities. He held his arms wide as he strode across the room, Annie requiring both hands to push herself up as she rose to greet him. Her brother-in-law was a broad-shouldered, tall man, quite unlike her husband, yet his embrace was gentle and considerate of her condition. She laughed at his jollity and the refreshing air of honesty with which he could fill a room. She had been so looking forward to his visit. Even the limited social contact she'd had on Achill had been curtailed as her pregnancy advanced, and the brightness of Arthur's character would provide a pleasant contrast to Charles's reserve.

'My, oh my, Arthur. A major, no less.'

'Oh never mind me, look at you! As beautiful as ever you were. I believe that the Atlantic air has made you sixteen again.'

Annie sat, blushing despite herself. 'Sixteen indeed. More like a basking shark.'

Charles tapped his cane against the floor. 'Enough of this nonsense, Arthur. You and your smooth tongue. It caused you no end of trouble with Father.'

'I know it only too well, Charles.'

Charles yanked the cord to summon the housemaid, Deirdre, who appeared promptly.

'Bring tea for Mrs Boycott and a decanter of brandy, girl.'

Deirdre curtsied and fled without a word, and Arthur raised his eyebrows at the sharpness in his brother's voice. Annie dropped her gaze from his and pretended to straighten the folds of her dress over her knee.

Both men took armchairs, Charles sitting forward, his cane clutched upright between his feet. His face was suddenly alive with anticipation.

'So, Arthur. How was it? The Crimea, I mean?'

Arthur's boyish grin vanished. 'Really Charles, I don't wish to be rude, but if you don't mind I'd rather not discuss the war. Perhaps another time.'

Charles looked at Annie in search of support for his mild indignation but she quickly turned away and regarded Arthur from the edge of her vision. She was aware that twenty thousand young British men had perished in that terrible war, many through tactical blundering. She rushed to move the conversation along.

'How is Emily? She must be a young lady by now?' Annie asked of the men's sister.

Arthur's smile returned. 'Sixteen and very pretty. Quite the book reader. I believe she wishes to pursue a profession.'

'How wonderful.'

'Absolute rot. Father would have no time with such nonsense. I hope you've done your level best to dissuade her, Arthur.'

'Charles. I've been away for two years. And Father has gone to his heavenly reward. So I'm afraid if Emily, or William or Frances for that matter, decide on a thing there's little to be done. Anyway, it's not so rare these days, women taking a profession.'

Charles grunted dismissively. 'Where is that maid?'

'I'm afraid Charles doesn't like change. He believes in "the constancy of order", as he calls it,' Annie remarked.

'And I'm right!'

A gentle rapping on the door preceded Deirdre's entry. After a sharp reprimand from Charles for her slowness, she skittered away, tears near to the surface. Annie closed her eyes, fearful they would lose Deirdre, not least because she might need the girl's help as the day of the child's birth drew near, but also because they'd gone through four maids since their marriage.

'Do you know, Annie, I still cannot quite believe that my scoundrel of a brother persuaded a girl of your beauty to marry him. How on earth did he accomplish it?' Arthur said, handing Annie a cup of tea.

Annie laughed unconvincingly and dropped her gaze. She'd had occasion herself to wonder how he'd accomplished it. The truth of it was that while she had found some degree of contentment in her marriage, it was far from the fulfilling relationship of which she'd dreamt. His regiment had been posted to Queen's County, where she had then lived with her parents, and she had been first attracted to his uniform, his gentlemanly ways and his ambition. Her parents had thought him a fine prospect from a respectable background and so their influence had hastened her up the aisle at the age of nineteen, quite before she'd known where she was.

She forced herself to enthusiasm. 'Oh, you'd be surprised how charming he was. And he promised me that one day we'd be like a lord and lady of our very own manor. What girl could resist?'

The talk turned to the intervening years since Arthur had last seen them on their wedding day. Arthur's good spirits were infectious and Annie became effusive in telling humorous tales of their honeymoon in France and Italy. Her enthusiasm betrayed the remembered excitement of young lovers first granted the freedom to indulge their passions and she reddened a little when she glimpsed the smile on Arthur's lips. Yet the memory of those very early days was precious to her, when Charles had for once surrendered his innate reserve and opened his heart, at least a little, and in that respect the honeymoon was wonderful, new experiences of the mind and body tripping over themselves to delight, terrify and educate her.

Through all of this Charles sat with a vaguely embarrassed expression, yet

Annie could tell that there was a hint of pride in his occasional dismissive grunts, a satisfaction taken that he, the younger and less handsome sibling, was capable of impressing a woman so. Such was the nature of men, of boys, certainly of brothers.

'And how did you find things when you returned to, well, to this remote outpost of the empire?' Arthur smiled, unfastening the top buttons on his tunic.

'Well, I have to say that I was startled at the energy with which Charles set about the business of managing this estate, such a passion to succeed. Isn't that right, Charles?'

She was keen to entice him into the conversation, as she was fearful of being too open, he being of such a private nature. But on this occasion he seemed keen to impress.

'Well, I've always believed that if one wishes to succeed in an enterprise one must devote oneself to it with discipline and single-mindedness. Two thousand acres and sixty tenants demands a great degree of dedication.'

'Sounds like the Charles I've always known,' Arthur chuckled.

Charles rose with a decisive tap of the cane. He pulled his watch chain free of his jacket. 'And on that subject it's almost six o'clock and I still have work to do. If you'll forgive me, brother, I'll leave you in the good hands of my wife.'

Arthur rose and Charles snapped a military salute as though still a captain, a position he'd vacated three full years ago. Arthur returned the gesture and his brother spun on his heels and exited without further exchange.

'Charles still pines for his days in the army, I'm afraid.'

'Still wants to play at soldiers,' Arthur said reflectively as he watched his brother through the window, marching with purpose down the path. He turned to Annie, his expression abruptly serious. 'It can't have been easy for you, these last few years.'

Annie stiffened a little, then shrugged away his concern. 'Achill? Oh I know it's remote, but it's very beautiful. Just wait until you see the cliffs at Croaghaun. They truly are spectacular, highest in Europe some say. And Moyteoge Head is …'

'I'm not just referring to the island, Annie. I do hope Charles has been...' he stumbled over his words and Annie guessed he was about to drift into a well-meaning, but ill-judged heart-to-heart about their marriage and feared she might find herself in a position of acute embarrassment. She struggled to rise before Arthur could continue.

'Arthur, if you don't mind, I need to lie down for a time. If you would call Deirdre for me and perhaps assist me towards my room, she'll see to your needs.'

'Of course. You're worn out trying to entertain a fool soldier.'

'On the contrary, Arthur, I'm so pleased you're here. Charles is away from the house so frequently that when he returns I think for a moment a stranger has entered my home,' Annie said jokingly.

'Yes. I can understand that,' Arthur replied, but the smile, she noted, was absent from his tone.

***

Deirdre helped her to undress and she lay on the bed in her chemise, relieved to be free of the constrictions of her clothes; though they were designed for maternity wear, fashion and decorum still demanded a certain rigidity. The maid then arranged a jug of water and a bowl on the dresser and checked that the bourdaloue was conveniently placed beside the bed. Annie observed the girl as she fussed about without comment, gaze perpetually fixed in a downward slant. She was a timid, homely girl with a coarse complexion, and was missing several teeth. And despite being relatively well fed in her capacity as housemaid, she remained as thin as a rake, a legacy of a childhood lived during the famine.

'Thank you, Deirdre. That will be fine. Please go and inquire if our guest needs anything before preparing dinner.'

Deirdre curtsied silently and turned to leave.

'Deirdre...'

The girl stopped in the doorway.

'Deirdre...please don't become too upset when Mr Boycott raises his voice. He doesn't mean any harm. It's his army training, you see...he...' she was at a loss where to go, unsure even that she should make excuses for Charles with a servant, yet she was keen to retain Deirdre's services. The maid gave an uncomfortable nod, then withdrew.

Annie heaved a sigh and closed her eyes, opening them an instant later in response to a kick from within. She pulled up her chemise, exposing her drawers and the taut curve of her pregnant form. Her hand felt cool against the warm skin as she searched for contact with the unborn child. And there it was again. A gentle tap beneath her palm. Her own flesh and blood, not yet born to the world yet reaching out to her. Annie's smile turned to an audible laugh and then almost as quickly to a sob, yet she was at a loss to tell if she felt happiness or sadness. Her emotions had been chaotic these past months, but the doctor had assured her that during pregnancy a woman's mood was apt to shift with the frequency of the Achill winds.

The truth was that her emotional confusion had begun soon after she had married. Even now as she lay looking out through the grey evening light at the boggy field in front of their home, she found it hard to grasp she was where she was: married and pregnant. It seemed like she could simply blink and she would be a girl of twelve again staring out the window of her parents' fine country home with a view of their estate of some nine thousand lush, fertile acres – and not leased like this barren Achill Island earth, but owned by her family for centuries. Oh, the happy years she had spent there in the company of her sisters and brothers, or the times her father, Victor Dunne, had brought her along as he toured the tenants' homes. Quite unlike her husband, he had always treated the tenants with respect, and with great charity during those terrible famine years. But when she had witnessed the hideous suffering of others on neighbouring estates she felt a profound guilt at their wealth.

How she missed her parents now – how she wished her mother could have travelled to Achill and kept her company as her time drew near. But her mother had been ill these past weeks with an infection of the lungs sufficient to keep her bed-bound.

Through the walls she heard the sound of muffled voices. It wasn't Charles, whose voice carried through walls of any thickness, but probably Arthur talking to Deirdre. There was a clang, as though an enamel basin had been dropped, after which Arthur said something and she heard Deirdre giggling, the first time she had heard the girl actually laugh. Arthur, she reflected, was so unlike Charles it was hard to credit they had the same father and mother. As different as leaf and stone. Looks, temperament, tastes, all so at odds. Their only points of commonality being, as far as she could tell, that they each had a military connection and both had lengthy, twirling moustaches, but this hardly counted. Arthur was much the taller. At over six feet he positively towered over Charles's five feet, eight inches. In terms of looks, he towered no less, having been blessed with handsome, manly looks and blue, gentle eyes. Charles was neither handsome nor ugly, simply in between, unremarkable. And, as she was learning, he was a small man in so many other ways.

As she listened to Deirdre's voice, Annie considered that it was the brothers' natures that most set them apart, for her husband would never allow such familiarity with a servant. Arthur was charming, charitable and gregarious. Charles usually concealed any feelings he might have within a shield, only rarely lowering his defences, such as those early days of their courtship and the precious few times on their honeymoon. Or when she had told him she was bearing his child. As the months passed, he'd increasingly existed in a closed world where order and discipline were paramount and no quarter given to the enemy, whom she often suspected included most of the rest of humanity.

She heard a door close followed by Deirdre's footfalls and then there was silence but for the spits of rain that had begun to pepper her window. The baby kicked again. She wondered if, when the child came, she might be granted sight of another chink in Charles's armour, a fleeting beat of his heart that she could share. Perhaps, she prayed, the child's presence might open his heart as never before. She had heard such things were possible.

Annie closed her eyes and fell asleep.

***

Several days passed before the weather improved sufficiently to reveal the island in its natural glory. Charles, who had been avoiding giving him the grand tour, citing the demands on his time, finally agreed after his elder brother's repeated requests, yet Arthur had the distinct impression he was an inconvenience.

Their path took them in a winding curve up the steeply sided Croaghaun Mountain across a landscape of uneven, boggy earth and rock and Arthur quickly realised why his brother had selected a sturdy, agile Irish Draught horse for the journey. A number of times his Hanoverian almost stumbled, unused as it was to the terrain. The sky above was a mosaic of blue dotted with puffy clumps of white cloud and the April air felt crisp. The Atlantic wind had abated and the mist being absent, he was afforded a magnificent view across the expanse of Clew Bay towards Mayo's Sheeffry Hills and the mountains of County Galway beyond.

'It's majestic, Charles, this place. I fancy there are few places on this earth that could compete with such a canvas of sea, land and sky.'

His brother grunted. 'I need to make a brief stop,' he said.

Arthur's musings on the scenery were interrupted by sight of a crudely built cottage set into the hillside ahead. It appeared to be a single room, windowless and with a thatch of gorse through which a plume of smoke rose into the bright sky. A low wall of rough stones defined a field in front of it in which a lone man toiled, his back to them. As they approached, the peasant turned and Arthur recognised alarm on his face. A woman in a soiled dress stepped from the cottage and from within he could hear an infant's cry. Despite the natural wonder of the place, Arthur was struck by how different a view these people would take of their surroundings. The tiny field would barely support the needs of one man, let alone his wife and child, and he imagined every mouthful of food they ate must be teased and coaxed from the unfertile earth.

'Captain Boycott, sir,' the man said, removing his cloth cap. He threw a nervous glance in Arthur's direction.

'Kilbane. Clearly our conversation on the subject of your sheep made no impression upon you. Yesterday the wall bordering my turnip field was disturbed and two rows of new plants were either eaten or trampled. There were sheep tracks everywhere and they led directly up here.'

'But sir, there are five tenants with sheep on the mountainside. And besides, sir, with respect…' the man said, an audible tremble in his voice, Arthur observed.

'What?'

'Well, sir, ye graze a herd of sheep yerself...'

Charles rose in his stirrups, his face turning red. 'How dare you suggest that my animals were responsible! My sheep-herders assure me my flock was nowhere in the vicinity. And as I have informed you, the tracks led in this direction.'

'But I checked me four animals last evening and they were on the western slope, near the cliff. That's more than a mile–'

'Don't you dare contradict me.' Arthur's brother's voice carried far across the hillside. 'The penalty will be a fine of two days' extra rent, the first day to compensate me, the second as a deterrent to you.'

The tenant took several steps forward, his hand running over his head, alarm written across his face. He made a desperate appeal for leniency. 'But sir, Captain Boycott, I can barely meet the rent now and feed me wife and child.' He gestured towards the cottage. 'Please don't take the food from their mouths.'

Charles wheeled his horse about and looked over his shoulder at the man. 'You should have thought of that before you let your sheep roam wild.'

As the horse turned Charles found himself subjected to the admonishing gaze of his brother. For a brief moment the two men were children again in Norfolk, Arthur reproaching him for some ill-treatment of the local peasant children or for disrespecting the men who laboured for their father. Charles's resolve seemed to weaken and he dropped his gaze. He brought the horse about and looked down at Kilbane. 'This will be your final warning. One more incursion and the fine will stand, do you hear?'

'Thank ye, sir, thank ye.'

Charles grunted, kicked into the horse and took off up a barely discernible path, Arthur following with a shake of his head. The incident had revived uncomfortable memories of their father's domineering, intolerant nature.

Charles led the way, single file along the narrow track. They travelled in silence for several minutes before Charles spoke without looking back.

'I can sense your reproach, Arthur. You believe I was harsh with the man. But I have my reasons. The rules must be obeyed, discipline maintained, especially in an environment such as this. We're both military men. We both understand the absolute necessity of knowing one's station in life and acting accordingly.'

Arthur almost laughed aloud at his brother's categorisation of them both as 'military men'. Their backgrounds in that regard could hardly be more different. He'd left home to join the army aged seventeen to escape their father's determination that he should enter the ministry and follow in his footsteps. He'd travelled the world, encountering countless cultures, learning to respect them, seeing unspeakable horrors and unwavering courage from comrade and foe alike. With Arthur gone, Charles had become the focus of their father's ambition, but the reality was that Charles didn't have the intellect to succeed with the theological studies required. A visiting brigadier had persuaded their father that the army could provide the self-discipline that would help Charles stay true to the path to God. Having little or no say in the matter, Charles was enlisted in the 39th On Foot regiment at eighteen and remained in the army for three years. He never saw action, and hardly ventured beyond the drill yard aside from his posting to Ireland when he met Annie. But he did embrace army discipline like a man possessed. Essentially, Arthur reflected, the army had broadened his own horizons immeasurably and narrowed Charles's even further.

'The thing of it is, Charles, you're not in the army now. And your tenants are hardly the enemy.'

No response was forthcoming and the matter was dropped.

Their route took them above Lough Accorymore, a beautiful lake nestling in the mountainside. Charles paused briefly to point out the almost palatial Corrymore House below, where he hoped one day to reside. But Arthur found he had to muster enthusiasm in his response. Up still they went, the unevenness and gradient of the ground forcing them to dismount, until finally the land vanished and Arthur found himself staring out at the vastness of the Atlantic Ocean. He secured the horse to a rock and walked to the edge, his brother coming to his side a moment later as he stared dizzily down at the sea crashing with ferocity against the rocks two thousand feet below.

'The western edge of the British Empire, Arthur. Incredible when you consider it, really. One could travel east from this spot all the way to New Zealand and still be on British soil. The magnificent order of it all.'

Arthur turned and regarded him. He could tell that his brother took a personal pride in the part he played daily in maintaining that order. The view, if anything, exceeded what he'd experienced that morning but the joy of it was lost on him, the earlier encounter with the tenant having left an unsettling feeling in his gut.

'A tiny barren island on the most western fringe of the empire. Yes, Charles, you truly have isolated yourself from the world,' he said as he turned away.

***

After another of her now-daily afternoon naps, Annie awoke to the sound of knocking on her door, the threads of vague dreams of her mother unravelling as she realised that the room had grown dark and the air had chilled. She tried to sit up.

'Who is it?'

'Deirdre, ma'am, with your tea.'

The girl entered bearing a lamp, poured the tea and handed Annie a cup.

'What time is it, Deirdre?' Annie asked through a yawn.

'Seven, ma'am.'

'Are Mr Boycott and his brother ready to dine?'

'The gentleman's in the parlour, ma'am. Mr Boycott's just returned.'

'Only now?'

The maid shifted uncomfortably on her feet.

'Thank you, Deirdre.'

Arthur had been with them a week and yet the three of them had barely shared a meal together thanks to her husband's insistence on working until the last rays of sunlight had drained from the sky. Charles had made no effort to entertain his own brother and at times she suspected he'd tired of his presence, perhaps unable to bear Arthur's broad-mindedness and light-hearted manner. But then he was much the same when anyone visited. Even when her parents were here he'd seemed at the edge of his patience until they'd left. On a number of occasions she and Arthur had dined together and while she found his company most agreeable, once or twice talk had again drifted towards her marriage and she had hastened away from the subject. Why, she did not know. Perhaps because he was a man and men were not famed for their understanding of the female heart. Or was that simply an excuse she'd contrived? Was she embarrassed to reveal her fear that she had blundered terribly in marrying a man seemingly incapable of genuine love?

She washed and dressed, then walked towards the parlour, her gait awkward, a hand clutching at the underside of her belly as though to hold the baby inside. She was halted in the narrow hallway outside the room by the sound of somewhat upraised voices from within, their tones almost acerbic. Charles and Arthur were arguing. She lowered the lamp to a table, hesitated as her conscience was momentarily pricked, then leaned her ear close to the door.

***

'For God's sake, Charles, is there no Christian charity in your heart?'

'Charity and business don't mix, Arthur. You've been a soldier all your life, you've no idea of the realities of running a business, especially in a place like this.'

Arthur rose from his armchair and decanted a glass of brandy without bothering to ask his brother's leave. 'That's precisely it. The land here is extremely poor. As are the people who work it. And yet I've seen you treat them with contempt.'

Charles uttered a curt laugh. 'That's ridiculous. I no more hold the peasants in contempt than…than I could hold a sheep in contempt. I run this estate precisely according to the terms of the contracts of agreement. The peasants know what is expected of them, as do I. It's the pre-ordained way of life.'

Arthur sat again and stared at him. He sighed and shook his head. 'My God, Charles, you're turning into Father more and more each day.'

Charles raised his metal-tipped cane and cracked it down on the wooden floor. 'And what's wrong with that, brother?' he snapped.

Arthur fell silent for a time, twirling the brandy glass slowly in his hands as he stared reflectively into the amber liquid. Although their father had been dead some three years, the memory of his strict authoritarianism was still fresh in Arthur's mind. William Boycott, vicar, and Patron of the Living of St Mary's Church in the village of Burgh St Peter, had been a man of rigid self-discipline who had tried to impose his moral philosophy on every member of his family and congregation by means of verbal and physical intimidation. He had no time for anyone that he referred to as 'beyond his class or cloth', and treated the men and women who laboured in the small bakery and pottery workshop they kept as one would treat beasts of burden. Their labourers and tenants had once been so angered by his treatment that a near riot had ensued and over a hundred people had besieged the rectory before order had been restored. Several generations back, their family name had been Boycatt, French Huguenots who had fled the repression of their Calvinist beliefs by the Catholic Church, or so their father had reminded them incessantly. William Boycott not only preached strict Calvinist doctrine from the pulpit, or at least his narrow interpretation of it, but each day their family was told that only the special few had been predestined for salvation, relegating all others to the status of something less than human. Any questioning or dissent was rewarded with the birch and the strap.

Arthur frowned at his brother's readiness to leap to the man's defence. He recalled that as a child Charles had been taciturn, preferring his own company. But there were times when they played together in the meadows of South Norfolk, or spent long hours fishing on the banks of the Waveney River, when Charles had opened up, laughed, talked excitedly of adventures beyond the horizon that they might share when they grew to manhood. And then their father's shadow would loom over them and Charles would retreat within himself like a clam. Self-isolation increasingly became his sanctuary.

It was their father's passing and Charles's substantial share of the will that had provided him with sufficient funds to leave the army and take the lease on Achill. He had hoped that somehow, with their father's death, Charles might begin to find a better path. And when he met Annie it seemed for a time that this might come to pass. Her warmth of character, intelligence and generosity seemed to open the doors within Charles that their father had slammed shut. Then they'd moved to Achill and Charles had found himself in a position of authority and responsibility. Perhaps his only means of coping was to resort to his father's ways. And when he thought about his brother now, Arthur could feel only pity.

'Charles,' he said softly, 'our father was a very bigoted man and a tyrant.'

'How dare you speak of Father in that mann–'

'Oh stop it, Charles. You know I'm right. He turned Mother into a trembling shadow. I could almost see relief in her face when he went to his grave.'

'That is outrageous!' Charles rose and took several steps towards Arthur, levelling his cane at his brother's face. 'Withdraw that remark and apologise immediately, sir.'

Arthur didn't move. He met Charles's gaze and then a smile slowly crept into the corners of his mouth. 'Charles, do you really think you can bully *me*?'

Charles slammed the cane down hard. 'I won't have Father spoken of in–'

'Oh Father, Father, Father!' Arthur was abruptly on his feet, towering down over Charles. 'The great William Boycott, Patron of the Living,' he said with a mocking sneer. 'Patron of the intolerant, the despotic, the supercilious, more's the truth.'

Startled at the sudden vehemence in Arthur's voice, Charles took an involuntary step backwards, but didn't respond. He stood there open-mouthed, too shocked to speak.

'The people of the Burgh St Peter's feared and despised him in equal measure. So did our mother. And Emily and Frances and William. And so did I. That's why I left to join the army at so young an age. I didn't wish to be infected by his pathetic dogmatism. And at least Mother found some peace in her declining years.'

'What are you saying? That you were pleased at his death?'

'Yes, damn it!' He almost expected Charles to lunge at him in rage, well aware of the ferocity of his brother's temper. But he remained silent and instead presented his back to Arthur.

'I will never forgive you for that hateful statement.'

'You fool, Charles. You imbecile. You refuse to see the truth of what is happening in your own home. And if you continue along that road you will surely end up as Father did, despised by those closest to him.'

Charles turned then, his expression one of puzzlement and suspicion rather than rage. 'What are you talking about?'

'Annie, of course.'

'Annie? What has she said to you?'

Arthur laughed without humour. 'She's said nothing. She's too loyal or selfless to speak. But any fool could see how utterly lonely she is. Not only have you isolated yourself from the world here on Achill but you've even succeeded in isolating yourself from the woman who loves you and whose love you purport to requite.'

'That's preposterous.'

'Is it, Charles? I can see it in her eyes every time we speak. She deserves better.'

'I refuse to discuss matters of such a private nature with you. To be perfectly frank, our marriage is none of your damn business!' Charles made to leave the room.

'Charles, wait.'

He paused and Arthur heaved a sigh and forced himself, if only for diplomacy's sake, to become penitent.

'Charles, forgive me. I apologise for the statements I made regarding Father. They were said in the heat of the moment and I withdraw them.'

His brother regarded him as though weighing the sincerity of his words.

'I know how much you admired him,' Arthur continued, 'I've had enough enemies on the battlefield and I have no wish to make one of my brother.'

After some seconds his brother's features softened. 'Very well. But I'll thank you to not intrude on my private life.'

'Very well, Charles, but I must say one last thing. If you truly love Annie, I suggest you tell her so. Before it's too late.'

***

An awkward silence lingered over their meal that evening, even with Arthur mustering his best efforts to engage Annie in bright chatter about the months and years of mothering that lay ahead. Her husband, clearly distracted, barely uttered two sentences.

Annie had heard almost their entire exchange, stepping across the hall to the safety of their bedroom a moment before Charles opened the door. Her improper eavesdropping had yielded some reward, although she was already quite familiar with their father's legacy. What had surprised her was the vehemence with which Arthur had derided the man, and his accurate observation of her dissatisfaction with her marriage, which she had done her best to conceal for appearances' sake.

Later, as she lay in the darkness of their bedroom, she prayed that Arthur's prompting might produce some change in Charles, however small. The man who now slept soundly by her side had at least been made aware of her feelings, though in all likelihood his stubbornness would result in denial that any problem existed. She felt a moment of despair well up in her heart and then a brief stab of pain in her abdomen. She clutched at the point of pain just below her naval and moaned softly in discomfort.

Immediately he was alert and sat up. He reached out and touched her arm.

'Annie, dear. Are you ill? Is it the child?'

Annie was shocked at his alertness. She sought his face in the blackness of the room but could discern only a vague outline.

'No. I'm fine, Charles. This baby isn't ready to see the world just yet. It's just a small pain. I believe they are to be expected.'

'Very well. Goodnight then,' he whispered hesitantly and she felt the weight of his body press into the mattress once more.

The cold stillness of the night descended again. She sensed his wakefulness and wondered what thoughts he entertained. Was he contemplating the baby's arrival and speculating on its future? Or was his head, as usual, filled with columns of profit and loss? Or, given the argument that had passed earlier, was he reflecting on his father and his life under the man's fierce hand?

'Annie?'

His whisper, so soft she wondered for a moment if she'd imagined it, caused her to turn her head towards him.

'Yes, Charles?'

She felt a brief swell of hope in her breast, of expectation.

'I...'

Somewhere off in the folds of the mountain a wind swirled and growled, its sound lonely and desolate in the far-off darkness. Some seconds passed before he spoke again.

'I...nothing really...I merely wanted you to rouse me should you experience any further pain.'

'Of course, Charles.'

There were many forms of pain, she wanted to tell him, but she said no more to him that night.

***

Unused as he was to idleness, Arthur decided to avail of the following day's bright spring sunshine to escape the confines of the house, and at breakfast asked Charles if he would be good enough to guide him part of the way towards Saddle Head. His request was met with a frown.

'I really have rather a lot to do today, Arthur. Perhaps another time.'

'Such a shame not to take advantage of the weather, Arthur,' Annie sympathised.

Arthur gave her a confident smile and surreptitiously winked, then turned to his brother. 'Charles, I have some knowledge of the terrain but I wish you merely to guide me to the gap overlooking Lough Nakeeroge. I can find my way from there. That won't inconvenience you at all, will it?'

Arthur's forthright tone left his brother in no doubt that he wasn't about to take no for an answer. He muttered an irritated 'very well', rose from the table and stomped out.

Arthur grinned at Annie. 'Since we were children I've found that sometimes with Charles it's simply a matter of letting him know who's in charge, standing up to him. Remember that, Annie dear.'

Annie, somewhat surprised at the brief interchange, returned his smile.

'I will, Arthur.'

He kissed his sister-in-law on the cheek and hurried out to the horse pen before Charles's impatience got the better of him. He followed his brother on a path to the north-east around the lower slopes of Croaghaun Mountain, leaving Charles to his business after several miles (much to his brother's relief, he sensed) and continuing alone towards Saddle Head, where he luxuriated in the glory of the uninhabited landscape, gazing in awe back at the towering sea cliffs that plunged towards the indefatigable Atlantic waves. Much as he treasured the experience, he could not help but feel that it would be so much finer shared with another.

He felt a degree of pity for Charles because, although he might look upon such a scene, he would never truly see it or feel it stirring his soul as others might. Indeed, his brother seemed to regard the world through narrow eyes that never really saw anything but the fulfilment of his own purpose and ambition. His inability to perceive nature's beauty paled by comparison to his lack of appreciation for the plight of those who filled his life, and not only Annie, but the unfortunate peasants who had to endure his antipathy. Thanks to their father, Charles believed that the will of God had pre-determined his place in the world, a belief that sadly deprived him of the ability to ever imagine that world through others' eyes and granted him the luxury of an existence almost empty of compassion.

As he stood there a tall ship appeared in the distance beyond Achill Head, bound no doubt for America. Despite the famine's end some years beforehand, the exodus of Ireland's sons and daughters had continued on a massive scale, now escaping not famine, but the insidious grip of poverty. And he was reminded again that his own brother played an eager part in maintaining that hold. He sighed, growing weary of his own thoughts, and drew his horse about. It was time to leave this place, leave Achill. Poor Annie, he thought as he carefully picked a path across the uneven ground. He felt a tinge of guilt at abandoning her to her life here, to a life with his brother. He could only hope that Charles might mellow with maturity, but it was a vain hope, he suspected.

An hour later he came upon Charles again near the village of Dooagh, as he needlessly reminded an unfortunate tenant that he faced eviction if his rent was not paid on time. At a second cottage he informed the woman of the house that two of her chickens were to be confiscated as the birds had encroached on his fields and pecked at his seedlings. The woman's shrill pleas for leniency were waved away.

Clearly their argument the previous evening had had little effect. As they trotted away, Arthur's reticence finally prompted Charles to speak.

'You still believe I'm harsh with my charges, brother.'

Arthur could find no response that would not betray his continued disquiet.

'Look, Arthur, maintaining order out here demands the strictest observance of the rules. I've no wish to burden these people unnecessarily but if I let one tenant off lightly I'll have to let another. So I treat all of them with equality and they respect that. You know, I've only evicted a handful of tenants. Others have evicted many more. That's because my tenants know precisely what is expected of them. I can't say fairer than that.'

'That's all very well, but besides the stick, haven't you heard of the carrot?'

'Liberal nonsense. If you wish a peasant to do your bidding there is only one motivation they…what the blazes?'

Arthur turned in the direction of his brother's gaze and saw a rider approach at a gallop from the west of the island.

'I believe that's Cromwell! My finest animal. And by God that's the stable hand riding her into the ground. I'll have his skin!'

They watched as the rider veered off the road below and moved towards them.

'He's coming this way, Charles.'

A few seconds later the breathless youth pulled the animal to a lengthy skid, almost colliding with Charles's horse, causing it to recoil.

'What are you doing on that damned horse, you ignorant whelp?'

'I'm sorry sir, but the doctor ordered me te take the animal and find ye.'

'The doctor?' Arthur asked with alarm.

'What's going on, boy?'

'We couldn't find ye, sir. Been looking for hours,' the youth blurted out, trembling from fear and exhaustion.

'Calm down, lad,' Arthur said, 'what is it?'

'It's Mrs Boycott, sir. There's something wrong I think.'

Charles' jaw dropped open and he snapped his head about towards his brother, eyes wide with alarm. He may not have been as demonstrable about his love as his wife might have wished, but in that moment Arthur saw how very real it was. His brother took flight with such abruptness and energy that he sideswiped the stable boy's animal and sent it tottering on its side into a ditch. Arthur hesitated enough to see that the youth was unharmed, then took off in pursuit, praying to God that Annie and the child had been the benefactors of His mercy.

***

Annie's memory of the past hours was of her small bedroom awash with blood, and of dread, pain and the sound of her own screams. She lay there now, exhaustion trying to pull her towards sleep. But she so dearly wanted, needed, to see her husband, for in this moment she knew she would see the truth of his nature. But he was nowhere to be found.

Barely had he and Arthur departed that morning when, seated at the dining room table, she had been engulfed by a wave of agonising cramps. There followed a warm rush of fluid between her legs and, to her horror, the sight of blood seeping through her dress. Her screams went unheard by Deirdre, who had gone to pump a bucket of water, and Annie had tried to stumble her way towards the bedroom, collapsing on the floor in the doorway, pain coursing through her body, tears and snot streaming down her face, panic overwhelming her. She was certain she would die in that spot. Then Deirdre was there, screaming herself, and Annie had a vague memory of seeing the metal bucket drop from the maid's grip, sending a wave of icy water splashing against her.

'The midwife, Deirdre,' she moaned as the girl tried to haul her towards the bed. 'Send the boy…don't leave me…'

The hours that followed were an anarchic mix of pain and nausea, drifting in and out of consciousness, faces whirling about her, voices, sheets soaked red. She had a distinct memory of being suddenly possessed of an irrational certainty that the infant would emerge a misshapen, deformed creature. Then at some point she was pushing, wrenching against the will of her body. Deirdre's ugly face, God forgive her for slighting the girl, was almost pressed to hers, crying out to her. And then it was over, a relief so indescribable, followed at once by a terrible fear for her child, her flesh and blood.

There was a man then, but not her husband, not Charles. A tall, refined man with a greying moustache. There were flashes of metal and cold, probing things, and she felt a terrible violation as she swayed between oblivion and the light and life of the room, all the time crying for an answer, desperate to know if her child had lived or died.

***

'This is your daughter, Charles. This is Mary.'

Annie smiled and pulled the swaddling cloth free of the newborn's head, revealing a puffy red scrunched-up face, a few strands of black hair matted to its skull. He stood by the bed and stared down at the infant, his face an unfamiliar mix of fear and anticipation.

'The doctor says she seems healthy. She surprised us all, coming early…'

Her husband leaned forward and swallowed mother and daughter in a gentle embrace and Annie felt moisture as his cheek pressed against hers. He then fell to his knees at the bedside and clasped at her hand. 'My God, Annie, I almost lost you, they say. I can never forgive myself for leaving you alone in the house with just the maid.'

For the first time she could recall, her husband's voice was trembling.

'You had no way of knowing, Charles, Mary came almost three weeks early. Here. Take your daughter.'

He pulled back. 'I don't know how…'

'Just hold her like this, support her head.'

Annie pressed the infant into his arms and the child made a sucking movement with its lips. He laughed almost inaudibly and Annie could see the joy in his face, a face rarely lightened by any of life's events. He touched the baby's cheek with his finger.

'A daughter. And you named her?' He looked up at Annie now.

'I hope you aren't upset, Charles. These past days I've dreamt of my mother again and again. No other name but my mother's seemed fitting. But if you wish to…'

He was shaking his head. 'My grandmother was Mary. It's a fine name, dear. Mary. Mary Boycott.'

He handed the child back, his pride evident.

'Charles. I must tell you. Something went wrong during the birth. The doctor said there was something amiss inside, some rare condition. We were lucky to survive. But he says I can't have another child. I'm so sorry, Charles. I can never give you a son.'

'We have a healthy daughter and I have a healthy wife. That is my only concern.'

Arthur was permitted a brief visit and was typically effusive about the infant and in his expressions of joy.

'We'll leave you to rest,' Charles whispered as they turned to depart. 'Besides, I really should see the doctor and midwife as I owe them for both your lives.'

'Actually Charles, one of your tenants, the Ruanes, also had a baby born to them this morning and the midwife was occupied there. She and the doctor only arrived after the birth to help with…with other things that needed to be done.'

'So how on earth…?'

Annie reached for the bell cord above her bed and a few moments later Deirdre stepped into the room. 'Deirdre, could you return Mary to her basket, like a good girl?'

Deirdre whisked across and did as requested.

'Charles, it is this girl here, Deirdre Feeney, that you must thank. She brought your daughter into the world. Had it not been for her we would both surely have perished. Deirdre delivered her younger sister's baby last year and attended many other births.'

Charles' mouth hung open as he stared at the maid, who stood stock-still, a look of terror on her face. After a time, he nodded firmly. 'Well, thank heavens she was here.'

Annie glanced at Arthur, who met her eyes with a smile. 'Charles,' she said.

'Yes?'

'I believe you'll want to thank Deirdre for what she did. And reward her accordingly,' Annie said with authority.

He shifted from one foot to the other, inhaled sharply and set his shoulders back. It seemed to take an age before he could bring himself to meet Deirdre's eyes.

'Deirdre,' he finally uttered with an accompanying cough. 'I wish to thank you for your assistance this day. I'll…I'll see you are…rewarded…in your wages.'

'Thank ye, sir. Thank ye,' she replied and scurried away.

Annie smiled and then felt her eyes grow suddenly heavy. She yawned.

'I'll leave you, Annie. Warmest congratulations again,' Arthur said softly.

'And my thanks to you, dear Arthur.'

His brother departed and as Annie slid down beneath the blankets, Charles peered into the basket once more.

'Mary,' he whispered. 'Mary.'

CHAPTER 3

In a neighbouring union a shipwrecked human body was cast on shore; a starving man extracted the heart and liver, and that was the maddening feast on which he regaled himself and perishing family.

–J Anderson, Rector and Vicar of Ballinrobe, County Mayo, *The Times*, 23 May 1849

It is indeed painful to consider the state of Ireland. In a land teeming with plenty and abundance we have a famine. More than two million Irishmen are starving while we export more provisions than would feed five times our population. Our state would be much improved were those who derive large incomes from this country to expend at least a portion of it among the people from whom they receive it.

–*The Anglo Celt*, 1 May 1846

October 1848

A leaden sky hung over them as they manoeuvred the body into the shallow, sodden grave. Appropriately, funereal clouds shrouded the mountaintops all around them in a sombre grey, and a drizzle, fine and penetrating, moulded their clothes to their bones.

Fr Lally lurched up the hillside, Tawnyard Lough a barely discernible backdrop in the mist. Like most of his flock, his frame was gaunt and ravaged and his progress was interrupted time and again by the weakness of malnourishment and pauses for heaving breaths. They were lucky to have him at all. His duties of late demanded his recital of the last rites at a rate beyond measure, calling him to the gravesides of young and old spread across the entire parish of Oughaval.

Thomas and Owen set about completing the interment of their father in the boggy earth just a stone's throw from their home. Michael Joyce had died two days earlier, leaving his sons but one possession each in the world, that of a brother. They took turns shovelling the brown earth into the grave, the exertion of every swing of the shovel bringing savage protestations from their bodies. The soft beat of the rain on the tattered blanket that served as their father's winding sheet made a sound that reminded Owen of the distant patter of approaching horses.

'Stop, Owen.'

Thomas had fallen to his knees beside the shallow grave. He reached out and laid a hand on the cloth, wet and sagging upon his father's face, searching for a final mortal link, a last sense of Michael Joyce as a man and not some disembodied spirit or, perhaps worse, nothing but rotting skin and bones. The tears came again then. So profuse had Thomas's weeping been these last days Owen wondered how he had not withered and shrivelled like a dead flower.

His own tears had subsided soon after the end, replaced by numbness and near-insentience. For hours he'd sat and stared into eternity, even wetting his breeches in his utter torpidity. Fearful for Owen's state of mind, Thomas had tried to return him to consciousness by striking him hard across the face and Owen had a faint recollection of lying on his back, his brother astride his chest, his face a mixture of rage and grief. Strange, but it was the taste of his own blood trickling from a split lip that finally awoke Owen from his stupor.

It had seemed so long since any taste had enlivened his tongue. It was the most nourishing thing to enter his gullet in days.

And so he came back to the land of the living, or at least the half-dead. Thomas told him that they must bury their father. He rose from the floor and looked about him, for a brief moment expecting to see his father, mother and sisters, but there was no retreat this time, no soporific curtain to hide behind. They were all dead except his brother. The room felt as hollow as his gut. But there would be no more tears, for the well had run dry.

Finally Thomas rose from the grave, wiped his face with the back of his sleeve and in a blink replaced his wretched, grief-stricken expression with one of anger, his teeth showing through barely parted lips. He then began hurriedly to shovel the earth over the shroud until the last of the corpse had vanished under the Mayo soil. Owen caught a fleeting glance of his brother's eyes ablaze with hatred. Owen's retreat had been into senselessness. He now saw that Thomas had chosen refuge in a much darker cavern where his only company would be malevolence and loathing.

'Jesus Christ!' Fr Lally's unusual taking of the Lord's name in vain broke their gaze and the brothers turned in his direction. The priest's chest was heaving, his hand clutching at his heart. 'Why in God's name didn't you bury him in the graveyard yonder?'

The priest was referring to the improvised cemetery that had been established on the valley floor where the others of their family had been laid to rest.

'Sorry Father,' said Owen weakly, 'we hadn't the strength to carry the body.'

The priest shook his head and looked about. 'Are you boys alone now?' he asked.

Thomas glared at him with undisguised contempt. 'How could we be alone when there are two of us?' He tossed his shovel away. It clanged against a rock.

'Thomas...' cautioned Owen.

But Fr Lally simply nodded and pulled a crucifix and a book of prayer from within the damp folds of his robes. 'Forgive me, lads, but time prevents me saying a mass for Michael. I must be in Leenane by nightfall.'

The brothers said nothing. The reality was that they wanted the heartbreaking ritual done with as soon as possible. The priest made the sign of the cross and they lowered their heads respectfully as he began to speak in a deliberately mournful enunciation.

'O God, by Your mercy rest is given to the souls of the faithful, be pleased to bless this grave. Appoint Your holy angels to guard it and set free from all the chains of sin the soul of him whose body is buried here, so that with all Thy saints he may rejoice in Thee forever.'

Fr Lally turned a few pages in his Bible, leaning over it to shield its fragile paper from the drizzle, then resumed, speaking in Latin.

'*Requiem æternam dona eis Domine; et lux perpetua luceat eis. Requiéscat in pace.*'

Thomas raised his head. 'What does it mean?'

'It means: Eternal rest grant unto him–'

'No,' Thomas interrupted. 'It's meaningless. Everything's meaningless. You and your God.' He guffawed as though the very notion was hilarious.

'Thomas. Stop.'

The priest was calm. He wiped his face clear of rain again. 'Sometimes our faith is tested sorely, Thomas. Your father would–'

'Tested? *Tested*?'

Owen seized his brother's arm, restraining him.

'I'll finish up and leave you to your grief.' Fr Lally stepped forward and looked directly across the grave at the young man who mocked him. 'Jesus said to them, "I am the bread of life. Whoever comes to me will never be hungry and whoever believes in me will never be thirsty."'

So cold and cynical was Thomas's expression as these words were spoken that Owen saw the priest hastily avert his gaze. He added a final line to his jumbled, expeditious rite. 'Michael Joyce, *In paradisum deducant te Angeli*. May angels lead you into paradise. Amen.' He made the sign of the cross over the grave and put away his book. Owen blessed himself, while Thomas stood impassively.

'Goodbye, lads,' Fr Lally said as he began to depart, casting thoughtful glances around at their small patch of land. 'You know, lads, Harris won't let you stay now. You'll be evicted. You have to go to the workhouse, it's your only chance to survive.'

'There'll be no workhouse and it's no business of yours what we do. We'll starve before we go there,' Thomas snapped.

The priest sighed. 'Then you'll starve,' he said and walked away.

***

The rain stopped during the night and Owen now sat on a rock bathed in milky morning sunshine, staring at the small wooden cross that marked his father's final resting place. He wasn't feeling tearful or angry or guilty, only the colossal apathy of the inevitable approach of death by starvation. Cramps gripped him again and he tightened his arms around his stomach, expelling rancid gas from his behind. He remained doubled over for some time, head between knees, eyes fixed on the muddy ground between his feet.

Thomas's voice disturbed him. 'The fuckin' smell of ye. Here.'

He looked up. Thomas held in his palm about seven blackberries. He studied them as though they were illusory; most of them looked half-rotten and none was larger than the tip of his small finger. He grabbed the berries and devoured them as one. As he felt the painful swallowing convulsion, a notion struck him and he looked up sharply.

'Did you have some?'

'Doesn't matter now, does it?' Thomas fixed him with a judgemental stare, then turned away.

Their ears were pricked by the sound of approaching horses and they looked to the east where the road wound around the curve of the mountain. Two riders appeared and rested their horses a few minutes, the beasts worn from the effort of the climb up the steep, mucky road. Thomas pulled Owen to his feet.

'It's Harris, the land agent, and some other bastard. Listen, we'll go te the field and pretend te be workin'. Father's away visitin' a sick relative.'

'But–'

'If he finds Father's dead he'll evict us right now and *we'll* be dead in a week.'

Owen was too weak to argue. Thomas pulled him by the arm to the wasted patch of land that still exuded the stench of the blight. The hillside was scarred with long ridges known as 'lazy beds' – the soil was so thin and peaty that to grow anything it was necessary to place a seed potato on the surface and fold a sod of turf over it – and it was across these ridges that the two now stumbled, surrounded by the withered, blackened stalks of the blighted potato crop. Owen stood there like a scarecrow for a few seconds until his brother pushed a spade into his hands.

'Pretend to dig.'

He walked a bit away and did likewise, both of them watching the men as they approached at a trot up the slope. Two bays, black manes and tails, all muscle and sweaty fur, carried the men to the Joyces' threshold. The beasts snorted as their masters pulled back on their reins, hooves dancing in the mud.

Owen recognised Harris at once, the other man he assumed to be Burrell, his lackey. He mustered his strength and tried to turn over a sod.

'You! Boy!' Harris called to Owen, he being the nearer. Thomas walked over and looked up at the land agent with his striking amber eyes, his face a mask as he struggled to contain his animosity. Harris sported long sideburns and both men had wide, wispy moustaches, their ends curled in the popular fashion of their class. Burrell wore a formal short riding jacket and a shiny bowler hat, while his master's attire consisted of bright jodhpurs, a black short-tailed jacket and top hat. Owen thought both of them looked as out of place on an Irish mountainside as a snowfall in July.

'You, then. What's your name, boy?'

'Thomas Joyce.'

'Yes, yes, and your father is Michael Joyce? Fetch him immediately, boy.'

Thomas snarled. 'My name is Thomas Joyce, not boy.'

Without hesitation Harris raised his riding crop and struck Thomas across the chest. The horse danced away a little at the movement as Thomas staggered back clutching at his breast, his face aflame. Owen found the energy to speak as Thomas weighed his spade in his hands as a potential weapon.

'Our father's away, sir. Leenane. A relative is ill.'

'Away, is he?' Harris chuckled over his shoulder at Burrell, who didn't smile. 'He'll be away a great deal more, I venture, if he doesn't have his rent next week. Tell him that, when he returns. If not I'll be back with a force of constables to serve you with a lawful notice of eviction.' Though he spoke in answer to Owen, his eyes never left Thomas and a supercilious grin never left his mouth. Revelling in his elevated position, he manoeuvred his horse sideways so that he cast his shadow directly over Thomas. 'Remember what I said, *boy*.' The final word was protracted, designed to provoke.

'Sir, we should be on our way, we've much ground to cover,' Burrell interceded.

To Owen's surprise, Thomas simply met Harris's gaze and replied in a restrained tone. 'I'll let my father know ye were here.'

The land agent tutted in disgust and whirled away with a spray of mud.

Owen, swaying on his feet, said weakly, 'I thought you were going to hit him with the spade.'

'Some day the likes of him will get more than a spade,' Thomas muttered, turning his back and walking towards the edge of the once luxuriant field. He looked up and down the dying valley as though considering where next to turn. He heard a 'whump', like a pile of sacks being thrown on a floor, and looked around to see that his brother had collapsed face down in the mud and was lying there as still as death.

***

Thomas mopped his brother's brow with a rag soaked in bog water, fearful that Owen had been gripped by the fever. Like one skeleton dragging another, he managed with a monumental effort to haul his brother inside to the bed of straw.

Owen was alive, but for how long? He recalled again his father's final private words to him, emanating on a breath so foul it seemed his father was already rotting inside, the voice pleading with him to look after his brother. *'I love ye both, Thomas, but Owen...ponders too much...ye're the strong one...ye'll need to act.'* In the next breath he had begun to converse with his dead wife's imaginary form. Thomas had shivered at the notion of his mother's unseen ghostly presence, then dismissed the idea as imbecilic superstition more befitting of a keening old hag. Both brothers had watched as their father had faded from life in the flickering light of a candle. He'd given up life's struggle, Thomas considered, and simply allowed himself to slip away, perhaps in his mind to find his wife and children in eternity, unburdening himself of the mantle of family provider and protector, handing it to Thomas like a poison chalice. As much as he'd loved and admired his father, now he somehow hated him in equal measure.

Owen moaned and blinked awake. 'What happened?' His voice was like a rusty hinge. Thomas held a cup of water to his lips. He sipped and spluttered.

'Ye fell over in the field. It's not the fever though, not like the others. Ye're just...' Thomas was at a loss to offer an explanation other than the obvious. Owen tilted his head away and began to sob quietly.

'Stop it! Stop it!'

Owen looked at him. 'What are we going to do?'

Thomas didn't reply.

'Father Lally was right. We have to go to the workhouse.'

'Ye fuckin' thick. Not while I'm breathin'. And anyway you haven't the strength te walk te the door, never mind te Westport.'

Thomas rose and wandered around the room, absent-mindedly picking up his father's blackthorn stick. Without warning he raised the heavy stick and brought it crashing down on a cracked old earthenware jug, shattering it into a hundred pieces, projectiles shooting in every direction, the water spilling across the hardened earth.

Owen was startled into a sitting position. Thomas stared down at the mess, his back to his brother, and then he threw the stick to one side. It clattered across the floor, rocked for a moment on a protruding nub, and settled into the silence.

'I'll find us food.'

'But where?'

He swung about. 'How in Christ's name do I know?' He picked up his jacket and walked towards the door. 'I'll be back. You lie there.' He had to check himself from adding 'it's all you're good for.' He slammed the door behind him and it rattled in its frame.

Owen called after him as loudly as his body would permit, but Thomas was too far gone to hear.

***

Thomas had no clear idea of where he might find even a morsel of food. The lake below was as barren of fish as the earth was of potatoes. Even the sky had been near stripped of birds. Year on year as the famine progressed, the adult birds had been snared, lights thrust in their eyes in the bushes by night, a blanket thrown to forestall their flight, then their nests emptied of eggs, robbing each successive season of new young until they were all but obliterated. The lands were practically picked clean of wild edibles and you could only get by for so long eating dandelions, dock leaves and dog roses. He turned and started down the hill as the early evening approached, putting the sun to his back. He followed the road as it rounded the mountain, with a cliff dropping sharply into the valley on one side. He could just make out the point about two miles distant where the Glenlaur and Owenmore Rivers became one, flowing back through the Erriff Valley and far beyond into the Atlantic, a course he feared he might soon have to take himself, although he had no desire to depart the country he loved dearly, beyond being driven away by starvation. Fleeing on an emigrant ship, he felt, was like holding up a white flag and handing their land with absolute finality to a foreign tyrant. Thomas believed, as had his embittered father, that this had been their strategy all along, to deliberately use starvation to strip the land of people, of resistance, and leave Ireland ripe for utter subjugation.

He drank his fill of the Glenlaur River's icy mountain waters under Tullynafola Bridge, reflecting that this very spot had been the scene of the gamekeeper Geraghty's demise. The road now swung northeast, under the shadow of Tawnyromhar Mountain. He looked up the mountain slope, and much as he dreaded the mammoth effort of walking up a steep hill, its foliage offered a slightly greater chance of locating food. Tawnyromhar's slopes were also home to a few other tenant farmers, if any remained, and there was a chance he might beg a few morsels of food from them. He grimaced at the notion of how pitifully low he'd been dragged, stripped of the pride that his father and grandfather had handed down to him like they were passing on a fragile heirloom.

After a tortuous ascent up the slope, he paused and looked around at the foliage. Grass and heather, heather and grass. Up higher where the incline grew into another precipitous cliff he could see the brightly blooming furze bushes clinging to the rocks, their gay, yellow colours at odds with the mood of the land. Flowers all around him but not a bite to eat. Dismayed, he cast himself to the ground to rest and as he sat there gazing wearily across the depleted landscape, he spotted what looked like a gargantuan worm moving along the road that skirted the southern side of the valley. It snaked along the road that followed the base of Maumtrasna Mountain's vast bulk, seeming like some vile creature that had crawled from the earth to add to Ireland's woes. Suddenly the sound of a gunshot echoed with great clarity across the valley, over and over, bouncing from Maumtrasna across to Tawnyromhar and Tawnyard Hill and then fading to a whisper. He strained his eyes at the sight and realised he was looking at an immense caravan of men and carts. It had stopped moving, and he could identify tiny figures bustling about it, hear the whinny of horses and the barely audible sound of many voices shouting and laughing. Soldiers. Most likely assigned to guard the carts, probably filled with Irish grain and animals bound for ships in Westport. He'd witnessed these caravans before, although never on such a scale. When he realised what he was looking at, his bile rose once more. To consider the hunger pangs in his belly, Owen lying near death for want of a morsel of food, his family, his countrymen one by one starved into an early grave, to consider all that, and to watch as the English conveyed from Ireland enough food to feed thousands; he dearly hated that race and swore that if fate decreed that he should somehow survive he would pay them back in kind for all the misery and blood that dripped from their hands.

He began to walk again, his eyes drawn repeatedly to the caravan, fires now springing up along its length as they made camp for the night. He briefly entertained thoughts of attempting to steal food from one of the carts, but so well guarded were they, he would surely end up with a bullet in his head. They'd already let half the country perish, what was one more worthless Irishman?

Thomas followed the curve of the mountain until it arced around into the smaller Cregganmore Vale, an offshoot of the main valley. To his left, despite the fading light, he could see all the way along the vale, the waters of the meandering Owenmore River white in places where it bounced over rocks and boulders, the fields newly harvested of wheat, their riches probably long gone on a ship to a foreign shore. A few cottages nestled in boggy hillside, high above the fertile soils.

Exhaustion forced him to slump to the ground again, his bony rump sending a ferocious ache through his body. He could just close his eyes, he thought, and let the fading light take him, drifting off to death in harmony with the setting sun.

But he wasn't prepared to surrender yet. The sight of the English fires across the Erriff Valley was the impetus for renewed rage, as was the sight of Harris's double-storied, semi-palatial dwelling directly north across the vale, which was named Oughty House after the hill in whose shadow it rested. Oil lamps burned brightly in its windows, mocking his desperation. On the road below he could make out the school that had once held a dread for him as each day dawned. Yet if time's door opened that moment, he would gladly step back and embrace those days of thrashings and incoherent lecturing and hour-long treks in the foulest of weathers. Because those days offered one other inducement. Food.

His recollection of schooldays set him thinking of his brother and how he had thrived at learning, among a select few in school chosen for special attention. Thomas, on the other hand, despite possessing a reasonable intelligence, had struggled. His defiance of their teachers and their cruelties seemed the more important battle to wage than that against ignorance.

Owen had a way of looking at the world, Thomas could acknowledge, that he'd never consider himself. Almost everything Thomas knew had been drilled into him, but Owen knew things he'd never been taught. He reasoned and pondered until the answers presented themselves. That was all Owen ever seemed to do – spend his days staring into empty space, thinking, dreaming, dithering. His brother was smarter than him; this was indisputable. But Thomas believed there were all sorts of intelligence. There was the book-reading kind, the seven-times-eight-equals-fifty-six kind, the Latin and ancient Gaelic scripts and Brian Boru defeating the Vikings, and all of that useless horseshit that was battered into them in school. And then there was the intelligence of survival; the intelligence of the fox to outsmart the hound; the intelligence of understanding the nature of man himself, instinctively to sense friend or foe and to know when to deceive, to feint, and when to strike. Whether his father's seed had carried in it Thomas's looks or hair colour he knew not, but he believed it had carried his father's guile. The world may need its thinkers and dreamers but they owe their very existence to the doers, the workers and the fighters, all the people who clear the paths on which the dreamers tread in quiet reflection, considering the whys and wherefores of some old bollocks. The doers were people like his father, Michael Joyce. The man who would traverse the earth for his family, who would work all of God's hours to feed them, who would die for them, or kill for them. As he had.

Geraghty. The land agent's gamekeeper. It was as vivid in Thomas's memory as if it had happened an hour ago. He'd just snared a small deer, a rare sight, when he'd felt the cold muzzle of a musket on his neck. Geraghty had outsmarted him, his foul breath sniggering with glee at the back of Thomas's head, promising prison, transportation, flogging. The sadistic gloating had been interrupted by a loud crack and Thomas had turned, trembling, to see his father standing there with a heavy, bloodied branch. They would flee, he'd said, leave the area, run, get a ship. This was his father's startled thinking. Scurry away like rats, was Thomas's interpretation as he stood there, the Glenlaur River's babble a backdrop to the deepening coldness of his thoughts.

'We can't,' Thomas had cried. 'We've no money, nothing, nowhere to hide. They'll catch us and hang you!'

Michael Joyce had listened in silence then turned away and with his father's gaze momentarily averted, Thomas had lifted Geraghty's musket and swung it over his head, about to strike at the prone gamekeeper. His father had grappled with him then and forced him to the ground, pinning him, kneeling above him.

He'd raged and ranted at Thomas. No Joyce would ever commit that terrible sin and be damned to eternal hell.

It was the *only* way, Thomas had countered, over and over.

At which point Geraghty had stirred in near consciousness. Tears had spilled from Michael Joyce's eyes, falling on to his eldest son's face. He had shaken his head violently as if doing so would keep at bay the terrible conclusion that was rushing upon him. That his son was right. Should Geraghty live, they might well hang Michael Joyce anyway, or at the very least lock him up for the rest of his days, a living death, alive but tortured daily by the thought of his family abandoned in the world. He had exchanged a look of terrible conspiracy with his son, seized the musket, and with an agonised yell had beaten the final, clinging nuances of life from Geraghty's skull. Thomas remembered thinking, as he watched his father kneeling and sobbing beside the lifeless body, that now, finally, he and his father truly shared the same blood.

Darkness was near upon him. He turned his head and looked towards the cottages further along the mountainside, his last, desperate hope. The sun was gone but its afterglow still cast a faint light across the heather. But he had barely shifted his wearied legs when voices gave him pause. Fearful they might be Harris's men, he threw himself flat on his belly and crept behind a small boulder. Just down the slope, three figures stood with their backs to him, looking away towards the lamp-lit windows of Oughty House. One of the men turned and spoke, leaving Thomas in no doubt as to their designs.

'Harris may have an armed guard outside. The bastard might even shoot on sight. So we have to approach carefully. It'll be completely dark in twenty minutes so we should be able to get close without anyone seeing us.'

'What about Uncle Éamon?'

That voice, a boy's, rang familiar with Thomas. The man spoke again.

'You hurry to Éamon's and tell him to meet us at the schoolhouse at Drummin in two hours. We'll all make our way up the track to Oughty House together. The more of us there are the better.'

'What about me? I can come along and–'

'It's no place for a lad.' The other man's voice.

'Jimmy's right, son. Harris could start shooting before we get near his door. But that's a chance we have to take. It's this or we all starve.'

'But I–'

'Don't argue with me!'

Thomas's mind raced. They were planning to attack Harris in Oughty House. Maybe kill him. Jesus Christ! They hadn't a hope of getting away with it. Half the fucking English army was camped across the valley. Were they insane?

'Go now. Quick as you can. Remember, two hours, the schoolhouse.'

The young lad, a broad bulky youth, turned and walked away with a disgruntled mutter, affording Thomas sight of his face. Tim Walsh. He lived on the other side of Tawnyard Hill, in the Glenlaur Valley. His father was Pádraig Walsh, once suspected in the murder of Geraghty, a real rebel by all accounts. Éamon Walsh was his brother and Jimmy was probably Jimmy Burke, a neighbour of theirs. The bunch had hatched a plan to do away with Harris, probably with Burrell too. They'd leave no witnesses. Bloody murder would be visited upon their land again tonight. No, not murder; bloody justice.

Walsh and Burke set off down the hill, fading into the swelling mist. Thomas lay in semi-shock for some minutes before resuming his trek, his mind a confused miasma of fear, excitement and hopelessness. He staggered on until he stood in the focal point of a semi-circle of cottages, most black and dead to the world, their thatch hacked out or burned. Yet one cottage remained intact. A low glimmer of flickering gold danced on the floor beneath the wooden door. A shadow interrupted the fire's capering light. Thomas looked up and saw a whirl of smoke drift up through a hole cut in the thatch, enlivened by an occasional spark. And escaping on those rivulets of turf smoke was that other smell, aromatic in the dampening Mayo air, exotic, rare and priceless: the smell of roasting animal flesh.

He strode towards the cottage door, the other dead houses seeming to watch him, to bear witness to whatever act he might perpetrate, because some part of him had resolved not to leave this house without a fill of meat and he would do anything he had to to fulfil that resolution.

He pushed at the door and found it barred or bolted. The inhabitants had something to protect and he knew full well what it was. Thomas gritted his teeth and hurled his bony shoulder against the door, which shifted inwards a few inches and allowed a wider wedge of light to escape into the night air. The smell of cooking meat rushed at him like a surging wave, swelling his nostrils and lungs, startling his flimsy muscles into renewed life. He heaved again and the door swung inwards, the bench that had been pressed against it toppling sideways with a thud. He stepped into the room and stared to his left at the sight of a man of maybe thirty, maybe sixty, his age lost in the ravages of starvation. He stood with his back to a crackling fire. His left hand clutched a bone chewed almost to whiteness but for a few bits of ragged, burnt flesh that clung to its balled end. In the other hand he held a poker, still faintly glowing, its tip pointed at Thomas, though it wavered in his tremulous grip. The man's lips shivered too, despite the overpowering heat of the room.

Thomas took a step forward and the cottier gasped, his breath heaving as though in mortal fear that hell was about to claim him. Or already had.

'You've got food.'

The man didn't respond.

'You've meat. If you share it, I'll be on my way. I need food for my broth–'

'I had no choice. *Jesus*!' The man started to weep bitterly.

Thomas thought the man looked mad, driven to insanity through hunger. He glanced around for a weapon should he need it.

'Just give me some meat and I'll leave.'

The man raised the bone in his left hand and stared at it and Thomas saw his opportunity to strike. A small three-legged stool rested nearby – he could grasp it and brain the mad old bastard before he knew what was happening. But before he could lurch at the stool the man spoke again through a babble of sobs.

'May God forgive me...oh Jesus...but she was dead already...I swear before the Almighty...' With that he threw the bone into the flames, sending a shower of sparks skywards. He then raised his eyes and allowed them to flicker over Thomas's shoulder to the other end of the room.

Some awful truth began to seep into Thomas's consciousness, a terrible, sickening reality he desperately wished to deny. He looked behind the door where a mouldy, ragged curtain divided the room in two. A clattering startled him and he looked and saw that the man had dropped the poker. His entire body seemed to sag, shoulders slumping, chin almost to his chest. Thomas turned his back on the cottier and walked to the curtain. As he reached out he was conscious now of his own quickening breaths. He grasped it, stepped forward, pulled it to one side.

He didn't know how long he stood there. His mind was having difficulty processing what he was looking at; his heart was pounding. Shame, revulsion, terror, rage and a thousand other feelings swelled until it seemed his very brain might explode. On the floor lay a ragged, bloody mess. He could barely discern the remains of a human body entangled in a filthy, dark green dress, some parts of limbs still attached to the torso within the garment, other parts cleaved and hacked free. On the floor beside the body lay a bloodstained knife.

A mass of tangled black hair drew his eye and commanded him forward. He released the curtain, which fell back into place behind him, isolating him with the ghastly tableau. He reached down and pulled at the hair, turning the head to one side. It was a girl of perhaps fifteen or sixteen, wasted as were they all, but familiar nonetheless. Her eyes stared blankly out at nothing, her lips were slightly parted, as though in surprise. Her name: it was Etain O'Casey. She'd been one of the 'bright' ones in school that had been selected for special attention along with Owen. He released her hair and her head fell back against the ground with a faint slap. He picked up the knife, he knew not why, perhaps somewhere in his mind intent on imposing justice on the cottier for this abomination.

Then came a sob, imploring some release. 'I had no choice. May God forgive me.'

There was a shuffle and the clatter of something falling. Thomas flung the curtain aside to witness the cottier's final death agonies as he desperately scratched at the loop of rope around his neck, his feet kicking wildly as they tried to locate the ground. Thomas stood riveted, his shock too intense to motivate any attempt to rescue the man. He stood there, mouth agape, staring at the pleading face, now turning purple. The clawing at his neck, the kicking, the spreading stain on his crotch, the creaking of the rope against the timber, endured for what seemed an age until finally Thomas's mind snapped and he ran from the cottage out into the blessed relief of the black night air.

Three or four steps were as far as he'd progressed when his feet entangled in each other and he went sprawling onto his outstretched hands and knees. He remained thus for five full minutes, sobbing and gagging, atavistic moans escaping his throat as his mind struggled desperately with the scene to which he'd just borne witness.

Finally he calmed somewhat and sat up on his haunches, staring out over the pitch-dark vale, his breaths easing, dots of colour still dancing before his eyes. He ran his jacket sleeve across his face and erased some of the snot and spittle and wetness.

They had come to this, he thought, his race reduced to the wanton savagery of a wild animal, starved not only of food but now also wrung dry of all humanity. Robbed of their very dignity as men. Ireland had been thrust back into a primeval age where the only rule was survival and morality was revealed to be nothing more than a mask of convenience. The cottier had no choice, so he'd said. And after a while Thomas began to accept it as truth.

And he himself was no different. The hunger still remained in his belly, the weakness in his every muscle. Were his brother not dependent upon him, he too might consider the option of exiting this world to sweet oblivion. But he truly did have no choice. Whether madness was taking him, or his actions were those of the perfectly rational, he couldn't have said.

He rose to his feet and turned to face the cottage. Through the open door the dead man's shadow moved back and forth, ever so gently accompanied by the slow creaking of the rope on the beam, like the sound of a boat on a lough surface straining on its line.

He glanced down at the bloodstained knife he still clutched, walked back into the cottage and looked up at the dead man.

He had no choice.

CHAPTER 4

Since the days of O'Connell a larger public demonstration has not been witnessed than that of Sunday last. About 1 o'clock the monster procession started from Claremorris, headed by several thousand men on foot. At 11 o'clock a monster contingent of tenant farmers on horseback drew up in front of Hughes's Hotel, showing discipline and order that a cavalry regiment might feel proud of. They were led on in sections, each having a marshal and occupying over an Irish mile of the road. Next followed at least 500 vehicles from the neighbouring towns. On passing through Ballindine the sight was truly imposing, the endless train directing its course to Irishtown.

–*The Connaught Telegraph*, 26 April 1879

20 April 1879

He'd been little more than a pimpled youth when he'd first heard the term 'The Three Fs'. What had they been called, the crowd who'd first penned that snappy slogan? Tenants' Rights Brotherhood? Tenants' League of Something? He couldn't remember.

He stood staring at the poster on the wall at the side of Brett's store. A man in the massing crowd jostled him, but he barely noticed.

THE WEST'S AWAKE!
Down with the invaders! Down with the tyrants and landlords!
MASS MEETING
Irishtown, April 20th 1879
TO PROTEST THE BRUTALLY UNFAIR INCREASE IN RENTS BY MAJOR JOSEPH BOURKE IMPOSED ON HIS IMPOVERISHED 22 TENANTS
Assemble in Claremorris Market Square for orderly march to Irishtown.
Hear the words of John O'Connor Power, Esq., M.P., John Ferguson, Esq. Glasgow, and Thomas Brennan, Irish Patriot.
We demand the three Fs! Fair rent! Free Sale! Fixity of Tenure!
THE LAND FOR THE PEOPLE
GOD SAVE IRELAND

More people jostled him and still he didn't move. In many ways it seemed that he, and the rest of Ireland for that matter, hadn't moved from the same spot in over thirty years. He imagined a new generation of Irishmen reading posters promising an end to injustice long after he was in the ground. The cycle was as predictable as the seasons.

He turned and looked at the gathering throng in Market Square. He had to concede it was impressive. The swarm of people obscured even the ground beneath their feet. Horses whinnied and reared, unhinged by the unfamiliar sea of humanity. Hawkers yelled in competition to offload hot potatoes and bread, some more surreptitious, unburdening themselves of bottles of poteen, eyes watchful for constables and Fenians alike, who had forbidden alcohol.

Children scurried among the sea of legs, dogs scampering in their trail. Women remained largely on the periphery, murmuring in groups as they watched the proceedings as though assembled to bid their men farewell as they departed for war. The thought made him weary. In fact the entire business ached in his bones, whether it be a prelude to another pathetic armed revolt like in '67, or some more restrained initiative that sought to part the landlords from Irish land and the British from Irish life with mouthfuls of soothing Irish brogue. Some damn hope.

Talking was all very well, but they'd been talking to the British for centuries and where had it got them? He looked around at the crowd. Their energy was not so much founded in hope as in desperation. Last summer had brought yet another foul harvest, and to compound their problems their crops were worth only a fraction of those of previous years. Summer was approaching and he recognised the sense of foreboding in their eyes that, yet again, God would piss on Ireland for three months and their crops would rot in the ground. And still the landlords demanded their rent without mercy even though the tenant farmers' income was in freefall. The land agent who lorded it over his own smallholding, Captain Charles Boycott, was no exception. A deep sense of foreboding and memories of another time, when the dead seemed to outnumber the living, haunted people's thoughts. The farmers were becoming desperate and desperate men are capable even of actions they would normally consider to be within the realm of evil.

He stood watching a couple of young men, both about eighteen, sharing sips from a flat black bottle. The beverage was imbuing them with a recklessness that is the preserve of young men, as they laughed and loudly recalled nationalist glories for the benefit of a beefy member of the Royal Irish Constabulary who was within earshot. The policeman had shown admirable reserve thus far, calmly watching the young gobshites from the corner of his eye. One of the youths removed his tatty bowler hat, playfully hitting his companion in the chest with it.

'Hey Niall, what is it the three Fs stand for again?'

'Jaysus...let me think...fuckin' landlords...the fuckin' English...'

'Yeah. And what was the last one...oh I remember...' He turned towards the constable. 'Fuckin' traitors.'

The constable visibly snarled and started towards the youths, his right hand slipping around his baton.

Christ, Owen Joyce thought, that's all we need. He quickly stepped forward and touched the constable's arm. 'Excuse me, Constable, but there's a man over there selling poteen. I'm a devotee of Fr Mathew myself, but he'll no doubt corrupt many young men with his evil spirit. You'd be doing us a great service if...'

The constable looked nonplussed at the outpouring and paused. The youths continued to snigger away, unaware of being under the watchful gaze of another tall, square-jawed man whose expression was one of restrained anger.

'It's that man over there, with the floppy hat,' Owen pointed.

'All right, calm down. Go about your business. I'll take care of the hawker.' With a final threatening glance at the youths, he reluctantly headed towards his supposed suspect.

The tall man immediately sprang forward and before the youths realised what was happening, he'd seized them both by the hair and slammed their heads together with an audible crack. One sank to his knees, the other staggered back against a cart.

'You fuckin' gobshites! No trouble, you were told! And what the fuck is this?' He seized the poteen bottle and slammed it into the ground where it shattered in a spray of glass and alcohol, the fumes mingling with those of horse shit and sweat that permeated the air.

'Fuckin' drink will curse this country until damnation.' He grabbed the two youths by the collars and shoved, sending them stumbling forward. 'Get the hell out of here! Go home to yer mammies, ye stupid gobdaws.' He swung a substantial boot at the men's arses and they took off like skelped dogs. He shook his head. 'Could have been nasty if that RIC fucker had started batterin' them. Next thing we'd have a riot. Thanks for steppin' in.' He proffered his open palm. 'Donal Doherty.'

'Joyce. Owen Joyce.'

They shook hands and eyed each other in silence a moment, Doherty's expression hinting at some level of puzzlement, staring into Owen's deep-set, dark blue eyes.

'Are you a Mayo man, Joyce?'

'I am. From Neale, Lough Mask Estate.'

'From Ballinrobe myself, just up the road. Have we met?'

'Don't believe so. I think I'd remember you.' Owen smiled as he looked up at Doherty, a good four inches taller than him. He was about forty, Owen guessed, neatly dressed and standing stiffly erect, giving him a military bearing. Doherty was undoubtedly a Fenian; not that he wore a badge or anything, he simply had that air about him. And the Fenians' devotion to the gun was no secret.

Doherty laughed. 'Fair enough. Sure, people are always thinkin' they've met. So you're under Boycott's thumb? Another bastard we'll take care of one of these days. Anyway, I better get these mucksavages into order. Jaysus, how are we supposed to drive the English out with an army of ignorant Connaught farmers?' Doherty turned into the crowd and started yelling commands.

Owen's first instinct was to inform Doherty that he himself was an 'ignorant Connaught mucksavage'. But he let his vexation recede. Doherty was right. That's exactly what they were. Ignorant. And it was ignorance that kept them on their knees.

He looked about. Probably half of those present couldn't read, write or do simple mathematics. For all the armies of conquest, for all the brutal despots and their cannons and swords that the English had inflicted on his country through the centuries, nothing had been as effective in securing Ireland's submission as that simple weapon – the denial of the means to provide education on any meaningful level. What hope had a bunch of ignorant farmers from the back-of-beyond against the might of Britain's educated establishment and its manipulation of law to propagate its own profligate wealthy? They were caught in the insidious, malicious trap of ignorance. And escape from some traps, he knew, could only be rendered by brute force. He felt the acrid, bitter taste of a resentment that had long been stewing. At whom his anger was directed was harder to define. His countrymen, the British, or at his own self? He hadn't exactly distinguished himself for 'the cause' down the years. Maybe he might begin to rectify that today.

He began to make his way around the small square. The farmers on horses outside Hughes's Hotel, he guessed, numbered in their hundreds. Those on foot in their thousands. Yet no sense of chaos or lawlessness prevailed. The juvenile behaviour he'd seen earlier had been an exception. Tenant farmers, their youth eroded by exposure to the elements and poverty, moved about with a common purpose and sober determination that began to subvert his cynicism about the so-called Land Movement. He'd only reluctantly made the twenty-mile journey here from his home at the insistence of his wife, Síomha. Clearly though, unlike previous land-related meetings he'd attended, this one was not only on a much greater scale, but there was a sense that today was the beginning of something more far-reaching. Men had come from not just Mayo, but accents from Galway, Roscommon and even Sligo and Longford could be heard about the town. Donal Doherty and P. W. Nally, the well-known Fenian activist, along with a number of others, had donned green and gold sashes and, like drill sergeants, were organising crowds of men into divisions, readying them for the march to Irishtown a few miles away.

Still unsure what he thought of it all, he determined for the present to remain a detached, uncommitted observer. Rather than be caught up in the official march, he decided to retrieve his jaunting car from where he'd left it near the railway station and make his own way to the venue.

Two minutes later he was driving the car south towards Irishtown. He pulled a chunk of bread from his pouch and chewed it as he gently encouraged Anu, his ageing chestnut brown draught horse, along the dusty track. He couldn't help wondering how many more seasons the animal could haul a plough through the fields. He had absolutely no means of replacing her. The rents he paid Boycott ate up virtually all his cash and there was barely enough left to feed his family, never mind five pounds to buy a horse.

The large building rising out of the fields to the east interrupted his thoughts. He immediately felt a chill as sounds, voices, smells and pain resurfaced and begged his inspection, but he denied them and used the crop on Anu's rump with unintentional sharpness. The pony whinnied and upped its pace, and he turned his gaze away from the grim blackness behind the workhouse windows.

As the road unravelled before him, he looked out across the rock walls that defined the paltry plots of pasture so desperately clung to by his compatriots. The day was mostly overcast with occasional spits of rain and a mild wind rippling the immature crops. Here and there the shape of a collapsed cottage could be discerned, the occupants long departed from the world or Ireland. And no children filled the void they'd abandoned. He'd travelled this road long ago and could recall several villages of twenty or thirty homes, whole towns wiped from existence, almost from memory. A vanished generation.

The car trundled across a wooden bridge that spanned the Robe River, its deep, brown waters gently rolling by just as they had decades ago when they'd helped deliver him to freedom and a redemption of sorts. The turbid, peaty flow looked as benumbing now as it had felt then, and he didn't linger. The road took a sharp turn to the east and, at the bend, a patch of ground had been appropriated by countless other carriages, carts, horsemen or families keen to see the march. He decided to join them and watch the procession, manoeuvring the car about among them to face the road.

Twenty minutes passed before he heard the first rhythmic, drum-like sound of the approaching men. It echoed off the walls of cottages, accompanied by the rising, high-pitched cheers of women and children. They came around the bend of the narrow boreen in disciplined columns. A hundred men on horseback, Pat Nally to the fore, upright, rigid, his green sash resplendent against his dark coat, eyes fixed ahead as though he held but one destination, one destiny in his sights. Then came two columns of men on foot. They marched past for ten minutes before another group of horsemen spearheaded a second column of men. They walked with pride, self-command, ordinary men of the land, their faces betraying only a steely determination. Still they came, more groups of horsemen followed by marching men, casting their shadows along a mile or more of Irish country road. Donal Doherty, the Fenian he'd met in the town square, led the final group. Doherty allowed his eyes to drift ever so slightly to one side and he made subtle eye contact with Owen, tilting his head in greeting.

There then followed a protracted train of carriages, open-topped breaks, jaunting cars, drays and buggies of all measure. A beautiful sporty phaeton, yellow-sided with a leather hood and drawn by black ponies, led this cavalcade. Inside sat two gentlemen in dark topcoats and hats, one of whom he recognised as James Daly, the wealthy newspaperman whose *Connaught Telegraph* had passionately championed the tenants' cause. In the next carriage he recognised the distinctively ugly, pockmarked face of John O'Connor-Power, the MP loathed by many nationalists, who was sitting beside the avowed Fenian militant, Thomas Brennan. His curiosity was piqued at the sight of such strange bedfellows.

He quickly roused Anu and had her trotting among the hundreds of other vehicles towards Irishtown. A mile further and the accumulating collection of abandoned vehicles and horses had contracted together like a rockfall at the bottom of a hill. He secured Anu and set off through the crowds. The land about them was the private preserve of Surgeon Major Joseph Bourke, which fed the families of twenty-two tenants, a couple of whom had approached the Land Movement for help when Bourke had decided, despite a pathetically poor harvest, to up his rents, leaving them on the brink of eviction, even starvation. These tenants had begun the avalanche of support that had settled at Bourke's front door that day.

He drew nearer to a widening of the road, until the throng proved too dense to make any progress nearer the elevated platform impossible. He glanced about him as the confluence of male bodies swallowed him whole. Young and old men tilted their chins up in an effort to see and hear the address from the platform. The odour of sweat and the land rose up all around him, the crush and the heat making it difficult to inhale. James Daly was addressing the crowd, his introductory words drowned in a swelling, congruent roar of support. When eventually it had subsided, he introduced John Ferguson, barrister and ardent advocate of Home Rule. To a hushed audience Ferguson's Glaswegian lilt drifted out across the sea of faces. Owen strained to hear.

'…the land of Ireland, like that of every other country, was intended by a just and all-providing God for the use and sustenance of those of his people…'

Applause. Calls for hush. Coughing. Missing words. Owen cursed.

'…any system which sanctions its monopoly by a privileged class demands from every aggrieved Irishman an undying hostility, being flagrantly opposed to the first principle of their humanity – self-preservation!'

A huge cheer of approval.

John O'Connor-Power, who had in recent years addressed the United States House of Representatives, projected his voice to much greater effect, calling for a 'peasant proprietorship' to prolonged applause, and concluding with a fist-thumping demand for 'Irish land for the people of Ireland!' Men on all sides gritted their teeth and punched the air, as though their simmering anger was finally finding some release.

A man called Michael O'Sullivan, a teacher and land activist from Galway, was then granted the stage. He strode with purpose to the centre of the platform. O'Sullivan was tall and broad-shouldered and had piercing eyes. His clothes hinted at a man of lesser means than the other speakers and his West of Ireland lilt was a world away from the more refined tones of the MPs and barristers who had preceded him. With his uncomplicated enunciation and his unadorned statement of the facts, he immediately registered with his congregation. His Fenian leanings were also soon evident.

'The past two seasons have been very bad. Does any man consider that the tenant farmers of Ireland can afford to pay exorbitant rents for their lands, or that the lands are worth those rents?'

They responded as one. 'They are not!'

Nodding, palms held outward, O'Sullivan continued. 'It follows, then, that the present rents being too high, justice demands their reduction! But, judging from the past, we know that there are landlords in Ireland who do not look to what is just, but to what the law will permit.'

An old man waved a trembling fist skywards and shouted, 'Bastards!', provoking a mixture of laughter and ovation.

'If, then, the landlords who are now demanding exorbitant rents do not lower them to meet the tenants' altered circumstances, let the tenant farmers themselves consult together and settle among themselves what would be fair, equitable rent. And if that is not accepted by the landlord – why, let them pay none at all!'

A tumultuous cheer rose into the Mayo sky and some of O'Sullivan's ensuing lines were lost to Owen in its wake.

'...a great deal of thought. I have seen the Land Question in parliament brought forward with unanswerable eloquence, but with what result?'

The man standing to his right yelled out through cupped hands, 'It was kicked out!' Another voice called out, 'Waste of time!'

The speaker resumed, his voice rising as he progressed as though climbing a gentle slope, reaching an apex of pitch as he neared the end. 'What, then, are the people to do? They cannot pay unreasonable rents. They wish to pay what is fair and just. And it must be accepted. If not, let the landlords take the consequences on their own heads!'

Another exultation. O'Sullivan didn't wait for it to abate.

'It is fearful to contemplate those consequences in their fullness – extermination of the people on the one hand, and – *extermination of the exterminators on the other!*'

The acclamation left many hoarse and as O'Sullivan left the platform, the crowd heaved and Owen felt himself lifted from the ground and deposited ten yards nearer the stage, only for the surge to recede and sweep him backwards again.

A further handful of speakers addressed the crowd, including the Fenian militant Thomas Brennan, who suggested ominously that if the landlords didn't concede to the Land Movement's demands, they might face a French Revolution-type scenario. And with the sounds of bloody revolution still ringing in their ears, the thousands began to disperse back along the laneways, back to their patches of rough earth and tottering homesteads, but with a newly lit fire in their bellies.

A body of men, whose overlapping voices bustled with ebullience and rebelliousness, jostled Owen back to his car. What precisely was he witnessing, he wondered, as he watched the crowd drift away? Half the speakers today had been constitutionalists, Home Rulers, MPs: men like O'Connor-Power, who had sworn an oath of allegiance to the Queen and were accordingly loathed by the militant Fenians, with whom they had today shared a public platform. Had today been about a call to arms, a readying of the troops ahead of an insurrection? If so, why had there been parliamentarians present?

The narrow road at that moment resembled an overfed gullet and he didn't believe he'd be going anywhere for a while. Anu danced nervously to the commotion and Owen had to calm the animal as he stood watching the departing throng. He reflected that he felt a common bond with all those around him, yet was unsure, when it came to action, where precisely he stood. Ireland's MPs in the House of Commons promised much but hadn't delivered. He was aware that these things could take an eternity. On the other hand, armed revolution brought much quicker results – if you won, that was. The temptation was always there to take that path because, frankly, his family couldn't wait forever for Captain Boycott to lower the rent so he could put food on the table. And Boycott would undoubtedly be much more complicit with a shotgun barrel pressed to his temple. He shook his head, driving away the notion. He often felt like Ireland herself, who through the centuries seemed to swing like a pendulum, using violence one generation and peaceful negotiation the next, with each successive failure to secure autonomy ensuring the pendulum would simply swing back the other way. His wife, Síomha, called him a 'foosterer', mulling over everything so much that he could never make a decision. Sometimes it drove her to distraction; at other times she would laugh, saying that he was like a cart with a horse at either end, both pulling against each other and getting nowhere.

He was surprised to hear his name called over the heads of the crowd. A moment later he saw Donal Doherty dodge his way towards him through the thinning numbers.

'Joyce! Fancy a drink?'

Owen shrugged. 'Love one, but the pub here will be packed.'

'Not in the pub,' Doherty said without explanation. 'C'mon.'

Avoiding the eyes of two RIC constables stationed outside the graveyard wall, Doherty led him behind a row of cottages that lined the village street. Owen suddenly felt a little nervous. This man was an avowed Fenian and in the eyes of the establishment a violent subversive. Still, you could probably brand half of Ireland thus and he didn't want to back out, having already agreed. They arrived at a two-storey building and a glance along the side-entrance towards the street revealed a hexagonal red post box. As they slipped in the rear entrance Owen touched Doherty's arm.

'Isn't it risky for Fenians to meet in Her Majesty's post office?'

He smiled. 'Man called O'Donnell runs it. Paid by Her Majesty, employed by the Irish Republican Brotherhood, the IRB. Anyway, if you want to send the bastards a message, what better place than from a post office?' He laughed and took to a flight of stairs.

Owen's eyes struggled to adjust to the murky light of the upstairs room. After a few seconds he realised that there were three others present, sitting on stools or standing against the walls. His unease was immediate and he rebuked himself for stepping into a situation replete with unknowns.

'Relax, Joyce. You're among friends,' Doherty said, offering him a stool.

'No, I'll stand.'

'Suit yourself.'

Owen realised that he recognised one of the men, Mick Kelly. Like himself, Kelly was a tenant of Boycott. Besides the Lough Mask Estate where Owen farmed and where Boycott acted as land agent for the owner, Lord Erne, Boycott personally kept a smaller estate at nearby Kildarra. Kelly was a tenant there and a couple of years previously Owen had organised some men to bring in Kelly's harvest after he'd broken his arm and his pleas for a rent deferment had been brushed away by Boycott.

Doherty handed Owen a drink, the robust aroma of whiskey streaming into his nostrils. Its hit was instant and fiery.

'Mick there recognised you, Joyce, says you're a good man to have around.'

Owen acknowledged Kelly with a nod.

'So, what did ye think of today's big event?'

Owen looked at Doherty, scrutinising the man for some stratagem.

'To be honest, I don't know what I made of it. Parliamentarians and Fenians sharing a platform? What's going on there? More to the point, why have you brought me into this…whatever this is?'

'This is just a few friends sharing a drink,' Doherty laughed, then quickly grew serious. 'From what I hear you've no liking for landlords. I also hear you're an intelligent man, Joyce. But I can see that for myself. And we need intelligent men.'

'Who's we?'

Kelly answered. 'Anyone who wants the British out of Ireland.'

'What about my question?' Doherty interjected. 'Were ye impressed with today's event?'

'Very. It was the most disciplined, well-organised protest against landlordism I've seen. But as I said, why are parliamentarians and Fenian militants sharing a platform?'

'Well, we may have had a few decent Fenians up on that podium, but the reason there were parliamentarians there was that some of our leaders have gone soft.'

'What are you talking about?'

Mick Kelly slammed his glass down on a table. 'He's taking about Davitt and Devoy getting too cosy with the likes of Parnell. The fuckin' New Departure.'

Owen's interest was enlivened by the mention of the legendary Fenians John Devoy and Michael Davitt; the former one of the leaders of the American arm of the IRB, the latter a member of the Supreme Council of the IRB and one of the principle organisers of the mass meeting he'd just witnessed, or so he'd heard. Charles Stewart Parnell, on the other hand, was something of an enigma to Owen. A Protestant aristocrat from Wicklow by birth and a landlord himself, albeit a very humane one, Parnell had grown to be a fervent nationalist, become MP for County Meath and was spoken of as the next leader of the Home Rule Party.

Doherty resumed. 'As I was saying, Davitt and Devoy and others are talking about their New Departure, they call it. Y'know, I just came back with Devoy from America. I was there three years – raisin' funds we were – to support the rebellion back home. To buy weapons. Or so I thought. Now Devoy and Davitt cook up this New Departure bollocks. This means they're happy te do deals with parliamentarians like Parnell. We're supposed to give our backing to MPs, men who've sworn allegiance to the fuckin' Crown. That's why we had militants and politicians sharing a stage today.'

Owen nodded in understanding. He realised there would be huge advantages to moderate Fenians and constitutional nationalists, so long adversaries, uniting in a common goal. And any observer that afternoon would have come away with the feeling that a fuse had been lit. 'Still, it sounded to me like the Fenians had top billing today.'

Doherty dismissed this with a wave. 'This is just the beginning. Next we know it, Parnell and Davitt will be releasing white fuckin' doves and hoping the English give them a few scraps from their table. But the English only understand one thing. Blood. They've spilled ours long enough and some of us think now's the time to start spillin' theirs again. We could be waitin' a lifetime for this so-called New Departure to get us anywhere.'

Owen knocked back his drink and looked at the group of men. Outwardly they were playing along with their leaders like Devoy and Davitt, but in reality intended to pursue a much more sinister, private war. These men were killers, executioners. But hadn't he known that from the moment he'd accepted Doherty's invitation for a drink? Hadn't he really known all along that, as his circumstances had deteriorated, his own darker demons had begun to win the battle? He'd watched them all come and go – The Ballinrobe Tenants' Rights Association, The Tenants' Rights Brotherhood, The Mayo Tenants' Defence League. Christ alone knew how many more groups he'd heard spouting bombastic rhetoric, getting precisely nowhere. How many more years of inertia were they going to have to endure? When he'd entered this room he'd wondered what he'd stepped into. Now he began to believe that he knew exactly where he stood. He'd mused and vacillated for decades. Today he'd seen the fire in his compatriots' bellies lit and heard them stride away ready to do battle. Doherty walked to the window, reached up behind the pelmet and pulled down a revolver.

'The thing is,' Doherty said, eyes on the weapon as he reflectively turned it over in his hands, 'some of us aren't prepared to wait and see where all the talking leads. Some of us believe in more direct action.'

Owen felt his gut tighten at the sight of the gun and was suddenly aware that if it was offered and he took it, he would be crossing a line he'd always been careful to avoid.

'Most of the lads there today are in the same boat as you. Harvests getting worse, prices falling, and yet the bastards keep putting up the rents. The whole rotten system propped up by the British establishment. From what I hear of Boycott, he's a right fucker. Treats the Irish like we're some lower form of life. There's lots like him. So, Joyce, are ye willing te do something about it?'

Doherty offered the butt of the pistol up before Owen's face. Owen met Doherty's eyes and recognised there an icy remoteness that detached him from human compassion. He'd seen that look before, long ago and in another place, and it chilled him.

'It's the only way, Joyce.'

Why was he hesitating? Was he a coward at heart? He'd always secretly wondered. He took an involuntary step back and half-chuckled.

'You want me to become a revolutionary? I'm a fucking farmer. I've a wife and children to feed and a farm to run.'

'You're not a farmer, Joyce. You're a lackey of some English lord. You exist accordin' to English laws and English rules. You own nothin'. Not the land you work or the house your family live in. It's no way for a man to live. Especially for an Irishman.'

Owen glanced around at the grim faces watching from the room's shadows, then turned back to Doherty. 'I'll have to think about it.'

'You don't hav–' Doherty cut himself off mid-sentence and seemed to search Owen's face. 'Could have sworn–'

'What?'

'Where did you say you were from, Joyce?'

'I told you, Lough Mask Estate, near Neale.'

'No, I mean before that?'

'I lived near Clonbur for a good few years. Before that, in the Sheeffry Hills, west of Lough Mask. Tawnyard Hill. But that was a long time ago.'

Doherty uttered a barely audible chuckle and shook his head as though he'd been suddenly privy to some revelation.

'Of course,' he said, and laughed aloud.

Chapter 5

> They know the people have been dying by their thousands and I dare them to inquire what has been the number of those who have died through their mismanagement, by their principles of free trade. Yes, free trade in the lives of the Irish people.
>
> –Lord George Bentinck, leader of the Tory opposition, March 1847

> ...the produce of our own soil is being exported every day, exported from the very spots in which the people are allowed to famish. All this is done in an empire which calls itself the most civilised, the most powerful, the most Christian and the most charitable in the world.
>
> –*The Nationalist*, April 1847

October 1848

Never in his life had he felt such lassitude.

It was as though a mountain boulder sat upon his chest, pinning him to the bed of straw. A series of pangs brought him to his full senses, if only briefly. Pain sliced across the shrivelled muscle in his back, like someone was drawing a blade across his flesh, and he gripped at the cottage wall until it passed. Then the cramp, deep in his bowel, came again and he moaned aloud with the agony of it. He slid his palm down across the ridges of his ribs to his distended belly. In trying to soothe the taut skin he broke wind again, which gave pitiful relief. He pushed his hand down further into his britches, conscious of a nagging ache in his balls. He sobbed when he cupped them, for they had shrivelled like dried berries and somehow that was worse than everything else.

He shivered and looked to the door, praying that Thomas would step through and deliver him from his agonies. It sat slightly ajar and the gap had created a thin curtain of diaphanous light that divided the room. Within it dwelled a universe of dust specks and tiny winged creatures. In that light and through the partially open door he could also see something else: a hope, a belief even, that Thomas *would* return. In a subconscious movement he stretched out his open palm towards the light as though he might grasp it, and in that pose he drifted into sleep.

***

His mind was playing tricks on him as he awoke, casting him back to the time his mother was alive before the blight, when the cottage had been filled with the smell of cooking food. He cursed the cruel illusion of the aroma that filled his nostrils now. The light told him it was morning, just after sunrise, and Thomas was bent over their hanging pot by the hearth, steam sweating his face. Had the hunger conjured a dream to tease his senses? Thomas turned and saw he was awake, dipped a cup into the pot and drew up a steaming broth. He came and knelt on the floor beside Owen, lifting his head.

'Here, drink this, Owen. Be careful, it's hot.'

And then Owen was sipping a thin broth, scalding his lips and tongue, but he didn't care. It burned in his throat and he coughed. Thomas blew on the broth and offered him more. He reached for the cup greedily, but Thomas pulled it away.

'Take your time.'

It was a sensation he'd almost forgotten, the feel and taste of food in one's mouth. And it was accompanied by another experience long distant from his memory, that of Thomas smiling, and he realised this wasn't some hateful hallucination. It was quite real.

'We're going te make it, Owen. Didn't I promise ye?'

'Where did you–?'

'Later. First, you've got te get strong again. Because we've te go on a journey.'

'Where?'

'Little brother, we're going to America.'

***

Owen's eyes blinked open. The cottage door had been thrown back and warm sunlight was spilling through.

'Ye were calling for our mother.'

Owen pushed himself up on an elbow to see Thomas tying string around a bundle.

'I was dreaming.'

'Are ye feelin' better?'

Owen rose to a kneeling position and rubbed his eyes.

'I don't know, I think so.'

Thomas nodded towards the pot suspended over a smouldering fire.

'Have some more broth. Get your strength back, ye'll need it.'

Owen rose on unsteady feet, swayed a little and took a hesitant step forward. The weakness had abated and he found he could walk without the fear that his legs would founder. He found it amazing how quickly the body could revive with nourishment. He stopped and stared down at the pot of bubbling broth, a pale, translucent brown with what looked like bits of white meat floating on the surface.

'What's been going on?'

'Ye've been in and out of sleep since I got back, but ye've eaten three times.'

'But where did you get the food?'

Thomas didn't respond. He turned his back and walked towards the open door, standing in its frame, bathed in afternoon sunshine.

'We've got te leave. Soon. I have te get away from this place.'

'Where did you get the food?' Owen repeated, his voice betraying growing apprehension.

'It's just wild carrots, dandelions and dog rose. Father always said that dog rose kept away the scurvy. It'll keep us going for a while. We've a long walk ahead.'

His avoidance of the question only served to heighten Owen's anxiety. He dipped a cup into the broth, held it to his nose and walked over to Thomas, who still had his back turned, his eyes sweeping the valley below.

'There's meat in this,' Owen held up the steaming cup and his brother briefly allowed his eyes to flit across to it before he stepped outside. Owen followed. 'Where did you find meat?' He'd involuntarily raised his voice and without warning Thomas swung about, his amber eyes ablaze.

'What the fuck does it matter?' he raged, spittle flying from his mouth. 'If I hadn't you'd be dead now and so would I. Do ye think ye could survive on boiled piss-in-the-beds? All that matters is that we have food enough te get us te Westport. To a ship.'

Owen looked down at the broth. 'If it doesn't matter, tell me. Did you steal it from another tenant?'

Thomas swung his arm and struck the cup from Owen's hand, sending it twirling through the air, the broth briefly defining a spiral pattern before splashing onto the bare ground. They both stared at it in silence. Such an act just one day ago would have marked one as a lunatic fit only for the Connaught Asylum. Food was the currency of the starving, and Thomas had just thrown away a small fortune.

'Yes, I fuckin' stole it! There, are ye happy now?'

'Who from? Who has meat?'

Thomas seemed to calm a little. He breathed out slowly and met Owen's eyes. 'From the English army.'

'*What?*' Owen was incredulous.

'From a caravan. Thirty, forty carts. Most of them overflowing with wheat. The rest with pigs and sheep. They were heading for Westport, I s'pose, then on to a ship and off to England so the fat bastards can stuff their faces with our food while we starve.'

'But how…?'

Thomas looked along the valley. He watched as a giant shadow crossed

Tawnyard Lough and moved up the hillside towards where they stood, as though God had shifted on his empyrean seat and blotted out the light. The gloom spread rapidly as the autumnal sun vanished behind a grey, obese cloud.

'I looked everywhere. All I found were a few wild carrots and dog roses. Not enough to feed a sparrow. Then last evening I saw the caravan of carts on the road just below Carrowkennedy, heading for Westport, about a hundred soldiers guarding the carts. Bastards. They stopped for the night. Bedded down. I was only a shout from them, lying in the heather. The wheat was guarded like it was fuckin' gold, I swear. But the pigs were squealing te wake the dead and that was my chance, because they left them alone te get away from the noise. I got under a cart, reached up and slit a piglet's throat, pulled it down and hid under the wheels. The pigs squealed a bit louder but all I heard was some bastard shouting for them te shut up. Then I crept back across into the heather.'

'You stole a whole pig?'

'No, I couldn't carry it. I cut a few shanks off, as much as I could hold and had te leave the rest, worse the luck.'

'Jesus, Thomas.'

'Jesus is right. When they discover the pig gone they'll come lookin' and we'll be on a prison ship to Van Diemen's Land before the week is out. But it'll take them time. And that's why we've got to leave. Today. If we head west then north–'

'But how will they know it was you?'

'My only jacket's covered in pig blood. And they've got dogs. They'll probably be able to follow the trail right to our door.'

Owen closed his eyes and shook his head. He went to turn away and Thomas stayed him with a hand on his shoulder. 'We'd have te leave anyway, otherwise we'd starve. Now, at least, we have something in our bellies for the journey.'

Owen sighed.

'I did it for you, Owen. If I hadn't, you'd be dead, and I'd be waiting my turn.'

Owen nodded reluctant acceptance.

'Have as much of that broth as ye can swallow. We can't take it with us. I've cooked what meat's left and wrapped it in reeds, it'll keep it from turning for a while. If we can get some dog rose and nettles, we'll be able te make it.'

Owen turned away and stepped back inside.

Thomas stood there alone. The day was growing increasingly cool, and murky clouds over the Atlantic to the west weighed heavily on the landscape. Thomas closed his eyes and tilted his head back as though in desperate prayer to the heavens, but his faith had long since faded and he realised no salvation lay above. Any redemption would have to come from within, from whatever justification his own mind might contrive along the future path of his life.

He looked down at the ground where he'd knocked the cup of broth. A piece of soggy meat no larger than a thumbnail lay at his feet and he bent and picked it up, turning it between his thumb and forefinger, studying it. He could never in his lifetime, he believed, reveal to his brother the truth about the meat that had saved their lives. And he would never forget the night just past – never, until he breathed his last.

***

'You can't take them, ye gobshite. We barely have the strength te carry ourselves, let alone a bunch of books.'

Owen was kneeling on the floor about to fold a blanket around his few belongings, which included three books he'd been given by their former schoolteacher. One was a weighty tome entitled *A Collection of the Myths and Legends of the Culture of Ancient Greece*, while the others were both novels: *Robinson Crusoe* by Daniel Defoe and the fancifully titled *Travels into Several Remote Nations of the World, in Four Parts. By Lemuel Gulliver, First a Surgeon, and then a Captain of Several Ships*, by Jonathan Swift.

He was about to protest when Thomas reached down and seized them, shaking his head as he perused the covers. 'That bastard Mullany was always filling your head with this bullshit. Lot of good they are to us now.'

Mullany, their schoolteacher, had been hated by most of his sixty students, particularly because of his enthusiastic use of the strap and his fondness for calling the children 'illiterate Irish potato-diggers', despite the fact that he was Irish himself. Thomas's frequent defiance of the man had meant he'd suffered more than most. Owen too had often sported welts, but having been identified early on as one of the brightest of the crop, he and a handful of others had also been the beneficiaries of extra schooling from the teacher. Mullany, born in Mayo, was much travelled and had been educated in philosophy and the classics in Rome. His small collection of books had opened a door to Owen and when he had stepped through he'd discovered a world of infinite possibility that had taken him across horizons far from the valleys of Mayo. There had even been mention by Mullany of a wealthy Catholic merchant in Galway who each year sponsored the further education of a number of boys. There was great hope and optimism altogether. Then they'd awoken that September morning in '45 to the smell, creeping into their home the way an early morning mist creeps low across a meadow, seeping into their nostrils as they slept, rancid and choking like decaying flesh, but in many ways more repugnant. It had been the smell of the end of his dreams.

Owen couldn't count the number of times that being among the teacher's 'special' children had earned him beatings from the other boys. And almost in equal number had been the times that Thomas had waded in to his defence, usually sending the bullies scurrying away. Yet he too had always seemed to resent Owen's desire for learning, and as Thomas looked at the books now it was almost with relish that he seized the opportunity to be rid of them. He'd always borne a chip on his shoulder as regards Owen's brightness and here was a chance to assert his position as the one in charge.

'We could sell them,' Owen offered in dim hope.

Thomas looked up and seemed to hesitate, about to say something, then turned away and tossed the books into the glowing embers of the hearth. 'More trouble than they're worth. Get your stuff. We have te go.'

Owen watched for a few moments as the corners of the volumes began to blacken and smoke, filling him with an immense sense of loss, and not just for the books. It was as though the door that the schoolteacher had opened had finally and inevitably swung closed.

***

An hour later they stood looking up the hill at the cottage that had been their home for most of their lives; they would probably never see it again, nor their family's resting place.

'We have to go by Drummin graveyard, we have to say goodbye to our mother and Bridget and Pat and Sally,' Owen was saying, tears in his voice.

Thomas put a consoling hand on Owen's shoulder. 'We can't go that way. That's where the soldiers and police are. We'll walk straight into them. We have to go west to Doolough, then north to Louisburgh, then to Westport. It's longer but safer.'

'This place. It's all we've ever known. Tawnyard Hill and the valley.'

Thomas sighed. 'Fuck it, Owen, all this place has brought us is misery. Let's go.'

They turned and began to walk, a tied bundle of their worldly possessions slung over each of their shoulders. Three hours later they sat and rested at a point where the Glennumera River's hasty waters rushed into Doolough. Then they turned north towards Westport, cast a final look back along the valley to the east, and bade farewell to their childhood forever.

Chapter 6

Boycott, who I knew personally and met frequently, was a surly, cranky man ready to snap at anybody, friend or foe.

–Dr Connor Maguire, MD of Claremorris & Ballinrobe

Boycott was considered a domineering individual, very exacting in his dealings with tenants and workers, and devoid of all sympathy towards the people generally. But he was a courageous and resourceful man, and fought his corner with the true spirit of a plucky Englishman.

–Michael Davitt, founder of the Irish National Land League

On June 29, David Feerick, age 29, an agent for the Browne estate of Brownstown was shot ten times at Carnalecka while he was walking home. He said he had passed three men he did not know. They shot him from behind and then came around and shot him in the face and upper body. Each man had a revolver. He did not die until six weeks later.

–*The Ballinrobe Chronicle*, 3 July 1880

AUGUST 1880

Captain Charles Boycott pushed back the blankets and swung his feet on to the bedside rug. He glanced over his shoulder at Annie, deep in a contented slumber in their four-poster bed, her still-handsome face pressing lightly into the pillow, pompadour hairstyle confined in a satin net, the loose nightgown failing to hide the slender curve of her form. He was pleased that her forty-six years hadn't blighted her beauty too greatly, nor had three decades' exposure to the damp winds of the West of Ireland. He wished the years in Mayo had been as kind to him, he thought, as he ran his hand over a slightly bulging gut and recalled its gurgling disquiet the previous day, when he'd over-indulged in brandy. But he really he couldn't blame Mayo for that particular, self-inflicted malady.

He slipped on his soft leather night shoes and walked quietly across to the window. He parted the curtains and was pleased to see the sun's rising rays touching the tops of the Partry and Maumturk Mountains on the west side of Lough Mask. On Inishmaine Island, which partially obscured his view of the lough's expanse, he could just make out Inishmaine Abbey, a relic of antiquity, the top of the ruins painted a bright orange by the early light. In a field not two hundred yards away, across the narrow channel of water that separated the island from his lakeshore home, Lough Mask House, he could identify the figure of Francis O'Monaghan toiling away on his harvest. He had to give credit to the man for his early endeavour – though only moral credit, as monetary credit for any of Lord Erne's tenants was something he would never contemplate, he thought, stroking his full and frizzy grey beard, which extended down almost to his chest. This, Charles Boycott believed, was not because he was in any way unchristian, but precisely the opposite. It was his moral duty to insist that contractual engagements were fulfilled to the letter; to do otherwise was to encourage further abnegation of duty, further idleness among the masses.

He was jolted from his reverie by the sight of the housemaid, Maggie, crossing the garden below, arms full of turf, an empty-headed smile on her lips as she hummed some old Irish melody. He quickly pulled up the window and leaned out on to the sill.

'Maggie! Stop dithering, girl; hurry up and get that fire going!'

The girl almost dropped the turf at the unexpected bark from the window.

'Yes, sir, I will, sir,' she replied with a brief curtsey.

'And when you've done the chamber pots, run around and tell that idler McHale that he's to have Iron Duke saddled and ready in twenty minutes. Quick march, now, girl!'

As she skittered away he heard Annie's voice behind him.

'For heaven's sake Charles, how many times must I ask you? Is it really necessary to yell at the poor girl in such a fashion? And will you please close that window?'

He pulled the window down and turned to her. 'Yes, my dear, I'm afraid it is necessary. It's the only way to get any results out of peasants. That and a firm hand.'

Annie heaved a weary sigh as she rose and pushed back the blankets. 'Maggie is not a peasant, Charles, she's been in our household for six years, since she was fourteen. She's almost part of the family.'

He shook his head in exasperation as he stepped behind a screen to dress. 'She's an employee, Annie dear. She's Irish. Catholic. Born in a hovel outside Ballinrobe. By any definition, she's a peasant.'

'Oh really, please don't start, Charles. You'll put me off my breakfast.'

***

Mrs Loughlin, the cook, had prepared her normal weekday selection of porridge with salt or honey, scrambled duck eggs, and fresh bread served with preserves. Most mornings Annie limited herself to porridge and tea. Madeleine, her nineteen-year-old niece, was similarly inclined, but her nephew, William, like a typical growing eleven-year-old boy, was devouring his second helping of eggs in huge mouthfuls.

'William, I'm sure your mother didn't approve of you eating in that fashion.'

William, whose looks and thick, dark hair reminded her of Charles's long-dead brother, Arthur, immediately lowered the fork and dropped his eyes in shame. His sister giggled childishly.

'Boys, Aunt Annie. Disgusting creatures.'

William glared at her. 'I'm not disgusting!'

'That's enough, both of you,' Annie said firmly, then smiled at her nephew to let him know she wasn't particularly cross.

In truth, Annie was delighted to have their company. They'd been in Lough

Mask House since the beginning of the summer after they'd been made Charles's legal wards. Tragically, dear, dear Arthur, their father, had been killed on some obscure battlefield when William was still an infant, and when their mother, Isabella, died a slow and wasting death earlier that year from consumption, the responsibility of caring for them had fallen upon her and Charles; it was a responsibility Annie had gladly accepted. Madeleine and William filled a void in her life, in part because they offered her company, and also because they made up, in some small way, for her daughter's absence and a need to fulfil her motherly instinct. She knew they would both have to depart for schooling purposes in the coming months and she had become so used to their company that she dreaded the day they would leave. But that might be as far away as October and any amount of things could happen between now and then.

She could hear Charles's voice now, even before he opened the dining room door, expounding loudly upon his usual topic to Asheton Weekes. Asheton, her husband's only friend, was now accepted as a permanent resident, it seemed. Although a decade younger than Charles, they'd become friends in the military, Asheton having seen active service abroad. Asheton's parents had died when he was a young man, as had his only brother, and Annie believed that the military had become a kind of surrogate family for him and that he almost viewed her husband as a father. It had been Charles's suggestion that Asheton come and live at Lough Mask House when he left the army, although Annie suspected that Charles's invitation was motivated in part by Asheton's equine expertise, and in fact Asheton now oversaw the running of the stables. Annie liked Asheton, who was every inch the gentleman and had a gentle, kindly way and an even temper, the diametric opposite to her husband. She occasionally wondered, given their differences of temperament, how their friendship survived. The door opened and her husband went directly to the side table where he began to spoon scrambled eggs on to a plate, not bothering with a greeting.

'Don't trouble yourself too greatly, Weekes,' he said. 'We've had this kind of thing before. Last August I believe. It's that deuced Land League. Since Parnell became their leader he's been stirring things up. It's all hot air, I assure you.'

'Good morning all,' Asheton said with a respectful bow.

'The way of it is, Weekes,' Boycott said, gesticulating with a slice of toast as he sat opposite his wife, 'is that the Irish as a race, generally speaking, recognise their place in the world as a people in need of a guiding hand. And England naturally fulfils that role, geographically looking over Ireland's shoulder since creation, as it were. It's an established fact that Anglo-Saxons are favoured with a sharper intellectual and spiritual core than the Celts or Picts, particularly the Catholic Celts. Peasants the world over accept the state of affairs that God and nature has ordained, but the likes of Parnell or that troublemaker priest in the village, O'Malley, are always apt to stir disgruntlement.'

Annie sighed inwardly. Her husband had a way of sucking all the lightness from a room. Madeleine had fallen silent and was idly stirring the porridge in her bowl. The previously animated William looked bored and clearly wished to be excused. Even Asheton appeared weary as he struggled to concentrate on her husband's tired rhetoric. It was only eight o'clock in the morning, for the love of God.

'The likes of Parnell and that reprehensible terrorist Davitt actually believe we should just walk away and let the peasants run the country. Home Rule? The Irish are no more capable of ruling themselves than...well, it's like asking horses to run the stable.'

'Charles. Must every meal be accompanied by a political lecture?'

Boycott lowered his fork and allowed it to clink against the china. 'My dear, these are important matters. Our very way of life is–'

'I have to resume my studies, Auntie. May I be excused?' William whispered.

'You may, William.'

'As I was saying, what the Irish as a race crave is discipline,' he said, slapping the table lightly. 'Oh they'll try to hornswoggle their betters. They'll happily steal the wax from your ear while they whisper words of trust. And if such behaviour is allowed to flourish, there's no telling where it will end.'

'Please, Charles, that's enough! I'm getting heartburn.' Annie said with sufficient force to surprise her husband.

'If you'll forgive me, Annie, in Charles's defence, he has been rather provoked this morning,' Asheton Weekes offered tentatively. 'What with the note and such.'

Boycott waved a dismissive hand. 'Not in the least, I–'

'What note? Is it like the one last year? Where is it?' Annie asked with concern.

Boycott pulled a crumpled piece of paper from his waistcoat pocket and tossed it across the table as though it was of no consequence. Annie unfolded it to reveal a crudely drawn picture of a coffin, with 'Boycott, R.I.P.' scrawled across the top and a barely legible line written in pencil: 'We dimand a 25% abatement of rents now! Or you will pay anuther way. God save Ireland!'

'My God! This is a death threat. You must contact the RIC and get protection.'

'As I was telling Weekes here, this is just another idle threat. The priest O'Malley is filling their heads with this Land League nonsense.'

'Idle threat?' Annie was genuinely alarmed. 'What about David Feerick?'

Two months ago, David Feerick, a young land agent for the Browne estate near Ballinrobe, just five miles to the north, had been brutally gunned down by three men assumed to be extremist nationalists. Thus far no one had been charged with the murder. Incredibly, the wretched Feerick had survived for six weeks, but succumbed to his wounds a few days ago, or so they'd read in *The Ballinrobe Chronicle.* Feerick was the latest casualty in a long line of land agents, bailiffs and landlords who had fallen victim to agrarian terrorists. The previous spring, her husband had been granted RIC protection for several months after a series of threats, without any major incident.

Boycott threw his cutlery on to the empty plate hard enough to chip it. 'I'll not skulk in my own home because a few peasants have said boo!'

'Honestly, Charles, you're as stubborn as that horse you bought!'

'Precisely. But unlike Iron Duke, Parnell and his Land Leaguers will soon discover that Charles Boycott won't be tamed.'

A fraught silence ensued until Maggie knocked and stepped into the room, eyes down, nervously twisting her hands in front of her.

'Excuse me, sir. But em, em…'

'What is it, for heaven's sake?' Boycott yelled, the blood still high in his cheeks.

'I'm sorry, sir, but Mr McHale told me te fetch ye. There's trouble in the fields.'

'What trouble?'

'Pardon me, but I don't know, sir. He just told me te hurry.'

Boycott heaved an exasperated sigh. 'What now, in the name of God?'

***

Lord Erne's holdings beside Lough Mask amounted to a relatively small fifteen hundred acres, which were farmed by thirty-eight tenants over whom Charles Boycott acted as land agent, responsible for rent collection, enforcing the rules of tenancy and ensuring the general upkeep of the property. But the position he'd taken seven years earlier had also come with the lease of six hundred acres to farm at his will, a substantial acreage which could provide a healthy annual return. It was to this land that he and Weekes now drove their carriage, the rarity of the summer sun blessing the Mayo landscape with warming rays.

They were greeted by the sight of his twelve labourers gathered at the edge of a field of oats. Boycott leapt down before Weekes could bring the carriage to a halt. A murmur among the labourers faded as grim faces turned towards him.

'What in blazes is going on? Why aren't you at work?'

Martin Branigan, a broad-chested man of forty with wild black hair, emerged from the group.

'Captain Boycott,' he said without any due deference, 'we want te discuss the terms of our employment.'

'You what? There are hundreds of acres to be harvested.' Boycott swept his cane across the panorama of field upon field of ripe golden oats, mangolds and turnips. 'Get to it immediately!'

'You heard me.'

'What are you talking about, Branigan, you insolent lout?' Boycott asked with incredulity as Weekes joined him at his side.

Branigan bristled at the insulting language and took a step forward. 'There'll be not a tap of harvesting done until we get an increase in wages of two to four shillings, relative to age and experience.'

'How dare you speak to me in that–'

'What's more, we demand te be contracted until November the first, not just until the end of the harvest.'

'You *demand*!' Boycott was beside himself with rage. 'You're not in a position to demand anything!'

'Previous years you've driven the men like slaves te get the harvest in as quickly as possible so you could pay them less. The ten weeks until November is a reasonable time for twelve men te bring in such a large crop. That's the deal, take it or leave it. Until then, we're on strike.' Branigan threw the scythe he was holding to the ground, turned his back and walked away. The others mimicked his action and Boycott and Weekes stood watching as the men trooped from his fields.

'You'll never work in this county again, you treacherous scoundrels!' Boycott yelled after them, his face near to purple in colour. 'It's that Catholic traitor O'Malley put you up to this, isn't it? If I had my way you'd be flogged for insolence. Come back here immediately and get to work!'

He received no reply but the silence of their backs as they disappeared up the lane.

***

'This is the most outrageous, insolent act I've witnessed in my entire life. How dare a rabble presume to dictate terms to me!'

'Charles, calm yourself. There's no point repeating the same thing over and over,' Annie said. She shook her head and looked at Weekes.

'Annie's right, Charles. This is getting us nowhere.'

Annie had feared her husband might damage his heart, such was his state of discomposure. The three were seated in the drawing room, where they'd been for over an hour, most of the time spent listening to her husband spitting venom about the Land League, Fr O'Malley and Fenians terrorists.

'I wish to be alone,' he snapped.

'Very well, Charles.'

Annie knew better than to argue. She nodded to Weekes and the pair shuffled silently from the room. Thirty minutes passed before he entered the dining room to where they'd retreated. He began to circumnavigate the table, one arm folded behind his back, the other holding his cane, which tapped the wooden floor as he walked.

'I've come to a decision. And I want you both to do me the courtesy of hearing me out without interruption,' he said, his voice calm, his tone measured.

Nods of agreement followed.

'I've no doubt that priest, O'Malley, is behind this. He's been filling their heads with *ignis fatuus* notions about their social rights. In short, this is blackmail. And as an Englishman and a gentleman, I cannot be seen to submit to blackmail, particularly from a collection of indolent peasants. Were we to kowtow to the likes of the Land League, it would be the thin end of the wedge for all the law-abiding landowners from Kerry to Antrim. What we must do is show the blaggards what steel our class is made of. What we must do, in other words, is bring in the harvest ourselves.'

He slammed the metal tip of the cane against the floor for emphasis. Annie sat with her lips parted, praying she misunderstood his meaning. She glanced at Weekes who wore a similar expression. He nervously pushed his hands into his jacket pockets.

'Eh, if I may ask, Charles. Who, precisely?'

He looked at them as though the answer should have been apparent and then swept the cane in a high arc to indicate the household. 'Why, all of us. Myself, of course. You, Weekes. Annie, Madeleine, young William, Maggie, the Loughlin woman, McHale in the stable. Everyone.'

'Charles, you can't be serious.'

'By God I am, woman.'

'But I wouldn't have the first notion how to–'

He swept her objections away with his arm as he and strode towards the door. 'Don't worry. I'll teach everyone what to do. Remember, dear, this isn't just about saving the five hundred pounds of crops, there's a *principle* involved. Have everyone assemble at the north field in fifteen minutes.'

'You mean you want us to work in the fields *now*?'

'Let's make hay while the sun shines, my dear.'

His footfalls echoed along the hallway as Annie sat and closed her eyes against the world.

***

No further argument would be brooked. He'd hastily pooh-poohed each protest with a wave of his hand and when he'd insisted on the reasonableness of his arguments with a raised voice, Annie knew from experience that further objections would be pointless. So she dutifully succumbed, rounded up the others and brought them to the field. The only concession he made was to submit to Annie's demand that Mrs Loughlin and Mr McHale be excused as they were both in their sixties.

At the gate to the field, he explained the task ahead to the bemused household. It was not just because of the appalling financial loss they would incur, he explained, but it was their moral obligation to make a stand here today. And so the five were assigned duties, and after a brief lesson in the use of a scythe, they set about bringing in the harvest. None of them was particularly athletic by nature, their clothes were unsuited to the task and all found the labour backbreaking. Progress was pitifully slow under the warm sun. At three o'clock young Madeleine, sporting unseemly patches of perspiration beneath her armpits, fainted and had to be carried into the kitchen and fed sweetened water. An hour later the same happened to Maggie. William, initially the keenest worker, now complained incessantly of tired arms. Of the women and children, only Annie seemed indefatigable and she continued to swing the scythe until late into the afternoon, before pointing out that they had cleared just a tiny fraction of one of ten fields.

That evening Boycott mulled long and hard as the others bathed, ate and proceeded directly to their beds hours before sunset. He was seated at his writing desk in the drawing room calculating how much of the harvest they might hope to save and the potential financial damage, when Annie walked wearily in and plopped into an armchair.

'Charles, I don't think we can continue. We're not cut out to do this kind of work.'

He turned and shook his head, then tugged at the tip of his beard, which she knew to be a sign of uncertainty. It gave her a glimmer of hope that her husband might abandon his futile salvo in the direction of the Land League, for she was certain that this lay behind his action. Soon after the mass meeting in Irishtown in April of the previous year, Parnell, Davitt and others had formed the Irish National Land League. Each day since, they'd grown in strength, held larger and larger meetings, and had mass support, especially in the west of Ireland. And although her husband blustered about the futility of their speeches of defiance, she knew he felt deeply threatened.

'We must carry on. The financial loss if we lose the entire harvest is incalculable.' He waved paper covered in scribbled calculations at her. 'And the principle–'

She suddenly felt the bile rise in her throat. 'Oh Charles, please don't lecture me anymore about the principle. I'm simply too tired!' She rose again and strode from the room, slamming the door behind her.

Annie went first to William's room, and found him lying diagonally across the bed, the blankets and sheets kicked into a tangle about his feet. Sonorous snores escaped his open mouth, so loud it was hard to credit they came from an eleven-year-old. She smiled, despite her weariness of body and mind, and gently pulled the coverings up to his chin, kissed him on the forehead and slipped from the room.

Madeleine was similarly in the depths of an exhausted slumber and Annie sat by her bed a few moments stroking her hair, studying her face. Although Madeleine and her own daughter, Mary, bore little immediate resemblance to each other, the subtle curves about her niece's eyes were an undoubted shared trait, as was their laughter, the kind of nuances of character that she imagined only a mother could identify.

She was suddenly gripped by a deep melancholy and a need to escape her niece's room. She bent and kissed Madeleine lightly and hurried to her own bedroom. She washed and quickly changed into her night things before slipping between the welcome coolness of the sheets. She lay there, conscious of the aches in her body that she knew would soon heal and the pain in her heart that never would.

***

Dear Arthur, she thought, ten years dead. How she wished he could visit them now, lightening their hearts with his charm and humour, and relieving her burden with his insight and his sensitivity, as he had done on so many occasions during those early years of her marriage.

She had grown strong, as Arthur predicted, and learned to love her husband despite himself. She had found the strength to stand her ground, although a woman's position in society only permitted so much latitude in such matters. And, of course, it was so utterly draining to try to counter Charles's belligerence and intolerance on a daily basis that she often found it made life easier to grant him his way, as had happened that very day.

And his character had mellowed somewhat, at least for a number of years. Once, soon after Mary had been born, she had been shocked when unbeknown to her he had entered their chamber as she was breast-feeding the infant. His silent observation of her with her breast exposed had not been the source of her shock, however; rather it was the compliment that he had bestowed upon her, telling her that she was one of God's most beautiful creatures. She'd looked up in silence, taken aback, lips parted, and then he'd become embarrassed, muttered apologies and stomped away. How she wished she could have seized that moment, gone to him, embraced him, rewarded him for the effort it had surely taken to say those few words.

And she had been pretty then, beautiful even, coal-black hair and a perfect complexion, a blushing smile and shy, hazel-green eyes. To hear an acknowledgement of her prettiness from her husband, a man of incredible reserve, was priceless to her, especially as she'd never heard it repeated in the twenty-four years since that day. Yet he hadn't been so restrained in his compliments to his daughter over the years and that had compensated her a great deal.

Mary had slowly grown strong though Annie's nurturing and attention, and quickly developed a voice whose loudness and insistence was surely an inheritance from her father. And the child found a way into his heart that she herself had only glimpsed.

She had encouraged it at every opportunity. In those first few weeks, taking him unawares, she would press the infant into his arms. His discomfort was evident, his smile set directly atop a grimace that threatened to break through at any moment. Annie usually had the sense that he found the smell of the child offensive, whereas she relished each of her odours – her skin, her warm breath, and even those normally unpleasant to the human nose, they were just another part of her daughter's being. Given the trauma of her birth, Mary was a miracle indeed. But despite his distaste for Mary's bodily functions, she noted that he became increasingly reluctant to return the child to her arms.

Awkward with the helpless infant, he was to prove at ease with the walking child. As Mary's steps had grown longer and steadier, he had set about tutoring her on her place in the world. Annie had taken her own steps to ensure some balance was brought to this venture, as she had no intention of allowing her sole offspring to develop into the peremptory character that she had married. Charles would on occasion allow the stumbling tot to accompany him about the estate, witness to his shrill commands or flights of temper. Annie had schooled her differently, urging compassion and honesty, albeit in terms a child could grasp. She could recall times when she would hear her husband one moment yelling at some employee and in the next whispering nonsense talk to his daughter. At such times she considered that he was indeed capable of love, but it was conditional. To earn his love, Annie or his daughter must freely embrace his behaviour.

By the time she was six, he had succeeded in indoctrinating one small aspect of his character into Mary with absolute success, and it was one to which Annie had no great objection. That was his love of horses. Mary had been able to ride a small pony when little more than waist high. In those days, father and daughter had been inseparable. When the requirements of her schooling had inevitably come along, Annie insisted that she be sent away to boarding school as she wanted to make sure Mary had the opportunity to spend time in the company of others her own age. After Mary left, Charles had been disconsolate for weeks and had unburdened his temper on her and the tenants.

As Mary had grown, so had Annie's awareness of Charles's approach to running the estate. It was true that he often returned to the house in the evening in the foulest of moods, giving voice to expressions of contempt for his labourers or tenants, but in those early years, Annie assumed that this was merely the way of business. Yet she had little meaningful knowledge of the tenants' lives, of the precariousness of their existence or of the added burdens that, as she would subsequently discover, her own husband frequently placed upon them. When she reflected later from the comforting, judicious sanctuary of middle age, she had existed in a shell of naivety, perhaps deliberately so. It was easier to live in ignorance, not to discomfit her mind with craggy, prodding thoughts.

When Mary departed for boarding school, Charles's temperament had regressed, laughter only ever creasing his face when it was in celebration of another's misfortune. With each year he'd become increasingly detached, distancing himself from almost all friendships, even those of family. She subsequently learned that for his tenants and labourers there were fines for snapping the handle of a scythe, for collecting dead branches from his fields or for crossing his land without permission. Every petty sin against Boycott's law was penalised with venom. And, of course, there were evictions – wailing, clamorous and often unjust – and it disturbed her that he seemed utterly indifferent to the suffering these terrible events wrought. But it wasn't a woman's place to become involved in such things. Yet she still felt an unbridled shame.

And then Mary had returned home a young woman and Annie's heart had swelled with the hope that Charles would mellow again under her influence. And her hopes appeared justified as his love for his daughter seemed as great as ever, and Annie glimpsed again those elusive smiles on his face. But it was not to last. For Mary was no longer a child and the irony of it all was that a wilfulness she had inherited from her father would ultimately play no small part in driving them apart forever.

In late 1873 the carriage bearing Her Majesty's Royal Mail trundled up the rise to Corrymore House and Charles was handed a letter bearing the Earl of Erne's seal. He'd announced with rising excitement the offer to take up the position at Lough Mask Estate. It was the opportunity he'd always craved, he'd said. It was a much larger estate, with better land, a fine house, more prestige, more money. And the opportunity to flee the memory of his daughter, Annie secretly thought.

Annie had been reluctant to leave the place she had spent most of her adult life, and to which she was still deeply connected emotionally, not least because of Mary. But she had reluctantly acknowledged that the new position would serve his ambition and their futures well. Their new life and fortunes awaited them across the hills to the east. In Charles's mind the greater the remove in time and place from the memory of Mary, the better. Annie had silently taken quite the opposite view, that those events would haunt their every deed until their dying day.

Arthur had told her once that Charles held no contempt for the peasants. He distrusted them, certainly, but was emotionally indifferent to them, as one might be to a sheep. But as a result of that terrible affair involving Mary, and her tragic, lonely death at the age of nineteen, Charles Boycott's distrust of the peasant had turned to malice. And it was no longer the broad notion of the universal peasant at which his hostility was directed, but the Irish Catholic peasant. Annie believed that it was this secret malevolence of his that drove him now to rail against every utterance of the Land League and to treat his tenants and labourers with disdain. He would make them pay for the wounds that he would never admit he bore.

She supposed he took solace in his contempt of the Irish or of Catholicism; or if not solace, perhaps it acted as a shield. She could not bring herself to loathe an entire race, especially her own, because of what had happened with Mary. As the years had passed since their daughter's death, she had endured her husband's open bitterness only because she knew she had shared in its inception; she herself had played a significant role in Mary's estrangement. But unlike Charles, she refused to allow bitterness to harden her heart. Instead, she simply bore the guilt in silence, and prayed often to God and to Mary for forgiveness.

The world went along on its way, ever-changing, joys and tragedies adding more to its sum. But Charles Boycott remained locked in a prison of his rearing, his culture and his personal bitterness. His deep-seated prejudice became out-dated and unfashionable, even among Britain's ruling elite.

As an Irish-born woman of the ascendant classes and one who had witnessed the famine years close-up, Annie believed that she had a greater insight into the current Irish mind and character than all the politicians, strategists and intellectuals in Westminster put together. Back in the late 1840s the potatoes had failed year on year, but a seed was sown in every Irish man, woman and child that had survived that horror, and it had grown and flourished. The Irish people had watched as the kingdom of which they had supposedly been an integral part had all but abandoned them to the brutality of mass starvation, as sure a means of fostering discontent, hatred even, as any on this earth. Charles and most of his kind had grown up in England, far from the abomination of those years. She had witnessed it. The Irish had suffered it.

Of one thing she was certain: the famine had been a watershed. Change was coming by either fair means or foul. She could see it in people's eyes, hear its subtext in their voices and sense it on the wind. If Britain's rulers could grasp even a little of what she knew, they'd have the sense to hasten and to help that transition. If not, then revolution and bloodshed was certain, sooner or later.

Did she love him still? She wasn't sure that she had ever loved anything more than a dream, the wish for a man who, as the years passed, would grow dearer in her heart. But their daughter had died and all hope that she would ever find that man had vanished. Instead, she was left with Captain Charles Boycott. But for all his faults, and they were legion, he'd always provided for her, never struck her, to her knowledge and belief had been faithful, and, she suspected, were it ever asked of him, would lay his life down for her. And as was the duty of a woman of her class, she would stand by him to the end, come what may.

***

Dawn was just touching the horizon when Annie awoke to find herself alone in the bed. Worry gripped her as she pulled a robe about her and hurried down the stairway clutching an oil lamp, which threw long, dancing shadows on the floor and walls as she glided along. After an increasingly fraught search she finally found him seated at the table in the kitchen where the servants dined, a cup and pot of tea before him, along with several newspapers of various vintages. His eyes were heavy, his clothes dishevelled, the slump of his shoulders more pronounced. He looked up with surprise at her approach.

'Annie, dear, what are you doing down here?'

'Charles, I may more properly ask the same of you. Have you not slept?'

He shook his head and tapped the newspapers. 'Couldn't sleep. Was reading and came down to make some tea, revive me before I return to the fields. I felt I should get the day off to an early start. Show those blaggards I won't be trifled with.'

'But Charles, you can't possibly work without sleep! You'll kill yourself!'

He tapped one of the newspapers, as though he hadn't heard her. 'Do you know that terrorist Davitt has been encouraging the masses to blacklist anyone who takes up a farm from which someone has been evicted? It's sedition, if you ask me.'

'Charles!'

He looked up as if he was suddenly aware of her presence. 'Yes, dear?'

'What are you doing? It's five a.m.!'

He nodded. 'You're right. I should get to work. Can't let this blasted Land League get the better of us. You and the others follow when you've eaten.'

Annie grasped his arm as he started to rise. 'No, Charles.'

'What do you mean, no?'

Annie inhaled sharply and sat in a chair beside him. 'I mean Charles, that if you wish it still, if you wish your wife to work like a common labourer from dawn to dusk, I shall do as you ask. But I won't ask it of the others. I feel ashamed our own flesh and blood were dragged into it yesterday. I won't allow it.'

He clutched a handful of the newspapers.

'Won't allow it? But what of these Fenian scoundrels? And the financial loss?'

'Charles. Do you really expect your niece and nephew to work as labourers until Christmas? What of William's schooling? And the household? How are we to run it without Maggie? Consider the reality, Charles. You can't defeat Parnell and Davitt and the entire Land League on your own.'

He stared at her in silence for a few moments before grunting and turning his eyes from hers. 'I simply cannot submit to their demands. I cannot!'

Annie sighed and began to rise wearily. 'Then I suppose I had better go and change and ready myself for a day of hard labour.'

She was at the steps when his voice halted her.

'Very well then. Have it your way.'

She turned and met his eyes. The phrase implied his submission was her doing. It was the best she could expect, that much she had learned.

'Thank you, Charles.'

'Oh don't thank me, Annie. Once I acquiesce, it will simply encourage them and there'll be no end to their demands. It's just what he wants,' he hissed, tapping the name 'Parnell' in a newspaper headline. 'This, my dear, is just the beginning.' With that he scrunched the page in a ball and hurled it angrily across the room.

Chapter 7

I was wholly unprepared for the spectacle which greeted our eyes at Aughleen. Here were collected three or four hundred emaciated people in various stages of fever, starvation and nakedness; the majority of whom were evicted tenantry. Many, too weak to stand, were lying on the cold ground, others squatting on the bare turf to hide their naked limbs. Some of the children and old people were dying, and I was informed that the worst had not made their appearance, as many were too ill to crawl out of their hiding places.

–*A Visit to Connaught in the Autumn of 1847*, James H Tuke

In the neighbourhood of Newport a poor man named Mulloy was found on the roadside. His emaciated frame betokened that his death was the result of want. On the same day, the body of James Brislane was found at Kilrimmin. On Friday last a poor man died at Deradda of actual hunger, leaving a family to follow in rapid succession. During the past week Mr. O'Grady, coroner, held inquests on the following persons: Anne Philibin, Patt Hemnon, Francis Gannon, Jordan Morrison, Anne Teatum, Patrick Corey, Thomas Costello, Patrick Maughan…

–*The Mayo Constitution*, 19 February 1848

October 1848

They saw the first of the dead just a short step along the road to Louisburgh. At first they thought the man was drinking from the lough, lying on the shore, face pressed into the frigid waters. They were immediately cautious, as their meagre supply of food wouldn't stretch to feed another. But when the man didn't stir at their approach they exchanged nervous but inquisitive looks. Thomas approached him with halting steps and ventured a 'Hello?' but got no response. He reached down, took the man by his shoulder and pushed him over. They recoiled as one at the sight of the half-eaten face, ragged grey flesh, bone protruding from his chin. He'd come to quench a thirst and died there, the tiny water creatures feasting on his flesh for God only knew how long.

'Let's keep moving.' Thomas pulled Owen back towards the dusty track, almost having to wrench his younger brother's eyes from the scene.

They continued along the road, the day grey but dry. With each step Owen was aware of a growing sense of loss as he felt the only life he'd known slip away; a life which had, until the famine, been relatively contented.

The Doolough valley in which they walked was as magnificent a place as any man might wish to behold. The steep mountains on either side of the lough seemed immense to him. The lough ran two miles to the north-west, almost half a mile wide, bounded by the plunging rocky escarpments of Barrclashcame to the east, Ben Lugmore to the west and Ben Creggan to the south. To the north towards Louisburgh the mountains receded into gentler slopes and then an open expanse of flat lands until Clew Bay and the ocean beyond. In the past he'd marvelled at the valley's silent majesty and wondered at the depths of the lough, which reflected the jagged slopes, grey and green with splashes of yellow furze and purple heathers. Now as he walked, each tortuous step gave him cause to wonder if he'd ever see its like again.

Progress was slow. They covered barely a mile in the first hours, although the road they travelled was as flat as the lough's surface, hugging as it did her north-eastern shoreline, yet each step was taken as though they were climbing the precipitous slopes that surrounded them. So wasted were their muscles that they seemed to have forgotten the elementary function of walking.

'Look.'

Thomas pointed out into the lough, where a solitary boat floated, almost motionless in the still water. They listened, and for a moment all was so quiet that Owen imagined he could hear his own heart beating.

'There's someone in it,' Owen muttered, and took a step closer to the water's edge.

The arm of a black jacket was draped across the side of the boat and a skeletal hand protruded from it, the extended fingers brushing the water.

'Dead, whoever it is,' said Thomas dispassionately.

The broadening valley to the north presented a barren aspect: reed-like pockets of growth nearest the water, and beyond that a bog whose pale greens and browns were somewhat lightened by the occasional hint of heather. They trundled on mostly in silence, eyes peeled for any person's approach, but the road was strangely quiet. As a mist descended, they were given to remarking on imagined or real figures of people in the distance, dots of black that appeared and vanished like smoke in the wind.

Two hours further and the soupy mist had settled over their heads. The mountains behind them were all but invisible and the lower hills on either side just ghostly shapes through the grey vapours. Light rain dampened their clothes and the first chills of the evening air began to settle into their bones. They rested again at a narrow bridge that spanned the Carrownisky River and contemplated their progress, which had been pitiful.

'We'll have te find somewhere for the night,' Thomas remarked as he looked into the darkening sky, wiping the accumulated drizzle from his hair and face with the sleeve of his jacket. 'We'll eat then.'

'We could sleep under the bridge here.'

'I thought that, but there's a fierce wind here most nights, we'd probably freeze te death before morning. We couldn't even light a fire 'cause you'd be able to see it for miles. We don't want to attract attention.'

In matters practical, Owen conceded his brother's good sense, but he felt desperately tired and his stomach craved renewed sustenance. The awful burps of fetid air were beginning to recur and with them the sense of dying from within.

'We'll find an abandoned cottage and–' Thomas interrupted himself and listened to what they both heard with unmistakable clarity: the approach of a carriage.

'Maybe they could give us a jaunt to Louisburgh.'

'And maybe they're English soldiers who'll cut our throats. Under the bridge, quick.' Thomas was already up and clambering down the steep muddy bank to the fast-flowing stream, Owen skittering hastily down behind him. They huddled under the old stone arch, pressing tightly against the wall to keep from sight. They listened to the slow approach of the vehicle, the horse's tramp halting and irregular, the carriage struggling to progress in the muddy, rutted track. Owen could feel Thomas's body pressed against his back, could feel his breath upon his neck as he used to do when they'd shared a bed as children. Thomas placed a hand on his shoulder and he closed his eyes. At that moment he had no fear, but a sudden awareness that he loved his brother and that Thomas loved him, and all that Thomas had done was for his protection and survival. He opened his eyes and tilted his head a fraction to get a partial view of the track. The cloud that had settled was impenetrable to the eye beyond twenty yards and from this he saw a single horse appear, snorting in protest at its exertions. Then a voice called 'whoh!' and behind the animal came a jaunting car upon which perched two men, the driver attired in coarse clothing and flat cap with a deeply lined red face, the other a gentleman in a top hat, dark overcoat, and upturned collar and tie, with a blanket across his knees. Thomas gripped Owen's shoulder and pressed his head back against the cold stone.

The carriage started across the bridge when an Englishman's voice halted its progress. 'Stop here a moment, Mahoney. My back is throbbing from the bouncing and I need to stretch.'

The brothers listened as the two men dismounted. There were mutterings they couldn't make out above the rush of the stream and then well-heeled boots crossing the stones of the bridge over their heads. There was a muffling, like clothes being adjusted, then they watched as a jet of piss shot out over their heads accompanied by a groan of relief. Owen looked at Thomas, who raised his eyes to heaven. His business complete, the Englishman strode back across the bridge.

'Oh Mahoney, fill the canteen, would you?' He then chuckled, 'And be sure to do it upstream of the bridge.'

'Yes sir, right ho.'

Owen gasped as Thomas fumbled at his jacket and withdrew his knife. Owen shook his head vehemently, but Thomas hushed him. The driver appeared and clambered down the bank carrying a metal canteen. His back to them, he crouched by the river and allowed the water to gush into its narrow opening until it gurgled. He re-corked it, stood and stretched, gently massaging his lower back, then turned. He stopped dead on seeing them, his eyes startled, his mouth open. Suddenly he was clambering up the bank as though he'd beheld a spectre come to take him to his grave.

'Sir! There are men! They have a knife!'

'What men? Where are they?'

'Under the bridge!'

They hesitated before revealing themselves, until finally Owen shook his head and looked at his brother. 'Put the knife away. They're not soldiers.'

Thomas reluctantly did as prompted and Owen stepped out from under the arch, his bundle of possessions dangling at his side, Thomas at his shoulder. Above them stood the Englishman, a pistol drawn, Mahoney at his side. The gent seemed nervous as though he feared being done to death by a band of Irish brigands. But when the brothers emerged the tightness in his features eased and he half-smiled.

'It's not men. It's a couple of lads.'

'I'm more of a man than the likes of you,' Thomas replied sharply.

The Englishman chuckled. 'Perhaps you are indeed. Who are you? Are you going to the workhouse in Louisburgh?'

'No sir,' Owen replied, 'we're going to–'

'Where we're going,' Thomas interrupted, 'is none of your business.' As he said this they climbed up the bank and stood directly facing the stranger, who still held the gun cocked at the ready. He was a man of maybe thirty; slim with long sideburns, a wide, thin moustache, and inquisitive eyes.

Thomas nodded at the gun. 'What are you afraid of? Two scrawny Irish *lads*?'

The man tucked the pistol into a leather holster within the folds of his overcoat. 'My name is James Tuke and I mean you no harm. I'm here to see for myself the effects of the famine and to report back in England. I merely wish–'

'Tell them they're pigs and murderers.'

'Thomas!' Owen counselled.

Tuke remained unprovoked. 'If I encounter any injustice or misdeeds I will indeed report them, as I have done on a previous visit.' By now Tuke and the driver were clambering on to their car. He tipped his hat with practised politeness to the brothers, something Owen had never believed he'd see. 'I wish you God speed, wherever the road takes you. I cannot give you food, but perhaps you can purchase some along the way.'

He tossed a coin and Owen snapped it into his palm. He looked at the copper penny in his hand, stamped with the image and name of George IV. It was like a tiny treasure fallen from heaven and he looked back to Tuke to thank him. But Thomas seized the coin and called out, 'Hey, Englishman!'

Tuke looked around just as Thomas flung the coin back hard at him. He reacted quickly and seized it before it struck his face.

'We don't want your charity,' Thomas said bitterly.

Tuke frowned and turned away, and Mahoney flicked the whip to set the horse in motion.

Owen fumed. 'What's wrong with you? He didn't mean us any harm. And we need money.'

'Not from the likes of him. Fuck him and his kind.'

Owen grabbed his arm as he went to turn away and Thomas met his eyes sharply.

'Let me go, little brother,' he said with grim conviction and after a moment's hesitation, Owen complied. Thomas picked his bundle from the ground and set off along the road, the noise of the wheels of Tuke's car fading into memory. 'Hurry up. Rain's getting heavier. We'll have te bed down before it gets too dark.'

Owen heaved a burdened sigh and followed.

***

The village of Derryheagh loomed from the thickening mist not half a mile further along. The rain was heavier now and their clothes were soaked through, the fresh ruts from Tuke's car already filling with water. From the dim light they could guess that darkness would descend about them within the hour. They were chilled to the bone and the only warmth came from their exertions; even their toughened feet were near to numb. Only their youth held them upright.

There were perhaps twelve homes in Derryheagh, clustered together just off to the right of the track, surrounding a small clearing with a trough of stone at its centre. They approached with caution, terrified they might be set upon and their food stolen, but nothing stirred at their approach. The place seemed abandoned, as though its inhabitants had as one departed in the night. A few cottages had been burnt out, but seven or eight remained intact yet utterly silent. None had fires lit against the October chill and no candlelight flickered. But for the spattering rain against the mud, the silence was total.

'Maybe it's deserted,' Owen whispered.

'Be careful.'

They walked into the clearing, eyes darting to every side. Owen went to the first house to his right and peered through a crack in a shuttered window, but he could see nothing but blackness. He shook his head at Thomas, who was investigating the cottage opposite.

Owen turned from the window and stepped to the door beside him. He gently pushed, the door creaking as it swung inwards with little resistance. He took a hesitant step and at once his nostrils were assailed by a smell so vile and overwhelming that he was forced to clasp a hand over his mouth and nose. As his eyes adjusted he could see more, but dearly wished he couldn't, for six famished and ghastly figures were huddled in a corner on straw that was blotched with human waste. There was a woman, dead and open-eyed, her gaze locked for eternity on the thatch, a claw-like hand clutching at her breast, her legs bent at unnatural angles as though her final death throes had caused her to kick out. Beside her lay four children, all with the same grim countenance of death, their limbs and faces black, lips drawn back from yellowed teeth, and purple blotches on their skin, which was wrinkled like an old man's. The man, if that's what it was, lay against the wall, as though slumped there drunk, his chin resting on his chest, a vast stain of dried blood all about him where the flow from his throat had gushed forth. A knife lay beside his open hand.

A squawk escaped Owen's mouth and the rats that had been feeding on the bodies scurried into darkened corners. The man must have witnessed his family's agonised death and hastened to join them by slitting his own throat. Owen stepped back in horror and bumped against the doorframe, which caused him to yell and hurl himself out into the rain.

Thomas ran to him, his own face drained of blood, and grasped Owen's arm.

'Are ye all right?' Thomas's voice was shaking.

Owen bent to retch, but nothing came.

'I checked two others. They're all dead, far as I can see.' Thomas paused. 'Jesus Christ...But we have te check the rest, there might be an empty house.'

'I'm not staying here! It's a place of the dead!' Owen said through trembling lips.

'We have to! We'll freeze te death if we don't. They're just bodies. Come on.' Thomas started to pull Owen beside him.

'Just bodies? They're people, they're all dead.'

Thomas stopped and looked into his brother's face. He spoke tenderly, his voice quivering. 'Owen, I know. I'm scared as well. But we'll do this together. We'll be fine.'

Owen nodded after a time and they continued past the next two cottages, which had been burnt out. At the last one in the row they found a lone emaciated man, the carcass of a dog that had provided his final meal at his feet.

'Look,' Thomas whispered, pointing to a pile of clothing and shoes. 'He must have taken the clothes from his family as they died. Maybe te sell them.' He stepped into the hovel and gathered some clothes and two pairs of leather brogues, securing them in a blanket. They turned to go and were halted by a pitiful wail.

'Is that you, Father McHale?'

Owen and Thomas exchanged horrified glances as they realised the man by the hearth was still alive. They stood frozen to the spot.

'Who is that? Who comes into my house? Máire? Have you food? Is that you?' He was making pathetic attempts to push himself up on his elbow, which repeatedly collapsed beneath him.

'He's blind. Come on, we can't help him.'

Owen didn't argue and they both turned to flee. Another man stood in their path, silhouetted against the grey light.

'Who are you? Are ye Quakers? Have ye food?'

Thomas gasped. 'We've no food. We only sought shelter.'

Behind them the blind man continued to yell in semi-delirium. The wretched phantom in the doorway pointed at the blanket that Thomas had just bundled together.

'What's that? Is it food? Let me see. Open it.' He moved closer. Owen and Thomas glanced at each other and instinctively rushed at the man as one, their joint strength sending his paltry frame crashing to one side. As he fell to the ground they burst into the open air, only to be confronted by as many as ten haggard wretches. Some looked like old men, but most were women with children. One woman was naked from the waist up, her decency lost in the ravages of her starvation, ribs protruding through her skin. Imploring hands outstretched, they moved towards Owen and Thomas with the speed of desperation. The brothers looked about but they were at the wrong end of the clearing and beyond the cottages was a hill thick with brambles.

'We have no food!' Thomas screamed from the depths of his lungs, to no avail.

Thomas felt a hand on his shoulder and turned to see that the man they'd knocked aside was upon them. He swung about and planted his bony fist into the man's face; blood spurted from his nose as he collapsed.

'Run!' Thomas yelled.

They hurled themselves into the baying, wailing tangle of emaciated arms and struck out at the hands that tried to claw free their precious bundles. Crying children fell in the mud, women screamed murder at them and tore at their clothes. They'd almost broken through when Owen stumbled and fell. A woman was on top of him in an instant, tearing at his bundle with a ferocity that belied her corpse-like body. He rolled on his back and struck her in the mouth with his fist.

'Owen!' Thomas screamed.

He scrambled backwards on his arse and finally forced himself up to standing, then turned and fled with Thomas, piteous wails and curses trailing in their wake. They ran for a hundred yards before they collapsed by the roadside, chests heaving, hearts pounding, their bodies wracked with countless agonies. When finally their hearts began to slow, they both fell to sobbing.

***

They spent the night in the collapsed ruins of a solitary cottage on a hillside just south of another village known as An Cregan Bán, which meant 'The White Rock'. They sat huddled in the partial shelter of what had been the hearth.

In the depths of the seemingly unending black night, a wind arose and howled down the valley, spattering them with painfully cold rain. They'd eaten of their meagre rations, a piece of meat each and a handful of the soft red fruits of the dog rose. Their venture into the village had yielded only some rags of clothing, a blanket, and, most profitably, the shoes. Owen's fitted almost snugly, but Thomas's were too large and he had to stuff the toecaps with grass. Beyond that, Derryheagh had brought them only a collection of images that would dance in and out of their consciousness forever, their minds unwilling or unable to bury memories of such vividly morbid power.

Owen sat awake and shivering. Thomas had somehow found the resource to sleep but his rest was tainted by pitiful sobs. They sat with their bodies pressed together, arms clinging tightly to one another against the cold and in search of some vague, elusive comfort. Owen realised that these past years they'd ventured little beyond the townland around Tawnyard Hill, and for all the horrors they'd witnessed there, they'd lived in a relative cocoon, ignorant of the magnitude of the abomination all around them.

He was torn by conflicting feelings towards the people who had attacked them. As he listened to the wind groaning in the hillside hollows, one moment he would hate them for the murder he had seen in their eyes, and the next he would cry for their circumstance, abandoned by hope and waiting to die an agonising death, diminished as one of God's superior creatures and reduced to the level of a scavenging animal. He closed his eyes and whispered a prayer to his mother that somewhere along the path of his life he would find a place where he could be free of this world's harshest cruelties.

* * *

Thomas was shaking him awake and he blinked at the early morning light, the tenebrous cloud having surrendered the sky to the rising sun. He was immediately conscious of the cold and his lips trembled as though he was afflicted by a fever.

'The walking will warm us. Let's get going.'

The memory of the last village they'd encountered still vivid, they steered a course around An Cregan Bán, crossing a bog that opened into fields which a few years past would have been filled with men and women digging a rich harvest of potatoes. The fields were black as though a great fire had swept across them, covered with the stems of potatoes that had turned to a filthy mush beneath the soil. What remained of the leaves was dark and putrid, though some still carried the telltale flecks of white that foretold disaster. The smell almost defied description, akin to rotten vegetable matter coalesced with that of decaying flesh, yet sickly sweet also, and so pervasive and inescapable it made them want to vomit. They hastened their pace, tripping over the dead furrows in their effort to escape the stench.

'There's the track,' Thomas said, pointing north, and they were on the road again.

They skirted the village of Tully and several more nameless places. The track snaked through a wood, yellowed leaves showering upon them with each gust of wind, and when they passed beyond the trees they caught their first sight of the holy mountain of Croagh Patrick, where Ireland's saint had spent so much time in communion with God. The mountain, close to their destination of Westport, rose majestically towards the blue sky, although its rocky peak had yet to don its winter mantle of snow.

As they drew near to the town of Louisburgh they decided to abandon the road and move across country, avoiding any contact with people. An hour later and they glimpsed the sea as it washed around the countless islands that speckled Clew Bay. Its waters held the promise of their escape to a better world and the sight of it set Thomas to a quicker pace. As they ate on the slope of a hill called Kinknock, Thomas excitedly rose to his feet and pointed to a tall ship, its sails unfurled as it rode the waves out into the vastness of the Atlantic. Neither of them had ever seen such an enormous vessel and they both stood, mouths agape, watching as it navigated westwards. It was the first time in perhaps a year that Owen heard his brother laugh with joy.

'That'll be us soon, on our way to America. All this – it'll be behind us forever.'

''Twill,' Owen said with as much enthusiasm he could muster, for despite their hunger his stomach was beginning to fill with something else – a dread of the loss of all that was familiar to him.

'Look there,' Thomas said, pointing to a few hundred yards below, where they could see people moving along the road. 'More people on this road. All headed for Westport.'

Thomas's mood shifted a few minutes later as he assessed their rations. The journey had been arduous thus far and a huge drain on their resources, but it would probably be tomorrow evening by the time they reached Westport.

'We've barely a small bite left of the meat.'

They continued east, Croagh Patrick looming directly ahead of them. As evening drew near, they bypassed the coastal village of Kilsallagh and on its landward side spotted a copse of pines, from within which rose a plume of smoke, thick and dark from an abundant fire, unlike the wispy trails from a peasant's cottage.

'Let's have a look,' Thomas said.

'Why?'

'Let's just look,' Thomas barked with impatience.

They kept low through the trees, like prowling animals, and soon emerged at a wall of shrubbery. The aroma that suddenly assaulted their nostrils was surely one of the most exquisite of their lives. They both inhaled softly, with eyes closed, the scent of freshly baked bread. They crawled into the shrubs, ignoring the prickly branches that clawed at their clothes, and emerged at the rear of a grand, two-storied house, obviously the home of a person of wealth. There seemed to be nobody about.

'C'mon,' Thomas whispered to Owen and before any reply came, he had wriggled all the way through and was running, head and shoulders bent low, across the garden. Owen followed and joined him where he crouched behind a couple of water barrels. They were near the corner of the house and had a view of the rear and side, giving them at least some seconds of warning should someone approach. Thomas pointed down into a basement to a door with a couple of windows on either side. One window was pulled halfway up and through it they could see four loaves of bread cooling on a sideboard. From within came a mellifluous woman's voice, idly singing to herself to the accompaniment of the clatter of pots.

As I wandered through the townlands,
And the luscious grassy plains,
Who should I meet but a beautiful maid,
At the dawning of the day.

Thomas nodded for Owen to wait as he proceeded down the steps into the basement. He crept with the craft of a fox, maintaining a watchful eye on the upstairs windows. As his brother began to descend the steps Owen looked along the side of the house, and, whether it was a fleeting dance of the light or the sound of a gentle trickle of water, his curiosity was aroused enough to find himself drawn to a window a few yards away.

Thomas peered into the basement where he saw a matronly housekeeper of around sixty, well-fed by the looks of her, with a white bonnet tied about her head and a long, black housemaid's dress which touched the floor and created the illusion of gliding as she moved about. Her age and red face belied the sweet voice that he'd supposed belonged to some angelic young beauty. The kitchen was vast, to his mind, with a huge open hearth in which a man could stand and a large stove of black metal. In the centre was a table on which was laid a spread of food beyond even his dreams: a side of beef, another of ham, plucked birds, vegetables of all types, flour, salt and a block of butter the size of a Bible. There were devices whose purpose he couldn't even begin to understand: a box on top of which was a metal cup and a handle for turning; a U-shaped wooden gadget with two hand grips; a flat copper pan with a yard-long handle. The dressers were filled with plates, all with deep blue images of trees and flowers that captivated his eye, as he had never seen painted crockery. Thomas, in awe of the scene, had to snap himself to attention to renew his task, that of stealing the bread, of which the owners clearly had plenty. But if he was caught, it would likely merit transportation to the dreaded English penal colonies.

He waited until the housekeeper was bent over the stove, then simply reached in and plucked a loaf from the sideboard. He was tempted to take a second, so easy had been the theft, but decided not to tempt providence, and quietly slipped back up the steps.

Owen had crept to the window at the side of the house feeling as though his heart would rise through his throat and burst from his mouth. He could hear his own shallow breaths in the still evening air as he peered into the room.

Thomas might have been able to describe the kitchen with some accuracy. Owen, by contrast, saw nothing of the room, for all his attention was devoted to the girl who stood within, and his eyes swelled wide at her beauty. She stood half-turned from him, tinkering with bottles on a dressing table, on which also rested a large bowl and a jug of steaming water. She was about twenty, dressed only in a white garment that billowed out on each leg from her ankles to her waist, above which she was naked. She pulled a pin from her golden hair, allowing the long, shining strands to fall to her shoulders. Her face was slender with a small nose, her cheeks a gentle curve of skin with a hint of red, her eyes dark, her mouth small. But it was the perfect curve of her breasts, bare and white, that most transfixed him, and he felt himself aroused like never before. She hummed a tune as she leaned over the bowl and lifted the jug to pour the warm water over her hair. Her breasts sat forward and Owen almost gasped aloud. He watched as she applied something from a dainty bottle to her hair and began to massage it in, suds gathering about her head like those he'd seen at a river's edge.

His reverie was broken by the sound of Thomas's voice and he looked over his shoulder. His brother seemed fit to strike him as he whispered through gritted teeth, 'We have te get out of here! Now!'

Owen forced himself to turn away at the precise moment that the scream came.

'My beautiful soda bread! Thief! There's a thief!' The dulcet voice of the housemaid seemed to have been replaced by that of a witch, so shrill were her yells.

'Go!' Thomas shouted.

Owen threw one last look through the window where he was granted a final glimpse of the girl, startled by the yelling, standing with a towel clutched at her bosom, her hair a wet tangle about her face. Their eyes met for a fleeting instant, then he fled.

Thomas ran and dived into the hedge as though into a lake, his momentum propelling him through the gap. Owen followed, but his pants snagged on a branch, his legs protruding back out onto the damp grass. Thomas grabbed his brother's shoulders and heaved him through just as the housekeeper arrived at the spot.

'Come back, you thieving blaggards. I'll have the constable and the dogs after ye and ye'll be off to Van Diemen's Land! I'll whip ye from here to County Cork and back!'

But her threats were already fading in their ears as they fled through the trees towards safety.

***

They found a hollow in the slopes of Ben Goram, the smaller mountain that lived in Croagh Patrick's shadow, concealed themselves with branches and prepared to spend the night. A deepening chill was seeping into them and by dark a frost had begun to settle. The feeling began to fade from their toes and fingertips, so they were forced to risk a fire of heather kindling and a few branches, which Thomas started with their father's tinderbox.

'This hollow, it faces inland,' Thomas reassured Owen, 'away from sight of the road, and nobody will notice it.'

'Do you think they'll have the RIC after us?'

Thomas considered for a moment then shook his head. 'I doubt it. There's people on that road below each day heading to Westport. Any of them could've stolen the bread.'

Thomas produced the round of soda bread from his bundle and both of them stared at it as though it were priceless metal. There was still a little warmth left in it and the aroma beckoned to them. Owen salivated as he watched his brother break the loaf in two. Thomas put one half away and broke the other again, handing his brother a piece the size of his fist. Owen bit into it and moaned softly, its moist, crumbly texture and mildly sweet taste seeming like a gift from God himself.

'Eat slowly or you'll be sick.'

They washed the bread down with water, groaning in fulfilment as a man will after a feast, then rested back and allowed the fire to warm their feet. Frugal as their meal had been, it was the finest moment of contentment they'd experienced in months.

A million stars lighted the night and Owen lay staring at them for some minutes in idle contemplation of the relative fullness of his belly, until his thoughts strayed to the girl, near naked as she washed her hair. He felt himself grow hard and shifted away from Thomas to conceal it, reaching down beneath their blanket and sliding his hand inside his pants, taking his swollen penis in his grip. After a minute his youthful imaginings betrayed him to Thomas, who stirred uneasily beside him.

'Are you playing with your *pócar*?'

Owen rapidly withdrew his hand and sat there indignant in the dark. 'I am not. I was sleeping.'

Thomas laughed lightly. 'It's all right brother. I saw the girl too as I ran.'

Owen felt a rush of anger as though the vision of the girl had been his alone to possess, then saw the stupidity of the notion. He sat and meditated for a time, watching Thomas's face in the fading glow of the fire.

'Thomas?' he asked, his voice barely a whisper.

'Try te get some sleep.'

'I will but…'

'What?'

'Do you think that our mother can see us, y'know, when we do sinful things, or when we think bad thoughts? Or our father?'

There was a sniffle of amusement. 'Like when you're playing with yourself?'

He bristled with embarrassment. 'Yes…but not just that…y'know…'

'No, I don't. That's bollocks,' Thomas snapped, a little angrily.

Owen pulled the thin blanket more tightly and after a few minutes felt his eyes grow weary. But his progress into sleep was disturbed by Thomas's voice. 'Owen…you know the meat we've been eating?'

'What about it?'

There was no reply. His brother's face had all but vanished into the dimness, the embers of the fire having turned an ashy grey. 'It's just that…' There was a long silence, until finally his voice came back more decisively, '…just that it's starting te turn and we better eat it in the morning or it'll be wasted. Go te sleep.'

Owen didn't reply, but sat there mulling over the brief exchange until the night folded him into slumber.

***

The morning dawned crisp and clear, with a light covering of frost that faded quickly at the touch of the sun's warmth. Light cloud drifted in from the ocean and Croagh Patrick's summit was hidden in a veil of mist. Further out towards the horizon, grey, brooding clouds lingered and threatened to dampen the final trek to Westport.

Thomas tore the last piece of meat in two and handed Owen his share. Thomas ate his piece quickly and turned away to gather their bundles. Owen hesitated, looking at the scrap of cooked flesh in his palm, before biting into it. There was a vaguely unpleasant taste, as though it was beginning to turn, which he washed away with a mouthful of water.

They set about making a decent pace, following the curve of the lower mountain slopes; they rounded Ben Goram and then Croagh Patrick until they crossed the pilgrim's path that snaked a steep and rocky way from Murrisk on the shore all the way to the holy mountain's summit. This day no pilgrims made the journey and Owen imagined that pilgrimages were rare in recent times, as the energy-draining climb would have proven near impossible to starved limbs.

On the road just fifty yards below, they could see far more people now, mostly groups of three or four, some with carts carrying all their worldly goods, others with a simple sack across their shoulder, and all wretched in appearance, walking in near silence towards the port or perhaps the misery of the workhouse.

Thomas spoke: 'It's probably safe te go back to the road, so many people…'

The sound of horses' hooves silenced him. A small troop of soldiers appeared, red coats with a white 'x' on their breast, horses thundering along the road with great purpose, sending people scattering to avoid being trampled. Thomas instinctively pulled his brother behind a rock and they remained there until the sound of hooves had faded.

'On second thoughts, let's stay off the road.'

They pressed on for hours, the terrain around Croagh Patrick ridge at intervals boggy or rocky and constantly undulating, reducing progress to a crawl. In the afternoon they rested in the narrow channel between two tiny loughs and ate half their remaining ration of bread. As they sat there, the last patch of blue sky was swallowed whole by a murky swell of cloud and they felt the first few drops of what threatened to be a downpour.

'That's almost all the food,' Owen remarked.

'We'll get something in Westport.'

'With what? We have no money.'

'Trust me, Owen, I'll get us food and tickets.'

'But how?

'Jesus! Just trust me.'

There was no more discussion and they walked on two more miles, crossing the Owenwee River and turning north to follow the curve of the bay towards the town. They were in open countryside now, boggy and flat, with a lone squat tree protruding from infertile earth here and there. To the north they could see smoke from chimneys in the town. The rain began to fall in dank, grey sheets, dispiriting them further. They came across a track that ran from the south and in its muddy bed were the footprints of a group of people, mostly barefoot, women and children they guessed. They followed its course for an hour or so until they were brought to an abrupt stop as they crested a small rise in the land.

There were six of them, two women, two boys, a girl and an infant. They lay in a hollow by the side of the track, ragged, huddled together, arms clinging to one another in a desperate union. All were dead, the rain washing mud from their emaciated faces.

'How are they all dead?' Owen's voice quivered as he fought the urge to cry.

Thomas spoke as though in a trance. 'They must have been caught in the open last night...were barely alive anyway. The cold must have finished them off. Jesus Christ...'

'Let's go, Thomas.'

Owen took his brother's arm and pulled to break the hypnotic spell the dead seemed to have cast on him, Thomas looking back over his shoulder at the macabre scene until they rounded a bend and it was lost from sight.

Eyes fixed on the muddy track, Thomas's thoughts escaped him in a whisper. 'Some day I swear I'll make the bastards pay for all this. As God is my witness.'

CHAPTER 8

You must show the landlords that you intend to keep a firm grip on your homesteads and lands. You must not allow yourselves to be dispossessed as you were dispossessed in 1847.

–Charles Stewart Parnell, speech in Westport, June 1879

DAVITT SPEAKS OF THE IRISH LAND LEAGUE TO AN IMMENSE AUDIENCE

The envoy of the Irish National Land League to this country, Michael Davitt, created the wildest enthusiasm in his audience. Events are marching so rapidly in Ireland, he said, that he had determined before leaving America to tell her people something about the real objectives of the Irish National Land League. 'You hear about the League inciting outrages, and that the organization winks at assassination. The British Government knows that it is playing a trump card when it makes these grave and false charges. It knows that if it can make you believe them we shall lose your support. The truth is that the Land League has from its inception called on the people to abstain from violence of all kinds. The movement is an angry movement. It concerns the life and death of the Irish people, and for this reason the people have sprung to their feet and declared that, cost what it will, Irish landlordism must come down.'

–*The New York Times*, 9 November 1880

9 September 1880

Owen Joyce woke to the sight of Niamh, his ten year-old daughter, curled perfectly against his wife Síomha in their bed, as if they'd been crafted that way. During the night the child had wandered in from the other bedroom of their three-roomed cottage, the one she shared with her sixteen-year-old brother Tadhg, sleepily muttering about nightmares. He quietly slipped from the bed and pulled on his breeches. His own sleep hadn't been untroubled – it rarely was – and he had a vague recollection of a dream of ships and his lost brother's voice beckoning to him.

He shook the memory away and dressed in silence, taking his boots outside into the room that served as kitchen and living space, sitting at the table to put them on. From the other bedroom he could hear Tadhg snoring on, a heavy sleeper from the day Owen had eased him from his mother's womb.

He judged it to be about six o'clock as he stepped out into the morning air, which was unexpectedly cool. A cloudless sky explained the chill and also meant a fine harvest day ahead, thank God, for thus far the season had been extremely temperamental.

Owen walked around to the rear of the cottage and up the slight rise on which it had been built, the elevation keeping winter floods at bay and draining some of the damp from his floor. In the early morning stillness he could hear the gentle flow of the Bunnadober River a little to the north, and its sound reminded him of his business at hand, whereupon he stepped behind the stone wall that formed their privy and relieved himself.

He paused on his way down the gentle rise and looked south towards the trees that surrounded Lough Mask House, Boycott's home. The house was below his line of sight, but a stream of turf smoke already rose from its chimney and Owen could not help but imagine the man warm by a fireside, eating a breakfast of porridge, eggs, bread and tea, all paid for by the tenants' labours.

Trying not to let bitterness overwhelm him on such a beautiful morning, he went to the side of the house where he'd constructed a stone trough that caught the run-off from the sedge thatch. He washed his hands and then the sleep from his eyes. Síomha insisted that they wash every time they crossed her threshold, a rule the children especially found infuriating, but had eventually accepted. Owen returned briefly to the cottage and, with the aid of a pair of tongs, pulled a large potato from the grey cinders of yesterday's fire. He wiped the ash off with his sleeve and bit into the still warm flesh, washing it down with a mug of water. He moved outside as he ate, gazing down at the two fields just below him, as yet unharvested, turnips in one, potatoes in the other. His field of potatoes alone, he considered, was three times the size of his father's holding on Tawnyard Hill. In fact the thirty-six acres he farmed was almost twenty times the size of his father's land and the soil much more productive. By any standards he'd made huge strides from those far-off days three decades ago when he'd left their home on the hillside, like a walking sack of bones. His house here by the shores of Lough Mask was more than twice the size of the cottage on Tawnyard Hill. He'd built a second, small bedroom as the children had begun to arrive. And his cottage had furniture – beds, a table and stools, even a cabinet in which Síomha stored her crockery. Besides his pony Anu, who doubled as their car and dray horse, he owned a small flock of sheep, which grazed one of the rougher fields away from the lakeshore and provided them with wool to sell at market. He grew a multiple of crops, potatoes the largest yield, but should the crop fail, turnips, carrots and oats could fill their bellies through the year.

Yet he shook his head in wonderment that he could have all this and yet find himself on the brink of poverty and eviction, because after rent had been paid to Boycott there was barely enough food left to feed the four members of his family. By his father's pitiful standards he was a wealthy man, although the notion seemed laughable. The only riches he possessed, he believed, were the three human beings sleeping within the walls behind him, and, of course, his other son, Lorcan, gone in search of a more prosperous life in America.

He began to walk to Anu's small, irregular enclosure, bound on all sides by dry stone walls, built long before he was born by hands that had pulled each stone from the earth, rendering the soil tillable. Anu was happily grazing in the morning light. As he slipped the harness over her head she gently nuzzled at him as though in greeting and he smiled and stroked her face. He suspected Anu would be lucky to see another summer.

Owen led her down the slope to the potato field and harnessed her to the plough, fitted with a flat share in place of a moldboard, and with a row of prongs, angled to bring up the potatoes, which Tadhg and Síomha would gather later. He slapped Anu gently and the beast snorted and with an effort began to haul the plough across the field.

After two appalling years, this season's crop seemed a little improved, although the yield still threatened to be markedly down on their last decent year in '77. And therein lay the rub. A bumper crop in '76 and Boycott had used it as an excuse to increase rents drastically. Again in '77 he'd pushed rents up. Then in '78 and '79 the dark days of a threatening famine had blackened the horizon for all of Ireland's tenant farmers. Not blight, but bitter frosts had sought out the seed potatoes and turnips deep beneath the earth. The damage to the crops had been little less than catastrophic. Owen had barely survived the two hard years.

With each year his family had traded off a bit more of their material worth to stay alive. Half of their original flock of sheep had been sold or slaughtered to feed them through the winters; they'd had to pawn the only decent suit he'd ever owned; and then poor Síomha, although she hadn't shown her distress to him, had to sell the white dress that had served as her wedding dress as well as her Sunday frock. Now she wore her heavy winter shawl to mass, even in the summer months, to conceal her poverty. The clock her father had gifted her on their wedding had also been sacrificed, its pendulum ticking off the seconds of another's life now. One piece of their dignity after another had been sold in an effort to satiate Boycott. And despite securing a ten percent reduction last year, they had as little chance of paying this year's reckoning as Anu had of beating Boycott's thoroughbred in a race. If God had put a more obdurate, parsimonious bastard on his earth, Owen was yet to meet him.

'C'mon girl, whoh! Turn girl.' He pulled on the rein and Anu swung about. He glanced back up towards the house and could see Síomha standing near the water trough. She waved at him briefly before disappearing inside, no doubt to rouse her son with a kick in the rump. It amused her to do this, and it seemed to be the only way to set their son in motion each morning. Not that he was lazy, for Tadhg was as industrious and spirited a lad as any father could wish for. He reminded Owen in many ways of Thomas.

Two children and a wife to feed for a year, rent to pay, seed to be purchased for the next season, and even their clothes were threadbare, patches upon patches. He'd done the calculations a hundred times. Sacrifice this to pay for that. Rob Peter to pay Paul. No matter what way he weighed the problem, he knew he wouldn't be able to keep the wolf from the door unless they could secure a large rent abatement. But what chance of that?

What then to do? He knew better, as a man in his forty-eighth year, than to let his emotion rule his actions, which was probably just as well, as his emotions told him to brain Boycott with an axe. Not to say he'd abandoned the notion of direct action. But since his day in Irishtown last year, the Land Movement had made tremendous strides as a result of an unprecedented linking of parliamentarians and militant republicans. This coming together of the two strands of the Irish nationalism had been, Owen had to confess, a masterful achievement for Davitt and Parnell, a man still in his early thirties. But, ultimately, what had been achieved? While their aspirations were wondrous, to him they seemed like dreams plucked from some outlandish fairy tale. The Land League aimed to bring about a reduction in rack rents. Fine, who could argue with that? But they would also '*facilitate the obtaining of ownership of the soil by the occupiers*'. As if the landlords would surrender the prize they'd stolen hundreds of years before and upon which they'd grown fat and wealthy. Parnell had taken off on a grand tour of America, or so Owen had read in *The Connaught Telegraph*, where he'd met President Rutherford B Hayes, addressed the House of Representatives and raised almost £90,000 to support the League's aims. He'd arrived back adorned by the press as: 'The Uncrowned King of Ireland'. But as yet none of the 'king's' proclamations had had any noticeable effect on the lowly tenant farmers. The League's call to resist unjust rents was all very well, but how far would Parnell's £90,000 go to housing and feeding the countless evicted?

He sometimes wondered if armed revolt was actually the only way. The Land League disapproved of acts of violence, which was ironic in Owen's eyes, as one of the reasons he'd attended local meetings had been in the hope of running into the extremist Fenian Donal Doherty, whom he'd encountered in Irishtown. Not that he was keen to embark on a life of terrorism; whatever about an armed uprising, he wasn't in the habit of assassinating landlords, despite the violent notions he often nurtured about Boycott. But something about Doherty had fascinated him. The man obviously had courage and was utterly ruthless. He also had the will and the means, albeit violent, to rid them of Boycott. Perhaps Owen held the dark, guilty hope that he might encourage Doherty to direct his attention towards the land agent, leaving Owen without blood on his hands and with a relatively clear conscience.

But there was something else about Doherty. That day in Irishtown he'd had a strong suspicion that Doherty recognised him, although the man never admitted as much. He'd unsuccessfully racked his brain to recall when he might have encountered the rebel Fenian. The mystery still nagged at him.

He'd demurred when offered the opportunity to join their band of assassins that day. Out of his sense of responsibility to his family? Conscience? Cowardice? The latter notion troubled him. Perhaps he was a coward. As far back as his youth, Thomas had always hinted that he was chicken-hearted, without ever calling him a coward outright. Yet there had been times in his life when he'd acted with courage, though out of necessity rather than choice. But given the opportunity, would he really be prepared to risk his life in the fight against landlordism, or to fire a bullet into another man's head, for that matter? One way or another, did he have the guts? Maybe he would never know.

Doherty had let him go about his business that day, but not before suggesting they might call on him in the future. But the knock on his door had never come, which in many ways was a relief, as he would have incurred Síomha's wrath at its fiercest for consorting with such men.

'I've brought the cart around.' His son's voice startled him to reality. Tadhg was already working at the soil with a potato hook.

'Grand,' he replied, looking towards the cottage. Síomha was ushering Niamh towards the gate and school, and his daughter waved at him before scampering up the track with her satchel in one hand and a warm potato in the other. Síomha began to walk to the field to begin her day's labour alongside him.

He was suddenly struck by the terrible vision of his family cast from their home at the onset of winter, wandering the roads freezing and starving, perhaps forced to seek sanctuary in the workhouse. It brought a shudder of revulsion. Would Niamh survive such ordeals? And despite her strength, would Síomha? And what of Tadhg with his future wiped away? Owen was suddenly aware that his choices were dwindling, his hand being forced. Captain Charles Boycott was like a splinter of glass moving ever closer to their hearts, and he, Owen, had to find a solution to the problem of the land agent very, very soon.

If only Donal Doherty had turned up, done the necessary, and rid them of Boycott. But you could never find a decent Fenian killer when you needed one.

***

Captain Boycott tapped his heels into the gelding and leaned forward over her flowing grey mane, gripping the reins tightly. He could feel Iron Duke's tremendous haunches rippling beneath him as they hurled him towards the ditch, hooves throwing up sods at the pursuing riders. Duke launched himself into the air and sailed over the furrow, his forelegs touching down a good yard clear, before his hind quarters followed and propelled Boycott into the field. He grinned to himself, patting the snorting horse on the neck as the constable and Asheton Weekes followed suit. The fourth rider, a hired bodyguard, lost his nerve and brought his horse up short with a skidding little dance to the edge of the ditch.

Asheton pulled up alongside him as the constable rode past and stopped ten yards away, granting them due deference, not assuming he could be party to their conversation.

'That's a shilling you owe me.'

'I'm a dashed fool to accept these wagers, Charles. You're the finest horseman in Mayo,' Asheton said, panting from the effort of the race from Lough Mask House.

Boycott turned his attention to his temporary bodyguard, hired at Annie's insistence. He'd had to fork out three shillings daily to find an Irishman who was mercenary enough to accept the job.

'Get off up the field and cross there and be quick about it. I'm not paying you to have a day in the countryside.'

He drew the horse about, the tomfoolery over, his mind re-focused on the business in hand. A small flock of sheep scattered across the field at their approach. The constable trailed behind as they rode, watchful for any threat. All four of the men were armed with revolving pistols, and Boycott rather theatrically with an infantry officer's sword. Asheton had grinned inwardly upon seeing it, a weapon with which he was familiar: royal cypher on the guard, brass back-strap and pommel, indicating a sword granted only to officers of high rank in the field. *Captain* Boycott had never seen a weapon drawn in anger during his brief spell in the army. Still, Asheton was happy to overlook Charles's small contrivance. Perhaps it granted him the illusion of an officer leading a battle against the Fenian hordes.

The bodyguard rejoined them, riding alongside the constable as they followed a muddy track along the line of Lough Mask's shore.

'Who first?' Boycott asked.

'I've a schedule,' replied Asheton. 'If you wish to visit all thirty-eight tenants by tomorrow we'll need to keep up a brisk pace, fifteen minutes a sortie – though, I mean to say, do you really need to do this? It's not rent day until the twentieth.'

'Asheton, old chap, I'm sure you were a fine soldier, but I'm a businessman. It does no harm, believe me, to remind these peasants of their rent obligations.'

Asheton shook his head in mild befuddlement. 'You know, Charles, they have had a rotten time of it these past couple of years, with the weather and all of that. I doubt they need further inducement to maximize their yields.'

Boycott turned his head and stared at Asheton, his eyes narrowing. He drew Duke to a gentle stop. 'Asheton. I do believe your heart has grown soft. Either that or the peasants have been pulling that hat of yours over your eyes. Trust me, the Irish peasant will perform precisely the minimum measure of work he deems necessary to survive and not a scintilla more.'

'Very well, old boy, if you insist,' Asheton muttered, evidently chastened.

Boycott grunted, his irritation with Asheton evident. He knew the man wasn't a hardened businessman, but his expression of sympathy for the tenants' 'plight' had left Boycott cold. There was no room for sentimentality in commerce. He could barely believe that his companion was mimicking the very lies that the Land League spouted weekly.

Asheton nodded towards a field of unharvested oats. 'This one belongs to McGurk, forty-six acres. Then we pass up by Ballinchalla church, visit several holdings along the way – Higgins, McHale, O'Toole and then Joyce.'

'Joyce? Don't recall him.'

'Older man, married, several children. Owen Joyce.'

Boycott snorted. 'That's the trouble with the damned Irish peasant. They all look and sound exactly the same.'

***

Owen Joyce washed his face in the trough outside his cottage, then looked back at the field where his son still toiled. He smiled at Tadhg's industry, as many a lad his age would seize any opportunity to shirk hard labour. What a shame, Owen thought, that his son had never had the chance to devote his energies to a higher calling. But such was the lot of the peasant.

He and Síomha had both been unfaltering in their insistence on the children receiving a good and extensive education, having been denied the opportunity in their own youth, at least beyond the learning they had provided for themselves through book reading. Tadhg had disappointed them in that respect, his obvious intelligence never translating itself into scholastic achievement. But they suspected his academic failings were more a result of his stargazing nature and his inability to concentrate. In that respect, Tadhg reminded Owen of himself, and in many ways also of Thomas, with his fiery temperament.

His son approached now, brushing dirt from his hands. 'Going to the upper field to check the sheep.'

'The food's almost ready,' Owen said.

'Won't be long,' Tadhg said and disappeared behind the cottage.

Owen shook his head in bafflement, then walked around to grant himself a view of the field above, where he spotted a pretty girl of about sixteen loitering on the track by the fence. Check the sheep, my arse, he thought, and chuckled.

He was so grateful to have Tadhg still at his side, unlike Lorcan, their first-born, who was twenty-one now and whom Owen and Síomha hadn't seen in almost three years. Lorcan had fallen for and married a girl called Deirdre Conway from Neale. They'd initially been pleased, then Lorcan announced a few weeks before the wedding that he couldn't contemplate a life under Boycott's terms. He didn't intend to waste his life's energies struggling to pay high rents and gratuitous fines. He and his young bride would take the ship to America in search of a new life. There had been a certain inevitability about it; half the youth of the parish had already fled abroad. Youth offered a landscape of possibilities if one was prepared to pursue them across the horizon. Farming was all Lorcan knew but the plains of Montana and Nebraska held the promise of a life of bountiful harvests. So in January of '78 Owen and his family had found themselves in tears on the pier side in Galway as they watched their eldest son's ship fade into a winter mist. The scene had stirred long-buried memories for Owen of another age when he'd witnessed yet harsher dramas on another quayside. A part of him envied his son, yet he knew in his heart that he could never leave his homeland, come what may.

He turned at the rhythmic thumping of hooves, realised it was Boycott, and was initially struck with cold dread. But it quickly dawned that while their financial status might be dire, the rent had not yet fallen due and Boycott had no legal power to serve him a writ, at least not yet. The four riders pulled up about ten yards from his threshold as Síomha appeared from within, concern etched on her face. Boycott sat on the horse with shoulders back, chin in the air, the bearing of a man constantly staring at the world down his nose. Asheton Weekes he knew also, and didn't dislike. He considered Weekes a strange bedfellow for the land agent. He didn't, for one, think it beneath him to engage in conversation with peasants. He was a man in his thirties, handsome, dark-haired and tall, and like Boycott had served in the army, yet he had a way about him that Owen could only define as mellow, effeminate even.

The other two were a constable and a rougher looking, heavyset individual, probably a hired thug.

'What do you want?'

The agent glared at Owen with disdain. 'Your rent falls due in two weeks. Twelve pounds, nine shillings and four pence,' he added, glancing at the paper in Weekes's hand.

'We know what rent is due.' Síomha's irritation was palpable.

'What do you want, Boycott?'

The land agent's face darkened. He jolted the horse forward until he was towering over Owen and leaned down towards his face. 'It's *Captain* Boycott to the likes of you.'

Owen met his remark with grim silence. The very air felt taut as the threat of conflict hung unresolved for a few moments before Weekes moved forward and spoke.

'Charles, we're here to assess the property, don't forget.'

Boycott glared at him for a second before sitting upright again and slowly sweeping his eyes about. 'This land and buildings are the property of Lord Erne and I hold the right to ensure no abuse is being done; the misuse of tillage land, digging of wells without permission and so on, and to impose penalties if necessary. Also to make sure no undesirables are resident, to wit, Land League agitators or Fenian reactionaries.'

Owen looked at him incredulously. '*What*?'

Boycott glanced over his shoulder at the constable and bodyguard. 'Scout about.'

Owen looked at Síomha. The 'inspection' was a ruse. He'd never heard such nonsense and he realised that Boycott's visit was for the sole purpose of intimidation. The two men behind jostled their horses and began to move towards the side of the house. Tadhg chose that moment to reveal himself, a spading fork clutched in his hands, upraised as though to defend himself, fury in his eyes.

'You've no right to hound us like this! Get the hell awa–'

He never finished his sentence. The bodyguard instinctively drew his weapon and levelled it. Owen's heart stopped at the sight and Síomha screamed as the constable struck him in the side as a shot rang out. The bullet flew wildly away and ricocheted off a wall.

Owen and Síomha darted across and seized their son, tossing the fork to the ground. He was unhurt but trembling, yet rage still creased his face. Owen turned to Boycott and Weekes, both of whom seemed startled themselves.

'If he'd died, Boycott…' Owen spat through clenched teeth, leaving the unspoken consequences to the agent's imagination.

Boycott recovered his composure and resumed his overbearing tone.

'You should discipline your offspring to behave like civilized men.'

The horses, a little unnerved by the gunshot, were dancing to and fro and Boycott was endeavouring to steady the animal.

'I remind you, if your rent is a farthing short I'll see you off this land.'

Owen met Boycott's eyes. 'I suggest you leave.' He glanced at Weekes who, shamefaced, averted his gaze. And with that the four pulled about and made off.

Síomha was at his side then and Tadhg ran a little of the way after the intruders, hurling an ineffectual rock that fell harmlessly in the mud.

'Tadhg!' Síomha called out in admonition. She looked at Owen, his face set hard and bitter, staring after Boycott.

'I swear I'm going to kill that man.'

***

The three of them stood there silently for a few moments, then Síomha walked across to Tadhg, drew her hand back, and slapped him fiercely across the face. He took a startled step back and clutched his reddening cheek, eyes wide in disbelief.

'What in the name of Jesus, Mary and Joseph are you up to? Do you want to get yourself killed, you *amadán*!' Síomha's voice was clamorous in the still air.

'Jesus M–'

'Don't take the Lord's name on top of it all. What good will it do if you get yourself killed? Did you think about your sister?'

'At least we can say we stood up for ourselves. That we didn't let that bastard trample on us!' Tadhg protested, confused and enraged, near to crying.

'Get out of my sight with your foul language and get back to work!' She picked up the potato fork and thrust it into his hands, giving her son a shove to get him moving.

Síomha turned towards Owen with an expression of disgust.

'You're going to kill Boycott are ye? *Bíodh ciall agat*!' she yelled, telling him not to talk nonsense. She habitually drifted into Irish when her blood was up.

'You and your tough man's talk will be the end of us.'

'What are you talking about?'

'You. I'm talking about you and your Fenians who are going to save Ireland from the English. How? By murder and butchery?'

Owen swung away and strode into the house with Síomha at his heels. The room was awash with steam and the smell of burning potatoes. 'The pot's boiled away,' he said and went to lift it from above the fire. Síomha overtook him and kicked the blackened tureen from its perch, spilling half its contents on the floor, the rest into the flames.

'Christ almighty, what are you doing? We have little enough as it is!' Owen leapt to rescue the food from the flames and his wife stepped back and watched him, hands on hips, breathing slowly and deeply.

'Well, we won't need so much food if one of us is dead, will we?'

Owen absently tossed the potatoes back into the uprighted pot.

'Nobody's going to be dead.'

'No? I've heard the talk of the men after mass. I've listened to you when you've too much whiskey taken. Patriots the lot of ye. The saviours of Ireland, my arse!'

'Are you saying you're happy to live like this? As long as the English are in this country we'll always be treated like dirt.' His pride piqued, Owen's voice was near to shrill as he watched his wife stride towards a cupboard that housed their few precious books and a myriad other odds and ends. She rummaged and pulled free some newspapers, slamming them down on the table. She slapped an open palm on *The Ballinrobe Chronicle*.

'So this is your answer? To join the savages who murdered David Feerick not ten miles from here?'

'Who?' he muttered unconvincingly, looking away through the window.

'Don't play the ignoramus with me, Owen Joyce!' She held the newspaper up to his face. 'Feerick. David Feerick. You remember? Your so-called patriots hadn't even the guts to look the man in the eye. Shot him in the back. Shot him ten times! So these are the men who are going to lead Ireland to freedom, are they?'

He pushed the paper from his face.

'And last week they killed a land agent's driver in Kerry! An innocent boy of just eighteen, from a poor family like ours in Castlegregory.'

Owen turned sharply away to the window again. But Síomha strode over to him and took his arm, swinging him around to face her and nodding towards

Tadhg in the field below. 'And now you're beginning to fill your son's head with this dangerous rubbish.'

'I haven't–'

'Why in the name of God do you think he was ready to bludgeon Boycott? That boy will follow his father to hell and back, he'll happily step into your shoes with the first beckoning.' She turned her back on him. 'Just like you're willing to step into *your* father's.'

'What does that mean?'

'You know well what I mean.'

She met his eyes, her voice now barely above a whisper. 'You told me yourself. Your father was a murderer. He killed that gamekeeper...what was he called...Geraghty?'

They hadn't spoken of the subject in ten years. Owen sought to conceal his shame in an indignant yell. 'I never said he was a murderer!'

'No, but that's what you believe.'

'I told you it might have been an accident for all I know, there might–'

Síomha gripped his arm and, for the first time in their quarrel, her face and tone softened and she looked up into his eyes beseechingly. 'Owen. Where does it end?'

He looked away and Síomha held his arm more tightly.

'Where does the killing stop? Hundreds of years, you say, we've put up with the English. They kill us and we kill them and they kill more of us and the whole thing goes on and on, generation after generation, father to son.'

'It wasn't us who star–'

'Stop! You're becoming infected by it. Is this the path you want your own son to follow? Owen, you're not a man given to violence; if I know anything about you I know that. But I've watched you these past years, drifting more and more that way, letting the hatred into you. If you carry on it will be the end of us all.'

Owen pulled free and walked across the room, his back to her, head tilted up as though the answers lay in the thatch. He exhaled despairingly. 'What am I to do then? You know yourself that to pay the rent we'll have to sell almost all the crop. Our choice is either to be homeless or to starve. What would you have me do?'

'Sit down,' she replied.

'What?'

'Sit,' she repeated, pointing at the table.

He shook his head and complied as she returned to the cupboard. From an old piece of crockery she pulled a folded sheet of paper and joined him at the table. She opened it as she spoke. 'Mr Parnell's going to be in Ennis on Sunday week.'

Owen uttered a cynical squawk.

'Listen to me! Read it. Read what it says.'

'Síomha, I've been to Land League meetings. They've been blabbering on for years now. All they do is talk. If we're ever–'

'Read it!' She planted her index finger sharply on the poster.

Men of Ireland, Patriots and All Who Yearn for Freedom!
Mr Charles Stewart Parnell MP
President of the Irish Land League
Will speak on the subjects of
Landlordism, Rack-renting and the Freedom of Ireland
from her Oppressors.

To abolish landlordism would be to undermine English misgovernment and when we have undermined English misgovernment we will have paved the way for Ireland to take her place amongst the nations of the earth.

An End to Landlordism!

Hear the Uncrowned King of Ireland speak
from the foot of the Statue of O'Connell, The Liberator.
The Square, Ennis, Sunday, September 19th 1880

Owen turned his head away muttering a sceptical 'uncrowned king of Ireland', but Síomha sensed his interest. She grabbed at his shoulder and spoke with growing excitement. 'Isn't this what you want? An end to landlordism and the likes of Boycott? You've got to go and hear what he has to say.'

'Go to Ennis? Are you mad? Have you any idea how far Ennis is?'

'There's others going.'

He eyed her suspiciously. 'Who's going?'

'Joe Gaughan. Francis Murphy. Lots of them.'

'Where did you get this poster? Where did you hear about the others?'

'Father O'Malley gave me the poster, asked me to speak to you.'

'Jesus! God save this country from priests!'

Síomha's brow creased and her nose wrinkled as her ire was roused again. '*D'anam don diabhal* for disrespecting your religion! And besides, Father O'Malley's more a patriot than any of ye. He's going too, he's going to Ennis to hear Mr Parnell.'

'Parnell...' he sighed again.

'Owen Joyce. For an intelligent man, you really are a fool and a half.'

'What are you talking about?'

Síomha tapped the poster again. 'The English are afraid of Parnell, far more than they'll ever be frightened by the murder of a few landlords. Whenever that happens, they just send more soldiers and make new laws to put us down. But they *do* fear Parnell because he's done something that few Irish leaders have ever done. He's organised us. He's brought us together. Instead of fighting with each other he's getting everyone to sing the one song. You talk about your hundreds of years? The reason it's been so long is that the English have always conquered us by dividing us. But Parnell's changing that. That's what terrifies the English and the likes of Boycott.'

Owen rose and walked to the window again. He stood there staring out at Tadhg, driving the plough and taking out his humiliation with a stick on the unfortunate Anu's rump. Finally he spoke. 'Ennis? It must be seventy miles!'

Síomha smiled for the first time since they'd entered the house. 'They're all leaving at five in the morning and Fr O'Malley's going to say mass on the way. You'll be in plenty of time. I'll make you food for the day.'

Owen laughed lightly, thinking he'd been out-manoeuvred by a woman and a priest.

'All right, all right, woman! I'll go,' he said shaking his head. He stared reflectively down at Tadhg again. 'And Síomha...'

'What?'

He sighed. 'Prepare enough food for two.'

CHAPTER 9

The starving sick crowd into towns in the hope of securing help. From the town to Westport Quay, on the Workhouse line, the people are lying along the road, or in temporary sheds, constructed of weeds, potato tops, with poor creatures lying beneath them. On the Newport line, the same sickening scenes are to be encountered.

–*The Connaught Telegraph*, 1847

As the ship is towed out, hats are raised, handkerchiefs are waved, and a loud shout of farewell is raised from the shore, and responded to from the ship. It is then, if at any time, that the eyes of the emigrants begin to moisten with regret at the thought that they are looking for the last time at the old country – that country which, although associated principally with the remembrance of sorrow and suffering, is, nevertheless, the country of their fathers, the country of their childhood, and consecrated to their hearts by many a token.

–*Illustrated London News*, 5 July 1850

OCTOBER 1848

The town of Westport loomed ahead of them, the smoke from its thousand fires rising into the drizzle. The track led them back to the road, but so great were the numbers of fellow wretches walking its course that they were paid scant attention.

As they approached the town they saw men at work in an expansive field to their right and at first thought them farmers digging a crop. Their illusion was shattered when the workers lifted a lifeless body from a cart and swung the cadaver into a huge pit, where it found company with as many as six or seven others.

'The workhouse dead,' a croaky female voice informed them. A diminutive old woman in a black shawl concealing a face of loose, wrinkled flesh had paused beside them. 'They say they bury twenty a day.'

'Twenty?' Owen asked incredulously.

'Twenty, it's true. I'm bound for there meself unless...can ye spare a few pennies to save me from the workhouse?'

'We're as poor as you,' Thomas answered.

They rejoined the stream of human wretchedness as it trudged its way into town. A narrow lane split from the road and many parted from the rest here, moving towards the largest building the brothers had ever seen, four stories of cut grey stone and fifty yards in length, with maybe two hundred windows cut into its walls. A man informed them that this was Westport Workhouse, built to house a thousand inmates, but crammed with twice that number, its rooms straining at the seams with misery. Around its base the indigent homeless thronged, their baleful voices beseeching their masters for pity. The scene was in some ways worse than their encounters with the dead. At least the dead were silent.

A wall sign told them that they were travelling along Peter Street, a long and steeply sloping thoroughfare that widened at its centre into an open space known as the Octagon. Houses of two stories lined the street, some painted white but with no gap between the buildings, as though they'd been crowded together for want of space. The windows were hung with lace curtains and they occasionally glimpsed a face peering out at the trail of the disaffected and destitute.

In the Octagon, the clamour of voices, and of horses, sheep and pigs was deafening to ears used only to the hush of the countryside. The brothers had never seen so many people in one small space, had never seen so many buildings huddled so closely together. They walked the streets of Westport with lips parted and eyes wide, such was the strangeness of it all. Owen wondered at the sight of pigs and sheep, how these animals were present in such numbers while most of the people around lived an existence on the edge of starvation. He noted also that men bearing arms guarded each temporary livestock pen. Many of the people in the square were like themselves, penniless and ragged, seeking passage to America, England or some of the more distant, exotic places of which they'd heard. Some sat exhausted on the ground, taking their rest before going to the quayside.

'What now?' Owen asked.

'We'll have to spend the night here and try get on a ship tomorrow. Come on.'

They continued on until they arrived at a bridge across a straight stretch of river, penned in by plunging walls the like of which they'd never seen and lined with trees on either side. Thomas noticed a building on the opposite bank, outside which a number of men in fine clothing and wigs of grey curled hair were standing, black parasols over their heads to protect them from the rain. They were chatting animatedly and appeared to the brothers like a gaggle of women.

'They're barristers,' Owen said.

'How do you know?' Thomas asked.

'I've read about them. That's the courthouse.'

Thomas turned away and approached a man loitering in the doorway of a tavern. 'Sir, can you tell me the way to the ships?'

The man smelt of whiskey but was neatly dressed by their standards at least, wearing the clothes of a tradesman. He eyed them with distaste for a moment, then sighed and pointed. 'Take the track that follows the curve of the Carrowbeg – that's the river te yerself. Follow it until it joins the main road. It'll take ye all the way there.'

'Thank you.'

'I hear it's four pounds and six shillings for a fare te Am-er-i-cay. Have ye got that type of money?'

Thomas hesitated. 'Our father's at the quayside waiting for us with tickets.'

The man nodded doubtfully. 'Well, good luck te ye, ye don't look like ye've had any of late.' He turned and disappeared into the inn.

Owen took Thomas's arm sharply. 'Four pounds six? That's eight pounds twelve just for tickets? Where are we going to get that kind of money?'

'Let's go. I've an idea.'

They crossed the bridge and in a laneway found shelter in the deeply recessed doorway of a store that had closed for the evening.

'Wait here, I'll be back as soon as I can.'

'Where are you going?'

'To find food.'

'I'll come with you.'

'Just wait here!' Thomas yelled and took off before his brother could muster a reply.

Owen sat, shivering, as the evening turned to night, his thoughts on his brother and what mischief he was up to. He rebuked himself then for habitually assuming Thomas was up to no good. Hadn't Thomas kept them alive thus far? But he couldn't help but fret. Thomas was gone over two hours and by the time he returned it was dark, the laneway lit only by a dim streetlamp thirty yards away. Owen had been pacing, praying, unable to contemplate the notion of being left alone in this strange town. And then there were hurried footsteps, splashing through puddles.

'Jesus, where have you been? What's this?'

Thomas had a large brown paper parcel bound with string, dark spots of rain dappling the wrapping. 'Get in from the rain, ye eejit!' he cried.

He untied the parcel. Despite the darkness Owen could recognise clothing – shirts, pants and heavy jackets.

'Jesus, Thomas, they'll flog you to death for stealing all this. How did you…?

'I admit I had to steal, but not from a shop. I followed one of those barristers home. They're all rich, money made sending the likes of us to the gallows. I climbed in a window and took his wallet from his jacket. It was hanging in the hallway and I was gone before anyone saw me. He won't even know it's missing 'til tomorrow and by then we'll be gone. Change your clothes. We can't arrive in America like scarecrows. And here…'

He pulled a piece of salted beef from his pocket. The sight of the food adjourned any argument. Owen took the meat and ate greedily as he stripped and pulled on the fresh dry clothes, which felt comforting against his skin.

'How much did you steal?'

'Nearly fifteen pounds. Enough for the tickets, the clothes and food for the journey.'

'Jesus, Thomas, this is wrong. We weren't raised to be thieves. Our mother–'

Thomas grabbed him by his collar. 'We weren't raised te be downtrodden pigs either. This money will get us to America. Then ye can do a jig with your conscience all ye like. Until then shut up and thank Christ ye're still alive. Better still, thank me.'

Owen stared at him and felt regret welling up. 'I'm sorry, Thomas. I'd be dead if it wasn't for you.'

'And don't you forget it.'

When the rain eased they returned towards the Octagon, which was a great deal quieter now. In the light of a streetlamp Owen could see that their clothes had a well-worn look about them, but at least they were clean and warm. Thomas led him into a boarding house called The Old Mill, and they ate a bowl of stew accompanied by bread and ale, the first time either of them had tasted it. It was the finest meal they'd had in memory, and they both scraped the bowls clean. When they inquired about lodgings, they were informed that all the rooms were taken, but suspected that the old bat of a proprietress simply didn't like the look of them. She offered them the use of a shed in the yard for tuppence, which they accepted, and gave them each a blanket.

The shed smelt of animals, but it was dry and they were grateful for its relative comforts. At first light they purchased bread and bottles of dark ale and breakfasted by the river's edge before moving to Bridge Street, where they found a store that sold dried foods and biscuits the size of a man's hand and as hard as bone. With sufficient to last them a month, they set off towards the quay.

The track to the quay meandered in harmony with the Carrowbeg until their ways parted after half a mile, the river continuing its gentle roll straight to the sea, the path veering south towards the road.

'America lies at the end of this road, Owen.' Thomas smiled, his humour this morning as bright as he could remember, nurtured by the wonder of the horizon and the food in his belly. Owen's dread had been building since he'd first opened his eyes to the grey dawn light. His fear now, as they joined the hundreds of others on the road, was palpable, although of precisely what he couldn't identify. He'd heard that Atlantic crossings were perilous and many died before setting eyes on the New World, but he didn't believe he feared the journey. Perhaps it was simply the unexplored expanse of the future that perturbed him.

To the left of the path were fields, and in the distance Croagh Patrick rose majestically towards the breaking cloud, a few shafts of sunlight picking out the white rocks that described its upper heights. To their right was woodland and within its branches Owen could see birds and hear their chatter, a language that was near alien to him by now, yet its sound lightened his heart a little.

A mile further on, the road split and most people followed the sloping right-hand path where, above the bobbing heads, they could see several more towering buildings and beyond those the masts of four tall ships. A huge windowless structure with colossal doors bore the name Patten, Smyth & Co., Importers and Exporters, and through one of these doors they could see giant wooden crates which resonated with the sounds of bleating sheep and sacks large enough to hold a jaunting car spilling over with grain. Near the quay, a river of men worked to load these goods on to a ship, using giant counterbalancing machines which brought yet more wonder to the brothers' eyes and anger to their hearts.

'Look. Enough food for ten thousand and they ship it off te England while the Irish are left te rot. If ye didn't believe the tales we heard, believe them now, brother.'

Owen nodded and was about to reply when he froze at the sight of a face not ten yards away. Outside the front door of the company office stood a fine, open-topped carriage and in it sat the girl Owen had observed in near-nakedness just two days previously. Now she wore a long dress of pale yellow, which dipped below her ankles and was adorned with a lace-like frill around her neck. A broad-rimmed bonnet with a white band concealed her long fair hair, and her beauty once again transfixed Owen. She turned her head and immediately their eyes met, her lips parting slightly as recognition struck her. Owen's heart skipped as he stared back, awaiting her scream and the constables to descend upon them. But she remained silent, simply maintaining eye contact until an older man in a long coat and tall hat, most likely her father, emerged from the office door and climbed up to take the reins. The carriage moved away, back towards the town, but she turned her head again and sought out Owen. She never frowned, never smiled, never cried out; she merely seemed caught in a trance of her own secret thoughts until she rounded the corner and he never laid eyes on her again.

'What's wrong? Looks like you've seen old Duffy's ghost.'

'Nothing. I'm fine.' Owen shook his head and moved on. He decided the moment was his alone, as if some deeply private act had just taken place that was not for sharing.

They rounded the corner of the largest building, named the Custom House, where the expanse of the quay opened up to them and they looked in awe at the masses heaving on the dockside, which stretched beyond their line of sight. Besides the four tall ships, countless boats and barges jostled for position in the narrow channel, on the far side of which rose a tree-covered hill. Hundreds, if not thousands, milled about the quayside, mostly gaunt-faced emigrants carrying their possessions or huddling in groups awaiting the call to board. Cats snarled as they ran in pursuit of the many rats that openly scurried about. Owen marvelled at the sight of a man turning the handle of a modern metal device of giant interlocking cogwheels, which pulled a rope along a huge sloping beam of wood, underneath which an entire cow was suspended; he cranked a handle and the entire machine swung about, delivering the beast whole over the ship's open hold.

The smell of human and animal excrement was woven into that of the rotting marine vegetation and the noise was so great that Thomas had to shout to make himself heard. 'There's the ticket office. Come on.'

They fought their way inside the building, which opened into a hall the length of which ran a counter with steel bars protruding up to the ceiling. Behind this were eight men engaged in selling tickets. The crowds were shepherded into long queues where people waited their turn to purchase what they hoped would be a new life. The brothers joined one of these and an hour passed before they reached the seller.

'We want tickets for America.'

'Where?'

'America, I said.'

The seller, a man in his forties with spectacles and a wide moustache, rolled his eyes to the heavens. 'Baltimore, Galveston, New York, Charlesto–'

The names were so exotic and mysterious the brothers were momentarily baffled, but seized on the first name that they knew.

'New York.'

'Names of the passengers?'

'Thomas Joyce and Owen Joyce.'

'Ages?

'Eighteen and sixteen.'

'That will be eight pounds and twelve shillings.' Thomas fumbled over the money, unused to handling paper cash.

The seller slid the ticket through the bars. 'You must pass a medical examination before you may board. It's the *Destiny*, the second from last along the docks. Leaves at four o'clock sharp. Three tall masts, even *you* can't miss it.' He smiled ironically as Thomas grasped the ticket.

The Medical Inspector's office was next door and there they queued again as stewards attempted to maintain a semblance of order among the shuffling, noisome crowd. Two hours later they arrived at a table where a young, fair-haired man with spectacles and a loose, full-length brown overjacket looked up at them with weary yet, Owen judged, kind eyes. He took a strange instrument with an eyepiece from an array of such on the table and looked into Owen's throat, eyes and ears, then probed under his jaw with his fingers. Lastly he lifted another device, a flat disc joined to a tube that grew wider along its length, held the cold metal disc against the bare skin of Owen's chest and the cylindrical end to his own ear. Thomas looked at Owen and shrugged in mystification.

'Any fevers, sneezing, shivering, pus from the nose, red marks on the skin?'

'No, sir.'

'Very well. Badly malnourished, but who isn't?' He smiled faintly, then turned to Thomas. As he repeated the process Owen's attention was drawn to a pretty girl of about sixteen at the adjacent queue, who was travelling with two younger children. The thin, middle-aged man who examined them had a sneering expression and narrow, lascivious eyes, which he allowed to wander openly across the girl's body.

'I suspect contagion on you,' he stated. 'None of you may board the ship lest you infect the other passengers.'

The girl almost fell to her knees, pleading with him to allow them passage.

'Sir, I beg of ye,' she wailed as the little ones clutched at her dress, 'we have no disease! All our money is spent. If we don't get on that ship we'll surely perish.'

He feigned indifference and sighed. 'You must be inspected for the marks of contagion. Leave the children here and wait behind that curtain.'

The girl closed her eyes momentarily and then whispered to the frightened children, who sat on the floor. She disappeared behind the long row of heavy curtains at the rear of the room.

'Thomas...' Owen started, but realised that the doctor was studying a facial gash that Thomas had received when the starving villagers had set upon them.

'I'd better put something on that.'

They followed the man into a tiny curtained compartment with a single table covered in small corked bottles. He poured a liquid of a deep, violet colour onto a rag and Thomas flinched and inhaled sharply when he pressed this against the wound.

'You're lucky. Mildly infected. Wipe this over the wound for the next few days.' He handed Thomas the cloth.

Owen was looking with mild amusement at the large purple splotch on his brother's face when a grunt from the adjoining compartment drew his attention. He gently pulled back the curtain a few inches and stared with horror at the girl he'd seen outside, seated on a table with the top of her dress pulled down to her waist, as her examiner sucked at the side of her neck in a nauseating fashion. The girl's legs were parted and the man was writhing between them, brutish grunts escaping him. Her eyes found Owen, her face filled with revulsion and tears streaming down her dirty cheeks.

Owen had never been one to leap into conflict; he suppressed the notion that he was a coward, but fear usually gave him pause. Suddenly, now, a deep instinct surmounted all his fear and he made to move towards the man, his rage such that he was intent on beating him senseless, but the girl made the slightest of movements with her head, panic in her eyes, and he stalled. He was breathing hard, his heart torn, his stomach knotted in spasm. He briefly allowing his gaze to linger on the girl's pitiful eyes then withdrew to the presence of the others.

'Sir,' he whispered urgently, 'there is a man…an examiner...he's got a young girl…he's…'

The young man, shame in his eyes, placed a hand on Owen's shoulder. 'I'm afraid it is beyond my power to intervene. And yours, if you wish to board the ship.'

'But he can't just–'

'There's nothing can be done.' He stamped their ticket sharply and turned away.

Thomas seized Owen's arm and pulled him, protesting, to the exit.

***

They found a perch by a stack of barrels near to the *Destiny*. Owen told Thomas what he'd witnessed, then stared unseeing at the chaos around them.

'There was nothing ye could do. Forget about it.'

Owen meditated a little more before turning to Thomas. 'That bastard was Irish.'

His brother looked away along the dock. 'He's been corrupted by–'

Owen interrupted him. 'Maybe we're as bad as them. The English. Maybe we're up to doing what they do. Maybe if *we* had the power–'

'Maybe, maybe! Don't talk like a madman. He was one filthy oul' bastard who deserves te have his balls cut off. You always get rotten apples. But don't compare me te any Englishman. They're no better than the shit ye wipe off yer foot.'

Owen leaned his head against a barrel and rested there, unspeaking. Thomas, seeking to shift the subject, lifted the ticket and stared at it as though it was a map to secret treasure, then began to read: 'Grimshaw & Sons Shipping. Passengers Contract Ticket. Ship *Destiny*, of 450 tons registered to sail from Westport for New York on the thirtieth day of October 1848; ten cubic feet of space per–'

'The thirtieth of October,' Owen muttered and shook his head.

'What about it?'

'It's my birthday.'

Thomas laughed and slapped him on the back. Owen seemed indifferent. I'm seventeen, he thought. The experiences of these past few days and weeks he felt had aged him a decade. He'd grown up almost overnight. Desperation has a way of doing that.

He gazed across the quayside at the huge ship, where sailors bustled about loading supplies and readying the sails, and he felt as though he was about to board a vessel bound for a penal colony. He heard shouts rise high into the air back along the dock and saw the lower sails of one of the other ships unfurl as it slowly pulled away.

They both made their way to the quayside to witness the ship's departure, marked by the rising wails of mothers clutching at their breasts as they watched their sons and daughters depart forever.

'If she's six hundred tons, I'm the Queen of Sheba,' commented a man of undoubted seafaring experience, with a shaggy beard and a weatherworn face, wearing a heavy black coat and a broad-rimmed sailor's hat. His companion nodded in agreement. 'And I'll wager there's more barnacles eating at them timbers than there are people in China.'

Owen looked up at the emigrants clutching at the ship's rail, crowding over each other as they sought to catch a last glimpse of a loved one below. Owen spotted the girl from the medical office, and even at this remove he could see the lines on her face where the tears had drawn tracks through the grime. She gazed towards Croagh Patrick, blessed herself, then turned away and was swallowed into the body of the ship.

He stepped over to the bearded man. 'Sir, pardon me, but what do you mean about the ship's weight?'

He pointed to the waterline on the ship. 'See how she sits in the swell? Her usual waterline's out of sight and she's riding very deep.' He had a strange accent, not Irish or English but with a curious fluidity. 'A ship can only take three passengers for every ton she carries. She's bearing two hundred souls, so she should be six hundred tons. I'll wager she's not more than four-fifty.'

Thomas stepped into the conversation. 'You mean it's overloaded.'

'*I* wouldn't sail on her.'

The brothers eyed each other with disquiet as the ship moved away along the narrow deep-water Westport channel that led beyond Garvillan Point, after which it would navigate a path beyond the hundreds of islands that speckled Clew Bay, and out into the Atlantic.

They rested again near the *Destiny*, munching on biscuits hard enough to break teeth. According to the large clock on the face of the Custom House, they had one hour left in Ireland.

'Our ship's safe, I'm sure of it,' Thomas muttered unconvincingly.

Owen didn't reply.

A sailor, perched on the rail of the *Destiny* and clinging with one hand to the rigging, held up a board and began to read from it in a booming voice:

'All steerage passengers hear this...boarding of the *Destiny* shall commence presently...no passenger shall be permitted across the gangplank without a fully paid ticket stamped by a Medical Inspector. Each adult shall be entitled to a space of ten cubic feet for luggage. Any found in excess of this shall have the excess thrown overboard. Obedience must be observed of signage which indicates areas permitted to passengers, rules concerning latrine usage and cleaning, distribution of food and water and so forth. These rules are for your own safety. Penalties for breaking them include shackling and flogging. Berths are provided to accommodate...'

They never heard the rest of the seaman's discourse as distant screams turned hundreds of heads almost as one towards the ship just departed, which had moved just beyond the patch of land called Roman Island. Now the families of its passengers who still lingered were running along the quayside towards the ship, a few hundred yards distant, as the level of the screams swelled.

Owen and Thomas could clearly see that the ship was listing to one side like a young tree in a high wind. There was panic on the deck, sailors and passengers scuttling about, some leaping into the water while others, unable to swim, stood screaming at the rail, arms waving in frantic appeal; but no boats were near and they were too far out to cast ropes. The ship lurched and the mast leaned precariously over as a renewed surge of human terror gave voice.

A uniformed man came running towards the waiting crowd, his face red from the exertion and panic. 'Her hull gave way at the brush of a sandbank! Launch the boats! In the name of God launch the boats!'

'God Almighty have mercy,' a woman sobbed and crossed herself several times in quick succession.

Owen could only imagine the horror taking place even as they stood there, the timbers exploding inwards followed by a wall of water, crushing people in an instant, drowning others, some desperately clambering up gangways only to find themselves trapped on the deck, most unable to swim. He thought of the young girl and her brothers. This had been their reward for her sacrifice. Better she had walked away and thrown her fate in with Ireland's.

'All you people, listen to me!' The sailor on the ship's rail bellowed again. 'Have no fear for your safety! The *Destiny* is a new ship in good order. That ship was over-laden and ran too deep. This ship will not, I tell you, and you will all arrive safely in the New World, with God's grace, in one month's time. But we must commence boarding now or we will miss the tide. The gangplank will be lowered and you will board in an orderly fashion. Have tickets at the ready!'

Four men hefted the heavy gangplank across the gap to the quay. Immediately the passengers began to stream aboard, burdened with babies, bags, wooden crates and sacks.

'Jesus, Thomas.'

'It'll be safe, like he said.'

'It's not that. All those people.'

'I know. Come on.'

Owen looked to see the doomed ship almost on its side now, the screams diminishing as the icy water silenced their voices. Ten or more small boats rowed furiously to their aid but they'd be lucky if they saved a hundred. He prayed the girl was among them.

The brothers passed up the gangplank and were admitted on deck, where hands directed people down into the body of the ship. Owen had the briefest glimpse of the deck: three huge masts towering skywards, at base each as wide as a man, and from them was strung a mesh of heavy rigging. Rearward of the ship he could see men in dark uniforms on a raised platform, a large wheel at its centre, one consulting a chart while another viewed the sinking ship through a long metal eye-glass.

'Hurry along now and stow your baggage, you may come back to the deck when you've found a berth,' one of the hands repeated again and again.

They descended the wooden stairway into the dimly lit space below and were struck immediately by the ingrained smell of those who had inhabited this chamber before them, musty and lingering and mingled with that of the sea. They walked through the ship's belly looking at the cramped berths with loosely fitting wooden slats for sleeping, stacked three high, each space barely affording room for two adults side by side, but already in some cases crammed with whole families and their baggage. There were already a hundred or more people jostling for space. Thomas yanked Owen forward.

'Here. This one.' They clambered up into the tiny space and undid their sacks, spreading out the blankets they'd purchased, then turned and lay watching as the noise swelled in proportion to the numbers. Owen was on the inside, against the hull, which was covered with the messages and invocations of past travellers, mostly cut into the wood, but some in ink. He read a few. 'May God have mercy on us. Peadar 1846.' 'Infant Joseph, perished in fever, God watch over his watery grave.' Others were more prosaic: 'Bastards.' 'Fever. Dying.' Another of affection: '*Is breá liom Eilín.*' His own random thoughts at that moment still echoed the screams of the drowning, and the dread of the departure rested heavy in his heart.

After an hour, in which they barely exchanged ten words, he felt the boat shift beneath him. A deckhand appeared in the stairway and called out.

'You may go above to say farewell, but not all together as anyone falling overboard will be left to their fate.'

Seeming collectively to ignore him, almost every passenger clambered up and rushed to the stairway.

'You go. I've seen enough of Ireland,' Thomas muttered, shifting aside so Owen could pass.

Feeling despondent and confused, Owen joined the crush up the stair. He emerged to a brightening evening, just a few wispy strands of white in a clear sky, and pushed his way to the rail. A hundred or so people stood on the quayside below, waving, calling out, wailing. With none to bid him farewell, Owen lifted his gaze to the horizon where Croagh Patrick was cut out in sharp contrast to the rare blue sky. Far beyond the majesty of the holy mountain lay Tawnyard Hill, an insignificant bump in the earth, beyond his sight and fading with each moment into memory.

Men scurried about on the quay untying ropes as the lower sails were unfurled, and the ship lurched as it drew away from the quayside.

Not a soul to wave to, he thought. All the people he'd ever loved, bar one, lay in the boggy earth in the shadow of that faraway hill, and as he looked down at the widening gap between the ship and the quay wall he began to sob. He raised his arm and tried to wave, as though the spirits of his loved ones could see him. The ship was ten yards out now and preparing to set off along the channel, where they would pass the wreck of the last ship and look upon the bodies of the unfortunate wretches whose dreams had ended not a stone's throw from Ireland.

Ireland. They were abandoning her to her fate. She was dying under the uncaring ravages of nature, the scourge of indifferent English rule and the inhumanity of landlordism. It seemed all of life was ranged against her survival. And if, as Thomas believed, the English had been waging a war of extermination, soon they would stand triumphant over a kingdom only of the dead. He could take no more. He wiped his tears and walked down the steps to Thomas, who lay staring blankly into space.

'Thomas.'

'What, Owen?'

Owen shook his head. 'I can't go.'

'What? We've already left. We're free. What are ye talking about?'

'I can't leave Ireland.'

'Shut up talking madness. Ireland is dead to us. Everything we know is gone.'

'Even if every Irishman dies, I'd rather die with my own when it comes, and in my own land.'

'Lie down before they think ye've a fever,' Thomas snapped.

Owen took a breath, leaned forward and whispered: 'I owe you my life, Thomas. I love you. God keep you safe.' He kissed his brother on the forehead. 'Goodbye.'

With that he turned and bolted up the steps two at a time with his brother's voice echoing in the hold behind him.

'Owen! Stop! We've pulled away! Owen!'

Owen bounded on to the deck and looked back at the quay. They were maybe a hundred yards from the berth but only twenty or thirty from the quay wall. He screamed, 'Look out!', and ran full tilt towards the rear of the ship until he came to the rail, vaguely aware of a sailor yelling at him. A startled woman screamed an oath and the people at the rail, seeing him careering towards them, parted and revealed a gap. He leapt up, landed a foot on the rail and propelled himself out into space. He hit the water in an enormous splash and its icy claws immediately tore at his body, but he'd felt them before in the mountain lakes and knew he could bear them. He sank like a stone at first, deeper than he'd ever been, the light above almost blinking out, then at last felt the slow reversal of momentum as his buoyancy pulled him up to the brightness. He broke the surface and gasped at the cold and for want of air, his ears instantly filled with a single word, repeated over and over.

'*Owen! Owen! Owen!*'

He turned in the water and was surprised to see that the ship was already thirty yards away and receding quickly. On its rear he could read the name '*Destiny*' and beneath it 'Westport'. Near to aft, restrained by two sailors, he could see Thomas, hand outstretched as though he might still pull Owen back on board, his mouth working frantically as it called his brother's name again and again.

Owen gasped and spluttered at the shock and the foulness of the seawater, never having tasted it before, and felt his limbs going numb. He turned away from his brother's cries and began to swim for the quay. His swimming skills served him well as he pulled against the icy swell, and within minutes he was desperately trying to find a grip on the slimy rocks along the quay wall. A voice above was crying, 'Make way, make way!' and a rope suddenly lashed across his face. He grasped it and wrapped it around his arm.

'Help me, men!'

The men on the quay heaved and slowly Owen was pulled up to safety. He collapsed, coughing and shivering, on the quay, and someone threw a blanket around his shoulders. He rose, barely hearing the startled comments of the gawping onlookers, and stared after the ship in silence. By now it had passed the wreck and was sailing off into the bay, the figures on it indistinct, ants upon a stick. Yet he fancied he could still see his brother's face and hear his futile beckoning.

And with that he fell to his knees and sobbed.

PART TWO

• • • • • • • •

ODYSSEY

The souls by nature pitched too high, by suffering plunged too low.

–*The Mill on the Floss*, George Eliot

Chapter 10

We can see [in Mayo] the miserable denizens of the ninety-four thousand one-roomed huts in each of which families, a half dozen old and young, married and single, lie and rise in presence of each other, and strange is the apathy, the indifference, the neglect of the great body of the Roman Catholic clergy to this degraded condition of their flock.

–James Daly, editor of *The Connaught Telegraph*, 1880.

Fr John O'Malley deservedly enjoyed great popularity for his kindly nature, his devotion to the poor, and jovial disposition. No good cause could fail in winning his whole-hearted advocacy, while he was one with the people in all their trials and hopes, a loyal counsellor and a faithful friend.

–Michael Davitt

19 September 1880

'Curse of Cromwell on ye!' Fr John O'Malley hurled the Bible with great violence across the room. He looked at the scattering of books from his previous evening's study, realised he'd absently selected the Bible to pulverise the mouse and then cursed himself silently. As the creature made its escape into the shadows, he rose and went to retrieve the holy book, his middle-aged back creaking painfully as he bent.

'Forgive me, Lord, should have used some pagan tome,' he whispered and smiled faintly, as though the ache had been sent as penance.

He shivered against the dismal chill that filled the room. The clock on the mantle that marked the passage of his earthly existence with an infernal ticking told him that it was four-thirty in the morning; he prayed there were no clocks in heaven and that he might indeed one day get there. Conversely, he hoped that day was still some way off; he still had work to do here on the earth.

The priest reached for the copper teapot that nestled among the remnants of the fire and poured another cup of tea. He sipped it and winced. Mrs Loftus, his housekeeper, had made it the previous evening and by now it was stewed so dark in colour it resembled porter. But at least it was warm.

The mouse was back, brave little creature. He let it be. It had no choice but to risk its life in the pursuit of whatever crumbs he'd dropped from his table. Eat or die. Much like his flock. Their choices were few, and he held the rising dread in his heart that many would soon be willing to risk life and liberty in pursuit of their basic human needs, and if it came to it, to take life also.

He sighed and looked around the room. The yellow lamplight painted shapes and shadows and dark recesses that rendered the space wholly altered from the daylight hours. The theological books on his shelves seemed like a row of slanting black columns teetering on the brink of collapse. The clock on the mantle, with its dark body and white face, appeared as some grim, hooded visage. The tall cupboard, one of its doors ajar, black within, summoned memories of his fears as a child, of banshees watching him from the dark places in his bedroom.

'Banshees indeed,' he scoffed and went to the cupboard, banishing that particular nonsense by reaching inside for the poteen he kept secreted there in a bottle marked 'Holy Water from Knock.' It was a minor deception that he hoped the Lord might overlook, as he suspected Mrs Loftus did. He enlivened his tea with a substantial shot and sipped, delighting in its warmth. His indulgence could be taken to be drinking first thing in the morning or having a nip late into the night; he chose the latter interpretation.

He'd retired at eleven o'clock the previous night, judging that six hours' sleep ought to serve him sufficiently for the exertions of the long journey to Ennis. Yet he'd barely slept for two, tormented by insubstantial ghouls of fear and uncertainty, and he woke frequently in distress. Finally at around three he'd had enough, rose and dressed, preferring to face the shadows of guilt in wakefulness, on his own terms.

But the guilt was unrelenting and as he sat there it nagged at him like some old hag. He remained unmoving for a time, his thoughts on his faith and the terrible demons against which he'd been pitted down the years of his priesthood. The demons had names like cynicism, rage and, most discomfiting of all, doubt. He pushed back his chair and walked to the water-speckled window of the parochial house, staring into the night and hoping he'd see the first of the men arrive in readiness for the journey. But only a few minutes had elapsed and nobody would arrive for an hour. He cursed, for he would dearly love the company of any living soul to divert him from his clouded musings. The tip-tip-tip of Lilliputian feet reminded him that his only company was the mouse, which, as he watched, somehow squeezed through the tiny crack beneath the door to the scullery, a feat he would have thought impossible. But the proof was in the seeing.

Therein lay the nub. If only he could witness some act of revelation, some small, insignificant sign, like a dove on a tree or the wind blowing open the Bible to a particular page or the tealeaves in his cup forming a letter. *Anything.* But the proof that would be undeniable to his eyes never came. And here, now, thinking about such things sounded like absurdity. Tealeaves and doves, he thought, shaking his head. He might as well run into the night in search of banshees and *grogochs.*

He sat again and poured a neat shot of spirit. He knew he shouldn't, not today, but he'd definitely make it his last, as the men would be here soon. Those same men of the parish of Neale had built the very room in which he sat, had built the whole church – St John the Baptised Church and Calvary – in fact. Five years ago now, and he'd had the honour of laying the foundation stone himself. And on this rock they had built their church.

God almighty. He felt such a hypocrite.

They were fine men, and their women likewise. Tough, hardworking people, honest to a fault, astonishingly hospitable given their poverty – God's own children. Oh, they had their faults, like all people. They could be begrudging of others' fortune, but he could hardly blame them for that; they'd had centuries in which to practise on their Sassenach masters. And they were a terrible people for gossiping and tattling, men and women alike. And if no scandal existed, by Jesus they'd invent some. He suspected the drink played its part, of course, but considering he was sitting there drinking at five o'clock, he could hardly condemn them on that score.

But on the whole he loved them dearly, loved them since the day he'd first driven into the village. They'd welcomed him with open arms and he in kind had embraced them as his flock, come to know each and every one. Sunday masses, weddings, christenings, funerals; he'd watched them arrive in the world and overseen their departure, laughed with them and tried to comfort them through the pitiless grief of loss. They had rewarded him by building a new church, stone by stone with their bare hands. As if they hadn't enough work. And here he sat within the fruit of their effort, struggling with his faith, like a man struggles with a fish on a line, terrified the line will snap, leaving him alone with the knowledge that his life of prayer and devotion has been utterly devoid of meaning.

He could still recall, as a novice, strolling the grounds of St Patrick's Seminary in Maynooth, his mind a whirl of conflicting issues. By chance he'd come upon the Reverend Dr Patrick Murray, one of the college's most revered theologians, who had taken some minutes to listen to the musings and doubts of the young novice, whose faith even then had wavered. He'd reassured him that he could always expect periods of doubt, especially when confronted with a sense of impotence or hopelessness. Jesus himself on the cross had cried '*Eli, Eli, lema sabachthani*?', the great theologian had reminded him: 'My God, My God, why have you forsaken me?'

'Doubt is part of belief. To question our own thoughts and actions is the very basis of conscience. God does not require us to simply squawk the scripture like a trained parrot. He has given us reason and it would fly in His face to eschew it. But He also gave us His only son, born through divine intervention of human flesh, to guide us along the path of righteousness. Remember that in moments of doubt. Jesus was, *is*, as real as you or I standing here among the lilac trees. He came upon the earth so that we might see God's love in human form and in its infinite purity. And He will always be at your side.' Reverend Murray had patted him on the shoulder, then smiled, and walked away.

Fr O'Malley reflected on that now. He had to ask himself if he doubted that Christ had existed, or making the assumption that He had, was He the human manifestation of the Supreme Being? Or, God forgive him, was the Supreme Being as nonsensical a concept as the pagan gods of the Romans? The theologian had warned that the greatest challenges to his faith would at times of hopelessness or impotence. And by God he'd had a baptism of fire. As a young novice in County Galway in the last year of the famine, much of his time had been spent standing over the graves of countless parishioners, trying to offer some faint solace to grieving, emaciated families. The famine had brought him to question again and again God's plan, His intent, His mercy. It seemed to him that God always worked on the side of the man who wielded the bigger club. The weak and helpless seemed beyond His vision. Oh, he'd of course learned that we must endure life's slings and arrows and our reward lay not in this life but at His side in eternity. But many a time he'd looked at the world around him and considered that if one removed God from the equation, if one adopted for a moment the position that the Supreme Being was a fallacy, then the world would be just as he saw it every day: cruel, unjust and heartless.

So here he sat, praying for a sign, or even a moment's clarity that might relieve the trauma of his doubt and help him face his parishioners with an unquestioning confidence, in this, yet another time of desperation. He was gripped with an abrupt, overwhelming sadness and buried his face in his hands. A sob escaped his lips.

Fr O'Malley wiped at his eyes with a knuckle and sipped his drink. 'God almighty, what's wrong with me?'

It is the hour, he thought, the deep cradle of the night, when we are at our lowest ebb. His ruminations on the famine and his flock's struggles had conspired to bring him low. That and thoughts of the challenge that lay ahead. Hard enough, given that many of his own cloth, especially the hierarchy, railed against him.

He glanced across the table at the bundle of letters he'd received from bishops and even a few parish priests, condemning his open support of the Land League. Among them was one from Archdeacon Bartholomew Cavanagh, the parish priest in the village of Knock, not thirty miles away. Just over a year ago, on 21 August 1879, a handful of Archdeacon Cavanagh's parishioners had been blessed with precisely the kind of sign that he now prayed for, an earthly manifestation of God's majesty. Three figures, the Blessed Virgin Mary, St Joseph and St John the Evangelist, had appeared on the gable wall of Knock church. He'd visited the shrine since, of course, prayed for hours on throbbing knees, but had been granted no vision, no enlightenment, no balm to soothe his troubled heart.

Archdeacon Cavanagh had offered to have him as his guest for the night in Knock. He had mixed feelings about the man – on the one hand as pious a soul as one might encounter, on the other an outspoken critic of the Land League, which, prior to the apparition, he had roundly condemned from the altar. He'd accused the League of preparing the country for violent revolution and of being populated by fanatical Fenians. He'd so outraged the people of Mayo that a 'monster meeting of indignation' had rallied over twenty thousand to protest. They'd countered that the Archdeacon had been siding with the landlords all along and in effect accused him of being a traitor to the impoverished tenants.

That evening, Fr O'Malley had steered the conversation away from discussion on the Land League and towards the even more phenomenal apparition, on which subject the Archdeacon was naturally effusive. After the terrible ravages of the past decades, he'd insisted, the Lord had chosen to remind the people of Ireland that they had not been abandoned to His heart. One thing was certain, that in the wake of the apparition, Archdeacon Cavanagh had wrested back the respect of the people. Now, perhaps, his pronouncements on the subject of the Land League might not be met with monster meetings of indignation, but with open ears and hearts. But if that had been his hope, it hadn't come to pass.

It confounded Fr O'Malley's thinking why was the man was so openly hostile to a movement that sought to destroy the great evil of landlordism, and a movement that enjoyed such widespread support among the impoverished faithful? But, of course, he hadn't been alone in that regard; many of the Catholic hierarchy were behind him. As he had personally discovered the previous October.

That month he'd had the honour of being invited to chair a Land League meeting in Ballinrobe. He'd felt humbled to share a platform with the likes of the great Michael Davitt, who was his close friend, and one of the key founders, along with Parnell, of the Land League. It was also the first time he'd met James Redpath, the famed American journalist and author who was writing a biography of Davitt. It was from Davitt's lips that day that he'd first heard the idea of ostracism as a weapon to fight the seemingly unassailable power of the landlords. He'd urged the enthusiastic crowd to treat land-grabbers as traitors, not just to their fellow farmers but to Ireland itself, to snub them in all things, offer them no succour, leave them outcasts in the community. So social a beast was the human that no man could endure such a circumstance for long.

His presence at the meeting, however, had brought him a strong rebuke from the hierarchy. And he'd been personally summoned by Archbishop McHale of Tuam, who berated him for his actions. He'd been reminded that his calling directed him to save the souls of his flock, not their livelihoods, a job best left to politicians.

He had argued his case, much to the consternation of the old man. He had been vaguely threatened with some unstated punishment. But what could they do to him? De-frock him? Transfer him to another village and away from the land issue? Such a place didn't exist the length of Ireland. So the Archbishop's threats had fallen on deaf ears. And not just his, but hundreds of other local priests. Most of the senior clergy lived lives remote from the realities of daily existence. One couldn't simply sermonise on Sunday and have no truck with the people's grievances the other six days of the week; their capacity to live honest lives was hugely diminished by their perilous situation. If a man steals bread, he transgresses – if you can help destroy the reason the man needs to steal bread in the first place, you are surely doing God's work.

But, of course, there was another stone in the hierarchy's shoe – Charles Stewart Parnell, a man they distrusted deeply. He was a Protestant, first of all, and it surely rankled with them that a man of that faith might hold sway over the Catholic masses. He was also a landlord, albeit a highly just and generous one. And he spoke with a distinct English accent, anathema to their vision of a great Irish statesman.

In reality it was all about power. The Catholic Church's power and influence had waned sharply in the wake of the famine. And now comes Parnell and unites the country as rarely seen before. He could well understand why the bishops felt so threatened. Yet at least Mr Parnell had a vision, a cause for which he intended to wield his influence. But it saddened Fr O'Malley that his elders seemed to want their power purely for its own sake, not to guide the paths of their vast congregation. Power for its own sake was a dangerous thing. It had led to terrible corruption and depravity in the Catholic Church down the centuries and probably would again in the future. But for now he was happy to stand side by side with his parishioners in the glow of Parnell's leadership. This wealthy Protestant landlord would be their guiding light, not the vapid missives from the bishops in their palatial homes.

Today they had the opportunity to hear the great man speak, as would thousands of others, among them a handful of his own flock. He hoped, he prayed, that he could look into their eyes on the return journey and see a new-found spirit, for theirs had been all but quenched these past months thanks to the efforts of Captain Boycott, whose very name made his gut taut with indignation. The name had become a symbol to him of all that was wrong in their country. His calling had put him beyond the capacity to hate, but he was sorely tempted. Never in his life had he met a man so marked by an absence of compassion and so lacking in personality. Never a kindly greeting was offered by him when encountered in the road or the market. Never a 'thank you' or a 'good day'. Or perhaps he reserved these utterances for his own kind, believing the wider Irish population beneath such natural, instinctive exchanges.

He certainly held Fr O'Malley in contempt, which bothered the priest little. Boycott, he believed, viewed him as a rabble-rouser and an agent of the revolutionary. The man also nurtured a deep hatred of the Catholic Church, which the priest believed Boycott saw as a conspiracy to undermine British governance. Fr O'Malley knew all this because the man often spoke openly and loudly on the subject as he wandered Lough Mask Estate among the labourers and servants, usually in the company of Asheton Weekes, who, by contrast, seemed a man of much more considered views. In Fr O'Malley's mind, Boycott's very act of talking openly within earshot of the subjects he was deriding said a great deal about his disposition. How could you begin to deal with such a mindset, how could you begin to reason, to deliberate, negotiate and resolve? Ultimately, Fr O'Malley believed, you couldn't. Somehow, by some means, arms were going to have to be twisted.

He stirred from his meditations at the sound of voices and was shocked to see that it was almost five-thirty and that the first hints of light were already touching the eastern sky. The rain had stopped and just along the road he could see two men approach – Martin McGurk and another. McGurk posed an awkward task. A man in his late twenties but still hampered somewhat by the impulsiveness of youth. A bright enough individual but given to temper and loud pronouncements on the violence he would one day inflict on the likes of Boycott, which the priest could never endorse. And regretfully, McGurk was not alone in his thinking. But Fr O'Malley believed that such action would ultimately be counter-productive, besides the fact that it was contrary to God's teaching.

So he would have to convince them to follow a different path.

There were others arriving now, five or six approaching on jaunting cars. There would be ten of them in all, please God. But as yet there was no sign of Owen Joyce, he was disappointed to see. And the clock had moved past the appointed hour.

He gathered his coat and the tattered leather satchel, which bore the items he would need to perform a roadside mass, a lunch prepared for him by Mrs Loftus, and the money to finance their tickets on the ferry from Cong to Galway, which he'd borrowed from the funds supplied by the bishop for the purchase of new vestments. He stepped to the door just as one of the men knocked and opened it immediately, startling the man.

'Good morning, lads, and God bless you all for coming,' he smiled.

They responded with an almost perfectly harmonious 'Good morning, Father.'

McGurk spoke. 'There are three cars, Father, it'll be a squeeze, but sure it's only as far as Cong.'

'Perfectly fine, Martin.'

He looked around at the tired, expectant faces. The group seeming a little sinister in the silent grey light, like a band of men bound for a furtive assault.

'Anyone else coming?'

'Owen Joyce was supposed te be here. Must have changed his mind,' someone said.

Fr O'Malley sighed. If only one had come he had hoped it might be Joyce. He was an intelligent man, more than he knew himself, and a moral man to boot, but one also plagued by doubt. His troubles stemmed not from his faith, however, but the battle that raged between his baser instincts to do violence, his higher intellect, which suggested a better path yet could not find it, and the need to assert his masculinity in the eyes of his family. Furthermore, Fr O'Malley believed that Owen Joyce suspected himself a coward. Far too many men were of the mind that courage could be validated only by lifting a gun.

They climbed on to the three cars, nine of them in all. It was a tight squeeze and he pitied the two unfortunates wedged either side of him as his portly figure, his voluminous backside in particular, made for the prospect of an uncomfortable journey.

'Apologies, lads, I promise to starve myself next Lent.'

The men chuckled and the driver lifted the short whip to hasten the pony away.

'Father! Hold a minute,' came a call from behind them. All the heads turned to see a fourth car approach, and even in the damp, early light, the priest could make out the face of Owen Joyce and beside him his son, Tadhg.

He grinned broadly as they pulled up. 'I'm glad you came, Owen. And Tadhg too.'

'I'll admit I was in two minds.'

'And what decided you?'

'Father, if you had to listen to a tongue-lashing from Síomha at half-four in the morning you'd walk through the gates of hell to be free of it.'

All the men laughed, as did the priest. It was good to hear their laughter, such a rarity in these times.

'Let's be off, then. We can't keep Mr Parnell waiting.'

They rode in silence along the bumpy track, the birds awake to their daily hunt for nourishment, chirping as they reaped the harvest of worms brought to the surface by the night's rainfall. He hoped their own harvest today might be as bountiful.

He returned in mind to the night he'd passed, hours clouded by doubt and a wavering faith. His heart felt surprisingly lighter now, buoyed by the brightening sky, the company of men and the awakening sounds of the earth. Demons, when they came, preferred the lurking hours of darkness and his particular demons had seemed far more ominous in the still silence of the night than they did now. His crisis was not at an end, he knew. But whatever his doubts, he accepted the teachings of Christ as a design for life, and a fine one at that. And did he really need celestial doves or flashes of heavenly light to affirm that his faith was justified? So much better the immanent God who revealed Himself through the actions of the moral and just. He recalled the words of Christ: 'I am the way, the truth and the life. No one comes to the Father but through me.' And he would seek his answers by following in the light of His teachings.

A deer ran into their path, stalled and stared at the approaching cars, then turned and darted into the woods. He smiled as he watched it vanish into the shadows.

In the car in front sat Owen Joyce with his son at his side. Another soul troubled by doubt.

One of the proverbs proclaimed: 'Fear of the Lord is the beginning of wisdom.' He'd never liked that particular notion of a God of fear. He preferred to think of doubt as the beginning of wisdom, for when we doubt, we question, and only by our inquiries do we gain enlightenment.

He prayed dearly that whatever wisdom was gained on this day, on the odyssey that lay ahead, could help him bring some peace and offer some prospect to the men around him, and finally mollify the sense of helplessness and impotence that they'd endured far too long.

CHAPTER 11

Famine has added horrors to the misery previously unbearable. Fathers see those they love slowly expiring for the want of bread. Men, sensitive and proud, are upbraided by their women for seeing them starve without rescue. Around them is plenty; rick-yards, in full contempt, stand under their snug thatch, calculating the chances of advancing prices; or, the thrashed grain awaits only the opportunity of conveyance to be taken far away to feed strangers. Do the children of the soil hesitate to see the avarice of man, and do they not resent the inhumanity as treason to our common nature? But a strong arm interposes to hold the maddened infuriates away. Property laws supersede those of Nature. Grain is of more value than blood. And if they attempt to take of the fatness of the land that belongs to their landlords, death by musketry is a cheap government measure to provide for the wants of a starving and incensed people. This must not be.

–*The London Pictorial Times*, 10 October 1847

November 1848

The old man raised his eyes and regarded Owen's trembling form with pity, then reached down to the pile of turf gathered beside the hearth and with a grunt tossed a sod on to the fire, producing a spray of sparks.

He shook his head. 'Seen thousands jumpin' on them ships te get out o' this cursed country. Ye're the first I ever seen jumpin' off one te come back.'

Owen stared at him, unable to reply such was the chattering of his teeth, then turned back towards the orange glow of the fire. He was sitting on a stool enshrouded in a rough blanket, naked beneath its coarse material. The kindly old man occupied the position of watchman here on the waterfront and had helped to pull him from the icy waters of Westport Harbour. Luckily his position afforded him the use of a tiny stone hut near the warehouses, to which he'd taken Owen to dry off and regain his senses. That was an hour ago now and yet his body still trembled, perhaps as much from the realisation that he was now truly alone in the world as from the chill.

'Beef broth, it's good.'

Owen took the proffered mug and looked into the steaming, thick soup. It smelled exotic to his deprived senses.

'They pay me with food. Most valuable thing on earth. Sure, tons of it comes through here every day,' the old man offered by way of explanation.

It tasted wonderful in all respects, warming, flavoursome and filling. As he sipped it he thought of Thomas, probably not yet rounded Clare Island, which guarded the entrance to Clew Bay. He imagined his brother staring back at Ireland as darkness descended, wondering what had possessed Owen. He stifled a sob and lowered his head.

The old man stirred, likely uncomfortable with the scene, and pulled on an old coat. 'Be back in an hour. Need te do my rounds. You rest and help yourself te the broth.'

Owen was left alone. He sat there motionless, his head by turns whirling with thoughts and then slipping to blankness, the emptiness of burnt bridges and the unknown road ahead. The solitude allowed him the painful release of weeping aloud, letting the tears spill down his face, muttering disjointed incoherencies. The tears abated eventually, as did the shivers, and he rose to check the condition of his clothes, strung up on an old ship's rope. Despite the warmth of the hut, they were still damp to touch.

The man returned just then, immediately nodding at the clothes. 'It'll be morning before they're fit for wearing. Ye can sleep on the floor if ye like, but ye'll have te leave then, son. They find I'm keepin' someone here, I'm as good as out on me arse.'

Owen nodded. 'I'll go first thing.'

The man offered Owen a shot of spirits, which caused him to cough and splutter, but he relished the comforting warmth as it slid down his throat. Chuckling, the old man took the poteen back and drank, then sighed as he stared down the neck of the bottle.

'So, why did ye jump, if ye'll excuse me pryin'?'

Owen ruminated for a few seconds. 'I don't know. I mean, I'm not sure exactly.'

'Had ye family on the ship?'

'Just my brother, Thomas.'

'Was there ill-will between yis?'

'No…we were just different to each other I suppose, but I loved him. I just couldn't leave.'

'Leave what?'

'Ireland, of course. I know that sounds stupid…I can't explain…my mother and father and theirs before…even though they're all gone…I don't know, I just couldn't…' He shook his head dejectedly, his reasons sounding empty and foolish when stated aloud.

'You know I've seen thousands climb on them ships these past years, and everyone spends their last moments staring back thinking exactly what you're thinking. But…'

'But none of them were stupid enough to do what I did.'

'I was going te say none had the guts te do what ye did.'

They fell to silence for a short time.

'Though sometimes I wonder,' the old man said then, 'y'know, about feelin' tied to a place, to all those dead and gone. I lost me whole family te the fever long ago, God rest them. Sometimes I sit here on me own at night and I get a sense of them and I think I was right te stay. Other times I think all that is just a load of horse's bollocks.'

Owen sighed and the man patted him on the back. 'Count yer blessings, son, ye could have been on that other ship today. Terrible sight. Only fifty made it out alive.' He blessed himself as he turned towards the straw bed in the corner.

'What happened to the ones who were rescued?'

'Heard the English took them to the barracks. At least the bastards are good for something,' said the old man and closed his eyes.

***

He endured a night of fitful sleep, tortured by images of screaming women and children as the sea swallowed them up, and of Thomas watching them from the deck as his ship sailed past towards America. He opened his eyes to the old man bending over him.

'Things are beginning te stir. Ye better be going.'

He quickly rose and dressed, and at the man's insistence took a final mug of broth.

'Here, take these biscuits.'

'No I can't take your last…'

The man pushed the paper packet into his hands. 'Don't worry. There's plenty more where that came from. Take that old blanket as well and this box of matches.'

Owen offered his hand. 'I don't know how to thank you.'

'Sure, I only did it for a bit o' company,' the old man said. 'They say things aren't so bad in the east. Maybe you should head that way.'

'East Mayo?'

'East Ireland. Dublin, Meath, Wexford. I hear it's bad enough, but naught te compare with here.'

'That's near two hundred miles.'

He shrugged. 'Other than that, there's the workhouse,' he muttered, his tone suddenly grim.

'I didn't jump off that ship to end up there.'

'Well, good luck te ye, wherever ye end up.'

Suddenly alone again, Owen wandered back towards the town, walking against the early morning trickle of dockworkers and emigrants. He felt aimless, uncertain, not knowing what each passing hour would bring, no purpose in sight. He had no money, not a single penny, as Thomas had always kept the pilfered cash on his person. He could find no positive notion among his thoughts but for the fact that he was well fed these past couple of days, although he knew that sooner rather than later, he would have to find food or work were he to survive.

If for no other reason than the old man's remark that things were not quite so catastrophic in the east, he began to wander that way. He strolled along Altamont Street, with a man-made water channel of some description to his left, and a terrace of houses on his right, their windows still curtained against the early morning light. He passed a building marked 'Asylum' and entertained the notion that his actions qualified him to be an inmate.

He reached the edge of town. Beyond were fields, black and pungent with the stench of the blight. He could smell it even here and felt hesitant leaving the confines of the town, as though he was re-entering a landscape that had been cursed from the heavens. But there was nothing for him here except bitter memories. So he began to walk, the defiled earth stretching out to his right as far as he could see. On the other side, some fifty yards away, the Carrowbeg River followed the course of the road. It gave him some mild hope that he might be able to catch a fish in its cold, brown waters, although given the hundreds who tramped this path each day, it was probably as barren of fish as a tree.

He began to meet people along the road, all bound for the port. They stared at him sometimes, probably wondering where the solitary youth was going, walking opposite to the flow of the Carrowbeg and the stream of desperation. It occurred to him that given his relatively new clothes, some of them might consider him worth accosting for whatever money or food he might have. One or two did ask alms of him, but most of those he met were America-bound and the more fortunate of the Irish. These were the ones who had scraped together the money to pay the ship's fare, in all likelihood by selling their every possession, whereas most of the poor were so wretched they had to simply wait in their homes while starvation pursued them to the grave.

He saw another body around mid-morning and realised that he was becoming used to such horrors. A man lay on his back near the road, his open, sunken eyes staring blankly at the grey sky. Someone had divested him of his jacket and pants and his bare legs and grey shirt were spattered with the mud of the field. The indignity of such an end had been unthinkable just a few years ago, the Irish being so respectful of their dead. But the effort even of burying the dead was beyond many. Owen could do nothing but bless himself and murmur a brief prayer.

Around midday he passed a weir on the river and, close to it, a footbridge. He tramped through the stinking field to the riverbank and climbed beneath the bridge, which afforded him some level of secrecy from the eyes of the passing hungry. He unwrapped the four oat biscuits the old man had supplied. Each was a dark brown disc about the size of his palm, hard as rock but near impervious to turning bad. He tried to bite into one but almost broke a tooth, cursed, then scampered down to the river and with the biscuit cupped in his palms, allowed the peaty water to soak it. Although softened, the brown water rendered it repulsive to the tongue, but he ate it as he had no choice and it did relieve the rising hunger.

The river and road parted company at a place called Coolloughra. He stood on the bridge across the road, staring down into the water, and wondered should he take the tiny muddy track that accompanied the course of the river or remain on the road. He could see no life in the river beyond that of the weeds which danced to the river's tune, and he decided that whatever fate lay ahead of him was more likely found round a bend of this road. There was little logic to his thinking, he was aware, but also he realised that he was beginning to care less and less. At least on the road from Tawnyard the company of his brother had offset his misery.

Coolloughra was a village of about twenty cottages spread out along a hundred-yard stretch of the road, most of them abandoned. Mindful of his earlier encounter with starving villagers, he proceeded as quickly and silently as his energies would allow. Near the end of the street he passed a cottage, outside which a small boy with vacant eyes sat on a mound of freshly dug earth, which looked distressingly like a grave. The pitiful child didn't shift his gaze as he passed, as though Owen was some invisible spirit floating by.

As the evening drew in and the cold increased with the receding light, he had to draw his jacket tighter around him and turn up its collars. He saw few on the road now, though just before dark two mounted English infantrymen rode past at speed, bound no doubt for the Westport barracks. He found the ancient ruins of a castle and decided it would serve as his accommodation for the night. It was of simple design: square at its base, with three complete walls but no roof, which had long since collapsed. Ultimately all castles come tumbling down on the heads of those in power, he reflected, more in hope than certainty as he gathered twigs for a fire. He managed to get a flame going and huddled in his blanket under a projecting stone, hoping that the rains wouldn't come, and wondering if Thomas was thinking of him as he gazed at the dark vastness of the ocean. He prayed the ship would sail his brother safely to the New World, and then slept.

It remained dry, but the night sent a chilling frost and he awoke shivering and ravenous. Given his paucity of food, he bore the hunger and continued on his way. At a place called the Triangle, so named as roads on three sides enclosed its lands, he encountered an eviction party at its business. There were some uniformed constables and a number of hired thugs to carry out the deed. A man on horseback was reading loudly from a piece of paper, detailing the notice of eviction. Owen hid in a ditch and watched as a battering ram splintered the door of the cottage and the burly men forced their way inside. A woman and child screamed from within. Then came the sounds of a scuffle and a young man was hauled struggling outside and felled with fists and cracks on the head from the constables' truncheons. Owen could bear no more and crept along behind some shrubbery, re-emerging on the road about fifty yards beyond.

At the Triangle the road had forked, and he now found himself walking more in a southerly direction. It mattered little, he thought; one road was as hopeless as the other. But, in a pitiful concession to good fortune, he found a metal cup by the side of the road, probably the former possession of unfortunate evictees. And at midday, the find enabled him to stop by a tiny lough, fill the cup and soak a biscuit to some level of edibility. He scooped up the mashed oaten mush with his fingers, then refilled the cup with water and drank the remainder down, making sure not to miss a speck. He sat there a moment looking out over the small body of water, idly recalling his days of fishing and swimming in the loughs near his home. He looked at the cup, an infinitesimally small piece of luck that had come his way; perhaps it was the beginning of better things, he thought.

He heard first the sharp snapping of a twig and a moment later felt the crack of something striking the back of his head, and his world turned as black as the inky depths of the lough beside which he sat.

***

Owen was first conscious of the pain, intense and concentrated on the top of his skull, and his hand instinctively reached up to soothe it. He could feel his hair matted with dried blood, the strands clumped together, and touching his scalp antagonised the injury.

He attempted to sit up, had a sense of the world swirling about him, and had to lie back down against the long grass. He groaned in protest at the nausea and pain and after a few seconds the grey sky above paused in its dance. He became conscious of the light drizzle on his face and the cold that had penetrated his body. Using his arm to slowly prop himself up, he looked about. All was as serene as one might expect in such a place. The surface of the lough lay as untroubled as a sheet of glass, the scattering of trees about the water's edge rested motionless, a few leaves clinging to the skeleton of branches. Slowly he gathered his wits, the nightmare of what had occurred gradually dawning. His food was gone, as was his blanket and the matches, even the metal mug. The only comfort he could take was that they'd left him his clothing, but even that was by now soaked through. He managed to get unsteadily to his feet. The only evidence of the attacker's presence was a branch, its end stained by the blood from his wound. He looked towards the road, but the thief was long gone.

Tears falling from his eyes, he began to stagger back towards the road, despair overwhelming him. The food, the blanket and the matches had been a small crumb of hope, at least for the few days ahead while he sought some end to his journey. Now the pointlessness of his choices seemed greater with every step and he felt a clamouring urge to simply fall to the ground and lie there until death relieved him of his misery. He fell against the low wall that marked the roadside and rested until his sobbing subsided. He looked up and down the road, now muddied with pools of water, and massaged gently at his scalp. How he wished Thomas was here now to suggest a course of action, to make the hard decisions he'd always dodged or dithered upon. It occurred to him that Thomas would never have sat with his back to the road, openly eating the food that was as tempting to a thief as a bag of gold, and he once again cursed his stupidity.

With little other choice, he clambered over the wall and began to walk again, the movement at least generating some little heat within his body. Judging by the hardness of the blood in his hair, he'd lain by the lough for hours, but the grey, drizzling sky denied any attempt to identify the hour. So he walked on, resting on a rock or a wall every so often, not encountering a soul, the near-flat landscape abandoned and desolate.

Ahead to his right he could see the gentle rise of some hills, their tops shrouded in mist, and realised he had little true idea where he was at all, if even he still walked the roads of Mayo. His mind felt as numb as his hands and he could frame no coherent thought, no notion of where he might be going, no scheme to find shelter or food. He simply pressed one foot ahead of the next until darkness began to enfold the world.

He woke beneath a bridge to the sound of a stream, having no memory of how he'd come to be there, then shivered and hugged himself tightly. He cupped his hands into the icy stream to satiate his thirst, but lost all feeling in his fingers, the skin turning white and wrinkling. As he massaged the wound on his head he was conscious of a prominent swelling that felt like a stone pushing through his skull. Clambering back up to the road, he saw a stone marker that told him he'd passed the village of Killavally one mile back. If he had, he could recall no detail of it; not a cottage nor a person nor a single stone within the place.

He walked on in dawn's early light, the day free of yesterday's unrelenting drizzle, and his body heat worked to dry his clothes, albeit with tortuous slowness. An hour into the day a family approached pulling a handcart – a man, a youth and two younger girls. They eyed him with suspicion and veered towards the far side of the track as he neared them. He had no choice now, he thought.

'Please can you help me? I was robbed. I'm starving and freezing.'

They hastened their step, the youth lifting his small sister into his arms protectively. The man looked over his shoulder at him. 'Keep clear of us! Sure isn't everyone starving? And the state of ye.' This last was uttered with disgust.

As they receded on the road Owen looked down at himself. His clothes were spattered with mud and his shirt was torn at the chest, although he had no recollection of this having occurred. He held a hand to his face and felt its muddy grittiness. But was his appearance so different from the countless other wretches who wandered the roads?

He continued through the silent countryside, the hills to his right rising higher, a multitude of loughs, large and small, to his left. Where one almost touched the road he knelt and drank, then leaned over to observe his reflection. He was horrified to look at himself, for blood from his wound had coursed down as freely as a stream across his face, where it had dried hard. Little wonder he had repulsed the family earlier, the streaks of blood giving him the appearance of some kind of savage beast. He splashed water in his face and found he had to rub hard to shift it. When the ripples in the water began to subside he stared into his own eyes for some minutes, realising that he barely recognised the youth who stared back at him. Besides the obvious gauntness, something about his eyes had hardened, or perhaps it was hopelessness that he saw there, and he knew that the water would never settle enough to allow him see the reflection of the person he'd once been.

The hunger continued to wail at him as he stumbled along. The food he'd had in recent days had merely masked his starvation. No nourishment had been stored within him and the energies of that food had long since been burnt away with the effort of walking. He was now near the point of death again, as bad as during those last days on Tawnyard Hill.

He heard the approach of horses at his rear and turned to see four English infantrymen approaching at a gentle trot. Was it possible they were still looking for him and Thomas for stealing the pig? It didn't matter. Better arrested and transported to Van Diemen's Land than to die here. At least they had food on prison ships.

He stood in the centre of the track and watched their approach, their red jackets and peaked hats clearly identifiable some way off. They slowed and split as they neared him, two moving either side.

'Please help me. Please can you give me some food? Anything.'

They looked down on him as though he was some form of diseased animal, repulsive and potentially dangerous. A couple of them exchanged uncertain looks, and an officer who sported a wide, curling moustache briefly met his eyes before calling out: 'Be off! We've nothing for you.'

The horses stepped again into a trot. The officer turned and looked at him over his shoulder and Owen, feeling now also starved of his dignity, mustered the energy to hurl a mouthful of spit in their wake. The officer turned away and continued on his journey. Owen closed his eyes and exhaled a drawn, mournful sob, then finally looked again at the road ahead. He could see no point. He would take not a single step more. He had reached the end of his road and found no salvation. All he had done, all the effort and trauma of survival thus far, had been in vain. He moved to the edge of the track and allowed himself to collapse on the long grass that bordered it, and there he lay, the life slowly ebbing out of him, his spirit finally crushed.

***

He opened his eyes to voices and looked up to see the faces of a man and woman above him. The woman, a black shawl pulled tightly over her head, blessed herself at his stirring, and the man lifted him a little from under his shoulder and held a flask to his mouth, dampening his lips.

'Thought ye were dead.'

They were in their thirties, country people like himself, poor but better fed than most he'd seen. She wore all black, her face barely visible beneath the shawl. He was dressed in a knee-length coat that had seen better days, and had huge, bushy eyebrows the like of which Owen had never seen before.

'Have you any food?' In his desperation, he hadn't bothered with the niceties.

They hesitated a moment, then the woman turned towards a handcart and rummaged out a loaf of bread. She broke this in four pieces and handed Owen a section. He looked at it a moment as though it might not be real, then bit deeply. It was coarse and grainy, but wonderful. The man proffered the flask again and he managed a barely audible 'thank you.' Presently the man helped him up and they sat on some rocks by the roadside, each eating a portion of bread.

'We're going to Australia,' the man offered to Owen's near silence.

He looked up at them. 'Thank you for the bread.'

'Where were you headed?'

'Don't know. Wherever I ended up.'

The couple considered this but decided not to pursue it.

'We buried the last of our children two months past. We had food enough, but the fever took them one by one, God bless their souls.' They both blessed themselves. 'After that, we decided this place had no more use for us.'

'I'm sorry for your loss.'

They rose as one. 'Well, better make tracks before it gets too late,' the man said.

Owen offered his hand. 'Thank you…eh…where am I, by the way?'

The man smiled incredulously. 'Up ahead is the village of Cloonee, where we lived, and then the road meets another going south between Lough Carra and Lough Mask. That leads to Ballinrobe.'

Owen had heard of Lough Mask and Ballinrobe, but they were places whose names meant as much to him as the likes of Dublin or Rome. As the man lifted the cart handles and readied to leave, his wife handed Owen the final quarter of bread. 'Take it, we've enough for our journey,' she said and smiled.

'The tragedy is,' the man offered in parting, 'there's a ton of food not a mile down the road.'

'What food?'

'Oats. Four cartloads. Guarded by ten of Her Majesty's bastards. Moving it te Ballinrobe tomorrow. They were waiting for more men te guard it.'

The soldiers he'd asked for food, he thought.

'Are you sure?'

'I ought te be,' the man called back, 'I helped te harvest it.'

Half an hour later a stone marker told him that Cloonee lay ahead. To his right was a small rise speckled with trees. Up ahead he saw a soldier leading a horse across the track and decided to leave the road and walk up the gentle slope, although the effort nearly finished him. As he reached the top and emerged from a copse of trees, he was met by the sight of a large body of water a couple of miles to the south, which he guessed to be Lough Mask, and in which he could identify a scattering of islands and a coast lined by woodland. To the west, the hills cast their shadow across the lough as the evening drew in. On another day he might have savoured the beauty of the scene, but he had only a small piece of bread to sustain him and he was beginning to formulate a notion in his head.

He moved towards a point overlooking Cloonee across an open field. He could identify a large cluster of cottages, several of them abandoned or destroyed. On the roadside near to these sat four large carts piled high with what he assumed to be sacks of oats bound down with ropes. The soldiers were using the abandoned houses, a couple of which were without front walls, as temporary pens for the horses. Three tents had been erected on open ground in full view of the carts and a couple of fires blazed in metal braziers. Two soldiers stood guard by the carts and a few villagers looked on, their hunger probably heightened by the knowledge that so much food was so close yet out of reach.

He lay on the ground until night began to descend. When he judged it dark enough, he began to crawl on hands and knees across the fields until he reached the cottages. Owen's heart was pounding, his nerves on fire, fear burning in his gut, yet somehow he knew he would not turn away. The imminence of death was a powerful motivator and if he didn't get a supply of food that very night, he was as good as dead anyway. He skulked silently along until he reached one of the ruins that corralled the animals. A couple of the horses whinnied, perhaps sensing his presence, but didn't draw the attention of any of the men who were about thirty yards away. He breathed hard, glanced along the narrow road towards the guards, then quickly untied one end of the rope and crept around behind the ruin. The horses stayed put, much to his good fortune. He felt about him on the ground for a heavy stick, found just that and weighed it in his hand for a moment before hurling it into the air. It sailed down into the roofless building and a moment later he heard one of the horses howl in fright, rear up and take to its hooves through the unroped entrance, its companions hurriedly accompanying it in sympathy.

There was immediate pandemonium as the men guarding the oats cried out to comrades gathered nearby around the blazing braziers. Peering round the building, he watched as four soldiers set off on foot after the animals. A number of others ran to a second derelict cottage and began to saddle the other horses.

'Come on, come on...' Owen urged through clenched teeth.

At last the men guarding the carts abandoned their posts to assist the others and, bent low, Owen scurried along the side of the cottage. He went towards one of the middle carts, which offered him the most cover, and began to yank fiercely at a sack of oats from under the ropes, and after some seconds of wrenching it from side to side, it came free and fell to the ground. He could see the commotion still ensuing through the wheels of the cart, the guards watching as their comrades set off in chase of the runaways. Any moment, he knew, they would turn back towards their posts.

He hefted the sack over his shoulder and was shocked at its weight – or perhaps it was his frailty – and then took to his heels, moving towards the rear of the cottages, his intention to make his way into the withered fields beyond, hoping they might not notice their loss until the morning. He stared out into the blackness of the moonless night. In ten seconds he would be gone from sight. He hurried forward and stepped directly into the swinging fist of an English soldier.

***

For the second time in as many days, Owen roused from unconsciousness and was aware of a throbbing pain in his nose and lip. He groaned and went to touch his injury, only to realise that his arm wouldn't respond. As the grogginess cleared he saw that his hands had been tied to the arms of an old wooden chair, and as he raised his head he realised he was inside a large tent. Directly opposite him sat a man on a stool, dressed in a red army jacket that had been completely unbuttoned, revealing a collarless white shirt beneath. Standing over him to his left was a huge, broad-shouldered soldier, his hat held stiffly under his arm.

'Water,' the officer on the stool said curtly and his subordinate promptly produced a tin cup of water and hurled it into Owen's face. He recoiled at its icy sharpness.

'You idiot, Blake!' the officer snapped. 'Give him a *drink* of water!'

'Sorry, sir.' Blake refilled the cup and held it to Owen's lips. He swallowed a few sips then coughed, his senses returning.

He looked at the officer and recognised the same man who had passed him on the road that very day, the one who had told him to 'be off'.

Blake spoke. 'You were right, sir, about it being a distraction. Thievin' vermin.'

'That's enough, Blake. Go and fetch him some porridge.'

'Sir?'

'Is there something wrong with your hearing, private?'

'No, sir.' Blake whirled about on one foot and disappeared through the tent flap.

The man sighed. 'I'm Captain Ackroyd and you, my lad, are in a great deal of trouble. What's your name?'

Owen simply looked at him, too weak and disheartened to reply.

'Sooner or later you will be compelled to tell us who you are; if not here, then in some decidedly worse environment, such as a prison cell.'

The officer, who was in his thirties, spoke in a clipped English accent that reminded him of the land agent Harris, as did his moustache and greased hair.

'Listen. If you continue to refuse–'

'Joyce. Owen Joyce.'

The officer stared at him intently for several seconds. Blake re-entered the tent carrying a bowl of steaming porridge and looked at his superior for direction.

'Untie him, Blake, unless you intend to feed him like an infant. I believe I'm capable of defending myself against a bag of skin and bones.'

'Yessir. Of course, sir.'

Blake undid the bonds and handed the bowl to Owen, who, after a slight hesitation, began to eat the warm mush greedily.

'You may stand guard outside,' the officer ordered Blake, who departed post-haste.

Owen scraped every last morsel from the bowl, then instinctively began to mouth a 'thank you', but stopped himself, a reaction not lost on the captain.

'What were you planning to do with the grain?'

Owen looked at him incredulously. 'Eat it.'

'Raw oats?'

Owen shook his head in a show of pointed disbelief at the captain's ignorance.

The man nodded. 'Yes, I imagine in your predicament you would be capable of eating almost anything. I apologise for the naivety of my inquiry.'

His self-deprecating remark took Owen by surprise and he observed the captain with a slightly more open frame of mind.

'Of course, you realise you are guilty of a number of serious crimes. The theft of the grain alone would merit a sentence of transportation. Interfering with Her Majesty's property, to wit the horses, thankfully recovered, would be sufficient to merit a long sentence of hard labour.'

'What sentence does allowing Her Majesty's subjects to starve to death while you steal their food merit?'

The man was contemplative for a time. 'We're simply carrying out our orders. Which are, to conduct the consignment of grain safely to Ballinrobe. Beyond that, as soldiers, we have no latitude.'

'Have you no compassion either?'

The man looked away and sighed, then muttered absently to himself, '*Homines libenter quod volunt credunt.*'

Owen smiled cynically. 'I *don't* believe what I want to, Captain, just what I see with my own eyes.'

Captain Ackroyd lifted his head in surprise at Owen's grasp of Latin. He smiled faintly as he spoke. 'You're a bright one, aren't you, for one so young? How old are you? Eighteen?'

'Old enough to see you for what you really are.'

'And what is that?'

Owen met the man's eyes with a look of hatred and disgust. 'You passed me on the road today. I begged you for a morsel of food...begged an English soldier...' he shook his head. 'Anyway, I got my answer.'

'We have orders not to give our rations to peasants. We cannot feed every man, woman and child we encounter on the road. By God, we barely carry enough rations for ourselves.' His voice rose an octave in irritation at what he perceived to be Owen's obtuseness.

'Then you camp in a village with a ton of oats parked before starving people's eyes. What sort of cruel bastards are you?'

The captain's eyes blazed wide and for a moment Owen thought he might strike him, but he relaxed again and exhaled in exasperation. 'For the kind shelter of their village, we rewarded each household with a payment of four pounds of oats.'

Owen was stumped. 'I don't believe you.'

The captain shrugged. 'Believe what you will.'

They were silent again for a short while before Owen spoke.

'Why are we talking like this? Why amn't I tied to a wheel or bound up in chains somewhere? Why am I here in your tent?'

He shook his head. 'I suppose that...that I simply wished to talk to you.'

'Why?'

He hesitated. 'I've never spoken to any of the peasants, face to face. I've only been in Ireland a month. And when I saw you on the road today, I felt...' He didn't finish.

'I don't want your pity,' Owen said.

'It wasn't pity. I felt a sense of injustice.'

'Injustice?' Owen almost laughed.

'What?'

'Forgive me, I'm just a thick Irish peasant. But don't you really mean *guilt*?'

'I mean injustice at what providence has sent your people, not at any actions I have personally taken.'

'Why don't you go to hell?'

The captain rose in anger, fists clenched at his sides. He began to button his tunic.

'As I have indicated, you have broken several laws and it is my duty to deliver you to the authorities at an appropriate location. However, I must also make a judgement as to whether doing so might interfere with my assignment. I am required to return to Westport in two days and as I have no wish to become embroiled in the machinations of the law, I intend to present you with the choice of either the court's punitive sentence or to become a resident of the workhouse. Despite the current excess of potential inmates, I happen to be familiar with one of the guardians of the Ballinrobe workhouse and I'm sure I can secure you entry. I am aware they are grim places, but at least you won't starve to death. Blake!'

Owen sat there staring up at the captain as Blake appeared and snapped to attention. The officer stood over Owen, his humanity replaced with the cold discipline of a dispassionate soldier.

'Well, what's it to be? Prison or the workhouse?'

Owen lowered his head. This was where his journey had led. In hindsight it was almost inevitable, he thought.

'The workhouse,' he uttered in a despairing whisper.

CHAPTER 12

Parnell was the most remarkable person I have ever met.

–British Prime Minister William Gladstone, speaking in 1898

On 19th September 1880 Parnell attended a mass meeting at Ennis. There, in a speech that rang through the land, he struck the keynote of agitation; he laid down the lines on which the Land League should work. Slowly, calmly, deliberately, without a quiver of passion, a note of rhetoric, or an exclamation of anger, he proclaimed war against all who should resist the mandates of the League.

–*The Life of Charles Stewart Parnell*, R Barry O'Brien, 1898

19 September 1880

He was so used to the smell of horse shit he barely noticed it, except when it was presented at such intensity. This was his first impression of Ennis, but it was only fleeting, for the horses that supplied the fragrance had also brought a surging river of people who flowed past him, cacophonous, vibrant with the tingle of anticipation.

Mill Street, along which they now tramped, weary from the journey, was bedecked with bunting and banners; a thousand triangles fluttering overhead, endless rainbows of colours strung across the narrow street. Above the bunting the sky was blue, washed clean of the early cloud. Banners, carefully crafted by eager hands, bore messages of adulation and hope: 'The Two P's! Parnell and the People!', ''Tis near the Dawn', 'Landlordism = Tyranny'. Every street and alleyway had risen to the occasion of Parnell's visit and Owen hoped with conviction that all their efforts had been worth it.

After a brief jaunt to Cong on the Galway border, they'd taken a steamer ferry from the north end of Lough Corrib to Galway town. He'd never travelled on such a boat before, with its funnel belching smoke into the sky and the throb of the engine beneath his feet. The craft had been packed with men from Westport, Clifden, Claremorris and even from as far north as Ballina, all on the same mission: to hear Parnell in Ennis. At least for the ferry owner, Parnell was good business. The last time he was on a vessel of comparable size he'd leapt from its stern. It had set him thinking about Thomas, a pastime in rare idle moments, wondering if he'd survived and what had become of him. They'd probably both go to their graves wondering what became of the other.

In Galway, Fr O'Malley had arranged the loan from another priest of a cart and a jaunting car. Another five hours' journey to Ennis and his arse felt like two gargantuan blisters. And Christ, he thought, we still have to endure the return.

'Father! Here!' McGurk was beckoning towards Carmody's Flour, Meal and Bran Office, where he chatted with two men in short jackets and flat caps, one of whom had a narrow moustache. They shuffled over.

'Don't mind the sign, lads, Mr Carmody here does a side trade in porter and spirits.'

The moustachioed man beckoned the group inside. 'Only glad to be of service to our Mayo Land League brethren. Jaysus, lads, you've had a long haul–. Oh excuse me, Father, didn't see you there.'

'Don't apologise. Sure, I'm not Jaysus.'

The laughter followed them into a back room where a handful of other men sat drinking porter. Nods and greetings were exchanged and the group gathered around the largest of the tables. A shy girl of sixteen or seventeen served drinks, her hair tied back, a stained blue apron wrapped around her. Tadhg's eyes followed her as a cat's would a mouse, and she briefly glanced at him by way of reward. Martin McGurk aimed a playful dig at Tadhg's ribs, who shrugged him away to the sound of chuckling.

Owen watched his son, happy at least that he had food enough in his belly to indulge himself in the natural fancies of youth. He had a brief, unexpected flashback to the memory of the near-naked girl he'd seen through the window decades ago, stirring some unsettling emotion he struggled to identify, then experienced an inexplicable guilt as Síomha's face came to him. He shook his head and lifted his porter.

'Now lads, I'm not one to preach…' The men laughed at Fr O'Malley's unassailable good cheer, then he continued in a more serious tone. 'But we musn't forget why we're here. A couple of drinks and we'll be off.'

There was a general murmur of agreement.

'I know you know Davitt, Father. You ever met Mr Parnell?' asked Joe Gaughan, a man with a huge frame and a voice as soft as a demure child. He was also a trusted neighbour of Owen's.

'Sadly, no, but he's a formidable man, I believe. He must be, to have brought the political running of the British Empire to a virtual standstill,' the priest said proudly.

Parnell's Home Rule Party, nauseated by the lip service paid to Irish matters in Westminster, had developed a simple but tactically brilliant stratagem that for years had disrupted and undermined British governance. Parnell and fellow MP Joseph Biggar had begun a policy of obstructionism in parliament, speaking for hours on end on points of trivia, completely disrupting parliamentary procedure. The British establishment soon began to realise that Parnell and his supporters were not to be taken lightly.

'Maybe so, Father, but Parnell, the Land League, all that, it might bring about change down the road, but I'm more worried about tomorrow,' said a tenant called Cusack. A chorus of concurring voices joined him.

'That's right. Our rents fall due tomorrow. What are we going te do?'

'Well, I'm three pounds short.'

'I'm the same. The price of spuds and turnips is only half what it was.'

'I'll pay if I get a decent abatement.'

'From *Boycott?* Ye'd need a miracle.'

'English bastard,' Martin McGurk spat.

'We asked for an abatement of twenty-five percent, remember?'

'But Boycott convinced Lord Erne te give us just ten.'

'So what can we do?'

'I'm not paying. I can't. Simple as that.'

'You'll be evicted. We all will. Then it's starvation. Or the workhouse.'

A glass slammed down hard and the chatter was silenced. 'I know what I'd do.' It was McGurk. 'Fix the problem once and for all.'

Nobody spoke. It was as though some unsavoury character had entered the room and all were afraid to speak his name. Owen, who had been quietly observing the proceedings, looked at the young farmer. 'What would you do, Martin?'

He leaned forward with a conspiratorial mien. 'There are men out there, around Lough Mask, patriots – they'd do the job. And by God I'd help them,' he said in a hushed voice.

Fr O'Malley spoke now. 'You mean you'd kill Boycott? And these men you speak of, Martin, are they the same brave soldiers that murdered the lad in Kerry last week?'

McGurk was indignant. 'That was an accident, from what I hear. Anyhow, there's more here feel the same, just won't say it. What about you, Owen?'

Owen hesitated. 'To be honest, I haven't made my mind up.'

'Jaysus, do you ever? Why d'ye all think we're here? What d'ye think Parnell's up to? Why d'ye think he's making friends with rebels the length of the country? I'll tell ye why. All this time he's been secretly organising a revolution. Even the English know it. And why's he been traipsing around America raising money? Te buy souvenirs? Te buy guns, more like. Any day now, there'll be a call te arms. Maybe *today*. And I'll tell ye another thing: I'll be the first te put a bullet in Boycott's fuckin' head.'

McGurk had worked himself into a minor frenzy and a drip of spittle ran from the corner of his lip, which he quickly wiped away with his sleeve. There was disquiet at the vehemence of his rant and at the use of profanity in the company of a priest.

Eventually it was Fr O'Malley who cracked the still air. 'The best revenge is to be unlike him who performed the injury.'

'No disrespect, Father, but the Bible can't help us.'

'Actually it's the…never mind. But I dearly hope you're wrong, Martin,' the priest said and drank the last of his whiskey. 'I think we should go and get a decent spot,' he announced, wishing to escape the deepening shadows of violence.

The men knocked back their drinks and rose almost as one. Only Owen lingered at the table, his eyes fixed on the priest.

'I never had you down as a stoic, Father,' he said as the others drifted out.

'A stoic? Me?'

'The best revenge and so on. Not the Bible.'

The priest raised his eyebrows and smiled. 'You continue to surprise me, Owen.'

Owen sighed and looked away, clearly piqued. 'I expect the likes of Boycott to assume we're a bunch of illiterate peasants. Not my priest.'

'Forgive me, Owen, I meant no offence. I'm merely surprised that a man such as yourself has the time to study the likes of Marcus Aurelius. Or to have the means to buy books of philosophy.'

'We have libraries in this country, Father. And I'm a fast reader. So, my question.'

'Well, *philosophically* speaking,' he smiled, 'no, I do not believe we have no direct control over the world in which we live. Otherwise I wouldn't be here today. But I'm simply selective of the philosophies that suit the moment, I suppose, at least those that concur with non-violence.'

Owen rose and moved to the door with the priest. 'And if McGurk is right, and Parnell is fomenting an uprising?'

'Then philosophy won't be able to help us, Owen. Only God can help us then.'

***

As they moved north along Gaol Street, the O'Connell Monument loomed large ahead, the Liberator's perch atop the towering Doric column affording him a panoramic view of the people's approach along the narrow roads, a sight which sadly affirmed that the great man's vision was yet to come to reality. The task had now fallen into the willing hands of others like Parnell and Davitt and it was surely no coincidence, Owen thought, that

Parnell had chosen the foot of O'Connell's column from which to make his address.

The crush was almost unbearable in the square and at times Owen could hardly breathe. Glancing about he could still see crowds of bobbing heads converging along the streets, like a thousand footballs cast into a river. They'd become separated from most of the others, but he held tightly to Tadhg's arm as though he were a small child. Fr O'Malley was just in front, but the rest had been swallowed up in the sea of bodies. A wooden platform had been erected at the base of the monument, bedecked in resplendent green flags.

'Owen! It's Parnell!' the priest shouted, sounding for all the world like an excited child.

A group of men ascended the platform, among them the unmistakable figure of Parnell, who gave a brief wave before taking his seat, unsmiling, austere; a man intent on business. A rising cheer swept across the crowd like a wave.

Owen looked up at Parnell and wondered if a trembling fear was gripping his gut at the prospect of addressing such a passionate and in many ways volatile throng. He'd read that the man harboured a terror of public speaking and in his early days in the House of Commons had spoken in a tremulous voice with little projection, hardly the sign of a man bound for leadership of a nation. But through sheer force of will, Parnell had mastered the art of oration, though he had to mentally steel himself before every speech, and he'd pulled himself to the pinnacle of Irish and British political life. He'd already achieved what many considered impossible: not the defeat of the common enemy, the English, but a much more stubborn and complex adversary, the divisiveness of Irish politics. Now, for once, diverse strands of opinion – revolutionary and parliamentarian – stood largely side-by-side. As a result of his organisational brilliance, the Home Rule Party had won sixty-three seats in the recent British election and held the balance of power at Westminster. The British establishment, Prime Minister Gladstone included, now viewed him with fear and admiration in equal measure.

Parnell himself was said to be remarkably aloof: he had few personal friends, didn't suffer the company of fools, and was an autocrat who regarded his own supporters as tools with which he could fashion an end. And if a particular tool was not performing he would discard it as a farmer might a broken shovel. Yet his supporters worshipped the ground on which he trod, principally because he passionately believed in Irish freedom from British misrule and was prepared to sacrifice himself to achieve that end – one of the key factors, it was said, in securing the hearts of the more radical or violent elements of Irish politics. And yet, for all his and Davitt's tactical brilliance, millions still remained trapped in an existence of near-subsistence. Change seemed to come at the pace of a pallbearer's step and there remained a substantial body of men who believed that the only way of altering British vacillation and indifference was to put a gun to their collective heads and, if need be, pull the trigger.

Owen craned his neck as one of the top-hatted dignitaries stepped to the wooden rail surrounding the platform. He recognised the man known as 'The O'Gorman Mahon', an impressive octogenarian who had once enjoyed a reputation as an adventurer and duellist but now served as MP for Clare. Sporting a beard of grey, scraggly hair and a red rose in the lapel, he yet retained some of the bearing of his swashbuckling youth and spoke in a voice that denied his eight decades, swollen with enthusiasm and pride. The crowd hushed to an anticipative silence.

'Men of Ireland, it is my great honour to introduce the Leader of the Home Rule Party, Member of Parliament for Cork City…' Mahon's voice rose an octave, '…and President of the Irish Land League…*Mr Charles Stewart Parnell!*'

The roar that greeted Parnell's name was simply cacophonous: upraised fists punched the air, hats were waved aloft, throats screamed to hoarseness.

Just thirty-four years of age, Parnell somehow managed to convey the charisma of a veteran statesman. Tall and slim, with a full beard of dark hair and the prickly sharp eyes of one possessed of a singular passion, his handsome face was stern and unflinching, and he held himself proudly erect yet not stiff. He placed both hands on the wooden rail and allowed his eyes to travel the crowd in a measured, panoramic sweep.

'My fellow Irish men and women…for seven hundred years we have endured the misery that has been by turns English tyranny, misrule, incompetence and injustice. But the dawn of the day is at hand when we can put that black night of English oppression behind us and walk together in the light of freedom…'

Parnell's voice was calm, deliberate, without passion, yet the words were as sharp as a cold blade. His English accent carried across the silent throng, but it was evident that not one among them doubted that this man was Irish to the blood and marrow.

'My friends, you have endured the injustice of landlordism for years without measure. Your fathers and grandfathers the same. Many of them worked to the grave by the landlords' greed, millions were lost to the famine or to the enforced tragedy of emigration. Yet I must ask you to endure a little longer yet. Depend on it that the measure of the Land Bill next session will be the measure of your activity and energy this winter. It will be a measure of your determination to keep a firm grip on your homesteads…'

A unified cheer rose as Parnell continued:

'It will be the measure of your determination not to bid for farms from which others have been evicted and to use the strong force of public opinion to deter any unjust men amongst yourselves – and there are many such – from bidding for such farms.'

As shouts of 'hear! hear!' echoed around him, Owen sighed. For all its steely intensity, much of what Parnell had said was the same rhetoric he'd heard before, suffused with hope and aspiration but lacking in the specific means of bringing about change.

'If you refuse to pay unjust rents, if you refuse to take farms from which others have been evicted, the land question will be settled, and settled in a way that will be satisfactory to you…' Parnell paused and looked slowly around the sea of faces.

'Now, what are you to do to a tenant who bids for a farm from which another tenant has been evicted?'

There were several impassioned yells of 'shoot him!' and 'string him up!'

Parnell clasped his hands behind his back and shook his head slowly until the clamour subsided. 'I think I heard somebody say "shoot him".'

Fists punched the air to cheers of encouragement. Parnell waited until the voices ebbed away. His face was calm, his demeanour unruffled.

'I wish to point out to you a much better way – a more Christian and charitable way, which will give the lost man an opportunity of repenting.'

The crowd fell to silence; questioning glances were exchanged.

Parnell's resumed, his voice infused with zeal, his eyes filled with determination and an unwavering belief in his cause.

'When a man takes a farm from which another has been evicted, you must shun him on the roadside when you meet him – you must shun him in the streets of the town – you must shun him in the shop – you must shun him in the fair and in the market place, and even in the place of worship, by leaving him alone, by putting him into a moral Coventry, by isolating him from the rest of his country as if he were a leper of old – you must show him your detestation of the crime he has committed.'

Fr O'Malley glanced back at Owen, his eyes bright with energy and excitement.

'If you do this, you may depend on it that there will be no man so full of avarice – so lost to shame – as to dare the public opinion of all the right-thinking men in the country and transgress your unwritten code of laws.'

A huge cheer soared into the blue Clare sky.

'The feudal system of land tenure has been tried in almost every European country and it had been found wanting everywhere; but nowhere has it brought more exile, produced more suffering, crime and destitution than in Ireland. It was abolished in Prussia by transferring the land from the landlords to the occupying tenants. The landlords were given government paper as compensation. Let the English Government give the landlords their paper tomorrow as compensation!' A loud peal of laughter. 'If the landlords continue obdurate and refuse all just concessions, we shall be obliged to tell the people of Ireland to strike against rent until this question has been settled! And if the five hundred thousand tenant farmers of Ireland struck against the ten thousand landlords, I would like to see where they would get police and soldiers enough to make them pay!'

A surge of cheering bodies lifted Owen and the others and they found themselves carried forward then back, almost losing their footing before calm descended again.

'I must take my leave of you, but I ask you to resist the injustice of landlordism by these means, and not to resort to the gun or the knife. I tell you this, whatever burden you must bear these coming months, I would willingly bear it for you were it in my power, and I stand by each and every man who shuns the evil of landlordism!'

Parnell waved and turned away as a clamour of adulation rose and echoed off the walls of the square, bouncing away along the streets of Ennis. Owen himself felt his spirit rise with the cheer and had to suppress a swell of emotion within his own heart at the unity of purpose, the impassioned solidarity that Parnell had evoked.

Fr O'Malley forced his way to Owen and Tadhg, his face a picture of excitement.

'Are you all right, Father?' They had to shout to make themselves heard.

'I am, Owen, I am. By God I am! You heard what he said, didn't you?'

'About shunning blackleg farmers? Great idea. But unfortunately I'll have to lose my farm first before we can put it into action.'

'Oh Owen, you took him too literally. Why just shun farmers when we can shun the agents who give them the farms? Tell me, what man is the most singularly deserving of being shunned in the county of Mayo?'

Owen paused for the briefest of moments, glancing up at Parnell one last time as he disappeared from sight. Then he looked back to the priest.

'Boycott,' he said.

CHAPTER 13

About four hundred of the most destitute families have crawled to Ballinrobe every Friday for the last month, seeking admission to the workhouse or out-door relief, and yet, though they remained each day until night, standing in wet and cold at the workhouse door, craving for admission, they have got no relief.

–Letter from The Reverend Mr Phew to the Poor Law Commissioners, 1848

In Ballinrobe the workhouse is in the most awfully deplorable state, pestilence having attacked paupers, officers, and all. In fact, this building is one horrible charnel house, the unfortunate paupers being nearly all the victims of a fearful fever, the dying and the dead huddled together. The master has become the victim of this dread disease; the clerks have been added to the victims; the matron, too, is dead; and the esteemed physician has fallen before the ravages of pestilence. This is the position of the Ballinrobe house, every officer swept away, while the unfortunate inmates, if they escape the epidemic, will survive only to be the subjects of a lingering death by starvation.

–*The Mayo Constitution*, 23 March 1847

November-December 1848

The day had dawned cold and bright, with a razor wind at their backs that stung at their ears and sought to invade their clothes. The small convoy trundled along at pace, motivated by the wish to see their task done and sit by a blazing fire.

Owen was seated on the leading cart, sacks of oats stacked high behind him, a rough-looking Irishman holding the reins. His hands and feet were bound before him, dispelling any notions of escape. Once or twice Captain Ackroyd had trotted up alongside him, inquiring of his background and experiences, but Owen had been muted in his responses. He found it difficult to fathom the Englishman's interest. It was as though the captain was striving to dissect him, maybe even to understand what he himself was doing in Ireland.

The captain had also told him that if he didn't remain in the workhouse, the police would be informed that he was a thief who'd gone on the run and justice would take its inevitable course. And while the workhouse walls might not hold him, the fact that he'd starve to death outside them should. When he considered it, the man was probably right. In just three days he'd collapsed near to death, been robbed, had almost frozen to death, and managed to get himself captured. He wasn't even a competent thief. The fact was that, alone, he was as vulnerable to the world's cruel vagaries as a newborn lamb. Grim and shameful as the prospect sounded, the workhouse was probably his best hope of survival.

They passed more people on the road now as the tracks and boreens converged on Ballinrobe. Without exception, they all appeared utterly destitute and dejected. Unlike Westport, this town offered no potential escape over the ocean. With pleading eyes, they watched the food-laden carts trundle by, but the soldiers' weapons gave pause to any notion they might have of approaching them.

A call from one of the soldiers at the front made him lift his head and he was amazed to see a tower rising high above the trees in the distance, absolutely the tallest structure he'd ever seen, the height of maybe seven cottages stacked upon one another.

'What is that?' he asked the driver.

The man glanced up. 'The flour mill,' he grunted.

They passed a Catholic church on their left, around which were gathered perhaps a hundred people, some kneeling and praying, many more languishing under shelters of branches and rags.

'They're begging alms from the church,' his gruff driver muttered with a sneer. 'Too proud to go to the workhouse.' He nodded towards the adjacent graveyard. 'That's the only place they're going.'

A crowd began to drift towards the convoy, begging for food. Their numbers made the soldiers uneasy and one or two of the men used the butts of their rifles to push people back. The captain forced his way to the front.

'Get back, I warn you, back!' he roared repeatedly at the fifty or so bedraggled wretches crowding round the wagons, all of them imploring with outstretched arms.

'Clear a path there, I say! Clear a path!' the captain was yelling ineffectively. The next moment everyone was startled by the thunderous noise of a gunshot as he fired his pistol in the air. 'Hear me now! If any of you molest this transport, you will be shot!'

This had the desired effect and the people reluctantly fell away to the roadside. As the captain's horse sauntered near to his cart, Owen fixed him with a reproachful stare.

'Give them one sack for pity's sake. Whoever owns the oats could afford at least that.'

'I will not,' Ackroyd uttered curtly and passed on.

Five minutes later they entered the town of Ballinrobe, its terraced buildings reminding Owen of Westport. On his right rose the curving walls of the infantry barracks. Immediately the gates opened and about fifty soldiers trotted out and formed an escort either side of the carts. They set off along what Owen saw to be Bridge Street; indeed, up ahead he could hear the unmistakable sound of rushing water.

The captain appeared at his side. 'Do you give me your word that you will not try to escape?'

Owen nodded and the captain used a knife to cut his bonds in two swift, practised movements. 'In case there is any trouble,' he added.

People lined the streets watching as they passed, stares fixed on the oats. Owen felt perversely ashamed, as though he was one of those responsible for depriving them, a traitor. They crossed the River Robe, for which the town was named, and to his left he was granted a closer view of the high mill tower. From his elevated position he could see down into the river, its waters deep and brown, long stringy weeds swaying with the rhythms of the current. Owen noted that where the river passed the mill it ran fast and white, tumbling over submerged rocks, but when it emerged from beneath the bridge to his right, it flowed placidly away with barely a bubble breaking its surface.

'Bastards!' someone called out and a piece of dung struck one of the infantrymen. Instinctively the man levelled his rifle, but a yell from a superior stilled him before he might fire.

They went up a short rise and turned right into Market Street, the town's main, though narrow, thoroughfare. Some of the buildings were three floors high, occupied at ground level by shops and taverns. A raised footpath on the either side of the street was lined with people, but Owen considered it was hardly a mob to merit the presence of so many soldiers.

'Go home, ye Sassenach filth!' a woman's voice screamed from one of the windows above. Many people began to whistle in unison, a piercing cacophony that made Owen wince. Halfway along the thoroughfare he saw a rather striking house set back from the street, a wide lawn stretching up to the two-storey, ivy-covered building, and he wondered if the oats they now conveyed were destined to further enrich its occupants.

A few more insults were cast in their direction, occasionally accompanied by a handful of horse shit, but in general the threat seemed minimal.

Owen turned to his driver. 'It's hardly a riot, is it? All these soldiers. Are they always this scared of a handful of Irishmen and old women.'

The man uttered a derisory laugh. 'It not these they're scared of.'

At the end of Market Street they swung left, passing a road going south out of town with a stone marker indicating the village of Neale at some five miles, the road narrowing into the distant countryside to be swallowed by a falling mist.

He was suddenly aware of a swell of voices and odours, and realised that the broad, triangular-shaped space called Corn Market was awash with the starving masses. Hundreds of sunken eyes stared up at them, ragged wretches rising from the ground all around to implore them for charity. Men, women and children crawled from filthy shanties, constructed of wood and turf and dung, pleading for a share of their cargo. The soldiers raised their guns and a way was cleared, but not before many were beaten back or brushed aside by the horses' bulk. The stench was almost unbearable, as was the incessant, clamorous keening. Ireland in her death throes, Owen thought.

'Why are these people here? Why aren't they in the workhouse?'

The driver mocked him again with a snicker, then spat on the road. 'They say it was built for eight hundred and there's already two thousand inside. These will only get in when those inside come out feet first. But they'll all get their turn. A hundred croak it a week, is what I hear. In one door upright, out the other on their backs.' He guffawed.

Owen rounded on the man in a rage. 'How can you mock your own kind? It's only by God's grace you're not one of them yourself, you ignorant bastard!'

The man snarled contemptuously, then spat in Owen's face. 'Listen, ye little shit. As ye'll soon find out, God only helps those who help themselves. He doesn't give a fuck about those starving dogs. And the reason I'm here instead of out there is that I don't give a fuck either. I'm the only one I look out for. Do the same if ye want to live, not that I give a shit what becomes of ye.'

Owen wiped the spit from his face, then closed his eyes against the misery. He felt the cart trundle along beneath him and heard the cries pursue him. Tears ran from his eyes at the awful prospect that awaited him around the next corner.

'There she is, your new home,' he heard the driver snigger and opened his eyes. They had left Corn Market but the hordes still lined the street that led from the town. They crossed a stream and up ahead on his right, beyond some wintry, leafless trees, loomed walls of perhaps twelve feet, and beyond them he could see the upper floor of a sepulchral, sombre structure of near-black stone.

He could barely see the ground for all the people gathered outside its grim walls pleading for admission. Their convoy forced its way along and the soldiers continued to beat the clawing hands away all the way to the huge wooden doors. As they swung aside, a building was revealed of two stories in height topped by five triangular stone apexes. Six or seven suited or uniformed men and women stood at the entrance. The train of soldiers, horses and carts drew to a halt in the cramped space between the wall and workhouse, and he saw Captain Ackroyd dismount near the entrance.

He suddenly began to wonder why they were here. Surely they had not risked bringing the consignment of oats through the hostile mass just to deliver him to the workhouse? He had assumed they would simply have him escorted here. Captain Ackroyd disappeared inside the building with a portly, suited man. Presently he reappeared and stood at the top step, the portly man at his side.

'Right, men, let's get these sacks unloaded and carried to the storerooms.'

There was a general groan from the soldiers as they began the process.

Owen sat there in a confusion of emotion as the captain approached him.

'The Master has agreed to allow your admission. They are in need of educated staff as a result of recent losses through typhus, so you will not be one of the general inmates but a staff assistant. Good luck.'

He started to walk away but Owen called after him. 'The oats were always coming here, to the workhouse?'

'Correct. I was ordered to safely convey this stock to help relieve the stress the extra inmates have placed on the enterprise. Had you been successful, you would have been stealing from the mouths of the starving. Oh, and on that subject, it was a fine tactical move, releasing the horses. Really only blind chance we caught you,' he smiled faintly.

'Captain. How did you persuade them to admit me when there are thousands at the gates?'

He shrugged. 'The Master is my uncle.'

* * *

A clerk recorded his personal details: name, sex, age, marital status, occupation, religion and townland of residence, and he was then taken along a corridor that looked into a large interior yard. The man accompanying him was silent and bore a vacant expression on his drooping face. At each step Owen could hear cries and moans carrying through the walls, some sounding uncomfortably like the voices of children, others like the ravings of lunatics. The man, who was maybe thirty and wore a drab, grey uniform of coarse fabric, admitted him through a door marked 'Examination Room – Male'. The room was bare but for a long table in the centre and a single chair. Only a tiny square window of white glass admitted light. His apparently mute guide pulled at his clothes and nodded towards a tiled washing alcove off the room.

Owen reluctantly stripped, leaving his clothes in a pile on the floor. The washroom was perhaps ten feet square, walls and floor covered entirely in smooth white tiles. A single copper tap protruded from a wall beneath which sat a bucket of water. He'd never seen a room like it before. He turned at a sound and was struck by a wave of icy water, the suddenness of which caused him to lose his breath and fall back against the wall. As he stood there shivering, the man began to refill the bucket, then pulled a slab of white soap from a pocket and tossed it to him. It struck the wall and Owen watched it slide into the drain, still too taken aback to protest.

The man appeared to take no cruel pleasure; in fact, he seemed entirely detached from his task. Owen did as ordered. Soap had been a rarity in their home and mostly the girls had made use of it anyway. He was unfamiliar with the suds it produced and he briefly examined a handful of them before rubbing them against his body. Two minutes later the man re-entered, lifted the bucket and threw its freezing contents over him again, then tossed him a shabby towel. Trembling from the cold, he emerged to find the room vacant and stood clutching the towel in front of his privates, unsure what to do next. The light had faded and the room grown dim.

He squirmed with embarrassment as a thin, mannish woman of forty or so suddenly entered, clutching an oil lamp. She wore a dress of pale grey with a white collar, a white apron extending from her shoulders to her feet, and a white bonnet, which almost completely concealed her hair. She regarded his shaking figure with disdain.

'What is your name?'

'Owen Joyce.'

She walked directly up to him and perused him slowly from head to toe, holding the lantern close to his body. He pressed the cloth tighter against his groin.

'Turn around.'

He remained frozen to the spot. Besides his mother and his sister when he was a small boy, he had never been naked in the presence of a woman.

'I said turn around, boy.' She grabbed his arm with a surprisingly steely grip, forcing him to turn. Having closely examined his hind side she pulled him around again. She drew up so close to him that he could feel her breath on his cheek and detected a vaguely repulsive smell, like the stink that emanates from the very sick. She opened his eyes wide with thumb and forefinger and stared into them, then probed his mouth with a flat stick.

She told him to sit and handed the lantern to the man, pulled a comb from a pocket and proceeded to slowly drag it through his hair, separating it with her fingers and peering at his scalp. This mysterious task completed, she pointed to the table. 'Lie there.'

He awkwardly tried to conceal his nakedness as he climbed up. When he was on his back the woman grasped the towel and tore it away before he could react. He gasped and covered himself with both hands. She went to lift his hands and he instinctively grabbed her wrist, at which point she drew back and slapped him hard across the face.

'Don't dare touch me or I'll have you lashed. Remove your hands. Now!'

Utterly abashed and shamed, he drew his hands back and laid them at his sides. To his bewilderment the woman commenced to repeat the same procedure with her comb and fingers as she trawled his pubic hair, her face only inches from his genitals. When finished, she returned the towel to him.

'You may sit up.'

Shivering and feeling humiliated, he sat upright on the table's edge.

'Can you read?'

'Yes.'

'You will address me always as Matron. Now, can you also write?'

'Yes – yes, Matron,' he chattered.

'English and Irish?'

'Yes, Matron. And a little...Latin.'

'We don't get many Romans, fortunately. Quite enough to cope with,' she said without humour. 'Can you do arithmetic, add and subtract and so on?'

'I can do algebra and trig–'

'I don't require your academic résumé, Joyce. How old are you?'

'Sev...eighteen, Matron.'

'Hmm,' she muttered doubtfully.

She turned sharply to the man in attendance. 'Fetch him clothes. And a brown apron. He may assist in the children's dormitories and the male infirmary.' She turned back to him. 'The male medical assistant died three weeks ago, from typhus, we believe. You will have to help fill in.'

Owen shook his head. 'But I know nothing about–'

'We will train you, and let's hope you're as bright as the Master's nephew seems to think you are, as you will have to learn fast. You are not compelled to take this post. If you wish you may join the general workhouse population. But if you accept you will be accorded staff privileges, without remittance of course.'

The vacant-eyed man re-entered with a bundle of clothes.

'What is it to be?'

Owen nodded. 'Thank you, Matron.'

'You may not thank me in a few days, boy. Work commences at six-thirty. Flynn here will take you to the kitchens. Tell them that Matron instructs them to feed you.'

And with that she vanished with the lamp and left him in the darkness.

***

Owen followed Flynn along a long, central corridor. Not a single inmate could be seen. As they walked among the echoes of their own footfalls and the dancing shadows cast by a candle, he could identify open spaces beyond the windows to either side, hemmed in by more buildings, and he realised the workhouse was designed around four internal courtyards. They arrived at the double doors of the kitchen. Flynn knocked, then turned and walked away as a thin, vexed voice beckoned Owen in. Timidly he stepped into the yellow glow of the kitchen. To his left a man sat by a fire smoking a thin cigar, a bottle of whiskey on the floor beside him. He lowered a newspaper.

'What is it, boy?'

Owen glanced around the room where he could see an array of huge pots sitting on four brick ranges. Tall metal chimneys rose from these and disappeared into the ceiling. The rear wall was a washing area where a youth stood scrubbing a pot. He gave Owen a nervy, fleeting glance.

'The...Matron...said I was to be fed.'

'Did she now?' the man snickered. He was about forty, almost bald but for a few greasy clumps of hair. His narrow eyes appeared half-closed as though he was permanently squinting. His cheeks glowed red either side of a squat nose. But it was the scoffing smirk that most prompted Owen's instant dislike. The man rose and walked over to him. 'And who would you be that Matron sends te me after my kitchen has closed?'

'Joyce, sir, I'm to be an infirmary assistant.'

He laughed aloud. 'Joyce? Now would that be your first name, Joyce, my darling?' The man touched Owen's cheek, and he instinctively drew back.

'Owen Joyce, sir.'

The man nodded contentedly. 'I'm Mr Rice, Kitchen Superintendent. The rapscallion there is Patrick Mooney. Mooney! Give him bread and buttermilk and be quick about it. I'm off home now and if there's a mark on those pots tomorrow I'll thrash ye meself.'

He turned back to Owen. 'No hot food. Too late.'

'That's fine, I–'

But Rice had already grasped Owen's face, pressing soiled fingernails into his cheeks. 'Oh I know it's fine, Joyce. Whatever I say is fine, whether it's fine or not fine.'

He let go and Owen rubbed his face as Rice gathered his coat, hat and whiskey. He grinned and gave a mock salute as he departed.

'Goodnight, gentlemen.'

***

Mooney silently fed him four slices of stale loaf and a jug of buttermilk, responding to Owen's questions monosyllabically. After they'd cleaned up, the youth led him to a tiny, ground-floor room already cramped with men on bunks. Climbing into a lower bunk, Mooney turned away towards the wall. There were a couple of aged men, one as thin as a rake, snoring wheezily, the other so still he appeared dead. On another lower bunk sat Flynn, the apparent mute, his face hidden in the shadow cast by a candle. The man above Flynn swung around and allowed his legs to dangle over the side. He extended a hand to Owen.

'*Dia dhuit*. Mick Caffrey.' He was thirtyish and handsome, with unruly black hair.

'Hello. Owen Joyce.'

Owen sat on the remaining bunk, which had a torn, faeces-stained straw mattress and a single blanket.

'What's wrong with that man?' he whispered, nodding towards Flynn.

Caffrey frowned and made a twirling motion with his finger to the side of his head. 'Poor bastard. Came in six months ago with his wife and four young ones. Around August every one of them died of typhus. It's like his brain still works but his soul's departed us.'

They were silent for a while as Owen wrapped his blanket about his shoulders.

'Can I ask, Mr Caffrey…'

'Mick.'

'Mick…the Matron…she searched my hair…y'know, down below…why did sh–'

Caffrey chuckled. 'Yeah, me too. Our new "eminent physician", Dr Gill, has a theory that the typhus is spread by lice. Load of bollocks, ye ask me. Spread by rat's piss, most say. She was searching yer balls for lice.'

Owen nodded. Somehow the knowledge lessened his humiliation.

'Eh, Mick, where is everyone? All the corridors are empty.'

'In their dorms by seven-thirty. Lights out at eight. Anyone outside their dorm or room after eight gets caned or flogged. You're found stealing food or near the women's dorms, they'll flog you within an inch of your life. Don't upset these bastards. Obey their rules and you'll be fine. Where you workin'?'

'The infirmary.'

'Jaysus. *Oiche mhaith*, boyo. Better get some sleep, ye'll need it.'

***

He had been roused during the night by a pitiful sobbing, which he guessed was emanating from Mooney. Other than that he'd slept soundly. A piercing ringing, loud enough to raise the dead, startled him to life and the door was flung open.

'All up and about!' the bell-ringer yelled. 'Joyce? Joyce?'

'That's me.'

'Matron says ye're te do the boys' ward.'

'What?'

'Get the piss-pots emptied and conduct them te the dining hall.'

Caffrey pointed along the corridor. 'Up the stairs te the left. Dining hall's on the ground floor towards the back. Good luck.'

He donned the full-length apron bearing a black cross and hurried out. In stark contrast to the empty silence of the previous night, the place was suddenly crammed with male bodies, each dressed in the same drab grey uniform, sneezing and coughing their way towards the dining hall. He located the boys' dormitory and went through the door to a long, broad room, windows opened to the cold November air. There were hundreds of children in the dorm, yet only about fifty cots. Mattresses had been laid between each cot and along the central aisle. The stench of urine and excrement was almost overpowering. The children were still clambering from the mattresses; the smaller ones crying, their older brothers trying to comfort them. Two middle-aged women, dressed in similar fashion to the matron, were shouting above the clamour of small voices.

'Up up up! Lickety split!'

Owen made his way through the mass of small bodies to the nearest of the women.

'Who are you?'

'Joyce. Matron sent me to help.'

'Right. You may address me as Miss Smith. Make sure every mattress is stacked and every chamber pot collected and emptied in the yard, then return the pots to the dormitory and conduct the boys to their dining hall. Get about it.'

Small, expectant, frightened faces turned to him. Compelled to action by a bark from Miss Smith, he raised his hands and yelled above the din. 'Boys! Mattresses gathered, quickly! Then collect the pots. Hurry now.' Many were already carrying out his orders, used to the routine, and a line of boys aged from six to twelve formed at the door, each clutching an enamel bowl of piss and shit. He averted his eyes. They trooped down the stairs behind him, each one careful not to spill a drop for fear of some harsh rebuke. The pots were emptied in an enormous pit within an enclosed wall, which was half-filled with the foulness of a million deposits of human waste. When the pots had been returned to the dormitory, Miss Smith told him to escort the boys to the dining hall. About to depart, he noticed a boy asleep on the floor.

'What about him? Shouldn't I wake him?'

She was grim-faced. 'You'll have a task. He's dead. The Matron will want to inspect him. Get along now to the hall.'

He turned away dumbly, then conducted the boys down the stairs again and into a wide hall crammed with long benches and tables. The children clattered along in line to one side, each clutching a metal bowl and cup, into which was spooned a dollop of dark gruel and a drink of buttermilk. When all were seated, a man's voice bellowed for silence and was instantly obeyed. Prayers of thanks were offered and then with a clap the hundreds of boys set about scraping every morsel from their bowls with a thunderous clattering of spoons.

As a staff member, Owen was permitted to eat a larger portion of the same thin porridge, made no doubt from the very oats he'd tried to pilfer, at a side table with a few others. The meal ended, the boys were conducted to a number of schoolrooms where they would remain for the day.

A man informed him that he was required in the male infirmary and, after several wrong turns, he found himself in a walled path that led outside the main workhouse walls to the hospital building to the south. It was an H-shaped structure, considerably smaller than the main building, with the sexes housed in opposite wings. He entered the male ward and once again was struck by the swell of human suffering, the smell and the noise. The room, designed for thirty, currently was home to a hundred men, who lay on cots, on the floor, or simply lolled incomprehensive in chairs, some shrieking, others crying openly like small children. The room was almost icy and he saw that every window was open wide.

'Joyce!' It was the Matron, standing beside a bespectacled, balding man who wore a brown coat over a suit. As he crossed the ward, the hands of the sick clasped at his legs, pleading for help or in some cases, death. He pushed his way forward to the Matron. The man glanced briefly at him, his eyes weary, face drawn and pale as though he hadn't slept in a week.

'Follow me,' the Matron snapped.

She led him into an anteroom filled with bottles and wooden boxes and began to dispense white powder into cups. 'All the fever patients have a white X on their breast. This quinine can reduce the fever in some. Stir a spoon into water and give each fever patient a dose. Then you may assist Doctor Gill in applying poultices.'

'Matron, may I ask, why are the windows open?'

'To disperse the miasma.'

'What's that?'

She sighed impatiently. 'I suppose it's as well you learn. Miasma or bad air encourages the disease. It builds overnight so we must flush it out. Now get to your work.'

He'd experienced the fever at close quarters before. Here in this place, half the men seemed in its frenzied grip, screaming or mouthing profanities as they battled demons of their own making, their clothes and beds soiled. It took him over two hours to dose everyone. Some fought him off so violently in their madness, he was forced to simply ignore them. By the time he returned to the Matron he sported a bruised face and torn apron.

'Still wish to thank me?' she asked.

***

And that was how most of the days ahead passed. He assisted the application of poultices of oats to draw the noxious blood from festering sores. He applied cloths of icy water to the chests of the feverish. His hands became discoloured from the application of iodine to bleeding sores and rashes. He bathed and washed those most foully soiled. He even helped to splint the fingers of a man struck by a sledgehammer while breaking rocks in the yard. Owen had been required to sit on his legs to quell their wild thrashing.

The end of each day saw him fall exhausted to his bunk. He would barely exchange ten words with Caffrey before sleep took him, then the bell sounded and the foul ritual commenced again. His vocabulary expanded with words like scarlet fever, smallpox, syphilis and, worst of all, dysentery, which rendered its victim utterly incontinent, requiring Owen to swab away the hourly expulsions of chokingly fetid excrement. The only solace he took from those weeks was that he somehow remained free from fever and that with his increased rations he began to regain some shallow layers of flesh. He'd learned that Dr Gill, a Yorkshire man, had only joined the institution in August when the previous doctor had himself succumbed to typhus. The previous year an epidemic introduced by a new entrant had claimed the lives of two hundred inmates and staff. This had led to the introduction of the rigorous medical inspection upon entry, the humiliation of that experience now lost to him amid the memories of suffering on numberless faces.

He developed a respect, if not a liking, for the Matron, who seemed indefatigable and was not averse to fouling her own hands as she did battle with the egregious, squalid indignities of defective body function. She projected an outward coldness and only once ever did she display any overt kindness to him. He'd been called late to assist in the amputation of a man's gangrenous lower leg. The man had been given copious amounts of opium, under the influence of which he'd confided that he'd once impregnated a neighbour's daughter. Despite the opium, he'd screamed as though being roasted over hell's inferno and it had required five men to hold him still enough for Dr Gill to cut through the bone, the sound of which had caused Owen to shut his eyes as his legs turned soft. Afterwards, standing in the corridor, staring out at the moonlit burial ground, the Matron had appeared and handed him a small bottle of whiskey. Unsmiling, she'd said it might help him sleep, and then hurried away.

As November turned into December and Christmas approached, the workhouse was struck by a widespread outbreak of typhus. In a single week ninety-seven souls departed this earth. The following week eighty-two died and the men had been set to building coffins in the yard. The wails of mothers informed of their loss carried through the walls and the old women took to keening to ease the passage of departing souls. A terrible gloom, deeper and more foreboding than normal, descended over the institution. It was no longer a place of refuge, but of potential death.

Owen was assigned to a burial detail and due to a shortage of materials it was decided to bury three children to a coffin. Each day four of them brought the dead to a large field to the south-west of the workhouse. A shallow pit was dug and the coffins were laid and covered with the freezing Mayo soil. Every few days a priest would hurriedly murmur funeral rites over the fresh plot. No headstone was laid or even a wooden cross erected. The dead were forgotten, countless souls left to the fancies of the decaying earth.

Three weeks before Christmas the epidemic began to diminish. Unfortunately the funds to purchase wood for coffins also diminished and they were forced to bury the dead wrapped only in filthy sheets. Those were the hardest moments for Owen to bear, as the sounds of the soil covering the bodies of the men, women and children of the Ballinrobe Union brought vividly to mind his own father's burial and set him in a deep depression. Until that point, his work had served as a distraction; it left little time for contemplation. Now he found himself brooding constantly on his separation from Thomas, his family's deaths and the loss of his home on Tawnyard Hill.

At his lowest ebb he found himself sitting in the men's workyard, staring vacantly across the crowded space when the Protestant chaplain, Reverend Anderson, approached him. In previous encounters he'd struck Owen as an amiable sort. The vicar had written to *The Ballinrobe Chronicle* decrying the state of the workhouses and even to Parliament imploring funds. All save one plea had gone unanswered, which had expressed 'the British Government's reluctance to interfere with the natural economic order of Irish society.'

'Don't worry, Mr Joyce, I'm not here to proselytise.'

'Reverend.'

'May I ask what troubles you these past days?'

Owen looked up at him. 'You mean besides throwing dead children into a hole? Or seeing scavenging dogs dig them up again? Or watching men rot from...' He realised he had raised his voice sufficiently to turn the heads of nearby inmates. 'I'm sorry, Reverend, I'm sorry. I didn't mean to raise my voice. I apologi–'

'Fine, fine, one apology will suffice. As a young man I had a tendency to run off at the mouth myself. But I understand your anger. Yet for all the miseries of this place, at least you can survive here.'

'Survive? It feels like a living death, Reverend.'

'A living death you say,' the vicar mused as he looked across the yard. 'Francis Flynn. Now that's a living death. A man living *for* death.'

Owen looked across the yard, where a hundred men were engaged in pointlessly chiselling away at rocks. The vacant-eyed Flynn stood watching them, ignored by all as though he was a wooden post.

Owen felt shamed. 'Forgive me, Reverend, I just miss my own family. They're all dead. Or gone to America.'

'One day you'll be free of this place, Mr Joyce, and God willing you'll have a family of your own.'

Owen laughed cynically.

'You are still healthy and young! Do not give in to despair. Hope, young Joyce, is our greatest ally. But listen to me sermonising again. And I almost completely forgot. The Matron asked me to convey some good news to you. The medical attendant that we've been promised for so long has finally arrived. Though I believe the Matron will truly miss your services. She would never admit that, of course, it's not her nature.'

'Does that mean I'm to become an ordinary inmate now?'

He chuckled. 'Oh no, not at all. Young Mooney in the kitchen has taken ill. And Mr Rice complains daily that he can't cope. So you're to be transferred to him. The work is, let's say, less stressful. Well, I must be about the Lord's work. Good luck, Mr Joyce.'

'Goodbye, Reverend. And thank you.'

The cleric smiled and wandered off. As Owen watched him depart, he wondered if his life had just turned for the better or the worse.

***

'They've fattened ye up nicely since we first met,' grinned Rice when Owen reported to the kitchen.

Owen said nothing; he simply stared back, awaiting direction to his chores. He'd had the opportunity for a brief perusal of the kitchen. There were four people working at the giant ranges, two female, one of these a woman in her forties, the other perhaps twenty. He glanced at her but neither she, nor any of the others, so much as raised an eye from the pots and pans and vegetables.

'Hmmh,' Rice frowned at the lack of response. 'The bakery, I think. Hot in there, unbearably so at times. Follow me.'

He turned on his heels towards an adjoining door that opened into an expansive space and Owen was immediately washed over with a wave of stiflingly hot air. Two middle-aged men worked at a table kneading dough and he was surprised to see Francis Flynn mechanically throwing logs into an inferno beneath one of the huge ovens.

'Unfortunately I have to make do with peasant farmers for bakers and lunatics fit for the idiot ward.' He openly directed this at Francis Flynn, then stopped and looked at Owen. 'Ye can't wear that thing,' he said, gesturing in disgust at Owen's blood and faeces-stained apron.

He aimed a kick at Flynn's behind as he bent over the pile of logs. 'Looney! Fetch him a white kitchen apron.'

Flynn walked from the room without even a flicker of his eyes.

'Now, pay attention, Joyce darling.'

Rice spent twenty minutes expounding on the operation of the ovens, which rose higher than a man and were constructed of heavy, black metal. They singed the flesh at the touch, as he discovered when he inadvertently leaned his hand against one, much to Rice's amusement. Owen's job involved placing ten loaves of dough on a metal tray into alternate ovens by way of a wooden pole with a hook on the end, regulating the heat with 'damper' doors, which increased or reduced airflow, and removing the baked loaves after twenty minutes. If Flynn was unavailable, he was also required to maintain the fire.

'Where do I get the wood?'

With a curled index finger Rice beckoned him to follow. He opened a door to an exterior yard containing two mountainous piles of wood and turf. Another door, set into the exterior wall, allowed for replenishment of the supply without having to haul it through the main building. 'That door is locked at all times. We must keep the hungry hordes at bay,' Rice laughed, the source of his amusement lost on Owen.

In the first few days Rice didn't trouble him overly; the man spent most of his time reading trashy pamphlets and indulging himself in the workhouse's medicinal stock of whiskey. Rice maintained a closely guarded watch over its supply.

There was little opportunity for conversation, so stifling was the atmosphere and intensive the labour. He was always grateful to see the arrival of Flynn, not for his company, but for the alleviation of his workload. The man seemed to be assigned to various simple tasks about the institution wherever a deficiency of labour occurred.

Conversing with the women in the kitchen was strictly forbidden unless necessary in the course of one's duties, so in the first week he exchanged not a single word with them. At one point he asked one of the dough-makers what had become of Mooney, only to be met with a shrug of the shoulders and averted eyes.

On the Wednesday but one before Christmas, a bright and crisp winter's day, Owen was in the yard bent over a pile of turf when he suddenly felt a hand against his backside and a voice exclaim 'excellent!' He jumped, sending the turf scattering, and turned to see Rice's grinning face.

'The work, I mean. You're doing an excellent job. I think we'll get along fine.'

Owen stood there as Rice walked to the exterior door, a bulky satchel over his shoulder, and lifted a key from around his neck to let himself out. Trembling, Owen looked towards the bakery, but no one had witnessed the incident.

It was a week to Christmas when Rice announced that his presence was required at the Ballinrobe Union board meeting that very day. He announced with a swagger that many esteemed gentlemen would attend. Several nobles and businessmen of the locale had apparently supplied charitable donations of meat and fruit so that the inmates might enjoy a meal befitting Our Saviour's birth. He warned that extremely strict punishments would be inflicted should there be the slightest neglect of their work in his absence or if any food should go missing. Furthermore, there would be no discourse or other 'carnal misdeeds'. And so off he went in his finest suit, his head held high, a supercilious smirk on his face, an unwittingly comical parody of a gentleman of importance.

A huge sigh swept about the kitchen as he departed. A young man who was helping to chop vegetables asked what a 'carnal misdeed' was, which brought laughter and titters from the older men and woman. Owen sought briefly to engage the girl in conversation, but she shyly resumed her work with barely a word.

There was little opportunity to take advantage of Rice's absence. Producing each day's soup demanded the preparation of ten stone of turnips, ten of parsnips and two of onions. The bakers were required to mix, knead and bake two hundred loaves of black bread. Once the food had been conveyed to the nearby halls, preparation immediately commenced on the next meal of porridge. The returning vats and trays had to be scoured out in readiness for the following day and this often required one or two of them to stay beyond the normal hours, and a rota had been agreed in this respect.

But Rice's meeting was too good an opportunity to miss, certainly for the dough-makers. The elder of the two, a broad-shouldered ex-farmer called Felim, abruptly slammed a huge metal spoon against the table.

'Lads. I've had enough. That pig's bollocks isn't here. How about a little break?'

Owen looked at the other man, called Rory, who shrugged as if to say 'why not?' Felim disappeared into a small storeroom and emerged with a bottle of Rice's supply of whiskey.

'No, listen, Felim. He'll notice it's gone. We'll be flogged and expelled,' Rory said.

Felim ignored him, poured three measures into cups then topped up the opaque bottle with water. 'He'll never know. Bastard waters it before he gives it to the hospital anyway. And he's always leaving these lying about.' He smiled and held up three thin cigars. 'Let's get out of this fuckin' heat.'

Owen closed the oven dampers to prevent the bread from burning and followed them into the yard, where they sat on the pile of turf. Felim handed Owen a cigar, and he took it hesitantly, never having indulged. A match flared and was held to the tip, and he coughed as the smoke filled his lungs.

'Don't inhale so much. Youngsters can never control their urges.'

The tobacco made his brain swim a little, as did the whiskey, the taste of which brought to mind the old man who had helped him in Westport.

'How did you know where he kept the whiskey?'

'I've been here a year. Ye see things. In that storeroom there's a panel behind a shelf where the bastard has his hidey hole.'

'What's in it?'

'Whiskey for one. Loaves of bread. Little bags of oats. Salt. Medicine – I think one of his lackeys in the dispensary steals that. He robs the stuff and takes it outside to the poor bastards and exchanges it for money or...'

'What?' Owen asked.

'Nothing.'

'How do you know all this?'

Felim glanced at Rory, who took up the tale. 'Before I was admitted, I was one of the ones he offered it to.'

'Man's lower than a pig.'

Owen drew on the cigar, beginning to sense a pleasant dizziness.

'What happened to Mooney, used to work here?'

The two men exchanged a grim look.

'Don't know to be honest. But he didn't die of the fever.' Felim said.

'He's dead?' spluttered Owen.

'Sorry, thought you'd heard.'

'It was poison,' Rory said grimly.

'What?'

'Either he took it himself or that bastard Rice slipped it to him. As I said, he has a lot of medicine in his hidey-hole.'

'Why would he poison himself?'

'Te be free of that fucker, I s'pose.'

The door to the bakery swung open sharply and each of them jumped up as though stung. To their enormous relief Flynn walked out directly towards them and began to gather turf. They might not have been there at all.

'Come on. Fun's over. Back te work.'

***

In the spirit of the season, a local landlord had made a charitable donation of ten of his flock of two thousand sheep, and a collection among the gentrified ladies of the Ballinrobe area, organised by the wife of Mr Ormsby Elwood, who was the land agent at Lough Mask House five miles away, meant that the inmates would enjoy half an apple and a slice of cake on Christmas Day. Unfortunately the extra food increased the kitchen staff's workload immeasurably.

Felim was requisitioned to cut the mutton from the bone, which meant Owen had to help knead the dough and operate the ovens. Flynn, at least, had been assigned to maintain the fuel supply, which he performed in his adopted self-isolation.

Owen was alone late on Christmas Eve, the days' baking almost complete, looking admiringly towards the kitchen where the young maid was sweeping the floor. She briefly met his eyes and allowed herself the faintest of smiles, which Owen returned. In the next instant she grimaced and vanished from his line of vision.

'Would ye like her?'

Rice's voice from behind startled him.

'Mr Rice…I'll finish my work.'

Rice's satchel sagged limply against his leg; undoubtedly he was returning from his latest enterprise in exploiting the starving.

'She's yours, if ye like.'

'What do you mean?'

'Oh, let's be honest. I know the desires that drive young bucks. I can arrange for ye te…*purge* those desires in a most enjoyable way.' He snickered.

Owen began to move away, but Rice gripped his arm.

'Why deny yerself? You've earned it. You see, I can persuade that pretty little peasant te do whatever I ask. Because if she doesn't she'll be caught stealing, whipped and expelled, maybe even transported. Faced with that…' he shrugged, '…even *you'd* consent te do anything.'

Owen wrenched free in disgust. 'You're evil.'

Rice slapped him across the cheek and was about to speak when Felim abruptly appeared. 'I've finished the mutton, Mr Rice.'

Rice snarled and strode towards the kitchen, brushing past Felim, who glanced anxiously at Owen.

'You call this finished?' he heard Rice bellow.

He took a despairing breath and returned to his work. But Rice didn't bother him again. At least not that night.

***

Morning bell sounded even earlier on Christmas Day so that the staff could take turns to attend mass. A choir of female inmates sang hymns and the walls of the workhouse resounded to the rare melodies of the human voice raised in joy. Thanks were offered for the birth of Christ and the Master, although a Protestant, made a brief appearance at each service to offer a prayer of gratitude for the gift of their lives.

The priests and ministers having supplied spiritual sustenance, the kitchen staff laboured tirelessly from dawn to provide nutritional sustenance for the two thousand inmates. In recognition of their efforts, two measures of spirits were to be granted them at the day's end, courtesy of the board of management. It was a pitiful inducement.

By late afternoon the last vat of mutton stew was finally wheeled away and the staff were allowed to enjoy their own meal, including two bottles of sherry, taken at the bakery table. Normally the women would have been required to eat separately and were denied alcohol, but as Rice was attending the senior staff's meal they simply ignored the rule and had a brief flirtation with the pleasures of half-decent food and one another's company. It was the only occasion that Owen heard communal laughter in the workhouse.

Their enjoyment was curtailed with the return of the vats, which had to be scrubbed before they retired to their beds. The oven fires still blazed thanks to the increased demand for bread and Owen had to linger alone to ensure they were quenched before he could leave. He closed the first damper and in his tiredness pressed his hand against the oven door, yelped and scurried to soothe the glowing flesh under the tap. Yet it still throbbed with a dull pain. He breathed deeply and exhaled, his every muscle weary from the day's labours, then walked to the flour sacks at the rear of the room and sat, intending to rest there until the ovens cooled.

Already soporific from his efforts, the sherry had added to his drowsiness and he found himself struggling to keep his eyes open. At some point he succumbed, lolled over on to the welcome comfort of the sacks, and fell into a fathomless sleep.

***

He was conscious of warm, alcohol-laden breath against his cheek as he struggled to return to wakefulness and had the sudden repulsive awareness that a hand was working at his pants beneath his apron. His eyes shot open and he saw Rice's face not an inch away.

'Hello, Joyce darling,' he whispered in a lascivious, breathy voice.

'Get away from me!' Owen gasped in revulsion and made to push him away.

Rice drew back a few inches and with a primitive animal reflex swung a razor-edged kitchen blade up to Owen's throat. Owen allowed his head to fall back as Rice pressed the blade's tip against the soft flesh where the underside of his chin curved against his windpipe. Rice grinned gleefully as he twisted the handle ever so slightly and Owen felt a pinprick-like sensation of the skin breaking.

'Oh dear, look what I've done, I've gone and cut ye,' he whispered with mock sympathy.

'Let me go.'

He shook his head slowly from side to side. 'Can't do that. Ye see, ye're so *pretty*. And young. Just the way I like them.'

He began to slide his left hand beneath the apron again. Owen felt nauseous and powerless. He had to think fast, for what was about to befall him was beyond contemplation.

'Is that why you killed Mooney? He wouldn't go along?'

Rice paused, a little taken aback, and shook his head. 'Oh he *did* play along, but he never, eh, joined in the spirit of things. Stupid bastard. I didn't kill him. He found my little apothecary store. Swallowed half my stock. Cost me nearly ten shillings in earnings.'

'Stop now, Rice, or I swear I'll report what you've done and about you thieving supplies. You'll go to gaol.'

Rice laughed and pressed the knife deeper into Owen's neck as a hand slipped inside his pants.

'Ye'll tell nobody, Joyce darling. Ye'll do precisely what I want, just like the others before ye. Or, my sweet young friend, it will be you who ends in gaol. Or in the graveyard. Doesn't matter te me. See how much blood just a little cut brings. Now imagine how much there'd be if I was to drag this knife from one ear te the other.'

He was panting more rapidly now, the dark thrill of his crude violation arousing a brutish excitement. Spittle ran from his mouth, his eyes widened, his face moved closer as he went to plant his lips on Owen's.

But Owen could take no more. He seized Rice's hand, tearing it free from his pants. 'You'll have to kill me first, you fucking animal,' he snarled and spat in Rice's face.

Rice drew back as though slapped and ran the back of his free hand across his cheek to wipe away the spit, then slowly drew his lips back revealing a row of chipped, yellowing teeth. 'Have it your way ye little fuc–'

A rolling pin came down against the side of his head and he cried out in pain and outrage as he toppled onto the stone floor, a hand clutching at the bloody wound on his temple. Owen sprang up to see Francis Flynn throw himself on Rice. The two rocked on the floor in a violent embrace, Rice screaming obscenities. Startled, Owen watched as they rolled towards the centre of the kitchen, Flynn's thrashings eerily silent, then strode across to the grappling figures, each trying desperately to stand and gain an advantage. Owen planted the tip of his shoe in Rice's back and the man howled, but it seemed only to enrage and stimulate him, and he wrenched his arm free of the tangle and swung his knife with deadly intent. The long blade sank deep into Flynn's left side, just beneath his armpit, faltering only briefly against his rib cage before cutting into the wall of his heart.

Flynn went rigid, eyes wide, and he collapsed, open-mouthed on to his back, a hand clawing at the knife buried in his side.

Rice came fully upright and swayed on his feet, his breath coming in heaving gasps. The trauma of the violence had frozen Owen and he stood rigidly, surveying the bloody tableau, mind gripped by paralysis. As Rice swung unsteadily around and their eyes met, Owen's rage was uncorked and he sprang at Rice in a frenzy, his outstretched hands seeking solace in the grip of Rice's throat. He met the man at full tilt, his younger frame easily propelling Rice backwards in a grotesque dance across the floor towards the oven doors. They hit hard and Rice yelled out at the impact. He began to claw first at Owen's tightening grip, then dig his fingernails into his face, but Owen barely noticed the pain. He saw where they were, pressed against the black metal doors of the ovens and with a depraved pleasure, realised he'd left one of the damping doors ajar. The fire still blazed within. He released his right hand and grasped Rice's face.

'You evil bastard,' he hissed, then slammed his head back against the oven. Rice screamed as the heat seared through the thin layer of greasy hair and melted the skin on the back of his skull. Owen pressed harder and Rice screeched, kicking and thrashing wildly. Finally his eyes rolled up in their sockets and his entire body went limp. Owen released him and he crumpled like an empty suit of clothes, lying there moaning and twitching.

But the god of his loathing had not been satiated. The man still lived. He whirled and seized the rolling pin. He fell to his knees over Rice's spasmodic form and raised the pin above his head. At that moment he thought nothing of the noose around his neck, the trapdoor's pitiless creak as it opened and condemned him to a choking death. No consideration entered his head of man's rules of law and no dread of eternal punishment in hell's fires stayed his hand. All of these things were utterly remote to him.

Yet he desisted. He rose slowly and dropped the pin to the floor, watching as it rolled against the brickwork beneath the oven, his breaths quivering like one afflicted by fever. He stared down at Rice and tried to collect himself, then remembered Flynn and turned to see him lying in a great expanding pool of blood, which sought the cracks and furrows in the stone floor, a delta of deep red. He rushed across and fell to his knees beside the man.

'Flynn! Flynn!' he called in desperation, lowering his ear to the man's lips. He needed Flynn alive. Lunatic or not, he was the only witness to what had happened this Christmas night of 1848. 'Francis! Francis!'

The man's eyes flicked open and met Owen's. The merest trace of a smile touched his lips and then was gone, stolen away on his last breath. Owen uttered a terse, miserable cry and closed his eyes against the world. When he opened them again he reached up and drew his hand over Flynn's eyelids.

'You got your wish,' he whispered.

A groan startled him to action for Rice had passed into insensibility but might come to any moment. He rose and drew his bloodstained hands down across his apron, his mind racing, trying to force it to reason, to direct his escape from this calamity. Had anyone heard Rice's agonised scream? Surely they would have come by now? He tore off the apron and moved towards the door, bloody footprints following him across the room. He nudged the door open and peered through. The kitchen area was dark and silent and he proceeded across the floor to the main entrance. Owen looked out into an empty corridor, lit only by the half-moon that hung in the December sky. In a sense he'd been fortunate, as the kitchens were remote from the dormitories and offices. He gently closed the door and hurried back into the bakery.

Rice had not stirred, although his head twitched and an occasional groan escaped his lips. He had to move quickly. He ran to the storeroom and pushed aside bags of salt to reveal a wooden panel set flush against the wall. A small hole allowed a finger to prise it free. Inside the space he saw bottles of whiskey, small sacks of oats, four loaves of bread and even a cloth bag of sugar. There were also bottles of medicine he recognised from the infirmary. He looked about, spotted Rice's canvas satchel flung into a corner and seized it and began to fill it with the spoils of the man's corruption. He took all the bread, a bag of oats, the sugar and a bottle of whiskey. As an afterthought he also grasped the bottle marked quinine. He left the panel open in the hope that whoever discovered the scene would also discover Rice's thievery, producing some small measure of justice.

He returned to Rice's twitching form, bent and found the key to the yard entrance strung about his neck. He tore it free and Rice's entire body shuddered, his head lolling over and revealing the blistering and bleeding mess that was the back of his skull. Owen felt not a morsel of pity.

He was about to rise when he remembered he was wearing a workhouse uniform, identifiable a mile off. Rice on the other hand had a jacket of heavy winter fabric – as one of the senior staff he was entitled to wear his own clothing. Owen began to divest him of the garment and soon had it free. He pondered taking the man's pants, but given what had occurred he found the notion repulsed him. He donned the jacket and put the satchel straps about his shoulders so that the bag rested against his back, leaving his hands free.

He took one look around, blessed himself at the sight of Flynn, walked to the door with the oil lamp and then quenched its flame. He moved out into the cold night air and trotted across the yard, pushed the key in the lock and twisted four times in rising panic before he heard the mechanism's parts click and turn. He pulled the door inwards and stepped outside, locking it behind him, the walls of the workhouse forever at his back.

Chapter 14

We are threatened, every man of us, with eviction – which the Prime Minister has called a sentence of death – not because we are unwilling to pay our rents, but because we will not pay them to a man who had made it the business of his life to torment us with the worst forms of feudalism.

–Fr John O'Malley, PP, notice posted in Ballinrobe in 1880

21 September 1880

Despite having the company of a constable riding at either side, Charles Boycott exchanged barely ten words with his protectors during his early morning seven-mile ride to Ballinrobe's Market Street. Not even the pleasant chorus of birdsong penetrated his thoughts, and the occasional grunt he uttered to steer his favourite mount, Duke, was spoken instinctively, for his conscious mind was focused purely on the day's proceedings: securing eviction notices against a substantial number of Lough Mask Estate's tenants.

Although a magistrate himself, his position was compromised as the legal code prevented him enforcing laws upon his own tenants, which infuriated him. But the law was the law, so he'd been forced to make the journey to Ballinrobe, and he found himself loudly pounding on the office door of the local resident magistrate, a Mr McSheehy, at nine-thirty on this grey Tuesday morning.

A stout woman admitted him, angrily demanding to know if he'd been trying to break the door down, and having introduced himself brusquely, he was shown to the magistrate's office. From the room at the rear of the house he had a clear view of the placid waters of the River Robe just yards away, and beyond that the large ordnance ground that separated the infantry barracks from the cavalry barracks at either end of the town. About a hundred men were distributed about, engaged in marching drills or firing at targets. Playing games, Boycott thought, when the country was half-overrun by murderous Fenians.

McSheehy's entry into the room disturbed his musings. He was a tall, thin, middle-aged man, with grey hair and a moustache, and wore the stern expression that he reserved for meetings with Boycott. Their dislike of one another was common knowledge. With cold formalities observed, Boycott proceeded to put his case for the eviction of thirteen of his thirty-eight tenants. Of this number the rent had fallen due for fifteen the previous day, yet only two had paid up. The remaining twenty-three were not due to meet their rent obligations for a further month.

After several hours of heated argument and debate, McSheehy granted him eleven Civil Bill Ejectment notices for the non-payment of rent. The magistrate, much to Boycott's fury, insisted on allowing more time for the remaining two tenants as both families had recently suffered bereavements. Pounding the table, Boycott thundered that the date of payment or otherwise of rent could not be determined by acts of divine providence; it was incumbent upon the tenants to anticipate unfortunate events and make allowances for such. But the magistrate held firm and used language unbefitting his position as he escorted the land agent to the front door and slammed it behind him.

He hastened then to the home of Mr David Sears, an officially appointed process-server. As he wished to begin proceedings early the following day, he suggested Sears accompany him home that evening, where he could remain until the business had concluded. Despite the inconvenience, the public servant relented at the land agent's strident insistence.

Two hours later Captain Boycott rode back through the gates of Lough Mask Estate in the company of Sears and the two police constables. All were armed and even as they rode through the sublime calm of the estate, they remained vigilant, eyes peering into the shadows of the woodland, twitching at the sound of birds taking flight. Such had it been all the way to and from Ballinrobe; Boycott was convinced that an attempt on his life was imminent, particularly as many had known the nature of his business in the town that morning.

An evidently relieved Asheton Weekes greeted him as they trotted into the stable yard to the rear of the house.

'Thank heavens you're safe, Charles.'

'What's the matter?'

'I need to show you. Down by the boathouse.'

'This is Sears. I'll need to let Annie know he'll be staying the night. You go ahead, Weekes, I'll follow.'

'Very well, Charles, but it's important.'

***

Asheton Weekes stood watching a piece of driftwood as it tapped against a stone by the water's edge. A chilly breeze from the north, a sure sign of winter's approach, troubled the waters of the lough. He was troubled himself by recent events – Charles' intimidation of his tenants, the threats and the imminence of the evictions, abruptly brought into focus by the arrival of the process-server. He feared greatly that violence might ensue in the coming days, his worry heightened by the message left for them during the night.

He turned and looked towards the house and ruins of the castle beyond. The house had stood here for just forty years. The castle, he'd learned, had been there since the fifteenth century, home of the de Burgo or Burke family of nobles. Indeed, the remnants of the fireplace still bore the inscription 'Thomas Burke 1618'. He pondered the transience of man, of families, even of dynasties, as he stared at the ivy-covered ruin. The castle had endured for centuries until it finally had fallen victim to new ways and new rulers, and he wondered how long the power that the Captain currently enjoyed might prevail. As the door to the house opened and Boycott approached, he had a disturbing vision of Lough Mask House similarly covered in clawing wild ivy, an empty shell within. He shivered and pulled his jacket tighter against the wind.

'I thought you'd forgotten,' Weekes said. He'd been waiting fifteen minutes.

'Annie kicked up a fuss because I hadn't informed her I was bringing a house guest for the night. Honestly, women. As if I haven't sufficient to trouble me. So, what is it that demands my attention?'

'Over here. I found it this morning just after you'd left.'

They walked towards the large wooden boathouse that housed a couple of boats used primarily for leisure. As they rounded it Weekes pointed to a mound of freshly dug earth, crafted to resemble a grave, at the head of which stood a crudely assembled cross bearing the name 'Boycott'.

'They must have done it during the night,' Weekes said grimly.

Boycott poked at the earth with his cane. 'Huh. I've seen this type of thing before. Remember, they dug a hole in the ground last year and sent me drawings of coffins. If the ruffians put as much labour into their farms they'd have no trouble paying their rent.'

'Charles, you have to take this seriously. We have to tell the RIC and restrict your movements until they get to the bottom of this.'

Boycott looked at him directly. 'I'll do no such thing, Weekes. We'll go about our business as usual, show them the steel of which we're made. Make them realize that empty threats won't absolve them of their responsibilities.'

'Charles, this isn't just about you. You have to consider your family's safety.'

'Inform the RIC, I agree. The fools might increase the number of constables. But I won't have my running of the estate upset. It's business as usual as far as I'm concerned.'

Weekes knew it was pointless to remonstrate further. He shook his head. 'As you wish, Charles.'

'Damned Land League is behind this, you know.'

'Perhaps.'

'The sooner Parnell is arrested the better.'

Boycott took two strides forward and brought his cane crashing down on the cross, splintering its rotten wood to pieces. He turned and looked at Weekes.

'We'll begin serving eviction notices at eight a.m. tomorrow.'

***

Fr O'Malley stood and looked at the sixteen men crammed around the table in the parochial house, their faces grim and uncertain, yet expectant that he might shine a light on the path ahead. He looked at Owen Joyce, who met his eyes solidly, but he was unsure if the man's expression spoke of cynicism or support. Perhaps, as usual, Owen himself didn't know. He swept his gaze around each of them, his own face sombre, as though about to impart some ominous tidings.

'Gentlemen, I'm sure many of you here still believe that our trip to see Mr Parnell was a fruitless exercise.'

They glanced about at each other, unsure how to respond.

'Well,' he continued, 'at least in one regard, I can guarantee that it was very fruitful.' He turned away to a cupboard. 'Because, before we boarded the ferry in Galway, I slipped into a licensed premises and purchased these.'

At that he swung around clutching a bottle of whiskey in either hand, producing a spontaneous burst of laughter.

'Owen and Mick, would you be so good as to grab some glasses and if there aren't enough I'm sure Mrs Loftus wouldn't mind us borrowing a few of her china cups.'

As they set about organising the refreshments, Owen considered that the chubby cleric had lifted the veil of gloom masterfully in a single stroke. Suddenly it was though they had gathered to organise a hurling match rather than discuss the possibility that many might be homeless within days. Glasses clinked and the men chatted a while until Fr O'Malley sat and called them to order.

'Of course, men, as you all know, there is urgent business at hand. Boycott. What's to be done?'

'We hoped you might have some ideas, te be honest, Father,' said Joe Gaughan.

Another, Peadar Higgins, a tough, weather-worn man of sixty, shook his head. 'We've tried everything except threaten the man. We've asked him politely, we've explained that the harvest these past years has been brutal. Every man here knows the rents should be half what they are.'

'Not te mention chargin' us for gathering wood. The fines. Bannin' rights of way. We've even tried writin' te Lord Erne, ye drew up the letter yerself, Father,' Joe said.

'And look what happened. We asked for a twenty-five percent abatement and Boycott convinced the old man te only give us ten.'

Luke Fitzmorris interrupted the murmur of concurring voices. 'He thinks we're dirt. Won't speak to us unless it's to insult us.'

Fr O'Malley raised his hands to calm the rising swell. 'Yes, lads, I agree, he *is* obstinate and rude, and perhaps the most unreasonable man I've ever met. So how can we deal with such a creature?'

Matt O'Toole, the youngest man there, spoke for the first time. 'Martin McGurk has a few ideas.'

The room fell quiet and O'Toole took a hasty swallow of his drink, looking a little sheepish now, wishing he'd kept his mouth shut.

'Yes,' said the priest, 'Martin has plenty of ideas, most of which are against the law and against God's law. The reason he's not here this evening, in case you're wondering, is that I didn't invite him. Neither did I invite John Lavin or Francis Cusack and a couple of others. I asked you men because I know all of you to be reasonable men, not given easily to flights of temper or violence.' He glanced at the youthful Matt O'Toole. 'And while one or two of you are subject to the hastiness of youth, most of you are experienced enough to know that rash decisions taken on the basis of emotion, hatred in particular, have a way of rebounding badly on you. I pray that Martin McGurk comes to his senses before doing anything he regrets.'

Owen looked around. To a man they were hanging on the priest's every word.

'But what are–'

The priest interrupted Matt O'Toole with a raised hand.

'What are we to do? I'll tell you, men. Mr Parnell provided us with a weapon that will make us more powerful than Boycott can imagine.'

'You mean to ost…ost…' Luke Fitzmorris stammered.

'Ostracise,' offered Owen.

'Yeah, to ostracise anyone who takes our farms when we're evicted. With all due respect, Father, that's fine longterm. But in the meantime, we'll be out on our arses, beggin' yer pardon. Our wives and children will be living by the side of the road. And it could be years before the plan works. How are we supposed to survive?'

The priest shifted his considerable bodyweight on the chair, which creaked in protest, so that he was facing Owen. 'Why don't you answer that question, Owen?'

Owen, who had been listening intently to Fitzmorris, was startled by the request. All the faces in the room turned to him. He stared at the priest, who had only briefly discussed the subject with him, but was met by an expression that suggested Owen was his right-hand man. He opened his mouth intent on distancing himself from the limelight, closed it again, sat back into the chair and looked at the expectant faces.

After some consideration, he spoke. 'We'll ostracise land grabbers all right, but we start by ostracising Boycott himself.'

'What?' said Fitzmorris.

'Shun Boycott. Treat him like a "leper of old" as Parnell put it.'

'Sure that old bastard doesn't care if we don't speak to him,' said Gaughan.

Owen exhaled nervously and was spurred on by a nod from Fr O'Malley.

'Listen,' he said, warming to his subject and leaning forward, 'Boycott can't survive without the people in this parish. He buys his supplies in Ballinrobe. Our people cook his food and tend his horses and wash his sheets. Well, how do you think he'd fare if he woke up one day to find them all gone? Every last one of them. He wouldn't be served in the grocers or at the dairy. The farrier wouldn't shoe his horses. His servants would leave him high and dry and I don't imagine Annie Boycott knows how to boil an egg.'

There was a brief chuckle but he could sense a swell of interest. He glanced again at the priest, who simply smiled and raised his eyebrows. He resumed while he held his audience captive, not wanting doubt to creep into their minds.

'But most importantly, if we convince his labourers to abandon him altogether he'll be facing immediate ruin. He's got, what? A thousand pounds worth of crops still in the ground? What he makes from rents is a pittance. Almost all his money is in the farm on the estate. If he loses the harvest, he'll be facing bankruptcy.'

'What's that?' asked Matt O'Toole.

'He'll be broke,' Joe Gaughan enlightened.

Fr O'Malley, sensing the enthusiasm, began to pass the whiskey around, a subtle ratification of their newly found purpose. 'And remember lads, only last month Boycott gave in when his labourers went on strike for more pay.'

'Which shows how desperate he is to get his crops in,' added Owen. 'The fact is, Boycott's not a farmer, he's a businessman, and a businessman's first and last thought every day is profit. It's all about money. If we deprive Boycott of his money, he'll either give in or go under.'

'And personally I suspect that Boycott's not quite as tough as he pretends,' Fr O'Malley remarked with a sagacious air. He continued, 'I can't be here tomorrow, unfortunately. But we'll advise Captain Boycott of his new circumstances on Thursday. So we need to delay him a little. By law, a notice of eviction must be issued to the head of the household. Your good selves. He can't issue them if you're not there.'

He removed three large pieces of bright red silky cloth from a drawer and handed them out to Fitzmorris and a couple of the others.

'Make flags of these. Your farms occupy the highest points around; they can be seen from all over. You see Boycott coming, go to the hill and wave the flag and yell your lungs out. Warn everyone. Then, I want you men to vanish. As I said, if you're not there, he can't serve the notices.'

'Leave our wives te do our fightin'?' Fitzmorris asked, his pride piqued.

'There isn't going to be any fighting, Luke. Remember, that's why we're here.'

Fitzmorris nodded, then looked at the unusual red cloth, which was embroidered with a gold pattern. 'Eh Father, where did you got the cloth for the flags?'

Fr O'Malley looked a little embarrassed. 'I've been meaning to purchase a new chasuble anyway. Besides, Pentecost is a long way away.'

There was some bewildered laughter, then they fell to silence for a few seconds, pondering the permutations of the plan, until Joe Gaughan spoke.

'Father, the thing is, it all sounds good in theory, but are we going to be able to convince Boycott's workers and the others to go along? I mean, will they listen to us?'

Fr O'Malley smiled faintly at some notion, a personal joke maybe, then looked up from his drink. 'They'll listen to me, Joe. They'll listen to their priest.'

***

The meeting broke up thirty minutes later, while there was light enough for them to travel safely to their homes. Owen lingered, as Fr O'Malley had expected he might, and the pair sat in the sudden silence, nursing what remained of their drinks.

'As I said, Owen, unfortunately I have to travel to Tuam tomorrow to be scolded yet again like a little boy by Archbishop McHale for supporting the Land League. I hope he doesn't decide to take a birch to me as well.' He laughed aloud at the notion.

'Why is the Archbishop so against us?'

'It's complicated, but God bless him, the man is ninety and he's been a great patriot all his life. I believe he just doesn't like Mr Parnell, among other things. I can handle him. But what really troubles me is that I won't return until late in the day. I haven't had any time to organise. I mean, I'll need to be here to convince everyone in the parish and beyond to follow us. You'll have to hold the fort yourself, Owen.'

'*Me*?'

'Yes! You saw how they listened to you. They know a leader when they see one.'

Now it was Owen's turn to laugh aloud. 'I'm no leader, Father. It's you they look up to.'

'How can I put this? I may lead their souls, Owen, but you lead their minds.'

Owen shook his head at the notion of men looking to him for guidance. A thought struck him as he pulled on his jacket and moved towards the door. 'Tell me, Father, why did you drop me in the middle of this without discussing it with me?'

Fr O'Malley grinned. 'I was confident you'd have worked out all the details in your head since we talked in Ennis. And as to catching you off guard? Well, I knew if I'd asked you to be my partner in crime, so to speak, you would either have refused or dithered over the notion for days and eventually convinced yourself you weren't the man for the job. Whereas I knew you to be precisely the man I needed. I decided simply not to give you time to think about it. I was confident you'd do the right thing.'

Owen stared at him and said nothing.

'Sometimes, Owen,' the priest continued, 'it doesn't serve a man well to think too much. Moderation in all things, as we say.' And with that he refilled his glass.

'Good night, Father.' Owen smiled as he pulled open the door.

***

He stepped outside and looked along the road north towards Ballinrobe, where a swirl of autumn leaves danced in the rising wind. The sun was gone, but its dying light still lingered sufficiently to see him home if he hurried. At the sound of Anu's whinny he began to walk around to the trap, hitched to a post by the side of the church. As he walked he couldn't help but grin, feeling surprisingly heartened by the evening's events; not just the scheme to ostracise Boycott, but at the turn of events that had set him at the forefront of the plan. He imagined it was the kind of sizzling excitement experienced by the likes of Parnell after an oration, or the nervous thrill an actor feels as the crowd rises to their feet in applause. Such comparisons were ludicrous of course, as he hadn't earned any applause, but as the priest had pointed out, the others had listened with pricked ears as he'd spoken. He couldn't help but feel a swell of pride and could hardly wait to tell Síomha about the evening. He also couldn't help but imagine the two of them entwined naked in each other's arms in their bed and supposed one swell of excitement led naturally to another, at least for men, he thought with a smile.

Owen stopped sharply as he saw Anu and the trap. The old horse snorted and turned her head towards him, away from the figure of a man standing directly behind her. He heard the man try to calm the animal with a 'shhh girl' and by stroking her face.

'Who's that?'

The man lifted his head now, but the light was so dim his face was nothing but a haze of darkness.

'What do you want? Is that you, Martin McGurk?'

'It's not,' came the answer.

'What are you do–'

'Take it easy, Owen,' the man said, ducking beneath Anu's neck.

Owen stiffened as he approached. 'How do you know my name? Who are you?'

'Jesus Christ, Owen,' the man said as he stepped near enough for Owen to see his face. 'Do you not know your own brother when you see him?'

Chapter 15

Lough Mask, thy beauties free and wild
Have soothed my soul and oft beguiled
My thoughts from earthly care
I love the rocks thy wavelets kiss
Thy solitude is sweet. 'Twere bliss
To dwell forever here.

–'Lines on Lough Mask', Mary Pearle, 1915

DECEMBER 1848

He'd had no time to conceive a coherent plan of escape and, besides, he knew little of this district. The hospital building was fifty yards to the south. East was the main road and to the north was Ballinrobe; none offered a viable option.

Owen set off west across the fields, praying his decision might bring him some fortune. He stumbled and staggered through the near complete darkness, tripping over low shrubs and almost colliding with a boulder, the sticky earth sucking greedily at his shoes. He reached a chest-high wall and had to clamber over it, dislodging a stone on the top and almost tumbling head over heels into the next field. He began to lose his sense of direction not one hundred yards into his journey and looked back towards the outline of the workhouse to gain some bearing. At precisely that moment the moon drifted behind a cloud and the world turned black. With no choice he stumbled on, falling repeatedly against jagged rocks, stifling his cries as best he could. Five more minutes and the moon swept free of its veil, revealing another wall just ahead, this one bordering a track. Chest heaving, he paused and tried to gather his wits. To his right he could hear water, but surely not the River Robe, which was further to the north-west. He tried to think. On his arrival at the workhouse he recalled crossing a stream to the south of the town, probably a tributary of the Robe. Unfortunately, this meant that he'd inadvertently strayed to within a stone's throw of Ballinrobe.

Voices nearby caused him to throw himself flat on the ground. There were men on the track singing, and from the wavering intonations he guessed they were drunk. He remembered it was Christmas night and the men were probably heading home from a celebration in town. He listened as the words of 'The Croppy Boy' rose towards the night sky, a song he'd heard his father sing many times.

And as I mounted the platform high
My aged father was standing by
My aged father did me deny
And the name he gave me was the Croppy Boy

It was in Dungannon this young man died
And in Dungannon his body lies
And you good people that do pass by
Oh shed a tear for the Croppy Boy

It was then that he heard the woman shrieking across the darkness. He gasped and sank lower as the voices of the men fell silent. Across the fields he could see lanterns come alive in the workhouse windows. The confused shouts of men swelled the sound to a chorus and through it all he could define one word, screamed over and over: '*Murder!*'

'What in the name o' God?'

'It's comin' from the workhouse, Mick.'

'Sumthin's goin' on, begod.'

'C'mon. Let's find out the trouble.'

Owen heard their feet shuffling hastily away. One thing was certain; he had to get away from there or he'd swing as sure as the Croppy Boy of long ago.

There were more shouts on the track as others hurried into town to discover the reason for the commotion. Crouching, he began to move towards the sound of the water. Fifty yards on he came to the stream, which was perhaps ten feet wide, and slid down the steep bank. To his left he could just make out a bridge, and he advanced towards it along the narrow bank, one tentative step at a time. He saw men on the bridge now, clutching lamps, running out of town, perhaps already in search of the outlaw. In the distance he heard a horse running through the dark at a pace beyond all wisdom. He reached the bridge and saw that his narrow foothold had disappeared. Without hesitation he slipped down into the placid stream's dark flow and gasped as icy tendrils entwined his legs and privates. Tramping boots approached and he quickly ducked down and slipped under the nearer of the bridge's twin arches. The stream was to his waist now and he had to bend almost double to move under the arch, the satchel on his back scraping along the bridge's slime-covered underside. The lone set of heavy bootsteps thundered overhead, and he moved out from under the bridge and clambered up on to the far bank. He enjoyed a small stroke of fortune as he saw that the stream meandered into dense woodland and he hastened his step while the moonlight favoured him. He reached the trees and immediately sank to a sitting position against an immense tree trunk. Here he waited while his breathing and his pounding heart slackened. He listened. There were more horses now, their whinnies piercing the still

Christmas night air. Indistinct bellows chased each other along the streets of the town. A policeman's whistle screeched, protracted in its beckoning. It spurred him to action and he rose and moved with as much haste as the light and his outstretched hands would permit, crashing into trees, tumbling through shrubs. He kept the stream close to his path, for it offered his only possible means of escape as crossing open countryside was no longer feasible. And as if to verify the thought, he was stalled in his tracks by the sound of barking, multiple and frenzied, encouraged by the cries of handlers. He had little time left.

The sound of rushing water reached his ears – the stream spilling into the Robe. He removed the jacket and folded it into the satchel on his back, then slipped into the stream again. He passed under another low bridge, the noise of the water growing louder with each step. To his left he could make out a large structure and realised it was the cavalry barracks, a building of three stories, lamps ablaze in the windows. A single horse approached and he sought shelter against the bank. The rider crossed the tiny bridge bound for the barracks. He pressed on, lifting his knees high to quicken his progress. As the meeting of the waters drew closer, he felt an increasing pull as the flow gained momentum. He allowed the water to take him fully and felt his feet lifted from the riverbed, gasping as the freezing water enveloped him, frantically paddling to keep his head clear. Experience told him that he just had to bear the pain for a few minutes and his body would adapt.

The stream carried him over the edge and he fell head first, six feet down into the River Robe. He surfaced and frantically sought purchase at the yielding water, trying to regain control of his direction, fighting against the pull of the river as he sought to reach the temporary haven of a tiny islet in the centre. The Robe's apparent tranquillity concealed the powerful undercurrents that felt like tendrils eager to wrap themselves about his legs. But he endured, clasping an overhanging branch to pull himself up to the islet's bank. He caught his breath as he took stock of his position. The small waterfall drowned much of the noise from Ballinrobe, now fully roused. It was not often that on Christmas night they received word that there was a murderer in their midst. He could make out the tall tower of the mill against the night sky, the bridge before it alive with the comings and goings of men with torches and mounted soldiers mustered from the infantry barracks. In the direction of the Robe's flow was another bridge leading to the cavalry barracks, its single arch tall enough to accommodate a barge. A barracks behind and another ahead. He had little choice but to go with the current. He slipped back into the water and began to paddle, the shock not quite so intense now, but was immediately horrified to witness a troop approach from the barracks gate. They would cross the bridge ahead in moments and a single glance in his direction would mean his end. He began to swim faster, pulling desperately towards the bank. He reached out and grasped at the long grasses. Clumps came free in his hands and he clawed for purchase like a man in the grip of a seizure, until finally he found a hold and wrenched himself up under the bridge, just as the troop clip-clopped overhead. He lay there looking up at the dark curve of the arch, trying to quiet his breathing. He heard military barks and blurted orders and saw the reflection of burning torches in the black river surface as they paraded across the bridge. He froze and listened, staring up at the underside of the structure, where he could see by the torches' dim reflected light what looked like a hundred fingers of stone pointing accusingly down at him. The tramping diminished and he was about to move again when a strange voice stilled him.

'Fuckin' 'ell. Christmas night. The only night we get decent grub! And we end up 'ere watching for a bleedin' murderer. Isn't that police business?'

'Shut up, Charlie, if the captain 'ears ye, ye'll be in a right stew.'

'Besides, what do we care? Let them all murder each uvver is what I say. Then we can go bloody 'ome.'

'Didn't you 'ear? It wasn't just murder. Sarge said he burned the flesh off some other bloke's 'ead.'

'Jesus Chroist. It's like the Dark Ages or summin'.'

'So we're pitchin' in to 'elp. So shut your bleedin' face 'ole. And keep your peepers peeled.'

''Ere. What if we spot 'im?'

'Easy. We plug 'im. Bang!'

Immobile for so long, Owen was starting to shake badly. He clenched his arms about himself in an effort to stem the tremors. His teeth began to chatter and he had to bite so hard against his lower lip that he tasted blood. If he didn't get moving soon he knew he would freeze to death. He'd been there five minutes when a horse approached and a voice barked out.

'You two! They need more men to search the mill. Get moving!'

Owen exhaled with blessed relief as the pair trotted away. When he was certain they were beyond earshot he began to swing his arms wildly to stimulate warmth. A minute later he slipped back into the water and swam out a few yards, allowing the current to take him. The bag on his back, contrary to being an encumbrance, had trapped some air and gave him buoyancy.

The Robe curved gently along and he had neither sight nor sound of people on the banks as he moved further from the town. But he knew he couldn't stay in the water much longer; his entire body felt numb and his limbs protested at every stroke.

He drifted silently beneath a wooden footbridge but an instant later became aware of the roar of crashing water. It was a waterfall of some kind, which didn't seem possible in such a flat landscape, but he knew it represented danger and he had to get to the bank quickly. He began to turn and kick, but his limbs were so benumbed and weary that he made no advance against the sweep of the current. The water became choppier and his head began to go under. He gasped and spluttered as panic began to seize him. The clamorous roar of the water was only yards ahead, yet almost invisible in the inky black of the night. Then he was tumbling, wrenched on to his side, rolling over a weir and crashing into a mass of churning white. He went completely under, his body pivoting and whirling in the dark, violent undertow. Finally his head breached the surface and he heaved a series of convulsive breaths. He kicked and clawed at the white water boiling on all sides, then glimpsed an over-hanging tree on his left. He knew if he didn't catch it he would surely die, for his energy was gone, sapped by the exertion and the cold. He clawed desperately against the currents and at the last moment he threw both hands aloft and grasped at the bare branches. He seized one but felt his body pulled from under him as the river fought to retake him. He reached out with his other hand and grabbed another purchase, then pulled with every ounce of will until he drew himself into the river shallows. His feet found a hold and he clambered, spluttering, on to the muddy bank, where he fell gasping until he passed out.

He awoke to violent shivers and looked around, but the town was a mile behind now and not a soul was about. As far as he could tell, he was in an open field far from any road. But through the blind pain of the cold he knew that he was far from safety and he must keep moving, an agonising prospect. He pulled the satchel from his back and his benumbed fingers were barely capable of pulling the buckle pin free. Delving inside the watery mess, he located the hard surface of the bottle, pulled it out and removed the cork with his teeth, then drank long and hard. The sudden fiery rush in his throat induced a fit of coughing and dizziness. When it passed he began to beat his arms about him again, then stood with difficulty and massaged his thighs. Had it not been for the cocooning layer of flesh he'd acquired in the workhouse, he was certain he'd be dead. He sought out Rice's coat, but it was sodden, as was all the food. Nevertheless he dug his fingers in and ate a large handful of the mush of bread. When he'd repacked he got his feet moving and set off along the bank, aware that should his pursuers appear, the river still offered a possible means of removing himself quickly from sight.

After about an hour of tortured walking, he spied a cottage ahead, nestled in trees by the river's edge. His first thought was to skirt it, but then an idea occurred to him and he crept up to it slowly, trying to control the chatter of his teeth. As he'd hoped and prayed, by the river's edge sat two boats. He quietly pulled the smaller and less conspicuous of them towards the river. It was barely eight feet long, but it would suffice. He waded into the water again, peering over his shoulder at the cottage, but it was as silent and dark as a morgue. At knee depth he clambered in and almost upended it, but it righted itself and drifted gently towards the centre of the Robe. He took the single paddle and guided the boat with silent strokes; within moments, the river had taken charge and was carrying him away to God alone knew where.

An hour later his arms ached from paddling, but at least, he thought, he could feel the ache. His legs, by contrast, so long unmoving, seemed not to be there at all. The bank was lined with woodland much of the way and he'd seen no sign of the forces of law. The river meandered wildly and he had no knowledge of his direction. But now he saw the trees begin to diminish and the landscape broaden to open fields. He had to navigate an acute bend, but as he emerged from it he saw, spread out before him in the moonlight, the broad, calm waters of Lough Mask.

***

Owen could identify the hulking shapes of two large islands close to the shore, and he rounded these and began moving south about a hundred yards out. As the first hints of dawn began to put form to his surroundings, he saw that the lough offered a multitude of islands, any of which might provide sanctuary. Some seemed half a mile long, others much more diminutive, but he was troubled by their proximity to the shore. Yet he knew he would have to find land soon, necessitated by the growing light and his debilitation.

One island to the west sat in relative isolation. In the dim early light distances were difficult to measure, but he guessed it was a couple of miles out, too small and remote to be inhabited. He could see the mountains rising to the west, their tops the first to benefit from pale light of the rising sun. The sight of a figure on the mainland, a speck of black moving through a field, determined his choice and he quickly turned the boat's nose towards the open expanse of the lough.

He guessed it took him an hour to reach the densely wooded island. He rounded the small piece of land and saw that it was a few hundred yards long, shaped like a spearhead, and through the mostly leafless trees he could see the ruins of a structure of some kind. He guided the boat through the curiously rounded black rocks that speckled the shallows and tried to climb out, but found that his legs refused to comply. It was an unsettling moment. He tried to lift his right leg with his hands and realized he could not sense the grip of his own fingers. He rubbed his thighs to enervate them, but although it restored some sensation it produced only a spasmodic twitch.

He negotiated the boat about so that his back was to the shore, which was a brief band of grass, speckled with more black rocks. When only a couple of feet away, he turned and hauled himself over the stern, desperate to keep his upper body from becoming soaked again. He dragged himself on to the grass, panting with the effort. Using his hands, he began to lift and bend his legs, rubbing them intermittently, yet it took considerable minutes before he was rewarded with any sensation. He managed to kneel and then crawl, grunting, to a small tree where he hauled himself upright. There he remained in a frozen lurch until he found he could lift his calves and slowly revitalise them.

He staggered back to the boat and pulled it towards the shrubbery, a task that seemed to take an aeon as he repeatedly collapsed. Supported by a staff, he heaved himself with faltering steps through the stalks of the winter wood, ankle-deep in withered leaves, and after a time emerged in a long and narrow open space, mostly grass, at the centre of which were the toppled ruins of a church from antiquity. The entire island was ringed by a narrow band of trees, shielding its centre from curious eyes. He crossed to the remnants of the building, which was little more than three irregular walls ten feet high. Holy men had sought sanctuary here from persecution long ago, and their efforts might serve a similar purpose long after their bones had turned to dust.

He sat, leaning back against a wall, hugging himself against the chill. It had been a mercifully mild night and he prayed that the rain would remain prisoner in the clouds for this day at least. But, fatigued as he was, he knew that he couldn't remain sitting there. He pulled off the satchel and removed the whiskey, careful not to over-indulge. He cursed himself for not taking a second bottle, for his supply was reduced now to little more than a third of a bottle. He ate a few more handfuls of the sodden black bread and some sugar, then looked about.

What he desperately needed was a fire, but he had no matches or flint and no real idea how to produce a flame without one or the other. It flitted through his mind that Thomas would likely possess the necessary skill. He looked at the satchel and lying beside it was Rice's jacket. The Robe's waters still dripped from the sodden material when he lifted it. The outside pockets were empty excepting a single penny, imprinted with the image of a youthful Queen Victoria. He found a buttoned pocket in the inside breast and thrust his fingers into the envelope of fabric. His hand lighted on a small parcel and he was disappointed to withdraw a package of Rice's cigars, soaked and useless, even if he had desired one. The other pocket brought the reward of a box marked 'Allumettes'. He turned it over to see the heavenly words '50 White Phosphorous Matches.' Gently sliding back the tiny lid, he saw about ten yellow-tipped matches which appeared relatively dry, the waxed wooden box having afforded them a degree of protection. The following minutes were spent gathering a large pile of tinder and sticks. Arranging the tinder in a corner of the ruin, he knelt and removed one of the precious matches, crouching low over the tinder as he scratched the match against the wall. It barely fizzled with a greenish glow, emitted a pungent smell and turned black. He swore. The matches, although not sodden, were clearly damp. He tried a second time with the same result, cursed loudly, and sat back on his haunches, trying to think. He needed a flame to dry the matches and he needed the matches to provide the flame.

He was about to despair of ever lighting a fire when a solitary word occurred to him: friction. He picked up a fist-sized stone and began to scrape it against a flat stone from the ruin with as much power as he could muster. After a time he pressed his finger against the larger stone and smiled when he felt the warmth. He continued the action for a while longer, then drew a match across the warm patch. This time it sizzled green, there was a mote of flame, and it faded. He cursed to the heavens. His patience straining, he took two matches, held them together, scratched them across the warm patch of stone, and watched with disbelief as the flame buzzed green then orange and began to roll slowly up the stick. He almost hooted with joy, cupped his palm about it and held it to the tinder. It was leisurely in its passing of the flame to the twigs and Owen feared it might fail to take hold, but after a few nerve-racking moments, the twigs took possession of the flame and the tinder came alive with dancing tongues of orange.

He spent the next hour collecting a supply of wood and arranging his every possession on the rocks around the fire. The crackling timbers produced a substantial amount of smoke, but a light breeze dispersed it by the time it reached the top of the wall, so he hoped it would not be visible from the mainland nearly two miles distant. He also removed his pants and draped them across a stone, feeling faintly ridiculous as he stood there almost naked. Finally he lay down beside the fire, weary beyond measure, and rested his head against the satchel.

***

He spent four days on the island, discovering, courtesy of a rough scratching on a large boulder, that his temporary home was called Devenish Island. His food supply dwindled to almost nothing and his last meal required him to scrape the inside of satchel for the remnants of bread and oats. And, most troubling of all, when he awoke that first day he was seized with a terrible shivering accompanied by a constant flow of snot. It had abated a little when he dressed and softened his misery with whiskey and quinine, but all the time he'd felt a grave fever stalk his every move.

Many times he'd stood under the cover of the trees watching the eastern shore, expecting the approach of policemen, or even fishermen, but he'd only seen a couple of small craft and none had ventured near his refuge. At times he'd contemplated taking the boat out into the waters and trying to catch some fish, but his hands quivered so much he couldn't fashion a line or a hook from anything in his possession, and soon abandoned the notion. He was grateful at least to have dry clothes, but his matches were all gone now and should he allow the fire to dwindle to nothing, he would have no means of producing another. The realities had dwelt ever larger in his mind as the food diminished. He would have to leave the island the next day, for all he had left was a lump of sugar the size of an egg and two swallows of whiskey.

He wondered what had passed in Ballinrobe in the intervening days. Had the stolen boat been reported and had they connected it to him? Surely, if they had, he would have seen a boat patrol wandering the islands. Or perhaps they assumed he'd not lingered, but headed south to Galway or west to the mountains.

As the night closed in he built the fire again and tried to banish the trembling that racked his entire body, and he experienced the curious duality of profuse sweating while his innards shivered. He'd seen similar symptoms while working in the infirmary, but all of those men had been suffering from typhus or some such ailment and surely he couldn't be so afflicted out here? He took more quinine but had little knowledge of the drug other than the Matron issuing it for fevered men. Late that night he managed to fall into a horribly disturbed sleep in which he witnessed his dead family rising from the workhouse mass grave, his brother being hanged, and the sensation of him drowning, kicking madly as he was torn away from the light above down into the cold, black depths. He came awake with a terrified gasp and immediately sensed rain on his face. His every nerve was quivering and his hands shook so violently he could barely grasp the logs to maintain the fire. He cursed his lack of foresight for not building some form of shelter, and as the drops of rain intensified he reluctantly conceded that he would have to seek shelter. He heaped every last gathered branch on the fire in the hope it might outlive the rain and then stumbled to a copse of fir trees. There he sat, trembling yet absurdly hot, until the rain abated towards dawn.

When he finally returned to the ruin, all that remained was a pile of sodden ash. He had no choice now – if he remained here without heat and food, the fever would surely claim him. He would have to abandon the island.

Once more he found himself without a plan, an aimless wanderer in the wilds of Ireland, except this time he imagined that half of the country was looking to hang him. He could barely think through the burning delirium, and swooned and fell time after time as he returned to the boat. Dim early light stretched across the lough's troubled waters, for a north wind had roused their ire. But it determined his course, for he had barely the strength to paddle, let alone to fight the elements. With the boat dragged back to the water, he almost fell face down into it but managed at least to keep all but his feet dry. He began to paddle away from the island, allowing the wind to steer his course, although it tossed the tiny craft to and fro, adding to his nausea. Some miles ahead he could see the southern shore, but it seemed so distant, and his body was so impaired that reaching it felt like an impossible task.

'Watch where you're going, you *amadán*!' Thomas shouted at him.

He looked over his shoulder and his brother was sitting there smiling. He patted Owen on the back. 'You're in horseshit now, little brother. Should have come with me, my boat was much bigger.' He suddenly pointed ahead. 'Watch the rocks! Jesus, do I have to tell you everything! Paddle more on the left.'

Owen did as instructed then turned again to Thomas, whose face had become grim.

'What's wrong with you?' Owen asked.

Thomas didn't reply.

'Why won't you speak to me? Thomas! Do you want to tell me something?'

But Thomas sat there, hands gripping the sides of the boat, staring with dead man's eyes. Owen had to turn away to steer his course and when he looked back again, Thomas had vanished. He began to call out his brother's name over and over, his futile cries skipping across the choppy waters. His eyes grew suddenly heavy and he sank back into the boat, the paddle slipping into the water. The sky above, which had been a muddy grey, began to glow an intense, bright white.

***

A man's hand was gripping his shoulder, shaking him. He opened his eyes and looked at the face, shrouded in a soupy white fog. The man was saying something but it made no sense, a nonsense of words like the babble of a madman. He felt a slap against his cheek. It was a policeman, he knew that now. They'd known where he'd been all along, had just been biding their time. They were going to hang him. Make him dance to their tune. He tried to grasp the policeman, seize him to make him understand. They had to know the truth. But he found it hard to speak as an immense thirst had swelled his throat. How could he be thirsty in the middle of Lough Mask? It was almost funny. He forced his voice from his lungs with a mighty effort.

'Not me. Rice. Rice killed him…swear…please.'

But it was pointless. They were lifting him, pulling him from the boat, and he had no fight left. Let them do their worst, he thought. It will be a blessed relief.

***

'Muireann! Fetch your mother. She's in the high field. Tell her what's happened and te come quickly.'

'What's wrong with him Daddy? Why's he talking funny?'

'Go now, child, quick as lightning. Go!'

The little girl fled with childish enthusiasm away from the lakeshore. The man managed to get his hands under the stubble-faced, delirious young man and lift him. Although about the man's own height, he was considerably thinner and didn't prove a heavy burden. He carried the youth to his cottage just fifty yards away, and kicked open the door. The cottage was large by the standards of most, with entry into a living area and the hearth directly opposite the front door, and with a room for sleeping to either side. He turned left into his daughter's room and laid the unfortunate young man down on her straw mattress. He was unsure what to do, as his medical skills were paltry compared to those of his wife, Maebh.

The youth continued with his incoherent talk, the content of which troubled the man more and more. He hurried to the hearth next door, where he occupied himself building the fire until Maebh burst through the door, panic written on her face, her hair like that of a wild woman.

'Tim! What's the matter? Who's been hurt? Muireann said there's a sick man! Where's–

'Jesus, Maebh, will ye calm down, woman! He's in Muireann's room. I was fishing when I found the boat drifting. Thought it was empty but when I pulled it up there's this man. Only a lad really. He's feverish.'

He led the way into the room, just as Muireann arrived back. 'Wait there Muireann,' her mother said.

They crouched down at either side of the mattress.

'Listen, Maebh. He was ranting…kept saying he hadn't killed someone. That someone called Rice did it. I'm worried. You know what we heard, about Ballinrobe. Maybe this is…'

She looked at Owen for a moment, leaned over and placed a hand against his forehead, then pulled back one of his eyelids. Suddenly she sat back sharply on her haunches.

'Mary, Mother of God,' she whispered.

***

'Hello,' a woman said as she pressed a wet cloth against his forehead. 'Shhh. Don't try te move.'

'My throat hurts,' he croaked.

She held a mug to his lips. He spluttered and coughed and let his head fall back.

'Not surprised yer throat hurts, the blatherin' ye've been doin' these past days.'

'Where am I?' He glanced around the small room, lit by an oil lamp and the glow of a fire through a doorway.

'Ye're in our cottage. On the shore of Lough Mask. This place is known as Kilbeg, in Galway.'

'There was a man…'

'Ye might mean me husband, Tim. He pulled ye from the lough and brought ye here. The fever lasted until noon today and ye've slept since. It was bad enough, but I've seen worse.'

'What day is it?'

'Three days ye've been here. It's Monday, the first of January 1849, Owen.'

'How…do you know my name?'

'Sure 'tis a wonder half of Connaught doesn't know yer name, with yer rantin'. Not te mention Thomas and Bridget, Flynn, Rice and a whole crowd of others I can't recall.'

Owen turned his head away at the mention of Rice's name.

'It's all right, Owen Joyce. Don't fret.'

She called out towards the other room. 'Tim, bring Muireann.'

A well-built man appeared with a young girl in his arms. The man nodded at Owen as he set the child down.

'Muireann,' she beckoned, and the excited child skittered to her mother's side.

'Ye see, Owen Joyce, I already knew ye. From the first moment I laid eyes on ye.'

He looked around at the three faces, utterly mystified.

'Ye saved me Muireann here's life.'

'You're mistaking me for someon–'

'Tawnyard, isn't that what you called your hill? It was down the valley from where I used te live.'

His eyes came wide at the name of his home, but he shook his head, unable to place her in that setting.

'Me name is Maebh Connor.'

Some faint recollection stirred in the haze of his memory. The woman leaned closer. 'One day maybe six months ago, it's hard te tell, I was at me end and so was Muireann. We was starvin', as were thousands, God knows, and I knew if I didn't find food Muireann would perish. I was ready te lie down and die, had barely the will te take another step. And then I saw you and I begged ye for food. And I know ye were starvin' too and ye had a family who needed food as bad as me. Yet ye gave me a fish. And it kept her alive and gave me the will te go on. If I hadn't chanced upon ye that day, we'd both be dead.'

Owen drew in a slow, deep breath. The scene was suddenly vivid in his memory. An hour later he'd reached home to find his sister dead. He felt his eyes grow watery and he clenched them shut.

His conscience began to trouble him. 'There's something I have to tell you…'

'It's all right, Owen. Go back te sleep. Ye'll feel stronger in the morning and we'll talk then.'

She bathed his forehead once more and then they left him alone.

***

He sat by the fireside and Tim handed him a mug of tea. They were alone, as Maebh had gone on an errand and a priest from Clonbur was schooling Muireann and a handful of other local children.

'Thank you. For saving my life.'

Tim smiled. 'Sure, I only dragged yer boat ashore. Beside such, I owe ye far more, by all accounts.'

Owen shook his head. 'I did what anyone would have.'

'Not te my mind. Or Maebh's.'

They sat for a while in an awkward silence.

'How did Maebh and Muireann survive?'

'A group of Quakers found her the day after she'd met you and transported her te Westport, where she gained admission te the workhouse. I was working in England on a farm, where I learned about the growing of mangolds, carrots, turnips an' the like. The farm owner was a very decent man who had heard of the sufferin' in Ireland, and when I came te be paid he was very generous. I'd been sending money te Maebh but she never got it. I found out later that a postal worker had stolen it. Bastard. It took me weeks te find Maebh and Muireann and I thought they were surely dead. But thanks be te God they were both alive. I'd enough money te get a lease here, six acres, and we've been working hard te ready the land for next season ever since.'

'Mr Connor…'

'Tim.'

'Tim, I have to tell you. The RIC are looking for me.'

'Oh I know. For murder.'

Owen almost dropped his cup.

Tim smiled. 'They're not anymore.'

'What do you…?'

He sat on a stool on the other side of the hearth. 'We'd heard about the workhouse. It's not often there's a murder like that in Mayo unless it's of a landlord or such. With all the talking ye did through the fever, well, we can add two and two the same as the next. So I started te ask questions and found out that the police hunt had been called off, wasn't sure why until yesterday. Well, I tell ye, that set our mind at ease.'

The door opened and a gust disturbed the fire and set a ball of smoke rising into the room. Maebh closed the door against the chill wind and pulled off her shawl.

'I got it!' She pulled a sheet newspaper from the folds of her dress and handed it to her husband, who allowed her take his fireside seat. 'I can't read, but Tim's not so bad.'

Standing before them, Tim unfolded the single-sheet *Mayo Telegraph* of 30 December. He began to read in a faltering voice, stumbling over the words.

'Cons…tab…ulry call…off mur…der…pursss…'

Owen's impatience welled as his excitement grew. 'I can read,' he blurted out, embarrassed at his own rudeness. 'I mean, I can read…well.'

Tim frowned a little but Maebh gestured for him to hand the sheet over. Owen turned to allow the firelight illuminate the page. He read aloud: 'Constabulary call off murder pursuit.' Beneath this a smaller type dramatised the hunt: 'On Christmas night, he eluded one hundred soldiers, thirty policemen and as many volunteers, yet almost all his cunning was for naught.

'The search for the fugitive from justice Owen Joyce has been suspended as a result of new information that came to the attention of the Ballinrobe Constabulary. Joyce, who had formerly been a staff assistant at Ballinrobe Union Workhouse, had been sought for the murder of another inmate, an idiot called Francis Flynn, and also for the violent assault on the Kitchen and Stores Supervisor, Mr Barnard Rice, who, along with heavy bruising, had sustained burns to his head.

'However, as a result of testimony provided by Dr David Gill MD, of Ballinrobe Union, and that of Matron Margaret Mitchell, the grave charges against Mr Joyce have been dropped.

'Doctor Gill revealed to Sergeant Mulcahy of Ballinrobe RIC that in the course of treating Mr Rice's wounds, he had been obliged to dose the patient with opium to relieve his pain. On the second day of this treatment and in the presence of Dr Gill and Matron Mitchell, Mr Rice, under the sedating influence of the drug, had repeatedly spoken words that hinted at Mr Joyce's innocence and a wish to see Joyce hanged. Many of Mr Rice's other exclamations suggested a perversity of character and could not be reproduced in a publication of decency such as *The Mayo Telegraph*.

'When questioned by the constabulary, Rice maintained that Joyce had indeed killed Flynn. However, subsequent investigations revealed that Mr Rice had been engaged in the sale of workhouse supplies for personal gain, including precious medicines. A dispensary staff member, Joseph Cullen of Carrownalecka, confessed to having been in league with Rice in the immoral trade and has been arrested. Several workhouse staff testified to Joyce's character, including Dr Gill and Matron Mitchell, who expressed grave doubts about Joyce's capacity to commit such violence. In fact she praised Mr Joyce as...'

Owen coughed and lowered his voice as he hastened through the rest of the paragraph.

'...a young man of compassion, courage and intelligence. Given his ability to evade the combined forces of Her Majesty's Constabulary, cavalry, infantry and a pack of tracker dogs, we can hardly doubt the fact of his intelligence, at the very least.

'For anonymity's sake, your correspondent is unable to name the source of the information that will ensue. But a man of high rank in the RIC revealed that under severe questioning and threat of flogging and transportation, Mr Barnard Rice conceded that he had been forced to kill the idiot Francis Flynn in self-defence. He furthermore admitted that his burn injuries had been the result of pressing his head against the fiery oven doors during his struggle with Flynn. He subsequently attempted to attach the blame for the violence to Mr Joyce, against whom he had a bitter grudge, thereby forcing the young man to flee for his life.

'It is only by God the Saviour's grace that no harm came to Mr Joyce in his escape, at least none of which this correspondent is aware. Had such occurred, a grave injustice would have transpired, which would have weighed heavily on the entire community of Ballinrobe.

'It is believed that in lieu of his full confession, only charges of theft will be preferred on Mr Rice, a decision that many find outrageous.

'At the time of writing, Joyce's whereabouts remain unknown. Speculation abounds that he evaded the constabulary at Westport Quay and secured transport to the United States of America.'

Owen lowered the sheet and looked around him at the two smiling faces.

Maebh at once rose and embraced him. 'What did that lady say? His compassion and courage? I didn't need te be told that.'

Owen looked at the floor.

'Don't forget intelligence,' Tim said.

'Ah sure, what good is that if ye've no soul?'

'All right, woman, no need to snap! I was only singin' the lad's praises.'

'It's a disgrace that louse Rice isn't hung. Tellin' such a tale. Ye could 'a been killed.'

Owen raised his eyes to them. 'I know why. I have to tell you. He wasn't burned in the struggle with Flynn. I'm ashamed to say I did it to him. For what he'd done to Flynn. And to me and others. I think the police discovered the monster he was and made him a trade, made him let me off the hook and in turn he was just charged with theft.'

'What did he do?' Maebh asked softly, but Owen only looked into the flames.

'Doesn't matter anyhow,' Tim muttered in the uncomfortable silence.

'Tim, I also stole that boat.'

Tim shrugged. 'Sure, I'll ask around, say I found it driftin'. They'll think it slipped its rope.'

'I can't ever thank you both enough. And I'll be on my way as soon as I'm well.'

'Ye'll do no such thing,' Maebh said.

'But...'

'Ye can stay here. Muireann'll be delighted to have a big brother, especially as she lost the two she had,' she said matter-of-factly.

'I'm sorry.'

'Sure, we've all lost family.'

Tim crouched down in front of him. 'We worked it out. Ye should keep yer head low, I'd say, despite being in the clear. Call yourself Owen Connor. My nephew from, where is it? Tawnyard Hill. Nobody round here knows your face from a sheep's arse. We've a lot te do with the season ahead so you'll certainly earn your keep. Ye'll have te learn about other plants besides spuds too.'

'Well?' Maebh asked.

He felt tears sting the corners of his eyes. 'Both of you...you remind me of my mother and father,' he said, his eyes fixed on the floor. 'Thank you so much.'

Maebh leaned across and kissed him on the forehead.

'Right then,' Tim declared, 'that's fixed up. I've work te do, and so have you, woman.'

'Don't tell me I've work! I know full well I've work. Cheek of ye. Get on with ye out of that before I plant me foot in yer behind.'

Tim laughed and disappeared out the door.

'Rest today. If ye're well enough ye can start tomorrow.'

'Maybe…maybe as a payment for lodgings…you'd allow me to teach you to read?' He gestured with the newspaper.

She was taken aback. 'Me? Read? Who ever heard of such a thing?' she laughed as she set about busying herself.

The paper still aloft, Owen's eye caught a different article beneath the fold and eagerly began to read.

> TWO HANGED FOR OUGHTY MURDERS
> At Castlebar – In relation to the murders at Oughty, among them the prominent land agent, Robert Peyton Harris, and as we reported previously, the trial of those subsequently found guilty of the crime, the sentences of death were carried out at dawn on Friday the 29th day of December 1848. James Burke of Cregganmore Valley and Padraig Walsh of Glenlaur Valley were dispatched to the next life. May God have mercy on their souls.

Owen lowered the newspaper and slowly exhaled. So Harris had met a violent end. He experienced a moment of grim satisfaction that some measure of revenge had been exacted on the man, then immediately felt a pang of guilt and a deep measure of sorrow that Walsh and Burke, fanatical nationalists both, had paid for their vengeance with their lives. And yet, but for the will of God, the kindness of others, or sheer chance, *The Mayo Telegraph* might well be reporting the details of his final moments before they pulled the rope around his neck.

'What's the matter, Owen?'

'Oh nothing. I was just thinking of my home. And all the things that have happened since I left there.'

She walked over and placed a comforting hand on his shoulder. 'Well, you've a new home now. And your journey's finally over.'

CHAPTER 16

Should the Irish peasantry be tempted to use force against the law and should the refusal to pay rent be supported by an organisation of murderous terrorism, it will be the duty of the Ministry, at whatever cost and however reluctantly, to apply to Parliament for the largest and most efficient repressive authority.

–Editorial in *The Times*, 24 August 1880

MURDEROUS MOLLIE MAGUIRES

The trial of the murderers of Policeman Yost was made interesting by the complete exposure of the workings of the mysterious order, which under the name of the Mollie Maguires, has done so much mischief in this county, and heretofore so successfully eluded detection. The Detective James McParlan, who occupied the witness stand today, told how he became a member of the order by a sharp piece of strategy. The Mollie Maguires' real name is The Ancient Order of Hibernians, and branches elsewhere repudiate the lawless acts of the Mollie Maguires. The order has its origin and foundation in Ireland.

– Special dispatch to *The New York Times*, Pottsville, Penn., 8 May

21 September 1880

'It's Thomas. Your brother.'

The man extended a hand and Owen slapped it away. He was little more than a vague form in the descending gloom.

'Jesus, Owen. It's me. Thomas.'

'That's not possible.'

Owen started for the car, but felt a hand grip his wrist. He froze and tried to catch a glimpse of the man's eyes, but the shadows were impenetrable.

'Let me go.'

There was no response except the faintest of laughs. Owen twisted the man's wrist sharply, brought his free hand across and seized his arm, then jerked it against its natural bend and forced his opponent's arm behind his back. He shoved him face-up against the church wall.

'Christ, you've learned a thing or two,' the man gasped. 'Must remember that.'

'Shut up.'

'Listen to me, for Christ's sake.'

'I've had enou–'

'Our mother and father were Michael and Honor Joyce,' the man grunted. 'Died in the famine. So did Pat, Sally and Bridget. We lived on Tawnyard Hill. Is that enough?'

Owen was given pause and relaxed his hold, then quickly tightened it again. 'Any fool could have found that out.'

The man yawped in discomfort again. 'Christ. We walked te Westport. I stole money for tickets. A ship sank in the harbour. We got on board our ship but you jumped off. Are ye happy now? My fucking arm is breaking.'

Owen released him and stepped back several paces.

Thomas turned and massaged his upper arm. 'In a village in Doolough Valley we were surrounded by, what would you call them? The walking dead. Had to run for our lives. What else? You're a good swimmer and we had a teacher called, what was the fucker's name, Mull...'

'Mullany.'

'That's it. Right bastard he was. Liked you, though. You and your brains. Why don't ye use them now? You nearly uncorked my arm bone.'

They stood in the pitch dark. Anu whinnied, then the night was utterly still.

'Thomas?' Owen whispered.

He laughed. 'Yeah. Thomas. Look.'

A moment later a match flared and he held it up to his face, but the effect was only to create a dance of shadows in the yellow light. He stepped closer to Owen.

'Owen, *it's me.*'

Open-mouthed, Owen stared into the unmistakable amber eyes of his brother and noticed a scar running the length of his face. The flame died and a faint sulphuric scent rose to his nostrils.

'Thomas?' he asked again, belief in his voice accompanied by a rising joy.

'Owen. I've come home,' Thomas said quietly.

Owen laughed aloud and threw his arms around his brother, who responded in kind. Within their long, unyielding embrace they both felt the spill of tears.

***

Owen could not contain the questions as they trotted back along the moonlit track towards Lough Mask.

'Where did you go? Why didn't you write and tell me you were alive?'

'Whoh, brother! You'll run the poor old girl into a ditch.'

'I've driven this road so often I could do it asleep.'

He found Thomas's accent strange. Although he still retained a Mayo brogue, there were hints of exotic tongues having bent his ear, like spices thrown into a familiar broth.

'Never mind me. You're married! Síomha? Sounds beautiful.'

'She is. And there's Tadhg, he's sixteen, and Niamh's eight. Then there's Lorcan, followed your path. Went to America.'

Thomas was slow to reply. 'My path? Hardly. What does he do?'

'The railways at first but then he got land in Montana. Have you been there? You might even have met him.'

Thomas laughed and clapped him on the shoulder. 'Montana's five times the size of Ireland and America's maybe twenty times the size of Montana.'

'Jesus. I mean, I know that, of course. I've seen the maps. But you never think of it like that, I suppose, unless you've been there.' He shook his head and chuckled. 'I still can't believe you're here. I would have sworn you were dead.'

'I *still* can't believe you jumped off the ship in Westport. And I was *certain* you were dead.'

'Well, we both made it somehow.'

Thomas laughed abruptly. 'Do ye remember stealing the bread? We almost got caught because you were watching that girl washing her tits.'

Owen was taken aback at his brother's coarseness.

Thomas sensed it and turned to him. 'Sorry. Twenty years working on railways and in mines with the hardest brutes on earth, ye sorta become rough 'round the edges.'

'Forget it. Just don't talk like that around Síomha.'

'Jesus, what do ye take me for?'

'Besides, she was washing her *hair*. But I was *looking* at her tits.'

Both of them howled with laughter just as they saw the glow through the cottage window.

'Here we are.'

***

Síomha yanked open the door and took a step outside.

'Owen! Jesus Almighty? Where have you been? Driving home in the dark! I hope you haven't whiskey taken as well! I was worried out of my wits.'

She was gesticulating wildly at the figure that stepped into the overspill of light from the doorway. When a man with coarse stubble and a long scar materialised, she emitted a startled shriek.

'Who are you?'

Tadhg was suddenly behind his mother, pulling her inside. Niamh called out in alarm.

'Everyone calm down,' Owen came around the trap and placed a hand on Thomas's shoulder. The pair stepped into the cottage.

Thomas held his hands up, palms forward. 'I didn't mean te scare ye. Ye came out so fast–'

'Everyone. This is my brother. This is Thomas.'

Mother, son and daughter stood side by side, each of them with their mouths open wide as though waiting like infants to be fed.

Thomas extended his hand. 'Like your husband said, Mrs Joyce, you're a beautiful woman. But I wouldn't like te get on the wrong side of ye.'

***

There was a flurry of activity. Síomha issued orders to the children to tidy the place and fetch the whiskey. She vanished to her room briefly and re-emerged in a clean dress and with her hair combed. Throughout it all, Thomas pleaded for no special treatment. He was all charm to Síomha, admonishing her for dressing specially – 'no matter what she wore her beauty would brighten any room.' Owen told him to pull back the reins on the sweet talk or he'd be expected to talk like that every day. Niamh and Tadhg sat in awe of the exotic visitor. It was as though a character had stepped from the pages of a book. They had all heard the tale of their father's brother and had often dreamed of the adventures he might be having in the vast, mysterious expanse of the New World. And now here he was, the phantom of their father's past come to life.

Owen studied his brother. He'd grown tall and looked fit for a man of fifty. His hair was black and cut short and his skin was dark and weathered. Sadly, his most striking feature was a deep scar that ran almost from his hairline to his mouth.

'Where's my pack?' Thomas asked as they sat around the hearth, Niamh content to squat on the floor nearby, staring at her new-found uncle's face.

Tadhg lifted the well-worn pack. 'Here it is. It's heavy.'

Thomas rose and took it from Tadhg's grip. 'No, let me.'

He rummaged in the pack and pulled out a leather pouch the size of a large book.

'I honestly didn't know Owen here had a family or was even alive when I came back, otherwise I'd have brought some decent gifts…'

Síomha and Owen began to protest but he hushed them. 'Listen, I've been dragging bits and pieces from all over America for thirty years. Now, let's see. Ah, yes.'

Thomas lit up Niamh's eyes with a gift of a necklace of polished bone beads from a state called Colorado, the work of wild Indians called the Arapaho. Niamh rewarded him with a prolonged embrace, which provoked a hearty chuckle. To Tadhg he gifted an arrow whose shaft was broken mid-way, but whose head was of shiny black obsidian, informing him that he'd broken the arrow removing it from a friend's flesh, much to Tadhg's fascination.

From a shallow metal can that rattled, he removed a piece of rock no larger than a man's thumb and handed it to Síomha, informing her she was now the possessor of a nugget of gold. He waved away her vociferous protests, telling her it was worth just a few dollars and then only if one separated and smelted the gold. All eyes watched enthralled as Síomha held it up and caught the tiny specks of gold glinting in the lamplight.

Lastly he produced a flat, rectangular object wrapped of wax paper that he began to unfold with great care, eventually revealing a piece of paper, yellowed, stained and cracked.

'Be careful with it,' he said as he handed it to Owen.

'What is it?'

'Open it. Gently.'

As he unfolded it, Owen was momentarily mystified. Across the top, in heavy but partly obscured lettering, were the words: *Grimshaw & Sons Shipping. Passengers' Contract Ticket*.

He lifted his head, dumbfounded, and stared at Thomas, who smiled.

'It's really not even mine te give. It's yours.'

'Our ticket for the ship in Westport in 1848.'

'My God!' Síomha leaned in to study it. 'There are your names.'

'I think ye missed your boat,' Thomas joked.

'Why did you keep it?'

He shrugged. 'Only thing I had te remember ye by.'

Owen choked on his next word and Síomha laid a hand on his arm.

Tadhg, his attention returned to the arrowhead, disrupted the emotive silence. 'Uncle, you said you pulled this out of someone. Where did it hit him?'

Thomas hesitated. He looked at their faces, rose a little and patted his rump. 'Right in the bum.'

Niamh began to giggle hysterically.

***

Niamh and Tadhg were dispatched to bed under protest. Síomha sat awhile, studying the brothers' faces. The resemblance was unmistakable, although their eyes were markedly different. Owen's were dark blue, his brother's a striking amber. Despite the hour, she was keen to learn about her husband's mysterious sibling. His shadow had always flitted about their lives, an imagined character remote to them, but his influence on Owen somehow reaching across the decades and the ocean. She was desperate to put some flesh on bones long since thought buried.

'What did you work at all these years?'

'What didn't I work at, you mean.' Thomas inclined his head. 'Let's see, when I arrived in New York I worked on the docks. Then I took te the railways. They were busy then building tracks all over America. Still are. A few years of that. Worked up in Michigan in the north then did odd jobs: farm-hand, factory work…When the Civil War started I was in Illinois. The pay was good and ye got a hundred dollars just te sign up. Sounded great. Most of the poor bas…poor eejits didn't realise that getting it would cost them their lives, or their legs. Anyway, I had no work then, so I joined up.'

'You were a soldier?' Owen asked incredulously.

He nodded. 'Three years, maybe ten battles. My only injury was a bullet that went right through my arm. I was lucky. Oh and of course, you probably noticed this.' He turned his face to display the scar in its fullness.

'You're not going to believe where I got it. The Battle of Westport.'

'You're joking?'

'I swear. It was in Kansas. We charged them at this place called Brush Creek and many of the Confederates were out of ammunition. This huge fella comes at me screaming in an Irish accent. I fired and hit him but he still comes on and swings a sword down like he's trying to chop my head in two. I just pulled back in time. Though not far enough. A second later a bullet went through his head so I never made his acquaintance.'

'God almighty,' Síomha whispered.

'Thousands died that day alone. They were the lucky ones. I saw men without legs or arms. This…' he indicated the scar, '…this was only a nick, compared to some. The worst, though, was that it was only then I realised I was fighting Irishmen and I began te wonder what we doing fighting our countrymen in a foreign land. Especially when there were still battles to be fought at home.'

He sipped his whiskey and looked at Owen.

'After the war I went west. There were rumours of a gold find in a place called Pike's Peak in the Rocky Mountains. Fortunes were being made every day, we heard. Ye could just pick up gold off the ground. But what we didn't know was that the main rush had been five years before and the easy gold had long since played out. All that was left was the dregs. I made some money, not much. I certainly didn't become rich.'

The three sat there in the soft lamplight, imagination and memory creating a reflective silence.

'Thomas, did you ever settle down. With a girl, I mean?' Síomha asked.

He uttered a mirthless sniff. 'Yes I did. I was married.'

'You were married?' Owen could hardly believe it. The unfolding tapestry of his brother's life was bewildering.

'Yeah. Her name was Eleonora.'

'Eleonora? That's beautiful,' whispered Síomha.

'She was Swedish. And she *was* beautiful. Her name meant "shining light". And she was that. Golden hair, clear blue eyes...' He seemed to drift away for a moment at the memory. 'I met her in Arizona and fell in love in a blink. I had enough money from the prospecting te buy a small ranch, that's a cattle farm. Well, small there.'

'How small?'

'A thousand acres.'

'*A thous–*'

'Owen, ye could grow as much in an acre of Mayo soil as ye could in a hundred of Arizona sand. Besides, it was cattle we farmed.'

'Cattle? But did–'

'Will you shut your big gob and let your brother talk about his wife?'

'Sorry.'

'Well, we built a house, bought the cattle, had a couple of farmhands. We had te fight off Comanche more than once. They're native Indians. I must have shot ten of them and they still kept coming. Fierce warriors. And cunning too. But that was something ye had te accept if you wanted te live there. Anyway, we were six months married. We were happy. And then one day Eleonora was riding out te me and the horse takes fright, right before my eyes. Maybe a snake, I don't know. She landed on a rock and broke her neck. Didn't suffer at least. She was five months gone with our child.'

'Oh Lord, Thomas, I'm sorry.'

Síomha reached out and squeezed his arm. Owen stared at him, incredulous of the joy and tragedy that had coloured his brother's experience.

Thomas waved a dismissive hand. 'Hey, listen, that was all a long time ago.'

'What did you do after?' Owen asked.

He sighed. 'Well, I went downhill I have te say. I sold the land and ended up in San Francisco. Jesus, what an insane place; gangs, killings every day, bars, gambling halls, whorehouses...' He paused and looked at Síomha, fearful he'd offended her, but she just sat unblinking. 'I took te the drink. Went all the way te the bottom. I think, though, that sometimes ye have te reach the bottom before ye can appreciate what's good in life. Somehow I resolved te get myself out of there. I decided te head back east. Worked my way across three thousand miles te Pennsylvania, a place called Port Clinton, mining town. That was a…' He trailed off at the sight of Síomha yawning. 'I'm sorry, I must be boring you both te tears. Talking all night like this.'

When she realised what she'd inadvertently done, she was profuse in her apologies.

'Thomas, the last thing you've done is bored me. It's fascinating. It's just I'm not used to sitting up so late. In fact, if you'll forgive me, I think I'll go to bed. And there's a lot to do tomorrow. But I really do want to hear the rest of your story, everything.'

She rose and embraced Thomas, then kissed him on the forehead. 'I'm so glad you you're here. Now, I'll leave you two boys alone. Not too late though, remember about tomorrow, Owen. Goodnight.'

She disappeared through the bedroom door.

Thomas appeared curious. 'What's tomorrow?'

'Rent's due,' he explained.

'The battle never ends, does it?'

'Anyway, what happened in Port…?'

'Port Clinton…yeah. God. I got a job in the anthracite mines, thought I'd landed on my feet. How wrong could I be? The pay seemed good until I discovered ye had te pay the company for somewhere te sleep, for "security", for doctor care, even if ye weren't sick. You'd end up with next to nothing. And the mines. Hell on earth. Ye spent your day crawling down shafts, barely able te breathe. You'd dig from dawn te dusk. Most days you never saw daylight. And there was a quota: fill seven trolleys a day or ye didn't get paid.'

Owen was silently watching his brother, who appeared to be in a dark spell of his own conjuring, relaying his tale with a bitterness not mellowed by years.

'And the deaths. The bastards were too miserly te dig emergency shafts. So when there was a collapse or a fire, anyone trapped was left te suffocate. Once, over a hundred men died in a single fire in Luzerne County. But did it change anything? No. Ye know why? We were Irish and Catholic, the two things that made ye lower than a dog, in their eyes at least. The owners were mostly of English Protestant stock. Sound familiar? They murdered two million of us in the famine and forced the same number te flee and the world didn't even blink. So what were the lives of a few miserable Irish miners worth?'

Owen briefly considered debating the historical perspective, but decided now was not the time; his brother's blood had risen.

'Thousands were dying in the mines or being murdered by the Coal and

Iron Police, a bunch of thugs in the pay of the mining and railroad companies. Not so different from the RIC. They murdered innocent men and their wives, often raped the women. The Irish even formed a secret society called the Mollie Maguires so they could fight back.'

'Mollie Maguires?'

'Yeah. Like the Mollie Maguires here. Or the Ribbonmen. I suddenly found myself in the middle of another war. Murders, revenge killings, sabotage, beatings. A guy even tried to recruit me into the Mollies. Never forget his name. McKenna. James McKenna. Northerner, from Donegal or Derry. But after the killing in the Civil War, Eleonora dying, hitting rock bottom in San Francisco…I wouldn't have any truck with it. I'd gone east te escape all that, not te end up in the middle of another war. So I got out while I could. Took what I had and went back te New York. A few months after I got there, I read that the police had arrested half the Mollie Maguires. Five men went on trial for the murder of a police thug called Benjamin Yost.' He paused, shook his head in anger. 'And who's the main state witness? James McKenna. The very bastard who tried te recruit me into the Mollie Maguires. Turns out his real name was James McParlan, a fucking detective with the Pinkerton Agency. You heard of them?'

Owen's shake of the head was barely perceptible.

'They're a private detective agency. Famous, they are. The railroad and mine owners hired them to infiltrate the Mollies. Jesus, I was so lucky I didn't take up McKenna's offer. All five men were found guilty. Within a year they'd hanged twenty. But for the grace of God, I would have ended up with a noose for a necktie as well.'

'Jesus.'

The fire had dimmed to a faint orange glow beneath a layer of pale grey ash and the room had grown cold in the autumnal night.

'Yeah. Anyway, I thanked God for my good fortune and settled into a life in New York. Got a lot of help from the Ancient Order of Hibernians. They're a fraternal organisation who help Irish Catholics in America. One of them helped me a lot, got me a job in the storeroom of an Irish bar, found me a place to live. I hadn't been in New York for twenty years. But there were so many Irish there it was like coming home. We had respect; nobody walked all over us, not like Pennsylvania. And I think it was because I was surrounded by Irish again, I got te thinking about Ireland, about home. About you. I was sure you'd died in the famine, but I had te know. It's been like a splinter in my head for decades. After a couple of years I'd put enough money by te make the decision. Four months ago I got on a ship and returned to Ireland. Made my way from Galway te Mayo. Went home first. Tawnyard. The hill. The valley. Thought you would have ended up there somehow.'

'Tawnyard Hill? You went home? Our cottage? Jesus, I haven't been there since the day we left.'

'The cottage is a ruin. A few stones left. Found our father's grave. Overgrown, it was. But when I couldn't find you in the area, I moved on. Just drifted from town te town in Mayo. Doing odd jobs again. Searching. Asking everyone I met if they'd ever heard of an Owen Joyce. But the name Joyce is so common. I had a few dead ends. Westport, Newport, Claremorris, you name it, I've been there. Finally two days ago I reached Ballinrobe. Man in a shop tells me he knows of an Owen Joyce on Lough Mask Estate near Neale. I watched you in the field today. From a way off. Wasn't certain, but I began te hope. I went into Conway's bar in Neale. Overheard men talking about a meeting at the church tonight. Your name was mentioned. I watched you arrive. Saw ye close up. No doubts. Then I just waited,' he paused and smiled. 'And here we are.'

They were silent a while as Owen absorbed it all.

'So what now?'

'Now? I don't know for sure. It's just good te be back. I have some money. And there's a man down Cong way might be able te help with a job. I knew his brother in New York. We'll see.' He chuckled a little. 'You've had te listen to me all night. I never even asked what became of you. All these years in Ireland. How you ended up here.'

'There'll be time enough for that. Besides, compared to your story, it's a yawn. Speaking of which, I have to get some sleep.' Owen stood up. 'Listen, Síomha's left some blankets there. No mattress. Sorry.'

Thomas laughed. 'I've slept in worse places.'

Owen walked to his brother and embraced him, his mind a flurry of emotion and trepidation. So much in one day was overwhelming. And tomorrow was still to come.

'It's a miracle you're here, Thomas. Really it is. Anyway, I better get away. I've a lot to do tomorrow.'

'Boycott?'

Owen stopped at the door to the bedroom and looked back.

'How do you know about Boycott?'

Thomas shrugged. 'You'd want te be as deaf as a sod of turf not te know about Boycott in this place. Half the pub was talking about him.'

Owen nodded. 'Right. Anyway, goodnight Thomas.'

Owen closed the bedroom door behind him and stood in the gloom looking at Síomha's sleeping figure, one thought rebounding in his head, one for which he could find no real justification.

Something didn't quite gel.

Had it been a phrase, a look, an intonation? He couldn't be sure of himself, but the thought persisted nonetheless that something in his brother's story didn't quite ring true.

***

Thomas waited until there was no sound from Owen's bedroom, then filled his glass and took a deep swallow. It was good to see Owen again, good to know the Joyce family blood still coursed through his children's veins. For a long time he'd believed the bloodline would die with him and that the English who had wreaked such devastation on his family would have won, at least in that personal respect. But finding Owen alive was just a bonus really.

Almost everything he'd told Owen had been true. *Almost.* He'd learned it was a good idea when telling a lie to embellish it in as much detail as possible with the truth. Everything up to the point where James McKenna had tried to recruit him into the Mollie Maguires had been absolute fact. The only difference was that he had accepted McKenna's offer and become an active member. One of his first missions had been to kill Benjamin Yost, a police thug who'd beaten and killed miners. He'd put two bullets into Yost without the slightest twinge of remorse.

The mine owners. The industrialists. The *fuckers.* Like the English, they only understood the language of the gun. Eye for an eye. He couldn't actually remember how many men he'd killed in the Mollie Maguires' name. And he had done it all with a clear conscience. He'd doled out the only justice those bastards had ever seen. It had been a war just like any other.

Then, by sheer chance, he'd been tipped off that the police were rounding up Mollie suspects. He'd headed east towards New York, living like an animal in the wilds, picking up odd jobs, moving on every couple of days. Then one day he picked up a newssheet and read about the trial of five men for Yost's murder – about McKenna, the star witness, a fucking Pinkerton agent. And there was his name. Thomas Joyce. Still wanted for Yost's murder. He made it to New York, just as he'd told Owen. And a man had helped him there, just as he'd told Owen.

A man called Donal Doherty.

A member of Clan na Gael, the American arm of the Irish Republican Brotherhood.

Doherty had arranged the job in the bar, along with a new name and papers, but he'd also recruited him to the Fenian cause, and the possibility had opened up to him of finally bringing into being the war that had raged in his mind and heart for decades. The chance to pay the English back for their brutality, for the mass extinction he believed they had attempted. He'd nurtured the thought every day since his father had died. And as he'd crawled about trying desperately to find food all those years ago, he'd seen the English convoy carrying ton upon ton of food away and his hatred had swollen. Then the man in the cottage. Driven to cannibalism. The walk to Westport, the horrors they'd witnessed. With every step and with every breath his rage had grown until finally he could see little else but his need to make them pay with their blood. When Owen had leapt from the ship, the weeks alone on the ocean had given him the opportunity to distil his feelings to pure form, with no force working to quell his bitterness. And as the years had passed, his venom had helped to carry him through the Civil War, the battles with the natives, and in the mines of Pennsylvania.

Almost three years he'd spent working for the Fenian movement in New York. Recruiting, raising funds, buying weapons. He'd come to realise that of all the races in the city only the Irish cared about what was happening in their own country. Only the Irish still saw Ireland as their real home. The Italians? The Germans? The Scandinavians? They couldn't have given a damn about their homeland. But the Irish? It was like everyone was biding their time, waiting for the call to take their country back. In '68 there was an anti-English demonstration held in New York and one hundred thousand Irishmen marched. All the talk in the bars was of ridding Ireland of the English. And, Christ, they were willing to part with their money for the cause.

Then John Devoy, one of the Clan na Gael's leaders, returns from Ireland and announces that the organisation is teaming up with Davitt and Parnell. The 'New Departure' they called it. New Departure? What a joke. Davitt and Parnell intended to talk the English to death. Jesus, would they ever learn? How many centuries would it take before they realised the English race were not to be trusted? To them the Irish were subhuman. But they'd think differently if they were wallowing in their own blood.

Many Fenians saw Devoy's plan as a betrayal. Splinter groups were forming. And Donal Doherty was part of one. Thomas had been only too willing to join up. They'd go along, bide their time, make their own plans.

Doherty had been back in Ireland over a year when Thomas had the lousy luck to be spotted by a Pinkerton agent in the bar in New York. He was still wanted for murder. He'd always planned to return to Ireland when the time was right, but now his hand was forced. It was the only place he'd be safe.

He'd barely been back a week when fortune had smiled on him. He would almost have put it down to divine providence, if he believed in that horseshit. Every Mayoman or woman he'd met down the years in America, he'd asked if they'd ever encountered an Owen Joyce back in Ireland. Hundreds, he'd asked. Always the same answer. Sorry. With each shake of the head the certainty had grown that Owen had perished. Then Donal Doherty tells him about a man he'd met at a rally in Irishtown the previous April. He'd actually tried to recruit him. Name of Owen Joyce. Grew up in a place called Tawnyard Hill. Was the fucking image of him, Doherty had said.

His brother.

Better still, he's a tenant on Lough Mask Estate.

The cards could not have fallen more sweetly.

All he had to do was play the role of long-lost brother. And that wouldn't be such a problem as he did love Owen, even if he was still a naive, dithering idealist.

His only problem was that he often had to struggle to conceal his hatred and bitterness. His dark heart. And it was going to be particularly difficult here, in his brother's home, in these times, watching Owen's family suffer the iniquities inflicted by English landlords. But he must. He had to control his mouth and his temper until his work here was done.

Doherty, his immediate superior in their rebel splinter group, had gone south to scout out a landlord marked for execution. His job meantime was to blend in and get to know the area.

And, when the time was right, send Boycott back to England in a wooden box.

PART THREE

• • • • • • • • •

BOYCOTT

boycott [***verb***] withdraw from commercial or social relations with (a country, organization, or person) as a punishment or protest. -refuse to buy or handle (goods) as a punishment or protest. - refuse to cooperate with or participate in (a policy or event). [***noun***] a punitive ban on relations with other bodies, cooperation with a policy, or the handling of goods.

–*Oxford English Dictionary*

We will never gain anything from England unless we tread upon her toes; we will never gain a single 6d worth from her by conciliation.

–Charles Stewart Parnell, speech in Manchester, 1877

CHAPTER 17

On Wednesday last, Mr David Sears, a process officer, was pelted with 'gutter' as he served eviction notices near Lough Mask.

–*The Ballinrobe Chronicle*, 25 September 1880

Reporter: The men didn't fight?
Redpath: No. They looked on. The women gave cheers for the Earl of Erne (he had been a decent landlord before Boycott was his agent) and they gave groans for Boycott and the process-server. Suddenly they threw manure and mud at him and he ran off with the crowd of women after him, the constables vainly trying to protect him from the infuriated women.

–*Talks About Ireland*, James Redpath, 1881

22 September 1880

'Considering the threats made against you, Captain Boycott, I strongly advise against being present today. We don't need any *inflammatory* influences,' Sergeant Murtagh said in his most strident tone, hands clasped behind his back.

'Are you daring to suggest that my presence might provoke violence? It's a fine day when a man as upholding of the law as myself is regarded in such a fashion!'

'I'm simply–'

'As it happens, Sergeant, Weekes and I have business to attend to on my Kildarra estate. We are already late and I do not appreciate your insistence on detailing the remit of your duties. This is a simple matter of serving eviction notices on defaulters. Even a country clod should be able to carry out that elementary task.'

'Charles!' It was Annie who sought to soften the effect of her husband's caustic tongue. 'Please forgive him, Sergeant, he's been under a lot of strain.'

'Strain, my foot. The only strain I'm under is because of the incompetence that surrounds me daily.'

The sergeant exhaled slowly and looked around. Besides Boycott and his wife, David Sears, the process-server, sat by the drawing room window chewing his thumbnail and watching the assembled constables, sixteen in all, who loitered outside, chatting and smoking cigarettes in the milky light.

'I merely wish to point out, sir, that the RIC are *not* here to issue eviction notices, only to uphold law and order and make sure that no harm befalls the server.'

'Fine! Now, get on with your job, Sergeant, and allow me to get on with mine. Good day,' Boycott snapped and left them with the sound of the door rattling in its frame.

Sergeant Murtagh turned to Sears. 'Right, then, will we proceed to the first cottage?'

Sears stood up and ran his palms down his suit, as he was in the habit of doing. He was a slight man, thin and not particularly tall, in his early thirties, with neat brown hair and of a nervous disposition.

'Sergeant, do you really think there's a risk of violence? I mean, they won't mistake me for Mr Boycott, will they?'

'I assure you, Mr Sears, nobody on God's earth could be mistaken for my husband,' Annie said wearily.

***

'How did you get on last night? Were you very late?' Síomha asked.

Owen was naked, his back to her, fumbling about for his pants in the semi-darkness.

'Owen?'

He pulled on the pants and began to don his shirt. 'It was good. We had lots to catch up on. Anyway, more important things to think about today. Damn! I've buttoned my shirt wrong!'

'What is it?'

'The buttons are in the wro–'

'Not that! Did something happen? You didn't fight, did you?'

He sighed. 'No. We didn't fight. It's just that…'

'What?'

He yawned. He'd spent most of the night ruminating on his brother's return and found himself in a turmoil of conflicting emotions. There was joy, of course, and he could barely wait to rekindle their relationship in the days ahead. Against that, he was troubled by a nagging suspicion that something about Thomas's manner didn't quite fit. Perhaps it was just the disquieting nature of his tale. Besides, he had little time to mull on such things today.

'Not now, Síomha. Later. Listen, I'm going to need your help today. And the children's.'

'But Niamh's got school.'

'Not today. Let me tell you about the meeting.'

Síomha was up and dressing as he spoke. When she was ready she followed Owen outside. They both looked over at the corner where Thomas lay wrapped in a tangle of blankets, snoring lightly. The empty whiskey bottle lay at his side.

Owen picked it up. 'Half full when I went to bed.'

Síomha shrugged. 'Let him sleep it off.'

***

Sergeant Murtagh tried to reassure David Sears by flanking him with eight men either side, yet the process-server repeatedly cast nervous glances into the shadowy cloisters of the woodland.

'Don't fret, Mr Sears. There's nothing they can throw at us we can't handle. And I wouldn't be worried just yet.'

'Why?'

'We haven't even left the grounds of Lough Mask House.'

Sears nodded and the sergeant raised his eyes to heaven as they picked up pace.

They marched through the gateway and turned left on to a section of road that ran as straight as an arrow for a mile. As they moved along, the sergeant was a little surprised to see not a soul working in the fields as it was past nine o'clock. He also had to admit to a certain uneasiness as a result of rumours of Fenian activity in the Ballinrobe area. He touched the grip on his service revolver.

They drew near to Joe Gaughan's cottage, where he halted the group and addressed them. 'I don't know all of you, but any of you that know me know that I don't take kindly to constables crossing the line. In fact, I'll batter the ears off anyone who does. These are farmers, not thugs and ruffians. Remember that. Right, let's get on with it.'

They marched up a short, muddy lane to the cottage. Smoke drifted lazily from its chimney and a few chickens pecked about the entrance.

'Mr Sears?'

Sears emerged from the body of men with his satchel clutched to his chest, the flap open as he rummaged about inside. He extracted the first eviction notice and rapped on the door. There was no response and he knocked more forcefully. The door was finally pulled open by a short, stout-faced woman of about forty. She calmly wiped her hands on a rag as she looked at the mass of dark green uniforms. Sears unfolded the eviction notice in an officious manner. The sight of a middle-aged woman and not a burly farmer had bolstered his confidence.

He began reciting the legal niceties. 'Under the Landlord and–'

'And who d'ye think you are?'

'Now, Mrs Gaughan, the man's just doing his job,' said the sergeant, stepping up beside Sears.

Síle Gaughan regarded the sergeant with distaste. 'Just because you've Ireland's harp on your fancy badge doesn't make ye any less a traitor.'

He became grim-faced and turned to Sears. 'Get on with it.'

Sears read: 'Under the Landlord and Tenant Law Amendment Act 1860

(Ireland), I hereby serve notice of ejectment for non-payment of rent.'

She leaned against the doorframe. 'You can't serve that on me. I'm not the head of the household. At least not *officially*.'

Some of the constables laughed.

'Is your husband here?'

'No.'

Sears smirked. 'Actually, it doesn't matter anymore. The law now allows me, in the event of the head of the household being absent, to simply attach the notice to the front door of the dwelling.'

Síle Gaughan's confidence faltered. 'What? You can't do that!'

Sears's grin broadened as he pulled a pin from his pocket. She quickly threw herself against the door, frustrating the server's attempts to attach the notice. The sergeant nodded to a couple of constables, who quickly stepped inside the house and took her by the arms.

'How dare ye touch me, ye traitorous pigs! Get your filthy hands off or I'll have me husband bate the daylights outta ye!'

With the struggling woman removed, Sears pinned the notice to the door and stepped away. Released, Síle Gaughan seized on the first thing to hand, which happened to be a freshly laid egg. She slammed it into a constable's face, provoking a hearty chuckle from his comrades. Enraged, the constable raised his hand, but Sergeant Murtagh seized his arm mid-swing.

'Don't dare, constable. Besides, it improves your complexion. Now, let's get on with the next one.'

The humiliated constable wiped the egg from his face and, fuming, stomped from the cottage. The group about-faced and marched, military-style, down the lane, the profane execrations of Mrs Gaughan ringing in their ears.

***

'I don't have te go te school?'

'Not today. I've a special job for you.'

Niamh stared excitedly as Owen crouched in front of her.

'You know the little rise near the Holy Well where Mr Fitzmorris lives?'

She nodded.

'I want you to watch that hill from our high field. And if you see anyone waving a red flag on the hill, I want you to run back as quick as you can and tell us. Do you understand?'

'Why is Mr Fitzmorris going te wave a flag?'

'It doesn't matter, sweet. But it's a very special job and only you can do it. And do you see this?' He held up a farthing and her eyes opened wider. 'If you keep a good lookout, you get this for your pay.'

Niamh took off towards the field with the enthusiasm of a child on an adventure. Síomha and Tadhg walked up as he watched her depart.

'What are *we* going to do, Dad?'

'We're going to get in the rest of the turnips. We can't afford to miss a day's harvest.'

***

The next cottage drew no response to repeated knocking. The sergeant peered in the window, but could see only his own reflection in the glass.

'There's no smoke,' one of the others shouted.

He began to call out. 'Higgins! Peadar Higgins! This is Sergeant Murtagh. If you're there it's better for you to come out.'

Besides a flock of crows that took fright from a nearby tree, all remained quiet. Sears turned to the sergeant.

'You're a witness that all attempts were made to serve the notice in person?'

The sergeant nodded and Sears pinned the paper to the door.

'Easy as pie,' he said with a grin.

As they turned back to the road a young lad sprinted past, giving them a wide berth.

'Who's next?'

'Martin McGurk.'

The sergeant frowned.

'What?'

'Trouble.'

***

Síomha's back ached from gathering the turnips. She had no fear of hard work, but this was one of the few jobs she detested. Bend, pick, straighten, bend, pick. Hour after hour. Her thoughts of discomfort were interrupted by the sight of Niamh running down the hill like a hare in flight, and replaced with trepidation.

'Owen!' she called to her husband and Tadhg, working across the field.

Father and son hastily abandoned their work, Tadhg vaulting the wall,

Owen climbing it as fast as his age permitted. The child came to a stumbling halt, panting so much she had to bend double.

'It's Mrs Fitzmorris…on the hill…waving a red flag and shouting, but I couldn't hear…what she said,' Niamh said between heaving breaths.

Owen put his hand to his forehead and spun away, trying to order his thoughts.

'Dad?'

'Tadhg. Go up to the road, towards Boycott's house. Find out what's happening. Hurry! Go!'

Tadhg wheeled about and ran without a word.

***

'Have ye brought half the force with ye, Murtagh? You must be feeling very brave altogether.'

'Now, Martin. No need for trouble.'

'Don't "Martin" me. It's Mr McGurk te the likes of you.'

Murtagh nodded to Sears, who held up the notice to recite the legalities. Before he got two words out McGurk snatched the paper, scrunched it to a ball and threw it into the mud.

'Get off my land,' he said through his teeth. His wife, Teresa, who was heavily pregnant, appeared behind him and tried to calm him, but he shrugged her away.

Murtagh motioned for several constables to close in.

'This is not your land, Mr McGurk,' Sears said as he gingerly untangled the crumpled, soiled notice. 'It's the property of the Earl of Erne and your rent is overd–'

'The only thing wrong with my rent is that it's twice what it should be. Tell that bastard Boycott to come down here and I'll explain it personally. If he's man enough.'

'That's it, McGurk,' Murtagh said, standing nose to nose with the farmer. 'Either accept this eviction notice or Mr Sears will pin it to your door. That will suffice.'

'Let's see him try.'

Murtagh nodded to Sears, who hesitated, abject fear on his face, then eased himself towards the door. McGurk blocked his path, and Murtagh and three constables immediately seized him. His wife screamed as he was wrestled away, yelling obscenities. Sears hastily pinned the ragged paper up as McGurk's wife watched him with loathing.

'Bastard!' she spat at him as he retreated into the yard.

McGurk managed to free a hand and land a solid fist on a constable's nose, drawing blood. His colleagues responded by raining truncheon blows on the farmer. Teresa McGurk's shrill howling echoed about the farmyard. McGurk collapsed in the mud and the pregnant woman fought to clear a path to him through the tangle of uniforms.

'That's enough!' Murtagh roared, heaving his men away one by one. As he did, one of them swung his baton and inadvertently struck Teresa McGurk on her side. She screamed, then fell wailing to her knees beside her bloodied husband.

'Do we arrest him, sir?'

Murtagh shook his head. 'Are we finished, Sears?'

Sears, aghast to be in the midst of such violence, simply nodded.

'Let's go, then. Fitzmorris next.'

***

'I met Séamus Gaughan running down the road. He says that they served his mother an eviction notice,' Tadhg panted. 'Some fella in a suit said Mr Gaughan didn't have to be there, that he could just pin the notice to the door.'

'Jesus.'

'They're heading towards McGurk's. Probably then to Mr Fitzmorris.'

'What's going on?' Thomas had wandered out from the cottage, bleary-eyed, his clothes dishevelled.

'They've started serving eviction notices,' Owen muttered absently, then looked at the others. 'If they only need to pin them up…'

'…we can't stop them,' Síomha said.

'We could stop them quick enough with a few guns.' Tadhg kicked out at a bucket sitting in the yard.

'No, Tadhg. That would make things worse. Listen to me. Here's what to do. Go and round up all the women and go to Fitzmorris's cottage. But none of the husbands. They can't be seen. We're going to block their path to the door. The RIC won't want to be seen attacking women. We'll make a wall of people they can't break through. I'll meet you there.'

Síomha stepped closer to him. 'You can't be seen there either.'

'I'll stay well out of sight, don't worry.'

'You're going to send women to fight your battles?' Thomas asked.

Owen turned sharply to his brother. 'There aren't going to be any battles.'

He kissed Síomha on the lips. 'Go. And be careful. Tadhg, I need you to help too, son.'

Tadhg, who had been standing, head down, hands in pockets, nodded reluctantly and hurried away, leaving Owen and his brother alone.

'Anything I can do to help?'

Owen hesitated. 'Yeah, you could put Anu in her pen. Look, she's after dragging the plough arseways around the field.'

'Leave it to me.' He smiled at Owen and set off towards the field.

***

Sergeant Murtagh became aware of a strange babble of voices as they strode up the slope towards the Fitzmorris home. They rounded the curve in the laneway to be greeted by the sight of twenty or more women, arms linked, three rows deep in front of the cottage. He cursed.

The cottage nestled in a hollow in the slope of the hill, the space in front roughly circular and bordered by trees and low walls. More women were approaching across the fields, and he had the sense of entering an arena. As his men trooped up in front of the lines of women, they were assailed by oaths the like of which he'd rarely heard from the women of Ireland.

He walked among his men, the cacophony of hissing and abuse forcing him to lift his voice to be heard. 'None of you men is to dare use a weapon. Not even a truncheon. The Royal Irish Constabulary does not make a habit of beating women and I'll have your guts for garters if any of you takes any unprovoked action. Is that understood?'

There were a few reluctant mutters of obedience and he turned to Sears. 'We'll dispense with the formalities. They know why we're here.'

The sergeant strode up to the first line of women. At six feet three inches he towered above them. In the centre stood Mary Fitzmorris, her right arm linked to the woman he recognised as Síomha Joyce.

'Where's your husband, Missus?'

Mrs Fitzmorris was a short woman of about fifty, with fiery eyes, her jaw firmly set, and long black hair tied behind her head. 'He's not here.'

He lifted his chin and began to shout towards the house. 'Fitzmorris. Luke

Fitzmorris. This is Sergeant Murtagh. If you're in there, hiding behind these women isn't going to make things any better. Come out before someone gets hurt.'

Mary Fitzmorris rounded on him bitterly at the slight to her husband's manhood. 'My Luke never hid from any man. He's got more courage than all your big boyos here put together!'

A defiant cheer rose from the lines of women and the spectators.

'I warn you,' the sergeant shouted, 'we are attempting to carry out the law according to Her Majesty's Government and you are impeding us in our duties and will be subject to arrest and penalties accordingly, which may include prison.'

'Her Majesty knows where she can shove her law,' Síomha yelled loud enough for the entire assemblage to hear. This instigated a new round of cheering and abuse, which was less directed at the constabulary and more at British rule and the landlords, Boycott specifically.

Murtagh's frustration was evident in the rising colour in his cheeks. He wheeled away to his men, who gathered into a tight scrum and strained to hear what he had to say.

***

Owen stood behind a wooden gate in the Fitzmorris's horse enclosure, which overlooked the farmyard. Tadhg stood to his left, fists clenched by his sides, feeling shamed at standing by while his mother faced the threat below. Owen had to confess to similar feelings. When the police had marched into the yard, his instinct was to run down and stand between them and the women, but he'd checked himself. It would surely only provoke the kind of violence he needed to avoid. Yet when the sergeant stood facing Síomha, he'd found the opposing natures of his character pulling him apart.

He heard a scuffle behind and saw Joe Gaughan and his wife approaching, the burly farmer clearly bent on retribution, his wife, Síle, trying to calm him. Owen turned and blocked his path before he reached the gate and in doing so almost slipped in a pile of horse dung.

'No, Joe, that won't do any good!'

'Out of me way, Owen. Those bastards came into me house and one of them was going te hit Síle. They battered the brains out of McGurk. Now I'm going to batter a few brains meself.'

Owen grabbed Joe Gaughan, who was half again as big as him and tried to restrain him. He yelled to Tadhg, who ran to his father's aid.

'Joe, listen to me! There are nearly twenty armed men down there. The reason they haven't touched the weapons is because of the women. If you start something, they *will* use the weapons and Christ knows what'll happen. Remember what Fr O'Malley told us, Joe, please!'

Owen felt Joe's resistance weaken. His shoulders slumped and he looked away.

'All right, Owen. If you say so. For now I'll do nothing. But if one of those bastards raises a hand...'

Owen released him and turned back towards the scene below.

Thomas was suddenly by his side. 'Looks nasty. Could blow up any second, if I know Her Majesty's henchmen.'

'Thomas, this isn't your business.'

His brother pointed with his chin towards the drama. 'Jesus! Look!'

Owen looked down. The sergeant had formed his men shoulder to shoulder into two lines only a breath from Síomha and the others. He began to yell loudly.

'This is your final warning! You are obstructing the constabulary in the course of their duties. If you do not step aside you will be forcibly removed and subject to the full rigours of the law.'

A brief silence of expectation descended.

The sergeant abruptly grabbed Mrs Fitzmorris by the shoulders and tried to wrench her from the line. The flanking constables took his lead and began to grapple with the women. Owen saw Síomha's enraged face disappearing behind the broad shoulders of a constable. Pandemonium descended as the women screamed and hurled abuse, and the watching crowd yelled their outrage.

Owen's frustration began to boil over. Tadhg was readying himself to leap over the gate. Joe Gaughan grabbed the top rail and squeezed it until the wooden slat cracked.

'No! Tadhg! Joe! Don't!'

'We have to do something, Dad!'

Down below, the police had succeeded in wresting three of the women in the front line free. These were manhandled back to the second row of policemen to ensure they didn't return to the fray. Síomha was still holding firmly to Mary Fitzmorris, her face red, shrieking abuse.

'I know what I'd do,' Thomas said calmly. He lifted a stone the size of a man's fist and tossed it up and down.

'Yeah! That's it!' Tadhg roared.

Owen gripped his brother's wrist and met his eyes with a hard stare.

'No, Thomas.'

Thomas gritted his teeth. 'Brother, I'm not a man given to violence. But sometimes...when your wife is–'

Owen's face suddenly brightened, and to everyone's disbelief he said: 'Wait! You're right! But if we start throwing rocks we'll likely as not brain the women. We won't use rocks. We'll use something better.'

He looked to the ground at a large, fresh pile of horse dung. He bent and grabbed two handfuls.

'Síle! Are you ready to get your hands dirty?'

Síle Gaughan, standing beside her husband, grinned from ear to ear and quickly looked about her feet. She found a dung pile and took two handfuls, then called to the women nearby.

'Girls! Time te do your duty for Ireland!' And with that she let fly towards the melee below.

The first handful struck a constable's back, the second his hat. Owen followed with two more salvos and greater accuracy, striking a constable square in the face.

'Well, lads?' he asked of Tadhg and Joe. They were momentarily dumbstruck, then quickly moved to action, as did all the women, and within seconds a torrent of horse shit was spattering the constabulary, who tried desperately to shield their faces. But the cannonade of foulness virtually encircled them. Sixty or more of the locals were enthusiastically engaged in the bombardment, expanding the arsenal of projectiles to include cow droppings or sods of turf.

The serving of notices was abandoned in the hope of escaping the rain of filth. Bent low, arms crossed over their heads, the constables sought cover in a huddle. Sears, his suit tarnished beyond redemption, his face spattered with horse excrement, was near to tears as he tried to shield his head with his satchel. Sergeant Murtagh yelled instructions to retreat. Like some aberrant creation of nature, the crouching body of men began a tortuous shuffle towards the laneway, the mass of legs occasionally tangling and slipping on the mud. The women who had stood centurion watched triumphantly as the constables finally broke and fled *en masse*. As they scrambled and slipped down the laneway, rhapsodic cheers followed in their wake. The gallery descended and ran to embrace the women, who had taken a few misguided hits themselves, but cared little. Owen fought through the cheering melee to find Síomha, her dress smeared with horse dung, yet laughing wildly. She threw her arms first about Owen, then her son.

'Are you hurt?' Owen asked as he looked proudly at her.

'Hurt? It'll take tougher men than them to hurt me.'

'You've smelt better!'

'It's the best smell I've smelt in my life.'

The cottage door opened and out stepped Luke Fitzmorris. He stood with hands on hips and stared at the scene around him. 'Jesus, look at the state of me yard!' he roared, then grinned and embraced his wife so enthusiastically he lifted her off her feet. Another cheer rose to the Mayo sky, then all fell to laughing and recounting the battle.

In the field overlooking the yard, Thomas shook his head with scorn, turned and walked away alone.

***

Owen and Tadhg immediately resumed their work on the harvest for the afternoon and were thus engaged when Fr O'Malley's trap appeared. A well-dressed man of about Owen's age rode beside him. He had a round face and longish black hair, but an extremely high hairline. He also had a very full beard, which reminded him of Parnell. Instructing Tadhg to continue with the work, Owen hastened up to greet the priest.

'Was there any trouble today?' Fr O'Malley asked as they alighted.

Owen hesitated. 'Well...'

'What happened?' The priest looked worried.

Owen glanced at the stranger.

'I'm forgetting my manners. Owen, this is Mr James Redpath. Mr Redpath is a correspondent with the *New York Herald* and he has a particular interest in our situation.'

'Pleased to meet you, Mr Joyce.' His handshake was firm and warm, as was his smile. His American accent reminded Owen of Thomas's.

'Mr Redpath. Father. Let's go inside and I'll bring you up to date.'

Síomha was off collecting Niamh, whom she had deposited to the care of a neighbour that morning. He hadn't seen Thomas since the Fitzmorris farm. His bag was gone, but his spare clothing was neatly folded in a corner.

They sat around the small table and Owen laid out the events of the day, including McGurk's beating and the subsequent events at the farmyard. The American wrote copious notes of his narrative at a speed that astounded Owen. This was the first time he'd ever met a newspaper correspondent and he was instinctively wary of him. When he reached the climax, the pelting of the constabulary, the priest sat back with a look of bewilderment, then laughed aloud. 'Ah, God bless *Mná na hÉireann*.'

Redpath looked at him quizzically.

'Women of Ireland,' Fr O'Malley explained and Redpath noted it down, a habit that was beginning to irritate Owen.

'Of course, I'd have preferred completely non-violent action,' said the priest.

Owen shrugged. 'Best I could come up with at the time.'

'Well, nobody was hurt, I suppose.'

'Except the RIC's pride, I suspect,' Redpath said.

'May I ask what your interest is in all this?' asked Owen. 'It seems a little odd that a New York correspondent would be interested in the events in a small Mayo village.'

'Quite the contrary; in fact, I'm extremely interested.'

'James has written many books and articles about various peoples who have been plagued by injustice. He has campaigned on the anti-slavery issue in his own country and is famous for his outspoken writings on John Brown, the abolitionist. He's also written in support of women's rights and many other issues.'

'But why here? Ballinrobe? Neale?'

'If you'll forgive a measure of immodesty, I have a nose for finding history's fuses,' Redpath replied.

Owen shook his head, unsure of the meaning.

'I suspect what's going to happen here will be bigger than you imagine.'

'Why? And how could you possibly know what's going on in our little backwater? I doubt we're the talk of New York.'

He laughed. 'No. At least not yet.'

The priest leaned in. 'James was already here to write a book about Michael Davitt and has attended and, indeed, addressed, many Land League meetings.'

'When I arrived in Ireland, I had to confess a lack of knowledge of her history or her current plight. I'm of Scottish and English background and was originally educated to be a Presbyterian minister, so my upbringing would suggest a bias towards the ruling ascendancy. However, in the past year I've come to understand the terrible malfeasance of Britain towards her Irish subjects and the evil they've supported in the form of landlordism. When Michael Davitt first expounded upon the plan of ostracism that he'd concocted with Parnell, I was fascinated. Fr O'Malley and I have become friends these past months and I asked him to inform me if he intended to put the plan into action. When he told me he intended using it on somebody as prominent as a land agent like Boycott, as opposed to a mere land-grabber, well, naturally, my interest was stimulated.'

Owen mused a while, then turned to the priest. 'You knew about the ostracising plan before last Sunday? Before Parnell?'

'I did, Owen. Davitt told me.'

'So why go to Ennis? Why couldn't you have laid it out yourself?'

'Owen, I can't hold a candle to the lighthouse that is Mr Parnell. You and the others needed to hear it from him, in person, before you'd begin to believe it might work.'

Owen could only smile at the priest's wiliness.

'Well, Mr Redpath, I hope you find something worth writing about.'

'I know I will. Also that it will do no harm to bring your plight to the eyes of the wider world.'

Owen nodded, but wondered if the world cared a damn about the tribulations of a few tenant farmers in Mayo.

Síomha returned and was surprised at the sight of guests, but the first thing Owen noticed was that the joyful spirit of earlier had left her eyes. She ushered Niamh from the room and, introductions made, she sat.

'What's the matter?'

She closed her eyes briefly. 'The midwife, Mrs Miller, was called to McGurk's place at noon. Teresa was due in November. She was hit by a truncheon today and the child started to come early. They lost it. A boy. And Teresa lost a lot of blood. They had to get Dr Maguire. He's over there now. Martin's all bruised and bloody himself, but they say he's like a madman, crying one minute then screaming murder the next.'

'Dear God have mercy,' the priest whispered and blessed himself. 'I better get over there before Martin does anything rash. But listen, I must speak to everyone tonight, in the church. Especially now. It's five,' he said, consulting his pocket watch. 'Let's say in four hours. I need you to rouse all your neighbours once again, everyone with a concern in this, in fact. You come an hour early, Owen.'

'What's this about, Father?'

'It's about Boycott, of course.'

***

Thomas returned soon after the priest and Redpath departed – they had encountered one another on the road and exchanged greetings loaded with curiosity.

They were all gathered around the table eating a meal of potatoes and turnips. Owen was pouring from a jug of water when he saw Thomas. There were 'hellos' all round.

'Uncle Thomas,' Tadhg smiled.

'Tadhg.'

'We weren't sure if you'd be eating with us, but there's plenty,' Síomha said.

'Sit beside me,' Niamh said enthusiastically, shuffling up the bench that extended along the gable wall.

'Are you sure? 'Cause I can get food beyond in Conway's.'

'We wouldn't hear of it. One of our family eating in a pub like a stranger!' Síomha fetched another plate.

He squeezed awkwardly in beside Niamh and found a disproportionate share of the food heaped on his plate. 'No, no, Síomha, you're depriving your own.'

'It's all right, I've not got an appetite anyway.'

'How did you get that big scar, Uncle Thomas?' Niamh asked, her directness sharply altering the trajectory of the conversation.

Síomha and Owen rounded on her in harmony. 'Niamh! That's bold! You know you're not to ask things like that!'

Thomas laughed. Niamh was abashed, her head hung low. Tadhg was agog in the hope of an answer, as the scar hinted at far-off adventure.

'Ha! Thank God for the innocence of children. If we were all so honest, the world would be a better place.'

'Amen to that,' Síomha smiled.

Thomas inclined his head to the child to afford her the best view of the unnatural trough that ran contrary to the lines of his face. Its surface was hardened and dark.

'Run your finger down it.'

Niamh's eyes widened as though she'd been granted the Tooth Fairy's wish.

The tip of her index finger could almost fit into the groove as she traced a path from his forehead, jumping the hollow of his eye, down his cheek, all the way to his lip.

'Got it in the American Civil War. But there were so many casualties that day that the surgeon only had enough catgut to stitch the really bad wounds.'

'You fought in the American Civil War?' Tadhg asked, fascinated.

'That's enough, everyone. Let Thomas be. There'll be time enough to hear all his tales. Right now we're eating.'

Tadhg and Niamh frowned at their mother and resumed forking the food into their mouths, eyes frequently drifting to their uncle, an action not lost on Owen.

'So how did you spend your day, Thomas?' Síomha inquired.

'Oh, after all the excitement of this morning, I decided just to get to know the roads and fields round about. I think I upset someone though.'

'How so?'

'I wandered through some woods and a man with a shotgun told me to be off, that it was private property.'

'You must have crossed the estate. Probably met Boycott's gamekeeper.'

'Boycott. Your land agent? Not too popular by all accounts?' Thomas inquired, a mouthful of food hampering his speech.

'Up to a few years ago we had right of way across the estate and could gather windfall from the woods, so everyone had a supply of sticks for the winter,' Síomha explained.

Tadhg, eager to impress, took up the tale. 'Then Boycott brought in a load of rules, banning us from collecting wood, so now we have buy turf. And he also has fines for letting animals stray on to his land. And we're not allowed–'

'We get your point, son,' Owen interrupted.

'They never change, do they?' Thomas gestured with his fork. 'Landlords, I mean. It was just like this when we were Tadhg and Niamh's age. If they can find ways to swell your hardship, they will. And they can get away with it because the British government supports them. And it suits the British to keep us in poverty. Maybe they're going to try and wipe us out altogether again.'

There was a brief silence. The 'us' in Thomas's little polemic wasn't lost on Owen. Curious, he thought, as his brother had spent three decades half a world away from Ireland and her politics.

'Thomas, talking of landlords, there's a meeting in Neale tonight about Boycott. Maybe you'd like to come along, hear what Fr O'Malley – that's our priest – has to say.'

Thomas washed the last of his food down with a mouthful of water. 'Maybe another time, Owen. I was planning to visit that man I mentioned. There's a chance of some honest work.'

'Oh, who's that?' Síomha inquired.

'Just the brother of an Irishman I met in New York. Down Cong way. Told me to look up him up if I needed work.'

'What kind of work?' Owen asked.

He shrugged. 'Not sure. I know he has a store and some land. But I've done pretty much everything these past years. So I'm sure I'll be up to it.'

'Cong? That's five miles,' Síomha said.

'Ah it's only a short step.'

She looked at Owen, who nodded a little reluctantly.

'You take Anu and the trap. Sure we're only going up the road to Neale.'

'No, I couldn't ask.'

'You're not asking, brother, we've giving,' Owen said.

Thomas smiled and clapped Owen on the shoulder.

'You're just too good, brother.'

***

Boycott suspected something was amiss the moment he laid his foot on the first step of Lough Mask House. A broad trail of what appeared to be dung tarnished the stone. He pushed open the door and saw that the filth stained the width of the hallway floor.

He looked over his shoulder. 'What the devil?' he muttered to Weekes, who displayed a growing apprehension.

They hurried to the drawing room, easily following the trail and their noses. Within, they were met by the sight of Sergeant Murtagh and three constables, along with David Sears. Annie sat by an open window but rose immediately upon her husband's appearance.

'What in blazes is going on?' Boycott demanded in his usual forthright tone as he whipped off his army-style pith helmet.

Murtagh stepped forward and Boycott and Weekes were struck by the fact that his uniform was barely visible beneath a layer of horse dung. The others were in a similar condition. The smell in the room was near to overpowering.

'I'm afraid that we were subject to…an attack…by the locals and succeeded in serving only three of the notices.'

Boycott was – and it was a rare moment to observe – utterly speechless.

Weekes, incredulous, took up the inquiry. 'You were driven off by people throwing *horse manure*?'

'Hundreds of them!' Sears fumed.

'Now, sir, there weren't hundreds,' the sergeant cautioned.

'Look at the state of me!' Sears stood and turned to Boycott. 'I only have one suit for work. I expect to be fully compensated for this...this humiliation.'

At the suggestion of expense, Boycott found his voice. 'You'll get no such thing! It is you who should compensate me. Look at the state of my house! You and how many? Seventeen? Seventeen constables are incapable of serving notices on a few illiterate country louts! What sort of idiots are you?'

Murtagh's teeth were grinding as he strode to Boycott, who recoiled a little at the heightened intensity of the smell. 'Sir, how dare you insult me and my men when we've endured this on your behalf. Short of beating women with truncheons, we were powerless.'

'Use your damn truncheons then!'

'Charles! Language!'

Boycott swung his eyes about the room as if searching for something or someone to strike, fists clenched in rage.

'Calm yourself, old boy,' Weekes said, laying a hand on Boycott's shoulder, which was shrugged off.

'Listen to me, Sergeant, Sears. The Ballinrobe Quarter Sessions are approaching faster than a bolting horse. If the notices are not served before that, they will become legally invalid. So far you have only served three, was it? That leaves eight. At the current rate it will be November before you've finished.'

'I'm not serving another notice without more protection! The army or someone,' Sears yelled.

'You damn coward, it's only a bit of dung! May the Lord forbid you'll ever have to face bullets or the thrust of a sword!'

Weekes, who was aware that his friend had never actually faced either of these menaces, stepped forward to try to calm the situation. 'Charles. I don't think it's merited to brand the man a coward. He is merely a public official who would not usually be subject to this form of intimidation.'

Boycott locked his hands behind his back and strode across the room towards Annie.

'Charles, why not sit down and agree–' she began.

He swung away from her as though she were an inanimate object he'd encountered and she was cut sharply to silence.

'Murtagh, how many men can you muster?' he barked.

'Maybe ten more if I telegraph some of the other towns round about. Maybe twenty. Plus the men from today. That would be almost forty men. But the other sergeants and inspectors aren't going to be happy. They have districts to police. We have to ensure the rule of law everywhere in Mayo, not just here.'

'Frankly, I don't give a fig about the rest of Mayo. We're not talking about catching a couple of illicit stills or poachers here. This is a coordinated and planned attempt to interfere with Her Majesty's laws and I expect – no – I *demand* that you show these peasants that they are not above the law.'

'Sir, you're not in a posit–' the sergeant began.

Boycott ignored him. 'Sears, you hear that? Forty armed constables. Now, I will thank you all to get out of my house and take that stink with you.'

'Two replacement constables will remain overnight in the hut outside for the security of your good self, Mrs Boycott,' snarled the sergeant, pointedly indicating that he cared not a whit about anything that might befall Captain Boycott himself.

With that the five men stomped from the room and Annie and Weekes flinched at the reverberation as the front door was slammed in fury.

'What's wrong with these people?' Boycott mused.

'Frankly, Charles, your attitude swells the ranks of your enemies with each passing day. It's a wonder anyone is still standing by your side.' Annie Boycott's outburst was as unexpected as her departure, which was also accompanied by the rattling of a door in its frame.

'What in God's name is wrong with that woman? She would serve herself better to have those maids clean this mess. I honestly don't know why we pay these girls. It's an Irish thing, Weekes. They make entire careers from the avoidance of work, you know? Well, we'll show them tomorrow, by God. Tomorrow.'

***

When the church of St John the Baptised and Calvary in Neale had been built by the men of the parish, Owen included, they had envisaged a church that might accommodate a hundred or so. There were surely at least twice that number present this night, the women crammed uncomfortably into the pews, the men and youths lining the aisles and squeezed into doorways and recesses. Almost everyone from Neale was present and, thanks to the efforts of travellers on the road to Ballinrobe and the broader area, word had quickly spread that Fr O'Malley wished to address the tenants and traders about the issue of landlordism and the Land League. Within the crowd Owen could identify shopkeepers and tavern owners and even Ballinrobe's barber, men and women who recognised that the issue of landlordism had resonances far beyond the just treatment of those who actually worked the Mayo earth.

Owen stood by the wall near the altar now, Tadhg at his shoulder. Niamh had been left in a neighbour's care and Síomha was seated in the front pew. The priest had set three wooden chairs facing the central aisle.

Fr O'Malley and James Redpath appeared through the rectory doorway and walked towards the chairs. The priest genuflected before the altar, an act that discombobulated the American. The priest then beckoned to Owen. Head bent low, Owen walked across before the countless watching eyes.

'What is it, Father?'

'What are you doing, standing to the side? I need you here to explain the plan.'

The blood drained from Owen's face at the prospect of addressing such a multitude. 'Father, I assumed *you'd* do that. I don't know anything about speeches. And they've more respect for their priest than the likes of me.'

'Nonsense. Now, will you take your seat like a good man before they get bored and decide to go across to Conway's pub?'

Before Owen could protest further, the priest had turned away to Redpath. Owen glanced at the field of glinting, expectant eyes, then sat and stared at the floor. Fr O'Malley took a step forward, the sight of his rotund bulk and flowing black vestments before the altar promoting a descending hush. He had decided not to speak from the lectern: while he hoped this meeting had God's blessing, it was not intended as a sermon. He clasped his hands together and closed his eyes in prayer for the briefest moment, then looked at the assemblage.

'Tonight I speak to you not as your priest, but as your friend and neighbour. Indeed, it heartens me that I see here not only the faces of Catholics but several also of the Protestant faith.'

This prompted a number of glances over shoulders. The priest continued in his baritone voice, his companionable Mayo accent reverberating from the stone walls, the effect lending *gravitas* to the words.

'And that is precisely as it should be, for our troubles are not the preserve of Catholics but the concern of all on this island. It is not a question of Catholic Irish against Protestant English, as some would seek to argue and use to raise rebellion and cast us into violence. Some of the worst landlords are not only Catholic but Irish. And many tenants exploited by landlords are of the Protestant faith. Remember that. Our true enemy is landlordism and the political system that supports it. Our true enemy is injustice.'

He paused and allowed his eyes to wander across the sea of faces. A pocket of silence had been trapped within the cavern of the church, undisturbed by the shifting air and whispering trees that lay beyond the walls. The audience were rapt, expectant, eyes and ears wide.

'I ask you now to interrupt your thoughts about Captain Boycott and his ilk and to turn them to the tragedy that has befallen our community. As many of you know, Teresa McGurk, the young wife of Martin, lost her child this morning. Teresa still lies gravely ill and Martin is distraught with grief. I want to ask everyone here to make a small, personal prayer to God that Teresa will recover and perhaps in the years ahead come to the joy of bearing another child.'

He bowed his head and as one the audience followed his lead. A minute elapsed. Fr O'Malley raised his eyes again and inhaled deeply.

'Sadly, that tragedy came about, indirectly, through violence. And when we employ violence, it inevitably propagates *more* violence.'

He unexpectedly clapped his hands together sharply, causing a number of the crowd to visibly jump and Owen to raise his head.

'You hear that?' he whispered, his head inclined, hand cupped around his ear. 'Listen.' He repeated the action and the audience listened as the handclap echoed back and forth around the walls until it was finally soaked into the fabric of the building.

'Just as that sound echoes from these walls, every act of violence echoes back tenfold. And each of those echoes begets another bloody act, but unlike the echo here, they do not fade away but become so many and so deafening we must clasp our hands upon our ears in desperation for peace.

'There are some here tonight who believe that the gun is the way to freedom, that the violent actions of the British Government in the past and the landlords' callousness give us the right to reply in kind. Yet here we are, seven hundred years since the English began their oppression of Ireland and countless bloody battles later. Here we are. Where has all the blood that was spilled by those courageous men brought us?

'But other Irish men of even *greater* courage recognised the futility of violence. Why is their courage greater, you may ask? Because they cast aside the gun and the sword yet stood before an enemy of overwhelming numbers with just their belief in the unquenchable spirit of our race. It is only through the Liberator himself, Daniel O'Connell's peaceful, yet powerful enterprise, that Catholics are today free to practise their faith and to seek high office and political representation. Yet not a single shot was fired on O'Connell's behalf, nor a single mother left to mourn the loss of a son.'

A pew creaked on the stone floor. A single, muted cough sounded.

'In Mr Parnell and Mr Davitt we can perhaps achieve even more. They do not advocate violence. They advocate another approach on which Owen here will elaborate later. But I tell you this. That our only weapons will be the strength in our own hearts to endure, and the force of our community acting as one.'

The priest's voice had lifted now, buoyed up with emotion, impassioned and swollen with pride.

'And if we stand firm, I promise you we can bring about the beginning of the end of landlordism, not just here, but in *all* of Ireland!'

Fr O'Malley raised his arms in appeal. 'People of Mayo, I ask you, I *implore* you, to stand together as one and let us show the world how the voices of a few in this small place can raise such a tumult, such a cry for justice, *that it will echo to the very ends of the earth*!'

Owen watched in wonder as the crowd raised a cheer to crack the eardrums. The women rose from their seats applauding. The men, their arms upraised above their heads, cheered themselves to hoarseness. Fr O'Malley sat, clasped his hands and bowed his head in prayer.

With the cacophony abating, he rose again.

'But how will we achieve our goal? Beside me are two of my closest friends. Owen, many of you know. Please stand up, James.'

Redpath rose and smiled, the audience attentive to the mystery of the debonair gentleman. 'This is Mr James Redpath, who is a correspondent with *The New York Herald*.'

The rarity of so exotic a guest prompted a whirl of excited chatter.

'Mr Redpath has a deep understanding of our cause and through his good offices as a correspondent, the world will be watching us. We must endeavour to make sure, by every action we take in the weeks ahead, that the world sees us in a favourable light.'

Redpath then spoke about the power of the press and how it had helped sway opinions on manifold issues in his home country. But Owen heard little of it. Since the moment he realised he would have to address the crowd, his guts had been churning. He had no notion of what he might say and was convinced that the entire effort would falter on his weakness of character. He found he could not even meet Síomha's eyes and she sitting only yards away. He would make as big a fool of himself as any man ever had in history and tales would be told in pubs for years about his oratorical inadequacy and the blundering confusion of the scheme he'd devised to outfox Boycott. He silently cursed the priest. And then he felt Fr O'Malley's hand on his shoulder and knew the moment he'd been dreading was upon him. Even now, he felt like fleeing into the night and the comfort of his home.

'Ladies and gentlemen of the parish and beyond. I'm a priest, as you know, and Mr Redpath a newspaperman, but I'm going to turn now to someone who understands better than either of us what it is like to live under the evils of landlordism; a tenant farmer himself. Please welcome Mr Owen Joyce.'

There was mild applause as he rose, pausing to fix Fr O'Malley with a raging stare, but the priest only smiled and gestured towards the audience. His innards quivered as though he'd swallowed a nest of ants and, unsure what to do with his trembling hands, he first placed them in his pockets, then removed them and hooked them into his belt. Finally he joined them together in front of his waist.

'I've…eh…not em…had a chance…' he coughed. 'I've not had...eh...an opportunity–'

'Speak up, Owen!' a voice called from somewhere.

He tried to lift his quivering voice.

'I said I haven't had the chance to prepare anything.'

Pleased to have summoned a single, coherent sentence, he glanced at Síomha. She beamed with such pride he felt a lump rising in his throat, though whether in terror of shaming her or because of a renewed determination to succeed, he knew not.

'I'm not a great man for speeches. I leave speeches to men like Fr O'Malley and Mr Parnell,' he said to the silent, seemingly critical gaze of the throng.

'In fact, the only speeches made in my home are by my wife when I've had too much poteen.' There was a general outburst of laughter and he glanced again at Síomha, who repaid him with an encouraging smile.

'So I'm not going to make a speech. All I'm going to do is tell you how we'll defeat Captain Boycott.'

A cheer rose at the prospect and Owen began to find a reserve of confidence he had no idea he possessed.

'And what we will do, in a sense, is *nothing.*'

He studied the puzzlement on the faces.

'We will have nothing to do with Boycott, his family or his friends. He sees us as idle peasants that he could well do without. Well, let's see how well he can do without *us*. From tomorrow we will deny him everything – labour, food, post, our skills, everything! No baker will bake him bread, no dairy will supply his butter. No blacksmith will forge his horseshoes and no farrier will fit them. No post will be carried to his house and no butcher will sell him meat.' Owen looked again at the faces. Some smiled, others conferred secretly and with excitement. They were beginning to understand the power they held in their own hands. He spotted some faces he recognised and began to point to them in turn.

'Mary Twomey – you will refuse him your eggs and cheese.'

He found another. 'Mr O'Flaherty. Your hardware shop won't sell him a pot or a hammer. Not even a nail. Mr Johnson, deny him even a crumb of your bread. Mrs Murphy, if Annie Boycott comes looking for a hat, refuse her!'

Mrs Murphy, a thin woman around sixty, briefly rose and retorted, 'I'll eat me own hats before I serve her!'

There was a mixture of laughter and supportive applause.

'As Fr O'Malley has said much better than I can, we must stand together. There must be no weak link, for if even one of us deals with Boycott the other links will weaken and the chain will snap.'

A general outburst of eager chatter ensued as the people of Neale and Ballinrobe exchanged notions of the parts they might play in the unfolding drama. Owen turned towards the priest and Redpath, the latter furiously scribbling, the former nodding approval. He raised his arms for quiet. His inner terror had long been forgotten, miraculously reborn as a passion to elucidate upon their scheme.

'But we must do more than all this. Most important of all we must deny Boycott the ability to run his estate. He employs almost twenty people – maids, stable hands, gamekeepers and most especially the men who labour in his fields. We're fortunate that this situation has befallen us at harvest. Most of Boycott's income comes from his crops. If he cannot get his crops in he will be facing bankruptcy, like we are. I say we give him a flavour of how that prospect feels!'

There was a cheer at the notion of retribution.

'So we must convince his cook to abandon his kitchen, his maids to abandon his rooms, his ostlers to abandon his horses and his labourers to abandon his fields. We must convince all of them to abandon Boycott!'

The applause resumed but he tried to calm them with his palms held high.

'But we must not use threats of harm, which would be tantamount to violence itself. Nobody will raise a hand to Boycott's workers. Remember, these are our brothers and sisters. We will talk to them, persuade them by our numbers and our unity that it will be to their longterm benefit to leave their posts. We are asking them to surrender their earnings, and to relieve this situation, Fr O'Malley will take a collection on Sunday to support those at a loss. We can't pay their wages, but we can help put food on their tables. We all live in impoverished times but we hope you will donate anything you can. Every donation will be a small payment towards Ireland's freedom.'

Nods of approval and goodwill ensued.

'Tomorrow, the process-server will return and Fr O'Malley has learnt that maybe thirty or forty constables will accompany him. So we must ask you once again to gather here tomorrow morning at nine. From here we will walk to Lough Mask House and begin.'

A lone voice rose from the rear. Owen recognised Francis O'Monaghan, who farmed the island opposite Boycott's home. 'Owen! Can ye hear me back here?'

'I can, Francis. What's your question?'

O'Monaghan, a short, wiry man of middle age, stood in a side aisle nervously twisting his cap. 'We all know what happened today. They served three eviction notices. How do we stop them tomorrow if we're all at Boycott's house?'

'Good question. As you all know, Boycott uses the letter of the law to keep us down. Well, we're going to do precisely the same. We're going to stop him from serving the notices not with manure, but with the letter of the law.'

'How, in the name of God?'

'Everyone listen. Here's what I want you to do.'

***

At that precise moment, in a cottage six miles to the south-west, in the townland of Kilbeg, just half a mile from the spot where many years before Tim Connor had saved Owen from the lough, Thomas raised a glass of whiskey and drank it in a single gulp. He then pulled out a packet of Allen & Ginter American cigarettes and lit one from the candle flame.

Two other men shared the table. One was Cal Feeney, a sympathiser to the cause of armed Fenian rebellion. The other was Donal Doherty.

'Maybe they hope te drive the entire English army out by throwing shit at them,' Thomas said.

Doherty sat grim-faced.

'The gobshites. Throwin' shit won't sort Boycott,' Feeney snickered.

Thomas didn't like Feeney. He seemed dim-witted, and Thomas didn't like working with dim-witted men when his life might depend on it.

'We'll get to Boycott soon enough,' Doherty said. 'Did you reconnoitre the area?'

Thomas nodded. 'I did. Had a good look around. And I'd already had a word with a tenant who's a sympathiser. Martin McGurk. I told him te stand his ground if they tried that eviction shite. He did, by all accounts. And now he's rightly primed te help us.'

'I'm looking forward to puttin' a bullet in that fuckin' English bastard,' Feeney said. Slightly drunk, he was almost drooling at the prospect.

The other men exchanged a look of apprehension. Thomas stubbed out his cigarette directly onto the table.

'Anyway, Boycott will have to wait his turn,' said Doherty.

'Why?' Feeney asked.

Doherty lifted a Colt revolver from his pack and placed it softly on the table, then looked into Thomas's face.

'Because we've bigger fish to fry.'

CHAPTER 18

Meanwhile the people at the Neale assembled. There is a priest there greatly beloved of the people, a man of resolute character and highly educated and although he is naturally conservative, he has unbounded influence over every member of his congregation, from the fact that he neither tolerates outrages by his parishioners on landlords, nor outrages on them by the landlords. He addressed the meeting, praised them for asserting their rights, but urged them, if the constables should come again in force, to offer no resistance.

–*Talks about Ireland*, James Redpath

While Mr Sears, the process-server, was waiting for a stronger constabulary escort to arrive a curious scene was enacted. As if by one sudden impulse, the vast throng rushed towards Lough Mask House.

–*The Connaught Telegraph*, 24 September 1880

23 September 1880

Owen came awake to the sound of a horse he knew was not Anu. When he looked out towards the pen, he saw a fine black mare grazing near to his ageing workhorse. Síomha followed him into the living room, where they found Thomas stirring a pot of porridge over a fire of blazing turf. The sun had just risen and the room was a cavern of shadows.

'I thought it's about time I started earning my keep,' he smiled at them.

'Who owns the horse?'

'Oh, yeah, that friend in Cong gave me a loan of it. Gave me some work too.'

Owen raised his eyebrows. 'Nice friend. Fine animal,' he said with a hint of scepticism.

'Oh it's only a loan. Te get back and forth.'

'You found work?' Síomha asked.

'Loading sacks in a storehouse, that sort of thing. I did Cal's brother a few favours in New York so he feels in debt a bit. I've te go back on Saturday, maybe stay in Cong a week. But he might have something permanent soon. I'll be out from under your feet before you know it.'

'You're welcome to stay as long as you like,' Owen said.

Over breakfast Thomas offered to help with the harvest, but Owen was keen to have him absent if the police arrived, knowing his brother's distaste for the RIC. So he struck on the idea, now that Thomas was mobile, of asking him to ride into Ballinrobe for supplies. He also couldn't shake a nagging suspicion that there was something off-kilter about his brother's tale of storeroom work. But maybe it was his imagination.

***

Sergeant Murtagh sat at the front of a coach normally used for the conveyance of prisoners, which had been loaned by a sympathetic sergeant in Claremorris. Progress was slow due to the weight of men crammed in the canvas-tented body of the vehicle, causing the wheels to sink deep into the rain-sodden road.

Within the coach, twelve constables and David Sears jostled uncomfortably for buttock space. Behind them three more vehicles followed, carrying thirty-seven men in total. They would deposit the vehicles in the grounds of

Lough Mask House before they began, principally for security reasons but also because the sergeant felt obligated to call on Boycott and expound upon the effort that was being made on his behalf.

He halted the vehicles at the crossroads a few hundred yards before the village of Neale. The road to their right led directly to Lough Mask House and he ordered the trailing vehicles to wait at the spot while his coach made a detour into the village. There had been a minor exodus from Ballinrobe the previous evening and he'd heard word of a meeting organised by Fr O'Malley. He was anxious to discover the nature of the gathering and to forestall any repeat of yesterday's undignified travesty.

Although he'd been in south Mayo for years and knew most people hereabouts by name, most of them were at best suspicious of him, a state of affairs he felt to be most unjust. He hadn't been born in the area, but hailed from Clare. Given the light in which many Irish people viewed the RIC, to wit an extension of the occupying English army, constables were all assigned to places remote from their home as it was believed their own kin might view them as doubly traitorous. And yet he considered himself a patriot. He supported Home Rule, as he believed the English had as little an understanding of the cultural and historical mindset of the average Irishman as he had of the workings of his pocket watch. But try telling the locals he was a patriot and he'd be laughed out of town. These past months the situation had deteriorated to such a degree that he could barely go for a drink without provoking silence on entering a bar. And, almost exclusively, it was down to Charles Boycott. If only the man could display the smallest button of charity or understanding of his tenants' plight, things might not have swelled to bursting point.

But he was there to see the law was upheld, and it wasn't at the citizen's behest to choose to follow only the laws that suited him. Unfortunately, as it stood, Boycott had the law on his side, which effectively put the RIC also on his side, a situation the sergeant found detestable. His dislike for the land agent had grown at a rate disproportionate to the brief time of their acquaintance.

The road curved to the right, bringing the body of the village into view – a lean body at that, a scant collection of cottages, a small grocer's shop, Conway's pub, and, at the far end on the left, the largest structure, the Catholic church. The village was quiet, he thought, even for such a tiny backwater. A couple of tots sat playing with sticks and chestnuts outside a cottage, their bare feet blackened enough to give the passing glance the impression of shoes. Behind the window of another home sat a young woman he knew by the name of

Mary McHugh, dress off her shoulder and an infant at her breast. She held his look as he rolled by, unperturbed by any sense of modesty. He drew near to the church where the priest stood chatting to two old women, their faces shadowed in the hoods of black shawls. He had the driver halt and jumped down.

'Father,' he tipped the front of his cap. 'Could I have a word?'

The women exchanged a whisper and walked away in a huddle.

'What can I do for you?'

'Well, Father. I heard word you held a meeting here last night. Tensions are running high right now and I was wondering if it had anything to do with the eviction notices or the Land League.'

'Hmm,' the priest muttered, clasping his hands before him. 'You are aware that I have every right to hold a meeting about the Land League if I wish, Sergeant. Thanks to the likes of Daniel O'Connell, the British were forced to concede us that at least.'

Murtagh's frustration became evident in his rising tones. 'Look, Father, I'm trying to avoid bloodshed if I can.'

'Well, I appreciate your good intentions. And as a matter of fact I did hold a meeting last night, and I give you my word as a priest that I spoke in the strongest terms on the subject of violence and urged everyone there to avoid bloodshed at all costs. So I wouldn't concern yourself too much on that account, Sergeant.'

The policeman's shoulders relaxed. 'Thank you, Father. I'm very relieved to hear that. Good day to you, then.'

Murtagh climbed back on to the coach, which rattled back the way it had come. When it was out of sight, Fr O'Malley walked to the church door and pounded his fist three times. The doors swung open and the hundred people within quietly spilled out and spread about the grounds. Owen and Redpath walked across to the priest.

'Thank God Mary McHugh warned us he was coming or it could have spoiled the whole party. What possessed him to come into the village?' Owen wondered.

Fr O'Malley shrugged. 'The man seems to think that I'm planning something.'

Redpath looked around at the crowd. 'Whatever possessed him of that idea?'

***

Boycott met the train of coaches fifty yards inside the estate's gate. He was mounted on Duke and in his shadow rode Asheton Weekes.

'Captain Boycott. We're on our way to serve the remaining notices. You should know that through the efforts of many officers, we have managed to raise almost fort…'

'Well, what are you waiting for? Get the hell on with it!' Boycott snapped and whirled his horse away. He and Weekes were moving into the trees before the sergeant had a chance to respond.

'Christ, I swear I'll kill that man!' Murtagh hissed through his teeth.

He climbed down and cupped his hands around his mouth.

'All right! Everybody down and into formation. Sharp as you can, lads. Let's get this bloody job over and done with once and for all.'

***

'I meant to say, Owen, when I was visiting you yesterday I passed a man on the track to your cottage and there was something vaguely familiar about him,' Fr O'Malley said casually as the crowd lingered around the church.

Owen chuckled. 'That would be my brother, Thomas.'

The priest was startled. 'Your brother? I never even knew you had a brother!'

Owen gave the clergyman a brief résumé of his brother's reappearance after thirty-odd years in America.

'Well, I look forward to getting to know him.'

'Yes, Father. Me too,' Owen replied, unable to dispel the niggling doubts about his brother that were proliferating inside him like woodworm in a crossbeam.

The priest studied him a moment, but decided not to pursue it. He turned to the church where Tadhg had scaled to the apex of the entrance passageway, about fifteen feet above them. The youth shook his head. He began to fidget.

***

The thirty-seven constables, the sergeant, and David Sears marched northwards past the homes they'd visited the previous day. Fearful of another trap, Murtagh had decided to serve Fitzmorris last. They continued for another hundred yards towards a farm on Lough Mask's shore.

'What's this tenant's name?'

Sears, praying the Sunday suit he wore would remain untarnished, produced a sheet of paper.

'Joyce.'

***

Artists and the like regarded the landscape south of Ballinrobe towards Neale as generally uninteresting. The absence of hills or craggy rock faces deprive it of the wild starkness offered by the Partry or Sheffrey Hills on Lough Mask's western shore, or the Maumturks in Galway, whose steep boulder-strewn mountains entrap a multitude of mountain loughs and are beloved of poets and captured in countless oils. In fact, the area around Lough Mask Estate undulates only in spots and these high points rise a mere twenty or thirty yards towards the sky. The advantage that this presented for Fr O'Malley was that much of the area could be viewed from a relatively low elevation, such as the church's entrance apex, where Tadhg now sat, eyes fixed on the west.

A man drew up on a trap and alighted. His suit was respectable enough, if a little worn. He approached the priest, Owen and Redpath.

'Father, may I ask what's going on?'

'Who would you be?'

He stuck out his hand. 'McCabe. With *The Connaught Telegraph*. I was told there was some incident regarding eviction notices yesterday and…'

They were interrupted by a yell from above.

'Father!' Tadhg was pointing. 'The flag!'

His view revealed Luke Fitzmorris atop the rise near his cottage, waving the improvised flag.

'That's it! Everyone! Now!'

The crowd cheered and as one made an energetic stride towards Boycott's home. The sudden exodus astonished McCabe, and as Redpath moved by him he paused in a moment of professional camaraderie.

'I'll say one thing for you, McCabe. Your timing is perfect.'

***

The body of constables strode down the gentle incline of the lane towards Owen Joyce's cottage. Sergeant Murtagh was disturbed by the complete absence of people, although the men might have elected to absent themselves again. But women and youths old enough to work were also nowhere to be seen. It was as though the land had been swept clean of humanity by some virulent plague. He began to feel the certainty that they would be waylaid at some point, but had determined that if there was a repeat of yesterday's incident, truncheons would be drawn and arrests made. The policemen reached the Joyce cottage and turned into the yard. A lone man sat on the water trough to the right of the doorway, which was open wide. Murtagh sent a handful of men to scout around the immediate area and set the rest facing the cottage. He took a few steps towards the balding, middle-aged man, who looked vaguely familiar. The individual was smiling contentedly, a sprig of hay between his lips.

'Who are you? What are you doing here?' Murtagh asked.

'I might ask the same of you.'

Murtagh frowned. 'We're escorting Mr Sears here, as he is required to serve notice of eviction on Owen Joyce. Is he here?'

'No.'

'Where is he?'

The man shrugged.

'I know you,' Murtagh said.

'And I know you. At least I know yer head.'

'What in Christ's name are you blathering about?'

'Can't say I'm impressed with your powers of observation, you being a policeman an' all. I've cut yer hair maybe three times this year. Turlough Curran. That'd be of Curran's Barbershop, Ballinrobe. Sixpence a haircut, tuppence for boys under twelve.'

The sergeant tried to suppress his irritation. 'Where is Owen Joyce?'

'Owen had business te attend to elsewhere and I'm looking after his place, te make sure the law is adhered to, and so on.'

'I've had enough of this.' The sergeant called out towards the open door. 'Joyce! Owen Joyce! If you're present you are required by law to accept a notice of eviction.'

Nothing stirred. The barber sat idly, arms folded comfortably across his chest.

Murtagh turned to the others. 'Right. You are all witnesses to the fact that we tried to serve Joyce in person. Sears, attach the notice to the door and let's move on.'

The constables moved aside to allow Sears through their ranks. He fixed a nervous eye on the barber as he fumbled with the notice. He stepped through the cottage entrance to pin the notice to the in-swinging door. He stopped and appeared befuddled, then turned and faced the opposite direction, then looked back the other way again. Finally he kicked the doorframe in frustration and stepped out into the light, a high colour rising to his cheeks, lip quivering.

'There's no fucking door!'

***

The moment the constabulary had departed Lough Mask Estate, a boy of twelve had sprinted ahead to inform Luke Fitzmorris. It mattered little which cottage they chose to serve first; the eight cottiers under threat had that morning removed their front doors and eight witnesses were assigned to make sure the constabulary followed their own rules. Luke Fitzmorris had immediately hastened to the rise and signalled with the flag. It took Fr O'Malley and his followers thirty minutes to reach the estate, by which time Sergeant Murtagh had abandoned his attempt to serve Owen Joyce and was marching towards the next tenant on the list, unaware that he would find that premises also devoid of a tenant and his front door. By the time the hundred spirited residents of Neale marched through Boycott's front gates, the constabulary were two miles away.

A few hundred yards ahead, the open land disappeared under towering woodland. They passed the abandoned police vehicles and then a man appeared at the point where the track curved into the trees. He was about sixty, squat and pot-bellied, and Owen recognised him as Boycott's gamekeeper. He wore well-exercised tweeds and a deerstalker hat with the flaps tied up, and carried a breeched shotgun across the crook of his arm.

'Mary Mother of God, what's this?' he uttered in bewilderment at the throng who had disturbed the estate's serenity.

The priest stopped, Owen and Redpath to either side, and the crowd spread out behind them as though taking formation for battle.

'I'm Father O'Malley, Parish Priest of Neale.'

'Heard your name. From Clonbur meself. What's goin' on, Father?'

'Mr...?'

'Mick Lavery.'

'Mr Lavery. These people would like you to leave Captain Boycott's employment at once.'

'What?'

'Do you consider yourself a patriot, Mr Lavery?'

The man lifted his chin. 'I'm every inch a patriot, Father, me own father fought...'

'Then in the name of Ireland and justice we're asking you to leave your post.'

'But how in the name of God will me leavin' me job help Ireland's cause?'

There was a bit of a rumpus behind as Joe Gaughan pushed his way through.

'Hello, Mick.'

Lavery nodded. 'Joe. What's this business about at all? I just keep foxes at bay, watch for poachers and the like.'

'Mick, Boycott served me eviction notice yesterday. And his henchmen roughed up McGurk and his wife lost their child. In a few weeks, me and me family are out on our arses without a roof over our heads. That's unless we make Boycott change his mind.'

'But why do I have te...?'

'The Land League is ostracising Boycott. He'll have no labour, no staff – he won't even be able to buy a loaf of bread for ten miles.'

Owen leaned in. 'The same goes for anyone who works for him.'

It took a few moments before the implications dawned on the man. 'Ye mean I won't be able...' He ran a leathery hand across his chin. 'Doesn't look like I've much choice, does it?'

'It's up to you, Mr Lavery,' Fr O'Malley said.

'Well, Mick?' Joe asked.

He heaved a sigh. 'Ah sure, he's a cantankerous oul' bastard anyway.' He nodded, albeit reluctantly, and a small triumphal cheer rose from the crowd, their first battle won.

As Joe walked away with Lavery, Owen turned to the priest. 'We can't do this one by one. It'll take all day. The police will be back soon enough.'

'You're right. We'll have to split up.'

'I'll take the labourers. I know a couple of them.'

The priest nodded. 'Leave the house to me.'

Luke Fitzmorris stepped up. 'The head stableman is a friend of mine. If Paddy leaves, the others will follow.'

Owen shouted to the crowd. 'Anyone who knows Boycott's farmhands, come with me.'

The priest looked at Owen as he mustered his troops and grinned at the change that had come about in him. Just a short time ago the man had been torn and uncertain, fearful of grasping the possibilities of his own potential. Now he was fully cognisant of not only his destination but also the road that would take him there. He'd thrown Owen in at the deep end of the lough and he'd come up swimming like a fish.

Síomha stepped up to her husband. 'I'll go with Father O'Malley. I know Maggie, their housemaid. You be careful.'

Owen smiled, then turned and left the path, heading along the line of the trees to the open farmland on the estate. About thirty of the crowd followed. The priest beckoned the remainder on.

McCabe, the man from *The Connaught Telegraph,* trotted up alongside them, a little breathless. 'Father, what's going on?'

'Captain Boycott likes to exercise his so-called rights to evict people from their homes. We're exercising our right to evict Boycott from society.'

* * *

The twenty or so labourers were spread across a number of fields. Half of them were cutting Boycott's twenty acres of corn, some of which lay in sheaves about the ground waiting for collection in a hand cart. The rest were divided in twos and threes across eight acres of turnips, two of potatoes and seven of mangoldwurzel. The men in the cornfield, who were the nearest, lowered their scythes and began to murmur nervously among each other at the sight of the crowd tramping across the cut stems. Adhering to the principle of safety in numbers, they hurried to each other's company and, by the time Owen and his band had reached them, were standing in a tight group.

Owen recognised a man he knew only in passing as Martin Branigan, a tough but honest character. Branigan was a broad-chested man of forty with unkempt black hair, and he wore a defensive scowl. The labourers had grouped themselves loosely behind him.

'Hello, lads,' Owen called out. 'One or two of you know me and you all know one of those with me. Most of us are Boycott's tenants and you probably know that Boycott is planning to evict us. You also know that Boycott's been overcharging on the rent for years so we can never give ourselves a decent life. It's the same all over the country. Landlords have their foot on our necks while their henchmen steal the money we've earned through our own sweat.'

'What's yer point, Joyce? We don't need a history lesson,' Branigan asked, his scythe clasped in front of him.

Owen moved to within a couple of yards of the man. 'It's got to stop, that's the point. Starting today. We want you to drop your tools and abandon Boycott. Leave his harvest to rot in the fields unless he agrees to lower rents.'

Branigan stepped closer. 'Give up our jobs? Ye'll need more than your mob here, Joyce, te make me walk away. How am I supposed te live?'

Owen hadn't expected this to be easy, but if he wasn't careful Branigan might be the one rock in the field to break the plough. He looked at the faces of the labourers, their ranks swelling as more hurried over from the adjoining fields. The crowd behind Owen looked uncertain, their faith in the enterprise wilting a little. He didn't want to coerce the labourers with the threat of ostracising them. He wanted to persuade them. A handcart stood nearby, half-filled with cut corn. He took a couple of strides to it and jumped up.

'Branigan's right. Yes, you'll lose your jobs. But there are many of us who stand to lose much more than that. If Boycott continues to do as he pleases we're not only going to lose our livelihoods but our homes. I've a family. Boycott's going to evict us with the winter coming. The same for Matt O'Toole there, he's got a young wife. And Francis Cusack. You've four children, right, Francis? Two of them only knee-height.'

'That's right,' shouted Cusack. 'I raised me family in that cottage. Been there twenty years. Boycott's been bleeding me dry since the day he set foot here.'

One of the other labourers spoke up now. 'Yeah, but you still have crops ye can sell. We have nothin' but the pay Boycott gives us.'

'And if you remember the reason you have the pay you deserve is that Father O'Malley stood behind you and encouraged you to strike in August.' He pointed towards Lough Mask House. 'Right now, Father O'Malley is up at the house standing up for everyone in this country to get what's theirs by right. And he's also organising a fund to help any man or woman who loses their job.'

'Hey, Joyce!' Branigan shouted and appeared like a dog set back on its haunches, ready to pounce. 'What'll ye do if we say no?'

Cusack pushed his way to the front. 'Branigan doesn't speak for all ye, does he?' There was a murmur of approval from the crowd and one of the older women pointed to a young labourer.

'Mick Burke! I see ye there! Yer mother would be ashamed of ye for standing with Boycott if she were alive!'

There were a few other comments of a similar nature and a few sharp rejoinders from the labourers. It was beginning to get out of hand. Owen thrust his hands in the air and shouted above them all.

'Listen! We're not going to force anyone to leave.' He looked down at Branigan. 'And Branigan, I'm for sure not going to force you, because first, I wouldn't stand a chance if I tried, and second, you're your own man. Nobody tells you what to do. Fair enough. But let me ask you this? How old are you? Forty? Forty-five? You're old enough to remember the famine and so are most of the rest of you. And you younger men, you've heard what it was like. I lost two sisters, a brother, and my mother and father. There isn't a man or woman here who hasn't a similar story. We watched the people we loved wither away and die while the landlords exported the food to feed the English and to feed their own greed. Not content with that, they threw us from our homes without pity. They robbed us of our dignity. And they're still doing it. At this very moment Boycott has his man out serving eviction notices. How many more years will we let them walk us into the earth? How many more years will we let them profit from our sweat? Sooner or later we have to draw a line! If you won't do this for us or for Father O'Malley, then do it in the memory of the ones you loved and who were left to rot in the famine by these same landlords.'

He stopped, suddenly aware that he'd been shouting, and lowered the arm that pointed towards Boycott's house. Silence reigned, and he turned and stepped off the cart. He stood there between the crowd and the labourers, caught in a moment of uncertainty. He turned as Branigan walked across and stood face to face with him. The labourer met Owen's eyes for a few seconds, then abruptly flung his scythe to the ground, turned, and began to walk through the crowd and out of the field.

* * *

Boycott and Weekes stood by Lough Mask's shore about a mile from the house, their view of the estate interrupted by woodland.

'This is where Lavery caught that man wandering?' Boycott asked.

'It was.'

'Poacher most likely. Plenty of game in the woods.'

Weekes seemed sceptical. 'He had no traps or other accoutrements.'

'A Fenian scoundrel, you mean?'

'Remember the threats.'

Boycott nodded. 'Threats or no threats, I'll see those rents paid or the defaulters out.'

A prolonged cheer carrying across the tops of the trees startled them both.

'What the devil was that?'

Weekes shook his head. 'It came from the fields.' He turned his ear towards the house. 'Listen. What's that?'

Boycott stood perfectly still and realised he could hear raised voices coming from the direction of his home.

'It sounds like some sort of commotion,' Weekes offered.

Within seconds both men were galloping towards the woods.

***

The crowd swarmed about the grounds in search of anyone in Boycott's employ. Fr O'Malley, Redpath, Síomha and ten others climbed the steps to the house and rapped on the door. McCabe, the newspaperman, stood fascinated as the drama played out, his notebook bearing testimony to the events which would soon be read by half the households in Connaught.

A smartly dressed lad of about twelve opened the door. He seemed alarmed but adopted his bravest face.

'What do you want?'

'Young man, I wish to speak to Captain Boycott.'

'Who are all these people? What do...'

'William! Come away from the door!'

Fr O'Malley raised his eyes from the boy to see Annie Boycott sweeping along the hall in a fine, multi-pleated blue dress. She threw a protective arm around William.

'Aunt Annie, there are strangers running all about the place.'

'What on earth is this? What's going on, Father?'

'I'm afraid I need to speak to your servants urgently, Mrs Boycott.'

'Our servants? What business can you have with our servants? Has someone died?' The alarm in her voice was evident.

He shook his head. 'No, but I need to see them immediately.'

'You cannot. You'll have to wait for my husband. And when he gets here there will be hell itself to pay for this outrageous intrusion. William, quickly, go upstairs to your sister and stay there.'

'But, Aunt...'

'Now!'

The boy turned and fled. Annie went to close the door, but Fr O'Malley stuck his foot against its base and to her stupefaction, began to force it open. She stepped back with her mouth open, unable to comprehend that those considered their subordinates were forcing their way across her threshold.

'How dare you! Get out of my home!'

'I'm sorry, Mrs Boycott. I bear you no personal malice. But we've been left with no alternative.'

The group streamed inside and began to call out to the servants. Síomha met Annie Boycott's eyes, unable to deny a sense of pity for the woman, despite the depredations her husband had brought upon the tenants. Entering into one's home by force was a violation she herself would rage against, but it was unavoidable. She lowered her gaze and moved on.

'I'm warning you, when Charles returns he'll have all of you flogged!'

Fr O'Malley moved past her and down the steps to the basement as quickly as his bulk would permit, wanting this over and done with. It went against his nature to force his will on anyone and he was regretful that Mrs Boycott was an unintended victim, especially as he knew her to be a good-natured woman who was cursed by a loyalty to her husband and the societal respectabilities of her position.

On entering the kitchen he saw Maggie Cusack, the housemaid, and stout Mrs Loughlin, the cook, a simple woman in her sixties. Two of his recruits were remonstrating loudly with them.

'Father! This man and woman say we've te leave!' Maggie spluttered tearfully.

'An' what about me bit o' cookin', Father?' Mrs Loughlin croaked.

Mrs Loughlin had only been with the Boycott household a year or two, he knew. Maggie, a plain girl in her mid-twenties, had been there years and was probably almost part of the family by now, in a master-pet manner at least. His heart struggled with the weight of what he must ask them to do.

'There's just three servants, they told us, Father,' the man said, a shopkeeper from Ballinrobe. 'There's a chargirl upstairs.'

He nodded, placed a hand on Maggie's shoulder, and addressed her and the cook in a compassionate voice. 'Maggie, Mrs Loughlin, I know what I'm asking. But I'll do everything I can to help you find other positions.'

'But why are ye ostra…ostr...'

'Ostracising.'

'Why are ye ostracising Mrs Annie and William and Madeleine? They've done nothing wrong!' Maggie cried.

'I'm sorry, child. They're unfortunate victims. And you will be too if you stay. Nobody will have anything to do with you. You've must leave for your own good.'

She heaved a sob. 'I know the Captain is rude and shouts at us, but Mrs Annie and the others have always been good te me!'

'Maggie, dear. You'll have no life if you stay. No one in town will speak to you. Not even your brother. You'll be shunned in the streets, the shops, even at mass. Now go and get your things and help Mrs Loughlin with hers. Go on, child.'

The maid ran away, sobbing.

'What's to become of us all?' Mrs Loughlin sniffed, shaking her head.

Fr O'Malley inwardly begged God's forgiveness. His confidence in their strategy had been unshakeable, but he realised now that distance had numbed him to the realities, the way a general moves pieces about on a board, uncaring about the horror a slight movement of his hand will bring in the field of battle. He thought then that it was an apt comparison, for it reminded him that at least in this war, no blood would be shed.

He returned to the entrance hall to find Annie Boycott still remonstrating with Redpath and some tenants, her voice almost strained to hoarseness. Síomha walked by with her arm about an uncomprehending young chargirl's shoulders.

Owen arrived, exchanged looks with Síomha, then moved to the priest. 'The labourers are gone. And the herdsmen. And Luke says the same about the stables. Only horses there now.'

'Good. That's good news.'

Escorted by the locals, Maggie and Mrs Loughlin came up the stairs, coats covering their uniforms. Maggie was inconsolable. She suddenly broke free and threw her hand out to Annie Boycott, who grasped it tightly in both of hers.

'Oh I'm sorry, Mrs Annie, ye've always been kind te me. Please say goodbye te little William and Madeleine.'

'I will Maggie, I will.'

Maggie pulled away and left with the rest, a handkerchief pressed against her streaming nose. Annie Boycott rounded on the priest.

'I hope you're happy! How could you do this to the poor thing? What's to become of her now? And Mrs Loughlin? You should be ashamed, a man of the cloth!'

The priest's voice was subdued. 'I'd no wish it would come to this, Mrs Boycott. But we've been left with no choice. Goodbye.'

At precisely that moment Boycott stormed through the doorway, his face incandescent with outrage. 'What the blazes is going on?' he hollered.

Annie rushed to him and grasped his arm. 'They've made everyone leave, Charles. The servants, the labourers, the stablemen. Everyone.'

Boycott turned to Fr O'Malley. 'How dare you enter my home, you popish idolator!' He glanced sideways towards Owen. 'You and your peasant filth! How dare you interfere with my workers! I'll make you sorry you ever set eyes on me!'

Fr O'Malley took a step towards him. 'I'm already at that point, Captain Boycott,' he said calmly and went to depart.

'I'll horsewhip you, you Catholic parasite!'

Boycott swung his riding crop above his head but the priest was surprisingly sharp and grasped Boycott's descending arm. He came nose to nose with the agent, his mellow aspect replaced, Owen saw, with fury.

'Horsewhipping is just what I'd expect from you, Boycott. A horse can't hit you back,' he spat out, and Owen was shocked to see the priest's rising right hand clenched into a fist. He seized Fr O'Malley by both arms and pulled him towards the doorway. He led him past a startled, breathless Asheton Weekes and joined the departing insurgents as they walked, cheering wildly, towards the exit, a verbal stream of Boycott's contempt washing past their ears.

'We did it! Let's see how Boycott does without his "idle peasants",' Owen said.

But Fr O'Malley appeared distracted, gazing absently into the distance.

'Are you all right, Father?'

After some seconds the priest replied, meditatively: 'Woe unto you, scribes and Pharisees, hypocrites...for ye shall receive the greater damnation.'

'Father?'

'God forgive me, Owen, I was going to strike him.'

Owen didn't reply.

They followed the track through the trees, animated with the triumphant locals. Maggie's sobbing was the only discordant note, her face a mess of tears.

'I pray to God we've done the right thing,' Fr O'Malley said.

***

A celebration of their initial success might have seemed appropriate, but the demands of their lives meant it would need to be put in abeyance and, to a man and woman, the people of Ballinrobe and Neale dispersed across the roads and fields to resume their daily toil.

Fr O'Malley and Redpath returned to the church, where the American would reside as a guest for the duration of whatever transpired over the coming weeks. The correspondent adopted the priest's living room as his temporary office, setting about expanding on his notes as he sought to give life to that morning's drama for his readers. The priest spent an hour in contemplative prayer, kneeling alone among the silent, empty pews that just the previous evening had rattled with the certainty of their righteousness.

Upon their return, Owen, Síomha and Tadhg were all surprised to see Thomas at work alone in the fields, steering Anu through the furrows.

'You've been busy,' Owen said, clambering over the wall.

Thomas pulled the animal to a stop and wiped his brow.

'Ye've been busy yourself. I came back te find a barber minding the cottage and the front door missing! He told me what was going on. Any particular reason ye didn't want me around?'

Owen decided a measure of truthfulness was called for. 'To be honest, Thomas, I knew the RIC would be here and I know you've no liking for them.'

Thomas nodded and half-smiled. 'Can't deny that. They don't seem much different from the police thugs in Pennsylvania.'

Owen picked up a spading fork. 'Anyway, I see you haven't forgotten how to use a plough. You might be good for something, after all!'

Thomas grinned and playfully threw a small potato at his brother, which Owen batted away with the fork.

'Good for something? Watch and learn, brother,' Thomas said, grasping the plough's handles. 'Ye can follow behind and do the woman's work.'

Owen laughed as Thomas began to shove the implement across the black Mayo earth.

***

Much to the bewilderment of the constables and Sears, Sergeant Murtagh exploded into laughter upon seeing that the second cottage they visited that morning was also missing its door, simply unable to contain his mirth at the manner in which they'd been outfoxed. They had visited a third cottage but he'd known the outcome even before the building came within sight. So he abandoned their mission and decided to return to tell Boycott the bad news.

As they passed cheering locals on the road, he became increasingly concerned that some violence had befallen Boycott and hastened their pace. The inactivity of the estate brought him near to panic. But, to his immense relief, he found Boycott, his wife and Weekes unmolested. He dispatched Sears back to Ballinrobe under escort, his continuing presence pointless.

'I want O'Malley arrested, and Joyce, and the rest of the mob,' Boycott thundered, stomping around the drawing room, outraged at the incursion and smarting at the manner in which he'd been outmanoeuvred.

'Arrest them for what, sir?'

'Trespass, of course!'

'Sir, I cannot arrest over a hundred people.'

'Arrest the ringleaders.'

'Captain, as I understand it, no damage was done, nothing stolen or no persons harmed. I'm afraid they will claim they simply came here to speak to certain employees and then left peaceably.'

Weekes, who stood leaning against the huge, teak mantle, shook his head. 'Surely it is illegal to coerce employees to abandon their work?'

'Can you prove coercion took place? Besides, given the isolation in which you find yourself, I would rather put my mind to your family's safety and make arrangements for a larger body of men to remain here in case more violent nationalists decide to take advantage of the situation.'

Annie, who sat near to the fire, a glass of brandy in her trembling hand, lifted her head at the mention of danger. 'That never occurred to me. I would be grateful for anything you might do to protect my nephew and niece.'

Boycott was silently pacing the floor, as though fuming within like a sealed pot brought to boil. He finally paused to pour himself a measure of spirits.

'Priests and peasants,' he muttered.

Annie fixed him with a vexed stare. 'Well, Charles, it seems the ignorant peasants aren't quite so ignorant, after all.'

He stared at her and for an instant Murtagh believed the man might strike his wife. Boycott hurled the brandy glass into the hearth, where it shattered and produced a short-lived fireball, causing Annie to emit a startled yelp. He then stormed from the room and the house.

'I'll arrange for huts for the constables. You'll be perfectly safe, Mrs Boycott,' Murtagh said to ease the tension.

'Thank you, Sergeant, I would appreciate that,' Annie said with as much poise as she could muster, although her voice trembled like a poplar in the wind.

***

Thanks to Thomas's admirable industry, Owen managed to make up all the harvest time that had been lost through the Boycott business, and during the course of the day he related the morning's events and explained their strategy to his brother.

'I hope it works,' Thomas said as they entered the cottage. 'I'm sceptical, I have te admit. And even if it gets a reduction in rents it won't get rid of the landlords forever. But anyway, I'm growing tired of talking politics.'

'Amen,' Owen said. 'Now, let's eat.'

The evening was convivial and pleasant, spent swapping anecdotes of the missing years, both in Ireland and America. It was a fitting end to the day when they had finally found a tool that might leverage them some small movement against the colossal mass of the landlords' power. By the time they said their goodnights, Owen had even begun to feel that his niggling suspicions about his brother might be flights of his own imagination.

With Thomas asleep in the next room, he and Síomha made love with as much silence as their intimacies would allow. And then he easily drifted to sleep, for tomorrow was another day. And their work was really just beginning.

***

As Owen fell to sleep with hope in his heart, Thomas lay awake staring into the darkness, his thoughts on the futility of his brother's efforts and on his own mission two nights hence, an action that would resound along the corridors of London's political establishment a thousand times louder than the ostracism of an obscure land agent. Boycott's name would be forgotten inside a week, but he'd give them cause to remember the name of Thomas Joyce for generations.

***

'I'm bothered about a word,' Redpath said.

Fr O'Malley shifted his gaze from the burning turf to the correspondent. His mood had lightened as the evening had progressed; his unease at the housemaid's distress and his lapse of control when confronted by Boycott had abated under the force of the American's enthusiasm for the strategy they'd unloosed. Redpath had spent the day composing a lengthy article on the affair, which he hoped might soon be published in *The New York Herald* and *The Chicago Inter Ocean*, both of which had large Irish readerships.

'I'm sorry, James, I was a mile away.'

'I said I'm bothered about a word.'

'What is it?'

'Well, when the people ostracise a land-grabber we call it social excommunication, but we ought to have an entirely different word to signify ostracism of a landlord or an agent like Boycott. Ostracism won't do. Many of my readers and even the peasantry would not know its meaning and I can't think of any other.'

'No, ostracism won't do.' The priest began to tap his forehead as though attempting to knock loose a notion that was trapped in a corner of his mind. Eventually he shrugged.

'How would it do to call it "to *boycott* him"?'

'To boycott,' Redpath mused. 'Of course, right before my eyes. Tell your people to call it "boycotting" when the reporters come. I'm going to Dublin, and I'll ask the young orators of the League to give it that name too. And I'll use it in my correspondence with the American press.' He smiled in satisfaction. 'Father, I think the English language just expanded by one word.'

'Let's pray it's a word that has some meaning.'

Chapter 19

Les gais irlandais ont inventé un nouveau mot, ils dissent a present 'boycotter' quelqu'un, cela signifie le mettre en interdit.

–*Le Figaro*, November 1880

[The bright Irish have invented a new word, they are currently saying to 'boycott' somebody, meaning to ostracise him.]

24 SEPTEMBER 1880

Charles Boycott had known some form of isolation all his life. He'd grown up in the rectory of St Mary's Church in Burgh St Peter in Norfolk, his home largely surrounded by inhospitable marshlands, and the church itself was at some remove from its flock, most of whom lived in the village two miles to the east. Not that any of the natural seclusion had troubled him terribly. As a child he'd always been sententious and taciturn, preferring from an early age the company of horses. His family had lived in considerable comfort and their grounds had included extensive stables, a pottery workshop and a large bakery. So the place was usually a bustle, with workmen and women, maids and servants adding constant voice to the murmurs of the countryside. Yet he'd rarely interacted with them or with the commonality round about.

His father, William, had charted a pattern of behaviour for all his children concerning dealings with staff. He addressed all males by their surname, without even the bother of a 'Mr' to assign them some status. The females he was constrained by convention to address as 'Mrs' or 'Miss', although he generally avoided female company as one might avoid a man brought low with fever. Yells of 'illiterate wastrel', 'cretin' and 'ignorant oaf' frequently echoed around the rectory's outbuildings as the man made his inspections. The staff would be branded pilferers and riff-raff, the result of ill-breeding and immoderate and immoral living. Once, a senior baker, nettled at the implication that he'd stolen a loaf, had dared to take issue with the rector. William Boycott, in full view of Charles, had taken a rod to the man and driven him from the bakery and from his job.

Charles began to view this behaviour as normal, and by the time he was seven he had already taken to addressing men fifty years his senior as 'Jarvis' and 'Pilcher' or just plain 'You'.

In 1848, at the age of sixteen, Charles had his first true awareness of Ireland as a place existing in reality. He'd barely touched upon the subject in his historical studies, which had consisted of a few lectures about the glory of England's armies bringing a civilising hand into their backward culture. But in the context of the British Empire, it was an insignificant little island off Her Majesty's west coast. Then, in his sixteenth year, a man had called seeking donations for the relief of a famine that had sprung up there. He recalled the man had been English, well-dressed, of good breeding, a member of the British Relief Organisation, and had been invited in and served tea and biscuits while he made his case. His father had listened patiently before informing the man that he would serve his nation more surely should he devote his energies to raising funds for the propagation of the faith. The man's passionate appeal to William Boycott's softer side revealed only that he had none; the blight was God's retribution for pursuing a heathen faith at the behest of an anti-Christ in Rome. The man could take himself off, as could the Irish, a race of ungovernable sloths if ever there was one.

As the years had progressed, unfortunately Charles's studies hadn't. A more disciplined approach to his education was demanded and it would be found in the confines of first Woolwich and then Blackheath boarding schools, both nestling in the leafy countryside to the east of London. But at Woolwich, Charles soon found himself even more isolated. In adulthood he would only grow to a squat and thickset five feet eight inches, and as a boy his shortness was even more marked. And marked he was, for the bullies were soon ducking him in the pond and emptying inkwells into his pockets. His uncommunicative nature and poor scholastic record had him characterised in the teachers' eyes as given to idleness, resulting in frequent beatings at their hands. He took to spending his days in silence, a swelling bitterness within, imagining ghastly endings for his oppressors. His rare communications with other students consisted of muttering abuse in their direction. Depression overwhelmed him. Through his mother's petitions his father had allowed him to move to Blackheath Proprietary School, where much the same pattern ensued, most of his classmates regarding him as something of a country fool. The school was famed for its academic achievement and virtually all its graduating pupils were up to the measure of Oxford or Cambridge. But Charles fell well short of the demands of England's famed institutions of learning and contented himself with a very modest completion of his education. Besides a basic understanding of the principles of commerce, Charles' principal acquisition from Blackheath was his abusive tongue; he rarely had a good word for anyone.

On his return to Lough Mask House on that September day in 1880 to witness an invasion of peasants, every nuance and consequence of his upbringing and temperament had surged to the surface. The notion of a horde of Irish Catholic peons stomping about his house, defying him, daring to act above their station, railed against every fibre of his being. He deeply hated the Land League, but until then it had all been somewhat notional and far away. This was different. This was personal. And the rage that it evoked in him kept him tossing in his bed long into the night.

But one thought had steeled his resolve. He had never in his life depended on others. Not once. He had spent much of his childhood alone, and as an adult had first elected to dwell in the wilds of Achill Island and now in the relative isolation of Lough Mask House. Solitude was a part of his being. And by God he'd show the priest and his ruffians just how much isolation he could take.

***

He came awake with a start in the darkness and for a moment struggled to recognise where he was. He'd been dreaming of his childhood home, elements and characters of which had blended disconcertingly with his life in Ireland. His father had been commending his attitude as they'd stood inside a bloodstained room in the village of Dooagh on Achill. Annie sat in a corner, sobbing into both hands. He'd stormed out and mounted his horse, Ironsides, an animal from his childhood, and begun riding hard, his intended destination Lough Mask House.

The memory of the dream melted away as the reality of his situation dawned. He was deathly tired, having spent the day milking their six cows, then feeding the beef cattle and horses and carrying out innumerable other tasks. He and Weekes had ended the day filthy. He had resolved to teach the others how to do these jobs for he could not succeed in doing everything himself – though, if need be, he would die trying.

The high-pitched cry of an animal pierced the morning stillness and he realised that it was a distressed cow in need of milking.

'Damn it all.'

He heard Annie's sleepy voice through the dark. 'Charles, what's wrong?'

He hesitated before replying. Her suggestion that he bore some responsibility for their predicament had irked him greatly. But if they were under siege, he couldn't commence battling with those trapped within the walls.

'Four-thirty. The cows need milking again.'

'Now?'

'Yes. And everyone must learn how to do this so that we can share the tasks.'

He exited the room. Annie moaned in exasperation and fell back on to the pillow.

***

When Annie awoke two hours later she had to quickly use the chamber pot, her need making her forego the comfort of the downstairs lavatory. The previous evening, she had struggled so long to prepare food in the kitchen's stifling heat that she'd had to consume large volumes of water or she would surely have fainted. Charles wasn't the only one discommoded by their situation. And not even a day had passed.

She dressed quickly and hurried below, struck at once by the quiet. Usually the place echoed to the sound of Maggie humming as she went about her duties and the crash of pots from Mrs Loughlin's kitchen. She stopped in the hall and listened. No voices carried from the stables or fields, no horse hooves trotted past outside, no farm implement clanged in the distance. She sighed and went below to the kitchen again.

How long did one boil an egg? How much tea was added to the pot? Where was the bread? And the milk? The previous evening, in attempting to cook a joint of beef, she had put too much wood in the stove and burned the meat's exterior, its middle still running red with blood. Madeleine and William had picked at the undercooked beef and the overcooked mush of vegetables, and kindly Mr Weekes had declared it just as he liked it, but Charles had pushed it away, stating that he had no appetite. For so long she'd taken for granted the food produced with such regularity by Mrs Loughlin, considering hers the meagre skills of a peasant. But what countless tips and tricks had she taken with her when she'd been coerced into leaving?

Annie fell into a chair and shook her head at the sight of the pots and plates from the previous evening stacked high in the washing bowl. Sore and weary, she had abandoned all and retired to her bed, but saw the folly of that now. Unless she adapted quickly to the continuous cycle of cooking, washing and other household chores, she would fail her husband and the others.

Or, she wondered, had her husband failed them?

***

'What is this?'

'Porridge.'

'Where are my eggs? And toast?'

'I tried to boil them, but I burned my hand and spilled the pot on the floor.'

'You expect us to work a farm all day eating peasant food?'

'It's the best I could manage.'

'If we're to get through this, your best must become better.'

Annie took the bowl from under his nose and casually threw it on the dining room floor where it shattered into an unseemly mess. Boycott looked like he had been slapped across the face. The others sat in shocked silence as Annie helped herself to a serving of porridge from the dish.

'Have you lost your mind, woman?'

'No, but I imagine it won't be long before I'm committed to the lunatics' ward,' she said between defiant spoonfuls of bland porridge. 'Actually, this house already resembles a madhouse!'

'Madeleine, William! Leave us now!' Boycott barked.

'No!' Annie almost screamed. 'This concerns everybody!'

'Now hear me, woman, I have a responsibility to the Earl of Erne and to Her Majesty's Government to see that these seditious rebels do not succeed. By God, there's a principle of gargantuan proportions at stake here, don't you understand?'

'You and your principles! In all of this you have forgotten your chief principle and chief responsibility!'

'What are you talking about?'

'Your responsibility to your family and your friend, you stubborn fool! Asheton there, whose loyalty stays his tongue even though it's evident you compound your troubles every time you exercise yours. Madeleine and William, who would double their efforts to help if you only once paused and granted them a kind word. And I, who have borne years of your wilful pigheadedness and tried my level best to please, beyond any notion of wifely responsibility. And now you expect me to work as a charlady, maidservant, milkmaid and cook and to master all these things overnight. And worse, you expect all of this but also to bear your insults about my failings. How dare you! You are an insensitive brute, Charles Boycott, and unless you change your attitude this moment, you may as well hold your hands up to the priest in surrender, because we refuse to lift a finger further to help you!'

None of them had ever heard Annie speak to her husband in that manner. In truth, they had never heard anyone speak to him so. Weekes stared at the ceiling. The younger folk sat with their eyes fixed firmly on their laps. In her anger, Annie resumed eating her porridge sloppily.

Boycott appeared traumatised. His face displayed the shock of one startled by tragic news. The colour had faded from his cheeks and his mouth was set in a circle, a dark hollow amid the fuzz of his facial hair. Some time drifted by in the taut silence. Finally he rose and took a few steps away, his back to them, both hands still gripping his spoon tightly. A thousand venomous retorts stalled behind his lips. His gut prickled with nervous indignation. Yet his next words would determine the course of this thing, not just his relationship with his wife, but the entire conflict. In his heart he knew there was some truth in her diatribe. In the army, it had been common practice among his fellow officers to occasionally praise their men, thus encouraging them to excel in the future, although he had usually been parsimonious in even that. He forced himself to about-face and dropped the spoon on the table, realising as he did, that he had bent it almost at a right angle. Everyone looked up. Annie sat back, head held high and turned slightly away from him.

'This is difficult for me to say.'

A lingering silence ensued, so prolonged as to suggest it was so difficult, in fact, that he could not actually bring himself to say it.

He sighed slowly and lowered his head. 'I…I…wish to apologise. Especially…especially to my wife. To you, my dear. In my rage, I have been sightless. Instead of directing my anger at our enemies, I have trained my guns upon my allies. I hope you can forgive me. That is all.'

He sat. Annie rose calmly and set another bowl before him. She filled the ladle with porridge, which was by now cold and congealed.

'Would you like some, dear?'

He nodded and she dropped a solid lump of the porridge in his bowl with an unpleasant plop.

And so passed breakfast in Lough Mask House on the first day of what, although they were unaware of it at that time, would be known ever after by the name of the man at the head of the table. The first boycott had begun in earnest.

***

Tadhg passed his morning digging a pit three feet deep, twenty long and four wide near the cottage. The weather had turned damp, with fine droplets specking his face, soaking the heavy material of his jacket and hampering his progress

'Storage pit?'

He looked up to see his uncle standing on the rim of the pit.

'For the turnips and potatoes.'

Thomas picked up another shovel and jumped down beside him.

'I'll finish this end.'

'Thanks, Uncle Thomas.'

Tadhg was impressed at the rate at which Thomas shifted the sticky earth. For a man of fifty he was an impressive workhorse.

'You've dug pits before, Uncle?'

'I have. Earth. Coal. *Gold*. I'm well used to digging. Sure, when me and your father were your age we had to do the same. Three feet deep, ferns along the bottom. Pile the spuds to a peak,' he made a mountain shape with his hands, 'then cover them with more ferns, pile the earth on top and beat the soil so tight it would smother a worm.'

Tadhg nodded, impressed. 'How do you remember so well?'

'I remember everything about those times. *Everything*.'

They fell to silence for a time before resuming their toil.

'Of course, our farm was only the size of me arse and not half as productive.'

Tadhg laughed, then paused in reflection. 'My dad doesn't talk about the famine much but sometimes I think he's remembering things, y'know? I see him stopped, looking away at nothing when we're working in the fields.'

'Your father's always been a deep thinker, Tadhg.'

Thomas heaved the remaining few shovelfuls from his end and stepped out, taking a deep, relieving breath. Tadhg paused, resting on his shovel, his eyes wandering aimlessly over the field. At length he looked up.

'D'ye think what we're doing to Boycott will work, Uncle?'

Thomas considered the question a time.

'I've found that people like Boycott only respect you when you show them how strong you are. And how far you're prepared to go. These bastards only und–'

'Tadhg,' Owen's voice called out sharply from just ten yards away.

Tadhg jumped out of the pit. 'Yeah?'

'You've done a fine job. Now can you help your mother gather the ferns?'

'He's a grand worker, Owen. You should be proud of him.' Thomas clapped Tadhg on the shoulder.

Owen nodded. 'I am. And, Tadhg, when you come to stack the potatoes, make sure there's no bad ones among them before you cover–'

'I *know* that.'

'It's no harm reminding you. Just one rotten one could spoil the crop,' Owen said, glancing at his brother before turning away.

***

'Charles, you know, even if we start today, and with the best will in the world, I don't believe we're going to be able to harvest forty acres of crops. I don't even know much about the work and the others are certainly unskilled in that regard.'

Boycott and Weekes were in the stables forking hay into the bays.

'What would you have me do? Submit? Not a peasant for twenty miles will work here. We *must* bring in the harvest ourselves!'

Although still delivered brusquely, Boycott's pronouncements had their sharper edges dulled since his wife's indictment at breakfast.

The task complete, Boycott threw his fork aside and turned to leave. 'I'm going to fetch William and Madeleine. We'll start with the potatoes and then I'll teach the girl how to milk a cow. You might learn yourself, for that matter.'

Weekes groaned inwardly, yet had to admire the man's seemingly tireless industry. They trooped from the yard towards the house, where they saw Annie descending the steps, her sleeves pulled to her elbows, her dress soiled from breast to feet by kitchen work. With growing alarm Boycott realised her hands were also soiled with blood.

'Annie, what's happened? Were you attacked?'

She shook her head dismissively. 'Of course not. Madeleine cut her finger slicing potatoes. It bled profusely and I've had to bandage it. Would Doctor Maguire look at it? Surely he is not part of this preposterous business?'

'I suspect all of these Irish ruffians are against us. She'll have to live with it, dear.'

'No, Charles. She can't!'

Sensing the rising pitch of her voice, he backed off.

'You're right. Weekes can fetch him.'

'There's something else. Mrs Loughlin used to go to Ballinrobe every Friday to stock up. All we have left are some porridge and tea. There's no beef or salted pork, not even bread. I must go to Ballinrobe and purchase supplies.'

'No, it's too dangerous,' Boycott said, shaking his head vigorously.

'I'll take a constable.'

'I could go also, Charles. We could be back in two hours,' Weekes offered, grateful for the opportunity to avoid clasping a cow's tit between his palms.

Boycott relented. 'Very well, but take two constables. That will leave six here. And be careful.'

'And, Charles, regarding the constables, they've decided to dig a latrine behind a hedge very close to the rear windows. The stench is appalling and they've only been here two days. They'll have to move it to a respectable distance.'

He responded only with an exasperated grunt, then walked away.

***

'At this rate the harvest could be in by mid-October, thanks to your help, Thomas.'

'Just earning my keep, Owen, but I'll need te earn a shilling or two meself as well. So I need te leave tomorrow for that job.'

Owen nodded as Thomas hefted an armful of potatoes onto the handcart.

'Eh, by the way, by chance I heard you talking about Boycott with Tadhg this morning. Mind if I ask what you said?'

Thomas shrugged. 'Nothing really. Just that I have me doubts about the plan.'

'And what would you do?'

'Haven't given it much thought. It's just that I've seen the power men like Boycott have. In the mines in America. And during the famine here. Ostracising them is like…well, it's like trying to knock down a house with a broom handle.'

'Well, we'll see, but I'd appreciate it if you didn't share your views with Tadhg. He's at an impressionable age and it's up to us – me and Síomha – to guide him.'

Thomas nodded. 'I'm sorry if I was out of line. I just thought that, well, as we both know from experience, it's better to learn the truth about the world.'

'In my experience, truth looks different from one man's eye to another.'

'Fair enough.'

As they continued their work Thomas turned the talk to tales of wondrous sights he'd seen in America – canyons wide and deep enough to hold an Irish mountain, birds the colour of a rainbow, trees the width of their cottage, and Owen became comfortable again in their banter. Despite his continued doubts, he could feel a growing affection for his brother. It was as though the bond between them, while stretched and strained over thousands of miles and decades of disparate experience, had remained unbroken.

'But listen to me, I'd talk a man to the grave. What I want to know is what happened to you after Westport. How did you survive?'

Owen wiped the rain and sweat from his brow. 'Do you really want to hear? It's nowhere near as dramatic as your story.'

'Jesus, I'm fascinated. I never thought you'd survive wi–' He checked himself.

Owen laughed. 'I know. You never thought I'd survive without you. To be honest, neither did I. And I almost didn't. I came this close,' he held his finger and thumb a hair's breadth apart, 'to dying at the side of the road.'

'Let's hear it.'

'You're a glutton for punishment. All right, then. After I jumped off the ship...'

***

The moment their landau passed through the main gates, Annie, Weekes and nineteen-year-old Madeleine saw a large group of schoolchildren gathered along the roadside ditch, who took up a chorus of catcalling for almost fifty yards. The mounted constables did their best to frighten them away, but with little effect. Annie, who sat in the rear of the landau with Madeleine, put an arm around her frightened niece.

Weekes, driving the vehicle, glanced over his shoulder. 'We'll be beyond them very soon.'

'Hey, Mrs Boycott!' a boy of about twelve called out.

When she glanced in his direction he promptly turned his back, bent over and pushed his pants to his ankles, much to the amusement of the others.

'Dear God,' Annie whispered. It occurred to her that surely at just two o'clock their school lessons were not finished. She felt a deep perturbation that Fr O'Malley might have inveigled children into his unchristian scheme to force her husband to submit.

The remainder of their journey was not without incident. Farmers working in fields turned their backs upon them. As they passed through a cluster of cottages and a group of mostly women and youths, it seemed they were about to be trapped in another gauntlet of abuse, but most of them just turned away in silent rejection. There were a few catcalls of: 'Go home, English bastards!' and one youth threw a clod of earth, striking Weekes on the shoulder. Annie observed that the boy's mother quickly struck him on the back of the head.

She was shocked that their station in life had been brought so low in the locals' eyes. Just a few short weeks ago, and despite the general disapprobation with which her husband was held, she would have been granted the courtesy and deference that their position of relative wealth and influence merited. And she had always repaid that behaviour with an equal measure of modesty and charity. Now, it seemed, they were to be treated with the contempt commonly doled out to society's lowest elements – criminals, debauchers of women or traitors. It all weighed heavily on her shoulders and she dreaded the thought of setting foot in Ballinrobe, where the abuse might be multiplied tenfold.

They turned into the town's main street, which was busy with the sounds of enterprise, horses and carts moving to and fro, piles of horse dung lying along the thoroughfare. Barrels stacked higher than two men sat outside a public house and a towering arrangement of pots and pans indicated the location of the hardware shop. Men and women loitered or strolled along the narrow paths on either side – workmen in soiled clothing, tradesmen offering their services as cobblers, farriers and the like, a few men in the more refined clothing of a clerk or bank teller. Only a few women were visible and almost without exception they were dressed shabbily in skirts that appeared moth-eaten, and wrapped in dark, coarse, woollen cardigans and shawls. She saw a single lady of quality and looked admiringly at her pale yellow dress, with a hooped, satin skirt, ruffled breast and clinging sleeves, topped with a lacy, feathered hat and white parasol. When Annie tried to make eye contact, the woman looked sharply away. Annie glanced down at her own dress, stained from her trials in the kitchen. Her hair also hung bedraggled from beneath her poorly chosen hat. She'd not had a minute to pay her own appearance any attention and was convinced she must look a fright.

As they moved along the street a cobbler spat into the hard-packed earth of the road and several others turned their backs on the landau. A small child pulled a wicked face and his mother scowled at Annie. An elderly man pointed first to a mound of steaming horse dung, then directly at them. Madeleine sobbed gently into her aunt's breast, and Annie pulled her niece closer and lifted her own head high in defiance.

Weekes pulled up outside the surgeon's premises. As they dismounted, a female voice called out from an upstairs window: 'Go back te England and take yer thieving husband with ye!'

They knocked loudly on the door while the constables took up positions to protect the carriage. A spindly, middle-aged woman answered and recoiled at sight of them.

'What do ye want?'

'Have you not a civil tongue in you? We wish to see Doctor Maguire,' Weekes blurted out angrily.

'I've no civility for your kind. He's not here!' And with that she slammed the door in their faces.

Annie's heart sank. Madeleine's finger was swollen and deeply discoloured, and she feared the girl might be inflicted with a poison of the blood.

'What are we to do, Asheton?'

They were about to leave when they heard raised voices from within and the door was pulled open again. Dr Maguire, a man of late middle age in dark pants and waistcoat, beckoned them inside.

'Contrary to what my hot-tempered housekeeper may have said, I believe denying medical attention to anyone would be sinful. Please come inside.'

'I wish you would express those feelings to Father O'Malley, Doctor.'

'Oh, there's no need for that. He specifically informed me that that was his wish. Not that I needed any encouragement. Now, what's the problem?'

***

Asheton Weekes left the doctor to his ministrations to begin purchasing supplies. As he walked along the pavement he had to endure continual catcalls and whistles, but to one who had dodged bullets and spears, they had little effect. He entered Corcoran's bakery and interrupted the gossip of two women and the proprietress, who fell to immediate silence.

'Excuse me. I would like six wheaten loaves please. And four of soda bread,' he said, consulting the list supplied by Annie.

The woman behind the flour-stained wooden counter exchanged a conspiratorial glance with the others.

'We've no bread today, sir.'

'What do you mean? This is a bakery, is it not?'

'The bread's all sold. Try Claremorris.'

'Claremorris? That's two hours' jour... What about all those loaves behind you?'

'That's all promised.'

'But surely you...' He paused and looked around at the cold, hostile faces.

'Could you please sell me a sack of flour?'

'We've no flour. And ye won't find flour anywhere in Ballinrobe. Not even the mill. Try elsewhere.'

He ground his teeth and thumped the counter in frustration before turning to the door, a final comment following him.

'Yes, go on. Try elsewhere, like England.'

He slammed the door behind him.

***

He had the same response at the mill, and again in the dairy and in O'Keefe's grocery. Fuming, he hurried back to the doctor's office where one of the constables was helping Madeleine, now sporting a heavily bandaged finger, on to the landau. Annie turned an anxious face towards him.

'Asheton, Doctor Maguire told me we're blacklisted!'

He knew her to be a resilient woman, but he could see her resolve weakened in the first, glistening hints of tears. 'He's right. None of the blighters would sell me a crumb. Blast that priest! They're calling it "boycotting", would you believe?'

'Asheton, take me to Kilkelly's immediately,' she said with determination.

They left Madeleine with the constables and hastened to Kilkelly's butchers. The store was empty of customers, but a tall, bearded man in a bloodstained apron manned the sloping counter display of meats.

'I'd like to purchase these cuts, if you please,' Annie said, proffering a list.

The man folded his arms across his ample chest. 'I've nothin' on your list.'

'What do you mean? There, salted pork. And there, that's corned beef.'

'I've nothin' for *you*, if you want me te spell it out.'

'How dare you! We've been customers of this shop for years. You will sell me what I want immediately, do you hear?'

The man slapped his hands on the top of the counter. 'It's past the time we take orders from your kind. Yer high an' mighty days of rulin' the roost in my country are near done. Now, get out of me shop!'

'How dare you speak to a lady in that fashion, you ignorant oaf!' Weekes stepped forward, intent on striking the man with the back of his hand.

'No, Asheton! Please, let's just leave!' she said as she pulled the infuriated Weekes from the store. Annie paused to collect herself outside. Her hands were visibly shaking and now a tear did run the length of her cheek.

'What are we to do, Asheton?'

Weekes noticed that the overhead sign indicated Kilkelly was a licensed victualler, an official supplier to the army.

'Come on. I've an idea.'

They remounted the landau and made their way back along Market Street to a cacophony of whistles so loud that Madeleine clasped her hands over her ears. By the time they reached the end of the street, Annie felt her humiliation was complete.

***

'Jesus, that's some story.'

During the previous two hours, the detail of Owen's survival during the famine had been unearthed once more, like the potatoes that were now piled high on the handcart.

'The workhouse sounds a bit like the ship,' Thomas reflected. 'There were two hundred and fifty passengers, fifty more than they were supposed te carry. Thirty died on the way and were just dumped overboard. We got half the rations we'd been promised. I got by because of the extra food I had. And half the ship had a fever when we docked. Christ knows how many of the poor bastards perished.'

'We both had to grow up fast.'

'But at least I had some money, you had nothing.'

Owen laughed. 'And I wasn't much of a thief either.'

'What do you mean?'

'Well, I only tried to steal oats from the English soldiers because you'd already done it. I thought I'd try the same.'

Thomas looked confused. 'I'd already done what?'

'Remember you stole the pig from the convoy? The meat that kept us alive?'

Thomas hesitated and then his eyes opened as though he could suddenly see through the fog of memory. 'Oh yeah. So tell me, what happened after the Connors rescued you from Lough Mask?'

Owen had the strangest feeling of deep remembrance just then, of something untold, but it was so vague and dulled by time he could not bring it into focus.

'Well, even when I'd recovered from the fever, Maebh or Tim wouldn't let me leave the farm for a month, until things had quieted. I would have gone insane but I persuaded Tim to go into Ballinrobe library and bring me some books.' Owen laughed at the memory.

'What's so funny?'

'They were simple but honest people. Maebh couldn't read, although I taught her later, and Tim was barely competent. And then one day he's asking the librarian for *King Lear* and *Oliver Twist*.'

'I've become a bit of a reader meself over the years.'

'*You* have?'

'Yeah. Me. The family fool.'

'I'm sorry, Thomas. I didn't mean–'

'Relax. You're right. Had no interest early on. Got it later, though. But not literature. Political books. Marx and such. Anyway, go on with your tale.'

'Marx, eh?' Owen reflected briefly, then continued, 'well, we agreed on a story that I was Tim's nephew from the west but I didn't go into Ballinrobe for nearly a year, by which time the whole workhouse incident had been forgotten; not starving to death was more on people's minds. The blight finally ended in '50 but it was still a struggle running Tim's farm. Though our landlords weren't the worst. Not like Boycott or most of the others. There were about ten tenants and a man called General Booth, who was the Duke of Wellington's secretary, no less, bought the estate. He wasn't so bad. Built a big house called Ebor Hall.'

'Ebor Hall?' Thomas asked and leaned against the field's gate.

'Hmm. His rents were low enough to allow us get by, but I was a burden on them. Then I met Síomha. We married in '57 and with the help of her dowry – her father had a pub in Clonbur – we took up this farm. We lost two babies at birth and then in '60 Lorcan came along. Tadhg in '63, then another stillbirth and we thought Síomha's childbearing days were past. Then Niamh surprised us all in '72.'

'What happened te Tim and Maebh? And their daughter, Muireann?'

'Muireann did well for herself. Became a teacher and then married one. Moved to Dublin. I still get the odd letter.' He heaved a sigh. 'Maebh drowned in Lough Mask in '64.' He threw a fleeting glance out across the water. 'Tim refused to come and live with us here. He wanted to spend the rest of his days on the farm that he'd shared with Maebh. I visited when I could and he lived alone a long time. Died three years ago.'

'I'm sorry.'

Owen waved it away. 'In the years before he died he was actually on friendly terms with the new landlord, Lord Mountmorres. Mountmorres used to drive back from his magistrate meetings in Clonbur drunk as a lord, so to speak. Tim picked him off the road more than a few times and brought him back to Ebor Hall.' Owen chuckled and shook his head. 'Mountmorres – a pillar of the British establishment – even sent a wreath to Tim's funeral. Tim would've had a good laugh at tha– Are you all right, Thomas? You look as white as a ghost.'

'*Me*? I'm fine. Go on.'

'That's it, really. The next significant thing that happened in my life was you turning up.'

Thomas laughed. 'Hardly significant. But it's good te be home,' he said, gazing reflectively back across the gentle slope of the field, the earth exposed and bare. 'It never leaves ye, ye know that?'

'What?'

'Ireland. Mayo. I spent a lot of time working dusty earth under a scorching sun thinking about the mucky soil in Mayo. I imagined when I left that it would fade away like the memory of some *cailín* ye had a *grá* for when ye were young. But it never did. Maybe it was because you'd stayed behind, I don't know. Or maybe we've all got Irish mud flowing in our veins.'

He laughed, but there was a sad, mournful note in his voice.

'Don't be getting sentimental on me, a hard oul' rock like you,' Owen joked.

'You're right. Cold as stone, I am. Cold as stone.'

***

A handful of children still lingered near Lough Mask Estate's entrance, their crude jeers providing a fitting footnote to the day's events. When they reached the house, Madeleine took to the steps like one pursued by wasps, desperate to banish the outside world. Annie plodded to the door, her despair weighing her down.

Young William asked after her and then ran excitedly to Weekes, who was lifting a wooden crate from the landau's luggage rack. William studied the stencilled writing: Her Majesty's Forces. Garrison rations.

'Do you think you could carry one of these, William?'

'What's in it, Mr Weekes?' the boy inquired as he lugged the crate erratically towards the house.

'The only food we could get. Canned beef and pea soup. Army rations. I cajoled an officer in the cavalry barracks to give it to us using my army ties. Though the blighter gave me a hard time of it. Said it was forbidden to supply civilians. It won't last long, but I suppose we have our own vegetables at least. Where is your uncle now, William?'

Before the boy could reply Boycott himself provided the answer, stomping up with a pitchfork in hand. 'Weekes! Where the blazes were you? Have you any idea how much work we have to do?'

'Yes, Charles,' Weekes muttered to himself. 'Far more, I think, than we can handle.'

CHAPTER 20

It was the anxious desire of the Land League executive to discourage all violence, except where an eviction for arrears of excessive rents might justify resistance. Beyond this the purpose of the League was seriously injured by serious agrarian crime. Deeds of violence, no matter how originating, would be credited by British papers to the teaching of the movement, and these would offer the government an excuse for a resort to coercion, and thus render difficult, if not impossible the work of thoroughly organizing the country. Perpetrators of crime were anathema at the headquarters of the League.

–*The Fall of Feudalism in Ireland*, Michael Davitt

25 September 1880

A line drawn along the midpoints of Lough Corrib in Galway and continuing north through Lough Mask would measure almost forty miles, although compared to the sea-sized lakes that Thomas had seen in America, the loughs were like village ponds. A relatively narrow strip of land separated the loughs and near the centre of this nestled the village of Clonbur, or Fairhill, as the English gentry called it.

One of those gentrified persons, Lord Mountmorres, or William Browne de Montmorency, 5th Viscount Mountmorres, a man of forty-eight years, had purchased a fine residence near Clonbur some years before called Ebor Hall, which enjoyed a magnificent view of the islands in the waters of Lough Corrib. With it came an estate of fourteen farms of twenty acres each, one of which had once been home to Tim and Maebh Connor, and to Thomas's own brother.

Lord Mountmorres had not garnered for himself a reputation as a harsh landlord, despite having recently refused a request, like Charles Boycott, for a reduction in rents. His Lordship's refusal was motivated by his poor stewardship of the estate, for he managed his financial affairs badly. He also tended to drink to excess to dull his financial troubles and a vicious circle began to enclose him in this regard. To his credit, in the tenantry's eyes, he had not evicted any tenants for years, despite several of them falling behind with rent.

But that is not to say he was widely beloved, simply not widely hated. And for the most part, the antagonism directed towards him resulted from his position as a magistrate of the law. Most Irish people held the view that 'law' was an abbreviated term for 'British law', which they considered was formulated to keep them in their place rather than to keep the peace. Lord Mountmorres confirmed much of this view as his judgements and sentences were considered erratic, extreme and heavily biased against the peasantry.

In August of 1880, Mr Patrick Sweeney, who spoke no English and was employed as a herdsman by Mountmorres, was dismissed for failing to attend to his flock of sheep, several having been stolen. Mountmorres also wanted Sweeney removed from his 'cottage' – a dwelling consisting of a sloping roof of turf supported by stones, which even by the standards of the day would be considered fit only for housing animals. Lord Mountmorres sued for a formal decree of eviction at the Petty Sessions of Clonbur Court.

Petty it may have been in the eyes of the law, but to Sweeney it was his only home and he presented his case through a translator to the appointed magistrate, claiming he was an agricultural tenant and should be afforded equivalent rights. The evidence was ruled in favour of Mountmorres and Sweeney was evicted, subsequently sharing his view loudly and widely that a British magistrate would never rule against one of its own over an Irish peasant. It was this ruling and Sweeney's vociferous condemnation of it that brought Mountmorres to the attention of a violent faction of Irish nationalism and essentially signed his death warrant. Donal Doherty and Thomas Joyce were appointed his principal executioners.

The court in Clonbur sat every second Saturday, after which Lord Mountmorres was known to join his fellow magistrates for brandy and cigars, where they would discuss their disaffection with Gladstone's Liberal Party and his kowtowing to Parnell, as well as Britain's military progress in other territories across the globe. These debates frequently extended late into the evening, so it was often in an advanced state of inebriation that Mountmorres would set off erratically in his carriage along the one-and-a-half-mile route home.

It was in this condition on the night of 25 September 1880 that he approached the bend in the road at a place called Dooroy, where the land sloped gently down to the glassy, moonlit surface of Lough Corrib, not five hundred yards from Ebor Hall, and where three men of murderous intent lay silently in wait.

***

Donal Doherty sat with his back to the wall, checking his Schofield revolver for the umpteenth time.

'Why de ye keep doin' that?' Cal Feeney asked too loudly for comfort, a distinct tremble in his voice, which issued from his lips on a breath of alcohol.

'Keep your fucking voice down!' Thomas snapped.

Feeney didn't comply. 'Why? D'ye think there's a constable hidin' behind every rock?'

Doherty abruptly grasped a fistful of Feeney's hair. 'Yeah. That's right. That's why we've never been caught. Now shut yer fuckin' mouth or I'll shut it permanently.'

'Quiet!'

Thomas, who had been kneeling against the wall watching for Mountmorres, dropped sharply to the ground.

'Is it him?' came Doherty's anxious whisper.

'Man from the cottage.'

'Fuck!'

They saw a light approaching from the direction of the cottage about two hundred yards away. They also became aware of a woman's voice.

'Peadar! Peadar Flanagan! Will ye come home this instant? Ye have me out o' me mind with worry.' Her voice was breathless, as though she'd had to run to catch up.

They watched as shafts of lamplight slanting through the gaps in the stone wall advanced ever nearer.

'Leave me be, Nuala! I'm sure I heard a man talkin'. If there's sheep thieves out here I'll throttle 'em!'

'Jesus, Peadar, they might be armed. And you with a feckin' hurley to defend yerself. Come back before I'm driven te me mind's edge.'

The man heaved a sigh. 'Ah sure, they're probably well gone.'

The light and footsteps began to recede, then the man whispered something and they heard the woman giggle like a little girl. The three released their captured breaths and relaxed. Doherty turned to Feeney.

'Take a turn watching. Keep quiet and keep low.'

'Can't wait te plug the bastard,' Feeney whispered.

Thomas and Doherty exchanged a shake of the head.

Ten minutes elapsed in the moonlit silence.

'My father was imprisoned by Mountmorres, so this is personal,' Doherty whispered eventually. 'And if what your brother said about him being blind drunk every week is true, this should be easy.'

'It's him!' Feeney blurted.

The two men whirled about and peered along the narrow country lane, hemmed in on either side by the signature stone walls that divided Connaught into a million plots of poor land. Mountmorres too would be hemmed in, unable to turn left or right or retreat.

'Feeney!' Doherty snapped in a whisper. 'Don't forget. If the horse bolts, stop it, shoot it if you have to. We'll take Mountmorres.'

'But I–'

'Just fuckin' do it!'

They watched as the carriage drew near. The wheels criss-crossed the muddy ruts rather than following them and the horse whinnied continuously as though in protest.

'He's pissed. Just like your brother said.'

They waited until they could see the man's shape within the dark hollow of the covered carriage, about twenty yards away, close enough to see the landlord's distinctive top hat.

'That's him. Let's do it!'

All three rose as one and vaulted the wall. Feeney stumbled and fell on his hands and knees with a curse. Doherty and Thomas took three steps into the track and levelled their weapons. They heard an audible gasp as the drunken landlord realised what was about to befall him, and he had time to flick the reins hard and spur the horse to mow them down. The two men fired together, Thomas's shot going harmlessly through the black canvas hood. Doherty's shot struck Mountmorres in the shoulder and the landlord cried out in shock and pain as he reeled sideways and tumbled from the vehicle face down into the mud. As the panicked horse took flight directly towards them, Thomas and Doherty leapt to either side of the track.

'Feeney! Stop the horse!' Thomas yelled as it hurtled by. He witnessed Feeney's pathetic and unsuccessful attempt to grasp the trailing reins.

'Christ!' Doherty roared as they rose and turned towards Mountmorres.

The man lay on his side, his fine black dress coat covered in mud and blood, his top hat sitting upturned on the grassy verge like a beggar's waiting for alms. He was grunting in panic and pain, but surprised them by suddenly pulling a small weapon and firing. Thomas reacted first, the gun being directed at him, and two bullets passed each other in the darkness, one grazing the soft flesh of Thomas's left arm, the other tunnelling through the landlord's stomach and exiting halfway up his back.

Mountmorres' gun hand reacted spasmodically, snapping out straight and releasing the weapon. His only defence gone, and realising his mortal peril, panic took hold and he rolled over and began to crawl away through the mud, emitting desperate, wheezing grunts with each movement. He'd barely progressed one yard before Doherty pushed a toe under his body and rolled him over on to his back. He lay there a moment staring up wide-eyed at his assailants, abject terror written across his mud-streaked face.

'This is the only justice you've ever seen,' Doherty snarled and pointed his gun at Mountmorres's head. Thomas aimed at his chest and a moment later two shots in quick succession echoed across the wild landscape.

'Let's get to the horses,' Doherty said and turned, but as they moved away Feeney pushed between them and walked towards the body.

'He's dead, Feeney, let's go!' Thomas snapped.

But Feeney was not to be denied. He emptied three chambers into the lifeless corpse and then laughed.

'Feeney! For fuck's sake, let's go!'

Feeney turned away and ran to them, then all three vaulted the wall and started to run across the stony field towards a small copse of trees where they had secured their horses.

'Couldn't let you boys have all the fun,' Feeney snickered.

***

After a hastily applied binding to Thomas's wound, the three mounted their animals and began to ride directly west towards the hills. Thomas thought it appropriate that they were moving into the region known as Joyce's Country, another part of Ireland blessed with breathtaking natural beauty and cursed with poverty in equal measure. Roads were few and far between, but that tallied with their intent to vanish into the night. The pale moonlight lit their way sufficiently across the barren landscape, albeit at a frustratingly slow trot.

They skirted the northern slopes of Benlevy Hill, whose dark shape rose thirteen hundred feet before them, and followed a barely distinct track around Coolin Lough, a small body of water that had been cut into the hillside in eons past. When they deemed themselves safe in the heart of the wilds, they rested under the cliff face that guarded the lough's southern shore.

'Why the fuck didn't you shoot the horse, Feeney?' Thomas asked.

Feeney shrugged. 'What does it matter?'

'Because it'll have run straight back to Ebor Hall. By now the place will be crawling with police.'

'Talking of crawlin',' Feeney laughed, 'did you see the fucker trying to crawl away?'

The others eyed each other in bewilderment. The man seemed utterly oblivious to what had just been said.

'Wait until I tell Micko.'

'Who the fuck is Micko?' Doherty asked.

'A friend of mine from Cong. Good man. Sympathiser.'

'You didn't tell him about tonight? Or us?'

'D'ye think I'm fuckin' stupid?'

'No, of course not.'

Doherty nodded at Thomas as Feeney took a swallow from a hip flask.

'Feeney, take the horses down and water them,' Doherty said.

'Why me? Why can't he do it? Anyway, it'll make them sick if–'

'That's an order, Feeney!'

Feeney groaned and stood, sulking as he led the animals down the slope. At the water's edge, he was startled when Thomas appeared from nowhere and took the reins.

'Let me give you a hand.'

'Where did you com–'

A muffled shot echoed off the cliff as Feeney collapsed like an empty sack, half-in, half-out of the water, blood pouring from the hole in the back of his head. The horses reared a little in fright, but Thomas held the reins firm and soothed them.

'That fool would have told half the county inside a week,' Doherty said, unwrapping the gun from the folds of his jacket.

'Better get rid of him.'

They tied a couple of rocks to Feeney's body, then waded out into the shallows, pushing Feeney in front of them, Thomas holding the rocks aloft.

'Jesus, it's freezing.' Doherty shivered as the water lapped at his waist.

Thomas snickered. 'My brother used to be able to swim in water like this for ten minutes.'

'You serious? I thought ye said he was as weak as a spring fuckin' lamb?'

'Yeah, I thought that once,' Thomas replied, his voice contemplative.

'Still too shallow,' Doherty said. He took hold of the tails of Feeney's greatcoat, and flicked it as though spreading a blanket, trapping a pocket of air. 'Now!'

Thomas lowered the rocks onto Feeney's buttocks and between his shoulder blades and they pushed. The dead man floated out ten yards before one of the rocks toppled and the body sank amid a flurry of bubbles.

'Nice trick. Ye done this before?'

'Yeah, but it's all right, he was English.'

They both laughed and waded back to the idling horses.

'Where to?' Thomas asked as they climbed into the saddles, the spare horse tied to Doherty's mount.

'We have to stay low for a while. When word about Mountmorres gets out, the gentlemen of the British government will be choking on their quail's eggs. I know a safe house, under Ben Beg, middle of nowhere. Good man there, Bull Walsh, can be trusted to keep his mouth shut.'

A lone bubble breached the lough's surface and made them turn their heads, the final physical manifestation of Feeney's existence.

'Besides that little hitch, it was a good night's work,' Doherty observed.

Thomas nodded. 'Parnell and Davitt make a hundred speeches and no one hears a word. But pull a trigger out here in the wilds of Connaught and those bastards in London hear it loud and clear.'

***

Lough Mask, September 25th 1880

To The Right Honourable Earl of Erne

May it please your Lordship

We, the tenantry on your Lough Mask Estate most respectfully beg to intimate to you that we have no intention of paying your rent to Captain Boycott. But at the same time we have not the slightest objection to paying a <u>just</u> rent to any other person whom your Lordship's better judgment may recommend.

Several other landlords in the south Mayo area have recently granted their tenants abatements of up to thirty percent in light of the appalling harvests. But Captain Boycott refuses to afford us the same measure of fairness. What is more, the Captain has hurted our feelings and caused great offence to his tenants in recent years. He has denied us the right to take windfall to heat our homes, he won't let us cross the estate thus causing great inconvenience and time lost in our work, he has imposed fines on us for all manner of petty offences like knocking a single stone off a wall, and is impudent and rude to us. For instance, he never spoke of us in better terms than Irish swine; and for these manifold reasons we hold him in utter detestation and will have no further dealings with him. We further add that in support of our grievances his workers have abandoned him and the people of Ballinrobe and Neale will conduct no trade with him.

As previously stated, your humble and grateful tenants would be more

> than willing to pay a just rent and we respectfully ask that your Lordship would consider all of the above and remove Captain Boycott from your service.
>
> Yours sincerely,
>
> The tenantry.
>
> P.S. An early reply sent to Mr Owen Joyce (but not to Captain Boycott) is respectfully requested.

'What do you think?' Redpath asked as he finished reading the letter back to Fr O'Malley and Owen in the rectory living room. It was eight-thirty, the precise moment Thomas and Doherty were firing the fatal shots into Mountmorres's body.

'"Hurted" is good,' Owen smiled.

'I agree. The letter has to give the impression we're a bunch of poor, uneducated peasants who've been mistreated. It has to gain his sympathy,' the priest added.

'We *have* been mistreated,' Owen pointed out.

'Nobody's disagreeing, Owen,' Redpath said as he made a few changes, using blotting paper and a rubber eraser, deliberately giving it an unprofessional appearance.

'The letter's worth a try, I suppose, but the old coot is very old-school. Set in his ways of thinking about tenants knowing their place,' Owen mused.

'Well, it can't do any harm,' said the priest. 'And the sooner we can end this the better. I'm concerned about the possibility of violence.'

'From Fenians?' Redpath asked.

'Closer to home. Someone hung an effigy of Boycott from a tree near the entrance of the estate. Someone else opened a gate and let his cattle wander into the crops. And I've had to reprimand the schoolteacher.'

'Old McQuaid?' Owen asked incredulously. The man was seventy.

'He allowed the children off early so they could jeer at anyone going through the gates. Sergeant Murtagh told me one of the boys bared his behind at Annie Boycott.'

Redpath and Owen snickered, earning them both a frown.

'Gentlemen, it's not a matter of levity. It starts like this, little things at first, and then escalates until someone gets hurt.'

'Sorry, Father, you're right, it's just…I can imagine her face,' Owen said, grinning.

The priest grunted. 'Well, that lad won't be baring his behind again, considering the number of stripes McQuaid gave it when he found out.'

'What do you want us to do?'

'Just keep reiterating that we don't condone any threats or acts of violence. Or vandalism. Anyone who does that will have to answer to me and I'll have no hesitation handing them over to Sergeant Murtagh. I'll remind everyone at mass tomorrow.'

'We'll spread the word and keep our eyes peeled, Father,' said Owen.

'Good, the next week is vital. Just one bit of bloodshed and this whole thing could fall apart.'

CHAPTER 21

Mayo landlord, Lord Mountmorres (5th Viscount Mountmorres) was murdered on Saturday evening Sept. 25, 1880 on the road between Clonbur and Ebor Hall as he was driving from a magistrates meeting in Clonbur. He was shot six times at close range. The perpetrators presumably escaped over the hills. When the horse and empty carriage arrived at Ebor Hall the servants went searching for Mountmorres. The incident was believed to be associated with Land League activities.

–Supplement of *The Illustrated London News*, 27 September 1880

Lady Mountmorres has received from Balmoral a letter written by command of the Queen, expressing her Majesty's sympathy with her ladyship in her affliction, and inquiring kindly regarding her condition.

–*The Nationalist*, 16 October 1880

London, Sept. 27. – A tenant farmer named Sweeney has been arrested in connection with the murder of Lord Mountmorres, and has been remanded for trial. The murder has caused the greatest sensation. It is expected that the affair will induce the Government to take decisive steps to control the utterances of land agitators. The meeting of magistrates, which was attended by Lord Mountmorres just previous to his death, had passed a resolution calling on the Government to adopt coercive measures in Ireland.

–*The New York Times*, 28 September 1880

17 OCTOBER 1880

'This is precisely what we didn't want,' Owen said and covered his eyes with his hand, as though to banish the scenarios that might stem from Mountmorres's brutal killing.

'Not ten miles away. They'll think this place is a haven for Fenian killers,' Fr O'Malley replied from the other side of the wall that surrounded one of Owen's fields. 'And whatever sympathies we might have been earning for our plight with the more moderate British will be forgotten.'

'And we can forget any sympathy from Lord Erne. Extremists have just murdered one of his fellow peers. What are we going to do?'

The priest leaned on the wall and bent his head low, appearing to study the mossy stone surface with deep interest. After some time he stood erect, his expression resolute.

'We continue to do what we've been doing. We condemn the killing and get everyone to do the same, whether it's in the pub or in town or to the RIC. Or if the press come snooping around. We continue the boycott. We see this through. Especially now, because I suspect this wasn't just meant to make a statement to the British. This was meant to undermine the Land League. The extremists have always hated the New Departure. They're trying to destroy everything we've built up and start a war.'

Owen heaved a sigh. 'Where's James, by the way?'

'Typical newspaperman. The moment he heard he took off for Ballinrobe to telegraph New York. You know what they say. Bad news travels fastest.'

***

The laundress, a Miss Lucy McDonald, was a short, irascible woman of sixty with a pockmarked and shiny red face. She would normally call on a Wednesday, wheeling a large hand-cart, to collect the soiled laundry from Lough Mask House, and then return to her cottage two miles away, where she would scrub the clothing spotless, employing the plentiful waters of Lough Mask, flaked lye and a bar of Hudson's Dry Soap. The ironed clothes would then be returned by Friday. Ironically, the woman's language was anything but clean, and normally Annie Boycott dreaded contact with her. But today she craved her arrival. Almost all of the ladies' underwear had been used and the men's were in a worse condition as a result of their sweaty labouring. Annie had just one clean dress remaining, which she was saving for Sunday. The rest of her and Madeleine's clothes had been soiled with porridge, pea soup, grease, blood, manure and perspiration, rendering their appearance more like common beggars than ladies of polite society.

A constable, one of twelve now residing in the grounds, had agreed to go and inquire why Miss McDonald hadn't called. Annie had a vague hope that the woman might be excluded from their ostracism (she refused to accept the term 'boycott'), as Miss McDonald was a Protestant. But when the constable returned grim-faced, she had to bite her bottom lip to prevent herself from crying in the man's presence. Closing the door, she leaned back against it and sobbed into the silence of the hallway. Cleanliness had always been of paramount importance to her and by now she was beginning to feel not just dirty, but defiled.

Since they'd learned of the Mountmorres assassination she'd also had to add a genuine dread to her general discomfort. She feared greatly for her husband's life and the constabulary's presence did little to soothe her worries, especially as Charles still insisted on going openly to work in the fields and riding the roads around the estate. She spent most of her days performing the household tasks while carrying a grim anticipation that every knock on the door would bring news of her husband's murder.

She quickly mopped her tears at the sound of footsteps, as Charles had insisted they must maintain a dignified, unflinching front. William appeared and saw her by the door, her eyes red. She forced a smile.

'Are you all right, Aunt Annie?' he asked with the concern of a boy on the first edge of manhood.

'I'm fine, dear. Dust in my eye.'

William, in his naivety, accepted her explanation without further ado.

'Auntie, em...I came to tell you...' His drooping features suggested something was amiss.

'What is it now?'

'I heard Mr Weekes talking to the sergeant and they said that the postboy refuses to handle our mail or deliver our telegraph messages.'

'Dear God, we're completely cut off.'

At the sound of her despair, William straightened his shoulders and clasped his hands behind his back. 'I'll walk to Ballinrobe with our letters, Auntie.'

Annie smiled through her tears, wrapped her arms around William's head and pressed it to her breast, holding him so for several minutes.

***

When Madeleine Boycott's mother, Isabella, had died earlier that year, the extended Boycott family had convened to discuss her future and that of her brother. And as the family was the product of several generations of rectors, and therefore of a deeply religious nature, among the considerations for Madeleine's future life had been to ensure that she be raised in an environment that would keep her from 'temptation's path'.

And so it had, Madeleine thought, for there were no remotely suitable young men in the vicinity of Lough Mask House, and her uncle's bad manners generally discouraged visitors. The only man of class around was Asheton Weekes, and although she liked him, he hadn't, as least as yet, displayed any great interest in her. Perhaps he felt their age difference was too great. Or maybe he simply didn't find her physically attractive, which was a notion that troubled her somewhat. Worse still, their current predicament meant she was denied the occasional excitement of a trip to Galway or Dublin, making her isolation all the more oppressive. And she never in her wildest flights of fantasy had envisaged spending her days pulling at the teats of cows and forking hay in the stables, her fine clothes reduced almost to rags.

These thoughts were swirling in her mind when the head of her pitchfork came free and shot over her shoulder. Her exasperation got the better of her and she beat at the stable door with the shaft, causing the horse inside to rear away in fright. She stopped and rested her shoulder against a wall until she could soothe her nerves. Presently, she picked up the three-pronged head and tried to reinsert the shaft, but without success. She wandered from the yard in search of assistance and walked towards the castle ruin, near which the constabulary had erected their huts. A tree stump offered her the prospect of a rest and she sat there, idly looking about.

It was a bright September afternoon, a month which always made her melancholic, for though she was past her schooling the sense of gloom remained that the long months ahead held no promise of summer walks with young men along the Waveney River or glances from the chaps after church on Sunday morning. These glances she stored away like secret treasure, for she considered herself pretty and shaped to the right proportions.

A loud male chuckle from beyond the constables' huts drew her attention, where a separate wooden partition had been erected, and in front of it she saw two of the constables sawing at a long plank of wood suspended across two upended crates. They each sported heavy moustaches and wore white shirts with the sleeves folded to their elbows. They obviously would not have been deemed suitable company for a lady of her class, but they were both young and handsome in a rugged way and an admiring glance was an admiring glance, whoever cast it. She smoothed her dress about her hips, picked up the parts of the fork and sauntered across with her best impersonation of innocence.

On seeing her approach, they halted their work and turned to face her, tipping their foreheads and bowing slightly.

'Miss,' they said in unison.

'I'm terribly sorry to disturb your work but would you mind awfully helping me to repair this?'

'Certainly, miss, my pleasure,' the nearest of the two said and took the fork. He lodged the end of the shaft on a rock, forced the head down over it and then hammered it up and down until it had slipped snugly all the way on to the pole.

'I'll put a nail through the hole here, miss, stop it coming off again.'

'Thank you, that's most considerate,' Madeleine said with a coy smile.

The young constable did as promised and returned the fork to her.

'Good as new,' he said.

Madeleine thanked them again and then realised she had no further reason to linger. She glanced at the plank they had been sawing, which was about twelve feet long and a foot in width, and saw they had cut out several large U-shaped segments from one side.

'Whatever are you doing?' she inquired brightly, pointing at the curious shape.

The two men looked uncomfortably at each other.

'Is it a shield of sorts? And you fire your guns through the holes. Is that it?'

One of the constables scratched his nose and looked away and the other stared at his feet, but neither responded to her inquiry.

'Is there someth–' she began, then stopped dead. Several thoughts rushed at her as once – the separate partition, her uncle telling the sergeant to move the latrine away from the house, the wooden plank with the holes. The embarrassment was so sudden and inescapable it was like the kick of a mule. She felt a sharp, warm rush of blood to her face and a droplet of perspiration tickle a track from her underarm. She yawped in mortification, then turned on her heels and ran, casting the fork aside as she fled.

Annie was still in the hall with William when Madeleine burst in from the rear of the house, fleeing towards the sanctuary of her bedroom, tears streaming down her cheeks. She glanced at her aunt and yelled at a tremendous pitch: 'I hate this place!'

***

It was the last day in September but it was unseasonably warm. Weekes lowered the scythe and leaned on the cart. He had removed his jacket and waistcoat and his shirt was soaked with perspiration. He was no longer a young man. Until he'd resigned his army commission some years previously he'd considered himself fully fit and able-bodied, but a life of relative leisure hadn't been kind to his physique. Now he found that the labourer's work cruelly exposed his physical limitations. He wiped sweat from his brow and felt his vision sway.

Boycott lowered his scythe and looked about him at the field of corn, a third of which had been cut. 'Damn fine luck with the weather.'

Weekes rose to walk towards Boycott, but immediately felt his knees go weak and his head swim, and he collapsed on the ground on his hands and knees. Boycott cast his scythe aside and rushed across.

'Are you ill, old man?' he said with evident anxiety.

Weekes registered the concern in his friend's voice, something so rarely expressed it helped to restore his energies.

'Just a faint, I think, Charles.'

Boycott helped him onto the end of the handcart and brought a flask of water.

'We can't do it, Charles,' he said presently.

'Can't do what?'

'Even if the weather holds, we'll never get all the corn cut, gathered and threshed.'

'We must, Weekes, we *must*!' Boycott slammed his palm against the cart.

They were silent for a while, Weekes looking across the field at the two constables standing guard. They provided no great comfort, so exposed were the two men in the open fields, but Charles had insisted the remainder protect the house and perimeter. Yet ten men spread over several miles were like a net with a mesh so large a whale might pass through.

'Damned shocking about Mountmorres,' Weekes said.

'Man was a fool and a drunk, by all accounts.'

'Charles–'

'I'm sorry, Weekes, but he rode alone at night with no constabulary. And I knew the man. Too soft with his tenants. Mountmorres showed the peasants too much leniency. And now one of them has been arrested for his murder. It's a deuced shame, don't misunderstand me. Outrageous, *The Times* called it. But much as I regret Mountmorres's demise, it could work in our favour. There are calls for new coercive measures and we might finally see the army off their behinds in Ballinrobe. They could round up all the Land League agitators in a week. In the meantime, I had the sergeant convey a message to that fool magistrate, McSheehy. He's contacted the Chief Secretary's office in Dublin Castle and made an official request for more constables and huts. What with Mountmorres's murder, I'm certain we'll get them.'

Weekes gestured towards the field with his chin. 'Yet it doesn't solve our central problem, Charles. Could you not hire labourers from Dublin and bring them by train? I know it would be expensive but–'

'I cannot.' Boycott said decisively, then looked away.

'But it makes sen–'

'I'm almost bankrupt.'

Weekes was shocked. He knew that Charles Boycott was not a particularly wealthy man, but had always assumed he had reasonable financial resources.

'I'm behind with the mortgage on the Kildarra estate and with the land agitation its value is a fraction of the original mortgage.'

'I didn't realise.'

'Weekes...Asheton...I'm on a financial knife-edge. If we don't save the crop I will be bankrupted. Disgraced. We'll lose everything.'

Weekes had never heard such utter wretchedness in the man's voice.

He mused on it, then said cautiously: 'Charles, you could end this by meeting the tenants halfway.'

The land agent was on his feet in a blink, shouting defiance. 'Absolutely not! I categorically refuse to submit to their threats!'

Weekes, in the face of Boycott's obstinacy, was moved to anger himself. 'Very well, Charles, but you must do something! Sell the herd, raise some cash and then we can concentrate on the harvest. As it is, Madeleine only milks the dairy cows to relieve them. Most of the milk is thrown away, a waste of money! And as for the cattle–'

'Very well!' Boycott shouted.

Weekes was so shocked that Boycott had agreed to his suggestion, he was momentarily dumbfounded.

'I'm sorry?'

'I said very well. We'll sell the herd, keep one cow for milk. Now, shall we get back to work?'

'Of course.'

'And, Weekes, not a word of this bankruptcy thing to anyone. Not to Annie or anyone else. If that popish agitator O'Malley should get wind–'

'He'd be the happiest man in Ireland.'

***

Fr O'Malley slammed the newspaper on the table, his face red with rage. Redpath had just shown him a clipping from *The Birmingham Daily Gazette* which claimed that 'people danced in derision on the spot where Mountmorres fell and threw soil stained with his lifeblood in the air' and that 'those guilty of inciting these outrages are the most prominent of the Nationalist party.'

'It's outrageous! And hinting that Parnell and Davitt were behind it. I'm beyond speech!' he thundered. 'And you say *The Times* wasn't much kinder? Or *The Illustrated News*? It's a disgrace!'

'Calm down, Father, please.'

'Calm down? They've tarred us all as murderers. They'll use this as an excuse to enforce any measures they want.'

'Gladstone might be able to hold them off. He's got a comfortable majority, especially if the Home Rule Party supports him. The last thing he wants is war in Ireland.'

The priest poured himself a stiff whiskey.

'Perhaps you're right, but with the press calling for coercive measures, it can't be too long before the British army are marching past our door. These hothead British politicians and newspapers are playing right into the hands of the militants. Was there ever a bigger collection of jackasses in this world?'

***

Thomas looked in his wallet at the six five-pound notes. To his brother it would represent almost half of his annual income, but he knew Owen would call it the wages of sin or use some other pious rhetoric if he knew its source. Or its purpose.

He stood in the main street of the village of Cong, a tiny hamlet indeed, notable for the ruin of a medieval church, Cong Abbey, and a pretty, riverside setting. But Ireland had enough beauty to keep countless poets happy. What she didn't have in any measure was freedom from tyranny, he considered. And that was where men like him came in. And why her countless banished children were willing to provide the finance to bring about that freedom. Maybe two million had died in the famine. Another million had been forced to flee Ireland in search of salvation. In the years since, another two million had been forced to flee the economic tyranny of the landlords and the British Government. Countless other souls who had sought to remain had died an early death through poverty and neglect, forced to live in cramped cottages, half-starved and freezing. In thirty-five short years almost five million people had gone, either dead or scattered to the winds. Sometimes the notion of it overwhelmed him and he wished dearly to kill as many of the British assailants as possible before they would strike him down. His hatred was like a fathomless well, and no matter how often he drew up the pail it would never run dry.

Yet, ironically, he believed that the decimation of his countrymen would ultimately rebound on their British tyrants. For America had opened her arms to those pitiful refugees and in her embrace they'd been reborn. He'd witnessed the teeming masses of Irish grow strong again in America, and far from forgetting their homeland the ties grew proportionally stronger. Their American-born children were no different. Or their grandchildren. All of them were Irish first and American second. And all were willing to pay their nickels, dimes and dollars to support the cause of Irish freedom. Much of the money found its way into the coffers of organisations like the Land League, but even more went to the Irish Republican Brotherhood and other militant movements. And that money would be well spent. Guns, horses, information. And safe houses. Places where men could lie low until the day of armed rebellion. And Thomas, these past years, had finally found his way home and into the heart of the rebellion that had filled his dreams for decades.

Originally Boycott had been deemed a minor target compared to the likes of Mountmorres. Just a pathetic land agent. But thanks to the efforts of Parnell, the priest O'Malley and his own brother, Boycott's star was rising. According to Doherty, the press was starting to take notice as this was the first time a land agent had been ostracised. And he, Thomas, had been granted the honour of putting the bullet in Boycott's head.

His brother had inadvertently provided him with a safe house. And who would suspect a Fenian killer to be hiding under the thatch of one of the main instigators of the non-violent protest, and on Boycott's own estate?

But Owen wasn't stupid, far from it. Just naive and misguided. He knew that sooner or later Owen might link his absence with Mountmorres's murder. Somehow he had to kill that notion completely. He'd continue to worm his way into the family. He'd acknowledge the success of Boycott's ostracism and offer to support it, perhaps make a contribution to their relief fund. But he would start by blinding them all with his kindness.

He stroked his horse's nose and stepped up towards the ladies' dress store, his interest in the frocks earning him a couple of giggles from two passing girls. He smiled at them and saluted, then pressed open the door. It was time to put some of the hard-earned contributions of the emigrant Irish to work.

***

The three youths recognised William the moment he rounded the bend in the track. He paused at the sight of them but it was too late to duck, so he steeled himself and pressed on until he came face-to-face with them.

The previous evening he had heard his uncle and Mr Weekes discuss their frustration at the unsent mail in the bureau. Even if a constable had taken it to Ballinrobe, the postmistress would refuse to handle it. So he had conceived a plan whereby he would take the mail to Ballinrobe barracks and ask them to despatch it through the military postal system. The soldiers were English and would surely be glad to help. And William was determined to play a big part in helping his uncle.

He had decided that he must act like a clandestine spy, keeping his mission secret from everyone in the house. So he'd taken the letters from the bureau early that morning and slipped over the wall. Ballinrobe was just five miles away and he calculated that he could be back by noon with news of his success.

He'd been trotting along with seven letters in a leather pouch clutched at his side, seeing only an occasional farmer in the fields, his confidence growing with each step. Until the moment he'd rounded the bend.

They stood side-by-side, completely blocking his path.

'Excuse me,' he said with his well-practiced politeness.

One of them pushed him in the chest but he managed to stay upright.

'I wish to pass.'

'I wish to pass,' one mimicked with a sneer. 'Ye'll have te pay te pass.'

'Pay? I have no money.'

'What's in the pouch?'

William instinctively clutched the precious pouch. He couldn't surrender it at any cost or his endeavour would take a disastrous turn.

The boys looked at each other; the pouch was clearly worth investigating further. They abruptly rushed at him and pushed him to the ground, one of them landing a fist on his nose and drawing blood. They clawed and tore at his pouch but he clung to it tenaciously, even as the punches began to land on his stomach.

'Let go of it, ye little bastard!' one of them snarled at him.

William was beginning to lose hope and felt the first of the tears sting his eyes when a shape moved above his assailants and he suddenly saw two of them yanked away.

'Get off him! Get off!'

Owen, who'd been driving to Neale to meet Fr O'Malley when he came upon the commotion, pulled the third boy free and almost threw him across the track, then helped William to his feet.

'He's one of the Boycotts. Little bastard's running messages for them,' the tallest of them shouted as the youths re-grouped.

'We're only helping Father O'Malley,' another said.

Owen stepped up to them. 'I know what Father O'Malley's going to say when he finds out about this. And I know what your fathers will do. Not to mention your *mothers*.'

The boys looked nervously at each other.

'And remember what Father O'Malley said about violence? Well, I wasn't listening when he said that bit.'

Owen suddenly struck the leader a ferocious clatter across the ear and followed with similar strikes on the ducking heads of the other two. As they turned to scamper away, he planted a couple of painful boot marks on their backsides. The youths gone, he turned back to William and frowned, taking the lad's chin in his hand and turning his head left and right. Bloodied nose, swollen lip; nothing more serious. He handed a rag to the boy to mop his nose.

'You put up a good fight considering there were three of them.'

William's evident sense of pride bolstered his spirit. 'Thank you, sir, for helping me.'

'C'mon, I'll take you home.'

He helped the boy on to his rickety car and they set off.

'Does your uncle or aunt know you're here?'

William shook his head, then looked downcast.

'Where were you going?'

'To deliver my uncle's letters. Our post boy has stopped coming.'

Owen felt a twinge of guilt and they rode in silence the rest of the way, stopped only by a constable inquiring what was happening. As they approached the house he saw a group consisting of Boycott, his wife, Weekes and two constables. Annie Boycott was yelling in panic. When she saw William on the car she screamed his name and rushed across. Her ragged appearance, unkempt hair and filthy dress shocked Owen.

'William! Oh Lord, I was frantic with worry. What in heaven has happened to you?' She lifted him down with surprising strength and hugged him.

'What have you done to my nephew? It's you, Joyce, I know you! Constable, arrest this man for assault!' Boycott yelled.

Owen reflected that aside from his similarly unkempt attire, Boycott had changed little. He began to turn the car.

'No, Uncle! This gentleman stopped some boys from beating me! But he said I fought well, didn't you, sir?' William called out from within Annie's clasping embrace.

Owen smiled down at the boy and winked. As he began to drive away, Annie Boycott met his eyes and nodded almost imperceptibly. Her situation had rendered it impossible to express thanks, not that he sought any, but he saw it there nonetheless.

If there was any integrity within these grounds, Owen thought, it was to be found in the mind and heart of Boycott's wife.

***

The evenings were drawing in fast and Owen's working day was growing shorter. He wasn't particularly worried now about getting the harvest in, thanks to his brother's help, yet he was troubled that the situation with Boycott continued to go unresolved. He felt like Damocles in Cicero's tale, that above his head dangled a sword suspended only by a hair, which at any moment could snap and leave them homeless and without the means to survive the winter.

He washed his hands in the lough and began to walk back up to the cottage. There was still no sign of his brother and as the days passed he was becoming increasingly concerned. He wasn't worried about Thomas's safety – he'd survived for thirty years in the wild frontiers of America – but by the reason behind his absence. He had said he'd be gone a week but it was the third day beyond his expected return and much as Owen tried to deny the notion, he couldn't help making a connection between his brother's absence and the murder of Mountmorres. He had been very vague on the subject of the work he'd been hired to do and Owen regretted not having subtly pursued the details further. All he knew was that it was down Cong way, but Clonbur and the scene of the crime were in the same general area. The idea was too disquieting to contemplate and, besides, it had no solid basis in evidence. He knew Thomas detested landlordism, but so did nine-tenths of the population, himself included. Perhaps the entire notion was ludicrous and he was worrying needlessly.

As if in response to the thought, Thomas trotted into the farmyard on his black mare, a large bundle tied behind his saddle. He didn't notice Owen and continued past to the horse pen where he unsaddled the animal and returned laden with his knapsack, the saddle and the bundle.

'Owen!' he called out brightly.

'I was beginning to worry. You've been away ten days.'

'Tut tut. You're clucking like a mother hen.'

'Sorry. It's just with all that's been going on.'

Thomas laid the saddle against the cottage wall. 'Why? What's been happening?'

He watched Thomas's face closely. 'Surely you heard? Lord Mountmorres was murdered the day you left here.'

Thomas nodded, as though distressed at the memory. 'Of course. I'm sorry, I thought ye meant something had happened with Boycott.'

'You know about Mountmorres then?' Owen pressed.

'Jesus, who doesn't? I hear the papers in Dublin and England and every godforsaken place are full of it.' He shook his head. 'You know, I was stopped three times in the last few days by the RIC, asking me who I was, where I lived, what was my business. The last thing you need right now is the place crawling with the police.'

Owen couldn't fault his reasoning or his apparent truthfulness. Still though, something nagged at him.

'I've no love for the RIC, as you know,' Thomas continued, 'but it's as well they've arrested someone for the murder. Might calm things down a bit.'

This was news to Owen. 'Oh?'

'Yeah, some fella named Sweeney. I heard Mountmorres had evicted him.'

Owen was secretly relieved at hearing they'd caught the man responsible and it was with a lighter heart that he opened the cottage door.

Síomha stood by the hearth readying a stew of potatoes, turnips and carrots while Tadhg sat combing his hair repeatedly, clearly intent on some courting. Niamh sat on the floor doing her school homework. They greeted Thomas's return warmly and he then announced that he had something he wished to say.

'The good news is that the job down Cong way looks like it will work out well.'

'Great. What's your friend's name, by the way?' Owen asked casually.

'Feeney. Cal Feeney. Owns a good stretch of land. His father came into some money years back and he managed te buy about fifty acres. And he has a nice little business trading in oats and the like. Earns a decent income. Pays well too. So I won't be cluttering up your home much longer, just until I can sort out a place te live near Cong.'

'Thomas, you're welcome to stay as long as you like,' Síomha said.

'Thanks, but I know when there's too many sheep in a field. And now that I'm getting on my feet, I want te repay you properly for your hospitality.'

They began to protest but he held up his hand. He lifted his paper bundle on to the table, untied the string and pulled out a flowing pale blue dress. He held it up in front of Síomha. It was relatively simple in design with a pleated skirt and a darker blue bodice that buttoned to the neck, but it would certainly be the most striking item in Síomha's wardrobe. Niamh reached out to feel the softness of the material between her fingers.

'Oh no, Thomas, I can't.'

'I insist. And besides, I don't think it'd look very good on me. I had to guess the size, but it looks about right. So, please take it.'

Síomha exchanged a glance with Owen, who smiled softly in agreement. In one sense he was delighted at her joy at receiving a gift that reflected her femininity, yet he couldn't shift the feeling of wounded pride that his brother was the one to treat his wife.

She hugged Thomas and thanked him profusely. A pretty pink dress for

Niamh elicited whoops of glee, and he'd also bought a jacket for Tadhg, which surely would be worn to his romantic rendezvous.

'And, Owen, I do want ye te have this,' he said when the others had disappeared to try on their new gifts.

Owen was astounded to see his brother proffering a five-pound note. He raised both hands, palms out, in refusal.

'No, Thomas. Jesus, that's as much as I'd get for my carrot crop. And besides, you've more than earned your keep. But thanks, anyway. I appreciate the offer.'

'Owen, I want you to take it. For me.' Thomas turned away and stared reflectively out the window at the darkening sky. 'When I left you in Westport, I had all our money. I didn't trust you not te lose it, te be honest.' He chuckled at the memory. 'But when I was on the ship I kept thinking that if only I'd given ye a few shillings…I was certain ye'd die because of that. Clearly I was wrong, but I'm sure some money would have kept ye out of that workhouse.' He turned back to Owen, holding the money out again. 'I need ye te take this and put my conscience at ease. Please.'

Owen hesitated still. The very sight of five pounds was rare. For it to fall into his hands like a snowflake was unfathomable.

'Look, your poor oul' horse is on her last legs, I'm sad te say. What are ye going te do when she dies? And if ye still aren't convinced, take it for the fund the priest has for them that's left Boycott. I'm sure they could use it.'

Owen smiled and reluctantly took the money, studying it as though he'd found some lost, fabled manuscript. 'I don't know how to thank you.'

'Don't. Being home here with you is reward enough.' Thomas said and clapped his brother on the shoulder, confident he was safely back in the family fold.

***

Fr O'Malley strained to read the article from *The Times* of September 28th in the dim, yellow light cast by the oil lamp.

> The murder of Mountmorres has excited feelings of alarm little short of actual panic among all respectable classes. It is said on all sides with equal despondency and bitterness that there is no longer any security for life or property in Ireland, that no man can feel safe who ventures to discharge his duties in connexion with the possession, occupation, or

> management of land. The country is fast drifting into anarchy, and the arm of authority seems paralyzed and the Executive utterly helpless... It is in vain that the land agitators now repudiate all responsibility for the crime and speak of it in terms of horror. Let them unteach if they can the lessons of the last 18 months they have been impressing upon an ignorant and excitable people. Let them endeavour to retrieve the principles of honesty and the instincts of humanity, which they have helped to stifle by appeals to the base passions of cupidity and revenge. They may then hope to get some credit for at least sincere repentance and an earnest desire to lead the misguided people back into the paths of reason and justice. A land meeting was held at Clonbur yesterday at which the Rev. Mr. Harty, PP, presided. Among the speakers were the Rev. Messrs J. O'Malley, PP, and Messrs. Redpath, Daly, J.D. Walsh and J Sheridan. It is needless to observe that the non-clerical speakers have been among the most violent in their platform speeches on other occasions. They now thought fit on the part of the Land League to disclaim all connexion with the crime. The country will now hold the agitators accountable for the atrocities, which have been the natural result of the inflammatory language which they have delivered and the pernicious doctrines they have taught.

He lowered *The Times* and looked at Redpath. It was Thursday, 7 October. A full two weeks had elapsed since the boycott had begun and while he'd heard reports that Boycott and his family looked like a collection of beggars, the stubborn brute had refused to concede a thing. On top of that, they'd had a curt reply from Lord Erne stating bluntly that the rents were fair and he would decline even to look into the matter. The priest was frustrated too at the increasingly insulting depiction of the Land League and the tenantry in the British press, and the unfounded insinuation that the terrible recent violence was as a result of their peaceful efforts to find justice.

'What do you think, Father?'

'This is almost ten days old. By now they've probably tried and sentenced us.'

'*Pernicious doctrines.*' Redpath brandished the newspaper in the air. 'This propaganda is the true pernicious doctrine. And the worst of it is that many British people will believe it.'

Fr O'Malley laughed.

'What's so funny?'

'They say we're an ignorant people. At least we're not so ignorant that we don't know how to spell "connection".'

***

They sat around the table in grim silence, waiting for Annie Boycott to enter. In normal times their dinners were much anticipated and enjoyed, when the day's experiences could be shared over fine meals of roast beef or lamb chops, roasted potatoes and gravy, and then sweet puddings of apple and pears. But as so much time had passed since they'd been abandoned by the world, those days seemed like they belonged to another life.

From the condition of Madeleine's dress it looked as if she had been rolling around in the mud and straw. Attempts by Annie to wash their clothes had proven disastrous. Her soap supplies were exhausted and she had taken to boiling all the clothes together in a kitchen vat. Unfortunately the colour had run from several items, turning the white shirts a greenish yellow, while the dresses emerged with ugly white patches between the pleats and their colours faded. And many of the stains had proven as stubborn as her husband.

Their supply of meat had long since been exhausted and a few days ago Boycott had grown so weary of the bland servings of unseasoned vegetables that he had decided to slaughter a sheep so they might enjoy a mutton stew. He'd shot the creature and brought the ungutted carcass to the yard behind the kitchen, so revolting Annie and Madeleine with the sight of all the blood and brain matter that their niece had retched and Annie had immediately ordered him to remove it from her sight. Only young William had the stomach to assist his uncle to carry the beast to the stable yard and to watch while he attempted to skin, gut and cut it. Boycott had returned with a ragged, hacked-off leg of mutton dripping with blood, which had been cooked and eaten, but such had been the trauma, waste and effort that no further livestock had been slaughtered.

As well as the dreadful food, there was an appalling smell in the house, though it was evident only to visitors such as Sergeant Murtagh, as they had all become accustomed to one another's body odours and the stench from the accumulating grime about the building. But when the sergeant had cause to enter, his face would be seen to contort instinctively as though he was trying to clench his nose shut. Once, as he'd stood in the hallway talking to Boycott, a piercing scream had issued from the dining room, and they'd discovered Madeleine taking refuge behind a chair while a rat happily nibbled on a morsel of potato beneath the table.

The area around the house offered little immediate relief in terms of the stink. There were by now eighteen constables permanently resident, living in two huts that had been supplied by Dublin Castle. A large latrine had been excavated to facilitate this group. Mingled with the noxious odours from this, the proximity of so many extra horses made for a positively nauseating stench around the immediate environs of the house. The presence of so many mostly young men patrolling the grounds had furthermore been a huge invasion into the family's privacy. On one occasion Madeleine had absent-mindedly wandered to the rear first-floor bedroom window garbed only in her underwear and met the shocked eyes of a group of four uniformed constables. She had run and hidden beneath her blanket, red-eyed and red-faced for an hour.

One of Sergeant Murtagh's visits had been precipitated by Boycott's request that the RIC secretly purchase the supplies for the family in Ballinrobe and deliver them to Lough Mask House. The sergeant had pointed out that were such a subterfuge to be discovered, it had been intimated that the boycott would be extended to the constabulary and that they could ill-afford to further antagonise the public in such dangerous times. Several sympathetic constables had made small gifts to Annie and her niece, such as bars of soap or chocolate, but their contributions, while gratefully received, were but a drop in the ocean of their needs.

Due to their inability to communicate with the outside world, the sergeant had agreed to secretly post any urgent correspondence of Boycott's. But he was, as he'd stated openly to the land agent, a decorated officer in the RIC, not a postman.

These last days Weekes had worn the face of a man weary of life itself. Bags had formed beneath his eyes from exhaustion. His hope that this troubling business might all end soon had vanished and he often found himself thinking the unthinkable: of leaving Lough Mask House forever. His plan to sell the cattle had proven impossible, as sufficient constabulary could not be supplied to escort the herd to Claremorris and the cattle train bound for the Dublin market. But his hopelessness stemmed principally from Captain Boycott's apparent inability to see any course of action other than the one upon which he was bent, expressly continuing to resist the war of attrition in the belief that when the peasants realised his pertinaciousness, they would eventually relent to his will. This, Weekes believed, was a truly short-sighted and ill-conceived strategy. All further attempts to serve notices of eviction had been abandoned due to the incendiary nature of the situation, which meant that the tenants could continue to go about their business without any immediate threat looming. They had no reason to desist in their action and could probably carry on through the winter.

Charles Boycott, though verbally as defiant as ever, looked drained in the face, his flesh pale and his eyes heavy. His beard had not been trimmed for two weeks and was thick and tangled. The few hairs that he normally combed across the top of his head were frequently allowed to dangle to one side, giving him a particularly dishevelled appearance. His hands were rough and his skin split in several places around the knuckles, exposing angry-looking red slits framed by ingrained dirt.

All in all, the group that sat down to their meal on the evening of Thursday, 14 October, was dispirited and strained to the point of snapping.

Annie Boycott entered with a steaming pot and placed it in the centre of the table, having long since dispensed with the niceties of using a serving dish. She began to ladle soup into the diners' bowls.

Boycott looked down at the thin, off-white liquid, which had small solid lumps floating on the surface.

'What is this, Annie?' he asked, his voice non-confrontational, by now cognisant of her limited resources.

'Potato and oat soup.'

His lack of response spoke volumes.

'The turnips you brought were rotten,' she explained. 'Perhaps they were in the ground too long. The carrots and mangolds were all used yesterday and nobody brought me a new batch. All I had left were potatoes, some oats and milk. So this is the best I could do today.'

Nobody responded. They simply ate their food, which, despite its blandness, was welcome nourishment that might restore some of their energy, if not their spirits. For the next ten minutes the only sounds were the click-clack of spoons on crockery and the heavy rain beating against the windowpane. No words were spoken.

When he had finished, Boycott sat back and looked around at the fatigue etched into their faces. He drummed the table with his fingers while the others finished eating.

'Thank you, Aunt Annie. That was most tasty,' William said dutifully. Following the boy's lead, a few more muttered thanks were offered.

Boycott rose sharply and startled everyone, his chair almost toppling behind him. He turned and walked towards the door with purpose.

'Where are you going, Charles?' Annie inquired.

'I'm going to write a letter.'

Chapter 22

To the Editor of *The Times*

Sir, - The following may be interesting to your readers as exemplifying the power of the Land League. On September 22nd a process-server, escorted by a police force of 17 men, retreated on my house for protection followed by a howling mob. On the ensuing day the people collected upon my farm and some hundred or so came to my house and ordered off, under threats of ulterior consequences, all my farm labourers, workmen and stablemen. My blacksmith has received a letter threatening him with murder if he works for me and my laundress has also been ordered to give up my washing. A boy who carried my post bag to and from the town of Ballinrobe was struck and ordered to desist from his work, since which time my little nephew, on 2d of Oct was stopped on the road, struck and threatened. The shopkeepers have been warned to stop all supplies to my house and the telegraph messenger was also threatened. My farm is public property; people wander over it with impunity. My crops are trampled, carried away in quantities and destroyed wholesale. My gates are thrown open, the walls thrown down and the stock driven out on the roads. My ruin is openly avowed as the object of the Land League unless I throw up everything and leave the country. I say nothing about the danger to my own life, which is apparent to anybody that knows the country.

Charles C. Boycott, Lough Mask House, Ballinrobe, Mayo, October 14.

–*The Times*, 18 October 1880

18 October 1800

Bernard H Becker reposed in the small nook in a corner ofYe Olde Cheshire Cheese pub in Fleet Street and sipped his Fuller's porter, the cloudy, dark ale beloved of workingmen and newspapermen. He wasn't by habit a daytime drinker, but he'd badly needed a tipple to soothe the residue of nausea with which he'd awoken that morning, his previous night having been spent in the company of several hard-drinking correspondents from *The Illustrated News* and *The Telegraph*.

He resolved just to have the one, as he would need to be at his sharpest later that afternoon when he put his proposal to his employer, Frank Harrison Hill, editor of *The Daily News*. Hill wasn't a bad sort, he thought, but he had been known to lose his temper or change his mind between diametric opposites in a blink and you could never be certain what might set him off.

Becker looked around the pub. It had been here a couple of hundred years and was said to have been a regular haunt of Dickens, Twain, Tennyson and the Irish writer and poet Oliver Goldsmith, or so he'd heard, although he himself had no grand literary illusions of following in their footsteps or finding inspiration by sitting in the seat once occupied by the great Dickens buttocks. Yet the thought of Goldsmith returned his mind to things Irish, a land of great possibility, he considered, for a man of his talents.

He had spent much of the previous week in the company of an Irishman, Detective Sergeant William Melville, a rising star in the newly created police division called the CID, the Criminal Investigations Department. The detective was an ambitious man who clearly knew the value of press publicity and had proven both entertaining and informative. He'd been working on a story that typified those 'human interest' articles that littered *The Daily News*. It concerned the decline of London's Soho area, once the location of choice for the upper middle classes but in recent decades deteriorating like an apple left to rot. Nowadays it was the location of choice only for drinking dens, gambling pits, music halls and countless whores. Melville had conducted Becker safely through the area's darkest pits of indigence and depravity, along narrow, unlit lanes and alleys where drunken figures lurched in doorways and the grunts of purchased sex sounded behind curtains flickering with lamplight – a maze of human corruption.

Afterwards, Becker had treated Melville to dinner and drinks, and the conversation had drifted towards the current unrest in the detective's country of birth.

Most Englishmen, Becker among them, knew or cared little about their island neighbour. All the Irish appeared to do was whine interminably about their impecunious predicament, disrupt the British parliament, and terrorise the unfortunate Englishman at every opportunity. The Irish were viewed as an uneducated, violent and backward lot, and his colleagues in the press generally endorsed the view. Melville had enlightened Becker somewhat about the current internecine struggle between those who wished to pursue Home Rule (or outright independence) through parliamentary means, or those who sought a resolution through violence. Charles Stewart Parnell had managed temporarily to unify the constitutionalists and more moderate militants, but a well-equipped number of extremists had maintained a campaign of terrorism, particularly against landowners such as Lord Mountmorres. Becker could certainly sympathise with the landowners, who had been virtually abandoned to defend themselves against the forces of terror by their government.

And now this letter had appeared.

Through the haze of cigar smoke around him, he could see the assembled members of the press laughing and exchanging stories about their assignments, their glasses clinking and tongues clacking about their humdrum stories. Becker himself was fed up with London, with the squalor of the stories that illuminated *The Daily News*. His recent assignment in Soho had given him an urgent want to run to the nearby countryside and breathe deeply of some untarnished air. Unlike the dailies, the misleadingly titled *Daily News* appeared only once a month, which meant the stories were more deeply researched and less frantically prepared, which suited his style. But they also tended to focus on the underbelly of life. This was understandable, considering that Dickens had founded the newspaper. The current editor, Hill, and all of the editors in the intervening years since 'Mr Great Expectations', maintained that ethos, and Becker felt that this could work in his favour regarding the potential project upon which he had just stumbled.

He lifted *The Times* and brought his focus to bear on the letter written in the West of Ireland not four days ago. He then quickly skipped to the lengthy editorial, inspired directly by this Captain Charles Boycott's letter, a singular honour indeed. In his treatise, *The Times'* editor encouraged the immediate arrest of Parnell, Davitt and other Land League leaders as a means of shutting them up and undermining the movement, claiming that these men, through their inflammatory language, were directly responsible for the violent outrages against the landlord class. It also suggested that the government was being driven into a position where they would be forced to purchase all of the landlords' land and then simply hand it over to the tenantry. The article posited an alternative – that Forster, the Chief Secretary for Ireland, should take whatever coercive measures were necessary to destroy the Land League. Parnell's arrest should only be a 'first step'. Becker could well imagine what the second step would be.

The article then went on to directly reference this Boycott fellow and painted a grim picture of what existed in a part of the British Empire not five hundred miles distant:

> The state to which some parts of Ireland have been reduced by the terrorism of the Land League is described in a letter from a gentleman in Mayo, which we print today. A more frightful picture of triumphant anarchy had never been presented in any community pretending to be civilized. The persecution of the writer, Mr. Boycott, for some offence against the Land League's code is an insult to the Government and to public justice. If such monstrous oppression cannot be put down by the 'Constitutional powers', Mr Forster must, however reluctantly, proceed to the alternative he has already recognized.

Becker knew full well what that alternative was – mobilisation of the army, troops patrolling the streets of Ireland and scouring her hills in search of militants. In effect, *The Times* was calling for aggressive suppression. But better than that, his newsman's nose smelled a story that would prove much more compelling than thousands being slaughtered on some battlefield. People weren't interested in reading about the fate of thousands.

But the heroic resistance of *one* fascinated them.

***

An hour later he entered Frank Harrison Hill's office and approached the cluttered desk. The editor was a man headed for sixty, almost completely bald and rather pudgy. Hill didn't look up from what he was doing, which seemed to involve butchering some unfortunate correspondent's prose with a broad-nibbed fountain pen.

'What is it, Becker?'

He set *The Times* on Hill's desk, folded to show the Boycott letter.

'What's that?' Hill muttered, yet to raise his eyes.

'Something I think we should pursue in the interests of our readership.'

Hill paused, looked at Becker, and sat back in his chair, his instinctive cynicism evident. 'Becker, you've never pursued anyone's interests except your own.'

Becker said nothing; he felt like the acrobat he'd once seen walking a tightrope above the Alhambra Theatre's stage in Leicester Square, terrified to lean even an inch to one side or the other. After a few moments, Hill picked up the paper.

'Yes, I saw this. What of it?'

'Did you notice *The Times* also thought it worthy of an editorial? It looks like this whole Land League thing is going to explode. *The Times* is effectively calling for blood.'

'What do I care what the Conservatives' mouthpiece calls for?'

'Gladstone's going to have to act. Every second conversation these days is about the Mountmorres murder. There's a fuse burning in Ireland.'

'Save the metaphors for your articles, Becker. Anyway, most people here don't care a hoot about Ireland. This publication is struggling to survive. Filling it with stories about Irish politicians isn't going to help. Nobody cares.'

'They'll care that one of their own, a fine English gentleman and his family, have been under siege in their home and are battling – outmanned and outgunned – against the forces of anarchy.' Becker risked a subtle smile, his pitch now on the table.

Hill tapped his pen against the desktop meditatively. 'You know, Becker, not everyone believes the Irish peasants are in the wrong. Some of these new unions would see them as comrades battling the forces of capitalism. And many in the Liberal Party think they've been handed a raw deal.'

'Have you Irish blood in your veins, Mr Hill?' Becker grinned.

Hill furrowed his brow. 'No, Becker, I've got human blood in my veins. Maybe you should try one of these new blood transfusions and get some yourself. Anyway, how do you know this Boycott isn't exaggerating? And what about the other point of view? Not, by the way, that I've agreed to this.'

'Hear me out. If you give me this assignment, I promise to give you every side of the story, not just Boycott's, but the peasants' as well. But you have to admit, the idea of an Englishman under siege by a mob, abandoned by the empire, would have a genuine attraction for every blue-blooded Englishman.'

Hill relaxed into his chair. 'How long would this assignment take?'

'Well, for a full picture, I'd need to travel the west coast of Ireland. A police friend of mine from Kerry has given me a few contacts there. And this Boycott chap is in Mayo. I'd start there. I'd say a couple of months.'

'*Months?*' Hill thundered abruptly, causing Becker to flinch.

'But if I can get our readers hooked on the Boycott story, they'll want to know more.'

'As I said, Becker, this publication's nearly broke. And you want me to finance two months' holiday for you in Ireland?'

Becker sat in silence. After a minute or so of idly staring out the window at the bustle of Fleet Street below, Hill turned and picked up *The Times* again.

'If I think this isn't working, I'll drop it and you come back. And your copy had better be good enough to sell to other publications; it's the only way we can afford the expense.'

Becker could barely conceal his delight, but he limited himself to a nod and a 'thank you', then walked to the door.

'Becker.'

The journalist paused with his hand on the doorknob. 'Yes, sir?'

'Have the Soho story on my desk first thing tomorrow.'

CHAPTER 23

Off the main track there are no houses, only hovels as wretched as any in Connaught. It is quite evident that the poor people who inhabit them cannot buy much of anything. Men, women, and children, dogs, ducks, and a donkey are frequently crowded together in these miserable cabins, the like of which on any English estate would bring down a torrent of indignation on the landlord.

–Bernard H Becker, Special Commissioner of *The Daily News*, 23 October 1880

20-23 October 1880

On the Thursday following the publication of Boycott's letter, a fellow ex-officer of Weekes, Captain Raymond Jephson, made an unexpected appearance at Lough Mask House. In his company was his attractive, dark-haired 'housekeeper', Miss Reynolds.

Jephson was an incorrigible playboy, was enormously rich, had been married twice, and spent his days in the jolly pursuit of life's pleasures. The captain had read of Boycott's plight, knew Weekes resided at Lough Mask, and had decided that he 'couldn't leave a comrade to perish at the hands of the natives.' Bound for a ship from Galway to the United States, he had left his Dublin estate at Brooklawn House in Kimmage and taken a diversion to Mayo to help 'relieve the siege'. With him he brought a cartload of supplies, such as tinned meats, preserves, biscuits and soaps, which brought no small measure of joy to all. Most importantly, from Annie's point of view, Miss Reynolds had volunteered to remain as their housemaid until the 'siege' ended, causing Annie to literally hug the girl, which Boycott found unseemly.

Boycott and Weekes entertained Jephson over brandies and the ex-officer produced a copy of the previous Monday's *Times.* Boycott was overjoyed to see his letter in print and that he'd merited an editorial. Weekes updated his friend on the news that Dublin Castle had agreed to increase by twenty the number of constables guarding the house. Given the uniqueness of their predicament, they'd also ceded to Boycott's request to use the RIC's internal mail system.

'So, Jephson, has there been any other comment about my plight?'

'Dublin and Westminster are positively awash with discussion about it, old man!'

'But are they going to damn well do anything?'

Jephson shrugged. 'Not for me to say, old chap. But Gladstone's said to be sympathetic to the Irish. But politics and all that aren't my *forte*. More a cricket devotee!'

Boycott sipped his brandy. He was grateful for the jolly fool's help but the crops still lay in the ground unharvested. His letter might well have made him rich in terms of support, but the hard reality was that soon he might be bankrupt in terms of all else.

***

Bernard Becker dispatched the first of his letters to the editor of *The Daily News* in late October from Westport. His preconceptions of a country amid the throes of violent anarchy had already taken several knocks. But his brief stay in Dublin had, if anything, reinforced his fears, as a perception existed there of the west as a wild and lawless place. The air of disquietude lingering over the city had been rendered all the more chilly as a result of Boycott's letter to *The Times*, which had confirmed the worst fears of the British gentry there, who believed that soon they would be under siege in their own homes. A gentleman at Becker's hotel, upon hearing of his travel plans, had considered him mad and had conducted him to a gunsmith's in Dawson Street, where the proprietor had persuaded him to purchase a double-barrelled carbine, the intention being to ensure one could fatally hit the frequently-drunk assailants even at thirty yards. He was warned also that he might well be murdered by one of these drunken killers simply because he *looked* English.

A few days later, sitting in his room in Hughes's Hotel in Claremorris, Becker recorded that 'the sense of alarm and insecurity diminishes, to put it mathematically, as "the square of the distances". Even after a rapid survey of this part of the West I cannot help contrasting the state of public opinion here with that prevailing in Dublin. In the capital, the alarmists appear to have it all their own way. I was told gravely that there was no longer any security for life or property in the West...yet I have found the people here to have an absolutely delightful manner, and their kindness, civility, good humour, and, I may add, honesty, are remarkable.'

It was when Becker sought out two English peers who resided in the Claremorris area that he gained his first experience of the dichotomy between the landed gentry and the general populace. The gentlemen informed him that not only was a rising imminent, but that it was set for 31 October. Mayo and Galway were beyond the law, they said, and when he mentioned that he had witnessed no evidence of this, he was ridiculed. The killers were everywhere, every man and woman he met was a potential murderer, 'their minds poisoned by the Land League'.

But he'd been largely disappointed with his experiences thus far. Much of what he'd seen had been a revelation rather than a revolution, and revolution made for better copy. Where were the soldiers pursuing armed marauders across the mountains? Where were the running battles between the locals and police, the villages ablaze, the hordes of drunken assassins killing indiscriminately? He recalled a line from *The Times'* editorial: 'A more frightful picture of triumphant anarchy has never been presented in any community pretending to be civilized.' The nearest thing he'd seen to anarchy had been when a guest at the hotel had requested toast and Joe, the black-haired Celt in attendance, had cried 'toast?' as though a request had been made for broiled crocodile. The truth was that, after a few days, he had little to write about.

Having travelled on to Westport, he hired a car and driver and set off beyond the limits of the town in an attempt to get a more accurate picture of the countryside round about. The land, after all, was what all the trouble was about, so he was keen to see what had so riled the peasantry.

Collapsed houses speckled the countryside, their walls home to nesting birds, their floors grown through with foliage. His driver informed him that most were the remains of cottages abandoned during the famine. Becker had little knowledge of the famine of which the man spoke. As a boy he'd heard vague talk of thousands perishing in Ireland, but his knowledge was scant. Sharing his thoughts with his driver elicited a hollow laugh after which the man had informed him that it had been 'millions more like, than thousands... and it has not been forgotten.' Whatever was implied by that remark was lost on Becker, who assumed that 'millions' was an exaggeration. Experience had told him that tragedy and exaggeration often went hand in hand.

Spotting a plume of smoke some distance from the road, Becker requested they turn off along the 'boreen', a wretched track consisting of large stones and mud ponds. Eventually it deteriorated to the extent that they were forced to continue on foot, a short but precarious journey that left the skirts of his long overcoat infused with brown mud. He realised they were approaching a small collection of hovels, as the word 'cottage' failed to adequately convey the repugnance he felt as he drew near. His driver informed him this was the 'village' of Cloontakilla. Some women nearby fled in terror at the sight of them, probably fearful he had come to evict them. His driver called out to a lone girl and with the fearless innocence that only a child can possess, she hurried to them with a sprightly skip, her mass of fair hair fluttering wildly in the cutting wind. The child, though evidently as pretty as a mountain sylph, was thin and scantily clad. Her legs and feet were bare and a faded red petticoat and 'shirt' of some indescribable hue, on which dirt largely predominated, formed all her visible raiment.

Enquiring of the child if they might visit one of the homesteads, she happily conducted them to that of a Mr Browne. Here Becker had his first insight into the multifold motives of Messrs Parnell and Davitt. The effect on him was profound and that evening, huddled over a dressing table, and by the light of a flickering candle, he wrote:

> It has been my lot at various times to witness the institution known as 'home' in a state of denudation. It is not necessary to go far from London's Whitechapel Church to find dwellings unutterably wretched. But Browne's dwelling, when arrived at, exceeds the wildest of nightmares. Part of the wall has fallen in, and the two rooms that remain have the ground for a carpet and miserable starved-looking thatch for a roof. The horses and cattle of every gentleman in England are a thousand times better lodged. The chimney has long since 'caved in' and vanished, and the smoke from the turf burning on the hearth finds its way through the sore places in the thatch. In a bed in the corner of the room lies a sick woman, coughing badly; near her sits another woman, huddled over the fire.
>
> Now, I have been long enough in the world to be suspicious, and had it been possible for these people to know of my coming I might have suspected a prepared scene. But this was impossible, for even my car-driver did not know where he was going till he started. There are no indications of cooking, and, besides an iron pot, a three-legged stool and a bench, no signs of property are visible. There is nothing at all to feed man, wife, sister-in-law, son, and daughter during the winter, and the snow is already lying deep on Nephin Mountain. The tenant, Mr Browne, is a sorrowful man; but, like all Irishmen, is not wanting in loquacity. He shows me his 'far-r-rum', as he calls it, and it is a poor place. An acre of oats and mayhap a couple of acres of potatoes and cabbages. Of beasts he has none, except an ass, the unfortunate creature, who is made to drink the dregs of any sorrow falling upon Western Ireland. The poor animal is a withered phantasm.

A few days later a telegraph from his editor informed him that, while the dispatches thus far had been received with reasonable interest, they had hardly blazed a trail of pioneering reportage. *Daily News* readers were well acquainted with accounts of squalor. Hill wanted to know where the hell was his Boycott story?

Banishing from his mind as best he could the appalling sights he'd witnessed, he refocused his attention on the subject of Boycott and began to make inquiries of the peasantry and townspeople.

But even in Westport, at over thirty miles' remove from the man's estate, Becker quickly met a wall of silence. Not a soul knew a thing about him, or so they claimed. The mention of Boycott's name in any store or public house drew every eye upon him and terminated all conversation. His inquiries greatly exercised the curiosity of a few as to his identity and precise business. When one man offered to take him quietly down a lane and impart some information, Becker was immediately given pause, fearful they might murder him and dump his body in a bog. But his journalistic curiosity won the battle over his fear and he had taken up the local's offer. Boycott, he was informed, had been required to attend a hearing of the Bessborough Commission in Galway, which was an attempt by Gladstone to get a true picture of the conditions of Ireland's tenantry. Becker's informant told him that the land agent was planning to return tomorrow via the steamboat up Lough Corrib to Cong, and then by car from there. How the man possessed such an intimate knowledge of Boycott's travel arrangements was unclear (he suspected loose lips within the RIC), but he sounded genuine and Becker rewarded him with a shilling. The man departed with a warning that he might be careful not to be mistaken for Boycott, who was by now despised the length and breadth of Mayo.

The following morning Becker packed his bags, his double-barrelled carbine and his notebook, and set off in search of the story of his career.

***

Fr O'Malley recited the funeral rite as the coffin touched the bottom of the grave with a crunching sound that was brutal in its finality. He had performed the service countless times, but few occasions had the personal resonance as that of Teresa McGurk, wife of Martin, who had succumbed to what the doctor believed was blood poisoning, a condition that found its beginning with the loss of her child.

Martin McGurk, already embittered, now appeared to have receded into a world of his own, a world, the priest feared, haunted by the vile spectres of blood and vengeance. A comforting hand on McGurk's shoulder provoked no reaction. The man simply stared into the dark rectangular hole in the ground, the final resting place of all his love and dreams.

As Fr O'Malley walked away to a chorus of wailing, he was joined by Owen, Síomha and Owen's brother, Thomas, whom he had never met properly. They were introduced at a suitable distance from the mourners.

'I can't help but feel responsible in some way,' the priest said.

'From what I know, Father, the only people responsible for this are those bastards, the RIC,' Thomas opined.

'Thomas. Now's not the time,' Owen muttered.

'Sorry, Father, I just say things as I see them.'

'Sadly, Thomas, every pair of eyes sees things differently.'

'Not every pair. The English all see us as vermin.'

Fr O'Malley eyed him with a troubled curiosity, but didn't respond.

That evening they reconvened in Owen's cottage and were joined by Redpath, who had brought a collection of newspapers, including *The Times*. The nationalist press, such as *The Freeman's Journal* and *The Connaught Telegraph,* did report positively on the boycott but in general gave more weight to refuting suggestions that Parnell and Davitt had encouraged recent outrages and murders. But when Redpath read aloud Boycott's letter to *The Times* and then the editorial, several upraised voices battled to profess their anger.

'We never threatened his workers,' Owen protested. 'We talked to them.'

Fr O'Malley sighed. 'I suppose one could argue even that was a form of intimidation. I know that I felt I had intimidated the servants.'

'You're not defending Boycott, surely?' Síomha asked.

'Of course not. No threats of violence were made as Boycott implies. No one threatened his blacksmith with murder. Not that I know of, anyway. And he says the shopkeepers were warned off as well. Half the shopkeepers were in the group who invaded the estate. No, it's full of half-truths and exaggeration. But from another point of view it could be interpreted as intimidation.'

'And that's the view the English will take,' Thomas remarked reflectively.

Fr O'Malley nodded. 'What really bothers me is this stuff about his crops being stolen and destroyed, cattle driven out on to roads and so on. Sure, it's impossible. Even if we wanted to, we couldn't get near his fields for all the constables roaming the place. He's portraying us as a band of violent thugs and ruffians.'

'Father, I think you've more te worry about than that,' Thomas said.

'Why?' Owen asked.

He shrugged. 'You've had a peaceful protest. How do they respond? They call for the army to be sent in. I've seen this sort of thing before when we tried to form unions in Pennsylvania. They answered us with guns. I'm guessing the English will do the same. It's their nature. The hard fact is that, sooner or later, Ireland's going to have to answer like with like.'

The room fell to silence, Thomas's viewpoint settling upon them like a grey cloud.

'Thomas,' the priest mused, 'even if, God forbid, we choose that path, they will always outgun us. And besides, it's not a Christian way of–'

'I'm not a very religious man, Father. But that aside, you're forgetting that they also say they're Christian. And, in my experience, God always sides with those with more guns.'

'I'm sorry you feel that way.'

Owen was troubled by his brother's sudden interest in the situation and his apparent championing of revolution. Having said that, Thomas was just expressing a view that was widely held across Ireland.

'This is a setback,' Owen said, 'but it doesn't mean we should abandon the boycott.'

'Owen, you really think the English care about your so-called "boycott"? They'll simply send in the army and that'll be the end of that.'

'Perhaps. We'll see.'

Thomas abruptly rose from the table and reached for his coat and knapsack.

'Are you going out?' Síomha asked.

'Yeah, I thought I'd go into Ballinrobe for a drink.'

The others eyed each other, surprised at the suddenness of his decision.

Thomas paused by the door. When he spoke his tone had softened and his shoulders slumped. 'Listen, I'm not trying to dishearten you…I think I'm just upset at seeing that girl buried today. Died for nothing, she did. Anyway, look, I'll say goodnight.'

He turned and exited into the cold evening air.

***

Thomas rode hard in the fading light, wanting to get as far as possible from the cottage before the blanket of night was pulled over his head. But he knew, deep down, that his incessant prodding of the horse was motivated also by anger, as much at himself as the priest's saintly championing of peace.

In his frustration, he'd shown too much of his hand. He couldn't risk them suspecting his true intentions. Sooner or later the truth would out. It certainly would after he'd killed Boycott, but by then it wouldn't matter as he'd either be dead or gone. He found it strange but comforting that neither prospect troubled him much.

Sometime soon he would have to get back to Bull Walsh's safe house, where he'd lain low in the aftermath of Mountmorres's murder; he had to contact Doherty and find out what exactly was going on. He'd been back here for more than two weeks and there hadn't been a word.

He'd used that time to plan Boycott's assassination, considering every possible approach: while the land agent was working in the fields; or by concealing himself in the dense woodland; disguising himself as a constable, even the possibility of firing from a boat on Lough Mask, but each presented its own problems, particularly of escape.

And every plan he conceived required the help of at least two men. He needed Doherty and Bull Walsh and perhaps even another. But Doherty had been as uncommunicative as a dead man these past days. His frustration was rising, a hint of it surfacing in the cottage that evening. And the odds were that soon the army would build a bulwark of men and guns around Boycott, impenetrable to any plan.

He approached Ballinrobe and slowed to a trot. He had a contact here, a butcher, who might be able to get word to Doherty about the changing situation.

Thomas looked across the fields at the lights flickering in the windows of the British cavalry barracks. Its presence on Irish soil repulsed him, stirred the violent soup of his soul. He had but one thing in common with the men within its walls. He was a soldier. But unlike them, Thomas Joyce knew he fought for the army of the just. And only English blood could balance the scales.

***

The morning of Saturday, 23 October dawned chilly but bright with a stiff breeze cutting in from the Atlantic, swirling the fallen leaves along the Mall on Westport's riverside. In a laneway just off the Mall, where thirty years beforehand Owen and Thomas Joyce had sought temporary refuge, Bernard Becker located the services of Mr Conn Costello, a man with an uncovered carriage who was more than willing to drive him the thirty miles of meandering road south to Ballinrobe.

The going was slow and cold, even with his heavy ulster coat and cape pulled tightly around him. The road was almost deserted and they met but a handful of men or women driving or riding a donkey laden with panniers of turf, which they offered him for sale for fivepence. He declined, of course, but did notice the scantiness of their clothing and wondered at the hardiness of these people to endure such cold while they toiled for pennies, making him a trifle abashed at his own discomfort. They veered south and crossed what seemed like an interminable peat bog where the wind was particularly biting. Costello informed him that the snow-capped hills rising to the west were the Partry Mountains, which hugged the western shore of Lough Mask, the mention of which heartened him, as surely they were drawing near his destination. His spirits were dampened again when he learned they still had ten miles to go. Yet his companionable driver persisted happily with his chatter, at times informative and at others amusing, indicating points of interest along the way, such as monuments of tall, upright stones that pre-dated all known history, or recounting stories of battles and legends from aeons past. He found some light relief when Costello pointed to an islet in Lough Carra called Pleasure Island, where an ancient prince had reputedly taken countless virgins for 'deflowering', accentuating this word with a gentle, conspiratorial 'man-of-the-world' nudge into Becker's ribs. Ever since that time, Costello said, the island had been incredibly fertile and the trees there always grew tall and erect, never going limp. Costello had concluded this tale with a peal of laughter, which Becker shared.

By the time they reached Ballinrobe, the wind had faded and the temperature had risen to an unseasonable warmth, to the extent that Becker was forced to shed his overcoat. Here he bade farewell to Costello, who made some excuse about having to return to Westport, and he was unable to find a driver to carry him the remainder of the way. After numerous enquiries, he realised the problem lay in his revealing his destination, as nobody would have anything to do with Boycott. Finally he succeeded in hiring a car by claiming he was an English writer of travel books.

Late in the afternoon he drew near to the Lough Mask Estate, the source of all the recent fuss among the readership of the London *Times*. The heat was now oppressive, he found, for he still wore several layers of clothing. He came to a tall, iron gate that marked the entrance, behind which stood three constables, each with a hand resting on a holstered weapon, ready to respond with deadly force should he prove to be a covert assassin of some kind. He informed them of his name and intent, but they were steadfast in their refusal to admit him and told him to 'be on his way' in no uncertain terms. He wasn't put off quite so easily. He saluted them cordially and remounted his car, trotting off until a bend in the track put him beyond sight of Boycott's guardians.

As he rounded the corner he came upon a sight that he considered unparalleled. He sat on his car and observed for some time in astonishment, then withdrew his notebook and began to write furiously:

> Beyond a turn in the road was a flock of sheep, in front of which stood a shepherdess herding them back, while a shepherd was driving them through a gate into an adjacent field. Despite the work she was engaged upon, it was quite evident, from her voice and manner, that the shepherdess was of the educated class, and the shepherd carried himself with the true military air. Both were obviously amateurs at sheep driving, for shepherd and shepherdess were only doing what a good collie would achieve alone and unaided. Behind the shepherd were two tall constables with carbines loaded who shadowed him everywhere at a distance of a few yards. All his backings and fillings, turnings and doublings, were followed by the armed policemen. This combination of the most proverbially peaceful of pursuits with carbines and buckshot was irresistibly striking, and the effect of the picture was not diminished by the remarks of Mr. and Mrs. Boycott, for the shepherd and shepherdess were no other than these.

He beckoned to Boycott, prompting the constables to whirl about at the strange voice and level their carbines at him. For a moment Becker feared his assignment – and his existence – might come to a premature end, but Boycott stayed their hand and inquired who he was. His *bona fides* having been established, the land agent admitted him to the field with enthusiasm and introduced him to his 'fellow workers': his wife, Mrs Annie Boycott, a fine-looking woman of early middle age, his pretty niece and young nephew, and his friend Mr Weekes. Mrs Boycott, while courteous, seemed particularly worn and unwilling to engage in conversation, so resumed her toil.

Becker had seen many sights as a press correspondent but never one to match that of members of the English upper class toiling like common labourers. It was simply an unthinkable state of affairs. He could already imagine the popping eyes of the gentry back in England as they perused his account.

He explained that he'd been dispatched to recount the depredations that had brought the land agent to such a cruel nadir and assured him that it was very much in his interests to relate the 'human tragedy' of his story. Boycott had only been too eager.

'Well, back in August, some local rabble stirred up my workers and forced them to strike,' he explained as they walked about the fields, constables in tow, Becker scribbling notes as Boycott strode along, occasionally striking the ground with his cane to emphasise a point. 'One of these new godless communist ideologies at work, I suspect. However, I was prepared to hear their grievances and make generous concessions, after which they willingly returned. But when several tenants defaulted on their rent, the entire tenantry rebelled, no doubt incited by the anarchists in the Land League and their local agitator, Father O'Malley. I was shocked! Hell and confound it, man, until then my tenantry and I were going along nicely. Since I've been at Lough Mask I've invested vast amounts of money on improving the estate and the general neighbourhood. It is as though one had a friend for many years and he suddenly slapped you across the face.'

Boycott stopped near to Lough Mask's shore and stared across the water, shaking his head in apparent sad reflection.

As they returned towards the cornfield he expressed the view that the Land League wished to 'hunt him out of the country'. Becker learned that they were reduced to one domestic servant as everyone else had been forced to abandon him, to a man or woman expressing sorrow and in some cases weeping openly at having to part from his employ. And no tradespeople for ten miles around would deal with him. He could not sell his herd or even the corn that had been cut, and he had no means of winnowing the corn anyway. He had five hundred pounds worth of crops still in the ground, and if they were not harvested within the next month they would rot and he would be ruined.

Becker thought Boycott a man with a short fuse and curt manner. He found several of his questions cut off before he could finish them, as though Boycott wasn't listening. But he recognised that the land agent's position was intolerable and the strain of this past month must have been enormous, so surely this accounted for his manner. He also formed an impression of Boycott as a resolute and quite valiant individual, instilled with a rigid self-discipline.

As they drew once more within sight of Mrs Boycott and the others labouring under the autumnal sun, their faces streaked with perspiration and soil, their hair awry, their clothing tarnished with every class of dirt, he could not suppress a sense of outrage at the predicament of a fellow Englishman. Yet he felt a surge of pride at seeing the Boycotts at their toil while armed policemen stalked along in their shadow. Boycott's first-hand telling of events had made him realise he would need little hyperbole to sculpt a stirring tale for the readers of *The Daily News*. Reporting the Boycotts' predicament would, in fact, be his patriotic duty.

Becker said his goodbyes, promising to return and to bring Boycott's plight to a wider audience, at which point the agent nodded, grunted and turned abruptly away.

It crossed Becker's mind, as his car reached the main road north to Ballinrobe, to take a detour to visit the tiny hamlet of Neale, home to the priest whose name had been spat from Boycott's lips. But the excitement of recounting the scenes he had witnessed was too great, so he quickly flicked the reins and pulled to his left, steering the horse towards Ballinrobe. Bernard H Becker's subsequent report would include no mention of any viewpoint on the situation at Lough Mask House other than that of Charles Boycott.

CHAPTER 24

Sedition, conspiracy and murder are abroad, life and property are in peril; the era of government in Ireland has passed away. The Government must put an end to the existing terrors *coute que coute* [at all costs]. Propose Coercion Acts; proclaim martial law! Ireland needs to be ruled with an iron fist.

–*The Daily Express*, 1 October 1880

MISS FANNY PARNELL, sister of Charles Stewart, to her countrywomen:

Our nation stands on the brink of a tremendous conflict between English colonist and Irish serf. Which is to win? The struggle will be a life and death one. Let Irish women put their shoulders to the wheel, for the war that must be waged will be for the cause of women and children. There is but one body in Ireland endeavouring to help you in your hour of agony – The Irish Land League. Extremists find fault with the League because it does not use physical force. I believe that the League is right to confine itself to moral force alone. Someone has said that suffering belongs especially to women. I entreat my countrywomen here not to belie the reputation of their sex. Have you heard what happened at Carraroe, when the women – as nobly as the old heroines of Rome and Sparta – threw themselves in front of the bayonets of the soldiery and saved their husbands and children? I fear that this winter heroic women as well as heroic men will be wanted in Ireland.

–*The Nation* and *The New York Irish World*, 12 August 1880

24 October 1880

Síomha stood looking at the ivy-covered sweathouse on Inismaine Island, the structure appearing little different to her now, some twenty-four years after she'd first made love to Owen within its ancient walls.

It was Sunday afternoon and like the day before, it had become pleasantly warm. Owen had lingered after mass to meet with Fr O'Malley, Thomas had disappeared to Ballinrobe without explanation, Tadhg had gone to play hurling and Niamh was at a friend's cottage. Finding herself alone, she'd decided to take a reflective stroll across the shallow waters out to Inishmaine Island and the precise spot where their life together, to all intents and purposes, had been conceived.

Monks from nearby Inismaine Abbey, now but a tumble of stones, had constructed the so-called sweathouse. They used to light fires inside and lie within, the swirls of heat and smoke allowing them to commune more closely with God, or so some said. It had certainly brought her closer to Owen, and the memories of those days had come crowding back like a flock of sheep channelled through a narrow gate by a sheepdog, clambering over each other to get through. And she'd let them come, allowing the indulgence of immersing herself in their sweet nostalgia. Just as she had immersed herself that day, long ago, naked, in the waters of the lough.

She quailed at some of her recollections as she began to stroll back towards the mainland – stripping naked in the open air, pretending to bathe at his favoured fishing spot, knowing he would soon be along to cast his line out among the silvery flashes of fish. She'd sinfully used her body to tempt him, coax him to make the leap she knew he couldn't make alone, to cast aside his indecision and fear and to give his heart to her without condition. As he had emerged through the bushes, she had allowed him the indulgence of caressing her with his startled, aroused gaze, before feigning affronted modesty, rushing from the water and clasping her dress. He'd sputtered profuse apologies and turned away as she dressed. She had grinned to herself like a mischievous sprite behind his back, then touched his shoulder and told him not to be sorry. She wasn't.

Yet she had known, even after they had kissed by the lakeshore, that Owen was still capable of changing his mind, of spending days mulling over their relationship and possibly backing away from commitment. She'd often over-heard the farmers say on market day during the barter of an animal that a drink afterwards would 'seal the deal'. That line had played in her mind as she'd led him to the sweathouse and crawled on hands and knees ahead of him into its dark and cool interior. Not a drink, but the conception of a child, would seal the deal on their relationship.

The risk, the rashness, the brazenness! What a little minx she'd been! But despite her self-reproach, she couldn't help but smile. Perhaps if she hadn't done what she'd done her life might have taken a wholly different path, one not so blessed, she thought; for, despite their poverty, she did feel blessed.

But to this day she bore a scar of guilt. She told him of her pregnancy a month later and they married hastily, raising the eyebrows of more than a few. But she need not have feared the whispers that would have accompanied a baby arriving just seven months after wedlock, for the child was stillborn, its life ending before it saw the light of day. Perhaps it had been God's punishment for her selfish ploy.

Síomha lifted her skirts to her knees and waded the short distance back to the shore. Feet on dry land, she replaced her shoes and turned to see one of the tenant farmers, Francis O'Monaghan, some distance away. She returned his wave.

She recalled that she had once regarded men like Francis as 'turnip pickers' – their days were spent discussing the trivia of village life while hers were spent in the endless limits of an imagination fuelled by books and learning. She was a publican's daughter in Clonbur, better off than most, and she'd been the brightest of her class at school, though none of the male teachers or her classmates would admit as much. It was their shared passion for books that had first brought her and Owen together. But what an intellectual snob she'd been, keeping the locals at arm's length for fear their company might taint her. After her marriage and the beginning of their life as farmers, she had quickly come to have a deep respect for the ordinary folk who surrounded them. They were tough, honest to a fault and dedicated to their families. And they would come to a neighbour's help without prompting.

And Owen had grown to be the man she knew he would be. He had never escaped the bonds of the land, but in many ways, although he often dreamed aloud of unfulfilled hopes and wishes as they lay in their bed, she believed in her heart that he hadn't really wanted to be anything other than a farmer. Perhaps it connected him to his own upbringing or to his family's memory, or perhaps it attached him in a real, tangible way to Ireland. She frequently ribbed him that he dithered over everything. He had dithered especially over her and only asked for her hand when he had no choice. The one time he had been decisive, she had told him with a smile, was when he'd leapt from that ship at Westport and swum back to shore. Ireland was his true mistress, she'd said, the one lady he could never be parted from and that could bring him to take action. He had rebelled at her suggestion, but 'he doth protest too much', she'd thought.

She had lost another baby in their second year and had begun to despair. A year later and she was pregnant again, her days filled with dread that another horrible loss would afflict them. But Lorcan had come alive into the world after a terrible battle that had raged an entire night. When Lorcan had, as a young man, taken a wife and departed Ireland forever, she'd been given to weeks of deep melancholy, haunted by the same awful sense of loss that had accompanied the stillbirths. And although Owen had been sorrowful, she could never convey to him the emotional depth of her privation as a mother robbed of the fruits of her womb.

When Tadhg's time to enter the world had come, she had undergone even greater agonies, and but for Owen, the child would surely have perished. He came four weeks early and day turned to night as the midwife's hands probed and prodded, the walls echoing back Síomha's screams. Owen, pacing frantically beyond the door, had finally burst in, earning a torrent of abuse, the midwife ranting about the indecency and outrage of his daring to intrude on a ritual ordained by nature for the eyes of women only. But he pushed the old crone aside roughly, calmed Síomha with tender words, knelt between her legs and reached inside her. He had delivered a hundred lambs and foals in his time and after a minute or so he turned to the midwife and yelled that she had the child 'arseways'. The woman insisted his interference would only do harm and that everything was in God's hands now. Owen muttered some profanity and began to press gently into his wife's swollen abdomen, probing and manipulating the unborn child inside her, trying to manoeuvre the child's head towards the opening.

He'd reached inside her then and begun to move the child with his hand, and what an eternity that seemed to take. But finally she felt something shift, a release, as though she had been probing about in a darkened room and finally her hand had fallen upon the door, and she pushed and pushed, and within minutes Tadhg's head had appeared and then the body, and then he had cried at the flick of Owen's finger. Owen took the infant and pushed it on to her breast, and as the rankled midwife muttered her disgust and left, they clutched each other in a tight embrace and cried.

She had lost one more child early in pregnancy and then, when she was aged thirty-six, Niamh had arrived. This time no call had gone out for the midwife. Thanks be to the heavens that, for once, all had gone well and they had been gifted their only girl, Owen having played no small part in not only the conception of two of their children, but also their birth.

But Owen wasn't perfect; she wasn't foolish enough to believe that. Like everyone else in the world, he was afflicted with flaws. He still ruminated on everything, even after all these years, and she often found she had to give him a kick in the backside, metaphorical or otherwise, to force a decision out of him. He'd sometimes allow a blackness into his soul, particularly when it came to landlords and the English presence in their country, and he had in the past, in anger, expressed a view that they would only ever be rid of the foreigners through war. And while he would give his life for his country or his family, she knew he'd never truly believed in bloodshed as an ultimate means to an end.

Over the years he had also been given to bouts of melancholy, when his mood would darken and he would snap for no reason at her or the children. He would often wander about the farm or sit staring across the lough bearing a sombre face, shoulders slumped. In the early years the bouts might last for days, but he had largely outgrown them, time closing the darkest pits of memory. Much of his sadness emanated from his experiences in the famine; she herself had lost two of her five brothers to fever. Everyone had lost someone. But he had been cursed to lose everyone either to death or to a foreign land. He had cause enough to feel mournful.

But her husband loved her and their children as much as it was within the ability of a man to love. And that, she considered, was her greatest blessing, and she prayed daily that God would not see fit to take him or any more of those she loved from her bosom for a great many years to come.

***

When Síomha arrived back home it was still early in the afternoon. There would be neither sight nor sound of any of them for some time yet, she imagined, and the preparation of their meal could be put on hold for a while. She picked up a week-old copy of *The Ballinrobe Chronicle*, which she set on the table, but her mind was distracted before she read the first line and she sat, chin on hand, staring out the window for a time.

She rose presently and went to the bedroom, her thoughts intent on drifting back to times past and that outrageous day on the shore of Lough Mask. She permitted the immodest thought that she had indeed been beautiful then, but life, babies and time had taken their toll. She stood before their old second-hand mirror and looked down at the dress that Thomas had given her and that had earned so many compliments after mass. She ran her hands along the curve of her hips, measuring them against memory, and frowning a little. Then she opened the buttons and allowed it to fall. She undid the lacing on her pantalettes and pushed them down, stepping lightly from them and standing there naked. She cupped her breasts, lifting them to ease the annoying sag that child nurturing had brought, and turned from side to side to determine if even a little of her beauty remained. She tilted the mirror forward for a better view of her lower body then turned to peer at her backside over her shoulder. It had lost the tightness and gentle curve of youth, but her skin was still smooth to touch, her flesh soft to press. Lost in her thoughts, it was in this pose she stood, when, too late, she heard the voice beyond the door.

'Síomha, they're saying Boycott's got the police posting his mail and–'

As he pushed the door open he froze at the sight of her, the words severed from his lips, his mouth dropping open, hand still gripping the door latch. So startled was she that she made no effort to cover herself and, for a moment, as his eyes wandered over her body and then rose again to her eyes, they were both transported to an earlier time, a youthful day that lived only in the privacy of their souls.

'What are you…?'

'Owen, I'm…'

He pushed the door closed behind him, took her in his arms and kissed her, all thoughts of Boycott and Parnell and landlords banished from his mind.

Owen lifted her from her feet and carried her to the bed, lay her down and almost fell on top of her. Síomha laughed aloud and pretended to push him away.

'Owen, it's Sunday, we've just been to mass. We can't…'

He was awkwardly, desperately pulling off his jacket.

'I'm sure God will give us his blessing,' he said.

And they made love as they had almost a quarter of a century before, their passion and their unqualified love undimmed by the passing of the years.

***

Their mood was upraised for the remainder of the day and their son and daughter were bemused at the air of gaiety that pervaded the cottage. Thomas returned late from Ballinrobe after they had retired keenly to bed and they listened as he mooched about, assuming he'd had too much drink taken, whispering their worries about his increasingly furtive behaviour.

The next morning, with Niamh at school and the men engaged about the farm, she began an overdue sprucing of the cottage. She carried their thin mattresses outside and beat them thoroughly with Tadhg's hurley, washed down the smoke-blackened windows and swept the floor of every room. As she was poking the broom under their bed, a mouse skittered across her bare foot and she yelped aloud. She made a lunge with the broom after the scampering rodent but it fled towards the living area. She quickly set off in chase, making several unsuccessful strikes as it fled past the hearth.

'Come here, you dirty little beast!' she yelled and swung the broom in an arc that sent a tureen clanging to the floor. In its terror the creature turned and ran directly across the room towards the corner where Thomas had folded his blankets and piled his possessions. The mouse now sought refuge behind these and she hurried across before it might escape into some hollow within the walls. She pulled Thomas's blankets and clothes away and saw the creature dart beneath his knapsack. Broom at the ready, she grasped the knapsack and threw it aside and was immediately conscious of its weight. It landed on the floor with a loud thud and her pursuit of the rodent stopped suddenly. The creature vanished as Síomha, the hunt forgotten, turned her attention to the knapsack.

She hesitated a long time, staring down at the crumpled bag. It wasn't in her nature to pry into people's personal possessions, but something disturbed her about that bag. He'd said he only carried a few clothes and mementos from America, but the weight of whatever lay inside was not that of pants or shirts – and his recent behaviour, disappearing suddenly into Ballinrobe, implying the boycott was all but useless, all conspired to set her mind ill at ease, and she soon found her hand reaching for the bag.

It landed with a thud on the table. She cast a quick glance through the window to check that no one was nearby, then began to undo the straps, fear rising in her breast. She folded back the flap and peered inside, then removed some shirts, pants and a small, flat metal can. There was a book by Marx, another by someone called Malthus and a bundle of pamphlets on Irish nationalism and anarchism. Troubled somewhat by the sight of these, she rummaged further but could find nothing to explain the bag's weight, and began to think she was imagining things. She lifted the knapsack again and allowed it to fall. Again it thumped down hard, yet she had removed everything. She glanced over her shoulder, her pulse racing and droplets of perspiration popping out on her forehead.

Síomha pressed her hand flat at the base of the bag and allowed her fingers to explore the edges, finally locating a cleverly concealed flap held in place by straps. She undid these blindly, fumbling with the tiny buckles. She lifted the flap to reveal a compartment holding a rectangular box of dark stained wood, its surface scuffed and worn, which she removed and set on the table. She lifted the small latch. There was a tiny metallic click and she trembled as the hinged lid rose in her hands, confirming what she had feared in her heart all along.

On the inside of the lid was a label, yellow with age, with the legend 'E. Remington & Sons Manufacturers of Arms and Ammunition, Armory, Ilion, N.Y.' The box was divided neatly into sections, lined with a soft, deep-red material, and within it sat a revolver with a barrel perhaps eight inches in length. The metal was black and it had a dark wooden handle grip. The other sections contained pliers, a small circular can labelled 'caps' and about twenty bullets. A shock of cold passed through her as she lifted the weapon, as though she'd stepped from a warm room directly into a frosty morning. The tremble in her hands was visible to her own eyes as she examined the gun, its cold metal surface giving her the same grim sensation she'd experienced when touching a corpse lying in wake.

But what to do? Should she call out to Owen this instant? Was it possible there was some explanation for Thomas having such a thing beyond what she feared?

'What are you doing?'

The voice made her jump and yelp. Síomha swung around and saw Thomas in the doorway. The fear in her heart was palpable and chilling. She'd had no notion of his approach, no hint of a footstep or a shadow. She had a sudden urge to open her bladder but fought it and with all her strength lifted her shoulders and stood square, facing him.

'You searched my bag,' he said. It wasn't a question.

Síomha could hardly deny it and could not invent any plausible explanation. Then she realised she had no need. She had been wrong to do as she had but her action had been outweighed by a far greater wrong.

'You brought a *gun* into my house?'

'It's just a–'

'Where my *children sleep*?'

He took a step forward and extended his hand. She could tell he was struggling to control his anger.

'Give me the gun, Síomha. It's not what you're thinking.'

She looked at the weapon, which she cradled in front of her. She had never held a gun in her hands before, had no knowledge of weapons. If she just pulled this trigger, would that cause it to fire? Or was some other action needed? Why was she even considering these things? Did she really believe she was in danger from Thomas? From Owen's brother?

He took another step closer. 'Síomha. Listen to me. It's a gun I had during the Civil War. It's just a memento. Haven't fired it in twenty years. I didn't tell anyone as I was afraid Tadhg or Niamh might become curious about it and do themselves harm.'

His voice had become softer, more conciliatory. He almost sounded like he was pained by guilt. And his explanation had some plausibility. She desperately wanted to believe him. She raised the gun in both hands, one on the grip, the other clasping the barrel, and took a deep breath as she tried to reason this thing out.

And it was then that she noticed the smell.

It was hard to define. Schoolroom blackboards. Chalk dust. Burnt paper. And the subtle scent that lingers when a match has been drawn across a surface, in the moment when the flame balloons. And though she had no experience of guns she knew in her heart and soul that this one had been fired in the recent past.

'A souvenir? When did you fire it last?' Her voice was trembling.

'Síomha, put the gun down.'

'Answer me!'

He stepped closer. He was just three yards away. She tried to back away but her backside struck the table. Thomas's face grew harsh again and he stretched out his hand.

'Give me the *fucking* gun.'

And then he lurched at her.

CHAPTER 25

To rescue the aristocracies from censure, to defend the monstrous oppression of Ireland, our contemporary rulers lay the blame on nature or God. Since Mr Malthus first published his book [*An Essay on the Principle of Population*], for the purpose of vindicating governments from the charge of causing the misery they pretend to relieve, a principle of population had been made the scapegoat for ignorant and oppressive rulers and they have cast all their own sins on the benevolent ways of nature.

–*The London Telegraph*, 23 January 1848

The Murder of Lord Mountmorres has excited feelings of alarm little short of actual panic among all respectable citizens. Private accounts represent the state of the West as very alarming. It is well known that other landlords are marked out for assassination and will be shot the instant an opportunity is presented. Quantities of arms have been brought into the country. The savage malignity of the assassins who gave the coup de grace to Lord Mountmorres may be inferred from the fact that so close was the revolver to his head that some of the powder was found in his eyebrows.

–*The Times*, 1 October 1880

25 October 1880

Thomas grasped the gun and tried to wrench it from Síomha's hands, the struggle sending the table cracking against the gable wall. She emitted a startled yell but clung to it tenaciously.

'Let go, you bitch!' he snarled.

Such was the venom in his voice that for the first time she had a glimpse into the blackness in his soul. All was revealed in an instant to be a pretence of decency, a mask concealing some darker purpose. And she was sure he would kill her if he seized the gun. But her grip was waning in the face of his savage, feral rage and she felt the barrel slowly rising towards her chin.

There was a noise, something clattering to the floor and Owen was suddenly behind his brother, his hands clamping Thomas's shoulders and heaving him away, his strength trebled by the sight he had come upon. Thomas fell face down in an ungainly crumple, his shoulder striking the tureen Síomha had dislodged earlier. He yelled out in pain.

But Owen's action had sent the weapon skittering across the floor towards the hearth, just yards from Thomas's grasp.

'The gun!' she screamed.

Owen launched himself towards it just as Thomas began to rise. His hand fell agonisingly short and in a moment Thomas was upon him, beating with his fists, and they became locked in a frenzied, rolling embrace. Síomha hurled herself on to Thomas's back, but he struck out blindly, landing a knuckle on her eye and she collapsed backwards, clutching her face.

Thomas brutally butted his brother twice with his forehead, drawing a stream of blood from his nose and causing Owen to loosen his grip. Thomas wrenched himself free, clambered up and took a step towards the gun before Owen seized his ankle and he went sprawling again. But his action had been in vain for his brother fell with his hand just inches from the weapon. He seized it, rolled over and aimed.

'No!' Síomha screamed.

But he didn't fire. He sat up, backed away on his rump and pushed himself up against the wall beside the hearth, his breath heaving. Owen clutched at his bloodied face and Síomha hurled herself to him, throwing her arms about his neck.

Thomas chuckled through gulping breaths. 'Ye could never beat me in a fight, little brother.'

Owen ignored him and held Síomha back to allow him look at her. Besides an already swelling left eye, she appeared unharmed.

'Are you all right?'

She nodded, her voice now lost to shock.

'Get up,' Thomas said, gesturing with the gun.

They both stood, Síomha clinging to her husband's arm.

'Close the door and sit behind the table.'

'Do as he says,' Owen whispered.

They sat with their backs to the gable wall, watching as he fetched a bottle of whiskey and drank from the neck, his eyes never straying from them. Besides, they were virtually trapped behind the table and by the time Owen might extract himself, Thomas would have ample time to do whatever he pleased. Owen took a small pleasure in lifting his brother's shirt from the table and mopping the blood from his face.

Thomas pulled a chair across and sat facing them, clutching the whiskey with his free hand.

Síomha abruptly gripped Owen's arm. 'Tadhg...if he comes inside–'

'It's all right. I sent him for seed. He'll be gone an hour.'

Thomas shook his head slowly. 'I didn't want this. Really. I'd have been gone soon and ye wouldn't be any the worse. But ye had to stick your woman's nose into my business. Christ! Do ye always search visitors' belongings?'

When she didn't respond he barked, 'Well?'

'I was chasing a mouse. I moved your bag and felt something in it. It was too heavy to be clothes or anything.'

'So you searched it? Just like that? What a nosey bitch.'

'Are you going to kill us?' she asked.

'Kill you? My own brother and his wife? What sort of man do ye think I am?' he snapped indignantly.

'I don't know, Thomas. What sort of man are you?' Owen asked.

Thomas didn't answer, just sipped his whiskey for a while, staring intently at them. Eventually he gestured towards the items on the table.

'Put them back in the bag while I think.'

They did as ordered. When they had finished he rose and lifted the bag, placing it beside his chair as he reseated himself.

'I s'pose your whole story about America was horseshit?' Owen asked.

He shook his head. 'No. It was all true. The war, my wife, the ranch, the mines. Not a word of a lie. I swear. But I did leave a few bits out.'

Owen studied him. His every gesture, the look in his eyes, the barely concealed triumphalism in his smile, his tone, they each were the traits of a different being to the one he'd welcomed into his home just a few short weeks before. It was as though the character he'd presented to them was a chimera he'd conjured and the true Thomas had finally revealed himself. What a fool he'd been. Blinded by his own love, his own wish fulfilment. He'd spent decades imagining the possible scenarios of his brother's life, hoping that one day he would reappear and they would embrace and exchange tales of their different lives, laugh and share a drink together as brothers. And Thomas had walked back in and stepped perfectly into the portrait of his imagination.

Except Thomas hadn't filled it perfectly. And Owen had simply chosen to ignore the flaws in the picture. Like Thomas disappearing for days, unlikely tales of jobs on farms, the money, the horse, trying to bend Tadhg's ear to his political leanings. None of these things alone had amounted to much, but collectively he should have recognised that his brother was not all he appeared to be. Yet, despite the warning signs, he could never have believed that Thomas would attack Síomha or that he'd ever look into his own brother's eyes and see murderous intent. He hated himself for his naivety, for putting his family at risk so he could fulfil some vain wish for an end to a distant chapter of his life. And he felt shame that it had fallen to Síomha to reveal Thomas for what he was. He could have searched the knapsack weeks ago!

'I know what ye're thinking, Owen,' Thomas said as he deftly removed and lit a cigarette with one hand. 'Ye never saw it coming. Ye're feeling guilty. Don't. I would have fooled anyone. Ye know why?'

'What's the point of this?' Síomha asked.

'I'll tell ye why,' he continued, ignoring her. 'Ye see, most of it was true. I didn't turn up here just te use ye. I never stopped wondering about ye all those years. I was happy te see ye, to find out what had become of ye. Ye can believe it or not. It doesn't matter anymore.'

'Why don't you shut up and tell us why you're here?'

He dragged on his cigarette and smiled at them through the wispy, blue-grey smoke. 'Oh now I get it, brother. It's not guilt ye're feeling. Ye think you're so fuckin' smart and I'm so fuckin' stupid and ye're as mad as a bull that I put one over on ye. That's it, isn't it?' He uttered a loud, terse laugh.

Síomha tightened her hold on Owen's hand.

'Anyway, it's of no matter now. I'm the one in control and your big brain can do nothing for ye. That's what ye never understood. Ye think ye can reason all this out, fight your enemies with clever words and speeches. But ye can silence any speech with a single bullet. That's where the real power lies.'

'Power? Is that what you want?'

'Yeah. But not for my own ends. For my country. The power te rid us of the English. And your landlords.'

Síomha leaned forward a little. 'And when you've achieved that, what then?'

'Then we'll be free, Síomha. Our destiny will be our own.'

Owen laughed mirthlessly. 'You've been gone thirty years. You know nothing about this country. What's your plan? Rule it through the barrel of a gun?'

Thomas bristled and threw the cigarette on the floor.

'Don't fuckin' insult me! I know far more about this country than you'll ever know. And I'm prepared te do more than your band of peace lovers ever will.'

'Fine,' Síomha said. 'Why don't you leave and get on with it?'

'No, no, missy. Not yet. There are a few things my self-righteous, arrogant brother needs te hear.' He swallowed another mouthful of whiskey. 'Now, where to begin? Time for some home truths.'

'Truth? You don't know the meaning of it.'

'Shhh, brother. Truth, as your priest will tell you, is a matter of perspective. And ye may find your own perspective changed. Let's see now. Pennsylvania. I'm afraid I told a little fib there. I *was* in the Mollies and I *did* actually kill the man just like they said in the posters. In fact, I killed plenty. But not one of them was murder. No more than killing in the Civil War was murder. It was just a different war.'

'You sound like you're proud to have killed,' Síomha whispered in disgust.

'Oh I am. That's the job of a soldier, to kill. But let's move on. Circumstances forced me to abandon that battle. But then, by chance, when I'd fled to New York I met a man who handed me the opportunity te fight the fight I'd always dreamed about. Te fight the English on my home soil. He introduced me te Clan na Gael, the American arm of the Irish Republican Brotherhood.' He grinned. 'It was that same man who brought us back together, Owen. A man you've met.'

Despite his anger, Owen's interest was piqued, but he was utterly mystified.

'His name is Donal Doherty.'

Owen's lips parted at the recollection of Doherty, the Fenian he'd met at the

Irishtown rally a year and a half ago. Doherty had actually tried to recruit him.

'He recognised you at Irishtown. He's a friend of mine, saw the resemblance straight away. I'd told him all about us. We couldn't be certain it was you. Joyce is a common name in Mayo. But when he told me, I knew. I felt it. Same area, same name, almost the same face.'

'Who is this Doherty, Owen?' Síomha asked.

'An assassin. They're terrorists. Not even part of the regular IRB. Extremists. He wanted me to join them. But I couldn't...' Owen glanced at her and shook his head.

'No, ye couldn't. That's always been your problem, Owen. Ye could never do what needed te be done. Make the hard choices. Which is why I'm here.'

'What do you mean?'

He made a dismissive wave with the gun. 'You and your boycott. The New Departure. Parnell, Jesus! Worse still, Davitt? Christ, how could a freedom fighter like Davitt get roped into this bullshit? While you make ripples we make waves with a single attack. Look at the English after Mountmorres, scurrying about like frightened rats.'

'You killed Mountmorres?'

'Me and others.'

'And what about the old herdsman they arrested for his murder? Is he part of your plan as well?'

'Had nothing te do with it. He'll probably get off. And if not...well...he's a casualty of war. Sometimes sacrifices must be made.'

'So what other "sacrifices" have you made?' Síomha asked.

'Listen to the pair of ye. Judgemental to the end. My conscience is clear. A man can only be true to himself. If he makes mistakes he has te live with them. That's war.'

Owen shook his head in dismay. 'Christ! Call it what you want but you've so much innocent blood on your hands.'

Thomas stared at them with a look of incredulity. He rose then, shook his head and to their surprise turned his back on them and walked around the room, his fingers to his forehead. Owen and Síomha exchanged a look: Owen considered this might be their best chance to overpower him, but Síomha, with an expression of dread, shook her head sharply.

'Jesus Christ, listen te what you're saying!' Thomas seemed to suddenly remember the situation and levelled the gun at them, but relaxed when he saw they hadn't stirred. He stood, observing them with perplexity. 'You're talking about a few deaths, innocent blood and the like. Fuckin' incredible! Have you forgotten what they did to us?'

'What are you talking about?'

'What am I…? The fuckin' famine, of course. The English tried te wipe out our entire race. Mass extermination. Nearly two million dead. The same number had te escape te the four corners of the earth. There are five million people less on this island than thirty years ago, do the sums.'

'It was a famine, Thomas, the potato blight, remember?'

'You no more believe that than I do.'

He walked forward and planted both hands on the table, the gun still pointed directly at Owen.

'Well?'

Owen averted his eyes.

'Ye see? You know as well as I do that the blight had nothing te do with it. The only reason the bones of millions are rotting out there in the fields is because that's exactly what the English intended.'

He backed away and sat.

'You're talking nonsense. Your hatred has warped your reason.'

'Nonsense, is it? Ye know what? You were always the smart one, the book reader. Over the years I became a book reader myself. Oh not like you, not your Shakespeare or Dickens. But things that mattered. I read Marx and Engels and others. Men who cared about the way the common man is treated like a dog. I also read a lot about the famine. About what was really going on. Their brutality. I've had thirty years te catch up. And I've got the rest of my life te repay them. And that's what I intend te do.'

He picked up a book that had fallen to the floor during the struggle and sat again, appearing to meditate over the worn, leather-bound volume.

'Y'know, during the famine, while everyone in Ireland was looking for help in the Bible, this was the bible the English were reading. Their handbook for our extermination. It allowed them te justify what they were doing.'

'What is it?' Owen asked. He had started to think that the best course was to indulge his brother's need to explain his motivations, as it might diffuse some of his apparent rage.

Thomas abruptly threw the book towards Owen, who had to block it with his hand to prevent it hitting his head. He picked it up from the table and read the title aloud: *An Essay on the Principle of Population as it affects The Future Improvement of Society*, by Robert Thomas Malthus.'

'You heard of it?'

'Vaguely.'

'I keep it to remind me. Just in case I ever feel any compassion towards an Englishman. Huh, some chance. That book reminds me what they are and what I have te do. Let me summarise it for you. Here's what they mean by "The Future Improvement of Society". Malthus believed that as the population grew, the ability of the earth te sustain it faltered and that God would intervene with famine and pestilence te restore the natural order. That was the basis of the English Government's policy towards Ireland during the famine. Their Prime Minister, Russell, was a big admirer of Malthus, as were all his cronies. In particular, the man handed the task of organising famine relief, the Assistant Secretary to the Treasury…'

'Trevelyan.'

'Thank you, brother. Ye know that much at least. Charles Edward Trevelyan. The greatest mass murderer in history. He's still alive, you know? He's number one on my list.' He drifted off for a moment, staring into space, then snapped back to reality.

'But where was I? Oh yes, Trevelyan. Ye know that Malthus was actually his teacher in school? And he learned his lessons well. The only problem was that he only applied his economic theory to Ireland. Not te Scotland or India or anywhere else the English had their murderous fingers. He hated us. Like we were dogs. So did they all. They no more cared that we all died than you'd care about killing a nest of rats. One of their great historians came to Ireland during the famine, Kingsley his name was. Do ye know what he wrote? He said he was daunted by the sight of all the human chimpanzees on the road. *Chimpanzees.* That's how they thought of us. Animals of a lower order.'

'You can't hold the whole English race responsible for the stupidity of a few politicians,' Síomha said, but Owen nudged her. He wasn't keen to get into a debate.

'The government represents the people. Or don't you believe that? Besides, it wasn't just them. It was the newspapers, writers, clergy, lawyers; their whole establishment conspired te wipe us out. Trevelyan and Russell said they had te have a "laissez-faire" approach to Ireland. Ye know what that means? It means not interfering with Ireland's economy. This despite the fact that we were supposed te be *part* of Britain, part of their economy. They decided te let nature take its course according te the best Malthusian policy. So when the blight struck they saw it as a godsend. Trevelyan actually said about the famine, and

I'll never forget this, he said that the judgment of God sent the calamity to teach the Irish a lesson. *Teach us a lesson*!

'One of his first acts when he got the job of famine relief was te stop all relief programmes in case they interfered with trade. That allowed the fuckin' English merchants te double the price of everything so that other food couldn't be bought by the Irish.'

'The merchants were Irish too, Thomas,' Owen pointed out, unable to resist the temptation.

'That's true. And the traitors' day of reckoning will come too. But the real effect of Trevelyan's efforts not te interfere with trade was that all the other food in Ireland was exported te keep the landlords rich. Do ye know how much food the English exported from Ireland during the famine? Enough to feed every single person. Not one Irish man, woman or child needed te die. Not one! '49 was actually a bumper year for corn. Millions were being turned into walking skeletons and the bastards were exporting the food grown in Irish soil before our eyes. On land they'd stolen from us. The English weren't only exterminating us but had the bonus of getting rich while it happened. Did ye know the same blight hit Scotland? The Highland Potato Famine. There were hundreds of thousands of tenant farmers there just like us. Ye know how many died? Ye could count the number on your fingers and toes. Ye know why? Every man, woman and child was given a daily ration of two pounds of oats.'

Thomas laughed bitterly. He appeared to be distracted, removed from the moment. He was being carried along on the swirling winds of a lifetime's bitter reflection, talking as much to himself as to them.

'What ration did Her Majesty's Government give her other subjects, the Irish? Nothing. Zero. They wanted us te rot inside our own clothes. And ye want more proof it was an extermination? If you accept Malthus's theories, ye allow the population te starve once it gets too big. The English Government claimed that Ireland's population had become so big the land couldn't support it. Which is strange, because Ireland had precisely the same number of people for every acre as England. Did they apply Malthusian theory te their own? Of course not. You know why? They *wanted* te wipe us out and the famine gave them the perfect weapon. Think of all the bullets it would save them. Civilisation? The English don't know the meaning of the word.'

'I know what Trevelyan did. But that was thirty years ago. We can't keep–'

'Thirty years? Ye think thirty years is enough to wipe out the murder of *two million* people? A thousand years wouldn't be enough. Ye know why? Because there's never been anyone called to account. There's never been any justice. Well, we'll give them justice all right. The only kind they understand. Ye know what the English did? Right in the middle of the famine when things were at their worst? They made Trevelyan a fuckin' *knight* for services to Ireland. Their highest honour. That's English justice.'

'Thomas. Stop! Tadhg could be home any minute. What are you going to do when he gets here?' Síomha pleaded tearfully.

'Shut up. Listen and learn. The problem with you and your band of pacifists is that you don't know your enemy. If ye did, ye wouldn't have bothered your arses with your boycott. That bastard would be dead now. You know what Marx called Malthus? The agent of the landed aristocracy. Mountmorres. Erne. Lucan. *Boycott.* The thousands of others. They're all devotees of the same Malthusian principles. The same war is still raging. They're still trying te exterminate us.'

Owen recognised his delusional state for what it was. His brother's years of hatred had distorted all reason and he was given to making vast leaps of judgement, all of his humanity abandoned as an encumbrance that might temper his need for vengeance. His own fear was also mounting that Tadhg might soon return.

'I'll tell ye what's going to happen with your boycott. The English are going te send in a few hundred troops, put guns te your heads and force ye te pick Boycott's crops. Then they're going te evict ye and let ye starve. Ye want te stop them? Kill them before they kill you.'

Owen shook his head at his brother's repeated mantra of bloodshed as the answer to all ills.

'Ye shake your head like I don't know what I'm talking about. After all I've said, ye still believe I'm wrong and you're right?'

'Let me ask you something that's been bothering me.'

'Be my guest.'

'When you had your ranch, in Colorado or New Mexico, I can't remember...'

'What about it?' He was puzzled by the sudden alteration in the course of the conversation.

'Why did you have to kill so many natives?'

He shrugged. 'If we hadn't they'd have torn us to pieces. They were savages.'

'But why did they attack in the first place? Was it because you'd taken their land?'

'We got the land by right from the state government! We put down a claim and got it all legal.'

'Don't avoid the question. The white men came and invaded their lands. They'd lived there for thousands of years. You got it legally? Don't fool yourself. The natives were doing exactly what we've been doing for hundreds of years. Fighting for the land that was taken from them. And you were killing them. You were doing exactly what the English did to us. You're no better than the men you vilify!'

'Shut your fuckin' mouth! There's no comparison. There was so much land millions could have lived there. All we had was a tiny scrap. All I did was defend it. Just as I'm prepared to kill te defend us now.'

'No matter how you try to justify it, it still sounds hollow.'

A grim smile crept across Thomas's face.

'Well, let me tell you something before ye judge me, *brother*. Our father knew what had te be done. He told me as much on his deathbed because he knew you were too fuckin' weak te do what was needed to survive. You hadn't the balls for it.'

'What are you talking about?'

Thomas finally had his brother's complete attention. Owen felt Síomha's fingernails dig into his arm.

'Like father like son, isn't that how the old saying goes? I kill because I know that's the only way out of all this. And so did our father. He killed too because he knew that was what had te be done.'

He was talking about Geraghty, the landlord's gamekeeper when they'd lived on Tawnyard. Owen had always suspected he'd been killed by his father, but had also harboured a hope that he was wrong.

'You know who I'm talking about. I can see it in your face. Geraghty. Our father, Michael Joyce, gave that bastard exactly what he deserved.'

'Our father killed Geraghty?'

'He did. The man was a pig. An agent of the Crown. So he just waited for him one evening and beat the fucker te death with his own gun. Bashed his brains to a pulp.'

'I don't believe you.'

'What? You don't believe he killed him?'

'If he did, it wasn't like that, there had to be a reason. He wasn't a killer. He wouldn't kill anyone just because he worked for the landlord. You're lying.'

Thomas took a swig of whiskey and lifted the gun, studying it for a few seconds, weighing something up in his mind. Then he grinned.

'You're right. Ye got me. It was a little fib. But he *did* kill him. Geraghty caught me poaching one evening. He had his old musket pointed at my head, promising me I'd be sent to Van Diemen's Land. Then suddenly our father knocked him out with a branch. He wanted te let Geraghty live. But when I pointed out that we had no choice, that it was either transportation for me or leave no witnesses, he did what had te be done. With Geraghty's own musket. So ye see, Owen, at least some of the men in our family can make the hard choices when we have to.'

'It was your fault, then. You got caught and left him with no choice.'

'He would have done the same for you, Owen, if you're been caught fishing. Who knows, maybe you'd have ended up the Fenian assassin and I'd be the nice family man? Our circumstances make us what we are, ye wouldn't argue with that, would you?'

Owen stood up with no thought of the threat of his brother's gun, fury swelling his heart. Thomas pointed the weapon directly at his chest.

'You bastard!' Owen shouted. 'The difference between me and you is that I would have taken whatever the law threw at me rather than force my father to kill to save me. And worse still, you've been using what you made him do to justify your own brutality. Whatever I am now, for good or bad, no circumstances could have made me like you – a bitter, twisted fucking killer blinded by hate. You're no better than a common murderer! You fucking animal!'

'Owen!' Síomha yelled, terrified the situation was going out of control.

Thomas slowly rose and levelled the gun at his brother's head, a narrow snarl creasing his mouth, breaths hissing through clenched teeth.

'Whatever you are now? You're a fuckin' coward is what you are. And the only reason you're even alive now and living with your fuckin' wife and children is because of me. If ye think I should feel guilty, then ye've just as much guilt on your shoulders. Let me tell ye the rest of the story about how we survived when we walked te Westport.'

'What story?'

'The food we had that kept us alive those few days.'

'What about it?'

As he asked the question all three of them were distracted by the sound of a car pulling into the yard.

'Tadhg!' Síomha stifled a scream and clutched at her husband.

'Nobody move!' Thomas hissed and ran to the window.

He watched as Tadhg drove past the cottage towards the pen.

'What are you going to do?' Owen asked, dread evident in his voice.

Thomas didn't answer for several seconds, then backed away to the hearth. 'I don't want te hurt him. Get rid of him. You. Síomha.'

'What do you mean?' she asked.

'He mustn't find out what's happened, ye stupid cow. Get rid of him.'

'And what about us?' Owen asked. 'We know you can't let us go.'

'Oh but I can. I should kill ye both. But I don't want to. Wouldn't help my mission. You're going te keep your mouths shut. Just tell everyone I went on my own merry way. But if the RIC or the priest or anyone else finds out about me, well, I'd hate te think of the consequences.'

He glanced in the direction of the pen, towards Tadhg.

'*You bastard!*'

'It's my insurance. If you two open your mouths, well, as I said, this is war, and I'd hate te see your son or daughter become casualties. Now, go and get rid of him. Tell him you're having a lover's quarrel, tell him te go squeeze some *cailín*'s arse, I don't care, just get rid of him. When he's gone, saddle my horse and bring it te the door. Your husband here will stay with me as a guarantee. And don't forget, I'll use this if I have to. Stay calm, and tell him ye hit your face on the door if he asks about the bruise.'

Síomha squeezed past Owen, meeting his eyes briefly, then exited the cottage. The two brothers stood facing each other.

'Don't look at me like that, brother. It's just the way the cards fell.'

Thomas picked up his knapsack and sat it on the chair. He added the remainder of the whiskey to the bag and closed the straps.

'Are you going to kill Boycott?'

'Not just yet. But when the time is right. Might be next week, might be a year. Who knows? But we'll get them all in the end.'

Owen was silent a moment, then pointed to the wall above the hearth. 'There's something I want you to have. There's a tin behind that loose stone. It's not a trick, don't worry.'

Thomas eyed him suspiciously, then backed up and reached for the stone. He pulled it out and revealed a large, partly rusted tin, illustrated with children happily eating biscuits and the title 'Jacob's & Co, Superior Biscuits.'

'Open it.'

Thomas pulled the lid off. There were some coins, half crowns and shillings mostly, a few letters, and a lease agreement.

'May I?' Owen asked.

Thomas placed the tin on the table.

Owen removed the aged ticket for America that his brother had returned to him. 'This. The sign of the "unbreakable bond" you feel with me.' He lifted the ticket in his two hands and tore it down the centre.

'No, don–'

'We were always destined to go on different journeys, Thomas.'

Owen repeated the gesture several times and then threw the pieces at his brother, the fragments of yellowed paper fluttering to the floor like some tainted snowfall. Thomas stared grimly back at him.

'You might be right, Thomas. Maybe it will take the gun to free us. But what worries me is what fanatics like you will do with my country afterwards.'

Thomas was about to reply when they heard the sound of horse's hooves outside. He moved to the window, smiled at the sight of his saddled horse and pulled open the door. He gestured at Síomha to come inside.

'Well?'

'I told him to go and collect Niamh from school. He argued, but he went.'

Thomas turned his back to the open door and looked at them.

'Sorry it worked out this way. Don't worry, you'll never see me again.'

'I hope that's a promise,' Owen said coldly.

'Goodbye, Síomha. Goodbye, brother.'

He backed out the door and pulled it shut behind him.

Síomha and Owen locked each other in a long, unyielding embrace.

CHAPTER 26

…he [Boycott] is unquestionably a brave and resolute man, but there is too much reason to believe that without his garrison and escort his life would not be worth an hour's purchase. There are few fairer prospects than that from the steps of his home, Lough Mask House, a comfortable and unpretending edifice. Yet the potatoes will rot in the ground and the cattle will go astray, for not a soul in Ballinrobe dare touch a spade for Mr Boycott. Personally he is protected, but no woman in Ballinrobe would dream of washing him a cravat or making him a loaf. All the people have to say is that they are sorry, but that they "dare not". Everybody advises him to leave the country; but the answer of the besieged agent is simply this: "I can hardly desert Lord Erne, and, moreover, my own property is sunk in this place." He cannot sacrifice his occupation and his property. There is very little doubt that this unfortunate gentleman has been selected as a victim whose fate may strike terror into others.

–Bernard H Becker, Special Commissioner of *The Daily News*, 28 October 1880. Part of an article reproduced in a wide number of prominent publications in Britain, Ireland and beyond.

25 OCTOBER-1 NOVEMBER 1880

Bernard Becker sat in the Old Mill Boarding House dining room, enjoying the final spoonful of a hearty lamb stew. The food had partially restored his spirits but his body still ached from almost a week's constant travel about the wilds of Mayo. He had developed a thorough dislike of Irish cars, vehicles seemingly of a construction designed to transfer all of the wheels' impacting over bumps and potholes directly into one's skeletal frame. But his lassitude was as much of the mind as the body, for his recent experiences had exposed him to vastly opposing views of Ireland's strife, and by turns he was sympathetic to the Irish peasants and disdainful of their reasoning.

He had been enthralled, depressed and confused in equal measure during a visit to the village of Tiernaur on the north side of Clew Bay. The scenery had mesmerised him: the countless islands of the bay, Croagh Patrick standing watch over it to the south, and a chain of rugged mountains embracing it to the north. All about he had seen evidence of *An Gorta Mór*, as they called it – the Great Hunger – and of continuing evictions. Numberless tenant farmers had either perished or been banished and their lands let in blocks of several square miles each to Englishmen and Scotsmen, who employed the earth for grazing and grew not a turnip or a potato. It was much more efficient, Becker considered, but expression of such a notion brought a torrent of disapprobation upon his head as countless thousands, he'd been informed, had been left with no means of subsistence.

He refrained from stating that the people could be better employed in the new, modern industries of the Age of Steam and that grazing made the best use of infertile land. But the Irish clung to their patches of rocky soil, he thought, like a mother clings to a deformed or idiot child. It was, to him, an astonishing perversion of patriotism endorsed by their priests. All and sundry seemed to believe that because they were born on a piece of land it should be theirs by birthright. To Becker, this was as alien as a flock of parakeets in Hyde Park. Since time immemorial, almost all farmers in England had been tenants to a wealthy landowner and were happy in their lot. But for the Irish, it seemed, their roots in the land went as deep as those of the mightiest oak.

The proprietress of the Old Mill now approached Becker with a deferential air. She was a handsome woman in her thirties with a harried deportment as though she was burdened by six tasks, all requiring urgent attention.

'Excuse me, sir, Mr Becker, but a boy's come with this from the post office.'

Becker accepted the envelope. 'Thank you, Mrs Neary, and may I compliment you on the delectable meal. As good as any I might enjoy in Chelsea or the West End.'

Mrs Neary flushed with pride and hurried away.

He removed two folded sheets from the envelope bearing the logo of the Electric and International Telegraph Company.

> Becker,
>
> You are aware that I had expressed my doubts as to the appositeness of your assignment. But it is with some surprise that I can relay the news that your recent submissions, particularly the one pertaining to Boycott, have aroused considerable interest among our readership and in political circles. Word is that *The Times* editor is kicking himself for not pursuing the angle, but the man deserved a good kicking anyway. Furthermore, letters of support for Boycott have been pouring into the associate publications and there is talk of a fund to send an expedition to assist him. There are rumours that five hundred men loyal to the crown in Ireland's northern counties are arming themselves for an invasion of Mayo. The Chief Secretary for Ireland, Forster, has openly expressed his fears that Ireland might be on the verge of civil war. I believe the army may soon be dispatched to your locale to quell any trouble.
>
> I require continuing updates on the situation and in particular, on any developments directly concerning Boycott.
>
> F. H. Hill, Editor, *The Daily News*.

Becker didn't know whether to feel elated or downcast. He was pleased of course that his reports had been so well received, but by the same token troubled at the escalation of events. But wasn't that precisely what he'd intended when he'd conceived the notion of Boycott under siege? Rousing his countrymen to action? He could hardly deny it. Yet the thought of war or violence troubled him. Especially the notion that *he* might have been the spark that ignited the powder keg that was Lough Mask Estate.

***

Friday October 29th, 1880

To the Editor of *The Daily Express* of Dublin

With reference to your recent excellent article by Mr Becker on the travails of Mr Boycott and the unwarranted attack on him by the Land League, it seems to me that it would be a most cowardly act indeed to abandon Mr and Mrs Boycott to be starved out. It is also a disgrace that Mr Boycott's crop should be left to rot in the ground, especially in the light of recent poor harvests. This is a shameful waste and tells us much about the mentality of the Land League's leaders.

It is my proposal, therefore, that a fund should be established with the aim of raising £500 which would finance a body of men to travel to Mayo to save Mr Boycott's crop and bring relief to this heroic gentleman and his family who is standing firm in the face of Land League intimidation. Furthermore, I would be happy to offer my own services as the leader of such an expedition.

I am, sir, your obedient servant,

Combination, County Dublin.

'Combination? What sort of an idiotic *nom de plume* is that?' Fr O'Malley asked of Redpath as he lowered the newspaper. They were sitting in Gallagher's bar in Ballinrobe.

'A contact in Dublin told me his real name is Manning. It won't come as a surprise that he used to be a land agent for the Lucas-Scudamore Estate in Monaghan.'

'Hmm. *Manus manum lavat*.'

'Eh, Father, my Latin isn't what it used to be.'

'One hand washes the other.'

Redpath nodded as he took the paper. 'And did you see the leading article supporting his call? And all the other letters?'

'This newspaper is the daily gospel for unionists and the landed gentry. They've printed countless unjustified attacks on the Land League and Parnell. And Becker's article was good, I'll give him that. He's portrayed Boycott as a symbol of everything the readers of this paper represent.'

'A symbol that's under attack.'

'But what if it happens? Hundreds of armed men invading Mayo! God help us all.'

***

Owen Joyce mechanically picked the potatoes from the handcart and placed them one at a time in the pit. It was necessary to ensure that no diseased potatoes were included, so each had to be examined by sight and touch.

Síomha watched her husband and Tadhg at work from a short distance away where she was tending to their small crop of cabbages. In the week since Thomas had departed, Owen's mood had been sullen, his temper short and his appetite almost non-existent. They'd told Tadhg and Niamh that their uncle had to leave for a job in Galway, a lie that had at least purchased them some distance from the terrible events of the previous Monday. Tadhg may have been just sixteen, but the nature of their lives brought a hastened maturity and she could see the doubt in his eyes.

An hour after Thomas had departed, Síomha had torn to shreds the dress he'd given her, taken the colourful rags to their latrine and dumped them, an act of childish symbolism, but satisfying nonetheless. Of the other gifts, the five pounds had already been donated to Fr O'Malley's boycott fund. They had allowed the children to retain their gifts to avoid questions.

Yet after the initial shock had waned, Owen had quickly lapsed into self-recrimination. Síomha had knelt and thanked God that no harm had come to them, trying to put the nightmare behind her. But no words could rouse Owen from his torpor. As she watched him slipping into his familiar proclivity for brooding analysis, she had promoted work as a remedy for all ills. She knew him well, knew he would recall each sentence shared with Thomas and dissect every action taken. Much of this was to be expected, as Thomas was his only brother and they had parted on the worst terms imaginable. But she knew also that her husband's self-analysis was without focus or purpose.

He had repeatedly told Síomha that she could be dead because of his inaction, and despite her reassurances that neither of them had seen it coming, the guilt continued to stab at him. Then there was also the disturbed, hateful being that had been unmasked behind his brother's face. He could barely countenance the idea that he shared the bloodline of such a man. Add to this the awful confirmation of what he had always suspected of his father, that he had killed. It had been just another blow that had served to cast him into a well of despair.

'You've put two in here that are half-rotten.' Tadhg was kneeling over the pit, holding the pair of offending potatoes in his palms.

'Don't tell me how to fill a pit! You must have put them there yourself, you eejit!' Owen yelled petulantly.

Tadhg responded to the unwarranted accusation by rising sharply and flinging the potatoes on to the ground.

'I didn't put them in! You're not looking at what you're doing!'

Síomha rose quickly and ran across as Owen angrily turned to face his son.

'Don't you dare talk to me like that!'

'*Stad sin anois*!' Síomha shouted as she pushed them apart, her face set in anger. 'We've had enough fighting in this family, don't you think?'

Owen fell silent. Tadhg turned to his mother. 'What fighting?'

'Never mind.'

A voice calling from the track turned their heads. 'God bless the work!' Fr O'Malley was steering his car through the gate.

'Oh Christ,' Owen whispered with annoyance.

'What sort of talk is that about your priest? *And* your friend?' Síomha snapped.

'I'm not up to talking to him.'

'You have to. Come on. Tadhg, get on with the pit.'

Síomha took Owen's arm and literally pulled him along as one might a reluctant child. They greeted the priest and entered the cottage. The men sat at the table while Síomha busied herself making tea.

Fr O'Malley soon sensed the prevailing air. 'What's wrong, Owen?'

'Nothing, Father. Everything's fine.'

The priest nodded and glanced around. 'Thomas not about today?'

Neither replied for a time, then Síomha turned and faced him. 'I'm afraid Owen and his brother had a falling out, Father. He's left.'

'I'm doubly sorry to hear that, Owen. But that's often the way with brothers, or sisters, I'm sad to say. Do you want to discuss it, Owen?'

He shook his head. 'No, Father.'

A notion struck Síomha. Her husband's despondency had not been eased by his decision to maintain only an inner debate. She had hoped that the distraction of work would help, but the mundane tasks of recent days had not taxed his brain. He needed something more; he needed to involve himself in the boycott again. And, as if on cue, Fr O'Malley raised the subject.

'You haven't been to the meetings this past week, Owen. We need your help. The other tenants take their lead from you. And there's trouble brewing. That's why I'm here. I need you to come to Ballinrobe this afternoon. We have to keep a lid on any potential disorder. I've received word that–'

'Father,' Owen cut in sharply.

'Yes, Owen?'

'I can't be involved anymore. You'll have to do without me.'

The priest set his shoulders back, clearly shocked. 'But I…but you're a part of it. What's happened? Owen?'

'I'm sorry. I can't help. I mean, I've too much to do on the farm. Sure I have to have that pit filled today, I can't be running off to Ballinrobe.'

Síomha put the copper teapot on the table with a thud.

'Owen, we have to discuss this. Now. Before you drive yourself insane, not to mention the rest of us,' she said.

Owen looked at her as though she'd lost her mind, conscious of his brother's threat to their children. She met his eyes with steely conviction, then turned to the priest.

'Father, Owen wants to make a confession.'

'*What*?' Owen almost shouted.

'What confession?' the priest asked, bewildered.

'No, Father, I mean he wants the sacrament of Confession. Can you do that here?'

'Yes, of course, but why–'

'What the hell are you doing?'

She placed a hand on his shoulder. 'Owen, you are going to confess everything that's been troubling you. You are going to tell Father O'Malley everything that's happened. *Everything.*'

'But you know what–'

'Father, could you remind Owen about a priest's duty regarding confession? You would be condemned to eternal flames if you broke your vow of secrecy? Is that right?'

'Well, I'd be excommunicated. Almost as bad. But you're right, the sacramental seal is inviolable.'

Owen was silent, clearly still uncomfortable, or perhaps unwilling, to relinquish the bitterness in his heart, and she feared he harboured vengeful intentions. She didn't allow him to ponder.

'I'll be helping Tadhg,' she said, and stomped from the cottage.

***

'Listen to this one, Charles,' Annie Boycott said, excitedly lifting *The Belfast*

News Letter from the patchwork of newspapers on the dining room table. She read aloud.

> ...I would further like to make the point that vast sums of money are pouring into the country from America, which is funding the opponents of law and order, to wit, the Land League. Ergo a fund to save Mr Boycott's harvest would indemnify him against his losses. If we don't act now, the despicable methods employed by the Land League will undoubtedly be repeated, but should all lovers of law and order rally to Mr Boycott's side and save his crops, the method would be rendered impotent.
> Your obedient servant,
> A Lover of Law and Order

Her husband listened with mild interest, but not the enthusiasm she had expected, considering he'd set this in motion through his interview with Bernard Becker.

'Here's another one,' Weekes said keenly. 'It's from the Reverend William Ross.'

'Let's hear it, Asheton,' Annie urged.

Boycott sighed as Weekes read letter after letter of support. When he could bear no more he rose sharply.

'I have to attend the Ballinrobe Petty Sessions hearing. Another deuced waste of time.'

'Charles, I'm puzzled. I thought you'd be delighted with all the publicity, but you don't seem terribly interested,' Annie asked.

'Frankly, I find this washing our linen in public a trifle distasteful. All I had hoped for was the Government to send the army to assist with the harvest and also to put the Land League blaggards in their place. I've written to the Chief Secretary several times in that regard, but as usual with these deuced civil servants I've only had a vague reply stating that they were studying the matter. And now all of this happens...' He made a sweeping gesture across the mass of newspapers, his face contorted in disgust.

Annie slapped the table sharply. 'Really, Charles, all of these people are rallying to your support and you talk of them like they were a scourge. You should be grateful to them. There is no pleasing you, Captain Boycott, sir! None whatsoever!'

***

'Did they have a fight?'

She knew she would have to respond honestly to Tadhg or else he would continue to probe and grow more suspicious. She stopped working and looked towards the cottage. They'd been in there an hour.

'Yes, they did, Tadhg.'

'What about?'

'Oh, things from their past. It's private.'

'But what could–'

'Tadhg. It's private. Maybe someday your father will discuss it with you. Until then, leave it be. Besides, you and Lorcan were always at each other's throats. These things happen.'

He was unsatisfied, but thankfully asked no more.

The door to the cottage opened and Fr O'Malley emerged. As she hurried up to him, he sighed and smiled faintly.

'What happened, Father?'

'I cannot discuss matters from the confessional, Síomha, even with you. But you have my sympathies. I don't know if unburdening himself has helped. Perhaps in time. But he isn't prepared to resume his…his involvement in the boycott. And on that matter, I must be off.'

'Father, please wait a while.' She touched his arm and he hesitated, nodded and then feigned annoyance.

'Actually, I must admonish your son, who I observed whispering to young Teresa Kelly during mass last Sunday.'

'Thank you, Father.'

She found Owen was sitting with his back to the door, elbows on the table, his splayed fingers pressed against his forehead as though trying to support the weight of his troubles. She walked silently across and sat next to him.

'Owen?'

He didn't respond, except to clench his hands over his eyes. She looked down at the table then and saw the stain on the wood, an irregular dark blotch, and felt a heave in her breast. She reached out with both hands and pulled at his wrists until he succumbed and allowed her to look at his face. Tears spilled from his eyes, male tears, a sight she had rarely seen past the age of twelve, even in grief. Struck by conflicting emotions of pity and joy, she knew it would trouble him to be seen that way, yet also knew his tears were like waters of redemption, cleansing his troubled soul of the malevolent stain that his brother had left. She ran a hand across the tangled mop of his hair, but said nothing. He angled his head away, unable to meet her eyes. After some time, she heard him whisper.

'I'm sorry. I couldn't stop thinking that if you'd died…my life would be empty now…and I'd have been the cause.'

'I didn't die. What might have been…we can't live our lives like that.'

'I know that now. But there's something else. Something I really did have to confess to Father O'Malley. Thomas. I've been wishing I'd killed him that day. I've been guilty of murder a hundred times this past week, in my mind. Thirty years I spent hoping that somehow he was alive. And now he's returned, all I want is him dead. I wasted so much time on him. Jesus Christ almighty. He may be out there somewhere but he's dead to me now in all the ways that count. And I'm the last of my family. My brothers, sisters, father, mother, all gone.'

'Except you're not the last.'

He wiped at his cheeks with his sleeve and turned towards her.

'What do you mean?'

Síomha nodded towards the window. 'You've a son out there. Another in America. A beautiful daughter. They're your family now. And me.'

He reached a hand up to touch her face and she took it in both hands.

'You said you wasted all that time thinking about Thomas. Well, now that you know the truth, it's time you stopped looking into the past and started looking to the future of the family you have now.'

'I'm doing my best for them...' he protested mildly.

'I don't mean raising them or schooling them. I mean the sort of world you want them to grow up into. Will it be Thomas's world or the one you would have? Teach best by example, isn't that what they say? Show Tadhg bitterness and hatred and that's what you'll get in return.'

He heaved a sigh.

Síomha glanced through the window where she saw Fr O'Malley walking towards his car, disappointment evident in the slump of his shoulders.

'Father O'Malley's leaving.'

'I thought he was long gone.'

'Well, he's not gone yet…' she said with sudden brightness and a hint of sarcasm.

'You expect me to go with him? *Now*?'

She stared squarely at him. 'No time like the present.'

He turned away and felt her eyes boring into his back, then looked at her again.

'He *needs* you, Owen.'

He shook his head and for the first time in a week – and although it came through a pretence of irritation – he uttered a clipped laugh.

'Jesus, you never stop your nagging. I suppose if I don't go I'll never hear the end of it.' He rose with a grunt. 'Where the hell did I leave my jacket?'

***

Ballinrobe Courthouse was a fine if rather unspectacular building of two stories of plain stone, topped by an apex into which had been set a clock. The building, on the corner of Market Street and Bridge Street, had originally been built as a market hall, and the odours of that commerce in oats, wool, goats and sheep still lingered within its walls, or so some maintained.

Charles Boycott believed that he was the victim of a gross injustice perpetrated by malicious individuals who had conspired to avoid payment of their rent. He also believed that his refusal to pay Martin Branigan, his former labourer, the wages he claimed he was due was also morally right and that the man was merely seeking to 'turn the screw', probably at the behest of the priest. Branigan's contention, ludicrous in Boycott's view, was that he was paid by the day and was therefore due three days' wages up to the Thursday he abandoned his duties. Although the amount was trifling – seven shillings and sixpence – he had refused to pay it on principle.

The District Courtroom was packed on the day and, although he had been conducted safely to the venue under escort of six constables and then admitted covertly by a side entrance, he could sense a swell of hostility within the large courtroom. To his right was a dark wood-panelled structure, which allowed about twenty of the public to view the proceedings. A similar structure stood to the left housing six plaintiffs, waiting to be heard on issues as varied as the underpayment for the sale of five sheep, a woman whose sense of decency had been affronted by the sight of three soldiers swimming in the Robe wearing only long johns (which roused a few titters), and a Protestant man defending himself for 'breach of the Sabbath', having been accused by Mr Brownrigg, the Rector of Ballinrobe, of whitewashing his cottage on Sunday. Branigan stood first in line.

The Resident Magistrate, Mr McSheehy, sat in a high bench at the head of the room, a junior magistrate to either side. Below them the court recorder huddled over a table scratching shorthand notes, and a bailiff sat at his side.

Correspondents from *The Ballinrobe Chronicle* and *The Connaught Telegraph* stood to the rear of the courthouse recording their own version of events. The gathering was completed by the presence of eight constables, six more than would normally be deemed sufficient to maintain order.

The court bailiff beckoned Branigan to approach the bench, while Boycott stood at by the side of the room. Branigan was sworn in and stood craning his neck up towards the elevated magistrate.

'Please state your name and petition.'

'Martin Branigan, your honour.'

'You may address me as "sir".'

'Yes, sir.'

Martin Branigan was a large, tough and proud man, normally intimidated not a whit by any situation or figure of authority. Yet on this day he appeared nervous and deferential, his shoulders slumped, twirling his cap between his fingers, continually dropping his gaze to the floor.

'My petition, sir, is that Captain Boycott owes me three days' wages for September the twentieth to September the twenty-second, as I worked those days, but he refuses to pay me.'

The magistrate looked around the court. 'Is Captain Boycott present?'

Boycott strode across the floor, eyed Branigan with distaste, and swore an oath on the Bible.

'Captain Boycott, why haven't you paid this man's due wages?'

'Because, sir, the man left his employment without due notice and abandoned my crop to rot.' He delivered this with customary impatience, as though the reason should be obvious to all but a fool.

'I did not, sir, that's a lie,' Branigan quickly countered.

'You most certainly did and how dare you accuse me of lying, you scoundrel!'

'Stop this at once! Neither of you will speak unless I address you. You, Captain, as a magistrate, should know how to conduct yourself.'

Boycott met McSheehy with a cutting glare.

'What do you say to Captain Boycott's charge, Mr Branigan?'

'Sir, if you please, but about sixty people came into the field and well, sir, they frightened me.'

'Frightened you in what way? And please speak up.'

'Well, sir, they said I had to leave Boycott's employment at once and I felt intimidated, sir. There were so many of them.'

There were a few titters from the public gallery, as most people were aware that Branigan was probably the least likely person in Ballinrobe to be intimidated by anyone.

'Did they threaten you with physical harm?'

'Not in so many words, sir. But they said it would be safer if I left. I mean, sir, how would you have felt?'

'Speculation on my reaction in such a situation is irrelevant, Mr Branigan.' He turned his attention back to Boycott. 'Captain, if this man was intimidated into leaving, surely you would sympathise with him and pay him his due, as the Christian thing to do.'

Boycott looked as though he had been punched.

'*Sympathise with him, sir*? Have you any idea of the condition of my farm since these thugs invaded it?'

'Yes, Captain, I believe the entire world knows of your situation by now. But, if, as you say, thugs invaded your estate, then surely that supports Mr Branigan's claim.'

'Sir. Mr Branigan left of his own accord!' Boycott was struggling to keep his voice down. 'He is a Land League sympathiser and deserves not a farthing.'

One of the junior magistrates interrupted proceedings by bringing McSheehy's attention to a document. Having perused it, the magistrate peered down at Boycott.

'Captain, did you not testify at the Bessborough Commission that your labourers had been driven off under threat of "ulterior consequence"?'

Boycott opened his mouth to speak but nothing emerged, as though his facial muscles had been momentarily paralysed, then he cracked his cane against the floor.

'Sir, that submission has no relevance here!' he shouted.

McSheehy replied in a calm voice. 'Captain Boycott, this is not the Supreme Court and I shall be the judge of what is and what is not relevant.'

He conferred briefly with his colleagues, made a note in his ledger, then looked down at Boycott and Branigan.

'I rule in favour of the plaintiff, Mr Branigan. Payment to be made before departing the premises. Next case.'

With that he slammed his gavel down, prompting a cheer from the public gallery. Boycott's face went deathly pale as Branigan turned to him, his posture suddenly appearing to straighten, his sheepishness vanished. He grinned wickedly at the land agent, an act that inflicted infinitely more injury on Boycott than the judgement.

'Sir, there's a bit of a crowd outside. We'd better go out the exit into Bridge Street and take you to the barracks,' a constable whispered, distracting Boycott from his fury.

'The barracks? A crowd? What crowd?'

***

'You were right, Father, and most of them look fit to kill.'

'Stop here, Owen, we have to calm things down before anyone gets hurt.'

'It might be too late for that. How did you know this might happen?'

The priest was heaving his considerable frame from the trap in Ballinrobe's Market Street.

'The postmistress told me.'

'The postmistress?'

The priest elaborated as they hurried towards the crowd of several hundred.

'She told me that the journalist Becker received a telegraph in Westport saying that Boycott has organised an armed invasion of Mayo by Orangemen, and that he's also persuaded the Chief Secretary to send in the army.'

Owen grimaced at the memory of his brother's prediction of just such an outcome.

'The postmistress in Westport forwarded Becker's telegraph here, to warn us, I suppose. It may be all just a rumour, but unfortunately by now half the county's heard.'

'Father, aren't telegraphs private by law?'

'They are, but you know how these things are. Anyway, never mind that, what in God's name are we going to do?'

The crowd was all around them now, becoming denser as men and women alike streamed towards the courthouse. So deafening was the chorus of 'Boycott out!' and so palpable the anger that they knew their task was all but impossible.

Fr O'Malley forced his way to the front of the courthouse, his hands held aloft, yelling himself to hoarseness in his appeals for calm. Those nearest paid some heed, but the crowd stretched away along the street, far beyond his vocal range.

'They're going to invade us, Father!' someone shouted.

'They're sending a mob of Orangemen!'

'We don't know that! But if Boycott's harmed, they'll have the excuse to do as they please!'

Owen saw a youth he didn't recognise wielding a fence post.

'Give me that, you *amadán*!' he yelled and wrenched the improvised weapon from the boy's grasp. He turned to the priest. 'Look at this! And some of them are carrying stones. I don't recognise half these men. They're from all over.'

'Dear God, Owen, I'm at a loss.'

The sight of Asheton Weekes approaching in Boycott's landau, a constable at his side, suddenly diverted the crowd's attention.

'Is he mad? He'll be torn to pieces,' Owen shouted. 'Come on Father! We have to get to Weekes.'

They battled their way through the crowd, the sight of the priest's clothing easing their passage. The crowd had surrounded the landau, cutting off Boycott's means of flight, and the young constable was standing with his revolver pointed skywards, appearing quite terrified. Weekes wrenched at the reins, trying to control the frightened horses. They finally reached the landau and Owen pulled away a man who was trying to dislodge Weekes. He hoisted himself up to the Englishman.

'Weekes! Help me get the priest up.'

'To what purpose?'

'Just do it!'

He and Weekes grasped Fr O'Malley's arms and pulled, fighting against the swell of bodies. They manoeuvred him into a standing position.

'Lower the gun, please, constable,' the priest gasped. The terrified man hesitantly complied.

Owen felt hands claw at his belt and was suddenly wrenched down into the crowd. A stranger squared up to him. 'Who the fuck d'ye think you are?'

With that he planted a fist on Owen's mouth, sending him reeling back into the embrace of bodies.

'Owen!' Fr O'Malley cried out.

Owen was conscious of several figures throwing themselves to his defence.

'Hey, keep yer hands off him!' a familiar voice yelled.

More punches were thrown as he struggled to his feet in time to see his neighbours, Joe Gaughan and Luke Fitzmorris, laying a number of men flat out.

'Stop! Stop it now!' Fr O'Malley appealed towards the melee. He turned to the crowd and employed the full volume of his capacious lungs to draw their attention.

'Everybody! Listen to me! This will not help our cause!'

'Go back to your holy water font, priest! This is men's work!' a voice cried out and Owen saw a scuffle as the heckler was tackled by several Ballinrobe locals.

The sight of a priest had calmed the crowd a little and the noise had dimmed, although there was still considerable tension in the air.

Fr O'Malley resumed. 'Please listen, I appeal to you, violence here today will be our undoing!'

'But Boycott's bringing a thousand Orangemen from the north and they all have guns! We only have sticks!' a man cried out.

'And Gladstone's sending the army to attack us! We have families to protect!'

The priest held his hands aloft. 'We don't know if any of this is true. What we do know is that if Boycott is harmed here today we'll have martial law inside two days. Now, please, for your own good, return to your hom–'

Fr O'Malley's voice was trampled under the sound of the boots of twenty running constables, led by Sergeant Murtagh, who surrounded the courthouse's side door, which opened into Bridge Street.

'It's Boycott!' someone cried.

Like a shoal of fish the crowd swirled towards the building and Fr O'Malley was forgotten, which at least freed the landau from the crush. Boycott's appearance was greeted by a cacophony of booing and hissing. The constables encircled him, batons held aloft, and the group began a tortuously slow journey towards the barracks. Fr O'Malley clambered down and Owen turned to Weekes.

'They're taking him to the infantry barracks. Get out of here, Weekes, until this quietens down. Go, now!'

Without any debate, Weekes pulled on the reins and drove the vehicle up Abbey Street and beyond sight. Owen turned his attention back to Boycott, who was skulking behind the constabulary, fearful a missile might strike him, although the only things thrown thus far were colourfully phrased insults. The booing was incessant and the constables struggled to hold the line as the throng heaved along behind them, but they worked themselves free of the crowd, courtesy of several baton swings, and began to run down the slope of

Bridge Street towards the river and the barracks beyond, the crowd stumbling after them in pursuit.

'I hope to sweet Jesus they make it,' Fr O'Malley said somewhat irreverently.

Owen and the priest began to follow the crowd, the slope of the street affording them a view of the entire scene. Owen saw a troop of mounted infantry emerge from the barracks and form two lines, creating a path into which Boycott and his escort fled. Immediately the soldiers closed ranks and began to retreat from the onward-rushing throng, backing their horses towards the barracks with great skill. Once they were inside, the gates were pulled shut. The crowd surged against them and began to hammer with fists and sticks, a few throwing stones over the wall. They saw a man climb on to the bridge wall to hurl abuse, but a passer-by brushed against his leg and he fell headlong into the Robe. A handful of friends hurried to his aid and pulled him out, freezing but unhurt.

'I'm terribly troubled, Owen,' said Fr O'Malley. 'After all we've done to keep violence out of this.'

'At least no one was hurt, not even Boycott,' Owen remarked.

'But for those constables, Owen, I fear they would have torn the man apart.' He shook his head in sadness.

'Don't despair, Father. This was a mob, terrified they're going to be invaded. Once a mob gets an idea like that in its collective head, it's impossible to control.'

They turned at the sound of approaching horses to see ten mounted constables escorting what looked like a high-ranking police officer and the magistrate, McSheehy, directly towards the crowd.

'What now?' Owen said.

The mounted constabulary ignored them and the few other stragglers, then halted on the bridge at the point where the crowd became too dense for them to proceed.

The senior officer drew his pistol and fired a single shot skywards to draw the crowd's attention. There were a few screams and yelps of fright, but when it dawned that the shot had not come from the barracks, but from behind them, several hundred faces turned at once. The RIC officer stood in his stirrups and began to yell above their heads.

'I'm Sub-Inspector McArdle of the RIC. You are all disturbing the peace and will disperse immediately. If you do not, force will be used.'

The silence continued briefly as the changed situation was absorbed. Then a chant started somewhere and began to spread like water spilt on a smooth surface.

'Boycott out! Boycott out! Boycott out!'

McArdle glanced at the magistrate and nodded. He fired a second and third shot and the chant faded again. McSheehy produced a document and began to read aloud.

> Our Sovereign Her Majesty Queen Victoria charges and commands all persons being assembled, immediately to disperse themselves, and peaceably to depart to their habitations, or to their lawful business, upon the pains contained in the act made in the first year of King George, for preventing tumults and riotous assemblies. God Save the Queen!

'Just what we needed, the Riot Act,' remarked Owen sardonically.

'The idiots! "God save the Queen". It'll be like a red rag to a bull!'

As if to confirm the priest's observation, the chanting immediately resumed, interspersed now with evocations of ancient Irish cries of freedom from tyranny.

'Father, quick, out of the way!'

As Owen pulled the startled priest aside, about fifty cavalry arrived down Bridge Street, having been dispatched from the barracks at the other end of town.

'They can't use soldiers! This is a civil matter!' the priest protested, the anger rising in his throat.

'They can if they judge themselves under threat. As soon as the crowd gathered outside the barracks–'

'My God, there could be killing.'

Owen saw a rock curve in an arc from the crowd and strike a constable's horse. The animal reared, throwing the man to the ground. McArdle quickly fired into the air again but rather than quell the crowd's rage, his action prompted a torrent of missiles.

An English voice yelled out: 'Forward! Do not fire unless ordered!'

The cavalry, guns at the ready, began a trot directly towards the crowd.

Screams rose from the women as the mass of people began to flee in all directions. At the same moment the barracks doors were thrown open and the mounted infantry reappeared, quickly followed by the twenty constables who had been guarding Boycott. Panic quickly spread as some of the crowd fled towards the edge of the town and more scampered down the banks of the Robe, while others sought shelter upriver within the walls of the mill. The constables now used their batons freely, seizing whoever they felled and hauling them away under arrest. A frenzied man wielding a stick sought to grapple with a soldier but was levelled by the butt of another soldier's rifle. Within two minutes the crowd had dispersed and all that remained were about twenty men, mostly sitting on the ground nursing bloodied heads, or simply dazed, but all under arrest.

'Thank God no one was killed,' the priest gasped.

A man with blood streaming from a wound on his face staggered towards them, reeling from side to side as though insensibly drunk. Owen ran out and tried to haul him from the centre of the street. He was suddenly aware of a looming shadow and turned to see the great bulk of a horse rearing over him. The constable atop the animal raised his baton high.

'Throw fuckin' stones at us, will ye?' he snarled and brought the baton down with all his strength.

Owen heard an intense buzzing and the world around him lost all cohesion, the buildings becoming fluid and swirling together. And then day turned to night.

***

From an upstairs window at the rear of the butcher's shop, Donal Doherty watched proceedings with a satisfied grin.

'That worked well enough.'

'It did. Pity Boycott got away, though.'

'Doesn't matter. Our orders for now are te stoke the fire, not throw gunpowder on it.'

'Hmm. Anyway, I'd prefer te kill the bastard personally, when the time comes,' said Thomas Joyce.

Chapter 27

On Monday November 1st, when Captain Boycott, a local landlord left the Court in Ballinrobe, a crowd followed him 'shouting and groaning'. He became so threatened that he took refuge in the infantry barracks. A servant trying to get to Boycott with a car was unable to do so because he was also 'shouted' away. Eventually the military was called out to clear the street. Stones were thrown at the military and police and 'the Riot Act' was read.

–*The Ballinrobe Chronicle*, 6 November 1880

Captain Boycott has described further persecution to which he was subjected at Ballinrobe on Monday, when 50 men of the 7th Regiment had to be summoned to the aid of the police to save him and a colleague. He states that the persecution is on the increase.

–*The Nenagh Guardian*, 6 November 1880

2-8 NOVEMBER 1880

'What did I tell you? What did I tell you? A mob intent on murder! But would my voice be heard? The Land League means to kill every law-abiding landowner and their agents or force us to flee to England. But, by God, all they've done is strengthen my resolve, I tell you!'

Boycott was pacing the drawing room, inflicting irreparable damage to the polished mahogany floor with the steel cap on his cane. His audience was limited to Annie, Weekes and Sergeant Murtagh. Annie had been terribly troubled by the events of the previous day. Her husband had been forced to spend the night in the infantry barracks and even now, a day later, appeared quite shaken.

'This sort of carry-on would simply not be tolerated in England. Murderous mobs roaming the streets at liberty to kill and maim. What sort of a police force do you have here? Well, man, speak up! How is this permitted? Answer me that, sir?'

'Sir!' the sergeant struggled to control his irritation. 'Thanks to my men, you did not receive a single scratch to your person and several of those men required treatment by the army medic.'

Boycott waved a dismissive hand. 'I don't want to hear excuses. The mob should have been dispersed before it could gather. And if you intend to arrest the chief instigator, you will find him scheming behind the walls of that Catholic den of agitators in Neale.'

'Sir, are you suggesting that Fr O'Malley instigated this disturbance?'

'Disturbance? *Disturbance*? The Riot Act was read, man! And that's precisely what I'm suggesting. O'Malley, the Fenians' local commander.'

'Charles, that's going too far,' Annie said.

'Too fa–'

Murtagh cut him off. 'Have you evidence for such an assertion?'

'Actually, Charles...' It was Weekes who spoke, his voice timid.

'What is it?' Boycott snapped.

In the face of Boycott's fury, Weekes quickly lost the battle with his own will.

'Nothing,' he whispered.

Annie fixed Weekes with a suspicious stare.

***

Síomha pressed the fresh, cold poultice of wet turf ash against the large bump on Owen's crown. He'd been taken home unconscious and poultices applied through the night to reduce the swelling. He groaned and began to stir, his hand instinctively rising to the source of the pain.

Síomha, who had been worried to distraction throughout the night, leaned over him. 'Owen. Can you hear me?'

Tadhg and the priest hurried in and knelt beside the bed. He struggled to raise his head from the pillow.

'Where am I?'

'You're home,' Tadhg said.

He moaned and massaged his head.

'You took a nasty blow. You've been out all night,' Fr O'Malley said.

'All night? What happened?'

The priest recounted the aftermath. The constabulary had wanted to haul Owen off under arrest, but Fr O'Malley had prevailed on the Sub-Inspector and Owen had been released. Joe Gaughan had brought him home in his cart.

Owen managed a smile. 'This peaceful resistance business is painful work.'

The priest snorted.

Síomha sniffled and held a handkerchief to her eye. 'This is my fault. I insisted you went. You might have been killed.'

Fr O'Malley stood up sharply. 'Don't *you* start!'

***

BOYCOTT RELIEF EXPEDITION

This publication continues to support the Boycott Relief Expedition and can report that the fund now holds in excess of £500. Mr Gladstone would do well to note the widespread support among loyal citizens for Captain Boycott. Among the contributors have been an elderly lady of limited means who has sent ten shillings, a retired ex-army sergeant who has volunteered to march to Mayo despite his advancing years and a schoolboy who has donated his paper round money. Thousands more loyal subjects are willing to help. As one letter writer to this newspaper so aptly put it – 'On to Mayo, boys!'

–*The Belfast News Letter*, 4 November 1880

***

Fr O'Malley returned in Redpath's company that afternoon. Owen asked Tadhg to sit in on their discussion, prompting a glow of satisfaction on the lad's face.

'What now, Father?' Owen asked the priest.

'What now? We start again. If the rumours are true about the Orangemen and the army, we've got to show even greater resolve in the face of provocation. We'll speak to everyone within five miles if we have to, door to door, and tell them to offer no threat to any invading force. At least we can point out the folly of mob rule now. Incidentally, Martin McGurk was arrested; he was one of the first to throw stones.'

'Y'know, there were a lot of strange faces trying to egg on the crowd. One of them gave me this thick lip.'

'Do you think it was coordinated?' Redpath asked.

He shrugged. 'Just a notion.'

'If Fenian militants are trying to stir up trouble, we'll just have to work harder to counter them. We really need your help in this, Owen.'

Owen glanced briefly at Tadhg and Síomha.

'When do we start?' he asked.

***

Owen, Fr O'Malley and Redpath spent the following days visiting every cottage and business premises in the broad locality, reiterating the need for restraint no matter what the provocation. There was general support and not a little embarrassment from some at having been drawn into the previous Monday's melee. Owen, not unmindful of Síomha's influence on his actions, suggested actively courting the mothers' and wives' support. The priest quickly recognised the value of this strategy and asked several of the women to take an active role, preaching the benefits of their tactics 'as far as their legs could carry them'.

As the three strolled along Ballinrobe's Glebe Street, a messenger boy approached and handed Fr O'Malley a telegraph, for which service the priest rewarded the lad with a halfpenny. As he perused the message, his face grew sombre.

'What's happened?' Redpath asked.

'Parnell and four others have been arrested.'

Owen and Redpath responded in mutual shock. 'Arrested?'

'For conspiring to incite tenants not to pay rents and, worse, for conspiring to exclude certain individuals from social and commercial intercourse.'

'They're trying to make boycotting illegal,' Owen observed grimly.

'They can't do that!' Redpath snarled. 'Who people have dealings with is their own business. They can't make it illegal not to talk to someone.'

'No,' Owen said, 'but they could make it illegal to conspire to organise a boycott.'

'Armed Orangemen. Threats of military force. Now the law. They're trying everything in their power to stop us.'

'You know this means we could soon be three law-breaking conspirators?' Fr O'Malley observed, crumpling the telegraph.

Owen grinned. 'It also means we have them really worried.'

❊❊❊

> The Freeman's Journal is pleased to report that our Defence Fund for Mr Parnell and his comrades' trial had been widely supported with handsome subscriptions from prominent citizens. Hitherto the Freeman's Journal has chosen to ignore the ludicrous suggestion that the Government might send troops to pluck some obscure landlord's crops in Mayo, but cannot remain silent at news of a planned warlike expedition by loyalists to assist this individual – organised by supposedly responsible publications. Furthermore, it must be pointed out that no newspaper favouring the Land League, including this one, has advocated the relief of suffering tenants by means of armed force.
>
> –*The Freeman's Journal*, 5 November 1880

❊❊❊

A letter was delivered to Boycott as he and Weekes continued their endless labours in the cornfields, the younger man having gained a deep appreciation of the average farm labourer's value, although he kept this thought to himself. Since the riot, they'd been under the constant watch of six constables.

Recognising the crest of the Chief Secretary for Ireland in Dublin Castle, Boycott eagerly tore at the envelope. 'It's from Forster's office.'

He began to read aloud.

> Dear Mr Boycott,
>
> The Chief Secretary wishes to inform you that your request for assistance with your harvest has been under consideration. Given the unique nature of the action taken against you by the local population, our original intention was to discreetly provide you with a workforce sufficient to carry out bona fide work and to escort said workforce to and from your farm with a small military force.
>
> However, given the widespread publicity generated by your situation, in England, Ireland and the United States, and in consideration of the fact that a large force of men is being privately organized to come to your relief, any intervention from this office has now been undermined. We stress that we oppose the incursion of a large armed expedition into Mayo and that this office will be not be in a position to provide this force with a military escort.
>
> Your most obedient servant,
>
> R. Jones.
>
> Signed on behalf of William Edward Forster PC, FRS, Chief Secretary for Ireland

'Blundering idiots!' Boycott fumed. 'If there's one thing worse than a civil servant it's an Irish civil servant. I've been asking for assistance for a month and they did nothing. And now they imply it's my fault they can't do anything to help!'

'I think, Charles, we've been overtaken by events.'

'Forster! Blundering Liberal Quaker. The man follows each miscalculation with a greater one. Heaven alone knows what idiotic, ill-considered move he'll make next.'

***

Most of the twenty or so press correspondents had never set foot inside a room quite so grand. In fact, several were wary of sitting on the elegant chairs for fear of soiling the embroidered upholstery with the touch of their workaday overcoats.

The Drawing Room at Dublin Castle had not been designed with men such as these in mind, but as the royal reception room of the Queen's representative in Ireland, the Lord Lieutenant. Any one of the three magnificent gas-lit chandeliers would have equalled in value the annual earnings of the combined group. The tall, elegantly curtained windows afforded the men a fine view of the Great Courtyard and the Bedford Tower, and those choosing to gaze around the interior could admire the intricate plasterwork or the ornate marble fireplaces crowned by gold-rimmed, ceiling-high mirrors.

They were an eclectic bunch, many of whom would normally elect not to share the same air as some of the others, but such had been the unprecedented nature of the message they had received through their editors that they had little choice.

Among them were correspondents of the staunchly loyalist *Dublin Daily Express*, *The Belfast News Letter* and *The Irish Times*. These gentlemen mingled uncomfortably with their politically diametric opposites of the nationalist press, *The Freeman's Journal* and *The Nation*. There was also a smattering of pressmen from *The Dublin Evening Mail*, *The Evening Telegraph* and *The Anglo Celt*, as well as correspondents from *The Times* of London, *The Telegraph* and a number of 'stringers' for the international press, an epithet they had acquired as they sold their correspondence by the column inch, measured with a piece of string.

Normally, news conferences with the Chief Secretary were strictly reserved for an event such as the onset of a war or the death of a monarch. And yet the subject of today's briefing was the tribulations of an obscure land agent in the wilds of Mayo. The so-called 'Boycott Affair' had moved into the realm of official Government business.

A stiff-looking man in tails entered through the door at the top of the room. He stood to the side of the lectern and clapped his hands as if summoning schoolchildren from play.

'Gentlemen of the press,' he announced pompously, 'Her Majesty's Most Honourable Privy Council, The Chief Secretary for Ireland, Mr William Edward Forster.'

The correspondents seated themselves as far away from their adversaries as possible, as though each felt they might be infected with the other's political leanings. A moment later Forster entered, unsmiling. The man bore a striking resemblance to Parnell: tall and thin, with a fine head of hair, and a full, squarish beard, although Forster was in his sixties while Parnell was still in his mid-thirties. But all similarities ended with his appearance, certainly to the nationalists. And if they viewed Prime Minister Gladstone as a well-meaning politician, Forster was definitely their enemy. Although nominally a Liberal, he held firmly to imperialist traditions and displayed little understanding of the present Irish situation or her history. He had earlier that year advocated the use of buckshot in shotguns when conducting evictions, as it would be more effective against crowds than ball cartridges, earning himself the sobriquet 'Buckshot Forster'.

The correspondents sat with notebooks and pencils at the ready. Forster coughed and placed both hands on the lectern.

'Gentlemen, as you are aware, it is not usual for the Government to communicate matters of news to the press. However, in agreement with the Prime Minister, I have deemed it appropriate, due to exceptional circumstances. The matter concerning the land agent Captain Boycott has received widespread coverage in the press throughout Britain, in America, Europe and, I am reliably informed by long-distance telegraph, in publications as remote as *The Times* of India and *The Sydney Morning Herald*. In the course of this coverage a great number of wild, exaggerated statements have been made and passions aroused, and it is my duty to set the record straight.

'When this unfortunate event began, the Government had been most anxious to assist Captain Boycott, and informed both him and Lord Erne that if they made arrangements for a small body of men to complete their harvest, we would be willing to provide military protection. These are the facts, despite accusations in certain publications of Government indifference to matters of law and order.'

He paused briefly to fix an admonishing eye on the Belfast *News Letter* correspondent.

'Unfortunately, events have moved on considerably, thanks in no small part to Captain Boycott's penchant for widespread publicity, thus inflaming the situation, precisely what we had hoped to avoid. It is our understanding that five hundred armed men are planning an expedition from the North of Ireland. Should this force be permitted to go to Mayo, there would undoubtedly be a very strong collision, the consequences of which I fear to speculate upon. It was *The Dublin Daily Express* that first mooted the expedition and this morning I informed the proprietor, Mr Robinson, that not five hundred nor even one hundred men would be permitted to travel to Mayo. In fact, a mere fifty men are all that is required to harvest Captain Boycott's crop. Sending five hundred would be an act of provocation. Should the smaller group of fifty be sent, however, we will provide sufficient troops to guarantee their safety.

'And it is to matters of security that I now turn. Following the unfortunate riot in Ballinrobe, I have ordered both garrisons there to be filled to capacity. I have furthermore ordered military patrols of the area, specifically the roads from Ballinrobe to Lough Mask House. I also intend to transport more troops into the general area and have asked the board of Claremorris Workhouse if they can temporarily house a large body of troops. And I have instructed that the telegraph lines between Dublin and Ballinrobe are kept free from interference. All Resident Magistrates in the Mayo area have been ordered to proceed at once to Ballinrobe to assist the local Resident Magistrate, Mr McSheehy, in the execution of his duties.

'Finally, gentlemen, it is in all our interests to avoid inflaming the situation. A war in Mayo is the last thing this country needs.'

Most of the correspondents nodded in acknowledgement, many thinking that from a newsroom point of view, a war was precisely what they needed.

'Well, gentlemen. Thank you for your attendance.'

As Forster turned to leave, twenty hands shot up at once.

'I hadn't planned to take questions. Perhaps one or two.'

In the interests of not appearing biased towards the loyalists, he pointed first to *The Freeman's Journal* correspondent. The man stood up. He was a young, intellectual type with spectacles and a well-worn tweed jacket.

'Sir, is it not the case that the charges brought against Mr Parnell and others relating to conspiracy to shun certain individuals, and the act of sending a large military force into Mayo, are both tactics designed to undermine peaceful attempts to bring justice to the impoverished tenantry?'

There were grunts of protest from some of the others. Forster squared his shoulders and inhaled sharply to convey his outrage at the suggestion.

'The events you refer to are entirely unconnected. And I would hardly call a riot and the intimidation of Captain Boycott "peaceful".'

He quickly pointed to the man from *The Belfast News Letter.* If he expected an easier time from a loyalist, he was sorely mistaken. The Belfast man was of a more experienced mould – middle-aged, rotund, well dressed, and with a fearless countenance.

'Isn't it true that it was only when men loyal to Her Majesty organised the Boycott Relief Expedition that the Government decided to act?'

Forster's voice jumped a notch. 'That is most certainly not the case! Captain Boycott is not the only one who requested help. We needed time to consider...'

'In other words, sir, your department dithered so long in offering help that it was left to *The Belfast News Letter* and its supporters to prompt the Government to action.'

'That is absolutely outrageous!' Forster slammed his palm against the lectern. 'This briefing has ended!'

With that he turned his back on the twenty men who scribbled and scratched their shorthand at a frenetic pace, their thoughts already turning to the following day's editions.

CHAPTER 28

IRELAND – THE LAND AGITATION

The Boycott expedition is the most exciting topic of the day. It has withdrawn attention from the prosecutions [of Parnell etc] and the agitation, and filled the minds of the public with mingled curiosity, irritation and fear. The refusal of the Government to permit 100 armed men to march through a district so disturbed is generally admitted by fair and reasonable persons to have been wise and necessary, in order to avoid serious breaches of the peace.

–*The Times*, 9 November 1880

I determined to pay a visit to Captain Boycott's house and see with my own eyes the true state of affairs at Lough Mask House. In marked contrast to the tasteful furniture of the drawing room into which I was ushered, was the appearance of Captain Boycott. He entered hastily, wearing an old shooting coat, which was bespattered with mud, and apologised for the condition of his attire, explaining that he had been 'dipping his sheep'.

–Press Association correspondent, 10 November 1880

9-10 November 1880

To Mr Bernard Becker, c/o The Railway Hotel, Eyre Square, Galway

Becker,

We've received information that the government is sending a thousand troops to Ballinrobe. They've also taken other emergency measures involving the police and judiciary. They've restricted the numbers of the 'Orange invasion' to fifty, but still fear a major confrontation. Westminster is rife with rumours that this could be the spark to start a civil war in Ireland. At least thirty other correspondents from Britain, Europe and the United States have been assigned to Mayo. The government is determined to break what has become known as the 'boycott', which they hope will also break the will of the Land League. This entire thing is being watched throughout the empire and beyond. Even the US Presidential Election and Ned Kelly's forthcoming hanging have taken a back seat. Boycott is the story everyone wants to hear about. Proceed immediately back to Ballinrobe and send daily dispatches. The fact that you have already established a relationship with Boycott should give you an advantage.

FH Hill, Editor, *London Daily News*. 11.00 a.m. November 9th 1880

***

'That's the third special army train today, full of soldiers and all manner of bits and bobs of equipment. Look at them guns they have, like they're readyin' for war. And the feckin' horses, they've covered me station in shit, excuse me language, sir, but I'll be a week cleaning the place.'

'That's quite all right. Thank you.'

Redpath snapped shut his notebook and tipped his cap to the discommoded stationmaster, who wandered off in a private grumble along the platform of Claremorris train station, trying his best to dodge the disembarking soldiers.

Keen to witness the huge influx of troops, the American had travelled the seventeen miles from Neale to Claremorris. Both *The New York Herald* and *The Chicago Inter Ocean* had that very morning telegraphed him requesting a detailed update on events surrounding the boycott. Interest in the story in America had snowballed and *The Chicago Inter Ocean* had, in fact, become the world's first publication (thanks to a report of his own), to use 'boycott' as a noun and verb – Fr O'Malley's new word had already moved into the vernacular.

Winter had finally broken on Mayo like a wave. The skies above were a blanket of dark grey and cold rain pelted down unremittingly. As he moved along the platform, his ears were assailed by an eclectic mix of English accents so diverse it was hard to credit that they all hailed from the same country. Horses whinnied as they were guided from the boxcars, men carted boxes of ordnance from the train and several covered ambulance coaches were being steered from an open railcar.

He dodged his way towards an officer sheltering under the platform roof and pulled out his notebook. The officer wore a scarlet uniform and stood in stiff military fashion, one hand behind his back, the second fixed rigidly by his side.

Redpath offered a 'good morning' and the man briefly flicked his gaze towards him without responding.

'Sir, forgive my intrusion, my name is James Redpath, correspondent with *The Chicago Inter Ocean*. Could I trouble you to inquire about the operation?'

The officer turned his head a little. 'An American?'

'Yes, sir, I am.'

'Sir, may I inquire, have you journeyed all the way from Chicago to report on this incident?' He seemed genuinely curious.

'Well, I've been here on assignment for some months. May I ask the scale of the current operation? Or is that a military secret?' He smiled in an attempt to weaken the officer's defences. To his surprise it worked. The officer relaxed and granted him an informal salute.

'Brevet Lieutenant Colonel Twentyman of the Hussars.'

His accent was clipped, his diction perfect.

'May I ask, sir, how many troops the operation involves?'

He nodded towards the men milling about under the incessant yelling of their sergeants. 'Well, sir, we've got four troops of the 19th Hussars, roughly four hundred men. Also a detachment of the Army Service Corps. In fact, where is he...?' He spotted another officer and called out. 'Major Reynolds!'

The major hurried over and snapped a salute.

'Yes, sir?'

'Major, this is Mr Redpath, an American newsman.'

Twentyman leaned towards Redpath and said with pride: 'This is Surgeon

Major Reynolds, VC, decorated with Britain's highest military honour for his service at Rourke's Drift in the Zulu war.'

The men exchanged greetings.

'Major Reynolds commands the Hospital Corps. Thank you, Major.'

Twentyman resumed his account. 'Earlier today, trains arrived with more men, rations, equipment, carts and so on, and this afternoon we will be joined by a further four hundred officers and men of the 84th Regiment. A formidable display of Her Majesty's forces, wouldn't you say?' Evidently Twentyman believed he was there to report on the impressiveness of the logistical operation.

Redpath decided to put at least one card on the table. 'Sir, you've brought heavy guns, explosives, cavalry, even famous military heroes. Isn't it a little excessive to keep thirty unarmed tenant farmers at bay?'

'Sir, I'm led to believe that the entire local population is working in league to intimidate Captain Boycott.'

'But they're unarmed men, women and childr–'

Twentyman's tone changed sharply. 'If you're implying I would order my troops to fire on women and children, I take that as an insult to the honour of Her Majesty's forces. But if necessary, we will defend an Englishman under siege from seditious reactionaries. And you may write that for your American readers. Good day, sir!'

Twentyman snapped an about-turn and walked away.

Redpath couldn't help but hope that if the time came, the Lieutenant Colonel would be able to tell the tenants from the reactionaries.

***

Fr O'Malley, Owen Joyce, Joe Gaughan, Luke Fitzmorris and young Matt O'Toole stood sheltering under a shop's canopy, watching as the soldiers approached down Bridge Street. Having marched the twelve miles from Claremorris to Ballinrobe, the troops were to a man soaked to the skin, their boots and legs muddied and their faces white with cold. Earlier the five men had watched an equally large battalion arrive and it was becoming hard to believe that the British Government had responded to Boycott's situation on such an extraordinary scale.

A shout went up from a mounted officer and the troops came to an abrupt halt. Even in the dim light cast by the street's gas lamps, Owen could see that they were all very young, most no more than twenty. They had the faces of poor men, their uniforms unable to conceal the fact that they came from the homes of labourers or miners, and probably joined the army to escape their own world of poverty. As he watched, he couldn't help but remember his brother's prediction, which seemed to be playing out with chilling accuracy: the English, he'd said, would simply send in the army to crush their pathetic boycott. He had to admit that when they'd started this he had never envisioned an invasion of English soldiers, but he hoped to God that the army were never given cause to spill blood.

Down at the barracks entrance they could see some commotion, with a number of officers on horseback exchanging words.

'What's goin' on?' Joe Gaughan asked.

The foot soldiers were craning their necks to try and ascertain why they'd been halted so close to their temporary home. Finally an officer rode back up and addressed the junior officers, having to shout to make himself heard above the pelting rain.

'Gentlemen. It appears that the Army Service Corps wagons have neglected to bring the tents or cooking utensils. And both of the barracks are already at capacity.'

A general peal of laughter started to spread among the locals who had assembled to watch the spectacle. The unfortunate, sodden privates did not appreciate their reception and aimed a few choice oaths at their audience before being reprimanded by a superior.

'Men! Until the tents arrive, you will break out and find shelter wherever you can. Be warned, this does not give you permission to enter private dwellings or premises by force. Fall out!'

The troops turned back towards the town and began to drift aimlessly in groups, each under the command of a sergeant. Within ten minutes they were huddling under canopies, crouching in alleys and standing in doorways. To add to their misery, they now had to endure the catcalls that emanated from several upstairs windows in the street.

'Have a nice nap now, lads!'

'Welcome te Mayo!'

'Jaysus, lads, yis shouldn't be out in the rain. Ye'll catch yer death!'

Joe had rigged a tarpaulin over his cart to provide some shelter. As the five men drove down Market Street towards home, looking out at the soldiers' miserable faces and listening to the chorus of taunts, Fr O'Malley cursed and shook his head.

'I wish they'd stop that. How many times do I have to tell some people? No provocation. These soldiers look fit to kill.'

They sat silently under the tarpaulin listening to the rain pattering down and the wheels churning a muddy rut beneath. Owen saw the dark shape of the workhouse across a field and wondered about the unfortunates still within its walls. The last time he'd had any direct involvement with the English army had been their pursuit of him when he'd fled that very building on a night almost as cold as this one.

They watched the dark, open countryside drift by. Soon they would all be home and warm in their beds, safe under the thatch they'd laid with their own hands. But Owen could sense what each of them was thinking. The army's arrival presaged bad times ahead. If the boycott could be broken and Boycott the man backed up with a military force, the day might soon dawn when the evictions would resume and everything they had worked for would be for naught. Their simple cottages would be taken from them and, alongside their wives and children, they would be cast out, huddling under winter skies like those soldiers, until either the workhouse or death claimed them.

'Y'know, Father, I'll go along with this, with you and Mr Parnell and Mr Davitt because I trust ye know what ye're doing.' It was Luke Fitzgerald who spoke.

'I'm glad to hear it, Luke.'

Luke looked out into the night reflectively.

'These fifty men coming from the north, the Protestant workmen, if they come down here and dig Boycott's spuds, then fine, I'm happy enough to not interfere. But if they come here bent on shedding blood because they know the English army will back them up, then I don't care how many there are, but I intend te defend me family.'

Joe Gaughan looked over his shoulder. 'I'm in the same boat, Father. If it's bloodshed they want, then that's what they'll get.'

'Maybe there'll be more than fifty. There could be a thousand. But them and the English can't just come into our county and walk all over us. I don't care if the English or the Orangemen have guns, I'll fight them with me pitchfork,' Matt O'Toole said.

'And you'll die with your pitchfork, young Matt.' The priest sighed despondently. 'Let's pray it doesn't come to that. And you, Owen, what do you say?'

Owen couldn't deny that the spectre that had once haunted his thoughts, of spilling blood, of war offering a path to justice, the very path his brother had taken, was beginning to stir again at the sight of the English troops. It chilled him even to contemplate the idea that he shared in some way the darkness in his brother's heart. But he knew he must face the stark possibility that they'd all been deluding themselves with their boycott. And if an English gun threatened his family, what would he do? What choices would remain?

'Would I kill, you mean? I suppose I'll find out when the time comes.'

***

A German man called John Valkenburg ran the Valkenburg Hotel in Ballinrobe's Market Street with startling efficiency – startling certainly to the locals, who generally adopted a more casual approach to commerce. Mr Valkenburg, by all accounts a most obliging and polite man, also knew how to maximise his returns, offering lower rates when he had empty rooms, doubling prices when demand was high and insisting on a level of punctuality that his Irish staff found baffling.

Maggie Cusack, the Boycotts' former maidservant, had been granted a position in the hotel thanks to Fr O'Malley putting in a quiet word with Mr Valkenburg. The German had been delighted to take her on, along with two other ex-members of Boycott's staff, as there had been a recent upsurge in business. In fact, he had never had such an influx of guests, not even in the summer when gentlemen flocked to Ballinrobe to indulge their love of fishing in Lough Mask's bountiful waters. It was boom time.

He had doubled up all of the rooms and had stratified the guests according to profession, as this seemed to his efficient mind the perfectly natural thing to do. So the top floor was filled to capacity with newspaper correspondents, and what a curious caboodle they were – Irish, English, Scottish, an American, a Frenchman and even a fellow German. On the first floor he'd put the military gentlemen, dispatched to the hotel due to the overflow from the town's two barracks. He appreciated the discipline and efficiency of the military and liked to watch them march about his hotel with their backs straight, riding crops and caps slung under their arms. Numbered among them was the overall commander, Major Coghill, then Colonel Bedingfeld, Lieutenant Colonel Twentyman and Surgeon Major Reynolds. He had crammed a host of other subordinates into the pokier accommodations; three to room, or in some cases, a bed, but at the same price, naturally.

On the ground floor there were only four bedrooms, but he'd turned a parlour and a smoking room into bedrooms, and the extra magistrates of the law occupied these.

Maggie approached Mr Valkenburg through the crowded reception area and handed him a telegraph.

'Maggie, all rooms done by noon, if you please. There is much preparation for dinner this evening,' he said, his German accent having been softened by the Mayo air.

Maggie nodded sullenly and turned away. Although he paid the girl more than she had earned in Captain Boycott's employment, she seemed permanently unhappy and wandered about the hotel with a faraway expression.

The telegraph was from Mr Bernard Becker, another newsman seeking a room. And although Mr Becker had stayed in the hotel recently, Mr Valkenburg could not accommodate him. Luckily he'd come to an arrangement with several townsfolk whereby they would absorb his overflow of guests and he would take a thirty percent commission for the referral. He would put Mr Becker with the Widow Barry, a wonderful woman with a large house who was already fussing over four officers of the Hussars.

Mr Valkenburg smiled as he wrote a note to the Widow Barry. This Captain Boycott was certainly wonderful for business.

***

Bernard Becker had taken *The Lady Eglinton* steam packet from Galway, which quickly conveyed him the length of Lough Corrib towards Cong. He had telegraphed ahead to the Valkenburg Hotel for a room and requested a car and driver to meet him off the ferry.

He had spent the past days wandering the landscape of Galway, particularly her coastline. While the county was rich in terms of natural beauty, sadly the good Lord had not bequeathed the people any level of prosperity. He'd formed the opinion that the Irish were unquestionably downtrodden but that much of this was due to a clash of cultures. He believed that the Irish as a race were given to prevarication to some degree, and procrastination to excess. Nothing was done at the snap of a finger if it could be deferred until some more suitable time, this 'time' residing wholly in their imagination. The Saxon, as opposed to the Celt, he considered, obediently and promptly does as ordered, and if he gives a command expects the same. Any Englishman would be apt to storm at procrastinators and shufflers. It would be natural in these circumstances that the unfortunate Irishman would view the Englishman as an imperious tyrant.

Yet for all that, he had seen the Irish peasant exploited to a shocking degree. He had written of the terrible neglect of the beautiful area known as Connemara, where, like Mayo, the bountifulness of the British Empire had yet to extend. Roads, piers, schools – whole villages in fact – were all in desperate need of investment. The entire place had simply been abandoned to the whims of the landlords. He had written of Connemara in terms of its general 'tumble-downishness'. He had visited cottages that were little more than hovels and had come across one seashore holding where the rents were not only appallingly high, but the English landlord charged the tenants for gathering seaweed to use as fertiliser. When he witnessed such exploitation, he knew that no clash of cultures could excuse it.

The rain had persisted for two days and even in the dim light he could see the white foam of countless crashing waterfalls on the distant mountains. He had learned that the situation in Ballinrobe was tense after the arrival of hundreds of soldiers and a body of constabulary sufficient to storm the walls of Troy. And their numbers were swelling daily, as evidenced by the presence of thirty-two RIC men on the steamer.

On disembarking, his driver was there thanks to the ever-efficient Mr Valkenburg and he greeted Becker deferentially.

'To Ballinrobe, your honour?' the man inquired.

'Yes, please, but I would like to go by way of Lough Mask House.' Although it was late and the rain still fell in relentless sheets, he was keen to renew his acquaintance with Boycott ahead of the hordes of other correspondents.

'It's not on our way, your honour.'

'I wish to call on Mr Boycott.'

'Sure, it's a different way altogether, your honour.'

This was precisely the sort of dithering that had inspired his 'clash of cultures' theory. He decided to adopt his strictest Saxon tone.

'Go that way, nevertheless,' he barked.

The man set off at a trot so gentle it would be midnight before they reached the house. Becker kept his frustration in check initially, but after thirty minutes his vexation at their snail's pace got the better of him.

'Can't you go any faster?'

The man pulled the car to a complete stop and turned to Becker.

'Your honour, if I may put it plainly. I've been engaged to drive you to Ballinrobe, which I will do with pleasure. But I will not drive you to Lough Mask House. It is not in the contract.'

Becker sighed. 'I'll pay you double.'

'No, your honour. Doesn't matter if you pay me a king's ransom.'

'Are you afraid? Is that it?'

'I am not, your honour. But I won't go against my countrymen. Mr Boycott is being boycotted, or haven't you heard? Now, you're welcome to walk if you want, only it's a good stretch of the legs. Seven mile or so. So what's it to be?'

Becker cursed inwardly. 'Ballinrobe,' he muttered.

An hour later they pulled into the town and Becker was further irked to learn that he was to be housed with 'the Widow Barry'. His competitors had beaten him to the bedrooms. His accommodation actually turned out to be very acceptable and the good widow had provided a fold-up cot for him in her front parlour, which actually offered him privacy to work. Having washed, changed into dry clothing and enjoyed a hearty meal, he set off around the town to gain an overview of the situation.

His first impression was of soldiers everywhere, wandering the paths and staring into the shop windows. The locals mostly seemed to be ignoring them or at least quietly enduring them. Yet the sight of so many armed men walking the streets of this small, remote place gave one the impression of a garrison town readying for war. The numbers of police added to the perception. They stood in twos or threes on the corners or patrolled in pairs along every street and alley, eyes nervous and suspicious. If anything, these men seemed more likely to come into confrontation with the locals. Perhaps, Becker thought, it was because they were Irishmen, regarded as being in league with the enemy.

He ran into the first of his competitors near the barracks – four of them, in fact. One he recognised from *The Times*, and felt a surge of annoyance. It was as though he felt this story and town belonged to him, having been the first to exploit the current troubles. He swore an oath and determined not to speak to the interlopers. He ducked down a set of steps to the riverside walk, which would take him parallel to the ordnance ground between the two barracks. He scaled a brief rise and looked across the open space with disbelief.

It was only here that the scale of the operation began to unfold. Spread out across the large ordnance ground were maybe a hundred tents, outside each of which soldiers grouped around blazing braziers. Men on horseback rode in every direction and sentries patrolled the perimeter, one of whom was eyeing him up and down as he stood there. At the far end of the green he could see carts trundling back and forth across the bridge that led to the cavalry barracks. Ambulance wagons were interspersed about the tents. Three pairs of soldiers hurried by, carrying what he recognised as those so-called 'machine-guns', capable of mowing down fifty men in seconds. He found the entire scene quite disturbing, especially as he felt he'd played no small part in bringing it about.

'Oo the 'ell are you?'

A soldier of no more than eighteen had come within ten yards of him, his rifle aimed directly at Becker's chest.

'Becker, press correspondent.'

'Let's see, then.' He held out his hand for some form of corroboration and Becker fumbled in his pocket for his accredited press documents. He held them up and the young private eased nearer to study them.

'All right, Mr Becker, sir. We can't be too careful with all these Fenians about.'

'That's quite alright.'

'But this area's off-limits to civvies, sir. You shouldn't be 'ere at all.'

Neither should you, he thought as he turned back towards the River Robe, tinged with the silver of the gathering moonlight.

Chapter 29

THE LAWLESS STATE OF IRELAND

TROOPS DISPATCHED TO PROTECT LABORERS AGAINST LAND LEAGUE

Four troops of Hussars were dispatched hence for Ballinrobe by special trains at 2 o'clock this morning. Four hundred infantry have just arrived at Ballinrobe and will encamp near Lough Mask House. These precautions are taken in view of the intention of the northern Orangemen to send laborers to harvest the crops of Mr. Boycott, Lord Erne's agent, for whom the local peasantry, at the instigation of the Land League, refuse to work. The Government will protect a moderate force of laborers, but refuse to permit anything approaching armed demonstration, which would certainly provoke a collision.

–*The New York Times*, 10 November 1880

L'AGITATION EN IRLANDE

D'après des dépêches télégraphiques arrivées à Paris dans la soirée d'hier, les hommes de la province de l'Ulster marcheraient sur Mayo, dans la province de Connaught, où se trouvent des troupes anglaises, commandées par le capitaine Boycott. L'intendant du gouvernement, dans le but de protéger ces troupes, a envoyé à Mayo des renforts de soldats dans la nuit du 8 au 9 novembre. La guerre civile paraît imminente.

–*La Presse*, Paris, 11 November 1880

11 November 1880

Annie Boycott emerged in her nightdress from behind the curtained screen as her husband entered the room. He had aged considerably these past months and she wondered if others thought the same of her. She had a permanent tightness across her chest, endured piercing and prolonged headaches, sometimes lasting an entire day, and often felt on the edge of reason. Dr Maguire had merely given her some powders and told her to find time to rest. What a monstrous joke! Although the household duties had eased greatly with the maid's arrival, she had been obliged to resume working in the fields until just a day past, when they'd received confirmation that fifty men were coming to relieve them. But even though she had escaped the backbreaking labour, the strain of living under siege, of contemplating their future, denied her the ability to relax in any meaningful sense.

He disappeared behind his own screen and she watched from the bed as his arms rose above the frame and pulled on his nightshirt. In recent days he had lost some of his famed truculence, only to replace it with a sullenness the like of which she'd never seen. He would never admit to being depressed, of course, as that would mean his spirit was wavering. And it was still possible to summon a cantankerous rant with a casual remark. But she was certain that he had regrets about his handling of the situation and that he disliked the surge of press attention, as he had pledged to talk only to that Becker fellow and one or two others. For despite the fact that when Charles spoke he could often be heard in the next county, he was largely a private man. What's more, he despised the notion that he was seen in England as a helpless little man who was being bullied by a few Irish brutes. His letter to *The Times* had brought him far more than he had bargained for.

Despite all that, she felt she must discuss certain matters with him.

'Charles, may I ask you about the coming days?'

He grunted an affirmative as he sat on the end of the four-poster bed, stroking his beard as he was in the habit of doing when ruminating on a subject.

'Fifty labourers are coming, is that correct?'

'Hmm. Arrive in Ballinrobe tomorrow night. Start work here on Thursday.'

'And how many soldiers will accompany them?'

'Why are you asking?' he inquired gruffly.

'Charles, I feel I've earned the righ–'

'About four hundred.'

'I beg your pardon?'

'Four hundred soldiers, or so I've been informed.'

'*Four hundred*?'

Annie had envisaged the labourers with a guard of twenty or so men to patrol the estate perimeter with the RIC. 'Are you saying…just a moment… surely they'll return to the barracks each evening?'

Boycott glanced over his shoulder, his expression suggesting her question was idiotic. 'Of course not. Organising the security to and from Ballinrobe on a daily basis would be impossible. They'll have to stay here until the job is done.'

Annie was sitting up straight in the bed now, the blankets gathered on her lap. 'And where will all these men sleep?'

'The labourers in the stables. The enlisted soldiers will camp in the open field beyond the woodland. The officers…' he hesitated.

'Go on.'

'The officers will have to stay in the house.'

'Here? *In this house*?'

'Of course. As an ex-officer, I cannot possibly countenance asking them to sleep under canvas.'

'How many?' Her voice was rising sharply.

'Six, perhaps seven.'

'Oh my dear God.' She put a palm to her forehead as she felt another headache swell inside her skull.

'It will only be for a couple of weeks, three at most.'

'Three weeks,' she said despairingly. 'After all that's happened, now I must turn my home into a barracks and surrender all semblance of privacy. Is this ever going to end? Answer me that, Charles.'

'I said three weeks, what else would you have me say, woman?' His tone suggested that he himself was not immune to lugubriosity at the prospect.

'And what about beyond that?'

'What do you mean?'

'I mean when the labourers are gone and the harvest sold, what then?'

He stood now, becoming his old belligerent self, but looking faintly ridiculous as he began to bluster in his nightshirt.

'Then we evict the blighters if they won't pay their rents and find new tenants! That's what we'll do, by God. They won't defeat me as long as I've air in my lungs.'

Annie wiped away a tear. She almost felt pity for him, such was his blindness to the obvious that had all his life prevented him from seeing the world as it really was.

'Charles. Even if we do as you say, no one will take up the leases. No one will go against the Land League for fear of being boyc– for fear of being shunned. Parnell has almost the entire country on his side.'

'Then we'll get them from England. Or Scotland. Plenty of proper, hardworking farmers over there, not like these Irish layabouts.'

'Charles, will you please listen? You won't get them. Not under these conditions. And let us say you succeeded. What then? Where will we shop? Who will work the farm next year and the year after that? Who will tend your horses? We'll still be treated as though we have leprosy. They'll never give in to us. *Never.* Is this to be our life?'

He slammed a palm against the bedpost, then turned and walked to the window where he stood peering out through a gap in the curtain at the starlight floating on the surface of Lough Mask. After a minute he walked silently to his side of the bed and twisted the small dial on the oil lamp, depriving the room of all light.

'Damn this place to hell,' she heard him whisper in the darkness.

***

She lay awake for hours watching the vague outline of his chest rising and falling. Every once in a while he grunted an unintelligible word and his head would turn from side to side, as though his troubles sought him out even in the realms of slumber.

What troubled him though, down there in the pit of his soul, in the places that only the inner eye of sleep could behold and recall to memory? The ostracism? His financial situation? Or did it go deeper, did his dreams force him to confront the events of those last months on Achill Island, the events that had finally set the mould on his character, forever shaping him as the belligerent, petty and vindictive man that most people saw.

When she asked him what they were to do after the crop was harvested and the enormous fuss abated, he'd blithely said that he would 'evict the blighters' and they would then carry on as before, as though the tenants were merely an infestation of woodworm and once banished, the problem would be solved.

In that simplistic assessment, she had heard an echo of another time, when he had carried out a particular eviction not because it was an 'economic imperative', as he would frequently justify the act, but as a means of leverage, and in shameful vengeance. And God forgive her, in her desperation, she had encouraged, even applauded the act.

When their daughter, Mary, had completed her schooling, including a year's educational travel through southern Europe, she had returned, aged almost seventeen, to live in Corrymore House on Achill Island. Her first months home had been relatively uneventful, although Annie noticed a growing hostility between Mary and her father. She had inherited much of his stubbornness and was also given to flights of temper. Where they differed, however, was her compassion and innate kindness, which itself was a source of conflict as Charles castigated her for her easy familiarity with the tenantry, as he had Annie when she was a younger woman. Yet Annie felt pride at sight of Mary's behaviour, as she believed it had been her subtle influence when Mary had been younger that had woven these sentiments into her daughter's nature. The one thing that had acted as a balm during these times of conflict had been Mary's own beauty, for she seemed as a flower sprung from the unyielding Achill earth: black-haired with intelligent blue eyes, arching eyebrows dipping to a dainty nose and a smile that went straight to the heart. Even Charles struggled to maintain his anger with Mary for any protracted period.

But her husband had not been the only one to suffer through Mary's recalcitrant nature. Annie also found her relationship with her daughter increasingly fraught. She displayed no interest in their home or general life, rebuffing as many social occasions as she could safely explain away through illness, eventually telling Annie that she had no interest in indulging in pointless conversations with stuffy individuals about matters of no consequence. Her year in Europe had been an experience of diametric contrasts, she'd explained; on the one hand the tedium of society's *politesse*, on the other the infinite expansiveness of the human mind revealed to her through Europe's, and in particular Italy's, museums, galleries and churches.

One evening her father had almost struck her when Mary had argued that Catholics had been responsible for the greatest period of human expression in history, the Renaissance, and that furthermore her time in Italy had exposed her to many members of that religion and, contrary to his lecturing, as a collective group they were no better or worse than any Protestants she knew. The allegorical straw had come when she'd expressed an interest in becoming a member of that religion, as she found the rituals and invocations 'were of a more spiritual, yet tangible nature' than those within Protestantism.

Only Annie's restraining hand had prevented him from using his, although he had screamed himself hoarse. Afterwards, Annie believed that Mary's interest in Catholicism had been largely about opposing her father, purely for the sake of it. But all of this was but a prelude to the chapters of strife, torment and heartbreak that lay in the months ahead.

Charles and Mary's one shared interest was their love of horses. And for her seventeenth birthday, he went so far as to purchase her a beautiful chestnut mare. Annie cynically suspected it was an attempt to bribe her into returning to his narrow fold, but she also believed it had been the final act of outright love in his life, for to act with such generosity in the face of what had gone before was surely a monumental struggle. So taken with the beast had Mary been that she embraced her father with tears in her eyes.

In the weeks after, all had gone exceedingly well and they had shared countless rides along Achill's beaches and around the lower slopes of Croaghaun Mountain. But the demands of the estate had parted them and eventually Mary had taken to disappearing for long hours alone, which often left Annie deeply worried, as Mary was impetuous and given to following paths that hugged the precipitous drops to the churning Atlantic. Yet she believed that the recent dark days were finally being put behind them and could be filed away as mere manifestations of burgeoning youth.

Such was Mary's brightness and exuberance by the early summer that Annie's suspicions were aroused, for surely the novelty of having her own horse had waned. Questioned, Mary seemed evasive, laughing away her mother's concerns. The frequency of her absences from home was also a concern, although Charles had barely registered these. It troubled Annie sufficiently that she determined to discover if her worries were unfounded, or merely the concerns of a clucking hen for her chick.

So she had told Charles she wished to freshen her own horsemanship skills and had followed Mary one day at a distance, her daughter's fresh tracks easily discernible in the soft earth. As she rounded a rocky crag near Lough Accorymore, at the east face of Croaghaun Mountain, she spied her daughter's horse grazing, but Mary absent. She dismounted and stole quietly up the hillside, peering into a small glade, where to her horror she saw Mary lying on a blanket locked in an embrace with a young man, who by his clothing she guessed could only be a peasant. The breath was stolen from her lungs as she surreptitiously observed their lips pressed together, the young man's hand cupped about Mary's breast. She prayed they had not submitted to the full temptations of lust – scandalous enough between those of the same class, beyond contemplation between people of such diverse breeding. She had returned distraught to her home, vistas of unimaginable terror opening up in her mind, for the truth would out sooner or later and there was no contemplating what Charles might do.

Upon Mary's return, with Charles absent, Annie had wasted no time confronting her daughter directly, doing what she had once prevented her husband from doing – slapping Mary forcefully across the face. Mary fell to the floor in shock and pain, clutching her scalded cheek, and lay there in tears as Annie revealed what she had witnessed. As soon as Mary recovered her composure, her defiance returned and she revealed the extent of the relationship.

His name was Francis Ruane, aged nineteen and son of Patrick Ruane, a tenant who leased fifteen acres of arable land near Dooagh and a further thirty on the slopes of Croaghaun that was suitable only for sheep. Francis was the herdsman for the animals, which facilitated the couple's trysts far from prying eyes. She had met him a couple of months previously when out riding.

Annie was enormously relieved at Mary's insistence that they had not had any sexual congress, at least none that would have consequences. Besides, they intended to marry, she'd brazenly revealed, after which it would be of no concern to anyone other than her and Francis.

Annie almost lost her mind with her daughter's blatancy, her naivety and her determination that her romance would continue. She loved Francis Ruane; it was as simple as that. Mary would not countenance any argument that they inhabited different worlds, cared little for the shame it would bring and was quite prepared to confront her father on the matter. As she put it, it was time someone in this household was prepared to confront him, a remark that earned her a further smack across the cheek.

In the coming weeks Annie tried everything she could to prevent the affair continuing. She locked Mary in her room, threatened her, and told her husband to deny her the use of the horse on some other pretext, terrified he would discover her true reason. But, as usual, Charles paid little heed to the goings-on of his own household.

Yet Mary had managed to escape to the hills on several occasions, returning footsore but happy and defiant. Knowing it was only a matter of time before the scandal escalated with a pregnancy, Annie began to consider the one remaining option. And one month after her discovery and at her wits' end, she decided to tell her husband.

All her pleas for him to remain calm fell on deaf ears. Her intention had been for Charles to warn the young man off, threatening his father with eviction or some such. What he had done was to first beat his daughter about their drawing room, leaving her face bruised and swollen and her back scarred by several frenzied attacks with his riding crop. With his daughter admonished, he'd located a pair of thugs and gone in pursuit of the young man, whereupon they had beaten him to within an inch of his life. Francis Ruane's father had been informed that should his son ever come within a mile of Mary again, he, his wife and four children would be evicted.

Mary was locked in her room for weeks and when allowed out confined to the house, the threats to her seemingly having effect. But though the swelling abated, her features never again regained their former beauty, for her smile was no more and her eyes harboured a deep hatred for her parents, especially for her mother, who she believed had so betrayed her.

A number of months passed without incident, but the approaching cold of winter was little beside that of the bitter chill that lingered in their household. In September, Charles received his offer to take up residence at Lough Mask and had been overjoyed. He saw it not only as an opportunity to advance his ambitions, but to extricate them from the place that had almost brought scandal upon their heads. He believed that Mary would soon forget about the affair when she was far away on the mainland, near to towns and railways and exposure to proper society. Annie had her doubts, which were confirmed when she discovered a box of letters beneath Mary's bed, many delivered within the previous few weeks, probably left on her window ledge by a sympathetic acquaintance of Francis Ruane. Another confrontation followed, but she was careful to avoid Charles having any knowledge of it. Mary told her mother she had no intention of leaving Achill, unless it was on a ship bound for America with her lover – her father would have to kill her to prevent it. Once again Annie found herself distraught, now suffering in silence for fear of the violence that might ensue. As it happened, she didn't need to confide in her husband, as one evening Mary stole from the house with a bag of clothes and her horse. She would never return.

Now desperate she would lose Mary forever, she had encouraged Charles to end the relationship with Ruane by whatever means, but begged him not to harm Mary. His first port of call, in the company of four burly transient labourers, was Patrick Ruane's cottage. Neither Mary nor her lover were present and the tenant swore he had no idea of his son's whereabouts, that he was equally opposed to the relationship, but that his son was infatuated. Despite his earnest pleas for mercy, they ransacked the cottage's three rooms, terrifying Ruane's wife and younger children. The following day Charles evicted the Ruanes, although he had no legal right to do so as Patrick Ruane had never failed to pay his rent. But her husband had means of circumventing the legalities and the family were abandoned to the whims of nature.

Two days of inquiries had led them to an isolated cottage beyond the village of Keel, where Francis Ruane's closest friend lived. Candles burned in both of the dwelling's windows. On her husband's instruction the men had shouldered the door open, the friend was bundled aside without debate and the door to the second room kicked in. And there Charles found Francis Ruane clutching a pole for protection with Mary standing at his shoulder, still defiant in the face of hopeless odds.

Ruane was quickly overpowered, thrown to the ground and subjected to a rain of blows and kicks. When Mary tried to interfere, she too suffered a number of strikes from her father's open hand before she was pinioned by one of the men. With her lover reduced to a bloody heap, obscenities spewed from her mouth and she swore that she would die before she ever again set foot beneath the same roof as Charles Boycott. When her captor's grip relaxed, she managed to wriggle free and grasp a knife, which she swept in a wide arc towards her father, clipping his arm and drawing blood. He struck out again instinctively, fiercely, and Mary collapsed in a corner, a tooth dislodged from her mouth, blood dripping from her chin, sobbing in utter despair.

The knife had severed the last bonds between them. She told him again through a mouthful of blood and a faltering, tear-laden voice that he would have to kill her to force her to leave and that if he didn't, every day that was left to her would be spent in contemplation of killing him. Charles Boycott had spat at her, told her she could have her peasant filth and that she would never set eyes on him or her mother again. He had aimed a final kick at the prone Ruane and left.

When he returned that night he had given Annie a complete account of what had transpired. His telling of the tale seemed in keeping with her daughter's character and he had not omitted any detail of his own behaviour. There was little reason to doubt anything he'd reported. When he was finished, he proclaimed that no word was ever to be spoken of the girl and her name was never to be heard aloud again under their roof. She had brought disgrace on his family, on her religion and her nation. She was a harlot, a whore no better than the painted women who haunted the docklands of Dublin, selling their sex for money. There was no end to the foul epithets he used. As far as he was concerned, his daughter was not just dead, she had never existed. He instructed Annie to wipe all trace of Mary from her memory, as though such a thing might really be possible. Neither of them would ever see or speak of her again. They would soon move to the mainland where none would have any knowledge of Mary's existence.

Soon afterwards he wrote to their relations informing them that their daughter had died from an unnamed malady. He said that it was too painful to speak of the matter further, did not wish to engage in any correspondence, and would be grateful if they respected his wishes. He removed the lone photograph of her from the frame on the mantle and cast it into the turf fire. He burned all her possessions, even the bed she had slept in. And then he threw himself into the running of his business, his treatment of the tenants on Achill in those last months bordering on brutality, yet remaining just on the correct side of the law.

Annie was in despair during those appalling months, her heartbreak accentuated by their departure from Achill. As the ferry crossed the narrow channel of Achill Sound, she felt that the cold Atlantic waters were the final, most impassable barrier that her husband had created against any hope of reconciliation.

And finally she had begun to let it go, to accept the inevitability of it all. She began to think of Mary as though lost to death, existing only in memory and in God's embrace. As the months drifted by she thought less and less about her and on occasion felt shame for having neglected her memory. But she had no choice but to live on and hope that her daughter too would survive and find a life of her own, separate from the woman who had brought her into the world and nurtured her with an intense love.

On the last day of October in the year 1875, two years since that terrible night, Annie Boycott received a letter at Lough Mask House. The letter was from Mary.

Dear Mother,

I am certain that you hate me and I understand why you might feel so, though before you throw away these words, please hear me when I say to you that I never intended to hurt you or to bring shame upon you. Nor was this my intention for my father, whom I always treated with respect until our falling out, and whom I always loved, as he did me, I believe.

Whatever you and Father choose to believe, my love for Francis was genuine, as was his for me. It was not some youthful flirtation and not pursued for lustful ends, but came from both our hearts, and it was our belief that because it was pure, it was therefore blessed by God.

After you departed, we were left almost alone in the world. Francis's father and his family were ultimately forced to seek shelter in Westport workhouse. Mr Ruane caught a fever there and died last year. I don't know what became of the others. But worse than that, as Father had rejected me, Mr Ruane rejected Francis, his first-born son, for the opprobrium and ruin he said that Francis had brought on the family. This was terribly hard on Francis as he had loved his father dearly and he never saw him again, and also I think there's a bond between fathers and sons that is seen almost as an eternal link through the generations. Perhaps it would have been better had I been born a boy and none of this would have transpired.

When Francis recovered from the injuries inflicted (I myself bear the constant reminder of a missing front tooth), he found a job as a labourer and I as a cleaning girl. Our intention was to marry and then travel to America in search of a new life.

This next part may be hard for you to bear (I am certain it would kill my father), but last May I converted to Catholicism. I know you may think this is just some foolish act of defiance, but that is not so, for it is a faith I have come to admire deeply, one that allows me find a greater spiritual connection with God than I ever did within the rigidity of my past faith.

We planned to marry in September and to commence our life together as man and wife. Even as I write these words, my heart is filled with lead and I feel tears rush to my eyes, for a terrible tragedy befell us. Francis left early for his labouring work just two months past and when he failed to return at night I became concerned. The following day a group of men went in search of him and found his body at the foot of a sea cliff near Moyteoge Head. No one knows what happened – perhaps he simply went there to stare across the ocean and dream of a better life in America or some silliness, and slipped on the soft earth. You know how dangerous that area is.

Oh Mother, I have been absent from my letter now for the past hour as the tears came freely when I recalled Francis' death, for I loved him so deeply, and in a way that is rarely seen in this world. Our love transcended all boundaries and bore no conditions; it was not an arrangement made for monetary or any other gain, or done because of social acceptance, but was given freely of our hearts, nothing more. I hope you can understand this, but I fear the conventions of society will prevent your ability to grasp it, and by that I mean no insult, merely a sadness that you have never known a love this pure.

My tale does not end there, for an even greater sadness is that Francis went to his grave unaware that come the spring, he would have been a father. My feelings now are terribly confused (perhaps that is why I got the notion in my head to write to you), for I am at once overjoyed at the thought of this new life springing up inside me and equally I am in despair that Francis will never see it except through the eyes of heaven, and also that I am terribly alone, more so than ever before in my life. I hear the women say that being with child plays tricks with a woman's mind and heart and perhaps that explains this pitiless aloneness that I feel, and perhaps the awfulness of it will pass. But I fear not.

Although the people here have been a great comfort to me and, despite their poverty, unfailing in their generosity and with their sympathies, I fear that when it becomes apparent that I am carrying a child, their compassion will wane under the weight of the shame they perceive. This too weighs heavily on my mind, as the road ahead seems so utterly empty of people, with no forks to offer me an alternative route.

Yet I don't write to ask for money or assistance of any kind. I beg only one thing from you, Mother, and it would be sufficient to bear me up as I journey along that long road. It is this. If you could see it in your heart to send me a note telling me you forgive me all the heartbreak I brought upon you, it would be sufficient a thought to carry me through. This is all I ask of you.

I never had the opportunity even to embrace you one last time before we parted and I know that was mostly my doing, but somehow I foolishly believed that it would all work out and we would be reconciled to each other in the end. In that regard you were right and I was naive in the extreme.

I know Father will never forgive me, and to be honest, I can never in my heart bring myself to forgive many of his actions, although I can understand his motivations to some degree. Therefore I do not ask his forgiveness, as it would be a fruitless gesture. But I have never forgotten the tenderness and attention he showered upon me when I was a child and for that he has my love, unrequited though it may be.

Please weigh my words carefully and believe me that everything I did was from the purest of motives, but the rules of this world dictated that that was not sufficient.

Take care of yourself,

Your eternally loving and respectful daughter,

Mary

A smudge stained the edge of the page, the words there faded to a paler blue where a tear had fallen from her daughter's eyes, and in the margin was a small print where Mary had inadvertently pressed her thumb against the fusion of ink and her own solitary teardrop. Annie touched the imprint and felt a tangible connection to her daughter, so long banished from their lives. Her own handkerchief was, by the letter's end, near to sodden.

What was she to do? Had it been her choice alone she would have immediately set out for Achill, galloping the car until the horse dropped dead if need be, not stopping until she found Mary and embraced her, swallowing her whole in her love and forgiveness.

But the choice was not hers to make. In truth, whatever her feelings, there would be no debate on the subject for there existed an autocracy in her home: the rule of Charles Boycott. Yet she resolved to speak to him of the matter in the hope that time had smoothed the jagged spikes of his memory. That evening after dinner, she softened his mood with over-filled glasses of brandy and tentatively broached the subject of their daughter. He sat in grim silence and listened, then turned an icy gaze upon her and pronounced in a voice of chilling calm that he was glad the Irish peasant dog had died, proof of the existence of a just God. He didn't care a whit for 'the harlot's' plight; she had made her choices and she could live with them, and in his vilest pronouncement yet, said that if he ever set eyes on her bastard child he would wring its neck with his own bare hands. And he reminded Annie that he had acted with her complicity on Achill. And then he departed the room and left her alone to wallow in her guilt and her dread of Mary's fate.

It took her a week to summon the courage to write a reply, in which she offered her forgiveness and expressed her own sorrow for what had happened. She told her daughter of her regret that she could not come to visit as this would leave her in an invidious position, almost certainly ending her marriage and leaving her cut off from all means of survival, disgraced in the eyes of the world, and incapable of assisting Mary anyway. She expressed her heartfelt love and signed the letter. As an afterthought she included ten pounds.

An envelope arrived a fortnight later containing a slip of paper with the words: 'Thank you dearly, Mother, love Mary', along with the two five-pound notes. That was the last contact she ever had with her daughter.

On the morning of 28 December of that year, Annie was embroidering a rose pattern into a white kerchief when a sharp knocking on the front door disturbed her. Maggie informed her that an RIC sergeant and constable were outside. The sergeant, a man in late middle age, seemed uncomfortable and hesitant in his greeting. He looked at her feet and asked for Mr Boycott. Annie informed him that her husband had left for Westport and would not return until evening, which discomfited the sergeant even more. At Annie's insistence, he finally delivered his tidings.

Did she have a daughter, Mary, resident of Dooagh on Achill Island?

Yes, she did.

Then it was his sad duty to inform her that her daughter had passed away two nights previously, on St Stephen's Day, 26 December, the cause of her death a medical condition of which he had no knowledge.

Annie had thanked the sergeant graciously, closed the door and fainted. Maggie roused her some minutes later, after which she sobbed at length in the girl's arms. Gathering her wits, she quickly wrote a note to Charles informing him in unadorned, matter-of-fact language that his daughter had died and that she would attend the funeral, never once using Mary's name. She would return as soon as travel arrangements permitted and he could rest assured that she would engage in no discussion on the matter upon her return. A promise she kept.

Then she departed for Achill.

At the funeral a peasant woman, Mrs Margaret Gaughan, expressed her sorrow at Annie's loss and explained that she had been in Mary's presence when she died. Her daughter, Mrs Gaughan explained, had spent Christmas Day in her company, as she resided in a room of her house, and it might be a comfort to her to know that Mary seemed cheerful and bright as they celebrated the day of the Lord's birth. Then during the night she had inexplicably begun to bleed heavily. No doctor could be called in time and Mrs Gaughan had done what she could, but the source of the blood was internal and beyond her skills as the local midwife.

Annie asked her if Mary had said anything in her final hours and Mrs Gaughan told her that she had repeatedly called out for Francis. She could recall no other words of significance. When a doctor did arrive early the following morning, some hours after Mary's final passing, he recorded her cause of her death as menorrhagia, or blood loss due to prolonged menstrual discharge. Mrs Gaughan had placed a hand on Annie's arm and told her in confidence that no other condition was recorded as a factor in Mary's death, in effect that no shame would attach to Mary's memory as a result of her secret, illicit pregnancy. The reality was that the miscarriage of her unborn child had killed her. She thanked Mrs Gaughan, who seemed a kindly woman, and Annie was glad at least that her daughter had died in the company of one such.

It being late December, no flowers could be found to adorn the grave, but the local children had gathered some pretty, coloured leaves and they brightened the dark soil somewhat. To these Annie added her tears and then left for home.

She was given to bouts of melancholy every now and again, when some chance remark, a slant of light or a turn of phrase would stir her memory and for the briefest of moments she would be back in the time when her daughter was a living, breathing, beautiful soul. But she found she could shed no more tears for Mary, as though the well had run dry. She had done as her husband had commanded and never spoken of Mary again, except in her prayers. She kept the letter with its solitary thumbprint secreted in a jewellery box, on occasion taking it out and gently stroking the final evidence of her daughter's existence.

She knew he thought of her too. His bitterness and stubbornness would not permit him to admit to it or ever to display any emotion on the subject, for his only emotion now seemed to be anger. Yet she saw him on occasion staring out at nothing and knew an image of Mary had flitted across his mind. Sometimes, too, he would look at Madeleine when he spied some tiny similarity to his daughter in her face or manner, and his lips would part in silence and he would pretend to cough, then his mask would return. These moments were among the scant few that allowed her to remain at his side all these years. For somewhere inside, she knew, he reproached himself, though his entire being worked in denial of this. She had no idea if there was any force on earth capable of exposing his inner truths.

* * *

It was 1880. Five years had passed since her daughter had shed her earthly frame. Annie rose from the bed after a tortuous night, unable to sleep for the greater part of it. Charles had long since risen and was about the estate already.

She removed her jewellery box from a drawer in her dresser and lifted the top section, revealing the only item of real value in the box. There sat Mary's letter, stained with her daughter's own tears. Many more of Annie's had dried into the parchment over the years. She lifted it and removed a yellowed kerchief that she had been embroidering on the day when the sergeant had come to the door with the terrible news.

She parted the curtains to admit the grey autumn light and sat by the window. They were in the autumn of their own lives, but she feared that a bleak winter lay ahead.

Annie looked at the half-finished embroidery on the kerchief in her lap and regarded the pattern of a rose, its outer petals complete, its red heart absent, eternally awaiting the threads of her industry.

Some roses could survive the cold and wind, enduring the harshest slights of nature, she thought, and still produce a blossom. Others were simply never meant to bloom.

CHAPTER 30

THE IRISH PEOPLE EXCITED – The escort for the Orangemen going to the relief of Mr Boycott will consist of two squadrons of Hussars and one squadron of Dragoons, 150 infantry, with two cannon, and 150 Constabulary. The troops have been strictly ordered on no account to fire on the people unless the people resort to arms, in which case the troops are to act as in actual warfare. Great apprehensions are felt here of the disturbance...numbers of peasantry are en route to Claremorris. Some of them are armed.

–*The New York Times*, 12 November 1880

The Orange Relief Party. London, November 12 – A relief party of fifty Orangemen has arrived at Boycott's farm, near Ballinrobe, from Monaghan today, unmolested. 7000 soldiers and police, with artillery, were sent for yesterday, for the purpose of maintaining order during the present excitement and are now between Ballinrobe and Claremorris.

–*The Brisbane Courier*, Saturday, 13 November 1880

'Bedad, sur, it's the queerest menagerie that ever came into Connaught.'

–Quotation from a London *Times* report, Monday, 15 November 1880

11 November 1880

Owen Joyce walked along Market Street in the company of Fr O'Malley, James Redpath and Joe Gaughan, brushing shoulders with English army privates every few steps. Many of the townsfolk still viewed the arrival of the soldiers as a great imposition and, worse, an insult to their good character. What did the British Government think? That they were all murderers or vandals?

'Did you hear the latest?' Owen asked of the others. 'The loyalists have sent an iron-clad ship bound for Galway and from there, a thousand armed Orange insurgents plan to seize boats and invade from the south up through Lough Corrib.'

Owen had been hearing wild rumours from the moment the army arrived in Ballinrobe, an event which presaged the imminent influx of what the papers were calling 'The Boycott Brigade'. The fifty labourers were due to reach Claremorris that evening. Owen and his friends had made a brief stop in Ballinrobe to assess the situation, after which they intended to continue to Claremorris to witness the much-reported 'invasion' and to try to keep a lid on the situation.

Joe Gaughan laughed. 'Didn't hear that one. There's another: that Gladstone has ordered an invasion of Ireland.'

'And the newsmen were in a right brouhaha earlier with a rumour that Boycott had cut his own throat. Heaven save us, but the rumour mill's more productive than the flourmill,' Fr O'Malley said wearily.

The others couldn't help but laugh.

Owen's laughter was suddenly stolen from his throat as he found himself not two yards from his brother, who had just emerged from the butcher's shop.

'Hello, Owen.'

Fr O'Malley looked anxiously at Owen, unsure how he would react when confronted so abruptly. Owen stood stock-still, fighting the instinct he felt to launch himself at Thomas and beat his face to a pulp. He made no reply.

'Come on, Owen, we've got to get going.' Fr O'Malley took charge of the situation.

'I'm sorry it worked out how it did, Owen, really,' Thomas said.

The priest began to tug at Owen's arm but there was a considerable resistance until he finally allowed himself to be led away.

'I told ye Owen. Didn't I tell ye? Look around ye. Our country is infected with the English,' Thomas called after him.

'Just keep walking, Owen.'

'What's going on, Father?' Joe asked.

'They had a falling out. Leave it, Joe.'

Thomas called out loudly, causing locals, RIC and soldiers to turn their heads. 'Owen!'

Owen looked over his shoulder at his brother, whose expression bore no triumphalism but was fixed with grim seriousness. As Thomas shouted his name the tone rang out with deep familiarity, but Owen could not recall exactly why. They were well on their way to Claremorris before it struck him. Despite the hatred he now felt, he could not deny the fact that Thomas's call had evoked a long-buried memory. His brother's voice had carried the same sense of loss as when he'd cried out his name from the departing ship in Westport harbour thirty years before.

***

One of the four constables guarding Lough Mask Estate's gates recognised Bernard H Becker and ushered him inside, informing him that Mr Boycott had been expecting him. As the journalist emerged off a deeply rutted track through some trees, he was somewhat taken aback at the sight of perhaps one hundred soldiers at work erecting tents and digging latrines. Horses and wagons crisscrossed the grassy field, churning up the damp sod. He recognised Boycott and his wife in the company of two officers. As he tied up the horse, Mrs Boycott strode off towards the house, head down, with a grim expression.

'Captain, officer,' Becker said as he approached the men.

Boycott glanced at him, then turned back to the military men who Becker later learned were Colonel Bedingfield and Captain Tomkinson of the 19th Hussars.

'So this is just an advance squadron, you say, sir?' Boycott asked rather testily.

Colonel Bedingfield swept his arm around in a wide arc. 'Captain Boycott, this is a large area with many potential access points. The labourers will be spread out over a number of fields and to ensure their safety it will prove necessary, I assure you, to bring in at least four hundred more men and establish a permanent encampment.'

Boycott nodded. 'Sir, please ensure your men don't help themselves to my crops.'

The land agent swung away sharply towards Becker, who noticed the two officers exchange a slightly vexed look behind Boycott's back. As he accompanied the agent to the house, he was conscious of the hugely increased numbers of constables and imagined that the thieves and other scoundrels elsewhere in Mayo must be enjoying a rare time of it.

Inside the house, he was immediately aware of a muskiness, as though food had gone off. There was also a tattiness about the place – pictures on the walls awry, ornaments coated in dust, and coats slung over chairs.

'Your piece in the papers certainly did the trick, Becker. Perhaps even overdid the trick.'

Was he being admonished? He was unsure. Boycott's tone was sharp, but he was forming the impression that it was permanently so.

'It was no burden to come to the assistance of a fellow Englishman.'

In the drawing room Becker took a seat without being invited to do so, as he was weary after an uncomfortable night's sleep on the Widow Barry's under-length cot. Boycott stood near to the bureau. Becker thought the man had lost weight in the few weeks since they'd met. His defiant attitude remained, but was it less forthright? The land agent's frame no longer stood quite so stiffly erect, but was bowed a little. His clothes were worn and downright dirty in patches. As he sat there, three constables walked by the window and looked directly into the room. A moment later he heard the crash of a falling pot followed by a blasphemous oath from a female tongue. Boycott didn't even blink at these small events. It was as though they had become normality.

'May I ask, sir, if you are displeased with what has resulted?' Becker asked.

'Well, sir, yes and no. I suppose it was beyond your control how much reaction the article would generate. My original hope was that the Government would simply send me a squadron of troops who might dig my crops and be gone. But now it seems half the army plan to encamp here and a band of men is due to arrive from the north. Truly I have no means of feeding them, except to let them eat my crops, which would seriously impair my profits, defeating the purpose of saving the harvest. Furthermore, we are still virtual prisoners, subject to daily threats from the Land League. Look at these.'

He rummaged in the bureau and as Becker waited, he saw a mouse running the length of the far wall and disappear behind the folds of a curtain.

Boycott handed him a number of notes and Becker flicked through them. There were crude drawings of coffins, hanging men, knives bearing Boycott's name, all with ominous threats like: 'You'll not hear the birds in spring', or another scrawl which read: 'Are you any way comfortable? Don't be uneasy in your mind: we'll take care of you. God save Ireland.'

The same hand had scrawled many of the notes, but one struck him as peculiar:

'An eye for an eye, a life for a life, Boycott – Rory of the Hills.'

'Who's Rory of the Hills?'

Boycott shrugged. 'One of O'Malley's thugs, I imagine.'

Becker found the note curious. While Boycott was clearly hated, as far as the correspondent was aware he'd never killed anyone.

'Sir, how can you be certain that the Land League is behind this and not some fanatic?'

Boycott snapped his frame to attention. 'Of course they are, Becker. And the Government believes the same. Why do you think they've arrested that seditionist Parnell? Why do you think they've sent hundreds of men here? Because of one or two lunatics? Of course not. But by God, I won't be beaten. I'll have my crop in and I'll laugh in their faces. Put that in your next report, sir!'

***

The Orangemen hailed from two counties, Cavan and Monaghan, and joined forces in Mullingar under the command of a Mr Goddard, a Mr Manning (he who had previously gone under the pseudonym 'Combination') and a British army officer, Captain Somerset Maxwell. In the final reckoning, all of the wild rumours had proven to be unfounded and the 'Orange Invasion' numbered precisely fifty-seven. They had, however, each been issued with a revolver, 'only to be used in self-defence'.

They were accompanied on the train to Claremorris by a collection of news correspondents, who reported being subjected to a chorus of booing at every stop. Every town, village and three-house backwater in Ireland was aware of the crisis in Mayo and turned out in numbers along the line to express their support for the Lough Mask tenants. Men waved pitchforks as the train hurtled past, women and children hurled dung against the windows, and banners proclaiming 'The Land League Forever' and 'Boycott All Landlords!' were held aloft.

The proprietor of *The Daily Express* had furnished the labourers with vast quantities of supplies, including hundredweights of oatmeal, ham, cheese, tinned meat and biscuits, not to mention fourteen gallons of whiskey and thirty pounds of tobacco. Unfortunately it had been impossible to procure tents, so the labourers' sleeping arrangements remained uncertain.

At three-thirty the steward on the train announced that they were approaching Claremorris. The labourers gathered their knapsacks, nervous glances flitting about the carriage as the slowing steam engine's hiss was forced to compete with that of the Claremorris residents massing outside the station. These people were denied access by one hundred and fifty men of the 76th Regiment, who stood shoulder to shoulder, with bayonets fixed, in a semicircle around the entrance.

Only members of the press were allowed on to the platform, but Redpath assured the RIC that Owen was his assistant. Fr O'Malley's cloth guaranteed his admittance. More soldiers and constabulary jostled for space on the platform, but the overall operation was still officially a civil one, which explained the presence of Mr McSheehy, the Ballinrobe magistrate.

Among the newsmen present, Owen noticed, was the wealthy owner of *The Connaught Telegraph*, James Daly, who had unashamedly used the columns of his newspaper to support the Land League's aims. After some lengthy discussion with McSheehy, Daly had secured permission, on the basis that no inflammatory language was used, to make a brief address to the arriving labourers, as their own leaders had addressed the Orangemen before they'd departed and therefore a balance must be struck.

The train hissed and hooted to a stop and the stationmaster cried out 'Clarrrrre-morrrisss' in a theatrical fashion. At the final grind of the wheels, a silence and a palpable tension descended over the platform and extended beyond the station to the crowd outside. The soldiers stood sharp, while the constables clamped hands on batons.

The carriage doors were thrown open and a handful of regular passengers alighted, looking about them in some apprehension at the sight of all the weaponry and grim faces. These were hastily directed into the station building. Next came the news correspondents, who quickly took up positions that afforded them a view of the reception.

Then they came, through several doors, blinking at the light, knapsacks slung across their backs. The first thing that struck Owen was how ordinary they looked. One might have plucked them from any farm in Mayo. They wore workingmen's clothing, worn and soiled with earth in places, and their faces had the same weather-beaten texture of those he knew who toiled for long hours in the rain, wind and sun. Their faces were also marked with fear. He had no idea what these men had been told to expect, but he suspected it had been greatly exaggerated. After all his fretting, on seeing them now, a collection of ordinary, ragged working folk, he almost had the urge to laugh.

They were organised into two lines, backs to the train, and Daly was granted his opportunity to address the men (under protest from their leaders Goddard and Manning). He stood facing them, hands on hips, head held high as he looked to his left and right along their lines.

'Men of Cavan and Monaghan. I can see by your faces you are worried. There is no need for this. I assure you that Connaughtmen will not soil their hands with your blood and soon you will return to your homes unharmed. I suspect you have been given a vision of Mayo and the Land League that has put the fear of God into you. But I can assure you that we have nothing but peaceful intent. All we pursue is justice and fairness, as is every man's right, yours and ours alike. And I believe that when you return home, it will be with an altogether different impression of us than when you arrived.'

There was utter silence for a time, the labourers giving each other sideways glances. Owen could sense a degree of bewilderment among them. From their point of view they were in a strange land, the heartland of the enemy, and they had no notion what the days ahead might bring.

One of them turned to Daly. 'What kind of bastard is this Boycott?'

Owen was surprised by the question at first, having assumed their loyalty to Boycott would have been secured. But then he remembered that they probably worked for a landlord themselves and many of them were likely as not to be subject to tough conditions and poor reward.

Daly shook his head. 'He is not worth all the fuss. He is a self-made martyr. The man has run his farm badly for years and when he got himself into a financial corner, he sounded the alarm bells so that ordinary men like yourselves would hand over your hard-earned money to extricate him. Whatever happens, Boycott will leave Ireland a richer man than when he arrived. Keep that in mind as you break your backs in his fields.'

Manning insisted on trying to counter Daly's arguments with a few bellowed statements about 'Land League lies' and 'Fenian usurpers'. In response, cries of: 'Go back to Ulster!' and 'Boycott's puppets!' began to sound from outside the station. Before things got out of hand, the men were marched outside to a cacophony of booing. The ranks of the soldiers braced themselves as the labourers grouped behind them, but the crowd restricted themselves to verbal missiles.

Almost on cue the heavens opened and much grumbling ensued as the cavalcade set off. The people of Claremorris followed to the edge of town but the narrowness of the road prevented them continuing and they returned to the warmth of their homes, leaving the 'Boycott Brigade' to tramp through the rain, mud and descending darkness.

Major Coghill led the cavalcade and behind him rode thirty Hussars, then the mounted constables, also about thirty in number, followed by fifty of their colleagues in carriages. Then came the men of the 76th Regiment on foot, who surrounded the drenched Orangemen to such an extent that the roadside spectators could barely see the tops of their heads above the spiked helmets and raised swords. After these came the ambulance and supply wagons, followed by the mounted Dragoons and then a curious collection of cars, covered carriages, farm carts and lone horses which conveyed the international press corps and various interested locals.

Women emerged from cottages with babes in their arms and stood gawping at the bizarre spectacle; dogs barked and nipped at the horses' hooves; farmers paused in their work and shook their heads in bewilderment; and birds took flight from trees at the sound of hundreds of approaching horses.

Owen sat beside Joe Gaughan on his cart. Redpath and Fr O'Malley were close behind.

'I've never seen such an oddball thing in me whole life,' Joe remarked at the stream of heads bobbing along the road as far as he could see.

Owen nodded reflectively.

Halfway through the twelve-mile journey, the cavalcade experienced its only casualty when Major Coghill's horse suddenly reared up and the officer was thrown with great force against one of Mayo's innumerable stone walls, shattering his fibia in two places. It took twenty minutes to manoeuvre an ambulance wagon through the massed ranks, by which time the unfortunate major had passed out.

It was past ten by the time the weary, sodden workers and soldiers trooped into Ballinrobe barracks. Owen and the others watched the procession snake its way inside for a full ten minutes, until finally the gates were pulled shut.

The priest pulled his coat about him to ward off the chill. He appeared a little disconsolate, standing in the light of the gas lamps, raindrops streaming down his face. 'I bet that blaggard Boycott is rubbing his hands at the thought he's beaten us,' he said.

Owen shrugged. 'I wouldn't say that, Father. In fact, I've been thinking all the way along the road that the government are playing right into our hands.'

Chapter 31

Nearly three weeks of painful excitement had made but slight change in Mr. Boycott's family. His wife and niece live under circumstances which would drive many people mad and the combative land-agent maintains a belligerent attitude, the grey head and slight spare figure bowed, but by no means in submission. On the contrary, never was Mr. Boycott's attitude more defiant... every feature of his extraordinary situation depicted in my first letter on 'Disturbed Ireland' is exaggerated almost to distortion.

–Bernard H Becker, Special Commissioner of *The Daily News*, 14 November 1880

THE LAND AGITATION

...but absurd as it may appear that a little army – horse, foot, and artillery – should be required to secure the safety of a number of labourers digging potatoes for an unpopular gentleman farmer, the affair has a grave aspect, by which the Government cannot fail to be impressed... it is impossible from the nature of the case to apply all over the country the remedy which may be found effective in defeating Captain Boycott's persecutors.

–*The Times* of London, 12 November 1880

12-14 November 1880

'My hope was to force Boycott to submit without violence. It would have been a fine symbol for all of the other oppressed tenants in Ireland,' said Fr O'Malley.

They were gathered at the side of the Ballinrobe to Neale road under a grey morning sky. Síomha and Tadhg stood beside Owen and the priest, and about fifty others loitered about, all keen to witness the labourers' arrival, and their accompanying escort.

Owen turned to the priest. 'We'll still defeat Boycott. He'll still be isolated after the soldiers have left. But can't you see what's happened, Father? This has gone beyond Boycott. The British Government are involved and the entire world is watching what's going on in our little parish. And they've made one huge blunder.'

The priest shook his head. Owen pointed to the approaching cavalcade. Necks craned, and children clambered up trees for a better view of proceedings.

'My thinking must be slow this morning, Owen.'

The enormous procession marched by, mostly watched in silence.

'Look at them, Father,' Owen continued, 'hundreds of soldiers, police, labourers from Ulster, horses, wagons, tons of provisions. The logistics must have been tremendous. How much do you think all of this has cost the English taxpayer?'

A grin touched the corners of Fr O'Malley's lips. 'I've no idea, Owen, but I imagine it's a pretty penny.'

'I'd say thousands of pounds. Perhaps ten thousand. To collect a crop worth five hundred. D'ye think that every time tenants boycott a landlord they're going to spend ten thousand to come to his aid? The British Exchequer would be bankrupt in a year. They've shot themselves in the foot!'

Síomha, who had shared Owen's thinking as they lay in bed the night before, now added her voice. 'This is a show they've decided to put on for the Land League, Father. But they can only afford one show. When it dawns on the world how much they've spent, they'll be a laughing stock. Far from discouraging other tenants to boycott their landlords, this will encourage them.'

The priest was smiling openly now. 'Jesus, Mary and Joseph, but I think you might have a point.'

'And it's too late for them to back out now. No matter what way they play the game, they lose,' Síomha added.

'There's just one thing that could destroy everything,' Owen said now, his tone more muted.

'What's that?'

'If someone were to kill Boycott.'

***

The cavalcade passed through the gates of the estate and the woodland to the field beyond. A halt was called and the correspondents leapt from their cars, Redpath among them, and hurried towards the front of the cortège, keen to record the moment of arrival.

They watched in silence as Boycott approached, Weekes by his side. Behind them, lingering near the house, was Annie Boycott, with her niece and nephew. The land agent carried a double-barrelled shotgun, locked in the firing position, and his companion a Winchester rifle. Redpath considered the display of weapons a means of reinforcing the image of a man under siege by violent insurgents. The fact was that since they'd left the road at Neale, they had not encountered a single other human being.

'Captain Boycott, I presume,' Manning said with great cheer.

'Thank you for coming to my assistance. This is Mr Weekes, my associate.' Boycott's greeting was delivered only to the expedition's leader, and in the most indifferent way imaginable. Introductions complete, he turned on his heel and began to walk back towards the house. The correspondents – from the nationalist press in particular – keenly reported that Boycott had failed to express a solitary word of thanks to the labouring men from Ulster who would rescue him from penury.

***

A trifle disappointed at the lack of drama accompanying the arrival of the expedition – violent drama in particular – most of the correspondents resorted to reporting on the vast encampment that had appeared in the grounds, which included five tents erected especially for the labourers. The nationalist correspondents once again gleefully recorded that the harvesting tools had been left at the barracks, which meant that no work could be accomplished that day.

Redpath strolled across to James Daly, who was laughing openly as about thirty soldiers struggled to keep two distinct factions of labourers apart.

'What's going on?'

'The Cavan and Monaghan men are at each other's throats because they have to share tents. Local rivalry or something. With any luck they'll beat the daylights out of each other.'

Redpath couldn't help but grin. Boycott's great relief expedition might well founder before a single turnip was plucked from the ground. It required the intervention of Colonel Twentyman to negotiate a peace, which involved putting different contingents in separate tents and splitting the workload according to county.

'Hardly an auspicious start to their great war of principle,' Daly said to Redpath as they walked away.

***

'How many?' Annie Boycott asked angrily.

'The officers, six I believe, along with four magistrates and Manning and Goddard.'

'Twelve people? You've invited twelve people to dinner without consulting me? My God, Charles, will you ever learn? I simply cannot take much more of this!'

They sat in fraught silence for a time until finally Annie stood, folded her arms across her chest and glared down at him.

'You'll have to request an army cook to assist the maid. Otherwise you may cancel the dinner.'

He went to reply but she cut him off before he managed a solitary word.

'Don't argue with me, Charles. Just damn well do it!'

She left him with his mouth hanging open. It was the first occasion in their twenty-six years of marriage he'd heard her swear.

He hastened to speak to Colonel Twentyman and within ten minutes a burly Yorkshireman with an indecipherable accent was dispatched to assist the maid. He turned out to be highly efficient at his job and in a few hours had prepared a meal of roast beef, gravy, potatoes and carrots, even supplying a pudding made from bread crusts, apples and eggs for dessert, which everyone, excepting Annie, agreed was splendid. Exhausted, she'd sat in virtual silence throughout. She and Madeleine had spent the previous hours washing the floors, scrubbing plates and cutlery, arranging table settings and then hurrying away to make some effort to improve their appearance.

The men crowded around the table now, sipping brandies, a number of them smoking cigars or cigarettes, and a fog of blue-grey smoke lingered overhead. Annie wasn't used to people smoking and found that it stung her eyes. By nine o'clock she was fit for bed but felt it would be rude to depart as these men had gone to such trouble to come to their aid.

'Eh Boycott, I hate to raise this subject after that wonderful meal, but I think it's better on the table, so to speak.' The speaker was Manning.

'What's that, Manning?' Boycott's apprehension was evident.

'Well, it concerns the labourers' remuneration.'

'Remuneration? You mean you expect me to pay them?'

'Well, naturally. These men were willing to risk their lives to come to your relief and it was assumed you would pay them, just as you would your own workforce.'

An uncomfortable silence mingled with the thickening tobacco fumes. Boycott began to tap the table staccato-fashion with his fingers.

'But I thought they would be paid from the relief fund,' he said at last.

Goddard joined the fray. 'The expedition costs have been enormous, I'm afraid, sir, and only succeeded through the generosity of the *Express* proprietor, Mr Robinson. I'm afraid the fund has reached its limits.'

Boycott slapped the table lightly. 'Sir, it is not that I'm ungrateful but I have been under enormous financial strain these past months. Some of my crop has already rotted in the ground. I mean, for heaven's sake, I didn't ask for fifty-seven men!'

Manning sat bolt upright. 'Well, sir, if you would prefer we shall return to our homes tomorrow!'

Annie squirmed with embarrassment. 'Mr Manning, what Charles meant was that he had only allowed for payment of twenty men. And he's been under enormous strain.'

Fifteen faces turned towards Annie.

Manning relaxed. It would be unseemly to continue the argument with a woman. 'Of course, madam, I'm sure the matter can be resolved to everyone's satisfaction at a later date.'

'Now if you will excuse me, I believe I will retire,' Annie said wearily. 'There's been far too much excitement in one day. Goodnight, gentlemen. Madeleine, would you accompany me?'

The men rose as one as the ladies departed. Once outside, Annie began to cry.

***

Overnight, a torrential rainstorm accompanied by high winds did its best to uproot the encampment's fifty tents. By morning the storm had softened to a light drizzle, a thousand muddy pools now speckling the area that two days previously had been an unblemished meadow. The labourers rose bright and early and were led to their respective fields: Monaghan men to dig mangolds, Cavan men to dig potatoes. At 8 o'clock precisely, the first of Boycott's potatoes saw the light of day. It was the first work done in the potato field in almost two months.

Despite the rain, the Ulstermen put their backs into the digging of the crops with the same vigour that would have marked their own harvesting. Eighty soldiers and constables wandered the perimeter and the labourers found it disconcerting to have men in suits observing them from the gate, scribbling notes or producing sketches for *The London Illustrated News* or *Harper's Weekly*. They knew little of the intricacies of newspaper writing, but they were all in agreement that surely there were more interesting stories in the world than reporting on labourers plucking potatoes from the Mayo mud.

'Have ye nothin' better te be doin'?' one of them finally shouted at the newsmen, Becker among them. After a few mutterings, the correspondents began to shuffle away.

The reality was that they actually had little else to be doing, Becker considered. But with editors baying for fresh news and the Fenians having failed to provide the predicted attacks, the sight of the labourers harvesting Boycott's potatoes was the most exciting event to report. The English public had been fired with the notion of rushing to a fellow Englishman's rescue. Unfortunately for their editors, this relief was being brought not by men unloading bullets at an encroaching bloodthirsty horde, but by the fifty-seven men rather undramatically wielding shovels against the mud.

Becker decided to abandon Boycott temporarily and return to the pursuit of more interesting stories in Galway. He would return to witness any drama that might accompany the conclusion of the expedition, but for now it seemed that the monster he had helped to create was as docile as a lamb and about as newsworthy.

***

Thomas pulled himself to the top of Lough Mask Estate's perimeter wall and listened. But for the pattering of rain on the carpet of autumnal leaves, all was quiet. He could see little through the darkness except for the distant glow of campfires through the trees. The RIC patrol was extremely accommodating in its regularity – having passed five minutes before, it would not return for thirty minutes, which provided ample time. He reached a hand down to Martin McGurk.

'Keep it quiet,' he whispered.

Having dropped down the other side, they remained crouching for a few moments.

'Which way?'

McGurk was nervous. There was a huge difference between writing threatening letters and actually going on a mission that might earn you a bullet. McGurk pointed towards the vague outline of trees.

'The field's just beyond those trees.'

Five minutes later they emerged from the copse and heard the low bleating of sheep. McGurk pulled out his knife.

'Make it quick and quiet.'

'I'd prefer if it was Boycott's throat.'

'Shut up and get on with it,' Thomas snapped.

***

Madeleine Boycott rose from her bed and rubbed her eyes. The clock on her bedroom mantel informed her that it was almost eight-thirty. The light on the curtain suggested a bright Sunday morning had dawned, which pleased her no end, as the weather of recent days had been foul. The presence of soldiers had robbed the woods of their stillness, but as it was Sunday she hoped to find some isolated spot that morning where she could read in peace and pretend briefly that this awful boycotting nightmare didn't exist.

She closed her robe about her and pulled back the curtains with a swish. It took a moment to register what she was looking at, then Madeleine screamed and fainted.

***

'Cut it down, ye fool!' Sergeant Murtagh yelled at the young constable who had been on sentry duty the previous night.

The constable drew his pocketknife and cut the rope, allowing the sheep to come crashing to the ground in a bloody heap. Its throat had been cut and it had then been suspended from an oak tree about twenty yards from the rear of the house. A sign dangled from one of its horns with the name 'Boycott' scrawled in blood.

'Take it to the camp and say ye killed it.'

'*I* killed it?'

'Listen, you idiot, it's bad enough that someone could get this close te the house, but the last thing I need are six hundred men with itchy fuckin' trigger fingers. Say ye were fed up eating tinned beef and ye fancied some mutton stew. Now, keep your mouth shut and get out of my sight while I try and calm Mrs Boycott.'

The sergeant walked to the house and admitted himself. He'd been summoned earlier when Mrs Boycott's niece had seen the animal. By sheer good fortune only the women had witnessed the incident, as Boycott, Weekes and the lad had gone out riding. Despite her distress, Mrs Boycott had the good sense to heed his advice not to inform her husband. He entered the drawing room, which was littered with blankets as it was now doubling as a bedroom. She sat in a corner, red-eyed, twisting her hands in her lap.

'Mrs Boycott. Once more, I want te assure ye this won't happen again. But I must appeal te ye again te keep a lid on this. I've got sixty constables I don't know out there, all twitching at the snap of a twig. I'm afraid this will make things worse. One thing could lead te another and we could end up with a bloody confrontation.'

Her voice trembled as she spoke. 'I can't take much more of this.'

He was surprised at her lack of anger. She almost sounded as if she was asking for a sympathetic ear.

'I understand, Mrs Boycott. How's Miss Boycott?'

'Oh she's had the most awful fright. I gave her some powders and she's sleeping. Why did they do that, Sergeant? What was the point?'

'To provoke, Mrs Boycott. Simply that. Do ye intend te inform your husband?'

Annie gazed through the window. She rarely kept things from him but she knew the sergeant was right. He would explode, demand more police, more soldiers, insist that every tenant be questioned. Their situation would just worsen, if that were possible. She would try to convince Madeleine also of the necessity of sealing her lips.

'No Sergeant. We'll keep a lid on it, as you put it. That's probably for the best.'

'Thank you, ma'am.' He nodded and left.

Annie decided on a course of action. It would require the assistance of Asheton Weekes. She had already made a decision to keep one piece of information from her husband; what matter then if she kept another?

***

It being the Lord's Day, the labourers loitered about the estate, the only diversion being a religious service held for them in the barn, after which a few engaged in foot races against their English protectors. Rumours abounded in the camp that there had been an incursion of some kind during the night and by evening the gossip had evolved into a certainty that a Fenian assault force had travelled from Tipperary and planned to attack as they slept in their tents. Colonel Twentyman believed the reports a fiction, but took the precaution of tripling the sentries, issuing passwords and requesting a further squadron of the 84th Regiment.

At the Sunday mass in Neale, Fr O'Malley again preached calm and non-violence, declaring that he'd heard from Michael Davitt, just returned from a fund-raising trip to America, and that the great man spoke of them in glowing terms. Every newspaper on the east coast of the US now wrote daily of their boycott and as a result, funds had poured into the Land League's coffers. The people could be proud that they had shown the world a way to defeat tyranny without the gun. But it would just take one random act of violence for the entire edifice to collapse.

Outside the church, people gathered as usual to gossip and converse. Fr O'Malley wandered across to Owen and Síomha and pulled a piece of paper from his pocket.

'Look at this.' He unfolded a poster, poorly printed, its message clear nonetheless.

People of Ballinrobe!

Are you prepared to let the English to invade your town?

Will you let armed Orangemen rescue Boycott?

Will you let Gladstone crush you while he
makes the landlords rich?
No! No! No!
Then rise up and take what is rightfully yours by force.
The soil of Mayo will only be yours
when you've darkened it with English blood!
God save Ireland!

'Jesus almighty. Where did you get this?'

'I pulled one from a pillar outside this very church this morning. Joe gave me six more that he'd taken down in Ballinrobe last night. It seems our Fenian friends are becoming more active.'

'Thomas,' Síomha said bleakly.

'Perhaps. But he and his band surely must know the people of Ballinrobe would be slaughtered if they attacked the British Army? I don't understand their thinking.'

Owen took the poster and stared at it reflectively.

'I do,' he said without lifting his gaze.

'What is it, Owen?' Síomha asked.

He looked at her and then the priest. 'Maybe that's what they want. A slaughter. A blood sacrifice. Everyone in Ireland would be outraged. And in America. The people here would be the martyrs. Ballinrobe, Neale, Lough Mask, they'd become a rallying cry to all of Ireland to mass rebellion. Parnell and Davitt and the League would be swept aside in the stampede for revenge. When you think about it, it makes perfect sense.'

'Perfect madness, more like,' Síomha said.

'My God. What sort of depraved minds could conceive such a scheme?'

'I can think of one, Father.'

They drove home across the gently rolling countryside washed by milky winter sunshine, Niamh squashed between them, both reflecting on the terrible vistas of Owen's speculation. Friendly nods in the direction of a passing patrol of mounted constables were greeted with cold stares. Everyone was a suspect, it seemed.

'There's that English man from the big house.' Niamh's voice roused them from their thoughts and they followed her pointing finger towards the gate of their farmyard.

Startled, Owen looked at Síomha. 'What the hell does he want?'

***

'Mr Joyce. Mrs Joyce,' Asheton Weekes said, removing his riding cap.

'What do you want?'

His tone was sharp, deliberately unwelcoming. He had no personal animosity for the man, but also knew that Weekes was unshakably loyal to Boycott.

'May I have a word with you?'

The horse unhitched and Niamh sent to play, they invited him inside.

'I'm sure you're used to grander surroundings, Mr Weekes,' Síomha said as they sat around the table, somewhat discomfited at the poverty of their home in Weekes's presence.

'I'd offer you a drink, but that would be breaking the boycott.' Owen smiled at him without warmth.

Weekes coughed. 'If I may explain. First of all, Captain Boycott is unaware I'm here. My presence is at the behest of Mrs Boycott.'

Owen raised his eyebrows. He could recall thinking that Annie Boycott was the one bedrock of sense in their household.

'Mrs Boycott is grateful for your having assisted her nephew and is aware that you are directly involved in…this situation. I must confess I was reluctant to agree to her request. It feels like...like a betrayal. But considering what is at stake...'

'What does she want?' Síomha asked.

'To know if we might open a dialogue with a view to ending this unpleasantness. Were you to agree to such, she would be willing to broach the subject with her husband. And I assure you, sir, such a gesture displays a great deal of courage on her part, as the Captain is a…a man of fiery temperament.'

'We know,' Owen said flatly.

'Frankly, Mrs Boycott has no wish to leave here. Until recently she was most happy here and enjoyed good relations with the locals.'

'We've no issue with Mrs Boycott – or yourself, for that matter. But we've never had any relationship with Captain Boycott, at least nothing better than that of a dog to its master.'

'It will not serve our purposes to trade insults. The issue at stake is rent. If Mrs Boycott could convince her husband to agree to a compromise on the abatement – say fifteen percent – and also to allow rights of way, the gathering of wood and so on and so forth, would you be willing to call off your action?'

Owen and Síomha looked at each other. They were both old enough to realise that compromise was usually the path to progress, yet they knew immediately they shared the same unspoken view.

Owen met Weekes's eye. 'The answer is no.'

He emitted a ponderous sigh. 'May I ask why? And should you not take the proposal to your companions before you decide?'

'They'll say the same thing.'

'How can you be so certain, sir?'

'Had Boycott offered this originally, we probably would have accepted it. But it's too late now. This has become bigger than any of us. All of Ireland, in fact half the world, is watching to see if a bunch of peasants in a small village can take on the most powerful empire on earth. This is no longer about the rent, Weekes. Or about me or Boycott. It's about justice. Because if the boycott succeeds here it can succeed in all the other farms in Mayo and Galway and Cork. Everywhere. In fact it'll be an inspiration to downtrodden people the world over.'

'You're losing control of your imagination, sir.'

'You think so? We'll know soon enough.'

'Please listen to me, I understand your grievances, I know its diffic–'

'But that's the problem, you don't understand anything.'

'Mr Joyce, I've lived here for many year–'

'Do you know why I'm certain that the others won't agree to your offer? Because most of them lived through the famine. That's what you and your countrymen don't understand. Back then we were almost wiped out. I lost my entire family. So did the others. It's not something you forget. *Ever.* Back then the landlords forced us on to the most barren scraps of land so they could still exploit us for rent and use the best land to grow crops for profit. When the blight came our food supply was wiped out. And when we couldn't pay our rent the landlords evicted us so that they could graze sheep on the land we'd tilled.'

Weekes coughed with discomfort. 'Sir, I've heard of that tragic time. But the variety of crops now means the danger of famine is greatly reduced.'

'For us maybe, but there are thousands of others on poorer land than this all over Ireland. What about them?' It was Síomha who posed the question.

'Ever watched a man starve to death, Weekes?'

He didn't reply.

Owen continued: 'Famine aside, eviction is almost as bad. How are a man and his family to survive by the side of the road? In the middle of winter?

That's what Boycott is threatening. And that's why his kind must be defeated. The landlords' power must be broken. What happened thirty years ago must never be allowed to happen again. You say the chances of famine are greatly reduced? If only a tenth of the numbers were to die, that would be more than a hundred thousand. So you see, Weekes, the stakes are much higher than you've imagined. Tell Mrs Boycott thank you, but it's too late.'

Owen rose sharply to indicate the conversation was at an end. Weekes was taken aback at the abruptness. He looked up at Owen for a moment, then rose wearily. He shook his head and turned away.

'Weekes,' Owen said to his back.

He turned around and saw with surprise Owen's extended hand.

'I don't suppose we'll ever meet again. I wish you good luck.'

There was a brief hesitation before Weekes took Owen's hand. Then he turned and left, the sound of the horse's hooves fading to nothing as he returned to tell Annie Boycott that her life in Ireland was all but ended.

CHAPTER 32

THE LAND AGITATION – BALLINROBE

Captain Boycott has received a threatening letter signed 'Rory of the Hills', threatening him with the fate of Lord Leitrim [who was shot], and calling him 'a —— robber'. It was illustrated with a coffin, a gallows, a representation of a man being stabbed with stakes and a death's head and cross-bones. Fr O'Malley, PP, of Neale, addressed the people today. He asked them to take no notice of the Orangemen and to show no sign of either favour or disfavour while they remained in Mayo. He says that the Orangemen have met with no molestation. But nobody who heard the savage hoots which greeted the arrival of the expedition can doubt that, but for the military, molestation would have been a mild term for the treatment they might have received.

–*The Times*, 15 November 1880

The Press Association Correspondent telegraphs that there is much dissatisfaction felt by the Ulstermen who volunteered to reap Captain Boycott's crops. It is complained that they received no welcome from the captain.

–*The Nation*, 20 November 1880

15-16 November 1880

Bull Walsh farmed eighty acres of land in a valley twelve miles to the west of Clonbur, in County Galway. His cottage lay on the slopes between Ben Beg and Bunnacuneen Mountain, and the nearest road was three miles from his door. The land was virtually worthless, so rocky and inaccessible on the steep mountain slopes that nothing edible would grow there, and most of his income came from sheep farming. The property was owned by a Lord Carruthers of Cornwall, though to Walsh's knowledge His Lordship had never set foot in Ireland, the annual rent of just twelve pounds being collected every March by an Irish land agent by the name of Thaddeus Kinsella, who, in Walsh's view, would sell his own mother for a shilling. Walsh was required to journey to the coastal town of Leenaun once a year, where Kinsella would receive his payment in the company of two bodyguards, as Bull Walsh's sobriquet was well earned, his bulk and near-permanent glower presenting a frightening appearance to even the bravest.

Beyond that, and by necessity to purchase supplies, he rarely ventured out of his valley. Since his youth he had grown used to his own company and would only tolerate visitors on rare occasions.

But Bull Walsh also left his isolated valley occasionally to kill people. The last of his victims had been four months ago, when he had stabbed a process-server seven times in the back as he returned from issuing an eviction notice. Before that he had been responsible for the murder of Thaddeus Kinsella's predecessor, whom he had shot in the head from close range. Despite his verbal reserve and generally uncouth appearance, Walsh possessed a deceptive level of intelligence, but the trauma of the famine years had robbed him of any wish to exploit it beyond his meticulous planning when an assassination was ordered. This, combined with the fact that he lived in the middle of nowhere, had ensured that not once had he been connected with a killing, and to his knowledge the constabulary weren't even aware of his existence.

Currently he was host to two fellow freedom fighters. As his guests were engaged in the same war as him, he could just about tolerate their intermittent presence, especially now that they had ceased their attempts to converse with him – and he *had* offered his cottage as a 'safe house', after all.

Doherty, the most senior, he disliked, but couldn't quite nail the reason.

Perhaps it was the way he ordered him to do this, get that, have this ready, and such. He had no objection to following orders such as: 'Kill land agent, Saturday, Leenaun,' the rest being left to him. But Doherty's continual commands to do petty things irked him greatly.

Thomas Joyce he liked, on the other hand, not an emotion he would ever openly express, but there it was nonetheless. Again, he wasn't sure precisely why. Perhaps he saw something of himself in Joyce, who was scarred on the outside and, he was certain, the inside as well. They also shared the skills of horsemanship and marksmanship, Joyce being particularly accurate with a rifle, which he had demonstrated by shooting a falcon from the sky. Despite the limitations in Walsh's knowledge of people, his basic human instincts also informed him that Joyce secretly hankered for a life less troubled.

'What time is he coming?' Thomas asked.

'The message said "after dark", which could be anything from six o'clock to eight the next morning.'

'Fuckin' great.'

Bull Walsh said nothing. He sat there peeling potatoes and throwing the damp peels on to the turf fire. He liked the way they hissed at first as though struggling against the flames, then eventually dried and supplemented the body of the fire. He looked at the other two, who both appeared unusually nervous. He himself was looking forward to the arrival of the commandant, who was his normal contact. The man operated out of Galway city, a long way away, so his trips to the wilderness were infrequent.

Their heads turned at the sound of a horse approaching at just above walking pace. Doherty lifted his gun and peered through a gap in the sacking that passed for a curtain.

'It's all right. It's him.'

'What's his name?' Thomas asked.

'Commandant,' Doherty said. 'The less you know, the better.'

The horse came to a halt and after a few moments there were three knocks, a pause and then a further three. Doherty admitted the man into the dim light from the fire and the solitary candle. Thomas hadn't been sure what to expect, but the character that crossed the threshold had enjoyed no remote place in his imagination. He looked more like an office clerk than a Fenian commander, wearing a dark grey greatcoat over a tweed jacket, a shirt and bow tie, his age about forty, though he was prematurely bald. He had narrow eyes and a pointed nose, which supported wire spectacles. He spoke with a Cork accent.

'Christ, Bull, I know ye like keeping te yourself, boy, but every time I come up here I nearly break me fuckin' neck.'

Doherty and Walsh had snapped to attention and saluted in military fashion. After a moment's hesitation, Thomas did the same.

'Commandant,' Walsh said simply.

'At ease. Have ye anythin' te drink?'

The men relaxed and Walsh produced a bottle of homemade spirits. Bull Walsh possessed no table or proper chairs, so they sat on two rickety old stools and a wooden crate, with Thomas resting his backside against the windowsill.

'You must be Joyce. I hear good things about ye.'

Thomas nodded faintly.

The man sipped his drink. 'Right. Te business. Ye've been busy in Ballinrobe and thereabouts, I believe.'

'Yes, sir, as ordered we've been keeping the pot simmering,' Doherty said and produced one of the posters he'd pinned up all over Ballinrobe, urging the people to rebel.

The commandant nodded. 'What else?'

'We've been generally stirring things up, killing Boycott's animals, breaking fences, although that sort of thing's dangerous now with all the security. We've been sending the usual threats, digging fake graves, and so on. The man McGurk that I told ye about, he's been sending Boycott letters calling himself 'Rory of the Hills'. Some of them have been reported in the papers.'

'And we stirred up a near-riot when Boycott was in court. The bastard was almost lynched,' Thomas added.

'Lucky for you he wasn't.'

The others exchanged looks of puzzlement. The commandant rose and began to pace the room with his head bowed and then turned back to them.

'Your orders now are to back off.'

Doherty stood up, his surprise evident. 'Commandant, we assumed ye were coming te order us te finish the job.'

The man raised his eyebrows, pursed his lips, and replied in an offhand manner. 'What you think is of no consequence. This comes from the top. Now, we can't be certain that Irish blood spilled in Ballinrobe would be enough te provoke a nationwide rebellion. Even if we provoked a battle, the army might only kill a handful. They've being showing restraint so far. Under orders from Gladstone. We need something bigger te rouse the whole nation.'

'Bigger?'

'We need coercion. The hotheads in Westminster have been demanding extreme coercive measures already. That means raids, arrests, beatings, intimidation. Perfect recruitment incentives. The people will be queuing te join up. And the money will roll in from America. We could mount a full-scale uprising within six months.'

'But how–' Doherty began.

'We leave this boycott to play out. Whatever happens, we can't lose.'

'I don't understand,' Thomas said.

'As you know, Davitt and Parnell have persuaded the IRB and Clan na Gael to work alongside parliamentarians, their New Departure shit. Those who oppose this, namely us, have only a fraction of their numbers and we can't win a war on our own. It's been decided the priority is te get men like Devoy, the other so-called moderates in the IRB and, most importantly, the people back on our side. If the boycott fails then the New Departure will fail. The IRB – and the people – will see armed insurrection as the only way.'

'And if Boycott is defeated? You'll never get the masses to abandon peaceful resistance then,' Thomas observed.

The clerk-like commander walked over to Thomas, removed his spectacles and began to clean them with a handkerchief.

'Boycott's now a household name in England. Their fuckin' hero. Even if he's defeated, if he was te die there'd be so much outrage that the British Government would have no choice but te introduce coercion. And you, my friend, your job will be te make sure that's precisely what happens.'

***

Four shots rang out in quick succession.

The horde of news correspondents, who were scattered about the encampment, spun as one on their heels towards the sound of gunfire. More shots ensued, followed by upraised voices as the newsmen converged upon the source of the shooting by the lough's shoreline. As they emerged through the trees, their expressions changed in a blink from a mixture of fear and excitement to outright gloom, as they realised that the salvo came from a group of bored soldiers competing to hit bottles in the water under the supervision of their officers.

The general air of frustration among the correspondents at the lack of incident immediately resumed. No attacks had occurred, no bombs exploded, no one brutally murdered, not even a fence vandalised. As a result, newspapers from Chicago to Sydney reported the fascinating news of the quantity of mangolds harvested by the men from Monaghan and the pyramid of potatoes built by the industry of the Cavan men. The disappearance of several of Boycott's sheep and the ensuing aroma of mutton stew was reported widely. As was his subsequent anger. When the soldiers and labourers requested some of Boycott's potatoes to add to their cooking pots, he duly charged them nine pence a stone. But the great enterprise was proceeding nonetheless, and it was hoped that the harvest would be completed within a week.

The only battles fought were those for the use of Ballinrobe's solitary telegraph line and with the elements, for it had turned bitterly cold again and ice had formed around the shores of Lough Mask. The encampment was one giant quagmire of half-frozen mud, yet the Ulster labourers never ceased their endeavours despite the hardness of the earth.

On a visit to the camp, Redpath learned that the army officers too were beginning to feel that their skills, finely honed on the battlefields of Afghanistan and the plains of Africa, were not being put to any substantial use. One of them privately acknowledged to the American that there was little honour in trying to suppress passive resistance by means of overwhelming military force.

On Monday evening Fr O'Malley was cheered greatly by news that the labourers and tenants on Boycott's Kildarra Estate had voluntarily joined the boycott. The tenants were demanding a twenty-five percent rent abatement and the labourers had simply walked off his land in unison, 'forgetting' to close the gates to his fields as they departed.

Boycott was granted an escort of Hussars to accompany him to Kildarra to round up his cattle herd, which were wandering the roads in the area. The following day, the sight of Boycott and twenty-five Hussars in their dark blue tunics with tall busby headdresses, galloping about the muddy boreens in pursuit of twenty cattle, was the cause of much mirth among the locals, as the soldiers were not skilled in cattle herding and much blundering about ensued, with two Hussars ending up in the mud.

When he had finally secured the cattle in a field and returned to Lough Mask, Boycott decided he'd had enough for the day, although it was only four o'clock. He considered asking Weekes to join him for a drink to debate their prospects, but upon further consideration he decided it might not be a good idea as the man had been decidedly reserved these past days, even appearing to avoid his company. Besides, he had enough on his mind.

He was unaware as he entered his home that he was about to have a great deal more.

CHAPTER 33

Our correspondent also reports that Mrs Boycott is suffering from an unspecified illness, likely brought upon her by as a result of the pressures of the past two months, and has been confined to her room for several days.

–*The Nation*, 20 November 1880

North Mayo Death Records

First Name: Mary

Surname: Boycott

Religion: Roman Catholic

Date of Death: 26 December 1875

Cause of Death: Menorrhagia (uncertified as no medical attendant at time of death)

Address: Dooagh

District: Achill District

Region: North Mayo

Age: 19

Status: Spinster

Occupation: Farmer's Daughter

Informant Name: Margaret Gaughan

Informant Address: Dooagh

17 November 1800

Annie Boycott lay on the bed, eyes closed tightly against the world. She could tell it was still light outside as a pinkish glow filtered through the membranes of her eyelids and she could hear the noise of industry beyond the walls. Was there any way she could banish the constant reminders that her life had once again been left in tatters? But this time her hands were unsoiled. This time the doing was all her husband's.

Five years ago she had seen her only daughter buried, leaving a hollow inside her that could never be filled. But she had survived the grief and guilt and come to accept a virtually loveless marriage, and despite it all found a place on the shores of Lough Mask where she had known some happiness. And once again her life was being demolished, trampled under the feet of a thousand British Army boots.

Annie opened her eyes, raised her arm and looked again at her daughter's letter, and the faded ink of Mary's heartfelt plea for forgiveness. In reality Annie knew that she had been asking for not just forgiveness, but rescue, and her mother had failed her. She recalled replying to Mary, telling her that circumstances prevented her from visiting. What a pitiful joke! 'Circumstances' was a synonym for Charles Boycott. She had been a coward, afraid of what he might do should she go. She had been afraid of the scandal of divorce, of being left with no means of support, no home, no life. And yet she should have gone. If she truly loved her daughter she should have taken her courage in her hands and gone, no matter what the consequences. The inward shame she felt now was so much greater than she would have had to bear had she allowed her conscience, rather than her husband, to dictate her course. And then, at his behest, to agree never to speak of Mary again. She prayed often that Mary, in whatever wisdom her heavenly host might bestow upon her, would allow her to see beyond her mother's denial of her existence, to see it for what it was – a means of survival. For the constraints upon wives were such that they could only march in one direction and that was by their husband's side.

Thank God for the presence of Madeleine and William, whose companionship had brought her a measure of happiness. As too had her life in Mayo. For she had no quarrel with the people here; indeed, she enjoyed their warmth and honesty and good spirits. She loved to chat with the women of Ballinrobe or Neale, who, while treating her with deference, responded openly to her almost as though she were one of their own. The innate disdain for formality was a distinctly Irish characteristic that she adored and Charles detested.

But now all of that was at an end. Two months of isolation had driven her near to madness. Her relationship with Madeleine and William had been skewed into some awkward thing by the unnatural circumstances. Her home had been turned into a barracks and the estate a giant army camp and latrine. She was trapped within the walls for fear of molestation, and butchered animals were left hanging outside their windows. And, worst of all, she could see no end to it. Especially now that her offer of an olive branch had been rejected. It had been a vain hope anyway.

At the outset she had made the instinctive decision to stand by him. It was a natural thing to do, to defend one's way of life and to demonstrate wifely loyalty despite her misgivings about the righteousness of his position. But now it wasn't just their home they were defending. They had to bear the burden of defending all of Ireland's landed gentry. They had become a symbol of resistance, or of tyranny, depending on one's viewpoint. Her husband's name had become synonymous with ostracism and was uttered in the streets of London and New York. The world was watching their every move, as though a giant eye hovered in the skies above their home.

There was great irony in the fact that her self-confinement these past days had been reported widely in the press and yet Charles had barely noticed. Since Asheton returned from Joyce's cottage on Sunday, all her hope had vanished for a future here in Ireland. Once again she must uproot herself and start a new life elsewhere, most likely in England. Yet her husband still stubbornly refused to accept this and clung to his delusional intention to defeat the Land League. He had already lost. He just couldn't see it.

Somehow, she had to make him see, because now they must begin to look to the future. She had to convince him to take the steps to ensure that they would have a decent home and a decent life elsewhere, where they could live out their declining years in peace. Otherwise she would wither away and die.

But what force did she possess to breach the walls of the prison her husband had built about them? His stubbornness and temper were the stuff of Irish legend. How could she possibly overcome it now after all these years of virtual submission?

She held the only possible means of doing so in her hand. Mary's letter. The risk she was taking was incalculable considering his threats should she ever mention their daughter's name again. But she would not deny Mary's memory a moment longer. She would do now what she had failed to do when Mary had reached out her hand for help and Annie had chosen to ignore it. She softly brushed her lips against her daughter's thumbprint in the letter's margin. She would stand up to him, come what may.

***

He rapped on the door and heard the faintest of whispers from within, then entered, promptly glancing at the drawn curtains and then at his wife, lying fully dressed on the bed, the back of her hand resting across her eyes.

'Why on earth are you lying here at this hour? Are you ill?'

Without asking, he drew the curtains sharply.

'Close the curtains, Charles,' she said with a sigh.

'But why ar–?'

'Just close them, for heaven's sake!' she snapped, and he complied. She lifted her head and looked at him. The strain was evident on her husband too. His beard was wild and untrimmed and there were bags under his eyes. His clothes hung loosely against his frame.

'How long have you been here, Annie?' he inquired, his tone softer.

'All day. And for most of the past week. Haven't you noticed my absence?'

'Well, I did, of course,' he stammered, 'but with all the goings-on I never realised you had become so…so…what precisely is the matter? Have you summoned the doctor?'

'A doctor can't help me. You're the only person in the world who can help.' Annie sat up now, swung her legs over the edge of the bed and regarded him carefully, just a couple of yards between them.

'What in heaven's name do you mean?' he asked, drawing back his head defensively.

'Charles. I can't bear what has happened to our lives. Being shunned, the filth, all the strangers, day and night, the English army camped on our lawn, the latrines, the stench, the–'

He interrupted her sharply. 'I've told you, in one more week they'll be gone and we'll have the harvest.'

'But what else shall we have, Charles? Our lives here are over and you have to begin planning for a new life somewhere else.'

'I'll do nothing of the sort! You're working your mind into a dither, my dear. This will all settle down soon, mark my words.'

Annie laughed aloud at his ability to see a cat and insist it was a dog, a necessary tool for the pigheaded and blindly pertinacious.

'Don't you understand, this will never settle down? Never. How have you lived in this country for decades and failed to understand a single thing about these people?'

'These people? The Irish are noth–'

Suddenly she yelled at him. 'Don't start your nonsense about layabouts and liars and that tomfoolery. It wasn't true the day I met you and it's still not true. It simply suited your narrow view of the world to believe it so! And frankly, Charles, hearing it for the thousandth time is boring beyond endurance!'

He slammed the tip of his cane against the floor. 'What's got into you? Why are you behaving like this?'

'Why? Are you insane? Our lives here are over! You've lost, Charles. Do you think the British Cabinet is going to send the army back every time you try to evict someone?' She was standing by the bed now, yelling, fists clenched by her sides. 'Do you honestly think we'll ever be able to go to Ballinrobe to attend church? Or to buy a dress? Or sell a cow? You have a harvest, to be sure, a harvest of bitterness and hate that you've been nurturing for years and all you've done is give it one final spurt of growth!'

'You know nothing about the matter! You're speaking from a woman's ignorance of such things. I've lost, have I? Not while I've air in my lungs!'

'And how long will that be? And how long before William or Madeleine or your wife takes a Fenian bullet meant for you? Or Asheton? And speaking from a woman's ignorance, I happen to understand a great deal more than you ever will. In fact, it was precisely because of that I made Asheton speak to Owen Joyce about the possibility of some kind of compromise.'

There was an abrupt silence as her words settled, drifting down upon him like a winter mist, slowly darkening his features.

'You *what*?'

She sat on the bed for support. 'I asked Asheton – no, I insisted he speak to Owen Joyce about settling this thing.'

'How dare you! How dare Weekes! I'll kill him, I swear it!'

'Don't blame Asheton! It was all my doing. I wanted to stop this before it went too far! The landlords and the British Army on one side, the Land League and terrorists on the other, and us squashed in the middle. It has to stop!'

He emitted a primordial roar and swung his cane wildly, shattering a large vase on her dressing table and sending a wave of fractured porcelain and water exploding across the floor. Annie instinctively covered her face with her forearms.

'You've betrayed me! You've betrayed your country! So has that scoundrel Weekes. I never thought I'd– And tell me, my dear Annie, what did your Fenian comrade say to your request?' His voice was mocking now and he inclined his head, stepping towards her.

Annie saw him approach and, chilled to the bone, she vacillated, wondering if she had gone too far. Then she recalled her earlier thoughts and how she had failed Mary, and from within that memory she found renewed courage to see this though to the end, whatever that might be.

She raised her head to look directly at him with defiant eyes. 'Joyce said they would have negotiated but that it had become too big now. And he's right. This has gone beyond you or me or them. And we have to make sure we have a life at the end of it all.'

'You stupid, stupid woman,' he hissed venomously and suddenly grasped the bun of hair at the top of her head. 'You think I'm going to run from a dog like Joyce, or the priest, or Parnell? You think I'll be beaten by a bunch of illiterate Irish peasants?'

The pain wasn't excessive, but he forced her head back so that her eyes were fixed on the canopy above their four-poster bed. She gritted her teeth as she replied with as much calm as she could muster: 'This is nothing to do with the Land League or the peasants. All of this, everything you've done these last months, everything you've brought upon us is about revenge. Don't spit your lies in my face about your lofty ideals because this has all been about taking vengeance on the Irish for stealing your daughter away from you!'

He released her abruptly and took a step back. 'What did you say?'

'I said this is all about revenge for Mary.'

'I told you never to speak that name again!' he screamed, then slapped her across the face, a fierce, malevolent blow that snapped her head back and threw her against the mattress. Annie fought to stay in her senses, forcing herself up and facing him again.

'Mary! Mary! Mary! Mar–' The screams of her daughter's name were violently interrupted by another blow, and this time she saw stars, tears involuntarily springing to her eyes, yet she swore she would not yield to them. She somehow managed to muster her strength and snarled through gritted teeth. 'MARY! MARY! MARY!'

Boycott threw his cane aside and leapt upon her with clawed hands, reaching for her throat. 'I'll kill you! I'll kill you!'

With her last breath before he squeezed her windpipe, Annie gasped into his face. 'Like you killed your daughter?'

He clasped his hands around her throat, but his grip loosened almost as quickly as it had closed and slowly he pulled away and staggered back, staring at his outstretched hands as if they had been afflicted with leprosy.

'What am I doing? What am I doing? God forgive me...'

Annie massaged her throat as she rose to sit again, needing her free arm to support her against the mattress.

'You couldn't bear that she would leave you for an Irish Catholic peasant and neither could I, may God forgive *me.* And she loved that boy more deeply than anything on this earth. That was what stuck in your craw. You'd been raised to despise Catholics and you viewed the Irish as illiterate good-for-nothings, but that was precisely what your daughter – our daughter, Mary – chose over you.'

He was breathing hard, his back against the window, his hands seeking the support of the sill through the curtains.

Annie pressed ahead; she knew it must all be faced now or it would forever haunt whatever was left of their life. 'We left her there with nothing but your hatred. And then when we heard she was pregnant and alone, you abandoned her for the final time and I was too weak to stand up to you and help her. But I was a coward, afraid of what I'd lose, afraid for my safety, if truth be told. My God, if only I'd known that there were much greater things to be feared in this world, like the inability to live with oneself. When she died, Charles, I felt as though I myself might just as well have plunged a knife into her heart. What kind of mother refuses the hand of her child when the child is clinging to life?'

He stood, but with his shoulders slumped, gazing absently across the room at some unearthly place. When he spoke, his voice was weak, mumbling.

'My behaviour towards you was inexcusable, not that of a gentleman. I beg your forgiveness.'

'What? My forgiveness? Haven't you heard anything I've said about the way we abandoned our daughter?'

'A man should never strike a woman as I did. I am ashamed.'

'I don't care that you struck me! Do you hear? It's a small penance for the way I treated Mary. But what about striking *her*? Do you feel shame about that? Or are you going to continue to boycott her memory?'

He looked at her now, but his rage had been exhausted and his expression was that of a man confronted by vistas previously denied.

'What did you say?'

She smiled mirthlessly. 'That's what they're calling it, is it not? All of this? They've turned your name into a word that means to shun someone. And that's precisely what you've been doing to your daughter all of these years, to her memory, her name even. You've boycotted them and forced me to do the same.'

He turned his back on her and walked to the dressing table where he idly began to pick at the shattered fragments of the vase.

'I didn't want her to die,' he said in a voice barely audible.

'But you did nothing to prevent it.'

'There was nothing I could do. I wasn't even aware she was ill.'

'No, but you knew she was alone and with child, and desperate. Even if God had determined to take her and returning her to health was beyond our powers, we could have been there in her last days, a comfort to her. We could have told her we loved her. And you did love her, didn't you, Charles?'

He didn't reply for some time, merely continued to gather some minute fragments of porcelain into a pile on the top of the dresser.

'I never revealed it to you,' he said finally, 'but I was...my heart was broken when she died.'

'You mean when *Mary* died. Say her name, Charles.'

'When Mary died.'

'No, Charles, but then you don't reveal anything to me, do you? Except your rage. Despite all that happened, despite you beating her and shunning her and the cruel way you evicted that boy's innocent parents in revenge, despite all of that, she still loved you.'

Annie fished the letter from her pocket. She stretched her arm out towards him now, the folded sheets between her fingers.

'Here, Charles, don't take my word for it. Take Mary's.'

He looked around and for a moment appeared confused. He took the letter and sat on the end of the bed, his back to his wife, and began to read.

Annie rose and lit an oil lamp as the sun had almost set and gloom had stolen upon the space without their noticing. As he read the letter in silence, Annie gathered the shards of porcelain from the floor and laid a sheet on the wood to soak up the water.

Presently she heard a sound behind her as she knelt mopping the last of the dampness. It was a sob, brief and stifled, but within that tiny sound she heard an expression of his grief, of the terrible pain of human loss. It was gone in an instant and she would never hear another, but Charles being the man he was, she knew that that miniscule expression of true emotion was a monumental leap.

She hunkered on the floor, the sheet gathered upon her lap, her back to him, waiting for him to speak. She heard the sound of paper being folded and a further silence ensued, not even their breathing audible.

'I've left the letter there on the bed, Annie. You should keep it, Mary sent it to you,' he said at last, his voice surprisingly even.

She didn't reply. She wasn't sure what more there was to be said.

'I'll not give in to them, the Land League and the others. I'll show them that they can take away my home and my livelihood, but they'll never break my spirit.'

Annie's heart sank at these words, although they were calmly spoken and lacked his usual venom. She stood erect and listened.

'I'll continue to be as forthright in my comments. But tomorrow…' He rose and walked to the door where he stood with his back to her. He heaved a sigh before he continued. 'But tomorrow, we'll leave for Dublin for a few days and while there I'll make enquiries about the possibility of a position in England. The break from this place will do you good anyhow. I will also make public our intention to leave with the expeditionary force for an extended holiday, although I intend to leave open the possibility of returning. At least in that way it will be a statement that I have not been vanquished.'

He opened the door, closed it softly behind him and she heard his footsteps recede.

Annie closed her eyes and arched her neck so that her face looked towards the unseen heavens. Then she smiled and whispered a single word.

'*Mary.*'

CHAPTER 34

Ballinrobe – Captain Boycott has expressed his intention of taking a holiday with Mrs Boycott after his crops have been reaped; but, having a lease of 31 years, he has at present no intention of throwing up his farm.

–*The Times*, 18 November 1880

Eene zonderlinge geschiedenis doet sedert eene week een eigenaardig licht op Iersche toestanden vallen. Een rentmeester van lord Erne, Kapitein Boycott, die zelf ook eene hoeve bebouwt, heeft zich vergrepen tegen de wetten der Land League door namens zijn principaal aan een pachter de huur op te zeggen en door een gerechtsdienaar tegen de woede der menigte eene schuilplaats te verzekeren.

–*Zierikzeesche Nieuwsbode*, Holland, 17 November 1880

CAPTAIN BOYCOTT DEFEATED

In today's paper is a letter from Captain Boycott to a Dublin gentleman warmly expressing his acknowledgement of the services rendered to him and stating that he intends with his family to leave Lough Mask with the expedition. The prospect before him, he says, is simply ruin.

–*The Daily Express*, 20 November 1880.

17-26 November 1880

'We've won.' Owen Joyce's expression was more of disbelief than joy.

'It looks like it.' Redpath smiled and then looked at the others gathered around the table in the Valkenburg Hotel, which was littered with a mess of newspapers and teacups. Besides Fr O'Malley and Owen, the rest were press correspondents, including Michael McCabe of *The Connaught Telegraph*, Seamus Duggan of *The Ballinrobe Chronicle* and Declan McQuaid, an intense, bespectacled young patriot from *The Freeman's Journal*.

McQuaid was more sceptical. 'But he says he won't give up the farm.'

'You don't know how stubborn Boycott is. He has to say something like that or he's admitting defeat,' Owen offered.

'I agree,' Redpath said, 'and if Boycott admits he's beaten, it's like admitting the entire British establishment's plan was a costly failure.'

McCabe piped up. 'The loyalist papers are still calling the expedition a "great success". And they're still getting money. The London *Telegraph* has just made a contribution of one hundred pounds.'

'Let them give as much as they want,' Owen said. 'No amount of money can finance this kind of operation all over the country. And it's spreading. Landlords are being boycotted from Cork to Donegal.'

'They've already admitted as much. Sure, two troops of Hussars are being withdrawn te Dublin tomorrow,' Seamus Duggan chipped in.

'Frankly, it doesn't surprise me,' Redpath said. 'They've begun to realise what a waste of resources it all was.'

Fr O'Malley had all the while been sitting pensively, sipping a cup of tea.

'You've been very quiet, Father,' Owen remarked. 'Aren't you pleased? You yourself said that when Boycott was gone, victory would be complete.'

He nodded. 'I did, I did, Owen. But he's not gone yet and we must remain vigilant until he's on the boat to England. This may be just the time that some hothead Fenian will decide to strike, when the shield the army have put around Boycott is lowered. It's wonderful news about boycotts beginning all over the country and to think we started it all here, but if any harm were to come to him, even now, it would be a catastrophe. It would be the final excuse the extremists in the British Government would need to force through coercion, and ironically that would suit the terrorists perfectly. They'd find their ranks swollen to bursting overnight. It's been seen a thousand times in a thousand places through history. Small rebellious groups can become armies overnight when an unpopular government uses extreme measures to suppress the masses.'

'But there's hardly even been a curse thrown in a week, Father,' McCabe said.

'And it troubles me that it's gone so very, very quiet.'

'But in the final shuffle, the Fenians want the same as the Land League. Why try to destroy that when we've come so far?' asked Duggan.

Caught up in his joy at the news of Boycott's departure, Owen had forgotten his brother's warning, that they would get Boycott sooner or later. He realised also that Fr O'Malley had been thinking precisely the same thing. Owen answered Duggan's question.

'Because the militants aren't prepared to wait. Even with all the boycotts, it might take two years before the British Government agrees to our demands and passes a bill. And besides, the Fenians' first priority is independence. Landlordism is just one issue to them. They want a war because war brings fast results. If they did drive the British out of Ireland they could pass any law they wanted overnight. The people in extremist groups are generally impulsive, impatient and violent. They march to a different drum. Believe me, I know,' he said and met the priest's eyes.

Maggie, Boycott's former housemaid, approached the table, bearing an empty tray and an acerbic expression. She began to gather the crockery noisily.

'How are you keeping, Maggie?' the priest asked softly.

She paused and looked directly down at him. 'What concern is it of yours?' she snapped and strode away towards the kitchen door. The priest shook his head, reminded that the boycott hadn't been without its innocent victims.

Their conversation continued in Gallagher's bar, the cups of tea replaced by more spirited beverages. There was general delight that even the weather was working in their favour. The ground in which the Ulstermen were digging was so icy that picks were needed to break the surface and the army tents had frozen so solidly that the canvas flaps could be swung open like a wooden door. Boycott's capitulation, as they chose to view it, was toasted repeatedly during the evening, Parnell's forthcoming trial was debated at length, and a final drink was raised to the citizens of Chicago with Redpath's news that they had named Parnell a Freeman of that great American metropolis. And then Owen and Fr O'Malley and Redpath, all slightly the worse for wear, began the journey home.

'Notice all those glum foreign correspondents in the pub?' Redpath asked as the car made its way along Market Street.

'Can't hold their drink,' Owen laughed.

'They expected a war and have spent a month writing about turnips. They're praying for a grand finale when the expedition leaves to get the world's attention again.'

Fr O'Malley pulled his collar up against the chilling night breeze. 'Then we'll have to make sure they have nothing to write about.'

***

Fifteen minutes after they had departed the Valkenburg Hotel, Maggie returned to gather the discarded newspapers. The room was quiet now but for a solitary man who had just arrived and ordered a meal. As she collected the papers, her eye fell upon a circled article in *The Times*. She picked it up and began to read, her heart sinking when she saw the line about Boycott's intention to leave Ireland. Somehow she had hoped that everything would work out in the end and she'd be able to return to Lough Mask House.

'Oh Lord!' she whispered and pressed her fingers against her lips to stifle a sob.

'Are you all right?'

The voice so startled her that she yelped aloud. She swung about to see the lone diner gazing down across her shoulder.

'Jesus almighty! What are ye doin' sneakin' up like that?'

'I'm sorry I startled ye,' Thomas said and smiled. 'I thought ye sounded upset. Was it something in the paper?'

Maggie slammed down the newspaper and spoke more to herself than the stranger. 'They're leavin'. And leavin' me high and dry!' she snapped and walked away.

Thomas picked up the article.

'Time is getting short,' he whispered.

***

'Didn't see you at mass, Joe,' Owen said as he and Síomha pulled up outside their neighbour's cottage.

'What are you, my priest?'

They both chuckled as Joe took Anu's reins and they climbed down. In his other hand Joe held an antiquated rifle and two bloodied rabbits.

'I was just returning the pick you lent me,' Owen said.

'Is Síle about?' Síomha asked.

'Took the boys to visit her sister in Ballinrobe. Thought I'd get a bit of huntin' in. You won't mention me missin' mass te her, now, will ye?'

'Your secret's safe,' she grinned.

Joe beckoned them across the yard. He nodded towards the south. 'Look.'

In the distance they glimpsed a convoy of Hussars and wagons laden with sacks.

'Boycott's corn. The army are moving it to Cong. Probably sell it in Galway.'

'On Sunday?' Síomha asked.

'They know that everyone will be at mass. Less chance of trouble. Boycott's gone on holiday and left everyone else to tie up his loose ends.'

'After all Boycott's work, the Ulstermen cleared the whole thing in two weeks.' Joe said. 'They're good men, good workers I mean,' he added, his respect evident. He laughed then. 'You hear that the RIC was ordered to drive Boycott's cattle to the Claremorris train? Sergeant Murtagh was so mad he was fit for the Connaught asylum. Then when the train got to Dublin, the drovers said they were boycotting the cattle!'

'There were five thousand at a meeting in Walshtown yesterday. They're going to boycott thirteen landlords. Soon there won't be a landlord in Ireland able to do business.'

'Holy Jaysus, Owen,' Joe laughed. 'What have we started?'

'You should thank Boycott too, boys,' Síomha said, prompting mystified looks. 'Well, if he hadn't been such a cantankerous ould git, none of this would have happened,' she laughed.

***

Only a week after they had departed for Dublin, Boycott and his wife drove their carriage secretly back into Lough Mask Estate under escort of eight constables and twenty soldiers. After seven years, just three days of their life here remained and Annie, despite being greatly revived with the break, was filled with a deep melancholy as they pulled to a stop outside the doors to her home.

While in Dublin, they had stayed at the Hamman Hotel and Charles had arranged several meetings with Englishmen of property to inquire into the possibility of a position as their land agent. The fact that his name was by now ubiquitous and that his countrymen saw him as a beacon of resistance to the Land League had helped his cause. As a result, the possibility had arisen of securing a position on an estate in Norfolk, very close to his birthplace, so at least for her husband it would seem like a version of home.

Home to Annie was here in Ireland, on Achill where Mary lay in eternal rest, or on the shores of Lough Mask, a place she had come to love and which she would soon leave behind forever.

***

Men of Mayo
In the name of the Lough Mask tenants, for the sake of the cause which they are so manfully upholding, you are earnestly entreated to permit the Orangemen and the English army to take themselves away out of your outraged county unmolested and unnoticed.
John O'Malley PP

(Notice posted by Fr O'Malley in Ballinrobe and Neale on 25 November 1880)

***

'Right, Mr Boycott, if you could just move a little to your left, that's it, behind your good lady wife. And Miss Madeleine, if you would mind not moving about? Sergeant Murtagh, isn't it? Perhaps with your cap on, yes, perfect. And Mr Weekes, could you maybe sit at the front alongside Mr Robinson. William, you go to the top step and you, gentlemen, on the right, please stand on–'

'Oh for God's sake, man, get on with it before we freeze to death!' Boycott shouted at the photographer.

Gerard Wynne normally did weddings and family portraits but had been hired by the proprietor of the *Express*, Mr Robinson, to record the conclusion of the Boycott Relief Expedition for posterity, or as Robinson had put it 'to forever capture the spirit of resistance to the forces of terrorism.'

He took one last look through the lens at the twenty people assembled on the steps of Lough Mask House, then dipped under the black hood to adjust the focusing bellows.

'Right. Remember: don't smile.'

He held the thermite flash bar up high and pushed the button.

And while all around him held their heads high, Boycott slumped and looked forlornly into the distance.

***

'They've given us the go-ahead.'

'Finally,' Thomas said in reply to Doherty, who sat warming himself by the fire in Bull Walsh's cottage. He'd just returned from meeting the Commandant in Galway.

Doherty continued. 'The Land League is claiming their boycott's a great success. And it's spreading like a gorse fire in August. There are boycotts all over the country. They think ruining a few landlords will change things. Fuck, we need te get rid of every English bastard on Irish soil. And there's only one way te do that. The tenant farmers are joining Parnell and Davitt's side in droves. We've got te stop it. Killing Boycott is the perfect way te do it. A few months ago he was a nobody, but now the world is watching the bastard. He's become a fuckin' icon te the British establishment. We kill him and the British will introduce coercion. When the farmers see the British trampling them into the ground te protect the rich arses of a few thousand landlords–'

'We'll have fifty thousand volunteers in a month,' Thomas grinned.

Martin McGurk took a step towards Doherty. 'That's all great. But he leaves tomorrow. How the fuck do we kill him when he's surrounded by five hundred soldiers?'

'Shut up, McGurk,' Doherty snapped.

'He's got a point though, Donal,' Thomas offered calmly.

With the aid of a tongs, Bull Walsh fished a couple of potatoes from the fire and dropped them at Doherty's feet. 'Have them. I'll get ye a drink.'

Doherty picked up one of the potatoes, its skin scorched black. He tossed it from hand to hand, wiped it clean and took a bite. He then turned to the others as he munched.

'The expedition leaves tomorrow. But we have information that Boycott won't be with them, although everyone's supposed te think he is. The bastards plan te leave a small force behind and then quietly sneak him and his family away at dawn on Saturday. They're going te use an ambulance wagon as a disguise so that anyone would think it's just the dregs of the expedition returning te the barracks. There'll be only twenty soldiers. And here's the good bit. There'll be just one wagon, so we'll know our target exactly.'

'Clever bastards,' remarked Thomas.

'We can't kill twenty soldiers! How do we get away?' McGurk asked nervously.

Doherty accepted a drink from Walsh and gulped it down in one go. 'We use rifles. Thomas and Bull, you're both good marksmen. We'll have te find a rise overlooking the road which gives us a good line of sight and has plenty of cover.'

'I know a place,' McGurk piped up, suddenly enthused. 'It's not a mile from me cottage, near the Holy Well. And there's trees there. It's about fifty yards from the road.'

'Good. You and Thomas scout it tomorrow. If it works, we'll escape across country on the horses, head south, then split up and meet back here on Sunday.'

'Hold on. How exactly do we do this?' Thomas asked.

'What do ye mean?'

'If we don't get Boycott with the first shot the wagon will be down the road like a hare. And what about the soldiers?'

Doherty discarded the last of the potato into the fire and brushed his hands. 'We all fire together. I'm good enough at that distance te hit one of the horses pulling the wagon, so it won't be going anywhere fast. McGurk, you're going for the soldiers, cause panic. If there's twenty of them, ye can't miss. Thomas and Bull, like I said, your job is Boycott in the wagon. Get off as many shots as you can.'

Bull Walsh, who was standing quietly with his back to a wall, turned and looked at Thomas, both thinking the same thing. Thomas stood up and stared down at Doherty.

'Ambulance wagons are covered. You said his family was going with him. How do we know where Boycott is inside?'

Doherty rose now and stared at him. 'Ye don't. But it's a good guess he'll be near the back, y'know, to help the women and children in, then climb in himself. Or we might get lucky and they'll leave the rear flap open. Ye might be able te see him.'

'And if we can't, we fire anyway?'

Doherty nodded. 'The women and children might be hit. Beyond our control. This is war, men. These things happen. If anyone's got a problem with this, let's hear it.'

He slowly turned and looked around. Silence descended on the room, disturbed only by the occasional crack of a spark from the hearth.

McGurk was the first to speak. 'The bastards killed me child before he was even born, me wife too. Eye for an eye, is what I say.'

'Bull?' Doherty asked.

'I've lost family te them as well. I don't like lowering myself te their level, but it's war, like you say.' Walsh's voice was barely audible.

'Thomas?'

Thomas was staring at the floor. He raised his head and looked at the others in turn, then shrugged. 'Fuck it. As far as I'm concerned, Boycott and his family are just part of the "surplus English population".'

Doherty went to gather up his greatcoat. 'Good. We meet early tomorrow at McGurk's. Everyone travel separately by dark. That's it, then. I'll see ye tomorrow. Come Saturday, all those newspapermen will be writing obituaries.'

***

Owen pulled his coat tightly around him as he stood next to Síomha by Lough Mask's shore. The mountains to the west had disappeared beneath a murky veil of cloud and a biting wind churned the lough into an expanse of white-peaked waves.

'There's a storm coming,' Síomha said.

'There is. And the British Government won't know what hit them.'

She laughed a little and pushed an arm inside his coat around his waist. 'And you helped to stir up the wind. I'm proud of you.'

He shook his head. 'I only did my bit. And so did you. Davitt, Parnell, Fr O'Malley – they're the ones who had the vision to conceive this whole thing. And not a shot fired. The press are saying the Boycott expedition cost twenty thousand pounds. Parnell said yesterday that every one of Boycott's turnips had cost a shilling to pick. And there are questions being asked in the House of Commons about the cost. It's the beginning of the end of landlordism.'

'Questions in the House of Commons,' Síomha said a little dreamily. She laughed. 'Mr Gladstone should have known better than to take on the Joyces from Neale.'

'Yeah. Sure you'd put the fear of God in anyone,' he joked and took her in his arms. They kissed tenderly as the wind rose around them, tossing Síomha's hair wildly about their heads.

Síomha looked up at the sight of an empty sack whirling high above them like a kite. She found she had to raise her voice to be heard clearly. 'If I didn't know better I'd say that God was sending Boycott a message.'

Owen grinned at her. 'Yeah, but you do know better.'

A surge of wind caught them, sending Síomha's shawl sailing out behind her like a flag in a stiff breeze. Owen caught her arm and gasped as the wind took his breath.

'Jesus, we'd better get everything tied down. This is going to be bad.'

As they hurried back in their cottage, Tadhg arrived along the lane, bent forward, battling against the wind. Owen had to shout to make himself heard above the intensifying screech. 'Tadhg! Get the car and the plough around the back of the house!'

Anu's frightened whinnying in the field off to their right caught their attention.

'What about Anu?' Síomha asked.

The animal was running about her small enclosure as though desperate for a means of escape. A couple of tall fir trees at the edge of the pen leaned at an angle, their branches aligned with the direction of the gale like a thousand fingers pointing away from the lough. They heard the distinctive cracking sound of a branch giving way and crash to the ground somewhere beyond their sight.

'I'll tie her up behind the cottage. She'll be out of the worst of the wind there.'

Niamh appeared at the door and Síomha scurried to get her safely back inside.

'Move, Tadhg!'

'Dad. What's going to happen to the soldiers in the camp?' Tadhg roared as his father began to stagger towards Anu's enclosure.

'I don't know. All I can say is, the poor bastards!'

***

'Colonel! Sir! The tree! The tree!'

Colonel Twentyman grasped at the private's arm in an attempt to remain upright.

'What damn tree, man?'

'Look, sir!' he yelled and pointed to the woodland. Through the darkness they could just make out the shape of a towering tree leaning ominously over the tents.

'Quick, man! Get them out of there now! Move!'

The private set off across the encampment, the gale giving his gait the appearance of a drunk. Colonel Twentyman tottered to the nearest tent, its pegs fighting to retain their purchase in the sodden earth, the glow of fiery braziers within the trembling canvas giving it an unsettling spectral aspect. He burst through the flap, admitting a howling gust. The ten soldiers within were clustered in the centre, sleeping rolls pulled tightly around them.

'You men! Get up! You and you! Go and help evacuate the men from under the trees. Hurry! The rest of you, rouse everyone and put down more pegs, otherwise the tents will never hold. Move, you bunch of dunderheads!'

The colonel found one of his captains and they careened through the chaotic encampment towards the wood. Men ran wildly about as they evacuated the tents beneath the ominously leaning tree. As they watched, a new sound struggled to be heard above the gale, a slow crunching at first that suddenly accelerated and swelled in intensity.

'It's going to go, sir!'

'Get everyone out! Get everyone out!' the colonel roared.

Men scampered from the remaining occupied tent, stumbling through the flap, some scrabbling away on hands and knees as the monstrous form of the fifty-foot-high tree surrendered its centuries-old hold on the earth and collapsed in a colossal wave of noise and destruction, flattening three tents entirely and ripping two others to shreds. As its branches settled into the mud, the colonel and captain searched for casualties, but thankfully, the evacuation had succeeded with only minor injuries. Another private fought for the officers' attention. 'Colonel! Ten horses have broken loose. What should we do?'

'Get the hell out of this damn country, that's what!'

'Sir?'

'We can't search in the storm. We'll find them in the morning.' He turned to the captain. 'In God's name, what else can happen?'

The captain stood with his mouth open, looking towards the churning night sky.

'Look, sir,' he gasped and pointed.

The colonel turned. 'Good God almighty!'

***

'Great God!' Annie Boycott gasped as she stared skyward through the raging storm, leaves filling the night air like black snowflakes. Her husband, Madeleine and William stood either side of her, the boy's face alive with excitement.

'Jeepers!' the boy yelped.

'What is it?' Boycott asked.

'It's a tent, Uncle!'

They watched in astonishment as an entire tent sailed one hundred feet overhead, a burning brazier trapped within the huge inflated canvas, filling the enclosed space with a ghostly yellow light, glowing embers spilling a trail of fleeting stars across the night sky. It floated beyond their view and a moment later the neigh of a horse sounded through the wind's keening howl. The riderless animal galloped past at full tilt, eyes blind to its destination.

'I've never seen a storm like it.' Annie observed with disquiet. 'It's almost as tho–'

The noise was sudden, grinding and deafening.

'Look out!' her husband roared, hurling himself at Annie as a giant, gnarled tree limb came crashing through the glass. Annie and Madeleine screamed as fragmented glass and wood showered the room.

'My God! Are you all right?' Boycott yelled, kneeling over his wife.

She nodded, staring in shock at the denuded arm of wood protruding through the shattered window.

'Madeleine? William?' Annie asked.

'Whoooeee!' William yelped with delighted, trembling enthusiasm.

'We're fine, Auntie,' Madeleine said, brushing down her dress.

Annie met her husband's eyes as he pulled her up. 'Charles…thank you.'

He smiled faintly and nodded.

'Those poor men in the encampment,' Madeleine reflected.

'Yes, dear. And the tenants, in those little cottages,' Annie said.

'To hell with the tenants,' Boycott replied.

***

Owen, Niamh and Síomha lay in the bed listening to the howling wind beyond their thatch, praying the roof would hold. The breeze whistled under the eaves and every door and window rattled incessantly. Added to the cacophony was Anu's terrified whinnying. The horse had been secured in the corner of the L-shaped rear of the cottage, protecting her from the worst of the gale.

'Daddy, I'm scared,' Niamh whispered.

Síomha pulled her tighter.

'It'll be all right. It might blow out soon,' Owen reassured.

He'd barely spoken when they were startled by a terrible grinding, followed a moment later by a tremendous crash. Owen was out of the room in seconds, almost colliding with Tadhg, who emerged from the rear bedroom.

'Dad! What was that?'

Owen was staring at the ceiling above the hearth as Síomha and Niamh crashed into him from behind. Where once their chimney had risen above the thatch was a gaping hole exposed to the rage of the storm.

'Jesus, Mary and Joseph!' Síomha screamed. Niamh began to cry.

'Light a lamp, Síomha, quickly, I better go and–' Owen stopped dead and met Tadhg's eyes as the dawning realisation struck them both.

'What's wrong?' Síomha asked.

'Why has Anu stopped whinnying?' Tadhg asked.

Father and son turned without a further word and ran from the cottage. Dressed only in long johns and tattered nightshirts, they stumbled barefoot through the blinding darkness. As they turned the corner Owen could just discern the hulk of the animal lying on her side. They fell on their knees in the mud beside the horse.

'Anu!' the youth cried out.

The horse had been directly under the collapsing chimney, struck by the full force of innumerable lumps of Mayo stone. The debris lay scattered everywhere. Owen placed a hand on the animal's nose and she lifted her head as if in thanks, then gave a barely audible whinny and laid her head back against the earth. She was all but dead.

Owen, his hands covered in the animal's blood, felt a catch in his throat. He'd toiled for years on end in the fields with the old workhorse his only company. Tadhg was crying openly, oblivious to the stinging rain and buffeting wind. They heard a scream and turned to see Síomha and Niamh approach with a lamp, their coats wrapped about them. Niamh began to wail as the lamplight fell across Anu's bloodied head.

'Tadhg!' Owen shouted, shaking his son by the shoulder. 'Tadhg! Take your sister inside. Go now!'

'What are you going to do?' he asked.

'Just go! Quickly!'

As the youth hauled Niamh away, Síomha fell to her knees beside her husband. 'Oh God, Owen! We should have brought her into the house!'

'Hold over the lamp.'

Síomha moved the lamp above the animal's head, revealing an ugly, gaping wound above her eyes. Her back and sides were brutally scarred by similar gashes. He ran his hand down the animal's nose.

'There, girl, there.'

Then he turned and lifted one of the fallen chimney stones. With both hands he raised it as high as he could above his head, briefly met Síomha's eyes, and the moment she looked away he brought it down with all the strength he could muster on the animal's head. He repeated the action twice. Anu gave a couple of brief kicks with her hind legs, but no more sound escaped her before she died. And for that he was thankful.

***

The waters of Lough Mask had contrived to grasp a fifteen-foot-long boat from its boathouse mooring and send it crashing against the wall, piercing the structure's side like a giant spear. Captain Tomkinson, who had briefly been accommodated in the boathouse, studied the strange sight of the boat's prow protruding through the wall like a giant nose and reflected that had he still been bunking there, he would surely now be lacking his head. He turned and started back towards the encampment in the bright morning sunlight. High in the trees he could see the remnants of a tent, its white canvas shredded to rags. In all they had lost six tents, either flattened by the falling tree or simply carried away whole into the sky. The tent that had taken flight complete with its brazier had been found in a nearby field, a mess of ragged, burnt canvas.

Twelve horses had fled the fury of the storm, of which eight had been recovered. Most had bolted to the relative sanctuary of the woodlands, but four were lost to them, an unintended gift from the British Army to some impoverished Mayo farmers.

The captain gazed across the scene of devastation. As far as he could see, not a solitary blade of grass remained. Wooden crates, pots, clothes and army packs lay strewn about the ground. Huge pools of water flooded the spaces between the battered tents and men dragged themselves about wearily as they dismantled the encampment. Lieutenant Colonel Twentyman approached and he saluted sharply.

'Sir.'

'Deuced mess.'

'Yes, sir. But at least nobody was seriously injured. Or killed.'

'Yes, a small miracle, I'd venture. Issue the order to have everything dismantled by two o'clock. Two tents will remain for the Hussars who will escort Captain Boycott and his family tomorrow. But the sooner we see the back of Mayo, the better.'

***

Beyond Lough Mask Estate, hundreds of trees had been uprooted and lay across roads and in fields. Seven of the tenants had lost at least part of their thatch. Joe Gaughan hadn't been so lucky. He'd seen the entire roof peeled away like the lid of a tin of salted beef. It was the worst storm in living memory.

For Owen, the loss of the horse was incalculable and left him fraught with worry. Where in God's name would he find five pounds to replace Anu?

He stood now in the bright sunlight, the blue sky overhead speckled with clumps of white, fluffy cloud, belying the malevolence of the previous night. He glanced down again at the dead animal, the unfortunate beast's mouth coated with white foam, then pulled the canvas sheet across her. A man from Ballinrobe would take her away, pay them a few shillings and then turn her into animal feed or some other abomination.

Despite Niamh's sadness they had sent her to school – an occupied mind dwelt less upon life's tribulations, and children were good at moving beyond such things anyway. Fr O'Malley arrived mid-morning and Owen explained what had happened.

'I'm sorry,' the priest commiserated as they prepared to repair the chimney. 'The church only lost a few slates, thank God.'

'At least we'll see the back of Boycott today,' Síomha said.

'Hmm. Even the darkest clouds have a silver lining. But that's why I'm here, Owen, to ask your help to make sure there's no trouble.'

Owen shook his head. 'Look, Father, I have to get this repaired. I'd love to go, but I've so much to do.'

'But after all the effort you've put in...'

'To be honest, Father, losing the horse, the damage...my heart wouldn't be in it,' he said with a sigh.

Fr O'Malley nodded, muttered muted farewells and left them to their work.

***

Niamh looked down into the water a few yards below at the reflection of the blue sky overhead. The low wall around the Holy Well was covered with a thick green moss, which felt damp beneath her bottom, but she paid it no heed as she was still so upset by Anu's death. She sniffled and wiped a tear away, then tossed a stone into the well. As it plopped into the water, sending ripples out to the walls, she quickly whispered a prayer that she would see Anu again in heaven.

She sighed, slid down from the wall and gathered her satchel. She would be late if she didn't hurry as she still had two miles to walk to school. But the sound of men's voices gave her pause again, especially as one voice sounded very familiar. She scampered across the uneven ground up a short rise towards some trees and there, about thirty yards away, stood her Uncle Thomas and another man she recognised as Mr McGurk. There were two horses nearby.

She knew that her father and uncle had a falling out, but people were always having fights and then making up – her mother and father did it every second week – and she wondered if that might be possible, as seeing her uncle again would certainly make up a little for losing their horse.

Mr McGurk was pointing towards the road and then her Uncle Thomas lifted a pair of binoculars and looked in the same direction. She was just about to call out when they turned away and disappeared into the trees. She briefly considered running after them, but suddenly remembered she was already late and could get into terrible trouble if she didn't hurry. She frowned, turned on her heel and ran, and by the time she reached the schoolyard all notion of her uncle had fled from her mind.

Chapter 35

The Boycott expedition, in which so much public interest has been centred, came today to a peaceful and honourable end. Its promoters can look back with satisfaction at the complete success of their sympathetic enterprise. The Ulstermen come back with characters unblemished and with the grateful thanks of Captain Boycott. The farewell was a fitting dénouement to a strangely vivid social drama. After a sleepless night, the uproar and fury of the storm keeping the men constantly employed in endeavouring to keep the tents from being blown away, the order to break camp was given. At length they marched round to Lough Mask House, headed by Captain Maxwell. Captain Boycott, with his wife, nephew and niece, were waiting on the steps to receive them.

–*The Times*. 27 November 1880

By the end of the week the Boycott episode will have ended. It was an extraordinary affair in more senses than one. The introductory music played up for it in the press by the landlord orchestra was the overture to an exceedingly serious tragedy. The piece itself, when the curtain rose, turned out to be a burlesque extravaganza of a very amusing kind... The most extraordinary preparations were made by the Government for the protection of 'Boycott's rescuers'. As for the conduct of the Mayo people, nothing could be better. They have offered no violence to the Orangemen or their protectors; they have in fact left them severely alone.

–*The Nation*, 20 & 27 November 1880

26 November 1880

Bernard Becker hurried towards the assembled throng in front of Lough Mask House and jostled with ten other newspaper correspondents for a decent position from which he might record any final drama. The low rumble of voices dwindled to naught at the sight of Captain Boycott emerging through the door and pausing on the top step. He was dressed in a tan safari jacket and pants, knee-high boots and a pith helmet, and would have looked quite the country gentleman had his clothes not displayed the scars of toil in the fields. He had also abandoned his customary cane in favour of a sheep hook, a prop, Becker suspected, to convey that he was one with the labourers.

The expedition leaders and financiers emerged from the crowd of about a hundred people. Captain Maxwell, who among others had spent the previous three weeks as guests of Lord and Lady Ardilaun in the luxurious surroundings of nearby Ashford Castle, led the delegation. Boycott shook his extended hand heartily, the contrast to the day of their arrival evident to all. After a few words exchanged in confidence, Maxwell nodded and accepted a handwritten letter. As he did, five more people emerged from the house. Asheton Weekes descended the steps and began to clasp hands all about him. Annie, Madeleine, William and the maid, Miss Reynolds, gathered around the top step.

Somewhat theatrically, Becker thought, Maxwell held the letter at arm's length and began to bellow out the words, as though he was a herald in the Roman forum.

> My Dear Captain Maxwell and Gentlemen:
> As leaders of the Boycott Relief Expedition, I cannot allow you to depart from Lough Mask without expressing my deep and heartfelt gratitude for the generous and timely aid you have one and all rendered me by saving my crops, and for the many sacrifices of comfort and convenience you have endured on my behalf. The difficult and unsolicited task you undertook, and have so fully and ably carried out in the face of many and great difficulties, would to men not possessed of your unflinching determination have proved insurmountable. With you and your worthy band of stalwart labourers, I am compelled, for reasons now well known, to quit with my wife a happy home, where

we had hoped, with God's help, to have spent the remainder of our days. Mrs Boycott joins me in again thanking you all from our hearts for the signal service you have rendered us, believe us, my dear Captain Maxwell and gentlemen,

Yours very faithfully,

CC Boycott

About five seconds of silence ensued, then a great cheer went up for Boycott and his wife, followed by several more for the expedition leaders, the army, the police and so on, and Becker began to think the celebration interminable. But he was quite surprised to observe Boycott, given his normally rigid reserve, mingling freely among the labourers, shaking hands all about, even cracking the occasional smile. It was as though some fundamental shift had occurred within the man, some weight had lifted from his shoulders, which Becker ascribed to his relief that the turbulent months were almost behind him. Further cheers went up for Mrs Boycott, who seemed quite moved and clasped an arm around her niece's shoulders.

Someone struck up a chorus of 'Auld Lang Syne', which was sung with gusto; there was much slapping on the back and more cheering before an officer brought the celebration to a close by ordering a blast of the bugle. Finally the procession got on its way, the labourers and soldiers in the belief that Boycott's family would soon follow them at the rear of the cavalcade.

Becker glanced over his shoulder one final time at the land agent and his family standing on the steps of Lough Mask House. Despite Boycott's good cheer, he couldn't help feeling that the man looked broken.

***

The hundreds of soldiers, labourers, policemen and correspondents trooped off like a giant snake slithering into the woodland, leaving only a handful of constables patrolling the perimeter and two troops of Hussars beyond in the muddied field.

Annie was immediately struck by a sensation she had almost forgotten, that of the beautiful calm and serenity of their home. Gone was the constant, distant chatter of hundreds of men, the horses clopping about, the hammering, the clang of tools, the yelling of officers. And she was suddenly struck by how unnatural it had all been. She listened, and all she could hear were birds and the gentle lapping of water on the lough shore.

'Well, that's that,' her husband said, cracking his sheep hook down on the step, as though putting a full stop at the end of a long sentence that had described the events of the past months. He entered the house, followed by Weekes and the others.

'I'll be along presently,' Annie said.

She began to stroll towards the lough, enjoying the brightness of the day and the calming silence, yet conversely weighed down by melancholy. This was her final day in her home, her last opportunity to open her senses to the beauty of the woodland and the sight of the mountains rising beyond the shimmering waters.

Had any good come of it all? For the tenants and the Land League, absolutely yes. They had their victory and would undoubtedly enjoy much more success on the road ahead. Her husband, on the other hand, was a man who viewed himself as belonging to the topmost level of society and acted out that self-image to the extreme, yet he'd been driven away by a handful of peasants. Despite rescuing his crops, how could he see it as anything other than a humiliating defeat?

She reached the shore and sat on a boulder, gazing into the water. In spite of her sadness, she felt that something positive had come from their recent trauma. Her husband would never admit to it, but a change had come about in him as a result of the boycott. As the expedition had made their farewells, she had witnessed something that she would never have believed possible: her husband moved to emotion – well, almost. Oh, he hadn't made a stirring address, principally, she suspected, because he'd been afraid his own voice might betray his newly born respect for the common labourers. Such a thing would have required too great a lowering of his mask of bombastic ascendancy. But the cheering had moved him sufficiently to go among them, clasping their hands and expressing his gratitude. Formerly he would never have demeaned himself – as he would have viewed it – in such a manner.

The boycott itself hadn't brought about the change in him, but it had certainly provided the stimulus; it had forced him to confront the tragedy of their daughter's short life and in that terrible private battle he had somehow discovered paths around emotional obstacles, around the immovable rocks of his warped and pretentious upbringing.

She washed her hands in the icy water, then began to walk back to the house. Tears stung the corners of her eyes and, strangely, she couldn't be certain if they were as a result of heartache or happiness; perhaps it was possible to experience both at the same instant. They would lose their home and their farm, for certain, but they would find another home, most likely in England, and life would go on. But they had also both gained something. Where before there had been merely a man and a woman, for almost the first time in her life she felt that now, just possibly, there might be a husband and a wife.

***

Two thousand boots tramped through the mud and storm debris on the narrow road to Ballinrobe. It was a spectacle as rare in Mayo as the sighting of an elephant, yet the only spectators were a handful of schoolchildren, Niamh among them, who had hurried across the fields to witness the labourers of Cavan and Monaghan, the constabulary, the 84th Regiment, the 1st Dragoons, fifty Army Service Corps wagons, several ambulance cars and a train of news correspondents. The children laughed and hurled a few insults, but that was the worst assault that the cavalcade had to bear.

Fr O'Malley had taken up a vantage point near to Ballinrobe, watching in the company of an aged widow by the name of Meehan, whose face had more furrows than a ploughed field. They stood behind the low wall outside her single-roomed cottage and watched the cortège approach. He found it difficult to suppress a sense of pride that his request for non-interference with the expedition's departure had been so completely observed, for the roads were virtually bereft of locals and not a line of newspaper text could be written in reproach of their behaviour.

'All this for one man, Father. Never seen the like in all me days,' the widow observed in a wheezy, withering voice.

'Well, at least they're taking him in the right direction. Away from us.'

As the covered wagons rocked unsteadily past, he wondered which of them contained the land agent. He would dearly love to have been able to look into Boycott's eyes and let him see the face of one of those who had brought the mighty so low. A moment later he lowered his eyes in shame at having entertained such a wish; he had sinned in taking satisfaction in the misery of another. It was unbecoming, especially for a man of his calling. He quickly muttered an Act of Contrition under his breath.

But the weight of self-reproach was lifted when he spotted Messrs Robinson and Manning at the forefront of the Ulster contingent, easily identifiable by their tam o'shanters. These had been two of the main instigators of, and propagandists for, the expedition. These were the men who had spoken of his beloved County Mayo in such disdainful and malicious terms. He simply could not resist the temptation and as they drew within earshot he turned sharply to the Widow Meehan.

'Did I not warn you to let the British Army alone?' he yelled. The unfortunate widow stared back at him open-mouthed.

The priest winked at her and continued: 'How dare you intimidate Her Majesty's troops? For shame, Widow Meehan! Be off now and if you dare molest these thousand heroes after their glorious campaign, I'll make an example of you! Be off!'

The old lady pulled her shawl about her head to conceal her chuckle. Robinson fixed Fr O'Malley with a furious glare, then hastened his step until beyond their sight.

'You're a terrible one, Father. Ye nearly gave me a turn,' she laughed through yellowed, crooked teeth.

'I am that, Widow, I surely am,' he smiled.

***

'What will we do about Anu?' Síomha asked, gathering the bowls from the table.

'The knacker's going to cut him up, isn't he?' Niamh asked.

Owen looked briefly at Tadhg and then Síomha, both of whom frowned. He stretched a comforting arm around Niamh's shoulders.

'We can't leave him out there, petal.'

Niamh nodded sadly and a moment later her eyes brightened. 'Will we be getting a new horse soon?'

'We'll see. Take the bowls outside and rinse them in the basin for your mother. Like a good girl.'

Niamh exhaled deeply through pursed lips, then did as requested.

'She's right, though,' Owen said. 'There's a knacker who passes through Ballinrobe on Saturday, pays for dead livestock that can't be eaten. You'll have to fetch him tomorrow, Tadhg.'

'All right, Dad,' Tadhg muttered.

Despite Boycott's departure, there was a general air of gloom in the cottage, principally because of the emotional and financial blow from the horse's death. The future was uncertain, even with Boycott gone. All the tenants had agreed to send their rents directly to Lord Erne, less the abatement they had demanded. He would have little choice but to accept them now. Yet even with the lower rents, the loss of the animal meant a large outlay of cash and they lived such a precarious financial existence already.

'We've visitors,' Síomha said, peering out into the darkness. Two cars had pulled into the yard and she saw Niamh run across to greet Fr O'Malley.

'It's Father O'Malley and Mister Redpath.'

Owen cursed. 'Jesus, I can't even afford a drink to offer them.'

Niamh ushered them in and, as though he'd overheard Owen's grumble, Redpath immediately produced a bottle of whiskey.

'I thought I'd bring this. It's a celebration, after all.'

All but Niamh gathered around the table and a toast was given to the success of the boycott.

'How did it go today?' Tadhg asked.

The priest grinned. 'Without a hitch. The road was deserted all the way to Ballinrobe. It was more like a funeral procession. I think they realise what a grand folly the entire thing was, though they'll never admit that, of course.'

Redpath refilled the glasses, Síomha intervening to prevent too much going into Tadhg's, much to his annoyance. The American raised his glass.

'A toast. To you, Father, not just for organising the boycott, but for adding an entirely new word to the English language.'

'I've a feeling we'll be hearing a lot of that word,' Síomha said, grinning.

'I don't know if that's a good thing,' Owen said. 'Boycott may be gone, but we'll have this constant reminder and he hardly deserves to be immortalised.'

The priest and Redpath exchanged a brief look.

'He's not *quite* gone, I'm afraid,' Redpath said.

'What do you mean?'

Fr O'Malley smiled. 'Worst-kept secret in Ireland. We were meant to think he'd left, but they're sneaking him out at dawn. You know what it's like trying to keep secrets in a small country village, Owen. One of the constables tells his wife, she tells her neighbour and so on. By now, half the press probably know he hasn't left. Still, I wouldn't worry. Most people will still be in their beds when he leaves.'

'In fact, a constable told me,' Redpath laughed. 'I've already included it in my latest despatch to New York. And talking of departures, I'm afraid I must make mine. I've to be up early tomorrow for the expedition's last leg to

Claremorris and then I'm off to Galway for a ship home.'

'We'll be sorry to see you go, James, your reports helped get us the attention we needed,' the priest remarked.

'It's thanks to all of you I had something to report. And I'm not finished yet. I intend to make sure that America knows what the people here achieved. I'm certain it will prove an inspiration for countless others.'

Redpath rose, offering his hand to all and a gift of a thruppenny bit to Niamh, positively the largest amount of money she had ever held in her hand. And with that, he drove off into the night.

'I'd better be off soon myself,' said the priest. 'There's a Land League meeting down at Cong tomorrow. The tenants there are planning to start their own boycott. And then there's the fund-raising for Parnell's defence. The work goes on.'

'I wish I could help, Father,' said Owen, his despondency returning. 'But with the loss of the horse, it's going to take all our time and effort just to survive the winter.'

The priest nodded and patted his friend on the arm. 'I understand, Owen, if there's anything I can do–'

'Why can't we borrow Uncle Thomas's horse?'

Four heads turned to look at Niamh, sitting on the floor by the hearth, gleefully shining her thruppence with her sleeve.

Síomha whispered a reply. 'Your Uncle Thomas has gone away, Niamh, I told you that.'

The child looked up with excited eyes. 'But I saw him today! And he had his beautiful black horse with him. I'm sure he'd lend us his horse for a little while.'

Owen looked at the priest, then turned on his stool to face her. 'Niamh, where did you see Thomas?'

'On my way to school.'

'Did he speak to you?'

She shook her head, a hint of concern on her face as she looked at the adults' grim expressions.

'Where was he, Niamh?' Síomha asked.

'I went to the Holy Well to say a prayer for Anu. He was there with Mr McGurk.'

'McGurk? Did they see you?' Owen asked with rising trepidation.

Again she shook her head. 'No. They were looking towards the road. I was behind them. They had those things for looking far away, bin…bin…'

'Binoculars?' Fr O'Malley asked.

'Yes, them. What's wrong, Dad?'

Owen sat with his back to the table, staring absently across the room, and as the seconds passed he grew ashen-faced.

'You don't think…' The priest's question hung unfinished in the air.

'Owen? What?' Síomha asked.

He rose slowly. 'Father. Boycott's leaving when, exactly?'

'Tomorrow. Early. That's all I know.'

'Daddy, did I do something wrong?' Niamh asked.

'No, petal. Tadhg. Get your coat and your sister's. And some blankets.'

'Why?'

'Owen, what are you talking about?' Síomha asked.

'Tadhg,' he said with deliberate firmness, 'do as I say and take Niamh into the bedroom now!'

The youth grunted in annoyance and took Niamh from the room.

Owen turned to the others. 'They're going to kill Boycott, I'm certain of it. And everything we've done will have been for nothing. Worse, the army will be back and this time they'll be using their guns every time they hear a twig snap.'

'How can you be certain, Owen?' Síomha asked, trembling as she spoke.

'They knew Boycott wasn't leaving today. McGurk's been swearing vengeance since the day his wife died. Thomas said he'd get around to killing Boycott sooner or later and if I know one thing about Thomas, he'll keep his promise. We should have seen this coming. Why did the trouble suddenly stop? Because they were waiting for the right moment – the army gone, Boycott on the open road with just a handful of soldiers. The road that runs right below the rise where Niamh saw them.'

'But you can't be sure of–'

'Why the hell else were they up there?' he almost shouted.

'Owen's right,' Fr O'Malley said. 'Dear God. And they'll blame us. They'll blame the Land League and everyone associated with it. And Parnell's trial next month…it'll be the end of him.'

'And the Land League. And all the other boycotts. The British will introduce coercion and anyone who looks cross-eyed at a landlord will be arrested. Thomas and the others, they'll get the war they wanted.'

The priest rose sharply. 'What do we do? Tell the police?'

Tadhg and Niamh entered dressed in their coats, each carrying a blanket and looking concerned at the frantic voices.

'We can't, Father.' A glance in the direction of his children expanded on his reasoning. His brother's threat echoed in his mind. He didn't truly believe that Thomas was capable of murdering children, especially his own blood, but he knew without doubt that he had associates capable of anything. And besides, it wasn't a chance he was prepared to take. 'And even if the RIC stopped them, news of the attempt would be almost as bad. It could destroy everything.' He paused a moment. 'I'll have to stop them.'

'No!' Síomha screamed.

'Mammy!' Niamh started to cry.

'I have to! And you're going to the church in Neale, you'll be safe there with Fr O'Malley.'

Síomha grabbed at the collars of his shirt and shook him. 'You can't! You're not even armed! What is God's name can you do? They're killers, these people. You're a fuckin' farmer!'

'Dad! What's going on?' Tadhg yelled.

Owen clamped his hands on his wife's wrists and prised her fingers free of his shirt, then looked into her face, glistening with the flood of tears.

'*I have to*, Síomha,' he whispered.

'No you don't,' she sobbed. 'You can't solve all the world's problems. It's someone else's turn, for God's sake.'

Owen let her go and turned away to the children. He hugged them both tightly and looked at his son. 'Tadhg, go now with Fr O'Malley. I need you to look after your sister and mother.'

'Where are you going?'

'To see Thomas. There are things we need to have out. Do you understand?'

Tadhg shook his head. 'No,' he said, but dutifully took his sister's hand and walked towards the door.

'Be careful, Owen,' the priest said and shook his hand.

'You too, Father.'

Left alone with Síomha he turned away to fetch her coat, but she pursued him into their bedroom.

'The sooner you go the better. I don't have much time.'

'Tell me again why you have to go!'

He faced her again. 'It's bad enough if Boycott is murdered, but if it's done by my own brother's hand, it's a thousand times worse.'

'Tell the police! Send them a message. Thomas won't know it was us. With any luck they'll kill your damned brother in the process!'

'Don't say that!' he shouted.

'That's it, isn't it? That's why you really won't tell the police. You don't want them to kill your precious brother! Even after what he did? After what he threatened?'

Owen shoved her coat against her roughly. 'It's not just that. I *am* afraid for you and the children. But there's something else...'

'What?'

'Thomas said I'd as much guilt on my shoulders as him. There are things I don't...' Owen shook his head. 'I need to know what he meant.'

He began to pull her back towards the front door by the arm.

'What exactly do you think you're going to do?' she cried.

He pulled opened the door and looked out at the others huddled on the priest's car.

'I honestly don't know,' he said. 'Please go, Síomha. I love you very much.' He pulled her close and kissed her softly, then gently ushered her towards the car.

'Owen. Please come back to me,' she sobbed and turned reluctantly away.

He watched as the car trundled up the boreen, four white faces against the black of night staring back at him in the yard. And then they were gone.

Owen was left alone in the darkness and experienced a momentary bridge across time to an indistinct memory. His brother's face lit by the fading embers of a campfire, a small hollow in a mountainside, the icy chill of a winter's night, their last morsels of food. But the flash left him only with questions. It was like an itch in his mind that he couldn't quite reach. He snapped from the reverie and hurried back inside, his own troubles discarded.

His troubles, after all, were mere trifles compared to Boycott's.

CHAPTER 36

BY SPECIAL CALOGRAMS – A national manifesto has been issued by the Irish Land League, calling upon the people to remain firm in their passive resistance to the tyranny of landlords such as Captain Boycott, but to refrain from overt acts of aggression, which would enable the British Government, by a display of military power, to crush the movement. The command given is 'Let the British display their despotism unheeded.'

–*The Southland Times*, New Zealand, 24 November 1880

THE EXTENSION OF BOYCOTTISM – The Irish Land League is extending the methods applied to Captain Boycott in such a way as to revolutionize society. Local attorneys who had been serving processes on behalf of their landlord clients have been called to account by agents of the League, and threatened that unless they abandon all such business they will be ostracized.

–*Sacramento Daily Union*, California, 26 November 1880

A correspondent reports that the Ulstermen left Lough Mask yesterday under a strong escort. There was no demonstration. The Hussars remained to protect Mr Boycott, who will leave on Saturday morning.

–*The New York Times*, 27 November 1880

27 NOVEMBER 1880

Five minutes of pacing the room, frantic in his thinking, like a caged animal desperate for a means of escape, and yet he could formulate no coherent plan. He was arrogant in his presumption that he had the wherewithal to intervene in his brother's malevolent designs. What in Christ's name could he do? Where to start, even?

Suddenly it dawned. There existed a solitary link from their world to his: Martin McGurk, his fellow tenant. He pulled on his jacket and was about to depart when he realised he was completely unarmed and heading into an unknown situation. All he had in terms of weapons were his farm implements, which were mostly too large and cumbersome to be of any use, although he did possess a sharp knife which he used for cutting ropes and the like. He rummaged in a wooden toolbox and produced the sheathed knife, removing it and holding it up before his eyes. In reality he didn't think he could bring himself to plunge a blade into another man's flesh, and he was about to throw the weapon down when it occurred to him that the knife might be of some use in terms of its threat value. He weighed it up in his mind a few seconds longer, then pushed the sheathed blade into the inside pocket of his jacket and ran out into the night.

McGurk's house was just off the road that ran past Lough Mask Estate. Owen trotted along the muddy trail as quickly as he could, but found his age and the squelching ground fighting against him, so that every fifty yards he had to pause for breath. The night sky was almost cloudless, stars beyond measure and a half-moon lighting his way a little, yet he stumbled ten times before reaching the short track that led up to McGurk's cottage. If the sky remained this clear, Boycott's departure in the early hours would be a frosty one in every sense.

He decided not to approach the house directly, but instead scrambled over a wall into a field and crept as silently as he could, bent low, towards the side of the cottage. A few low bushes afforded him some shelter from the curious eyes of anyone who might gaze out through the windows. He peered through a gap in the prickly shrubs.

The cottage seemed quiet, although a dim light glowed from one window and smoke drifted from the chimney. He wasn't sure what he intended to do now that he was here. He couldn't simply march up to the front door, ask if his brother was there and then try to talk him out of his plan. At best they'd knock him unconscious until their work was done. More likely they'd leave no witnesses.

Perhaps this entire thing was nonsense. For all he knew, McGurk was sitting quietly in there reflecting on his recent tragedy. He only had a child's word as evidence that his brother was with McGurk. Perhaps she'd mistaken some other man for Thomas.

Owen pulled back and knelt there, pondering the situation. He realised he was trying to invent an escape clause for himself, hankering for a scenario that had an altogether happier ending. But he knew in his heart he was right. If he didn't somehow intervene, disaster would surely follow.

Five minutes later he had scrambled through a tangle of undergrowth and emerged at the rear of the cottage. He lay flat on the cold ground and peered over a rock. Four saddled horses stood side by side, tied to a post at the windowless rear wall. They stood motionless, almost like equestrian statues, but possibly sensing his presence, one of them raised its head and snorted. He drew back sharply and listened, but all remained silent.

Yet here was the confirmation of his fears. Four horses, saddled and ready to leave at a moment's notice, waiting to convey their masters towards their dark purpose.

Four men. What on earth could he do? Armed only with a knife, he had absolutely no chance of stopping them. But he realised that that was a problem he could rectify: Joe Gaughan had a gun.

***

Boycott wasn't due to leave until dawn, which was hours away, yet it occurred to Owen that the sooner he intervened the better, as Holy Well, where Niamh had spotted Thomas, was likely just one potential place of ambush they might have scouted. Besides, he couldn't be certain of Thomas and his comrades' plans and, for whatever reason, they might abandon McGurk's cottage at any moment, so the sooner he got back there the better. He had a vague notion of using the gun to pin them inside or perhaps scattering their horses into the night. Either was a huge risk, but he didn't see he had any choice.

Fifteen minutes later Owen was still running along the main road that skirted Lough Mask Estate on his way to Joe's. He was breathless, his heart pounding, and he came to a gasping halt, planting his hands on the estate wall. He couldn't escape the irony that he'd spent so long striving to bring about Boycott's downfall and now here he was, stumbling about in the dead of night trying desperately to save the man's life.

'Don't move!' came a voice from behind him.

'Back away from the wall,' a second voice shouted in a Kerry accent.

Startled, he turned and saw two figures standing twenty feet away, handguns levelled in his direction. He groaned and stepped back from the wall. The men approached cautiously and he recognised the familiar flattened shape of their RIC caps.

'What are ye doin' here in the middle of the night, eh?'

'Looked like he was goin' to climb over the wall into the estate.'

'I was just resting there, catching my breath,' Owen offered in explanation, but this simply prompted further suspicion.

'Sure ye were.'

Suddenly they were on him, the Kerryman seizing his arms and pinning them behind his back while the other stood facing him, grabbing a handful of his hair and forcing his head up, using his free hand to search Owen's jacket. 'So where were ye in such a hurry to at this time of night?' The man searching him asked, his face so close Owen could smell cigarettes on his breath. The constable's hand inevitably fell on the knife in his inside pocket. 'What the fuck is this?'

'It's not what you think, it's–' Before he could finish, the Kerryman drew his truncheon and delivered a fierce blow to Owen's temple. A buzz exploded in his head as he fell to his knees, though he remained semi-conscious. He was aware of being hauled to his feet and dragged along for what seemed like an eternity, until finally he glimpsed a dim light and found himself pushed through a doorway and then shoved roughly into a chair. An icy splash of water startled him fully awake and he saw the unfamiliar faces of four constables gathered around him in a semi-circle. He groaned and reached a hand up to massage his head.

'Who are ye? What's yer name?' one of them yelled.

He was in some kind of hut with thin mattresses spread out on the floor at one end and a few chairs at the other. They'd sat him in a corner, the door at least fifteen feet away. The chances of making a rush for it were next to naught.

One of the constables slapped him hard across the face.

'Who are ye, I asked? Ye fuckin' deaf? What are ye doin' climbin' over Captain Boycott's wall armed with a knife?'

Owen blinked and tried to clear his thoughts. 'Owen Joyce. I'm a tenant.'

One of the others bent down and studied Owen closely in the dim lamplight. 'Yeah, I know him. You're one of the troublemakers, aren't ye?'

'Joyce, eh? Answer the question. Why were trying te get into the estate in the middle of the night armed with a knife? Ye Fenian bastard!'

His interrogator kicked out at his shin and sent a biting pain coursing up through the bone. Owen yelled and clasped at the injury with both hands.

'Ye were planning to kill Captain Boycott, weren't you? Thought all the army and police were gone. Stupid fucker!'

One of the others restrained him just as the man raised his fist. 'No Mick, stop! He's no use unconscious.'

'Listen please. The knife was in my jacket all day. I use it about the farm. My horse was injured badly during the storm and I was going to borrow a shotgun from Joe Gaughan to put it down. I couldn't leave the animal like that all night. That's where I was going when you saw me. I'm telling the truth!' Owen lied. 'And besides, Boycott's already gone, isn't he?'

'Quit the act. You should be in the Theatre Royal in Dublin with that act,' the Kerryman sniggered.

'What do we do with him?'

'Keep him here until they're gone, then take him to Ballinrobe. Right, let's tie him.'

Owen had to think quickly. 'Wait! Wait, listen! I know Mr Weekes. He'll tell you I'm just a tenant. He visited my wife and me in our cottage just a few weeks ago. I'm no Fenian. I swear!'

This seemed to give them pause.

'Just ask him!'

'He'll be asleep. It's one in the morning,' his principal interrogator said.

'I think they're still clearing out the house,' the other offered, earning him a frown from his colleague, who clearly wasn't too inclined to make the effort.

'Please! He'll vouch for me!'

One of the constables turned to the others and Owen heard him whisper, 'What if he's telling the truth?' They muttered among themselves until, with a wearisome sigh, one finally agreed to go to the house and report the capture of a possible 'Fenian assassin'. Owen sat under their gaze for over an hour before the man returned, by which time he was beginning to panic. Dawn was only a couple of hours distant and Boycott would undoubtedly be departing soon.

'We're te bring him to the house.'

A gun at his head, he was hauled through the trees past the ominous shape of the ruins of Lough Mask Castle towards the lighted windows of Boycott's home. A cart stood outside and two Hussars were busy loading trunks on to it. The last time he'd been inside the house, he remembered, was the very day they'd begun the boycott.

He was dragged into the drawing room, where the huge window had been boarded up. They sat him in a chair and another ten agonising minutes passed before the door opened and Weekes entered.

'Weekes, will you please tell these constables that I'm just a farmer? They think I'm some sort of assassin, for God's sake. You know I'm no killer!' Owen pleaded.

Weekes walked towards him and looked down. Constables took up positions either side of him. A third guarded the door.

'I don't know anything of the sort.'

'What are you talking about?'

'You've done everything in your power to bring Charles to ruin. Why would you not go a step further?'

Owen tried to rise but was quickly forced down by the constables.

'Weekes, whatever our differences, you know I wouldn't do that!'

'You are a peasant, Joyce. How could you possibly imagine that I might know anything of your motives?'

'Weekes. Listen. Don't try to exact petty revenge!'

'Petty revenge?' Weekes chuckled and turned away towards the door. 'It's nothing to do with revenge, Joyce. It's simply a matter of natural justice. Goodbye.'

Owen struggled to rise but was wrestled down by his guards. 'You sat in my home, Weekes. You came to me with an olive branch, remember? Would you have done that if you believed I was a terrorist? And what might have happened to young William if I hadn't intervened? Is this how you repay me? What sort of a man are you?'

Weekes had paused at Owen's outburst, but didn't turn or offer any response. The constable pulled open the door for him and he stepped out into the hallway.

'Boycott! Get me Captain Boycott, Weekes! Maybe he's more of a man than you are after all,' Owen almost shouted in his desperation.

Owen saw Weekes pause again for the briefest of moments, then the constable pushed the door shut and he was alone again with his guards.

Minutes ticked by. Owen looked around in search of a clock but the room was bare of adornments. Besides a bureau and some chairs, everything was gone. The walls bore the outlines of the hanging place of paintings, the mantel was empty of ornament, even the rugs were absent. Soon all trace of Boycott's presence at Lough Mask would have been erased. And unless he found a way out of this, Boycott's very existence might also be erased.

Another constable entered. 'We're te take him back to the hut. Waste of time, this.'

'No! Listen, get me Boycott, let me talk to him!'

They ignored him and hauled him to his feet under gunpoint. He was beginning to despair when the land agent entered the room and strode across to Owen, his cane tapping the floor.

'You!' he sneered.

Owen tried to calm himself. He'd been pondering the very real possibility that he would be left with no option but to tell the truth. This was likely to be his last chance to extract himself from the mess.

'Boycott. Listen to me. I had no intention of coming near you or harming you. That would go against everything we've been doing. I was on my way to borrow a shotgun to put down my horse, like I told the constables.'

Boycott laughed. 'You must take us for fools, Joyce. What happened, were you perhaps ploughing your fields by starlight when your horse broke its leg? It's of no consequence anyway. To be perfectly honest, I'm grateful to you. You've presented me with the opportunity to repay you and your priest for what you've done. I'm sure O'Malley will enjoy visiting you in prison. Thank you again for such a fine parting gift. It will considerably lighten the load of my family's journey.'

Owen closed his eyes for a moment. Events had just taken an even darker turn. 'Your family's still here?'

'Farewell, Joyce,' was Boycott's only reply.

'Whatever you do to me, Boycott, I beg you to send someone to check my story. Or are you the sort of man who'd leave a horse to a slow, agonising death?'

[illegible] He grunted, looked fleetingly at Owen, then turn[illegible] man to his cottage. If he's telling the truth, finish off the animal. In the meantime, get this peasant out of my house.'

***

Another hour passed, in which time Owen was transferred back to the hut and tied securely to a chair. Through the hut's small window, he could just identify the first, faint hints of the dawn. Whatever was going to happen, it would be very soon.

The door opened and a constable entered with Asheton Weekes.

'Your horse was already dead,' the Englishman said.

For a moment Owen believed they'd realised his subterfuge.

Then the constable said: 'I found her behind the cottage. Must have died while ye were here.'

Owen feigned relief, then looked up at them. 'I was telling the truth. Untie me!'

'Forget it. You're off to Ballinrobe Gaol,' one of the others said through a smirk.

'What? You know I'm innocent!' Owen began to struggle at his bonds and one of the constables slapped his head.

'Stop it!' Weekes shouted. 'Release him.'

'What? But Captain Boycott said we–'

'Release him now or I'll inform your commanding officer that you're conspiring to frame an innocent man. Do it now!'

After much discontented muttering, the bonds were cut.

'Whatever differences we've had, Joyce, I believe you to be an honourable man. And I don't wish to tarnish my own sense of honour with a cheap act of vengeance. You may leave. I doubt we'll ever see each other again. Goodbye once more, Joyce.'

Owen nodded at him. 'Goodbye, Weekes. And thanks.'

***

Joe Gaughan was alone in his virtually roofless cottage. Most of the thatch had been torn away by the storm and he'd worked until well after dark effecting repairs, but it would take weeks to return the cottage to its former state.

He'd sent his family to stay with his wife's sister and now lay huddled in the ruin under a sheet of ragged canvas that had landed in his fields the previous night. The former British Army property served as an improvised tent to keep the chill away, allowing him to remain, look after his few possessions and to keep scavenging animals from rummaging after his stores of food and seed. One of those possessions was a single-barrelled, breech-loading shotgun manufactured by W. Richards of Liverpool. It was at least forty years old, a bequest from his father, yet it was maintained in pristine condition. The gun now lay cradled in his arms.

But the predator he could hear stalking his homestead now was no fox, and no visitors came calling at such an ungodly hour. Only scavengers of the human kind. His cottage would be easy prey. Or so they thought. He quietly rose and pushed back the canvas, then crept through the darkness towards the remains of his front door, which lay at an angle, barely supported by one hinge. The man stood in the centre of his yard, bent over, hand on his knees, as though studying something he'd spotted in the mud. He braced the shotgun against his shoulder.

'Don't move an inch.'

The man ignored him and stood erect. Joe's finger instinctively tightened on the trigger.

'Joe! Thank Christ! I thought there was no one here.'

'Owen?'

'Yeah. It's me. My God. Your roof.'

Joe lowered the gun and hurried out. Owen was still catching his breath.

'The storm took it like a leaf. What's going on? Have ye been running?'

Owen took a step forward. 'Joe, I need to borrow that.'

Joe looked down at the weapon and then at Owen's dark form.

'The gun? What for?'

'My horse was injured in the storm. I thought she might be all right, but... I'll have to put her down.'

The big farmer nodded. 'Fair enough. I'll come with ye and do it. It's not so easy te kill yer own animal.'

Owen placed a restraining hand on Joe's arm. 'No, Joe. I'd prefer to do it myself.'

Joe nodded slowly. 'Fine. Here.'

As Owen's hands closed about the cold metal, he looked directly into Joe's face.

'Have you any more shells?' he whispered.

His neighbour didn't answer for several seconds.

'More shells? I know ye're a lousy shot, but even you couldn't miss a fuckin' horse at six inches. What in Christ is goin' on?'

'I need more shells, Joe.'

'Owen, are ye in trouble?'

'Will you please give me the damn shells?'

After a moment's hesitation, Joe turned away towards the cottage. He returned a few minutes later with two shells.

'That's all I have. We've been friends for years, Owen. Please tell me what's goin' on.'

Owen shook his head. 'I can't, Joe. I have to go. Thanks for the gun. I appreciate it.' He began to walk away through the debris scattered about the yard.

'Owen. Whatever it is, let me help. You've helped me enough in the past.'

'Thanks, Joe. But this is my business. I have to take care of it.' He paused near the laneway. 'There's one thing. If anything happens, do whatever you can for my family.'

'You know I will, but I don't like the sound of–'

But his words went unheard, for Owen had already fled into the fading darkness.

***

The first slivers of dawn's light speared the sky behind them to the east as the four men secured their horses in a copse of trees. Thomas emerged from the tree cover and looked around to make sure that their arrival had gone unnoticed, but at this early hour not even the industrious farmers of Mayo had stirred from their beds. The only thing of note he could see nearby was an ancient, moss-covered well. He turned back towards the west, which afforded him a dim view of Lough Mask, and below the rise, not fifty yards distant, lay the road along which Boycott's entourage would travel.

'Where's best?' Doherty asked.

Thomas led them towards the front of the copse of fir trees. 'Here,' he said, pointing to the road a short distance away. 'We can stay inside the tree line and there's a perfect view of a hundred yards of road. We can be on the horses and away without them even getting a glimpse of us.'

'Perfect. You happy, Bull?'

Walsh simply nodded, then began to check his rifle. McGurk brushed roughly past Doherty, irked that his opinion wasn't requested.

'Right, then,' Doherty said. 'Now all we need is Boycott.'

***

Weekes looked at the twenty mounted Hussars, who were attempting to align their horses into formation. In their dark, full-length winter great-coats and cylindrical shako hats, armed with rifles, handguns and swords, they appeared to him quite a threatening force, deterrent enough for any would-be attacker. Two horses had been hitched to the baggage cart and behind it stood the ambulance car, driven by four animals, the driver also a Hussar. The car could carry eight people and was covered in a tall curve of sturdy canvas. It bore the sign of a red cross within a circle on either side.

He looked in and saw that Miss Reynolds, the maid, had already boarded. Beside her sat William, looking a little sad but upholding the family tradition of keeping his head held high. Weekes smiled in at them and looked up at the house to see Annie emerging arm in arm with Madeleine. Finally Charles appeared, stopped on the top step and stared back into the empty hallway, his shoulders slumped. He pulled the key from his pocket and massaged it absently between his thumb and forefinger, then after a moment he grunted something incoherent and pulled the door shut. He locked it, then turned to see Annie and Weekes standing stock-still staring up at him.

'What the deuce are you waiting for? Let's be gone!'

He hurried down the steps, forcing himself to walk erect, head high, his strides long and deliberate. He took Annie's arm and helped her into the ambulance where she took a seat beside Madeleine. Weekes climbed in and sat to the rear, then Boycott entered last, sitting opposite him. One of the local magistrates, Mr Hamilton, who had been given official charge of the final departure, appeared on horseback.

'Well, Captain, if we're all ready, shall we proceed?'

Boycott nodded, a shout went up and the ambulance driver flicked the reins. Everyone rocked back and forth at the initial jerk of the vehicle. Madeleine blurted a brief sob, her previously expressed dislike of the place seemingly forgotten. Annie exhaled a long, trembling sigh as she looked back at her home. Her husband glanced sideways at her, placed his hand on her arm and squeezed.

Lough Mask House disappeared from view as they rounded a corner.

'That's that,' was Boycott's only valediction.

He reached up and pulled at the string to release the canvas flaps, which fell like stage curtains at the conclusion of a drama.

***

Killing a man was easy if you knew how, Thomas considered, as he lay on the dewy ground beneath the cover of the fir trees. Not in terms of which gun to use or where to plunge a knife, but in the sense of overcoming the burden of morality which society had inflicted on humanity. He simply had to remind himself of the lesson he'd learnt in his youth that morality was a façade, a contrivance of the powerful. Man's true nature was to be found in the battle for survival. The only moral was that the victor wrote the rules. Men discover this truism often in times of war, when human society's scabbed face is revealed and a selective morality adopted for expediency's sake. Where were the cries of 'thou shalt not kill' from the priests and politicians then, when war served their narrow ends? Were not the commandments absolute? It made a farce of the slavish observance of Christianity. And because he knew these things, he also knew he would have no hesitation pulling the trigger when the moment came.

The trees above him stood in conical stillness in the placid morning air. He trained his rifle from left to right from the point where the road appeared around a bend to where it disappeared behind a clump of bushes. It would take them a good minute to traverse the distance, an eternity in which to fire a shot, in which to end a man's life.

That he might also have to kill women and children had troubled him. But experience told him that it was just the old conditioning reasserting itself, the phoney ethics of those who, laughingly, described themselves as civilised men. Luckily he could see through that as easily as one could see through water, although ripples sometimes distorted his view. To do what he had to do was merely a question of detaching himself, removing himself in mind and spirit to a place where brute instinct took charge.

He looked to his left. Next to him was Bull Walsh, a man who appeared permanently detached. He liked Walsh, although he knew the man's brooding silence unnerved the others. But he seemed to have achieved what Thomas often longed for, a life uncluttered by false dogmas or scruples. He reminded him of the machines he'd seen in factories in America. You put something in one end, it did its job and produced the desired result at the other. It operated without pause and didn't require any inducements or cajoling. Still, he supposed, to achieve Walsh's state must have required the experience of some terrible trauma, combined with a life of isolation, removed from human kind.

Not a thing Thomas could easily contemplate.

Beyond Walsh lay Martin McGurk, the youngest of the four assassins. His motivation was revenge, pure and simple, and within this extremist Fenian cabal he'd found a convenient cause on which he could piggyback his hatred. Yet he seemed now to be filling the moments of anticipation with prayer, blessing himself often, lips moving in rapid, silent entreaties to his God or his dead wife. He wondered, when the moment arrived, would McGurk would be capable of pulling the trigger?

He looked the other way, past the trunk of a tree, where Doherty was lying, rifle at the ready. Doherty was a good man in many respects: he was decisive, he could think strategically and follow orders without question. But what bothered Thomas was that, in truth, he believed Doherty to be slightly insane. Or could one be *slightly* insane? Maybe no more than a girl could be slightly pregnant. He didn't howl at the moon or anything like that. It was just the look that appeared in his eyes on occasion, a lascivious anticipation of killing. Perhaps you needed to be insane to do the job he did.

'Here they come,' Doherty whispered as Thomas watched him. He turned his head and saw the first of the Hussars round the corner.

'Nobody fires until I give the order, got that?' Doherty said.

Thomas tightened his grip on the rifle. It was time to detach himself.

***

Owen felt as if his heart was going to explode. He pushed his hand inside his jacket and clutched at it through his shirt, fingers digging into his flesh as though he was trying to wrench it from his chest. He was on his knees, heaving huge breaths, sweat coating his face like an oily balm. In order to approach them unseen it had been necessary to skirt their position, but that had required over a mile of brutal exertion and he was no longer a young man. Although his daily labours had rendered him reasonably fit, the reality was that age had ambushed him as surely as Thomas planned to ambush Boycott. He grabbed the gun from the ground and rose. Should he have to fire, he prayed it would not be at his own brother.

The sound of tramping horses turned his head and across the fields he could identify the hats and plumes of the 19th Hussars bobbing above the bushes that lined the road. In minutes they would pass close to the rise near Holy Well and carnage would ensue. He looked ahead and saw that he still had almost a quarter of a mile to cover before he could reach the trees where Thomas and the others were most likely hidden. He had the sudden calamitous realisation that he had failed. Crossing the space between him and his brother in time was an impossibility, pure and simple.

'Jesus Christ!' he cried and began to run.

***

The road below angled away from the four assassins slightly, affording them a partial view of the rear of the ambulance car. In front and behind it rode ten Hussars, another driving the car. A cart laden with trunks followed at the rear. A civilian rode beside the leading Hussars, but they quickly realised it wasn't Boycott.

'The fuckin' red cross is like a target te aim for,' Doherty whispered with a chuckle. 'Anyone got a view of Boycott?'

McGurk shook his head. 'The flaps are down. He could be anywhere inside.'

'He's probably near the back,' Thomas said.

'Fuck. Well, there's nothing for it. We take the lot of them,' Doherty said. 'By the time we've done shootin', the canvas will look like a colander. Chances are we'll hit the bastard. Remember, I'll take one of the horses upfront. McGurk, you go for the troops. You all know what you have to do. This is it. Everyone, on my word.'

***

Hamilton, the magistrate, was a little startled at the sight of a girl running towards them through the pale morning light, her skirts covered in mud. She appeared frantic and red-faced and carried a small valise, which bounced and bobbed against her legs as she stumbled along the muddy track. Her free hand clung at her bonnet, which threatened to become dislodged at every step.

'Captain,' he said to the officer leading the troop, 'what's this?'

The captain, who had been busily surveying the surrounding fields, turned and saw the running figure, causing him to instinctively smack a hand against the butt of his pistol.

'Stop! Stop! Wait!' the girl cried out.

The captain raised his arm and yelled an order to halt. The girl staggered along the final few yards until she stood gasping, staring up at them over the horses' heads.

'Who are you? What do you want?' the captain snapped.

The girl gulped a couple of more breaths before finding the strength to reply, which came as a desperate, sobbing plea. 'Me name is Maggie Cusack. I'm the Boycotts' maid. I want te go with them!'

***

'Hold it!' Thomas hissed at the others. 'They're stopping.'

'What the fuck? I don't believe it,' Doherty whispered. 'Right where we want them. But what's going on?'

They watched as a girl appeared from the direction of Ballinrobe. She began to converse with the troops.

'Do we do it now?' McGurk asked with a trembling whisper.

'Let's see what happens. We might get a shot at Boycott. Be better in the press if we just kill *him*,' Doherty replied. 'Everyone wait.'

One of the Hussars dismounted and conducted the girl by the arm towards the ambulance. They could see one of the flaps being partially drawn back and there seemed to be a lot of talk.

'Have you a shot? Bull? Thomas?'

'Not yet.'

'Not for certain.'

***

'Mr Boycott, Mrs Annie, please let me come with ye! Ye're all I have since me Mam died years ago. Only one brother left and he's an oul' drunk. I've no one here. I'm all alone. I don't care if ye're going to England. I want te come. Ye know I'm a good maid, I'm a hard worker and I promise I won't let ye down,' Maggie tripped frantically through all of this in a wash of tears.

'Out of the question,' Boycott said. 'You should have thought of that when you abandoned us for those Land League scoundrels.'

'But I was afraid! I didn't know what else te do, Mr Boycott!'

'Charles! Stop it,' snapped Annie. 'I've had enough of this…this recrimination. Look at her, for heaven's sake. You can't take revenge on an innocent girl. I would have thought you'd have had enough of that!'

Boycott looked around at her and frowned.

'Sir, I'm uncomfortable stopped out in the open here,' the watching captain said sharply. 'I'd like to get moving at your very earliest convenience, sir.'

Boycott heaved a sigh of resignation. 'Oh very well. But you'll be on your best behaviour from now on.'

'Oh thank ye, sir, thank ye!'

He pulled back the flap and began to climb down to allow Maggie to pass. He stood on the track and helped her inside, where she immediately embraced Annie and continued to babble her thanks.

'Just be quiet, girl! And stop that deuced bawling!' he barked.

***

'Christ, that's him!' Doherty almost shouted. 'Thomas! Bull! Take him now!'

Thomas drew the sight up and fixed it very slightly to Boycott's left side, knowing the barely perceptible breeze from the lough would carry it all the way to the land agent's heart. He curled his finger around the trigger and began to squeeze.

'Nobody move! Drop the guns – now!'

The voice came from behind them and Thomas recognised it the instant the first word had been spoken. He eased the pressure off the trigger and looked over his shoulder.

'What the fuck?' Doherty cried out.

Bull Walsh lowered his gun. McGurk almost threw his away as though it was hot.

'Owen, brother,' Thomas said calmly, rolling over and sitting up.

'What the fuck are *you* doing here?' Doherty snapped.

'Throw the guns over here. Now!'

'Jesus, the state of ye,' Thomas said, coming to his feet. Owen's face was bright red, his hair wild, his face and neck coated with sweat. His clothes were mud-spattered and torn from brambles. His breathing was laboured, his hands shaking as they struggled to maintain the shotgun level. It was in this final observation that Thomas saw the chink of hope.

'I said throw the guns over or I swear to Christ I'll pull the trigger. At this range, I'll take at least two of you.'

The others were standing now. They reluctantly tossed the guns towards Owen. Doherty glanced over his shoulder and saw the soldier pulling the canvas flap on the ambulance into place and preparing to depart.

'They're getting ready to leave,' he said bitterly to Thomas. McGurk and Walsh stood immobile beneath the canopy of trees.

But Thomas barely heard Doherty, for he was walking tentatively towards his brother, Owen's gun pointed squarely at his chest.

'Nice stalking. Ye got right up to us without a sound. Hold your breath, did ye?'

'A trick I must have learned from you, Thomas.'

'Yeah, but have ye learned how te pull the trigger when you're looking into a man's eyes? Even if that man's your own brother? I would, Owen, without blinking. But not you. You could no more shoot me than sprout wings and fly.'

'Don't bet on it.'

'You never made those decisions. You needed me te do it for you. It's the only reason you're standing here now.'

'What the fuck does that mean? Don't come any closer.'

But Thomas ignored him and continued to take tentative steps, just a few yards away now. He smiled. 'I want te see, Owen. I want te see in my last breath if you've finally found the guts te do what has te be done. Go ahead and shoot. Right here, my heart. You can't miss.' He tapped a finger to his breast.

'Don't make me, Thomas.'

Thomas stopped with the gun six inches from his chest. 'Listen te me, I'm goin' te tell you how te get out of this, because you're my brother. There are four rifles scattered around your feet. All repeaters, fully loaded. You can easily have one in your hands before any of these boys behind me gets within five yards of ye. Then ye can do as ye please with them – kill them, for all I care.'

'What the fuck are ye tellin' him?' Doherty snarled.

Thomas ignored him. 'There's just one problem. First ye have te kill me. Your shotgun only has one cartridge. And if ye don't use it on me, I swear te Christ I'm goin' te take it from ye and use it on you. Now. What's it to be?'

Owen trembled, as much from exhaustion as the tension and dread. He searched within himself to find the strength to do it. It was almost as if Thomas wanted him to fire, wanted some release from the life of bitterness he'd wrought for himself. He met his brother's eyes and tightened his finger, felt the huge pressure of the trigger resisting as it was squeezed back; just one more tiny morsel of effort and it would click, the spring would snap free and the hammer would explode on to the cartridge, releasing a hundred deadly pellets into his brother's heart. It just needed that last effort of will to overcome the instinct that lay in his heart, the instinct formed from memories without number of the haunted, starving faces of his family – his mother, his father – and the countless thousands of skeletal creatures who had walked the land of his youth, because within the depths of that ocean of death and suffering, he had witnessed the survival of human compassion and human dignity. To pull the trigger would rob him of his own dignity, destroy the one thing within himself that had emerged unscathed from that terrible time.

He eased the trigger back into place.

'Boycott's leavin'!' McGurk suddenly shouted.

Owen flicked his eyes in McGurk's direction and in the blink of time it took to do it, Thomas had seized the barrel of the gun and forced it skywards. He launched himself at Owen, the gun between their bodies, four hands twisting and writhing as they sought to wrench it free of the other.

'Get the fuckin' rifles!' Thomas grunted. 'Get Boycott!'

The others ran forward to seize the weapons just as Owen, his body weakened and racked with pain, felt the shotgun begin to slip from his grip. Grasping at one last desperate thought before he surrendered his grip, he yanked down on the trigger and the deafening explosion of the discharging gun resounded across the landscape.

***

The Hussars turned as one towards the sound. The captain drew his horse about towards the rise, which was topped by a small copse of fir trees.

'Probably an early morning hunter,' the magistrate said.

The captain ignored him. 'Get moving now! Quickly! Pick it up there, I want us a mile down the road in five minutes! Move, you bloody galoots!'

The horses took off at a canter. As the ambulance moved past, the captain yelled a reassurance to the Boycotts that all was well, but when the last of the Hussars approached, he ordered six of them to scout around in the direction of the shot. The six men snapped a salute, swung their animals about and leapt the roadside ditch into the field, moving at pace towards the rise.

***

'Fuck!' Doherty shouted as, from behind a tree, he watched the ambulance disappear from view, conveying Boycott beyond danger.

'Christ,' Bull Walsh added, virtually his only contribution to the day's discourse. But Doherty saw that he was pointing at something else – the six mounted Hussars spreading out as they moved across the fields towards their position. He turned back to Thomas, who now stood over his prone brother, his rifle restored to him. He ran across the space and launched a violent kick into Owen's ribs. Owen screamed and curled into a foetal position, clutching his chest. Thomas instinctively pushed Doherty away.

'What the fuck are ye doin'?' Doherty asked. 'It doesn't matter anyway. We have te get out of here fast. They're comin'. Everyone split up, meet back at McGurk's place. You take him with ye. He's your fuckin' brother. And, Joyce, he's a dead man!'

Thomas poked Owen with the rifle. 'Get up, quick.'

Owen struggled to his feet and Thomas pulled him towards the horses. He pushed Owen up to the fore of the saddle and then mounted himself as the others peeled away and galloped from the trees and from sight. Thomas pressed a pistol into Owen's side as he seized the reins with his free hand.

'Christ, Owen. What a fucking mess,' he said and jabbed the horse with his heels.

***

There were just two horses at the rear of McGurk's cottage when Thomas pulled up fifteen minutes later. He dismounted and backed away, not bothering to remove the rifle from its saddle sheath. He pointed the pistol up at his brother.

'Get down.'

'What now, Thomas?' Owen said hoarsely as he clambered down, clutching his ribs.

Thomas shook his head. 'I feel like killing ye meself. Do ye know what you've fucking done? The chance we missed? You're a misguided fool. For all your brains, you've still no idea how the world works.'

'You know who you remind me of, Thomas?'

'Who?'

'Boycott.'

Thomas gestured with the pistol. 'Around the front. Inside.'

They entered to find Walsh and McGurk, but no sign of Doherty. Both men were drinking whiskey, McGurk from the neck of the bottle, a trembling cigarette pinched between his thumb and forefinger.

'Where's Doherty?'

Bull Walsh, who was sitting on a stool behind the door, gun on his lap, shrugged. 'Didn't make it back yet.' The man seemed perfectly calm.

Thomas pushed Owen into a seat in a corner and snatched the bottle from McGurk's grip, then poured a drink and sat. McGurk sat by the hearth.

'How did he know?' Walsh asked.

Thomas looked at Owen, who made no reply, then turned to McGurk. 'Have you been blabbing your fucking mouth?'

'Don't blame me, ye bastard!' McGurk roared indignantly, his fear palpable.

'It wasn't him,' Owen said. 'You were seen scouting the spot near Holy Well. When I heard Boycott wasn't leaving until this morning, it was easy to figure out the rest.'

'Who saw us?'

'One of the tenants. Can I have a drink?'

Thomas studied his brother's face for a long interval. Then he half-turned to McGurk. 'Give him a drink and give me a cigarette.'

McGurk did as ordered. Silence descended as Owen sipped from the mug they'd given him. What he really needed more than anything was water, but the burning whiskey was a happy alternative, soothing his quivering nerves a little.

'You fool, Owen. You and your stupid boycott. You think it's going te change anything? And then ye had the chance te kill me and get clean away and ye couldn't even do that. What is it? Are ye trying to atone for the guilt you've been carrying around all your life? Is that what this is all about?'

'What guilt?'

'Don't give me that bullshit. Like I told ye before, the only reason you're here is because of me. You'd have never even reached your seventeenth birthday if I hadn't done what I did.' Thomas dragged on the cigarette.

Owen laughed mirthlessly. 'Christ, you saved my life thirty years ago. How long do you expect me to keep thanking you?'

'Oh it's more than that, Owen, and you know it. It's the way ye survived, where the food came from when ye were just a skeleton held together by skin. Ye know full well that I didn't steal it from any British Army convoy. Do ye think I'm stupid enough to try that? You chose to believe it because it suited ye. But ye knew all along really, you knew there was something...*tainted*... about the food. But it suited ye te eat it because if ye hadn't you'd have died. In fact, ye didn't bother questioning at all, because ye didn't want to hear the answer. That way ye could keep your conscience clean. Let me do the dirty work, let my soul blot up all the sins, keep your jotter spotless.'

'I honestly don't know what you're talking about,' Owen said, but knew he wasn't being entirely honest. Something rang true about what Thomas was telling him. He could recall a suspicion that something had been amiss, an unsettling sensation, like a rumble in the gut when you've eaten food that's turned. But he hadn't pressed it. He'd told himself that it would do no good, his brother would simply have rounded on him, caused a row, the last thing they'd need on that journey to Westport.

'Huh. I can see it in your face. You're betraying yourself,' Thomas laughed.

'What the fuck is this?' McGurk suddenly blurted. 'Who cares about thirty fuckin' years ago? What about thirty minutes ago? Boycott got away – or have you forgotten?'

Thomas didn't even turn his head. 'Shut up, McGurk. What's done is done. And until Doherty turns up, we wait. They're the orders. Or have you something better to do?'

McGurk didn't reply. Walsh sat in his customary silence, staring vacantly into space.

'So tell me. Tell me what happened,' Owen said.

Thomas was suddenly grim. 'It's not a story I like. There are...elements... I'm not proud of. But I did what I had te do te survive, so you'd survive, just as I'd sworn to our father I would. Are you sure ye want te hear?'

Owen didn't answer.

'Do ye remember a girl called Etain O'Casey?'

The name had a vague familiarity, but that was all. He shook his head.

'I do. I'll never forget her, even though I barely knew her. She was in school with us. Ye had a *grá* for her, if I remember right. She would have been about fourteen.'

Now his memory stirred. Dark curly hair, round face, bright; the teacher had picked her as one of the children worthy of closer attention. She'd been one of the first girls his eye had fallen upon, one of the first girls to rouse his nascent male urges. Then the famine had come and such instincts were abandoned to the more urgent ones of survival. He hadn't thought about her for thirty years. He nodded at his brother, his curiosity stirred.

'That night I went looking for food I came to a cottage on the mountain facing Oughty Hill. Inside I found a man eating meat...' he paused and exhaled a slow, tremulous breath, 'except as I found out, it wasn't mutton or beef...'

He looked directly at Owen, allowing the words to hang in the air, allowing him to complete the picture himself. Owen's lips parted slightly as the realisation dawned.

'The man, probably her father...he said he hadn't killed her, she'd died of starvation. What was left of Etain was behind a curtain, just skin and bones, couldn't have been more than a pick on her. Barely worth his trouble for all the meat he got from her.'

'Stop.'

'What? Ye think I'm enjoying this? Besides, you only have to listen, I had te witness it. Anyway, the man hanged himself, couldn't live with what he'd done. With what he'd been forced te do. I witnessed that too. So there I was, in a house of death, starving, you even worse. I thought, if Owen is to live, I've only one choice…'

Owen shook his head in denial of what he believed he was about to hear.

'They'd reduced Ireland to that, the English, the landlords. Reduced us to cannibalism,' Thomas said bitterly. 'They got everything they deserved, in my book.'

'Who? Who are you talking about?'

'You've no idea what that experience was like. Seeing that. It changed me. Forever. But it also set a lot of things straight in my head. It was the first time I saw the world as it really was. And I did what I had te do, the only thing I could do.'

'You're talking in riddles.'

'Let me explain it for ye, then.'

CHAPTER 37

I was so maddened by the sights of hunger and misery...that I wanted to take the gun from behind my door and shoot the first landlord I met.

–Reflection of Capt. Arthur Kennedy, Poor Law Inspector in County Clare, from *Sir William Francis Butler: An Autobiography*, 1848

Britain has permitted, in Ireland, a mass of poverty, disaffection, and degradation without a parallel in the world. It allowed proprietors to suck the very life-blood of that wretched race.

–*The Times*, 24 March 1847

October 1848

Thomas rose to his feet and turned to face the cottage. Through the open door the dead man's shadow moved back and forth ever so gently, accompanied by the slow creaking of the rope on the beam, like the sound of a boat on a lough surface straining on its line.

Still gripping the bloodstained knife, he walked back inside and looked at the emaciated man dangling from the roof beam, eyes popping but unseeing, mouth open, bony limbs hanging limply. He righted the stool, stepped up and cut the rope, allowing the shrivelled body to fall, the sound eerily quiet, as though he'd merely tossed a few sacks on the ground. He climbed down and closed the dead man's eyes, as if he believed that even the unseeing eyes of the dead should not bear witness to the act he was about to commit.

He turned once again towards the ragged curtain and began to take slow, faltering steps until the filthy fabric was almost pressed against his face, and there he stood, blind to the world, as his breaths deepened and grew in rapidity while he sought to steel himself for the savagery of what he must do. Finally he reached out, grasped the curtain and flung it aside, revealing once again the brutal, blood-drenched sight of Etain O'Casey's butchered corpse. He uttered a barely audible sob, but one that had been born in the darkest recesses of his soul, for its quivering timbre betrayed not just his horror, but his own self-loathing. Thomas fell to his knees and reached out towards the dead girl's dress. One leg had been completely hacked free, the other partially, and he shoved the dress upwards until what remained of her wasted upper thigh was revealed. Although her body had already been pitilessly desecrated, he still suffered a bout of shame at exposing her intimate parts; it was but another terrible sin he would have to bear, another layer of guilt.

'Oh Jesus,' Thomas uttered in a wretched whisper, as he reached out with his left hand and grasped the cold, greying flesh above the girl's knee. He tried to summon the image of his dying brother, telling himself he had to do what he was about to do, searching for any scrap of justification, until at last he tightened his grip on the girl's leg, closed his eyes tightly and plunged the knife into the wasted layer of flesh on the underside of her thigh. The sound and feel of the knife driving into the emaciated muscle was sickening, yet he persisted, daring, finally, to look at the wound he'd made, while desperately trying to keep his eyes from drifting to her face. Although she surely had died in the last day or so, very little blood seeped from the gash as it had mostly settled in the lifeless veins on the underside of her body. He twisted the knife and was aware how easily it slid through the flesh. It occurred to him that in better times this knife had probably been used by the cottier for slaughtering sheep or gutting chickens, and here now he had reduced this young girl to the level of those beasts, merely a piece of slaughtered livestock.

A ragged chunk of human flesh fell free from the girl's body, no larger than a human thumb, and he paused and stared at it, as it lay on the hard-packed mud floor, its colour a faded pink, a hint of moisture glistening on its surface, a sliver of mottled skin just visible on its underside. Once again he braced himself, gritted his teeth, briefly allowed his eyes to flicker closed a moment or two, before he reached down and picked it up. He lifted it to his face and stared at it as though he held in his grip the essence of evil, a morsel of Satan's own flesh, which when consumed would forever damn him.

He felt that madness was taking hold of him, pulling him deeper and deeper into its insidious grip, and yet he felt powerless to take any other course. An involuntary shudder passed the length of his body as he raised the flesh to his lips, and he suddenly found himself engulfed in convulsive sobbing, akin to the wails of the bereaved. But these sobs were not for the girl, or her father, or any of those who had been claimed by the famine. Thomas was grieving for the death of his own humanity.

He face washed by tears, he finally opened his mouth and pressed the piece of human flesh between his lips, slowly bringing his teeth down on the raw meat, sensing its sinewy texture as he bit through it. But it was when he perceived the first, infinitesimally tiny hint of the taste, vaguely sweet, that finally his will was broken and the enormity of what he was about to do exploded in his brain.

Thomas yanked the flesh from between his lips and emitted a howl of revulsion and rage. He flung it beyond his sight, then planted his hands on the floor and spat repeatedly until his mouth ran dry. He gagged for a full minute 'til he felt only bile rise in his throat, for his gut was empty of all else.

He sat back on his haunches, and stared up at the thatch, gasping for breath. 'God forgive me,' he sobbed, conscious that he'd questioned God's very existence just days beforehand. He'd reached a line he couldn't cross. The dead man just ten feet from him had been forced to step over that line, reduce himself to animal savagery, Thomas would not, could not. And not because of some sense of outraged morality, but because the thought was forming that if he consumed that flesh it would be an admission of defeat. The British had reduced them to this state. No one else. They'd driven his countrymen to the edge of extinction. And God alone knew how many the length and breadth of Ireland had succumbed as had those who now lay dead in this cottage. But not him. Never. Death offered a more welcome path. Or revenge. Because he suddenly realised he did have another choice.

He rose to his feet and wiped his face free of tears and spittle. 'I'm sorry,' he whispered to the lifeless remains of Etain O'Casey, before pulling down the ragged curtain and throwing it across what was left of her body. Others would have to bury her. He had work to do. He turned towards the dead man lying in the centre of the room and stared down at him.

'You're forgiven, mister,' he said aloud, then turned with purpose toward the open door.

***

Thomas set off directly down the slope through the heather. Across the valley he could still see the lights burning in the windows of Oughty House, the home of the land agent Harris and his lackey Burrell, the bastards who had been threatening to evict them. He stumbled through the dark, down the uneven ground for thirty minutes before he reached the track that ran up the centre of the valley. As he continued on, he remembered the conversation of the men he'd encountered earlier that evening. They'd been hatching a plan to do away with Harris and Burrell. He recalled thinking that they were mad, so desperate they were prepared to risk ending up at the end of an English rope. But he knew differently now. Theirs was the only way to deal with the likes of Harris. Except he was going to beat them to it.

He'd overheard the men planning to meet in two hours. There had been two of them and a youth, but he had been sent away. They intended to meet up with another man to carry out their attack. Three of them in all. And he was merely one. Barely a man himself, and so weak from the hunger he was finding it harder and harder to order his thoughts, the trek across the rough, open countryside draining his last reserves, bringing spells of dizziness, inducing pains that felt like steel pins being driven into his legs. Yet Oughty House lay just ahead, lit like a beacon, beckoning him on. It was set a little up the slope of Oughty Hill, a low, twin-capped rise of less than a thousand feet. He came to a small brook, babbling white where it tumbled over rocks just visible in the moonlight. He rested and took his fill before commencing the final struggle up the slope to what appeared to Thomas like a palatial mansion. At least an hour and a half had passed since he'd first heard the men hatching their plot and unless the hunger was playing tricks with his mind, he reasoned he had thirty minutes to beat them to the kill. As he drew nearer the building he was suddenly, strangely exhilarated at what lay in prospect, enlivened by the fear that danced in his otherwise empty gut.

And there it was just yards ahead, a structure of two floors, five windows across the top, just one of them lit now. On the ground floor were two tall windows at either side of an entrance, framed by thick stone columns. All of the downstairs windows glowed with lamplight. To the left of the main house was a less impressive building – older, moss clinging to the gaps between its stonework, with a large wooden door whose timbers had seen better days. And as he crept closer to this structure, the unmistakable odour of animals confirmed it to be, as expected, the stables.

Thomas, bent low, crouching behind walls and shrubs, moved towards the doors, then skittered across an open space and pressed his back to the wall. He waited there while his breathing receded, trying to master the welling fear in his stomach, trying to still his trembling hands. He closed his eyes for a few seconds and listened. He could hear the faint shuffling about of the animals, hear their breaths seeping through their wet nostrils, smell their beastly sweat. He could discern a faint light at the gap just below the door. Somewhere inside a lamp burned, and he could now make out the muffled sound of a man whistling. He reached inside his jacket and pulled out the knife, the same blade that had already cut through human flesh. Thomas took a deep breath and pulled gently at the door handle, felt it resist and silently cursed. The old timbers gave just a fraction of an inch, but sufficient to allow him to peek through and see that all that secured the door was a simple hook-and-loop mechanism. Unhooking the catch was simplicity itself with the aid of the knife and he was inside and pulling the door shut behind him in seconds.

He found himself between two rows of four stable boxes and could make out the forms of five horses resting in near silence, but for an occasional soft snort. He began to creep past the boxes towards the far end of the building and the whistling, which seemed formless, random notes tripping over each other. As he reached the end of the row, the structure opened out into a tall loft on two levels, the upper part reached by a ladder, and beneath that was an area littered with the tools of the farrier. Fifty horseshoes hung on nails on the walls like ornaments, wooden racks were stacked with hammers and pliers and boxes piled high with horseshoe nails. And in front of all of these, on a rickety, three-legged stool, sat the whistler. It was an old man, half-turned away from Thomas, poking at a horseshoe with a small metal tool, working away contentedly by lamplight, oblivious to the danger that inched up behind him. Thomas tried desperately to still his quivering breaths, but he need not have troubled himself, for the man's hearing was as worn as his face and even though his attacker came to within inches of his back, he revealed no awareness of his peril. It was only when the hand grasped at his head of grey hair and he saw the knife glint in the lamplight as it came towards his throat, that he gasped aloud and dropped the shoe and tool, both of which clanged against the cobbled floor.

'Who are you?' Thomas whispered urgently, staying behind the man, not revealing his face.

The old man's lower lip quivered as he tried to respond, but such was his shock that no words emerged.

'Are ye Harris's stableman?'

The man breathed rapidly, and in between his desperate gasps he managed to squawk a disjointed reply.

'Michael Crean…handyman…please don't hurt…'

'Shut up! Ye work for that English bastard, don't ye? Fuckin' traitor. Tell me who's in the house. Is Harris there? And Burrell?'

The old man produced several tiny rapid nods in reply.

'They any friends with them?'

'No, don't think–'

'Where are they? Which room? Tell me or I'll cut your throat.'

He shook his head. 'Maybe the drawing room…at front.'

A door at the other end of the stable sat a few inches ajar.

'Can I get to the house through there?'

'Yeh. Across the yard te the back of the house. Please don't hur–'

He was crying as he spoke these last words and Thomas had to fight to suppress his guilt. But he steeled himself to carry on, to see the night through. He bent and seized the horseshoe that the man had dropped and brought it down hard on his skull, sending him toppling from the stool without even a cry. He lay quite still on the cobblestones, eyes closed, lips parted as though in a contented sleep.

Thomas looked around for a gun, but could see nothing. The only thing of benefit he found was a half-eaten apple, and he devoured this greedily, almost choking as the lumps of fruit fought against his constricted gullet. A minute later and he was approaching the rear of the house, which was in darkness. The windows offered no clue to the layout, such was the depth of blackness within. The rear door was locked. He cursed and tried to conceive a means of proceeding, trying to fight the urge to flee, finding strength in the thought of exacting revenge for all the misery he'd witnessed, and the prospect of at last finding food. As he stood there, he heard the sound of a door creaking inside the house, then footsteps. Lamplight danced to and fro about the room. There was the remote sound of laughter and then a voice calling out.

'Which one did you say? Very good. Just give me a minute.'

He heard the clink of bottles and a man humming absently. As surreptitiously as he could, he bent low and crept to the window, listening, trying to gauge where the man was, and then cautiously rose and peered over the sill. It was Burrell, the land agent's subordinate, a man of about thirty, with oiled black hair and a wide, curled-up moustache. He was removing the cork from a bottle. Burrell began to turn suddenly and Thomas dropped low in a blink. He realised the time had come. He must make his play.

Towards the centre of the rear wall stood a stone water trough, about three feet high, built to catch the run-off from the slate roof. He crept to the door, rapped his fist against it, then took off and ducked behind the trough, the knife clutched tightly in his right hand. He watched from the darkness as the door creaked open a few inches.

'Hello? Crean? Is that you?'

Thomas felt about on the ground until he located a small stone, then tossed it high into the yard. It landed with a sharp crack and skittered away.

'What the devil? Crean? Hello?'

The door was pulled shut again and Thomas swore. What the hell did it take to get this bastard to come out? But as the very thought was formed, the door opened again and he watched as Burrell stepped out into the night, his right arm held high, clutching a lamp. In his left hand he held a pistol.

Thomas ducked low as the man emerged fully and looked around.

'Hello, Crean? Is there someone here?'

Burrell was about five yards away, his attention drawn for the most part towards the stable. He took another few tentative steps into the yard and stood now with his back to Thomas, holding the lamp towards the stable door, which had been left ajar. Thomas took a sharp breath, clenched his teeth, almost painfully so, stood up and darted towards Burrell. Just as the man began to turn at the sound he swung the knife in an upward arc and plunged the blade deep into Burrell's back. The Englishman's body arced and his head shot back as though he was trying to look at the night sky, a guttural bawl starting to spring from his open mouth before Thomas's hand clamped tightly across it. Burrell's lamp arm shot rigidly out to the side and the lamp went sailing across the yard, landing in a crash of flame and glass. The gun fell harmlessly at his feet as he tried desperately to claw over his shoulder at his assailant. Thomas heard a sickening gurgle and experienced the sensation of warm, sticky blood spouting from the man's mouth; in his revulsion and his desire to see the deed ended, he pulled the blade out and plunged it in again. He heard a low, choking moan and finally felt the body go limp, felt its weight transferred to his own arms as though the man was dying from his legs up. He loosened his grip and Burrell slowly slid down his body, seemed to kneel for a few seconds, like he was making a final prayer, then fell forward and landed face down with a thump.

Thomas gasped aloud and had to suppress the urge to sob. His entire body shook at the horror of the act he'd just committed, and still there was more to do. That thought brought him to action again and he looked towards the open door, certain that Harris would burst out at any moment, roused by the noise of the lamp, the remains of which sat in an eerie pool of flame in the cobbled yard. He pocketed the knife and seized the gun, then peered around the doorframe, the fading light from the burning oil allowing him to see that it was a large kitchen. The door at the far end remained closed and he could not see or hear any sign of Harris. His left hand was entirely covered in blood and he quickly wiped this in Burrell's clothing, desperate to rid himself of its repulsive stickiness.

He looked at the gun. He had little hands-on experience of guns but he knew enough to recognise it as a revolver, a weapon that could fire maybe six shots.

Thomas leaned against the doorframe and closed his eyes. He'd done it now. Stepped over the cliff edge. And no force on earth could pull him back to safety. And his task was not yet complete, for Harris was the real enemy. To truly exact some small revenge for his family's deaths, for all the evil that had befallen his country, he would have to face the land agent and take his life also. He stepped into the kitchen and moved past a table covered in food: plates of meat, bread and fruits. Incredibly at that moment, despite the starvation that racked his body, he felt no desire to reach out and seize any of it. Yet the sight did fully restore his appetite for blood, and he steeled himself.

Suddenly there was a voice on the other side of the door, drawing near, a cheery voice that called out in feigned irritation.

'Harold, dear boy, where the devil are you? Did you break another of my bottles? Well, you can damn well pay for it if–'

Harris opened the door, lamp in hand, and was met by the sight of Thomas, revolver levelled at his chest. He stopped dead, the smile melting from his lips as his eyes widened, his initial surprise turning to anger as he realised his home had been invaded.

'Who in the name of–?'

'Shut up!' Thomas snapped. 'Turn around, back the way ye came, slowly, or I swear te Christ I'll kill ye the way I killed that other bastard.'

Harris's mouth opened at the realisation that Burrell was dead, the peril of his situation dawning in an instant.

'You'll hang for this, by God!' he whispered.

'Turn around!' Thomas snarled.

The land agent did as ordered and Thomas followed him along a narrow hallway that led through an open door into a large room lit by several lamps. Two towering windows were curtained against the prying eyes of the outside world. The room was luxuriously furnished with a divan and three other single armchairs, a bureau, and a table on which rested a flower vase and a lamp. Giant paintings, portraits mostly, decorated the walls. In one wall a vast marble mantel enclosed a hearth, in which blazed a turf fire.

The man swayed on his feet a little as he crossed the room and Thomas guessed that he and Burrell had been drinking heavily, most likely after they'd stuffed their bellies to bursting.

'Put the lamp down and sit.'

Harris was in his mid-thirties, medium build, about six feet, with short fair hair, long sideburns and, like his dead friend, a handlebar moustache. His narrow-set eyes betrayed a mixture of fear and rage. The land agent sat in one of the leather-upholstered chairs and gripped the wooden arms.

Thomas allowed his eyes to wander around the room. 'Nice house. This must be what ye get for living off the backs of the starving.'

'Who are you? What do you want?'

'Who am I?' Thomas shook his head in disbelief. 'Ye spoke te me this very day and ye don't even recognise me. We're nothing te ye, are we? Ye don't even see us as humans.'

A glimmer of recognition flicked across Harris's face. 'Joyce? From Tawnyard?'

'That's right. Michael Joyce was my father. He's dead. Left te starve te death like most of the rest of my family. Murdered by you.'

Thomas moved closer, just two yards away now, staring down the slope of his arm past the gun at the land agent's eyes. Harris made no response, his grip on the chair arms so tight that his knuckles were bone white.

'Have ye nothing te say, ye murdering dog?' Thomas snarled.

The fear abruptly vanished from Harris's eyes to be replaced by defiance. He replied through gritted teeth. 'All I have to say to you is go to hell.'

Thomas calmly took a step backwards. He dipped the gun and pointed it at Harris's gut.

'This is for my father,' he whispered and pulled the trigger.

The bullet ripped into Harris's stomach and the land agent immediately started to convulse, hands clutching at the wound, legs flailing wildly like he was doing some crazed dance, his entire body writhing as his agonised screams echoed about the house. Blood spouted between his fingers and sprayed wildly in every direction and his eyes strained wider than Thomas had imagined possible.

'Oh holy Jesus!' Thomas cried out.

The grotesque spectacle refused to end and, desperate for release, he levelled the gun at the thrashing figure and pulled the trigger again, this time hitting the land agent in the head, all but erasing the upper half of his face. The writhing stopped abruptly and Harris fell dead, sliding downwards and flopping to the floor, his upturned head coming to rest on the bloodied upholstery.

'Mother of God,' Thomas whispered.

And that was when the door opened and the Irish maid, in her night robe, stepped in and screamed. Thomas turned and instinctively fired from five yards away, hitting her in the throat and killing her in the blink of an eye. The young girl fell dead in the doorway.

Thomas gasped and fell to his knees, sobbing. 'Oh Jesus, Jesus, Jesus! Fuck it fuck it fuck it fuck it!' he yelled into the wooden floor.

Slowly he rose, desperate to collect his wits, sweeping his sleeve across his eyes, realising his time was short. He had to think quickly. Other men would be coming at any minute.

Thomas overcame his revulsion at the sight of the man he'd just murdered to reach inside Harris's jacket. Nothing. He began to rifle the bureau and found not a farthing. He stepped over the dead girl's body and raced up the stairs, leaving a trail of bloody footprints behind him. Having located the master bedroom, complete with blazing fire, lamps, four-poster bed, wardrobe and a tall chest of drawers, he began to search wildly, finally uncovering three five-pound notes and four single notes, nineteen pounds in all, more than all the money his father could earn in two years. He'd never even seen a piece of paper money before this moment, but he knew he was holding his and Owen's ticket to America, if they could survive that long.

He ran down to the kitchen and found a small sack that he filled with enough bread and cooked pork for the journey, desperately stuffing handfuls of bread into his mouth as he worked. Burrell's uncorked bottle of brandy still rested on the worktop where the Englishman had left it. Thomas took a long swig, then fled towards the main entrance.

Emerging from the light, the darkness was intense. He strained to see if there were any witnesses to the terrible malignancy that had just transpired, tried to identify any ill-fitting sound, but his only reward was an accusing stillness, a silence that allowed the voices in his head to scream to their fullest. With the door pulled closed behind, he hastened down the track, arrived at the narrow dirt road and ran across it into the relative safety of the grass, heather and rocks of a wild, untilled field. After a few minutes of shivering, of breathing in raspy gulps, he managed to restore his nerves to some level of calm, reminding himself over and over that what he'd done had been right and just.

The sound of distant voices stirred him to action. It was the sound of men approaching, not skulking or whispering or plotting, but talking openly and drawing nearer by the second. He turned away and fled across the field towards the mountains, towards his home, where he would restore his brother to life as he'd sworn he would to his dying father. He would feed him, clothe him, protect him and carry him to the safety of the New World, free from the baleful, vengeful hands of the English. Thomas would abandon the country he loved in search of freedom and life. And perhaps on that far distant shore the memory of this night might finally begin to recede.

Chapter 38

HOW EXECUTIONS WERE MANAGED IN THE PAST

There was much brutality witnessed in those days with public executions, with the corpse dangling on the rope, *coram populo*, for 30 minutes, as required by law. I grew up in 'a hanging country' – in Ireland – and I have in my mind one of these hangings in triplicate. Through the swinging traps in the floor of the iron structure called 'the drop' I saw in my boyhood dozens take the jump into the dark future. The condemned stood with heads covered, awaiting the springing of the bolt, which was to cast them into eternity. At last the bolt was drawn, three iron trap doors swung open with a hoarse screech and the three fell, writhing and plunging in the agonies of strangulation. Warders supplemented the judicial hanging by laying hold of the legs of the still living wretches and swinging from them until the plunging ceased, and a few convulsive shudders told that all was over.

–*The New York Times*, 14 September 1879

The work of the Boycott relief expedition is completed. The Ulstermen, escorted by Infantry, marched from Ballinrobe to Claremorris, a distance of 13 miles, where they took the train northward at seven o'clock this morning. Almost before daylight, Boycott himself with his wife, niece and nephew, left Lough Mask in a covered ambulance wagon and escorted by a number of Hussars, was driven rapidly to Claremorris.

–*The Montreal True Witness*, 1 December 1880

27 November 1880

'That was how it started, I suppose,' Thomas said, staring at Owen. 'I came to realise after a while that what I'd done had been the right thing to do, the *only* thing to do. It was our only chance to survive. As the days passed, as we walked to Westport, when I knew we were going to make it, it troubled me less and less. And I saw that the only way this country would ever be free was to do it a thousand times over, until every last Englishman was driven from Ireland. And I swore to myself that one day I'd return and carry on what I'd started. It just took me a lot longer than I expected.'

Owen's disquiet, his revulsion, was overwhelming. Since the day Thomas had revealed his true nature in the confrontation with him and Síomha, he had been under no illusions about his brother's capacity for violence. Yet to hear this now, to learn that even in their first flush of youth when, as he'd supposed, their fundamental human dignity had survived the ugliness around them and they had resisted their baser urges to seek bloody retribution, Thomas had even then submitted to the darker recesses of his heart.

'What about the girl, the maid? What about her?' he whispered.

Thomas shook his head slowly and lowered his eyes. 'It was an accident. I didn't mean to…I didn't intend…if I could have avoided it I would. Besides, I only killed three people. They killed two million. It was a small sacrifice in the name of justice.'

'Justice? You bastard!'

'Now why do you say that, Owen? Is it because you realise at last that you have to face the truth you've been avoiding all your life?'

'What truth?'

Thomas laughed mockingly as he gestured to the world beyond McGurk's cottage. 'All of this, this fucking boycott stuff, peaceful resistance, all that bollocks. Your entire life is founded on spilt blood. If I hadn't done what I did, if I hadn't killed those bastards, taken their food and money, you'd be long dead, rotting in the ground, never have seen a day past your seventeenth year. You're alive, Owen, because *I killed*. Síomha? Ye would never have met her. Your children would never have been born. Tadhg, Lorcan, Niamh? They all owe their lives, their fucking *existence* te me. Everything you are is built on bloodshed. And, like I said earlier, ye knew all along. You knew when we were walking te

Westport that the food ye were eating was "tainted". Ye just wouldn't admit it te yourself; ye wanted *me* te carry the burden of it so your damn conscience could remain clear. If I've any guilt on my shoulders, you share it in equal measure.'

Owen's mind spun as the words fell from his brother's lips, as he desperately tried to make the pieces fit, to put some order and sense back into his perception of his own life. His emotions tumbled and tangled in an unseemly brawl, wrestling for clarity, with rage ultimately gaining the upper hand. He leapt from the chair, but Thomas was expecting him and stood up sharply, pulling his gun up in a blink, holding the barrel inches from Owen's snarling face.

'Don't, Owen. I'll kill you if I have te, I swear.'

'You bastard! You fuck! Don't try and make me a part of your sick world. Everything you did, you did for yourself. You know what I am?'

'What?'

'Just another one of your victims! How many more are there going to be before you've satisfied your blood lust?'

'As many as it takes to free Ireland, something all the boycotts in the world will never achieve–'

'Walsh? What the fuck are ye doin'?' McGurk's voice took them by surprise, as much from the fact that they'd almost forgotten the presence of the others as from what he was saying.

Owen and Thomas turned their gaze on Bull Walsh, who had been sitting in complete silence beside the door, hanging on every word spoken by Thomas, yet his eyes appearing vacant as they looked not at the walls about him, but across the landscape of his memory. Now his large, imposing bulk stood erect, his arm extended, gun pointing directly at Thomas.

'Drop the gun, Joyce.'

'Are ye fucking mad? What are ye doing?'

'Drop it or I'll kill ye where ye stand.'

Thomas lowered the gun to his side and allowed it to drop to the floor. Owen now stood almost by his side.

'If your brother's been living a lie, you've been living one a hundred times greater.'

It was the longest sentence Thomas had ever heard the man speak. He shook his head in confusion. 'What are you talking about?'

'What did you say was the name of the house? Oughty House? Where your land agent lived? Harris?'

Thomas nodded. 'Yeah. That's right. What about it?'

'Let me finish yer story for ye. The men ye heard coming up the track as ye were leavin', that would have been Pádraig Walsh, Éamon Walsh and Jimmy Burke. I wanted te go with them, but they wouldn't let me. Tim. That's my name. Tim Walsh. Pádraig Walsh's son. Éamon was my uncle. Jimmy was a neighbour. They were going up te see Harris te ask him te defer the rents, not te kill him. They weren't even armed. The front door was open and they went in, saw the bodies and ran. But the old stableman, or whatever he was, he'd come to, woken up. He was walkin' around the front of the house when he saw the three of them running out the door. He put two and two together and got five. When the RIC questioned him, he identified me father, me uncle and our neighbour as the three killers. Jimmy tried te get away to America. He was arrested on Westport Quay. They shot Éamon dead near his home when he resisted arrest. Me father and Jimmy were put on trial. They swore their innocence. But me father was known te be nationalist. And they had an eyewitness. That was all they needed. They hanged them in Westport. I watched. They left them hanging by their necks for half an hour after they were dead, so all the world could see the dead faces of the murderers.'

'Bull, wait. I didn't kn–'

'Ye knew. Ye knew they were going te Harris's house that night. Ye knew that they'd get the blame.'

'No, I couldn't have known there'd be a witness. I thought they'd go there and then just run.'

'Ye were fuckin' counting on it, you bastard! Ye were counting on them getting blamed, so you'd have plenty of time te get away.'

'No! You're wrong!'

Walsh emitted a small laugh and shook his head almost imperceptibly.

'I swore after I'd watched me father die an innocent man that I'd make the English pay. I spent my entire life doing just that. Killin' them, one after another. It became as easy as wringin' the neck of a chicken. They weren't even human te me. And all that time, I was hatin' the wrong people. All that time, it should have been you. You. Ye as much as put the rope around me father's neck and pulled the lever. And me uncle. And Jimmy. All their deaths were down te you. You fuckin' evil bastard!'

Walsh raised the gun an inch, pointing it straight at Thomas's heart. Thomas didn't move, simply stood there blank-faced, as though in acceptance that his time had come.

'Wait! Walsh! Don't!' Owen shouted and went to move in front of his brother. Thomas pushed him roughly away and he slammed back against a wall.

'Listen!' McGurk shouted, as the sound of a horse coming to a stop reached their ears. 'Is it Doherty?'

They stood in silence for a few seconds as a shadow flitted past the window. The door was pushed in and Donal Doherty stomped brusquely into the cottage. He stopped in the centre of the room as he realised the scene didn't meet his expectations, then looked behind him and saw Walsh standing there with the gun levelled at Thomas.

'What the fuck?'

'Where have you been?' McGurk asked, his voice fraught with dread, perversely hoping Doherty's return would herald some measure of sanity.

'Fuckin' horse threw me when I was tryin' te get away. What's goin' on? Bull? What are ye doin'?'

'Get out of the way.'

Doherty was almost directly in Walsh's line of fire. He looked around at Thomas and Owen.

'Why are ye pointin' that at Thomas? It's the other bastard ye should be... why is he still alive, for that matter?'

'Shut up, Doherty,' Thomas said.

'What? I've had enough of this. Let's get this over and done with.'

Doherty brought his pistol sharply up towards Owen and fired, denying him even an instant of contemplation of his end before the bullet struck him. As he spun about and fell across the chair, which collapsed beneath his weight, he was conscious of a sudden explosion of pain – he was conscious too that Thomas had thrown himself at Doherty as he'd fired. Otherwise he would surely now be dead. He rolled on his back and clutched instinctively at the wound in his shoulder, and felt blood oozing between his fingers. Above him he watched as his brother and Doherty struggled for control of the gun, their bodies pressed together, hands wrenching at the weapon, which Owen could see was angling ever more towards the side of Thomas's head. His brother was losing the battle.

'You fuckin' traitor, Joyce... all of you, traitors!' Doherty hissed venomously as he watched the tip of the barrel slowly move against Thomas's temple. 'I'll kill every last fuckin' Joyce in Mayo... startin' with you...'

Doherty felt his finger tighten against the trigger. That was the final sensation of his life.

Bull Walsh took a single step forward, pointed his gun at Doherty's head and fired. The Fenian's eyes snapped wide and uncomprehending, his lips forming a perfect circle as though he'd suddenly witnessed something startling, and he fell face down against a small table, upending it and shattering the McGurks' small collection of crockery into a thousand shards.

'What are ye do–'? McGurk roared as he desperately scrambled to train his own gun on Walsh, but his sentence, like his life, ended prematurely as Walsh put two bullets in his chest. He collapsed back into the hearth, sending a small cloud of cold grey ash swirling about his lifeless face.

Walsh took a step forward, long, slow breaths escaping his lips.

Owen struggled to stand but only managed to get up on one knee. Thomas stood with his back to him, facing Walsh.

'Walsh…don't…' Owen croaked.

'Nobody's going to deny me this. Not Doherty, not McGurk, not you.'

'Do it, Bull. But leave my brother out of it,' Thomas whispered, his eyes fixed directly on Walsh's.

'This is for me father,' Walsh said through a snarl.

'No! Walsh! Don't fire! Walsh!'

But Owen's cry was lost in the gunshot's odious screech, the terrible sound replete with sickening finality. Thomas's mouth shot open, his eyes wide, as his body was thrown back against the wall, hands clutching at the gaping wound over his heart. Owen screamed and threw his arms about his brother's falling body, as though catching him might somehow prevent the inevitable end. Thomas slumped to the floor, Owen's arms swathing his body, tears flooding his face, his fingers digging into Thomas's flesh as he tried to cling on to his brother's life, to wrench him free of death's grasp.

'Thomas!' he cried.

Thomas turned his head to Owen. His lips tried to form a word, a valediction, but no sound came. His eyes met Owen's for a brief moment and then the life slipped from them, and they saw nothing.

Owen pressed his face against his brother's and softly sobbed, unable to deny the terrible loss despite all that had passed between them. Then he remembered that Walsh still stood over him, a gun pointed in his direction. He turned his head despondently and looked up at the man.

'It's over,' Bull Walsh whispered. He turned his back and departed the cottage. A minute later Owen heard the sound of a horse take off at a gallop and he was left alone with his brother's lifeless body.

***

He had no idea how much time passed before Fr O'Malley's shadow fell across the cottage floor. He heard the priest utter a gasped exclamation of shock before he felt hands pulling at his jacket and shirt.

'Owen! Thank God you're alive!'

Joe Gaughan's face was there then, and he felt Joe's hands exploring the wound.

'Bullet went through,' Joe declared. 'I've seen this before. He's lost blood, but it's not bad. Father, get a cloth and water. Owen, can ye hear me? We're going te bind the wound.'

Owen nodded. 'I'm all right,' he whispered, then grasped the priest's wrist.

'What is it, Owen?'

'Father. Joe. We have to get out of here. The police.'

'First we have te fix ye up.'

They spent ten minutes washing and binding the wound with torn strips of a bed sheet. As Joe wrapped the cloth painfully about Owen's chest and shoulder, the priest looked about him at the vacant stares of the dead.

'Holy God,' he muttered.

He turned first to Thomas, knelt and drew his palm down across his eyes to close them, made the Sign of the Cross on his forehead with his thumb, then, head bowed and hands clasped, he recited the words:

> 'Requiem æternam dona eis Domine; et lux perpetua luceat eis.
> Requiescat in pace. Amen.'

He repeated the ritual with the others, differing only with McGurk; just a couple of months beforehand, he had been a young man living in expectation of the child his pretty new wife would deliver to him. The priest shook his head and laid a hand on McGurk's forehead. 'Oh Martin. How does it profit you now?' he whispered.

He turned to the others.

'Can ye stand, Owen?' Joe was asking.

'I think so.'

'Father, help me,' Joe said and they managed to get Owen on his feet.

'Joe…' he said. 'I need you to do something. My brother. His body. Take it away. Maybe to the church.'

'Whatever ye want,' Joe said, looking uncertainly at the priest.

Fr O'Malley nodded. 'I'll take Owen home. You take the body in your cart. There's a small room for the repose of the dead behind the sacristy. I'll meet you there in an hour,' he said, as they stepped out into the early morning sunlight.

***

Síomha screeched as she ran from the cottage with Tadhg and Niamh at her side, and they enveloped him in a tangle of arms as he climbed uneasily from the priest's car.

'My God, you've been shot!'

'I'm all right. I'll be fine. Oh God, Síomha!' He clasped her in as tight an embrace as his wounds would allow.

'What happened? Oh Jesus, Owen, I was certain you were dead,' Síomha cried, Owen's face cupped in her palms.

'Daddy, are you all right?' Niamh cried.

'Let's get him inside, Síomha,' Fr O'Malley counselled.

Owen lay on the bed as Síomha redressed the wound, Fr O'Malley and the children running to and fro with basins of boiled water, bandages and a bottle of Harper's Tincture of Iodine, whose application actually hurt Owen more than being shot. When, finally, the treatment was complete and weariness began to overtake him, he clutched at his wife's hand, rested his head back and met her eyes.

Síomha glanced over her shoulder at Tadhg and Niamh. 'Your father needs to rest now. We'll be out in a few minutes.'

With the children gone, Owen looked towards the window and spoke in a voice barely above a whisper. 'Thomas is dead. Don't ask me what happened,' he sighed. 'I'll explain everything later.'

She nodded and clenched his hand tightly. 'Jesus, Owen, we were frantic all night. We didn't know where to look this morning. The Holy Well, around the estate. We met Joe and he told us about the gun. Then Father here suggested McGurk's. He wouldn't let me come. I was sure you were...'

Owen felt the swell of a sob and pulled her face down to his as he sought to conceal the conflicting emotions of his love and grief.

Fr O'Malley, who had been standing behind her, took a step nearer.

'Owen. Did you–?'

Owen shook his head. 'I didn't kill any of them, Father. It was another man. He's gone now.'

'How many people?' Síomha asked.

'Thomas, Martin McGurk, a man called Doherty, a Fenian.'

Síomha blessed herself. 'Mother of God.'

'Owen, how are we going to explain all this?' the priest asked.

Owen looked at his friend and Síomha.

'We're not,' he said.

Chapter 39

AN EVICTION BY THE LEAGUERS

Mr Boycott, to whose aid the Orangemen went to near Ballinrobe, has quitted his residence there for England.

–*The Sydney Morning Herald*, 30 November 1880

Look at the case of Captain Boycott the other day. (Cheers) It is perfectly impossible to resist the five million people of the country, and the Government cannot do it if you are organised and determined. He was a very plucky man, and yet the Government of England was obliged to employ something like 7,000 soldiers and police for a whole fortnight to save £100 worth of turnips and potatoes. (Laughter) Well, now, this one example should be sufficient to show you how utterly impossible it is for the oligarchy of the country to contend with the organised power of the masses. I believe that we have forces sufficient to achieve our ends and we call upon you as one man, if you believe in us, if you believe in our honesty, to stand by us and to help us with the ability, with the genius, which God has given to Irishmen, confident in ourselves and in yourselves and the future of our common country. (Great cheering).

–Charles Stewart Parnell, speech in County Cork. *The Times*, 5 December 1880

6 December 1880

'It's beautiful, Owen,' Síomha whispered almost to herself as she looked down into the valley on a bright, crisp winter's morning. Tawnyard Lough glinted in the sunlight, the glassy surface reflecting the almost cloudless sky, its small cluster of islands overflowing with fir trees and wild shrubs, and Maumtrasna's great bulk rising behind it.

'A view I used to wake to every morning. I haven't seen it in over thirty years.'

'Why didn't you ever come back, Owen?' Fr O'Malley asked.

He shrugged and simply smiled. 'Never had the time.'

They had travelled the previous day and stayed the night in the home of the local priest, who had gladly submitted to Fr O'Malley's request on condition that the now-famed Master of the boycott tactic address his parishioners. Tadhg, Niamh, Fr O'Malley, Owen, Síomha and Joe, who had conveyed Thomas's remains in his cart, had managed to cram themselves into two tiny rooms in the priest's cottage. But it sufficed, and besides, they'd all known much greater discomforts in the past.

The land that Owen's father had farmed on the side of Tawnyard Hill had lain untilled since the days of the famine, sheep its most frequent visitors. After the land agent Harris's death, it had gone through many hands and now belonged to yet another absentee landlord who had never set eyes on the place. His land agent, however, had agreed to permit a burial on the hillside, his compliance spurred no doubt by the presence of Fr O'Malley.

'Right, we've a bit of work te do,' Joe said as he stared up the slope from the track, where they'd secured Joe's cart, the jaunting car and Thomas's horse.

***

Despite his protests, Síomha refused to allow Owen to assist as Joe, Tadhg and Fr O'Malley hoisted the simple pine casket from the cart and began to climb the slope. Owen's wound was healing well, but any serious strain would undo all the work of the past ten days. So he led the way, and Síomha and Niamh, holding hands, following closely behind them. Thirty minutes later, after several gasping stops, the slope eased and flattened, revealing the area where Owen and his family had struggled to coax a meagre existence from the poor earth. Above them, Tawnyard Hill rose up another thousand feet towards the blue sky.

'Mother of Jaysus, Owen,' Joe gasped, clutching at his chest as they rested Thomas's coffin on the ground. 'Couldn't ye have had a childhood home a bit nearer the road?'

Only Tadhg, in his youth, seemed untroubled by the exertions. Fr O'Malley was red-faced and perspiring profusely.

'Sorry, Joe. It's steeper and further up the hill than I remember.'

'Ye were like Tadhg there the last time ye came up that hill, for God's sake.'

Owen laughed, despite the sadness of the occasion. He clapped Joe on the shoulder in gratitude, not just for his exertions but for everything he'd done in the past days. He had removed Thomas's lifeless body and transferred it to the church in Neale, where Fr O'Malley had arranged to have two local women quietly prepare him for burial. Joe had then built the casket and, despite the enormous amount of work on his own plate, had volunteered to help Owen conduct his brother to his final resting place. Considering what Owen had helped to do for the tenants, he'd said, it was a mere pittance in repayment.

Word had reached the constabulary that same day, courtesy of Joe, that shots had been heard near McGurk's cottage, and upon investigation two bodies had been discovered, one of them a known activist in the militant republican movement. The RIC were currently working on the theory that some factional dispute had resulted in the men being murdered by a third party – not too distant from the facts. But they as yet had no clue who the killer might be and considering the secrecy in which these groups operated, it was Sergeant Murtagh's view that they were unlikely ever to catch the culprit. No involvement of Owen or his brother was ever established or even considered. Tim 'Bull' Walsh was never heard of again.

A week after the events at McGurk's cottage, Owen had trotted his brother's horse to a quiet spot beside the shore of Lough Mask and pulled out the rifle that would have been the instrument of Boycott's death. He had a vivid recollection of his father hurling a musket out over the waters of Derrintin Lough where he used to fish as a boy. A musket with which he'd killed. Owen took his brother's weapon and, with his good right arm, repeated the action, watching as the rifle twirled in an arc across the sky, Lough Mask's placid waters claiming it forever. Events had come full circle, he thought, as he watched the ripples fade and disappear.

'It wasn't the famine or hatred of the English that made my brother what he was,' he'd said to Fr O'Malley over a drink that evening. 'It was my own father. He may have had no choice, and he was normally a peaceful man, but when he killed that gamekeeper before Thomas's eyes, he set his son on the violent course of his life.'

The priest nodded. 'We must measure what we bequeath to our children in far greater terms that the material things we leave behind,' he said.

A few days later they'd read in the newspaper that Boycott and his family had made it safely to Claremorris, overtaking the huge military cavalcade as it conducted the labourers from Cavan and Monaghan to the train station. From there, Boycott and the men who had laboured to bring in his harvest went their separate ways. The military escort then broke up and returned to their separate barracks in Dublin, Ballinrobe and Kildare. No protests greeted the Boycotts either in Claremorris or upon their arrival in Dublin, Fr O'Malley's counsel reaching all the way to the east coast of the country. Yet it wasn't quite the end of Boycott's troubles in Ireland, for the proprietor of the Hamman Hotel in Dublin's main thoroughfare, Sackville Street, received several warning letters, some threatening a boycott of his premises, others from militants threatening his life should he continue to house the Boycott party under his roof. The Boycotts were requested to vacate the hotel and Charles, Annie and the others took the mail boat for England on the morning of the first day of December 1880. Boycott's long and troubled involvement with Ireland had finally come to an inglorious end.

***

'Here it is,' Owen called out to the others, who had been scouting about among the long grass in search of his father's grave. There was little trace of his childhood home left; that sad little one-roomed cottage had long since tumbled to ruin and only a handful of stones remained stacked upon one another. All the others had fallen and been swallowed whole by the earth and nature's unrelenting growth.

He beat back the foot-high grass to reveal the vague shape of a grave, fifty or so moss-covered stones, most of which had collapsed into the earth as his father's body had been reclaimed. He had stood there another day, in another life, his brother at his side as they'd listened to the priest perform the funeral rite. Now, at last, Thomas would find a final resting place beside the father he had loved so dearly.

They dug the grave and lowered the coffin into the soft, peaty earth. Fr O'Malley said a mass and finished with the final rite of burial. 'O God, by Your mercy rest is given to the souls of the faithful, be pleased to bless this grave. Appoint Your holy angels to guard it and set free from all the chains of sin the soul of him whose body is buried here, so that with all Thy saints he may rejoice in Thee for ever. Requiem æternam dona ei Domine; et lux perpetua luceat ei. Requiescat in pace.'

In her innocence, Niamh sobbed profusely as she looked into the dark hole in the earth, but Owen felt no sting of tears as he cast a handful of soil on to the coffin. He had none left to shed.

His brother had said that he and his family owed their very existence to an act of violence. But Owen had pondered this during the inactive days of his recovery. He asked himself: was there a living soul on earth who could say any differently? We are all the product of some violent confrontation, some war or battle, ancient or within memory, that had steered and determined the course of our lives, all the way back to when man had first emerged from his primordial lair. But now, more than ever, Owen believed that bloodshed was not necessary to chart the paths of our lives. Humanity's blossoming was proof not of the success of violence, but the success of its avoidance.

He watched as the others followed his lead and cast their small handfuls of Mayo earth on to his brother's final place of rest, at his father's side.

'You're home, Thomas,' he whispered as he felt Síomha's arm slip inside his own.

A lone bird took flight from the heather nearby and Owen watched as it soared away across the valley and the bountiful waters of the lough far below.

Historical Epilogue

A system has been instituted in the Limerick locality of 'Boycotting' local solicitors to prevent them from acting professionally for plaintiffs in eviction cases.

–*The Limerick Chronicle*, 23 November 1880

The Land Agitation is spreading to the North. We draw attention to the Land League's warm reception in Ballyshannon, Enniskillen and Derry, which has resulted in the formation of local branches, while the most successful of last week's demonstrations was in Cavan, one of the counties that supplied the men for the Boycott expedition.

–*The Nation*, 27 November 1880

Mr Walter Lambert, a large landowner and magistrate at Athenry has been 'boycotted' by his neighbours.

–*The Irish Times*, 27 November 1880

The agent of an estate at New Pallas has been boycotted after the tenants offered to pay their rent according to Griffith's Valuation and were declined.

–*The Nation*, 4 December 1880

Lord Clanricarde's tenants near Loughrea have refused to pay rent beyond Griffith's valuation and the local Land League threatened he shall be 'Boycotted'.

–*The Nenagh Guardian*, 5 December 1880

Photograph of the so-called 'Boycott Expedition' taken on the steps of Lough Mask House at the end of November 1880. Charles Boycott is in the back row, fourth from right. Annie Boycott is seated in front of him. William and Madeleine (face blurred) are to his right. Asheton Weekes is in the front row, centre, wearing a tam o'shanter..

The practice of boycotting spread almost with the same virulence as the blight that had once ravaged Ireland's potato crops. By the end of December 1880 boycotts had sprung up in every county in Ireland, including the loyalist north, where Parnell had partially succeeded in separating the issue of landlordism from nationalism. The Chief Secretary for Ireland, William Edward Forster, wrote to Gladstone: 'Unless we can strike at the boycotting weapon, Parnell will beat us.'

Under huge pressure, primarily brought about by the use of the boycott, within a year a new Land Act was passed by the British Government, finally granting the Irish tenantry 'The Three Fs' that they had long sought: fair rent control, fixity of tenure on leases, and freedom of sale. This Act and further Land Acts in the decade that followed allowed tenants the opportunity to purchase the land they farmed, returning the land to Irish ownership for the first time in centuries and signalling an end to landlordism in Ireland. They were also granted a rent abatement of twenty-five percent in cases where the tenant was in financial difficulties. Parnell and Davitt's Land League was a victim of its own success, however, and the League ultimately outlived its usefulness. Yet it had been the single greatest instigator of agrarian reform in Ireland's history.

***

The trial of Charles Stewart Parnell and many other Land League leaders took place just weeks after Captain Boycott's departure from Ireland. In a sense it was the Land League itself and the tactic of boycotting that were on trial. The defendants were acquitted and Michael Davitt remarked that, 'We have beaten the Government to smithereens...nothing contributed more to the victory than boycotting.'

A Coercion Act was introduced in 1881 in an attempt to bring an end to boycotting. Parnell, Davitt and hundreds of other Land Leaguers were arrested without trial. But British Prime Minister Gladstone quickly realised that coercion was hardening Irish attitudes and negotiated a deal with Parnell while he was in Kilmainham Gaol – nicknamed 'The Kilmainham Treaty' – in which Parnell won further concessions to the Land Act and an end to coercion. Davitt and Parnell were released in early 1882. Parnell would bring Ireland to the brink of Home Rule before the scandal involving Kitty O'Shea, another MP's wife, destroyed him politically. He died in 1891, aged just forty-five.

***

Michael Davitt continued to work for land reform in Ireland, Wales and Scotland. He campaigned tirelessly on behalf of workingmen everywhere, Britain included, for universal suffrage, for the underprivileged, against anti-semitism, and was one of the founding members of the British Labour Party. He died in 1906, aged sixty, always maintaining to the last that violence was self-defeating. Mahatma Gandhi attributed the development of his own mass movement of peaceful resistance in India to Michael Davitt and the Land League, and successfully adopted the strategy of boycotting. Despite the vast contribution he made to Irish freedom, Davitt has never been granted the accolades he so richly deserves.

***

Although Lord Mountmorres's former sheep-herder, Patrick Sweeney, was initially questioned about the landlord's murder, no evidence could be found linking him to the killing. He was also believed to be incapable of having carried out the assassination given his age and limited intelligence. Considering the planning and clinical nature of the atrocity, it was widely believed that several individuals had been involved, most likely extremist nationalists. No one was ever charged with Mountmorres's murder.

***

Bernard Henry Becker continued his travels through Ireland, and given the partisanship of most newspaper correspondents at the time, his reports to *The Daily News* of London displayed a good deal of impartiality. He visited the homes of landlords and tenants alike in Mayo, Galway, Clare, Limerick, Kerry and in late January 1881, boarded a ship in Cork and returned to England. Later that year he published his collected accounts under the title *Disturbed Ireland – Being the Letters Written During the Winter of 1880-81*. He continued to write for *The Daily News* and the well-known society journal, *The World*. He also travelled widely in the cities and towns of northern England and brought the plight of the impoverished there to a wider world. He died in 1900, aged sixty-seven.

***

James Redpath returned to America where he continued to promote the Irish cause through the columns of *The Chicago Inter Ocean* and *The New York Herald*, in which he wrote a passionate condemnation of landlordism and of Captain Boycott himself, as the former land agent was, at the time, on a visit to New York in the company of his family. In 1881 he released a book entitled *Talks about Ireland*, which covered the famine, landlordism, enforced emigration and, of course, the original boycott itself. His contribution to the causes of anti-slavery in the USA and Haiti was recalled in *Forgotten Firebrand: James Redpath and the Making of Nineteenth-Century America*, by John R McKivigan (2008). He died in 1891, aged fifty-eight.

***

Fr John O'Malley continued his work with the Land League, speaking at countless meetings and encouraging the practice of boycotting as a peaceful means of achieving justice. He also continued to condemn violent acts carried out by extreme nationalists. Much loved by his parishioners, he was not just an inspirational force in the struggle for tenants' rights, but a generally caring and humanitarian man who did all in his power to help the unfortunates of the world. He continued to minister in Neale until his death on 30 May 1892 at the age of fifty-seven. He was buried at the foot of the high altar in St John the Baptist Church & Calvary in Neale, which his parishioners had built and which still stands today. Beside the building is a monument in the form of a church bell, erected in 2000, inscribed with his name, suspended on stone taken from Neale's original church. The Fr O'Malley Millennium Park in Neale also honours his memory.

***

Arthur Boycott's character is a composite of several people – primarily Arthur himself, who later became a vicar, and Charles's younger brother, Tom, who served in the Royal Navy, as well as Charles's army colleagues, most of whom, unlike Charles, had seen active service in far-off lands.

The portrait of Charles's father, William (and his influence on Charles's personality) is similarly a composite. As a young man on Achill Island, Charles was a close acquaintance of a man called Edward Nangle, an imperious, domineering figure who utterly detested Catholicism and believed that the Pope was the Antichrist. Nangle had set up the Achill Mission with the specific ambition of proselytising the Catholic population. Charles and his siblings did grow up in a strict Protestant household with a rigid line drawn between the 'gentlemanly class' and the so-called 'lower classes', and Charles's father may or may not have been like the authoritarian figure portrayed. In a curious portent of events fifty years later, his tenant farmers once rioted and besieged his rectory because of excessive tithes, and the rector was forced to concede to their demands.

Asheton Weekes eventually became a clergyman and cemented his bonds with the Boycott family by marrying Charles's niece and ward of court, Madeleine. Young William also studied to be a clergyman; he married and became the final rector of Burgh St Peter to bear the name Boycott.

***

When he left Ireland, Charles Cunningham Boycott took up a position as the agent for Sir Hugh Adair's estate in Flixton, Suffolk, not far from his birthplace in Burgh St Peter, Norfolk. During and after the boycott in Mayo, £2,000 was raised in England by public subscription in sympathy with his plight, a vast amount of money to the ordinary man (representing, in today's money, about £800,000 in earnings, the equivalent of £150,000 in spending power today). He also eventually managed to offload the lease on Lough Mask Estate, though for considerably less than it was worth. He retained his smaller Kildarra Estate and, when the political situation calmed in the following years, he often returned there with Annie for summer holidays. Despite his apparently handsome financial situation, he proved to be as poor a businessman in his later years as he had been in Ireland, and when he died he left Annie with huge debts, which required the sale of most of his remaining assets, including Kildarra. His health declined rapidly in the mid-1890s and he died at his home in Suffolk in June 1897, aged sixty-five.

Although there are no references to the Boycotts having had a daughter (biographies refer to them as childless), an Achill Island death certificate was issued for a Mary Boycott, who died on 26 December 1875, aged nineteen. This puts her birth year at 1856, just a couple of years after Charles and Annie's marriage. At the time they were residents in Achill Island. Furthermore, there was a strong tradition in the Boycott family of handing down names through the generations and Charles's grandmother and great-grandmother were both called Mary. The name Boycott is rare enough in England, so the odds of Mary not being a close relation to Charles and Annie are astronomical. The cause of Mary's death was listed as menorrhagia. There was 'no medical attendant'. She was recorded as being a spinster, a farmer's daughter, and, most surprisingly, a Roman Catholic. No family member was present at her death, which took place in the cottage of a Margaret Gaughan.

***

Although the strategy of ostracism had been employed before 1880 in different parts of the world, most notably the National Negro Convention's refusal to support slave-produced goods in 1830, the boycott only truly came into its own when it proved so effective on a national level during Ireland's Land War. The widespread, almost global publicity of the 'Boycott Affair' ensured that the efforts and success of the villagers of Neale and Ballinrobe, County Mayo, were known the world over and were an inspiration for countless other movements that sought to redress injustice by peaceful means. Among these were the famous Montgomery Bus Civil Rights Boycott in Alabama, the United Farm Workers' Grape Boycott (which was among the most successful in US history and which won Mexican and Filipino grape workers significant labour rights), the Indian boycott of British goods organised by Gandhi, several anti-apartheid boycotts against South Africa and countless others.

At the time of the original boycott in County Mayo, Lord Randolph Churchill, Winston Churchill's father, said of the act of boycotting:

'It is better than any eighty-one-ton gun.'

BIBLIOGRAPHY

Charles Boycott & The Land War

Althoz, Josef L., *Selected Documents in Irish History* (M.E. Sharpe 2000)

Beresford Ellis, Peter, *Eyewitness to Irish History* (John Wiley & Sons, New Jersey 2004)

Boycott, Charles Arthur, *Boycott - The Life Behind the Word* (Carbonel Press 1997)

Campbell, Fergus J.M., *The Irish Establishment, 1879-1914* (Oxford University Press 2009)

Davitt, Michael, *The Fall of Feudalism in Ireland* (Harper & Brothers 1904)

Dixon McDougall, Margaret, The Letters of Norah on her Tour Through Ireland (Series of letters to *The Montreal Witness* as Special Correspondent to Ireland, 1882)

Jordan, Donald E., *Land and Popular Politics in Ireland: County Mayo from the Plantation to the Land War* (Press Syndicate of the University of Cambridge 1994)

Marlow, Joyce, *Captain Boycott and the Irish* (History Book Club 1973)

'Miracle at Knock, and a Disturbed County Mayo', article, *The Galway Advertiser*, 13 August 2009

The Erne Papers – Public Record Office of Northern Ireland

'The Neale Heritage Walk', pamphlet issued by Mayo County Development Board

'The Role of the Church in the Land Movement', article, *The Galway Advertiser*, 20 August 2009

Vaughan, William Edward, *Landlords and Tenants in Mid-Victorian Ireland* (Clarendon Press 1994)

Young, G. M., and Handcock, W.D., *English Historical Documents 1874-1914* (Eyre & Spottiswoode Ltd. 1977)

Websites:

http://www.ricorso.net/ Archbishop John McHale

http://www.knock-shrine.com/ Archdeacon Cavanagh

http://en.wikisource.org/ Bernard Henry Becker

http://www.generalmichaelcollins.com/ Buckshot Forster

http://www.achurchnearyou.com/burgh-st-peter-st-mary/ Burgh St. Peters

http://www.historicalballinrobe.com/

http://www.historyireland.com/ The Catholic Church and Fenianism

http://en.wikipedia.org/wiki/Daily_News_(UK)

http://www.spartacus.schoolnet.co.uk/ The Daily News

http://www.lib.utexas.edu/ Frank Harrison Hill

http://en.wikipedia.org/wiki/James_Patrick_Mahon

http://landedestates.nuigalway.ie/ Lough Mask House
http://www.theneale.com/
http://maggieblanck.com/Mayopages/ Obituary of Archbishop Mac Hale of Tuam November 12, 1881 The Illustrated London News
http://www.clarelibrary.ie/ The O'Gorman Mahon, Duellist, Politician, Soldier and Adventurer
http://www.maynoothcollege.ie/ Past Figures - Dr Patrick Murray

General Reference

'A Sweat-house at Inishmaine, Near Ballinrobe', article for the Mayo Historical and Archaeological Society (2005)
Kurtz, Lester R. & Turpin, *Jennifer E., Encyclopedia of Violence, Peace and Conflict* (Academic Press)
Lewis, Samuel, *A Topographical Dictionary of Ireland* (S Lewis & Co. London 1837)
Ruttledge, Robert T., 'Devenish Island', *The Irish Naturalists' Journal* Vol 2 No. 6, 1928
Sheppard, F.H.W., *Soho, Its History and Architecture in the Survey of London* (English Heritage 1966)
The Most Rev. Dr. Healy, Archbishop of Tuam, 'Two Royal Abbeys by the Western Lakes Cong and Inismaine', The Journal of the Royal Society of Antiquaries of Ireland, Vol. XV. Fifth Series Part 1 (Dublin University Press 1905)
Wilde, Sir William R., M.D., *Lough Corrib its Shores and Islands with Notices of Lough Mask* (Glashan & Gull, Dublin 1867)

Websites:

http://en.wikipedia.org/wiki/Allen & Ginter Cigarettes
www.archive.org/
http://en.wikipedia.org/wiki/Colt_Single_Action_Army
http://en.wikipedia.org/wiki/The_Dawning_of_the_Day
http://www.dublincastle.ie Erin Room, Dublin Castle
http://www.capitalpunishmentuk.org/hanging1.html
http://en.wikipedia.org/wiki/Hanoverian_(horse)
http://www.tcd.ie/history
http://www.1articleworld.com/ The Irish Draught Horse
http://www.libraryireland.com/
http://www.maggieblanck.com/Mayopages/
http://irelandgenweb.com Oughaval Civil Parish
http://en.wikipedia.org/wiki/Remington_Model_1858
http://en.wikipedia.org/ The 17th On Foot In The Crimean War
http://www.bog-standard.org/ Victorian Toilets

http://blog.aurorahistoryboutique.com/tag/victorian-toilets/
http://en.wikipedia.org/wiki/Ye_Olde_Cheshire_Cheese

The Great Famine

Carleton, William, *Valentine M'Clutchy, The Irish Agent* (James Duffy, London 1845)
Gray, Peter, *The Irish Famine* (Thames & Hudson)
Hays, J. N., *Epidemics And Pandemics: Their Impacts on Human History* (ABC-CLIO, 2005)
Houstoun, Matilda, *Twenty Years in the Wild West* (J. Murray, London 1879)
Krakauer, Jon, *Into the Wild* (Villard 1996)
Litton, Helen, *The Irish Famine, An Illustrated History* (Wolfhound Press 1994)
Malthus, Robert Thomas, *An Essay on the Principle of Population* (Oxford University Press 1999)
Mitchell, John, *The Last Conquest of Ireland (Perhaps)* (Glasgow, Cameron Ferguson 1876)
O'Donnell, Ruán, *A Pocket History of the Irish Famine* (O'Brien Press 2008)
Póirtéir, Cathal, *Famine Echoes* (Gill & Macmillan)
Redpath, James, *Talks about Ireland* (J.J. Kenedy 1881)
Scally, Robert James, *The End of Hidden Ireland: Rebellion, Famine & Emigration* (Oxford University Press,1995)
Tuke, James H., *A Visit to Ireland in the Autumn of 1847* (Charles Gilpin, London 1848)
Whyte, Robert, *The Famine Ship Diary, 1847* (Mercier Press)
Woodham-Smith, Cecil, *The Great Hunger, Ireland 1845-9* (Hamish Hamilton London 1964)

Websites:

http://multitext.ucc.ie/ Charles Edward Trevelyan
http://www.irishhistorylinks.net/ Contemporary Reports & Images of the Great Famine
http://www.mayo-ireland.ie/ Famine in Mayo: Letters & Reports To The Ballina Chronicle
http://maggieblanck.com/Mayopages/Famine.html The Great Famine 1845 - 1849
http://en.wikipedia.org/wiki/Great_Famine_(Ireland)
http://xroads.virginia.edu/ Irish Views Of The Famine
http://www.irelandoldnews.com/ Mayo 1849

Lord Mountmorres

New York Times Archive 1880
The Gentleman's Magazine, Volume 103, Lord Mountmorres

'The Irish Canadian', article on the Parnell Commission, 1 August 1889
The Times Archive 1880

Websites:
http://maggieblanck.com/Mayopages/LandIssues.html Lord Mountmorres' Murder
http://www.thepeerage.com/
http://en.wikipedia.org/wiki/Viscount_Mountmorres

Charles Stewart Parnell
Boyce, George D., and O'Day, Alan (Editors), *Parnell in Perspective* (Routledge, Chapman & Hall Inc 1991)
O'Brien, Richard Barry, *The Life of Charles Stewart Parnell, 1846-1891* (Haskell House 1898)
O'Connor, T.P., *The Life of Charles Stewart Parnell* (Ward, Lock 1891)
Parnell Howard, John, *Charles Stewart Parnell: A Memoir* (H. Holt and Company, 1914)

Websites:
http://multitext.ucc.ie/d/Charles_Stewart_Parnell
http://www.libraryireland.com/HullHistory/Parnell1.php Parnell and the Land League

United States of America
Brown, Dee, *The American West* (Simon & Schuster 1995)
Kutler, Stanley I. (Editor), *Dictionary of American History* (Charles Scribner's Sons 2002)

Websites:
http://en.wikipedia.org/wiki/Ancient_Order_of_Hibernians
http://en.wikipedia.org/wiki/Apache
http://en.wikipedia.org/wiki/Battle_of_Westport
http://en.wikipedia.org/wiki/Clan_na_Gael
http://en.wikipedia.org/wiki/John_Devoy
http://www.historynet.com/ Molly Maguires
http://en.wikipedia.org/wiki/Molly_Maguires
http://en.wikipedia.org/wiki/Pike%27s_Peak_Gold_Rush

Workhouses
'Ballinasloe Poor Law Union Archives Collection 1842–1931', document, Galway Library.

O'Connor, John, *The Workhouses of Ireland: The Fate of Ireland's Poor* (Anvil Books 1995)

'The Workhouse Diet and Its Effects 1845–1850', document, Waterford County Library

Twining, Louisa, *Recollections of Workhouse Visiting and Management* (C. Kegan Paul & Co., London 1880)

Websites

http://www.workhouses.org.uk/Ballinrobe

http://www.askaboutireland.ie/building-milford-workhous/

http://maggieblanck.com/Mayopages/Ballinrobe.html The Workhouse & Famine in Ballinrobe

http://www.institutions.org.uk/workhouses/ireland

Museums & Libraries:

Clare County Library, Ennis, County Clare

The Clew Bay Heritage Centre, Westport Quay, County Mayo

The Dunbrody Famine Ship & Museum, New Ross, County Wexford

The Jeanie Johnson Famine Ship & Museum, Dublin

The National Library of Ireland, Kildare Street, Dublin.

The National Museum of Ireland – Country Life, County Mayo

Waterford County Library

Wicklow Gaol, Wicklow Town, County Wicklow

Contemporary Map References:

Bald, William, Map of Maritime County Mayo, 1830, Mayo County Library

Ordnance Survey Ireland Map of 1829-1842

Newspaper Reports and Sources

The Anglo Celt

The Ballina Chronicle

The Ballinrobe Chronicle

The Belfast News Letter

The Belfast Telegraph

The Birmingham Daily Gazette

The Brisbane Courier

The California Daily Alta

The Chicago Inter Ocean

The Connaught Telegraph

The Cork Reporter

The Daily Express (Dublin)
The Daily News (London)
Le Figaro (Paris)
The Freeman's Journal
The Illustrated London News
The Irish Canadian
The Irish Times
The Los Angeles Herald
The Mayo Constitution
The Mayo Telegraph
The Melbourne Argus
The Montreal True Witness
The Morning Herald (London)
The Nation
The Nationalist
The Nenagh Guardian
Neue Freie Presse, Austria
The New York Irish World
The New York Times
The New Zealand Tablet
The Pall Mall Gazette
The Pictorial Times (London)
The Press Association (London)
La Presse (Paris)
The Quincy Daily Whig (Boston)
The Sacramento Daily Union
The Southland Times (New Zealand)
The Spectator (London)
The Sydney Morning Herald
The Telegraph (London)
The Times (London)
The Trawley Herald
The Tuam Herald
The West Coast Times (New Zealand)
The Yorkshireman
Zierikzeesche Nieuwsbode (Holland)